ORPHAN MAGE

ERIK JENSEN

CHICAGO SPECTRUM PRESS
LOUISVILLE, KENTUCKY 40207

CHICAGO SPECTRUM PRESS
4824 BROWNSBORO CENTER
LOUISVILLE, KENTUCKY 40207
502-899-1919

Printed in the U.S.A.

10 9 8 7 6 5 4 3 2 1

ISBN: 1-58374-124-0

Cover art by Willie Peppers
Cover and book design by Dorothy Kavka

This book is dedicated to my parents, without whom *Orphan Mage* would be naught but a dream.

And to the Sacred Gods, without whom my dreams would be empty.

–Erik Jensen

BOOK ONE OF *THE FIFTH* TRILOGY

SUMMARY

 he Balance is shifting, and the Forces of the Dark are massing, led by an immortal Sorcerer who will stop at nothing to see Chaos reign supreme. All that stands in his way is a friendless boy plucked from obscurity by an ancient Foretelling. Accompanied by a young group of outcasts, he will be thrust into a world of intrigue and danger on a journey through exotic lands and magical races as he becomes the most powerful Soldier of Order the Forces of Light have ever sent forth. To overcome the ever-expanding tide of Darkness and to save Midgarthe, he will have to become the Orphan Mage.

CONTENTS

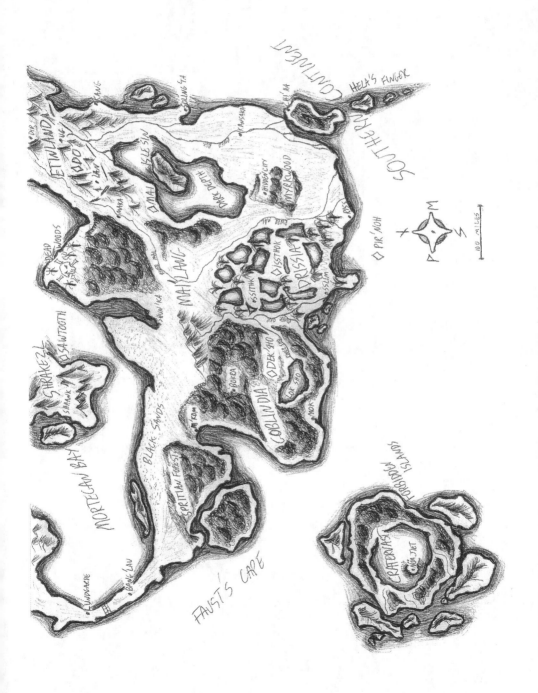

PROLOGUE

More than two millennia before, an immortal named Dak'Verkat—the Dark Tithe—was born to a Mai'Lang King. He grew to become a Sorcerer of limitless potential, one of the most powerful men to inhabit the Midgarthe since the Gods had walked the world. Wealth, power and immortality could never fill his insatiable desire for more, however, for there were others like him. Immortals, wielders of the elements. Sorcerers bent on power and Chaos, and Magi devoted to peace and Order. The Sorcerer became obsessed with amassing more and more power and wealth and of devising a way to rule them all. After more than a thousand years, he finally discovered the means to do so.

Fyrdn Dokksbana was High Mistress of the Elven Mystic Order of Vyzardn and the greatest warrior of her time. A weapons master of unparalleled prowess, a weapons smith of unequaled renown and a Mystic of unrivaled power, she had forged the three Oracles in an effort to rid the world of the Dark magic wielded by the Order of Daemonika, her hated enemies once and for all. There was an Amber Oracle, forged from the Light magic of Midgarthe, an Obsidian Oracle forged of the Dark magic of Midgarthe, and a Jade Oracle forged from Midgarthe herself. Separate they were little more than shiny marbles, but together, united, they were a source of almost limitless power.

Through deceit, manipulation and carefully planned treachery, Dak'Verkat managed to steal the Oracles from Fyrdn and once he had taken possession, she could no longer hope to recover them. Undaunted, Fyrdn sacrificed herself for the good of the world, vowing that Evil would never control the Oracles. She channeled all of her power, knowledge and her very essence into a sword forged from the stars. Fyrdn—in the guise of an ancient bone's thrower— delivered the magnificent blade to Dak'Verkat as an act of homage. However, when the Sorcerer attempted to take the sword, Fyrdn's curse was triggered and the Oracles erupted in such a devastating blast of power that everything as far as the eye could see was destroyed.

The Oracles were scattered to the far edges of the continent with the curse that should they ever again be united, only the wielder of the sword, the immortal son of an immortal would be able to harness their power. This referred to an ancient Foretelling about a boy who would bring the Gods back to Midgarthe, the Champion of Order, the Sapphire Son. Fyrdn herself disappeared, along with her all of the Elven Mystics, both Vyzardn and Daemonika. The sword was lodged in a huge blue sapphire and buried in the heart of the world, where it would remain for centuries until it was discovered by Dwarven miners.

Dak'Verkat did not die, for he was immortal, and soon he became more obsessed than ever. For the next thousand years he scoured the continent for the Oracles, oblivious to the changes occurring in the world around him. Not long before the beginning of the Great War, Dak'Verkat once again united the three Oracles of Fyrdn and discovered their curse. Through his triumph, disappointment, and subsequent rage, the Sorcerer once more became part of the world. As he plunged it into Chaos, he began a new quest, this one for the Orphan Mage, the boy who would become the Sapphire Son.

PART I

JOURNEY TO MIST PEAK

PART I:
JOURNEY TO MIST PEAK

 disturbing vision awoke me from my slumber late last night. I don't know its full detail, only that it was set in the far future. I'm not sure what disturbed me most about the vision—the massive, continental-scale war taking place or the simple fact that I was not present, a severe blow to my immortality's pride, to be sure. Dreams, however implausible and vague at times, will surely be the downfall of the one who pays them no heed.

However, I did find it most gratifying that my progeny will come to play such a prominent and benevolent role in that future. Unfortunately, so will the brood of my dread counterpart. Such will always be the case, I'm afraid. Light cannot exist without the accompanying darkness. Endless day is not much more preferable to endless night.

Perhaps it is just a trick of the moonlight, but as I look out upon this land that I have called home for centuries, I feel as if I can actually watch the world slowly evolve. Will it be thus for my descendants? It is the epitome of irony that to learn the great truths of life, one must first die.

I often wonder when the Sacred Gods look down upon us, do they see our lives for what they truly are, or merely as a spark on the crest of the horizon? When our lives finally do burn out, does the next life hold all that we have been promised? Where does one such as myself fit into the carefully woven fabric of fate the Norns have decreed?

And what of my enemies, the teeming hordes of Darkness? Are they entitled to the same afterlife as I? Or perhaps they train for Ragnarok in their own way. For aren't Good and Evil merely words used to describe two sides of the same spectrum? Justice is viewed through a prism: each angle holds a different perspective. Whatever the case, I will continue to fight for the cause I believe to be right, which in the end **makes** it right, does it not? Perception varies greatly from one man to the next; mine simply seems the only logical view.

—Archives Magus Gellar

This Sacred Year 87

Age of Mystery

CHAPTER 1
THE BREAKING

It is said that there is a place in Midgarthe where time bows before desire, and was is but a word, a place where happiness can be measured by the number of stars in the sky on a clear Summer night. But that is not this place. In this place, Evil lurks within every shadow, and even children must beware the notice of the Dark...

he young boy ran through the thick tangle of undergrowth, heedless of the thorns and brambles that tore at his skin and clothing. His lungs were on the verge of bursting as he gasped for air, but he pushed his small frame on. Clutching a single-edged shortsword in a death grip, Danken tried in vain to hack away at the blurring branches that snagged his ripped, dirty grey woolen clothes. He made a sharp turn in an effort to throw off his pursuers and twisted his ankle. Stifling a cry as he pitched forward onto the hard forest floor, he felt panic threatening to overtake him.

Danken furiously tried to hold his ragged breath and strained his ears for any sound of pursuit. He could hear rough, guttural shouts and cracking branches behind him and off to his left, closing in around him. The unearthly growls and snarling of the fear hounds that had been chasing him for more than a day filled him with an indescribable dread.

Using the stout trunk of a tree for support, he painfully pulled himself back up, testing his sore ankle. Sweat burned his eyes and left rivulets in his dirty face. The forest was becoming dark. As the sun descended below the horizon, Danken knew that his advantage over the creatures of the Dark was no more. Whimpering softly, he pushed away from the tree and began running again. Overhead, he could see the silhouette of a *terykt,* its huge leathery wings outstretched and its toothy, dog-like muzzle simultaneously growling and screeching. A Goblin Rider on the *terykt's* back yelled harsh commands at it. He studied Danken with glowing yellow eyes the same as those of the *terykt*. Danken felt a cold shiver run down his spine.

A decaying log protruding from the foliage tripped him and sent him tumbling. He landed with a dull, breathless thud. Danken sprawled motionless with his eyes closed, sure he had died, until the blissful numbness gave way to burning pain once more. Danken's eyes snapped open. He was confused by the fact that his surroundings were suddenly tinted blue. It was as if he was looking through a blue glass in the midday sun. Danken held his dagger up. In its reflection he saw two burning blue candles where his eyes had been. His first thought was that it must be dawn already until he heard the ever-closer sounds of his pursuers. He glanced up to the starry sky to confirm his suspicions. Danken's vision blurred as if each star was a massive bonfire. Somehow his eyes were using the stars to create light to see by.

The changes within him both frightened and exhausted him, but Danken had no time to ponder how they had come about. He doggedly stood up from the bushes once again. Danken had not even gained his feet when a huge, snarling form slammed him back to the ground. All he could see were jaws lined with uneven teeth that could rip a man to shreds.

As Danken fell, he thrust his shortsword into the coarse, sickly green and gray fur of the beast. He struggled against its crushing weight, trying frantically to avoid its acidic saliva that could burn through stone. Abruptly he ceased thrashing as he realized that the sticky, foul smelling liquid pouring over him was not his own, but the black blood of the fear hound. He scrambled out from beneath it with a cry of disgust, eyeing it as if any moment it would come back to life and attack him. Its wicked, glowing yellow eyes hazed over in death.

"There he is! Get him, you idiots!" a woman's voice shouted in a tongue Danken could barely decipher. The forest exploded with sudden action. A wiry green, rough-skinned Goblin, not much taller than he with odd grey and brown tufts of hair, a long, pointy nose and a mouth full of sharp, rotting teeth, broke from a bush ahead of him. The creature released a bolt of yellow fire at him from its clawed, crooked fingers that charred a tree nearby. Its evil yellow eyes narrowed in anger as it raised its dirty, jaggedly curved blade.

"Comes tos a us, little a Sendar," it croaked triumphantly.

"Leave me alone!" Danken squeaked as the creature rushed in.

Danken dove under the Goblin's swing, barreling into a second, fat Goblin in the process. He cried out and slashed the fat Goblin across its ugly face. The wiry Goblin kicked Danken in the gut, dropping him to the ground in a breathless heap. The fat Goblin, who had been swinging his jagged-edged blade at Danken, instead caught his wiry kin across the throat. The Goblin pressed a crooked hand frantically to its throat, unable to stem the flow of black blood.

"Yousa is a traitors, yousa is!" it gurgled at the stunned fat Goblin.

Taking full advantage of the Goblin's confusion, Danken ran from the grisly scene. Daring a look behind him, he saw a black-haired woman burst forth from the undergrowth. Her pupil-less eyes widened in rage as she took in the two injured Goblins. Flipping open a metallic black fan with a razor edge, she decapitated them both. "Neither the boy nor the girl were to be harmed, only captured, you filthy vermin!" she screamed at their corpses. "What use are they to me dead? We don't even know if he is the one from the Foretelling or just some Faerie boy with white streaks in his black hair!"

Danken shut out her voice and barreled ahead, trying to discern the meaning of her words. What had she done with Wytchyn? Had she escaped? He prayed to the Gods she had and that the Goblins were only pursuing him.

Danken could feel the Goblins and fear hounds all around him and behind him, now, like a fungus on his skin. He heard a rumbling ahead. What could be making such a noise? The rumbling suddenly became a loud thunder, and a damp, cool breeze touched his hot face. Abruptly, he came to the edge of the treeline. Running all the faster for fear of being caught out in the open, Danken almost didn't see the massive waterfall cascading into the river hundreds of feet below.

With a cry, Danken skidded to a stop at the edge of the precipice. He watched with wide eyes as a few tiny rocks went careening into the

ravine. Danken backed hastily away. His stomach lurched as his pursuers emerged from the forest, their faces contorted by wicked,
drooling grins. Yellow eyes burning maliciously, they advanced slowly.
Danken had nowhere to run. They laughed and floated insults at
him. The snarling fear hounds strained at their bits, their Goblin
masters struggling to maintain control. The *terykt* glided far above
him, its Goblin Rider watching for any escape route. The white-eyed
woman stood at the center of the attackers, black lips parted in a
triumphant smile. Her twin bloody black fans snapped open.

"Come little one. With me to guide you, you need never know
fear again," she told him seductively in a staccato accent. "If you are
the Sapphire Son, you can shape the world in your image. You and
your sister can rule the world."

Danken didn't understand her meaning, but had the feeling that
death would be preferable. Fearfully, Danken looked over his shoulder to the foaming waters far below. He swallowed the acid in his
throat. The shortsword in his hand was shaking so badly that he knew
it would be useless. He thought of his mother, blissfully unaware of
his predicament. He felt a pang of sadness that he would never see
her or his sister Wytchyn again. With a renewed determination,
Danken stared his enemies in the eye.

"I will never give you the pleasure of killing me, nor will I end up
in your cook fires this night!" he shouted over the roar of the falls.

The boy took a shaky breath to steady himself and sheathed his
blade. The Goblins suddenly stopped smiling and regarded him curiously under their heavy brows. He gave them a smile of his own, far
more confident than he felt inside. He closed his eyes and said a prayer
to the Gods.

"Odin, may your Valkyries accompany me to Valhalla if worthy
you judge me. May you watch over my sister and keep her safe from
harm until the Norns see fit to reunite us."

With a graceful leap, he plummeted down to the churning waters
below.

"It is not!" Danken squinted his eyes at the black-robed woman
leading a huge wagon towards the city.

"It is too!" Wytchyn squealed, dancing away from her twin's playful shove as they left the fortified confines of the port city of Rakshoal, headed for home.

"Elves don't wear black, Wytchyn, and—"

"You don't know that," she protested, sticking her tongue out at him.

"Aye, Bjorn said it was so, and he's been to their realm. Besides, Elves have glowing green eyes. Everyone knows that," Danken declared.

"It could still be the Elven circus, though," Wytchyn pouted, pointing a finger at the approaching cart. "Look at her wagon. It's not like any Sendar cart I've ever seen."

"Aye," Danken noted the way the cart appeared to be made of entirely living wood, a trademark of Elven crafting. "But it looks too ugly to be."

"No it doesn't!" Wytchyn swung a bolt of the cloth they had traded for in the city at Danken's head before darting off across the parade ground to get a closer look. "Last one there is a Troll's dinner!"

"Wait! No fair!" Danken took off after her.

The woman stopped as the two children raced up to the cart, dismounting elegantly to regard them, but her face was hidden in the shadows of her cowl.

"Are you with the circus?" Wytchyn asked. "The Elven circus?"

"Why, I most certainly am, child. Would you like to see the rest of the performers?" the woman asked in a foreign accent.

"Oh, aye!" Wytchyn nodded happily, Danken doing so less enthusiastically.

"Come, then child." The woman led them to the back of the huge wagon, and Danken began to grow uneasy. Something felt wrong abut the whole thing, and the team of a dozen horses pulling the cart veritably reeked of fear. As they came around to the back, a strong northern breeze brushed back the woman's cowl just enough to reveal black lips and pupil-less white eyes. Danken froze.

"Actually, we're rather late as it is. I've need to get back home," he grabbed Wytchyn's arm and began pulling her towards the forest at the edge of the clearing.

"Danken, What—?"

"Hush," he hissed. "Don't you feel it?"

"Feel what?" Wytchyn stopped cold, feeling Danken's sudden terror well up inside of her as well, for they had always shared this bond.

"Don't run from your destinies, children," the woman's voice became seductive. "You can have everything you ever dreamed of if you will just come with me. You can rule the world. I will teach you of power beyond your wildest dreams. Come with me."

"Flare that!" Danken shouted, and he and Wytchyn broke for the forest.

"Get them!" the woman shouted, and two-dozen short, cloaked figures with burning yellow eyes and half again as many hideous dogs leapt out in pursuit. "Don't let them escape! I want them alive!"

Danken and Wytchyn ran for all they were worth, which was considerable, as they had been born in the forest and knew it like they knew their own backyard. They shed the heavy packs full of goods they had acquired in Rakshoal, hoping it would slow the ferocious dogs down some. It worked, and the twins used it to the fullest, employing every trick they knew to throw off pursuit. For more than three turns of the glass they ran, never stopping, never checking their direction. They ran until the sounds of their pursuers faded away into nothing.

The two collapsed in a jumble of limbs, struggling to regain a trace of the breath they seemed to have lost forever ago. The sun was beginning its descent into the West and the shadows cast by the trees were long indeed. The children looked at one another with wide, haunted eyes, each still too afraid to speak and sure the thundering of their hearts would give them away. Danken reached over and took his sister in his arms, trying to reassure her even though he himself was about as unsure as could be.

"What were they?" Wytchyn whispered after a long while.

"I don't know. But the woman was Mai'Lang, I think."

"Mai'Lang?" Wytchyn inhaled sharply. "But how?"

"It doesn't matter. She's gone. We're going to be all right now."

"Aye, Thor will protect us."

"Aye, he will," Danken agreed. "We are safe."

Just then two of the cloaked figures leapt out from the shadows and grabbed them from behind. Wytchyn screamed as they were hauled to their feet and the figures laughed cruelly, their breath stinking of rotten meat. Danken kicked up behind him, catching his captor in the groin and dropping him to the ground. Danken grabbed a sharp rock off the ground and hurled it at the creature holding his sister, blasting it in the head. As she fought her way loose, two more figures jumped in between she and Danken.

"Wytchyn, run!" Danken yelled, throwing another rock at the two to draw their attention before bolting off in the opposite direction. All four creatures took up after him, and soon he could hear their dogs as well. His mind blanked as he ran, only Wytchyn's face burned in front of his eyes.

Wytchyn ran until she broke out of the forest and onto the beach. Oh, Gods, she had run the wrong way! Home was in the opposite direction. She sat down heavily in the sand, tears pouring forth from her purple eyes. What had happened to Danken? Was he all right? He had to be. She would know it if something was wrong with him, just as he would with her. It had always been that way with them. He was her best friend and her mirror in every meaningful way. To be separated from each other even for short periods of time was a pain neither would willingly endure, and this was pure agony.

Through her tears, Wytchyn saw the Mai'Lang woman materialize from thin air not two feet away from her. She tried to rise, but the woman's strong hands clamped down on her shoulders. Wytchyn cried out in pain as the woman's hands rose to her face, and then her thoughts started to become blurry. She struggled in vain against the powers warring within.

"Your powers will be mine, child, no matter how hard you fight. I will mold you into my image and make—" the woman's breath caught in her throat as a beam of white fire blasted the tree just to her left. Wytchyn's vision went black as the woman's hands fell away from her face, taking her memories with them.

A loud explosion woke him with a start. A white muzzle softly grazed his face. The horse snorted again and Danken rose slowly to regard the magnificent creature. The gigantic white stallion eyed him defiantly, and Danken knew it was a wild horse, untouched by man. He approached it slowly, his hand opened in what he hoped was a gesture of friendship.

"Can you help me?" Danken asked. "I need you to take me back home, but I don't know where I am." Through that need, an unfamiliar power surged within him. Suddenly a thin cord of blue energy erupted from his fingertips into the horse. Danken could feel his intentions flowing through the energy and the horse's emotions flowing back. His name was Bolt.

At first, Bolt seemed unsure about this new development. Danken reassured him by gently stroking the proud stallion's muzzle. He scooped up his damp clothes and tried to jump on the horse's back.

"You're too tall. I can't get up." In response, Bolt lowered his front legs until Danken could leap on. Without further ado, the horse negotiated the narrow path out of the canyon and back into the forest on the opposite bank.

"I have to find Wytchyn, Bolt. Maybe she made it back to the stead, or maybe she's still out there somewhere."

Through their strange new communication, Bolt negotiated the forest confidently. Danken was content to go along for the ride. With his stomach lurching and growling, Danken fell in and out of a restless sleep, the swaying motion of the horse's easy gait like a sedative. Sometime before dawn, he jerked awake, instantly alert to danger. The dark forest was once again alive with Goblins and their fear hounds. Danken felt his hope turn to ashes. The black-haired woman was nowhere to be seen, but he knew she was near. Danken's blue eyes flared dangerously. "I am not yours! Do you hear me?" his voice cracked.

Like a lightning bolt, an angry Bolt slammed through their ranks, viciously kicking several of the Goblins and fear hounds. Danken drew his dagger. Through the blurring haze, he thought he saw a long pearly horn erupt from the horse's forehead. The boy hung on for dear life. He stabbed at anything that moved. Two pairs of rough hands flung him from Bolt's back. Danken landed with a painful thud and was immediately set upon. He felt as if his soul was being wrenched from his body.

"Yousa are's gonna gets it a now, Sendar!" he heard a Goblin giggle.

"Yousa is a gonna serves the Mistress a now, yousa is!" another hissed.

A blinding flash of light disintegrated the two Goblins to sparkling yellow dust. Danken looked up to see a massive golden-maned horse float down into the clearing, an ethereal glow emanating from its body and fiery eyes. Sitting astride the golden-armored horse was a tall, astonishingly beautiful red-haired woman with glowing white eyes. She wore a golden helmet, armored brassiere and a plated golden skirt. Her knee high golden boots and intricate gauntlets complemented her huge glowing broadsword.

The Goblins and their fear hounds cowered in unmoving terror as the majestic woman settled onto the ground. She fixed them all in her powerful, ensnaring gaze. Two of the Goblins' hearts stopped beating from sheer panic, and they collapsed.

"This one is not yours," she said, and her voice seemed to shatter the silent forest. Danken thought he would never hear a more beautiful sound. "His time is not yet come."

She pointed at the huddled Goblins with her fiery sword.

"But yours is now." With a sweeping arc, her sword disintegrated the Goblins and their hounds, leaving a smoldering pile of ash where they had stood.

Though the boy was barely ten years old, he knew the woman for what she was.

"A Valkyrie," he whispered in awe. When her gaze fell upon him, he was suddenly very aware of his nakedness. With a warm smile, she took off her dark blue leather cloak and wrapped it around his shoulders. "Thank you," he managed, surprised that his voice was not shaking as the rest of him.

"You are far from home, little one, but not without friends."

"Friends?" Danken echoed.

"You do know what a friend is, do you not?" The hint of a smile tugged at her lips. Danken shrugged, embarrassed. "Well, now you have one. Agreed?" She placed an armored hand on his shoulder.

"Aye," he answered, wide-eyed.

The Valkyrie looked away momentarily, focusing on a large black raven that winged its way angrily from the scene, as if fleeing the sunrise. Bolt whickered softly behind him, obviously just as enthralled with the Valkyrie's horse as Danken was with its rider. His pearly horn had vanished as if it had never been.

"Do you have a name, child?" she asked in her impossibly sweet voice.

"You don't know it?" he blurted, then went red in the face as he remonstrated himself for his ill manners.

"I know only what you are called in Asgard, not your name here."

"I'm sorry. My name is Danken Sariksen."

"I am Tersandi."

"Thank you, Tersandi," the boy said, trying the powerful name out on his tongue. She smiled slightly and pointed to a folded cloth on the ground that had magically appeared.

"Inside is enough food to get you home. Worry not for your sister, Danken. The Gods have sent me to watch over her and protect her. She now walks a path separate from yours. Be pure of heart and strong of mind and someday you will meet again. It is hard, I know, but it is as the Norns decree. Your prayers have not gone unanswered."

"Gods be with you, Tersandi," Danken told her with tears in his eyes and a thousand questions about Wytchyn on his tongue. He could do little else as she began to float into the early morning sky.

"The Gods *are* with you, Sariksen," and with that, she was gone.

Danken ate ravenously as he and Bolt began their journey back to his stead. With the sun's first rays, his eyes switched out of the "starlight" spectrum and the blue tint disappeared. Little did he know that the danger was now coming from within.

From the blackness of Dark Depth, the spectral, shadowy figure of Dak'Verkat rose. Murky water streamed from his cloaked form as if fleeing from a doom unfathomable to beings of flesh. So still did he hover over the gently flowing waves that a passing observer would have dismissed him as a trick of the moonlight reflected off the water. Floating imperceptibly, as if unconcerned by the natural order of time and space, Dak'Verkat reached the shore, letting his feet touch the ground for the first time since the previous night.

Somewhere within the impenetrable recesses of his cowl, the Sorcerer's red glowing eyes flared in anticipation of a day he had been awaiting for centuries. An eerie light pulsed rhythmically from his gloved hand. Dak'Verkat slowly unclenched his fist to reveal three perfectly spherical orbs the size of marbles. Each gave off its own unsettling light, like a dark rainbow of dread. One green, another gold and the last black, burning as if they were on fire.

These were the Three Oracles of Fyrdn.

Now, after all these long years, their time had come. With a deep breath to steady himself, Dak'Verkat hurled them to magically predestined owners across the continents. Their owners would not know what it was they had found, only that they must not lose it. Two of the owners were inconsequential. Who they were or what they did mattered not, only the first. Her location would remain a mystery, but it was not really important anyway. It was a condition of the magic that he'd had to accept. He would have to wait for the Sapphire Son to find his sister, and with her the first Oracle. Only then would the Sorcerer's carefully devised plan fall into place.

From there it would set in motion a chain of events that would change Midgarthe forever.

Waiting on the shore, the black cloaked woman shook her head.

"You take a grave risk," Hrafna scowled, her white eyes glaring accusingly at him. "The boy and his sister can still be taken." She fanned herself with one of her black metal fans. "We were lucky to find them this time. It is only a matter of time before we find their village. Though they split initially, they will doubtless return to be together. They are twins, and moreover they are entwined by Fate. The boy at least can be taken and his sister cannot have gotten far; not after what I did to her."

"With a Valkyrie watching over them? Not bloody likely. Besides, they are lost. My scouts have scoured every village within seventy-five miles of Rakshoal. The cursed Magi have detected our presence there. We can no longer move about safely, and my magic will no longer be of use there."

"And if the Oracles fail?" she asked.

"Follow your orders and they shall not," Dak'Verĸat said icily, a menacing shadow in the moonlight.

"It will be so," Hrafna bowed. Without another word, she morphed into a raven and flew into the night.

Wytchyn woke to the lap of salty waves against her face. The grey sky above seemed far too bright as she pried open her eyes. She pushed back her jet black hair and wrung it out, leaving two shockingly white strands of her bangs hanging down over her sand-encrusted face. By the Gods, her head hurt. She took off her grey cloak but left her grey woolen skirts and her white undershirt on, mindful that many would take advantage of an unclothed young girl all alone. Wytchyn did, however, take her boots and stockings off as she made her way along the shoreline. The wet sand felt good on her blistered feet. How had they become so? She wondered. Along the way she began to cry and did not know why.

There were no people or houses in sight along the forest-edged beach. Only trees, sand and blue-grey ocean waves. Wytchyn tried to force herself to remember how she'd gotten here, or even where "here" was, but the effort only made her head hurt worse than it already did. The only thing she could remember was a boy yelling, "Run, Wytchyn!" Who was the boy? And what had she been running from? Was the boy in trouble? Gods, she was hungry. Her stomach growled fiercely.

Wytchyn had been walking for nearly two turns of the glass, shivering, tired and hungry when she came upon a hut just visible beyond the tree line. Seeing no other options, Wytchyn carefully surveyed the area. Only the calm lap of the waves broke the silence. Nothing moved save the gentle sway of tree branches in the breeze. Wytchyn realized she had been holding her breath and exhaled slowly. Cautiously, she made her way towards the well-kept hut. The windows were dark. No smoke rose from the chimney. She glanced up at the darkening sky. Perhaps the hut was deserted. Hesitantly, she knocked on the wooden door. No answer. She knocked twice more to no avail. She tried the doorknob. Unlocked. Wytchyn winced as the door creaked.

Once her eyes adjusted to the gloom, Wytchyn stepped into the spartan hut. It contained only a sooty stove, a simple bookshelf, a table and an unassuming bed. Something about the hut made her uneasy, as if she were not alone. She fumbled about the table to strike a match and light a small lantern. As light filled the room, she stumbled, nearly knocking the lantern over.

"Gods!" she gasped. On the bed was an ancient man with a peaceful look on his wrinkled face. Something in her memory took in the pointy ears and registered them as Elven. "I'm sorry, sir Elf. I didn't mean to—Sir?" She touched his arm and found it cold. Wytchyn jerked her hand back reflexively. The Elf was dead. Her first instinct was to run. But to where? Instead Wytchyn continued to back slowly away from the Elf until she bumped into the table, knocking several bags to the floor. She bent to pick them up and realized they were filled with oats and crystallized fruits. Darting an uncomfortable look at the Elf, Wytchyn began to eat ravenously. It was only afterwards as she rubbed her hands together for warmth that Wytchyn noticed the small pile of wood next to the stove, which she lit. Despite the warmth, Wytchyn shivered.

"Run, Wytchyn!" the boy's voice startled her awake. She jumped up and dashed outside of the hut to find him. There was no one there. A cold sweat stung her eyes. Wytchyn glanced up to the sky but the stars hurt her eyes. It was like staring into a purple sun. Confused, she stepped back into the hut. The lantern had gone out. Her glowing purple eyes lit the interior as well as a hundred lanterns. How was this possible? She blinked rapidly. Could the Elf have something to do with this?

Wytchyn began looking around the hut once more, thoroughly this time. She needed answers. She needed something to hold onto. Something that would explain why she could remember certain things, but nothing of herself. Had her eyes always been like this? Wytchyn felt so frustrated and alone. She was unable to stem the flood of tears that came once again. Sorrow and confusion threatened to overwhelm her.

"Stop it!" she raged at herself. "Crying will get you nowhere!"

Wytchyn angrily wiped away her tears. A glint of metal wedged between the wall and the Elf caught her sight. How had she missed it before? Avoiding looking at the Elf, she took what appeared to be a spear from his grasp. Hefting the feather-light handle with a long blade curving opposite directions from either end, she twisted her wrists slightly, and the handle unscrewed. Wytchyn realized that it had been two swords together at the hilts to form a sort of sword-staff.

Wytchyn caught her reflection in the shiny metal. She touched her face, seeing herself for the very first time. Gods, her eyes really *were* glowing. I'm pretty, she thought. How old am I? Not very, she decided. Though the swords made her feel comfortable and safe, she had no idea how to use them. Wytchyn looked for a place to hold them in her own garments, but they were little more than rags. She swept up the Elf's long black-hooded overcoat hanging near the door and put it on. There were several leather hoops sewn in about the back and waist that would suit her purposes perfectly. With this task accomplished, Wytchyn cuffed the ends of the sleeves, as the over-coat was far too large for her.

Wytchyn quickly packed a leather satchel full of supplies. As an afterthought, she took two books off the bookshelf that seemed far-less dusty than the rest. Wytchyn was about to leave the dead Elf to his peace but some sort of custom prevailed. Solemnly, she drew the Hammer of Thor over the Elf's body.

"May Thor protect you. May your Fylgia guide you to safety. May you walk through the Gates of Valhalla and rejoin your ances-tors in everlasting honor." Where had that come from? She wondered. Was it even the right thing to say?

Leaving the Elf and her questions behind her, Wytchyn set off along the beach away from the hut.

Wytchyn had not been walking along a narrow path just inside the tree line for half a day when four men emerged from an intersect-ing path on horseback. Each wore a knee-length coat of shining mail armor under a bright purple, yellow and red tunic and molded steel knee-high boots over tight purple breeches. Their polished helms left their faces clear but arched down the backs of their necks to end in a sharp point, while a single purple plume protruded from the crown. Each carried a wide double-edged broadsword at his waist and a curved triangular shield with a purple falcon set against a red and yellow checkered background. Their large horses were well brushed and shod with polished shoes.

Wytchyn stopped to stare in awe of the riders as they fanned out to check for dangers. A big brown-bearded man fixed her with hard eyes that took in her two swords and odd appearance. As he edged his horse towards her, a large carriage driven by a stately old man and surrounded by six more armored riders came onto a well worn path just inside the tree line. At a beckon from the brown-bearded man, the entourage came to a halt and soon the other three lead riders came to surround Wytchyn, who stared up at them with her wide, sparkling purple eyes.

"What is your name, girl?" the brown-bearded man asked gruffly as he dismounted and came to stand before her.

"Wytchyn," she answered in a tiny voice.

"You are far from any homestead I know of, too far for one so young. Where is the rest of your group?"

"My group?"

"Aye. Where are your parents, girl?"

"I don't know," she answered hesitantly. "I am alone."

"Then who do these two fine swords belong to?"

"They are mine." Wytchyn touched their hilts unconsciously, and the four men laughed loudly in response.

"Aye, I'm sure they are, lass, why don't you just give them here until we can find out who you and they belong to," smiling widely, he reached for them. Wytchyn stepped back quickly and drew both swords, narrowing her eyes to cover her uncertainty and resting the point of the blades against the soft forest floor to keep from shaking.

"I said they are mine, and I belong to no one," came her surprisingly strong voice.

"Aye, so you did, girl." The brown-bearded man smiled widely and put his hands up to show her he meant no harm. "So you did," he chuckled, but there was ice in his eyes.

"What is going on here?" a deep voice asked from the carriage. A strikingly handsome blond man stepped out. He was dressed in similar but markedly finer fashion to his retainers. The sword at his waist had a gold crosspiece and the pommel was set with a large amethyst. His bright blue eyes fixed on Wytchyn with the amusement of a fox hunter who has just sighted his quarry. His intensity made her uncomfortable and his smile was even worse.

"We were trying to determine the girl's identity and purpose, First Heir. She says her name is Wytchyn."

"You believe her to be a threat?" the blond man asked lightly, looking her up and down like one would livestock.

"No, First Heir, but possibly a diversion. She claims to be alone and of no ancestry or upbringing," the brown-bearded man answered, with an arched brow as the blond man stepped forward.

"I am Gjaldi Jorgensen, First Heir of House Sorndral. You realize you travel the lands of House Sorndral with no escort or permission?" he asked with a predator's gaze that made her look away, uneasy with his mannerisms.

"No," Wytchyn shook her head, unsure of what the man was speaking of.

"And what is your purpose here, then?"

"Purpose?"

"Aye, girl, your reason for being here," Gjaldi said, with a cold smile that made Wytchyn shiver. "For delivering yourself to me."

"I—" Wytchyn looked at the ground, trying to keep the tears from flooding from her eyes once more, for she had no answer.

"Be calm, child," Gjaldi put a hand on her shoulder. "We mean you no harm, and it is obvious you have no malicious intent towards us. Perhaps you wish to accompany me back to Sorndral Manor?" Wytchyn looked up at him then, nodding her head slightly, unsure of how to refuse such a man. *"Dwei."* Gjaldi smiled. "Come on then. It's not much farther." He gently helped Wytchyn into the plush carriage where she sat across from two tan, motherly-looking blond women in fine silk and lace dresses, with elegant makeup that made them appear far younger. As the carriage began moving again, Gjaldi introduced them. "Wytchyn, this is my mother, Head Mistress of House Sorndral, and my aunt, Second Mistress of House Sorndral."

"What an interesting child," his mother declared. "Purple eyes like an Orcan's." She shook her head in wonder.

"I have never seen the like," his aunt agreed. "Not in all my years, but she does appear to be Sendar."

"I am sure you have many more years and many more things to see yet," Gjaldi said charmingly. Wytchyn only blinked back and forth at the two women silently. The First Heir placed a hand possessively on her thigh.

"Surely—" his aunt preened just as a silver-fletched arrow cut through the silk window curtains and slammed into her neck. Before the shock had worn off, a second identical arrow embedded itself into Gjaldi's mother and she, too, died instantly.

"Get out of my way!" Gjaldi shrieked. He threw Wytchyn to the floor of the carriage as another arrow stuck into the side wall where his head had been only a moment before. Wytchyn heard the sounds of rearing horses and shouting men. The carriage shuddered to a halt as the dead driver released the reins and the horse-team became entangled around a large spruce tree just beside the path. "Stay here and don't move until I give you permission to do so!" Gjaldi ordered as he drew his sword and barreled out into the open.

Wytchyn watched fearfully as he searched for the enemy but found only dead soldiers scattered along the path, each killed with a silver-fletched arrow. Suddenly a woman emerged from behind a nearby tree. She had green-flecked, fiery red curls of hair past her waist, almond-shaped, green eyes, pale, porcelain skin and silver-painted lips. She wore a blood red leather corset fastened at the neck with a dazzling ruby, silver-laced up the front to expose her ample cleavage and taut midriff. A low-slung, silver-belted red leather skirt clung tightly to her hips and flowed to the ground, split up the sides to allow her shapely bare legs room to move. She wore silver-worked knee-high red leather boots and archer's gloves that covered only the thumb and first two fingers, ending well above her elbow. A water-proofed red leather cloak was pushed back to reveal a bow etched in silver Elven runes, as well as a half-full quiver of silver-fletched arrows hanging from her back. Two glowing blue swords with red dragon pommels called dao rested easily in her warrior's hands.

"It cannot be. Even you could not have killed them all, Ariel Starvayne."

"Gjaldi Jorgensen," she smirked.

"Why?" he asked, his voice trembling. "I have done nothing to you. Who sent you?"

"You should know by now that a true assassin never reveals her reasons or her employer."

"When I am done with you, rest assured that you will beg to tell me," Gjaldi vowed, trying in vain to sound brave.

"I admire confidence but unfortunately, you have none, coward," Ariel smiled wickedly. "Shall we?"

With a roar, Gjaldi charged, swinging his sword with a fear-driven power Wytchyn thought for sure would cleave the woman in two. But Ariel moved like lightning, scoring two slashes to Gjaldi's back as she darted by. He cried out in pain as he attacked again. Once more she effortlessly sidestepped and dealt him two more gashes to the backs of his legs. It soon became clear even to Wytchyn that the assassin was taunting Gjaldi with her skill, leaving identical deep cuts across his cheeks and chest. Gjaldi cried out for mercy.

"I will double whatever you're being paid!" he screeched.

"*Tsk, tsk.* Now that would be unethical," Ariel remonstrated him, continuing her vicious assault until he was nearly unrecognizable.

"Please!" he begged. "Don't do this! Have mercy!"

"Hmm." She paused to consider. "No."

"Wait! No!"

Ariel calmly decapitated him. Afterward, she methodically cleaned her blades before sheathing them. Terrified, Wytchyn slunk away from the carriage and bolted for the forest. She ran for only a few short strides though, before the assassin materialized right in front of her, knocking her to the ground with a light swat. Wytchyn saw that Ariel had taken the time to collect all of her arrows, clean them and place them back in her quiver before giving chase. She felt foolish for even trying to escape, for the woman hadn't even broken a sweat.

"You are not of House Sorndral, or any of the Minor Houses. Certainly not any of the Great Houses," Ariel said softly, cocking her head to the side. Wytchyn was too scared to answer. "So why would you be traveling with them?" Ariel continued. "You are not an Orcan despite your eyes and hair, so that rules out a treaty with the Gilled Ones. Perhaps Gjaldi fancied you? You are quite pretty, though a little old for his tastes," she spat with a disgusted grimace. Ariel then smiled as the horror of what she meant dawned on Wytchyn, who unconsciously pulled her cloak tighter around her neck. "What, you didn't think he was helping you out of the goodness of his heart, did you? He has been 'helping' girls like you for years. I might have killed him for free if a rival House hadn't put five thousand gold on his and his mother's heads."

"Are you going to kill me, too?" Wytchyn asked as she stood shakily. Ariel drew in a sharp breath, her eyes narrowing dangerously as she spotted Wytchyn's sword hilts.

"Where did you get those swords?" she demanded. "And that cloak!"

"I—" Wytchyn's breath caught in her throat and tears sprung to her eyes.

"Where?!"

"From an old man down the beach," Wytchyn sobbed, pointing towards the hut she had left.

"You stole them?" Ariel's glowing green eyes blazed angrily.

"No!" She shook her head, clinging tightly to her only possessions.

"Then how did you get them? Caliosthro would never let another touch his shornstave, much less his cloak."

"He does not need them anymore!" Wytchyn cried.

"Why, girl? Did he choose *Hathal'Ankiar?*" she asked suddenly, fervently.

"I don't—" Wytchyn shook her head.

"Did he put away the blade? *Hathal'Ankiar,* The Hidden Blade. Is that what he did?" Ariel grabbed Wytchyn and shook her.

"I don't know what that is. All I know is that he was dead when I found him, so I gave him the Hammer Rite and took my leave."

"Caliosthro is dead?" the assassin let Wytchyn go with a shocked look in her eyes. "How?" And now she was the one holding back tears.

"In his sleep, I think," Wytchyn swallowed nervously. "I'm sorry if I hurt your feelings," she added after a tense moment. "He was your friend?"

"Aye, he was my friend," Ariel forced a smile before turning away and walking back towards the carriage. For lack of a better option, Wytchyn followed. What horses had not fled were grazing nearby and the assassin expertly mounted a large grey. Doing her best to imitate the woman, Wytchyn struggled to climb up the foot-holster and reins of a smaller black mare, who shied at her clumsiness but didn't buck. Ariel turned her mount back towards the ocean and continued until she had reached the shore before turning to regard her follower. "You don't have to follow me, girl. You can go home now."

"I have no home," Wytchyn said sadly. "At least, I don't think I do."

"You don't remember?"

"I don't remember anything but my name. Nothing before yesterday."

After a moment of contemplation, the assassin shrugged and continued down the beach. By nightfall, she reached the hut where Caliosthro had lived. Not wanting to interfere with the older woman's grief, Wytchyn waited outside. A bright green light began to emanate from the hut along with a beautiful melancholy song spoken in a language she couldn't understand until the hut erupted in green flames that seemed to consume and create at the same time. By the time Ariel emerged, the hut had disappeared. In its place was a single sapling growing out of a fresh patch of ground.

Wytchyn stared first at the sapling then at Ariel Starvayne. For the first time she noticed that the woman's ears were larger and pointed, unlike her own. Some part of her memory said that this was an Elf, but another part said Elves only had blond hair.

"Are you—?" she began.

"An Elf? Aye. Three-quarters at least."

"Why did you do that there?" Wytchyn pointed to the sapling.

"Elves are born of the Treemother. When they die, they are given back, though I'm sure your Hammer Rite was well-intentioned."

"This was your home?"

"Once," Ariel said with a far off look in her eyes. "But that was when I was your age. Caliosthro was my teacher."

"Why did you leave?"

"I was too angry."

"At what?"

"You ask too many questions."

"Sorry." Wytchyn looked away, but after a long moment Ariel continued.

"I was angry at the world for leaving me without a family, for making me a half-breed. Caliosthro tried to teach me peace and harmony, but I could never truly embrace them. Finally, I found someone as angry as I was and he taught me to be an assassin. At the time I was young and naïve and I thought I loved him, but Zorrid loves only himself. Still, Caliosthro tried to bring me back, but I was too headstrong. I just wanted to show him what I could do on my own, and now it's too late," she sighed sadly. "I should have listened to him."

"You can still listen to him. All you have to do is remember," Wytchyn said.

"You remind me of myself at your age," Ariel smiled, glancing at the swords Wytchyn wore crossed at her back. "You don't know how to use those, do you?"

"No," Wytchyn admitted.

"It is a two week journey to where I must retrieve my contract and then another month back to my home. If you still wish to accompany me, I will teach you along the way. Also, I will stop for awhile in order to let this blow over before I collect my fee, so I will teach you then as well."

"You would teach me to be like you?"

"No. I will teach you to *fight* like me. Who you become is up to you. Do you remember your name?"

"Wytchyn, I think."

"Well, Wytchyn, what is your decision?"

For the next thirteen weeks as they journeyed east and then back-tracked before venturing ever further south, Ariel taught Wytchyn the basics of swordsmanship. Though Caliosthro's blades were still too large for her, Wytchyn learned amazingly quickly. For all of Ariel's hard exterior, Wytchyn quickly grew to regard the Elf as an older sister and imitated her every move and mannerism. By the time they reached a hidden compound tucked into a rocky cove just west of the Elven city of Myr, the young girl was beginning to swing her blades like one who had been around them far longer.

Several sleek red-sailed ships sat at anchor in the harbor and a few sailors swathed in red could be seen tending to their duties aboard. The compound would have been unrecognizable from the large sea-smooth boulders scattered along the shore and the tall evergreen trees that grew in the spaces in between had Ariel not pointed out the entrance. It was guarded by two huge Trolls wearing red skirts and carrying their mighty battleaxes as if they were toothpicks. Wytchyn stared at their shiny green, heavily muscled torsos and was shocked when their glowing amber eyes accorded Ariel something verging on worship.

"Greetings, Ariel Starvayne," the larger of the two rumbled. "Word of your deed travels far and well."

"Greetings to you as well. Lost is the warrior with fear in their heart." She spoke the password.

"Be fearless and your path will be clear," the two Trolls moved aside and Ariel led Wytchyn inside.

The thin dimly lit entrance corridor soon became a huge under-ground cavern with three stories accessible by a winding stone pathway on the edge. Each floor held at least forty small cubbyholes that were just large enough to fit a cot and a washbasin. The lower floor was dominated by a massive weapons rack and two training rings all centered around a huge table that could easily sit a hundred people at a time. Red-clothed, heavily-armed men and women went about their business, but all had a respectful word or nod for Ariel. She led Wytchyn to the very top floor and an adjoining cavern. Inside was a large four-poster bed decked in red satin, plush red Langjian carpets worked with gold, two copper tubs, an ornate oak desk and a private dinner table.

Most impressive of all though, was the bald man in a red leather overcoat that reached the floor, exposing only the steel tips of his red leather boots. His pointed ears and glowing green eyes marked him as an Elf, but his size and black lips were those of a Mai'Lang. He was a half-breed as well, called a Lanalf. The twin red-dragon pommeled blades at his back were larger than Ariel's and double-edged. Wytchyn noticed he carried no bow, instead relying on several daggers along his waistline. He had the look and smell of absolute power and confidence about him as he seized Ariel by the back of the neck and kissed her roughly. Wytchyn was surprised to see Ariel respond likewise. Taken aback by this fearsome man, Wytchyn tried to make herself as inconspicuous as possible.

"Gods, I have missed you, my pet," he told Ariel before kissing her again.

"It has been long, Zorrid," Ariel nodded and stepped back as he attempted to undo her corset. "We are not alone."

"What?" Zorrid's eyes grew wide as he noticed Wytchyn for the first time. "You found her," he breathed.

"What do you mean? Found who?"

"My fortune," Zorrid strode forward and cupped Wytchyn's chin in his strong hand, ignoring her futile efforts to dislodge herself.

"Zorrid, what are you talking about? She's just a little girl I decided to train."

"No, my pet, she is so much more. While you were gone, a Mai'Lang woman paid us a call and promised one hundred thousand gold and a Lord's title and lands on the Mai'Lang mainland if I found the Sendar with black hair and white bangs with purple eyes-or her blue-eyed twin brother. And now she is mine. Maler!"

"Aye, Dragon?" a beefy Sendar with a patch over his eye and a thick black stubble came into the room.

"Send the carrier pigeon to Hrafna. Tell her we have what she is looking for."

"Aye, Dragon," Maler nodded and disappeared once more.

"What does this woman want her for?" Ariel asked sharply.

"What do I care?" Zorrid once again began kissing Ariel. Picking her up easily, he tossed her onto the bed. "We will be rich and never have to hide from the Mistgarde again. The Fearless will grow strong beyond our wildest imaginings!"

Ariel pushed him off of her with an effort. "Zorrid, anyone that rich and powerful must be connected with the Sorcerers. What incentive do they have to pay when they could just kill us all? Besides, she is of value to me."

"Leave the planning to me. Your work is finished."

"But—" Ariel began only to be silenced by a powerful open-handed slap and a hand tightly around her throat.

"Do not forget who you serve, pet," Zorrid warned. He lashed a foot out to catch Wytchyn in the stomach as she sought to come to her teacher's aid, that sent her flying. "Maler!" Zorrid shouted.

"Aye Dragon?" the Sendar appeared again.

"Take the girl to the dungeons and set four guards on her. If she is hurt or escapes, you and they will pay for it with a death that lasts for a year. And take her bloody swords!"

"Aye, Dragon." Maler grabbed Wytchyn by the collar and the waist and hauled her off as she struggled weakly, still trying to catch her breath. The last thing she saw before leaving the room was Zorrid ripping Ariel's corset lace open and taking her, her empty eyes never leaving Wytchyn's.

Maler unceremoniously dumped her on a filthy, greasy patch of rotting hay and slammed the iron-barred door behind him with a cruel laugh. The overpowering smell of feces and the cold stone floor was all Wytchyn could sense in the complete darkness even with her newfound starlight vision. She heard Maler inform the guards of their orders. Wytchyn cried silently until there were no tears left and her throat was dry and hoarse. Despite her sadness and situation, she couldn't stop thinking of what Zorrid had said. She had a twin brother with blue eyes. It had to be the same one from her memory. And the Mai'Lang woman must be the beautiful but evil face that flashed through her mind sometimes. If only she knew her brother's name, it might all be worth it, she thought grimly.

Wytchyn had lost track of time when a commotion outside her cell stirred her from her inward thoughts. She stood shakily as the sound of keys jangling in the rusty lock reached her ears. The torchlight that flooded in as the door opened noisily temporarily blinded her. Two hands grabbed her and then her swords were pressed into the scabbards on her back. It was then that she recognized the silhouette of Ariel Starvayne standing atop the bodies of four men. Wytchyn flung her arms around the Elf.

"Oh Ariel, I knew you wouldn't—"

"There is no time for that, girl! Follow me!"

The assassin led her to a large crack in the side of a winding tunnel deep within the compound. The sound of rushing water could be heard faintly and water dripped from the jagged mineral-encrusted edges. Without hesitation, Ariel shoved Wytchyn through and followed. It was a slick, smooth chute that took them sliding down into a small chamber lit only by filtered light of the ocean surging up through a small hole in the rock.

"There's no way out!" Wytchyn groaned.

"Aye, there is," Ariel pointed to the gurgling water.

"But—"

"When you come up, swim to shore and then run as far away from here as you can."

"What about you?"

"I have unfinished business," Ariel said grimly.

"Then I will stay and fight with you," Wytchyn declared as the sounds of men shouting reached them.

"This is my fight, and you will only be a hindrance. Now go."

"No, you are—"

"I am not your mother, girl! I am nothing to you! I have nothing to offer you," Ariel grabbed Wytchyn's cowl and pulled it over her head. "Listen to me, girl. This is very important. Keep your cowl up no matter what until you are sure you are safe. Do not take it down for *any* reason, understand? Just run until you are far away from here. I have taught you what I can. You must go out on your own now." Without further ado, Ariel shoved Wytchyn into the water before using her innate Elven talents to scale the nearly vertical, slick chute, coming out with blades flashing.

The eyes were everywhere, piercing into her. Wytchyn couldn't see them but she knew they were there. They were searching for her. Wytchyn couldn't hide from them, so she did what her brother and Ariel had told her to do; she ran. She ran even as the sun went down and her eyes began to glow. She ran even as her legs burned and grew leaden. She ran even as her lungs seemed ready to burst. Away from the eyes. Away from the darkness. She ran until a tiny cluster of lights in the distance gradually turned into a huge harbor with hundreds of ships and a city that stretched into the forest further than her eyes could see. As she passed under the huge white gates of the city, Wytchyn saw a few Sendar close to their big ships or near taverns. Mostly though, she saw Duah.

No one paid her even the slightest amount of attention and Wytchyn even had to dodge a few people who carelessly walked straight towards her. She could feel the city's heartbeat all around her. Green torchlight illuminated the winding streets. The beautiful buildings were *alive,* magically grown as a part of the forest. Through the ordered bustle of the city, Wytchyn moved, thrilled to be around people. She listened to several conversations and ever so slowly pieced together that she was in the Duah city of Sancor. A nice looking old Elven woman was sitting on a bench feeding several fat seagulls. Her green lips and glowing green eyes were wrinkled with age, meaning she must have been close to a millennium old, if not older. Her nearly white hair was marred only by the shiny green strands of all Elves.

As Wytchyn approached the ancient Elf, the seagulls scattered noisily. The woman drew back in confusion and peered around, her eyes flaring.

"I'm sorry I scared away your seagulls," Wytchyn said softly in her own language.

"What is that? Who is there?" the woman looked right through her and Wytchyn guessed she was blind. Her accent was sing-song and quite hard to understand.

"Sorry to disturb you, I didn't realize you were—"

"Ah, too many spirits for this old woman tonight," the Elf shook her head groggily. "First I hear voices and then I speak to them in filthy Sendar?" She shuffled off, switching back to her native Duah as she continued mumbling.

Thoroughly perplexed by this turn of events, Wytchyn made her way towards the docks. She narrowly avoided being trampled by a group of huge, green skinned Trolls. Wytchyn had the horrifying thought that they might be invaders. Thankfully they, like seemingly everyone else in the city, did not notice her. She saw two Sendar sailors at the end of a narrow pier talking and laughing as they loaded crates onto a large three-master ship. She felt strangely comforted by their familiar use of her native tongue. At least she knew that much about herself, she thought.

The two continued talking when she stopped not two feet away so she cleared her throat loudly. The men stopped abruptly, scanning the docks with perplexed looks.

"You 'ear somethin', mate?" one asked.

"Aye, an' I didn't like the sound o' it neither."

"Bloody Duah cities are filled with filthy flarin' magic. 'S why I'll be glad t' get underway tonight. 'S a long voyage but well worth it, eh?"

"Aye. Good ol' Breakwater never had no bloody magic wot t'scare a bloke with, right mate?"

"Aye, y'are." The sailor agreed. They began loading the last of the crates more quickly. "Breakwater's got all a Sendar could ask for."

Wytchyn was about to scream at them that it was impolite not to acknowledge someone when it struck her: They truly couldn't see her. She was invisible! How was it possible? What should she do? She wanted a place to stay but had only the meager coins Ariel had given her. Of course, being invisible, she might not have to pay for *anything*. For a child, this was a dream come true. But then, who was to say she had not always had this ability? How to control it, though? She could see herself but others could not. Somehow they couldn't see the clothes or weapons she carried either. Had Ariel ever noticed it? If so, why hadn't she said anything?

Thinking Breakwater sounded nice for a Sendar like herself, Wytchyn decided to stowaway aboard this ship. She shimmied up an unoccupied pulley rope and danced around the milling figures above-decks. The combination of saltwater, wood, leather and sweat provoked strangely intriguing smell. Wytchyn had never been on a ship before—at least, she didn't think she had. With boundless curiosity, she carefully explored every nook and cranny until she found a nice, comfortable berth for herself in the Captain's quarters. Wytchyn pilfered a blanket and pillow from one of the officer's quarters. Both were obviously *not* invisible so she had to be careful not to attract attention. Hoping it would escape notice, she stashed her bedding behind the large desk built into the cabin wall. As she snuggled into her bed and quietly ate her meager dinner, the cabin door opened. A hard-looking woman in a loose fitting white blouse, formfitting black leather pants and knee-high black boots entered. She couldn't hold a candle to Ariel Starvayne, but she was not a woman to be dismissed easily, either. She pulled off her red head scarf and shook out her long, curly brown locks. Several gold rings jingled from her ears, nose and lips. Wytchyn was awed by her aura of power. A shiny cutlass hung from a red satin sash at the woman's waist. Wytchyn hadn't known women could be Captains.

The woman was pulling off her boots when a light rap on the door heralded a grey-haired, barrel-chested man in a sleeveless brown vest. His waxed grey moustache bounced as he talked. Wytchyn thought this quite hilarious and had to stifle a giggle.

"Sorry t' be botherin' you, Cap'n Baeldotir, but we're provisioned an' ready t'ship out on your orders."

"Make it so Mr. Jamesen, you have the helm," she responded in a husky voice.

"Aye, Cap'n." He turned to go.

"Oh, and Mr. Jamesen, have Merid bring in a basin and some warm water, please."

"Aye, Cap'n." Jamesen left. Not long after, a tall, gangly girl entered the cabin. The girl was about five or six years older than Wytchyn and wearing identical clothes to the Captain. She carried a large wooden wash basin filled with what looked and smelled like hot sea water.

"Anything else Captain?" the brown haired girl asked.

"No. That will be all, Merid. Go enjoy the sights of the harbor while you can. It will be two months or more before we'll be calling port at Breakwater. The open ocean can be very monotonous and boring if you don't have your mind in the right place."

"Aye Captain." Merid lowered her hazel eyes in acknowledgement.

"Once we're underway, we'll resume your navigation lessons."

"Aye Captain." Merid hastened off.

After locking the door, Baeldotir stripped and began washing. Wytchyn felt intensely embarrassed and guilty about invading the woman's privacy. The woman's confident, brusque demeanor echoed Ariel's. Gods, Wytchyn missed the assassin. Would she ever see her again? She resolved to adopt a similar bearing, for both the Captain and Ariel had garnered respect and Wytchyn wished the same for herself. Soon Wytchyn was parroting the captain's every word and action, though Ariel was never far from her mind.

As the days rolled by, Wytchyn followed Baeldotir everywhere. She sat through her navigation, sailing and sword lessons with Merid and was a very fast learner. Though her training with Ariel had given her skills beyond her age, Wytchyn still learned much from the Captain. She adopted the ship's jargon quickly and even managed to stomach the terrible, monotonous ship's fare. Wytchyn had even mastered the roll of the ship. She stood the decks like an old hand. Wytchyn had also found that she could read people's base emotions and types of secrets simply by looking into their eyes. She became expert at determining who was hiding what and what they had done or would do, as if they'd told her themselves. The girl used this to her advantage every chance she got, though most times it was very vague and never completely accurate.

One night when the Captain was fully immersed and busy with some tedious bits of repair work, Wytchyn retired early to her "quarters." She was ready to call it a night when she caught her reflection in the wall mirror in the cabin. She snorted at the too-big cowl that obscured her features in shadow. Why had Ariel told her to keep it up at all times? She looked silly. Not like anyone would notice, though. How was it she could see her reflection and herself when no one else could?

Wytchyn noticed the steaming, unused washbasin in the corner of the room. She had not had but two quick cold rinses in the aft storage compartment. Wytchyn wasn't exactly sure about washing with sea water, but it had been hard enough for her to obtain fresh warm water just to wash her face and brush her teeth. The prospect of a warm sponge bath sounded utterly delightful. Had she ever had a sponge bath before? It certainly *looked* like it would feel good at least. Wytchyn hoped she had time, for she did not want to be an invisible form dripping water if the Captain returned early.

Carefully, Wytchyn placed her swords against the wall before disrobing. She continued to look at her reflection in the mirror as she touched the warm water with a toe. How had she gotten those two white streaks? Or her purple eyes? No other Sendar she'd come across had anything even remotely similar. So many questions, so few answers, she sighed. She washed quickly, then toweled herself dry with a small rag before getting dressed again. Sponge baths *did* feel nice. She had just finished putting her boots on and had one arm through her cloak when the door swung open.

Merid dropped the pitcher of water. Her mouth worked silently as she stared Wytchyn straight in the eye.

"Who—who are you?" Merid asked shakily. Wytchyn looked around before she realized Merid was talking to *her.*

"You can see me?"

"Of course I can see you. What am I, blind?" Merid quickly regained control of herself and looked to be on the verge of screaming out for the master-at-arms. Wytchyn glanced at her swords. What would Ariel do in this situation? She quickly finished donning her overcoat, pulling the cowl low over her face as if it were armor. Ariel had told her to do that, at least.

"My name is Wytchyn. I'm only—" she stopped as Merid's eyes went wide, and she frantically searched the room. "What's wrong?" Wytchyn asked, and Merid stopped cold.

"What happened? Where are you?" Merid asked.

"What are you talking about? I'm right here. You just bloody said you could see me! Which is it?"

"How did you do that?"

"Do what?"

"Become invisible."

"You mean you really can't see me now?"

"No."

"It's the cowl," Wytchyn whispered to herself. Ariel had known the cloak would make her invisible. So *that* was why she had told her to wear it! "Please," she begged Merid, "don't tell anyone I'm here. I don't mean anyone any harm. I just want to make it to Breakwater."

"I—I don't know…"

"Please?"

Before Merid could answer, she heard footsteps in the 'tween decks. In that instant, Merid made her decision. She dropped to her knees, beginning to scrub the floor furiously. Wytchyn darted over and grabbed her swords. She slipped into the corner of the cabin, where she stood as still as could be. Her heart raced wildly as Baeldotir walked in, nearly slipping on the wet floor.

"Merid," she scolded, hands on hips. "What is this mess?"

"I'm so sorry, Captain. I slipped and dropped the water. I'll have it cleaned and a new basin brought in within a turn of the glass."

"See that you do." Baeldotir admonished, closing the door as she left. Both girls heaved sighs of relief. Merid slid down the door. Wytchyn pushed her cowl back, becoming visible again. She still held the separate blades in her hands. Merid eyed them, then shifted her gaze to the younger girl.

"Do you intend to use those?"

"No," Wytchyn blushed, crossing them behind her back hastily.

"Gods, that was bloody close."

"Thank you," Wytchyn said sincerely.

"I don't know why I did it but you're welcome."

"Let me help you." Wytchyn dropped to her knees and begin scrubbing.

"Where do you sleep?" Merid asked when they were finished. Wytchyn showed her her hiding place. "You can stay in my berth if you wish. It's small but at least you will not have to hide."

"You would do that?' Wytchyn dropped her gaze so that Merid wouldn't notice the fresh stream of tears. She didn't want the older girl to see her weakness. Ariel had always said that the perception of strength was nearly as important as strength itself.

"Aye. I was a stowaway once, too. Much younger than you are though. A runaway from a bad home. But Captain Baeldotir adopted me and began teaching me the way of the high seas. She says in another year or so, I could be First Mate. But Mr. Jamesen will never retire." Apparently Merid was glad to have someone to talk to. Wytchyn was thrilled, just the same.

After replacing the wash water and clandestinely spiriting the blanket and pillow to Merid's berth, the two girls squeezed into the small hammock. They lay awake a good part of the night talking quietly about their past—of which Wytchyn was sorely lacking—and of the intricacies of sailing. Wytchyn fell asleep wondering when she'd last laughed. If she ever had at all. Ariel had not been one for humor. She wished she could just remember who she was. What was the blue-eyed boy's name? Where was she from? Was someone looking for her at this very moment? In spite of her lingering doubts about her past, Wytchyn had to think about her future now.

In time, Wytchyn and Merid became close, almost like sisters. Merid had been surprised when she realized she could see Wytchyn's reflection in the mirror even when she wore the cloak, yet when looking directly at her, there was nothing there. So from then on Wytchyn was careful around anything reflective.

During the quiet nights, the two girls would read from the books Wytchyn had taken from Caliosthro's hut.

One book was an account of the Great War a decade earlier and a detailed description of all the Light and Dark Races. They told the tale of how the Magi and Sorcerers had united the Forces of Light and Dark respectively from the dozens of tiny feudal states. The ensuing war had been great and terrible. In the end, the Northern continent, Sendar, had been populated by the Light, while the Southern continent, Mai'Lang, had fallen to the Dark. Out of the ashes, the great Nations of the Races had emerged.

The second book was a fascinating compilation of the ancient times during the Age of Gods before they had left the world and with them the Immortal Races. All but one: the Dragons, who ushered in the Age of Dragons, the birth of the Sendar and Mai'Lang and the separation of the Four Continents, (though the Eastern and Western had disappeared long before living memory). The ancient Ljosswyrm and Svartwyrm Dragon races killed themselves off in the cataclysmic wars of Light and Dark, leaving only the lesser—but still huge, terrifying and immortal—Gem and Painted Dragons in their place.

The Age of Mystery—of which the current year was 3117—had heralded the rise of the Mortal Races. Then there was the cryptic passage of the Foretelling. This stated that someone called the Sapphire Son, along with a powerful group of allies called the New Immortals would bring about the next age, which would be called the Age of Heroes. In his wake, the Sapphire Son would allow the Gods to once again return to Midgarthe.

By the time they rounded the Northern Peninsula of Mai'Lang, not only had both girls become well versed in the history of Midgarthe, they had become expert navigators. Wytchyn was beginning to feel truly comfortable with her weapons. The sun appeared to be just cresting the horizon.

Only it wasn't the sun. It was several tremendous lightning crashes that constantly lit the sky. Cracking thunder soon followed. The ship pitched violently. Waves twice as tall as a man slammed into the ship from all sides. For several turns of the glass, the noise and angry sea raged on. The ship became more sluggish by the quarter-glass.

"Full starboard rudder!" Baeldotir screamed over the deluge.

"She's not gonna make it!" Jamesen bellowed.

"She will!" Baeldotir grated. "She bloody has to!"

"It's too close!"

"All hands, brace for impact!" Jamesen called.

With a loud, jarring crash, *Rimrunner* lurched and then was abruptly still. Wytchyn and Merid were thrown to the deck.

"We've run aground!" Merid exclaimed. "Come on!"

Wytchyn and Merid scrambled atop decks. The dark loomed menacingly over them, slashed their faces.

"Look over there!" Wytchyn pointed to a rocky outcrop a few hundred yards away. All around them, the crew was already loading the shore boats, for it was readily apparent that the ship was damaged beyond repair.

As Merid was lowered onto the first heavily tossing shore boat, an invisible Wytchyn clung tightly to her back.

"Where are we, exactly?" she screamed over the tempest.

"Bloody Mai'Lang mainland!" the prowman back. "Flarin' storm did blow us right off course! Hold tight now!" He and four others began rowing toward the shore. The huge waves tossed them about. As they reached the shallows, Wytchyn saw the second shore boat drop into the water. Before it could be loaded, however, a massive fork of lightning stuck the main ship. With a loud groan of timber, *Rimrunner* began to list just as Merid and Wytchyn waded ashore.

The crew of the shore boat didn't get out.

"We've got t'go back for 'em! You stay here!" the prowman yelled. "Don't bloody move 'till we get back!"

They rowed out frantically, searching for survivors. Merid tried to run back into the surf but was leg-tackled by Wytchyn.

"I have to save Captain Baeldotir!" Merid cried.

"You can do nothing but die yourself!"

"No! I must—" A massive swell rose above the shore boat. As the sea spray cleared, Merid let out a strangled cry. The shore boat was gone, swallowed by the greedy sea. Only the masts of the main ship were visible above the foamy crests of the waves. The two girls felt as if their world was sinking along with it. "We have to save them!"

"They are gone," Wytchyn's words sounded odd to her ears. Her voice sounded very much like Ariel Starvayne's.

"She can't be!" Merid collapsed onto the sand, heedless of the stinging rain. "She was the only mother I ever really had. The only one that cared for me." She sobbed loudly. Merid did not remain defeated for long. She regained her composure and reassumed her commanding role. "We have to find shelter or we'll freeze to death."

"Aye," Wytchyn agreed, searching the shoreline. "There's bound to be something over there." She pointed to a forest not a hundred yards inshore.

They found a low hanging ewe tree branch and huddled together. Wytchyn was filled with despair. Did it ever stop? What would happen to her next? She certainly hadn't washed up on the beach north of Sancor with a shredded cloak, several bruises and a splitting headache as a form of relaxation. Unknown to Wytchyn, the Jade Oracle Dak'Verkat had magically bestowed upon her while unconscious was now sinking to the bottom of the crashing waves along with the wreck of *Rimrunner.*

Wytchyn started awake. What had woken her? Where was Merid? The sounds of boulders grating against each other was suddenly drowned out by her friend's piercing shrieks. Wytchyn leaped to her feet and frantically followed Merid's cries to the source of her distress. It didn't take long to locate either. Though the warm sun had returned, the sight of Merid's attackers made Wytchyn's blood run cold. Three Giants were arrayed on the beach. One held Merid five feet off the ground by the ankle like a rag doll. Wytchyn couldn't decipher their rock-crushing language but she understood all too well by their cruel, lewd gestures what they intended to do with her friend.

It took Wytchyn only a moment to realize she had slept in her cloak, which had likely saved her life. Without a second thought, she had her swords drawn and was rushing towards the terrifying scene. She studied the Giants as she ran. Each was over nine feet tall and well over one thousand pounds. Their completely hairless features were heavily over-exaggerated. They had huge lips and noses underneath tiny, beady white eyes. The beasts had no muscle definition, just pure bulk under bear-fur togas. The hand of the Giant that held Merid was nearly as big as she was. In his other hand he held a gargantuan stone club. What was she to do against such terrifying creatures?

Seemingly from thin air, a massive broadsword cut the closest Giant nearly in half. Wytchyn gasped, skidding to a halt. The Giant groaned as he fell with ground-jarring force, his severed bulk emitting a horrific odor. Wytchyn could hardly imagine a being strong enough to cause such damage until she saw the sword's bearer. Wytchyn thought she had never seen such an intimidating figure. The bald-headed man was more than seven feet tall and packed with hard, rippling muscle that bulged through his sleeveless, open chested black vest with each graceful movement. His pupil-less white eyes contrasted starkly with his black lips. Wytchyn marveled that he was able to maintain his grim smirk, even as he dodged death blows.

Following closely behind the warrior was an ancient man in full length, black satin baggy attire with a raised black skull cap that complemented his black lips. In one red-palmed hand he held a long, slightly curved blade wider at the tip than at the base. In the other he wielded a long curved dagger upside down so that it ran up the back of his forearm. Though he was clearly an ancient, he moved with feline grace.

Wytchyn watched, mesmerized. The old man dealt several deep, long gashes to Merid's captor. The brute dropped Merid with a roar of pain. Wytchyn ran forward, grabbed her friend and hustled her away from the fierce fight. Both remaining Giants let out shattering roars that preceded a dangerous magic spell called *Etinrage*. A Giant in the throes of *Etinrage* could continue to fight long after it should have been dead, even after its head had been cut off. Strangely, this only seemed to encourage the ancient and the warrior.

The big warrior met the second Giant eagerly, a vicious glint in his white eyes. He easily dodged the Etin's club and lopped off its thick arm with one graceful stroke. The Giant didn't so much as flinch as it swung its huge fist at him. The warrior ducked. With a triumphant shout, he buried his sword in the Giant's skull to the hilt. Wytchyn was shocked at the man's ferocity, and even more so as the Etin continued to thrash. The warrior did not seem surprised, though. He simply let go of his blade as it was far too embedded to remove safely. Wytchyn could feel the man's powerful confidence as he attacked the Etin with bare hands.

Wytchyn's attention swiveled to the breathtaking motions of the ancient then.

He danced about, laying gashes wherever the enraged Giant's defenses permitted, which was just about everywhere. Though the ancient's slices didn't do even a fraction of the damage of the warrior's, soon there were so many that the Etin was covered in its own black blood. The ancient seemed to be taunting it in some strange tongue. Wytchyn's mouth dropped open as the man actually began to *laugh*.

She couldn't imagine being so confident in battle, when she herself had to struggle not to run away. Run like the boy from her memory had told her.

Soon even the *Etinrage* wore off and the Giants' bodies had to admit defeat. The warrior and the ancient stood easily. From her invisible vantage point, Wytchyn observed the pair warily. They carefully scrutinized the sobbing Merid, talking between themselves in their foreign tongue, though Wytchyn noticed it was the ancient who did most of the talking. They began to approach Merid when the distinctive sound of Wytchyn's swords whipping through the air gave them pause.

Though she remained invisible, both men's hearing and training was so acute that they immediately picked up on her general position. The warrior's eyes narrowed while the ancient wore a thoughtful, considering expression, stroking his white moustache. Wytchyn tried to make her voice sound old and authoritative.

"If you killed them just to get her, you will not find me so easy a fight. I'm warning you now!" she said in Sendar.

"An invisible Sendar, eh?" the ancient spoke in a staccato-accented Sendar. "Well invisible Sendar, what makes you think we would want anything at all from her?"

"You want the same as those Giants wanted."

"Well *I* personally don't find you Sendar all that attractive. What about you, my friend?" he asked the big warrior, who arched a thick, black eyebrow and shook his head.

"Then why did you do what you did?" Wytchyn asked. "You're not like us. You're Mai'Lang. I know all about you. So why would you kill the Giants if not to enslave her?"

"Because they were filthy Etinspawn out of their mountains," the warrior spat in a low baritone. "These are our beaches, not theirs."

"But you *are* Mai'Lang, aren't you?" Merid spoke for the first time. Carefully, she retrieved her sword from where it lay in the sand.

"Aye," the ancient nodded with a calm smile.

"You are evil," Merid accused. "I know that much from my time on the high seas."

"And from books," Wytchyn added.

"Are we now?" The ancient laughed. A tiny smile pulled at the warrior's black lips. "Do you think the world is as black and white as the print on the page of a book? Tell me, invisible one, have you ever met a Sendar who was less than benevolent? Mean? Abusive?"

"Aye. I have," Merid answered quietly. "My father and mother."

"Then would it not stand to reason that not *all* Mai'Lang were Demonspawn?"

"What do you want?" Wytchyn cut in, feeling patronized.

"A thank you wouldn't go amiss," the warrior scowled. "Bloody ungrateful Sendar."

"To see who I'm talking to wouldn't be too much to ask, would it?" the ancient asked. Wytchyn hesitated before slowly lowering her cowl. "Very young to be on a dangerous continent alone, no? What with all the Darkspawn out and about."

"We didn't have much choice," Merid bitterly replied. "It's not like we chose to come to this Gods' forsaken continent. Our ship wrecked."

"I see, and where do you go from here?"

"To find a ship to take us to Breakwater."

"Ah, perhaps you are unfamiliar with the trade embargo between our two continents? You will find very few Mai'Lang ships that will approach anywhere *near* a Northern port. The Mistgarde navy would sink them in a heartbeat."

"We will find a way."

"Will you then? You haven't been here a day and already you've nearly gotten yourself killed. How much further before the next time? Or the time after that?"

"And what is this supposed to do? Scare us? Too bloody late," Merid sniffed. "We've already lost everything. We are not Mai'Lang. We are Sendar and we don't belong here, so we will leave."

"What is your point?" Wytchyn asked the ancient quietly. She was as grateful as Merid was trying not to be, but a Mai'Lang was a Mai'Lang.

"We can help you," the ancient said.

"How?"

"Keep you safe, give you a place to stay, teach you to use those." He indicated their weapons.

"We know how to use them," Merid said defensively.

"Of course. You know how to *swing* them. I can teach you how to *be* them."

Wytchyn used her gift to see into the men's hearts and was truly surprised to learn they did not lie. She looked back at the sullen Merid, who had been raised her whole life to hate Mai'Lang. The two girls shared a brief, knowing glance that said that they really had no other choice. Finally, they agreed.

"Excellent. *Dwei,* as you Sendar say. Am I correct?" he smiled.

"Aye."

"Give them some food, please," the ancient told the warrior, who dug in a large sack at the waist of his black buckskin pants and tossed them each a large piece of jerky. As they gulped it down, the ancient introduced himself as Duarta'Rhan, Dockmaster of Maka. The warrior was Katir'Tua, his adopted son and apprentice.

Over the years, Sendar would become a distant memory like so much of her past. Wytchyn dedicated her all to her new life as a Mai'Lang. She resolved that from this day forward, no one would see her face, that the past she didn't have could never recall her. Today was the first day of her new life. There was no yesterday.

CHAPTER 2
THE FRIENDLESS

anken headed out early that morning full of anticipation and not a little nervousness. Having just turned eighteen, this would be his first Autumn Finding Festival, and one of the few times he would actually set foot in the village. Though he was avoided by the people of Lok Tryst as an outsider, they would still allow him to compete, even if he didn't have any friends to cheer him on. Of course his mother Marga would have been there if he hadn't steadfastly refused, citing the enormous amount of embarrassment she would likely cause him as his lone supporter. No, he had decided he would rather compete to the tune of jeers or even worse, silence.

Danken repeatedly shifted his long bow across his back, attempting to affect just the right tilt to roll with his stride. Long and dangerous, he hoped. The lope of an experienced forester. He was an expert marksman, though so were all the men and most of the women who lived in the secluded villages of the Pixian Forest. Danken peered suspiciously over his shoulder at his shrinking stead in its tiny clearing, making sure his mother had not given over to any wild flights of fancy and decided to sneak after him. Marga was sly and stubborn, a combination that had caused him many tongue lashings and numerous sore backsides over the years.

Danken's blue eyes flared, enhancing his vision well beyond the normal range. Finally—although still cautiously—satisfied, he took the well-worn path through the ancient forest. The whip of the wind blowing and the smell of hay and cow manure ceased abruptly upon entering the peaceful shelter of the wood, to be replaced by chirping birds and an occasional chitting squirrel. These glades were Danken's sanctuary, the one place he was not an oddity, a spare part. Here he *was* a part. He had spent his life in these forests, often hunting, but always searching other villages and secluded steads for any sign or mention of Wytchyn.

Danken fingered the three throwing knives at his belt, reassuring himself for the dozenth time that they were still there. Chiding himself for his anxiousness, he rested his hand on the shortsword swinging easily from his hip. Its comforting feel steadied his nerves. Automatically, Danken picked his way through the undergrowth, leaving tracks only the most experienced tracker could pick up. He moved with the silent grace of one who had been born of the forest, avoiding dry leaves and seed pods, and effortlessly gliding around low hanging branches.

With the sun just cresting the Eastern horizon at his back, Danken reached the village of Lok Tryst. The townsfolk were already about their early morning business. Many women were returning from the creek with fresh loads of laundry. Shooing his two fat hounds out of his way, the baker bustled by, carrying a stack of steaming rolls and buns. The rhythmic clang of the blacksmith's hammer could be heard competing with two ancient, crooked men loudly complaining about something or the other.

Danken spotted Bjorn and his daughter Kierna, and headed in their direction. He halted abruptly when he saw the company they kept, however. Jetrian Torvaldsen was a month older than Danken and easily four inches taller. His long straight black hair shone magnificently in the early morning sun, pulled back from a face that drew the breath from women's lungs. His pale, mysterious grey eyes gleamed with the sparkle of a joke no one knew but him. A dozen women— some not so young and some married, Danken noted—hovered around the boy. Jetrian and Danken were rivals of a sort, having clashed often over a choice stag or a brace of hares. Kierna, with her blond hair tied into a ponytail and clean, grey riding leathers, appeared the only one immune to Jetrian's charm. Danken turned away rather than endure his nemesis' cockiness, only to be brought up short by Bjorn's authoritative call. One did not ignore Bjorn Svelgisen.

"Danken," Bjorn didn't even bother making a gesture. Repressing a sigh, Danken reluctantly came to join them, remonstrating himself for having jumped to heed the man like a child.

"Hailsa, Bjorn," he flashed a hesitant smile.

"Competing today, I see." Bjorn's red hair was tied back into a tight ponytail and his thick sideburns and beard were braided past his chest. His blue eyes were as sharp as daggers.

"Aye, that's right." Danken glanced quickly at Kierna, then Jetrian before greeting them likewise. Jet snorted loudly at the notion of Danken competing, but cut off quickly when Bjorn leveled a withering glance his way. Danken suppressed a snigger. Gods, how he hoped he beat Jet today.

"Hailsa, Danken." Kierna kept her icy blue-eyed gaze on something in the distance. Typical, he thought. There was always something more important to Kierna than him. Jetrian looked Danken hard in the eye. Suddenly, a deck of cards fanned out in the boy's hand, though Danken was sure Jet hadn't moved a hair.

"Pick a card, Sariksen," Jet said in his smooth voice. Danken's eyes narrowed, for Jet's tricks always left him looking foolish. Danken suppressed a growl as all around him women ceased their chattering and focused on him. He felt his face flush at their condescending looks. Trying to ignore them, Danken was forced to concentrate all his energy on his eyes to keep them from glowing. The townsfolk did not like to be reminded that he was not like them, though he doubted they ever truly forgot. Smoothing his face, Danken reached up and took a card. When he turned it over, he realized it was the 'Midden Tender,' the lowest card in the deck. He groaned inwardly.

The ladies burst out laughing. Danken felt like a scorned child. With a supreme effort, he avoided incinerating the card using his blue fire. It was a secret and not one he was particularly anxious to have known. Instead, he handed the card back to Jet, barely keeping his hand from shaking. Jet looked at the card in mock surprise.

"Only one of these in the entire seventy-two card Hierarchy deck. Odd, don't you think?" Jet smirked and Kierna rolled her eyes.

"Not likely with your tricks, Jetrian," Bjorn said wryly.

Jet laughed. "Maybe your luck in the Festival will be better, Sariksen."

"Good luck today." Danken forced a smile as the Mayor of the town took his place at the front of the crowd. The man's bald pate winked in the sun as he adjusted his suspenders importantly around his considerable girth.

"May I have your attention please?" he called in his reedy voice. "It is my honor as Mayor to declare this year's Autumn Finding Festival begun!"

The crowd cheered as the children competed in sack races and relays followed by the larger men participating in an eating contest. The women showed their skills at side-saddle and a fast-paced jig until only one was left standing. Danken was chagrined but not surprised to see his mother among them. A flute, pipe and fiddle trio started up a tune during the intermission, and all the village joined in to dance and celebrate.

Jet had so many offers to dance that it seemed he had a new partner at every turn. Danken had not a one. He stood off to the side busying himself with his bow as if it did not bother him. He saw Jet's father Torvald eye his son with simmering anger. Torvald's hands rested on both of Jet's younger sister's shoulders with a possessiveness that gave Danken pause. For all of his cockiness, Jet was nothing short of timid around Torvald. Danken had seen Jet's enormous skill at fighting first hand, so the bruises that were often on the boy's face were likely the handiwork of Torvald. Danken looked hastily away when Torvald made eye-contact.

Kierna was scowling at the proceedings, deflecting offers to dance with a twirl of her staff. Danken smiled and moved to join her. Her baleful glare did not slow him. He was used to it. She turned her attention back to her staff, dismissing him. Danken was not so easily put off.

"I thought today was supposed to be fun."

Kierna twirled her staff. "This is fun for me."

"Plenty of time for that soon enough. There is a dance going on in case you haven't noticed."

"So?"

"So, I think the point is to be...you know, dancing." Danken arched a brow.

"Like you are?"

"Not by choice."

"Not my fault."

"No. But it is your loss."

"My loss?" Kierna whirled on him. "What would *you* know of loss, Faerie. You never had anything to lose. You don't know my reasons nor my burdens. So bugger off."

"Is that the *way* of it, then?"

"Aye, that's the way of it."

"Sorry I tried."

"So am I."

Danken hid the sting of her words as he walked away. That had not gone as he had planned it. What burdens could she possibly have? It wasn't as if he'd asked her to jump off a cliff. And who knew better about loss than he? Kierna's generally foul mood seemed only to grow more so when he was near. Jet leveled a triumphant look his way as he danced with another beautiful girl. Danken gritted his teeth. How had he even *begun* to feel pity for him? Cursed be of he ever would again.

After the dancing and drinking had died down, the weapon's competitions began. First was the hammer throw, won by the blacksmith, then the tug-of-war, followed by the archery contest, which Bjorn won as he did every year.

Knife throwing was next. A new target was set up forty feet out. Only Danken and Jet were left to go before the previous Festival's champion, the village butcher. The contest was all a formality really, for Jet was the best knife thrower—and wielder—even the village elders had ever seen. When his turn came, Danken stepped carefully to the line. He drew a knife from his belt. Feeling its weight, he threw it with a graceful, if unorthodox twist of his wrist.

The knife thudded into the bullseye, just off center. Danken caught the butcher staring in amazement at the throw. Bjorn studied him curiously. Jet appeared completely unconcerned. He sauntered over to the line in the grass where Danken had stood and took ten long paces backwards. The crowd's excitement was palpable. With the same insufferable grin fixed on his face, Jet became a blur of motion. He tossed three knives from his belt consecutively thirty feet in the air. Then suddenly there were two more in his hands from some-

where in the recesses of his wide sleeves. These two he tossed simultaneously. Both points somehow embedded in the exact center of the
bullseye, hilts sticking out at impossible angles. Jet caught the air-
borne three in succession and threw them seemingly before they
touched his fingers. All three thudded with their points touching the
first two, making a five-pointed star out of the hilts.

Jet bowed deeply, and the butcher stalked off without bothering
to throw. "You should follow his example," Jet told Danken with a
condescending nod at the butcher.

"Kiss my arse on the way and you've got a deal," Danken retorted.

"Suit yourself, Faerie," Jet laughed as he walked off. The crowd
drifted off to observe the much-anticipated staff tournament. A large
stone circle had been placed in the middle of the green with two long,
dented wooden staffs inside. The competitors were divided into four
brackets of eight.

Danken easily made it past the first two rounds, defeating an old
innkeeper and another first year youth. The crowd was silent at his
advancement, but cheered wildly when it was learned he would face
Jet in the quarter-finals.

Twirling his staff expertly, Jet danced around Danken, making
odd faces and gestures which delighted the onlookers. Like lightning,
he darted in with a series of attacks that left Danken's hands numb
from blocking. One shot slipped through, catching Danken across
the knuckles. He dropped his staff in pain. A quick jab from Jet to
his face set Danken on his rear. Shaking his welted hand, Danken
picked up the staff. The judge awarded the first point to Jet.

Danken circled warily, launching a few testing attacks that Jet
easily countered. Following another seemingly useless flourish of his
staff, Jet suddenly swung in with the butt, catching Danken squarely
across the side of his face. Danken dropped. The crowd gasped, then
cheered again. After the stars faded from his vision and the noise
died down, Danken rose again to hear the second point awarded to
Jet. He spotted Kierna at the edge of the circle. She seemed surprised
that he was even able to stand. Danken thought he saw concern for
him in her eyes, but when she met his own, they faded to stony indif-

ference. Shaking thoughts of her from his head, Danken picked up his staff and began to circle once more.

"Give up, Sariksen, I don't want to kill you," Jet mocked. "At least not in front of all these people! Besides, it's not as if you have any chance of—"

Danken cut him off, dancing inside Jet's defenses and cracking him across the knee, followed closely by a hard butt to the stomach. As Jet doubled over, Danken brought his staff crashing down on Jet's head. Jet dropped like a bag of stones. He groaned weakly, trying unsuccessfully to rise. He tried to rise again and only managed to do so under the attentive hands of half a dozen women, each of whom shot Danken dark looks. He winced as he rubbed the side of his face gingerly. Bloody Jet.

Kierna and Bjorn approached. "You learned his style by letting him get the upper hand," Bjorn commented, as much for Kierna as for Danken. Kierna always seemed to study Danken intensely without ever showing the slightest hint of emotion one way or the other.

"Aye, I suppose I did."

"Try that with me and you won't rise after the first time." Kierna stated flatly before stalking off. Danken stared after her, confused. Bjorn snorted, patting him on the back before striding away to watch the next duel.

In their match against one another, Kierna was as good as her word. She gave him no opportunity to counter her blows. Danken did not even see the blur that was her staff, nor did he hear the resounding cheers that followed. Kierna kicked him in the side as he tried to rise. "That's it? You didn't even try to hit me!" she raged. Considering she could defeat men in the village in unarmed combat, it was no surprise. Farley the blacksmith dragged Danken unceremoniously out of the circle before his mother hurried over to help him up.

"Oh, my little Sapphire, the trouble you let your pride get you into." Marga shook her head. Danken came to in time to watch Jonaton, a hunter from the outskirts of the village, beat Kierna in the final round by a score of two to three. Danken staggered over to where she was nursing her wounded jaw and pride. He pushed his own blood-caked hair out of his eyes.

Kierna looked angrily at him as he approached, pushing her father's hands away from her face, where he had been tending to her. Bjorn put them back without even blinking, slightly rougher this time and she cried out in pain.

"What?" she grated. "Come to gloat? I still beat *you,* so keep your snide remarks to yourself!"

"Actually, I came to congratulate you on getting second place," Danken said quietly, avoiding her fiery gaze. "It's not easy to get that far."

In response, Kierna snorted and dismissed him from her attention. Danken felt a hand on his shoulder and whirled so quickly that his vision tunneled. He narrowly avoided retching.

"A fiery girl she is," Jet commented archly. Danken noticed he was keeping pressure off of the knee he had clubbed, as Jet guided him away from the fuming Kierna. "A shield-maiden if ever I've seen one, but I'd set my sights a bit lower, were I you," he laughed, immediately regretting it as he clutched the back of his head.

"My sights aren't set anywhere, Jet." Danken smirked at his adversary's pain, hiding his own.

"Aye, I'm sure, Sariksen. She is too *dwei* for you anyway. Besides," he leaned in conspiratorially. "I don't think she likes boys. Or men for that matter."

"Just because she doesn't like you doesn't make that so."

"Aye, it does. And don't think I haven't seen the way you look at her. You can't fool me."

"Sorry for hitting you so hard," Danken apologized insincerely to deflect his embarrassment.

"You got lucky on this day, Faerie. It will not happen again. Bet on it." With none too light a smack on the bloody side of Danken's head, Jet loped off.

Danken gritted his teeth and made his way back to the forest, avoiding his mother, who was now in a busy conversation with a score of other cackling mothers. After all, she was not a Faerie race like him so why shouldn't they like her? All such thoughts fled from his mind when a sharp pain at the base of his skull struck him like a hammer. The woods spun crazily and then he saw only black.

Was this a dream? Danken wondered as he stumbled through the forest.

Holding a rag to the side of his skull and trying not to breathe too deeply for fear of incurring the wrath of his bruised ribs, Danken felt the strange sensation of someone or something watching him. He had felt its like before, but never quite so bad as this. His stomach dropped as he realized it would once again be accompanied by a burning, lancing pain at the base of his skull. He dropped to his knees. He held his head tightly, eyes scrunched up in pain and struggled not to give voice to his silent scream. When the pain finally abated and Danken determined that somehow he was no worse for the wear, he detected a slight rustling in the nearby bushes. Determined to find out who was watching him and why, he mastered his nausea and crashed into the woods in pursuit of his tormentor.

Using every forest trick he knew, Danken ran full tilt while he followed a shadowy trail that may or may not have been from his watcher. Amazingly, his quarry always seemed one step ahead of him, anticipating his tricks and tactics and countering them before he had even employed them. Danken had run for more than half a turn of the glass and lost all sense of direction when he stumbled into a small clearing. A dilapidated wooden shack leaned precariously to the side. He could almost see the termites working to turn the entire structure into sawdust. Filthy, web-encrusted windows leaned at insane angles, and he doubted any light penetrated through. A thin stream of smoke puffed from a twisted chimney.

Danken shivered in spite of himself. Dusk had turned the sky an eerie red and the silence was broken only by unnatural sounds. And spiders! By the Sacred Gods why did it have to be spiders? He was about to ask why it couldn't have been snakes or rats or bats, but one by one, he picked out various specimens of all three lurking around the shack like guard dogs. He searched all around the clearing for the trail to resume, but it ended right at the door to the shack. Both the trail and the chimney smoke told him someone was home, and he *certainly* wasn't going to risk a look through the windows to make sure. Danken drew his dagger. For lack of a better plan, he listened to the goings-on inside.

For a few tense moments, he heard nothing. Then a scuttling, shuffling noise came from within. Warily, he pressed his ear to the door. He heard some sort of mumbling and what might have been a screech. Pressing harder in an attempt to make out the noise, he was caught off balance as the rickety hinge suddenly gave way. Danken sprawled face first on the floor, sending a cloud of dust into the air.

In a panic, he scrambled up and put his back against the wall. The dim candlelight highlighted a virtual horror shop of an apothecary. What might have been a fine oak desk a thousand years ago now stood on worn legs crisscrossed by centuries' worth of spider webs. Stacks of colored glass vials, beakers and jars filled with all sorts of shadowy things cluttered the top all the way to the ceiling. The walls were covered with shelves holding more horrific specimens. Dead animals freakishly preserved perched atop shelves, staring at him with dark, glassy eyes. Books covered in dust so thick they were unreadable were scattered everywhere, all open to one page or another as if someone might turn up to read them at any movement. A foot-long centipede skittered over his boots and into a crack in the floorboards.

A hunched figure in filthy rags shuffled out from behind the desk. It was an ancient woman older by far than any Sendar Danken had ever even heard of. Her thin, wispy tangle of white hair reached the floor and her pale, wrinkled skin was riddled with warts and liver spots. Her eyes were a milky, sightless white on either side of a large hooked nose and thin twisted lips. She headed straight for him. Danken drew back in disgust, clutching his knife tightly in front of him. Unconcerned, the old hag closed the door and mumbled something about catching a chill before turning to him and plucking a fat spider off of his shoulder, popping it into her mouth and crunching. Danken swallowed loudly as bile rose in his throat.

"He wants to know," the woman hissed to herself. She produced a decaying leather bag with a hair raising cackle. "He wants to know," she repeated as she crumpled to the floor and dumped the contents of the bag in front of her, revealing an assortment of small bones, trinkets and rocks. As Danken watched with morbid curiosity, the old hag began mumbling some sort of chant that he couldn't make out. A second high-pitched cackle caused the hair on the back of his neck to rise. "He wants to know, so he will know." She scooped up her bones, rising to point a crooked, knobby finger at his neck. "They are scrying for him, he feels it. Searching, always searching they are."

"Who is scrying for me? What do they want? What are they searching for?"

"For this!" she screeched.

Danken's neck began to glow blue, the pain at the base of his skull throbbed in pulse with the light. Danken felt his neck restlessly in an effort to isolate the source, but it faded and then was gone.

"What—what is it?"

"He doesn't know yet," she hissed, rocking back and forth with her disconcerting laugh. "He doesn't know, he doesn't." Her sightless eyes burned with sudden intensity. "But he will. He will, very soon."

"Tell me, please! Why am I different from everyone else?"

"He will know, aye, very soon." She cackled again and then shuffled behind her desk. Danken attempted to follow, but found only a long-dead skeleton in decaying rags covered in spider webs, sitting in a rocking chair. It rocked slowly back and forth, creaking disconcertingly.

Terrified, Danken bolted from the shack, a horrible cackling in his wake.

CHAPTER 3
BONDED

anken brushed silver and black strands of hair from his eyes. The blue orbs glinted in the late afternoon sun. He methodically laid antlers, deerskins and rabbit furs into his cart. This load was the last of what he had caught in the past three months. He clicked his tongue to get Bolt's attention. The horse dutifully followed Danken's lead into the barn. Tomorrow Danken would ride the goods into the city to trade for the supplies his mother needed. Unlike other boys his age, Danken didn't mind the work. Marga had been through enough since Wytchyn had disappeared.

He began to daydream as he often did while doing the numerous menial chores of a forest stead. Since that day eight years ago, he hadn't seen Tersandi again, nor any more Goblins. Those memories remained, burned into his mind. He often wished he could meet the beautiful Valkyrie again to let her know that she had changed his life. But most of all to ask her of Wytchyn. But Valkyries likely had more important things to do than talk to simple forest boys. Even if those simple forest boys were madly in love with them.

"Danken, dinner!" Marga called. Danken dropped his chores and ran into the house at the speed of a hungry eighteen year old, which is considerable, as all mothers know. "Go wash up, Sapphire," she reminded him as he entered. Danken hurriedly washed his hands and face before returning to the kitchen to watch Marga put the finishing touches on dinner. He loved to watch her cook. As poor as they were, she still managed to make everything taste as if it were a gourmet dish from one of the fine shops in Savhagen. They had only a small vegetable garden, a milking cow and what Danken could hunt, but it was enough.

"Are you ready to take the skins into the city tomorrow?" She asked.

"Aye. I'll leave at dawn," Danken quickly laid the ceramic plates and mugs on the table.

"Do you have the list I gave you?" Marga placed a venison slice and a heap of vegetables on a steaming piece of bread.

"Aye." After eating, he helped her wash the dishes and clean the kitchen, as he always did.

"Time for bed, my little Sapphire," she said, using the nickname given to him at birth by his grandmother, on account of his eyes, just as she had called Wytchyn her little Amethyst. His mother kissed him on the forehead. "Tomorrow is a big day."

She could not have known how right she truly was.

With the pre-dawn, Danken sleepily rolled out of bed and got dressed, as always donning Tersandi's fine cloak over his clothes. The cloak had faded to grey, which suited a hunter like himself just fine. His eyes glowed automatically to ensure he didn't bump into anything. He stumbled into the kitchen and devoured the bowl of cold cereal and glass of milk waiting for him. By the time Danken was ready to depart, the sun had risen. He tiptoed into his mother's room and kissed her on the top of her graying blond curls.

"I'll be back in a few days," he whispered, then quietly made his way out to the stables. Bolt was waiting for him, knowing as he always did when they would be going into the city. Though Danken had returned to Rakshoal to search for Wytchyn many times, he had never returned to sell his goods. He always ventured to Savhagen now, just to be safe. After fitting the cart onto Bolt's harness, Danken jumped up into the driver's seat.

"Ya!" he called enthusiastically to the impatient Bolt, and they were off.

The trail through the forest surrounding Danken's stead had always held many mysteries for him. Today was no different. The ancient redwoods towered into the air hundreds of feet, creating an enclosed feeling that scared most people, but that Danken had always liked. As a small boy, he had often tried unsuccessfully to climb these very trees. He and Bolt wove their way around the thick patches of undergrowth which grew in the rays of sunlight, creating the illusion of windows in the canopy. The cart's wheels made a soft rickety sound as they rolled over the packed foliage of the path.

Beautiful as the forest was, Danken knew it was dangerous. Gnomes, as well as Pixies, made it their home, and neither looked kindly on Sendar, especially those who came to harvest their forest. Most tales were the exaggerations of superstitious villagers though. Danken generally discounted such nonsense. He had lived his whole life in these boles and had rarely seen hide nor hair of either creature.

Danken fingered his shortsword out of habit. He had carried it since he was old enough to walk, and was more than proficient in its use. His father had left if for him when he had gone away, and his mother had made sure he received it, though she was always fretting about its uses and dangers, especially to him. Since the Goblin attack eight years before, however, she had no longer tried to dissuade him from carrying it.

Something was different today though; he could feel it. Sensing his rider's unease, Bolt trotted at a good steady pace. Danken could feel eyes on him. It seemed to be a rather common occurrence of late, he thought grimly. Abruptly, Bolt stopped short, snorting angrily.

"What is it?" Danken asked. In answer, Bolt's head shot over to the right. Danken immediately deciphered two gnarled figures crouching not fifteen feet from his cart. Gnomes. Small, evil creatures born of the forest, they stood barely two feet tall. Their dull green eyes were burrowed deep inside mahogany skin reminiscent of bark. Knobby little-fingered hands held small crossbows with poisoned darts.

"I am just passing through. I mean you no harm," Danken told them firmly. The Gnomes appeared not to understand. They muttered something to one another in their guttural language, never taking their eyes off of him. Suddenly, they raised their crossbows. Danken heard the distinctive click of the bolts being loosed. Exploding into action, he drew his blade and dove underneath the missiles. Bailing off the edge of the cart, he charged the Gnomes. Apparently, neither creature had anticipated their darts missing and were taken completely aback by this crazed boy with the flaming blue eyes.

Danken caught one Gnome by the back of its filthy neck, slitting its throat in one fluid motion. Green blood spattered across the forest floor. The other Gnome made a headlong escape into the woods.

Danken had nearly caught it when he heard a faint, pathetic whimper behind him that stopped him. The Gnome disappeared into the undergrowth. Danken turned to investigate the source of the noise. To his astonishment, he found a young Pixie locked inside of a cage. After scanning for any other signs of danger, he looked closer.

Villagers throughout the Pixian Forests always spoke of Pixies and how evil they were, inflicting horrifying tortures on supposedly innocent Sendar, but Danken had yet to see any evidence. Looking at this tiny creature, scarcely the size of his thumb and flecked with beautiful gold, Danken found such stories to be exaggerations at best. He decided to let the Pixie out. Warily, he sheathed his shortsword. He doubted it would be of much use against the darting creature anyhow.

"I'm going to let you out, so don't do…whatever it is Pixies do, all right?" he asked, but received no answer.

Reaching down, Danken took hold of the cage and bent apart the thin, rusty bars. The Pixie huddled in the far corner, its wings fluttering nervously. Danken reached in slowly, but this only seemed to frighten it more. Instead, he brought the cage over to his cart.

"What do Pixies eat?" he asked the tiny Nymph. She blinked. Danken reached into his pack and grabbed a tin of honey. Dipping his fingertip into it, he tried again.

Slowly, cautiously the Pixie inched forward, sniffing his finger. After deciding it was not a danger, the Pixie put its tiny hands on either side of Danken's finger. Its long, thin tongue snaked out tentatively, tasting the honey. Finding it good, the Pixie hungrily licked the rest off of his finger. Danken laughed at the tickling sensation.

"Can you speak?" he asked. The Pixie turned its huge golden eyes up to him blankly. Danken released a tiny spark of blue energy from his fingertips into its hands, telling the Pixie his name. After a moment of stunned silence, the Pixie released its own golden energy into him.

"This Pixie is T'riel. Thank you."

"I'm Danken. What happened to you?"

T'riel's eyes teared up. "Stupid Root Twisters killed this Pixie's parents. Root Twisters did plan to eat One," she explained.

In this simple exchange, each had taught the other to speak their basic language.

"Do you have a place to go?" Danken asked in Sendar, the common tongue of the Northern continent. T'riel looked at the ground and shook her head. Danken felt her pain. "Then you can come with me if you want," he offered. T'riel looked up happily and shot up his arm in a blink. She perched on his shoulder, chirping excitedly in his ear. Laughing, Danken once again took his seat at the head of the cart and signaled Bolt to go.

The next day brought with it a heavy fog. Danken heard faraway whispers harshly calling his name. He had slept fitfully, twice coming awake to the blinding pain that meant the nameless evil was looking for him. The old bones thrower's cryptic words echoed in his head. They were searching for him. Why? He wanted to shout. What had he done? What did they want from him? T'riel flitted about ahead as the day wore silently on, aware of the darkness weighing heavily on the forest.

Emerging from the forest was like stepping out of a closet. The late day sun assaulted Danken's eyes and T'riel, who had never been out of the forest, scampered into his robes to hide. It took many ticks of adjusting for Danken to coax her out. When she did, Danken saw that she was no longer glowing gold, instead closer to reflecting it.

Soon after, they crested the ridge that overlooked the city of Savhagen. The city's name meant "Safe Harbor" for long ago it had sat on the shores of Lok Brae. This was the largest city for nearly one hundred miles around and it bustled with constant activity. As it was a Sendar city, T'riel was best advised to go back inside his cloak. Sendar were generally uncomfortable around magic.

Savhagen was well-fortified with armed guards patrolling massive gates. They carefully scrutinized each passerby. Danken was no exception, though his wagon full of goods attracted more attention than he did. Or so it would have been, had one of the sentries not placed a beefy hand on his chest.

"Take your cowl off," he commanded. Danken slowly complied, revealing his crystal clear eyes, which seemed like blue marbles reflecting the sun's rays. Alone, they were cause for comment, but combined with his white bangs, Danken stood out sharply. The guard looked shocked for a mere second before recovering. A voice from the opposite tower called out.

"Relax, Sorg, Faerie boy lives west of here a ways. He's no one." Sorg didn't look so sure, but waved him along anyway. Danken put the cowl back over his head. Once they were out of hearing range, he spoke quietly to T'riel.

"I thought we'd had it for a second there, T'riel." She poked her tiny head out from his cloak's pocket.

"Shiny man would have been sorry," she chirped before withdrawing back to the safety of his cloak. Danken was confused as to her meaning, but let the matter drop as they pushed through the bustling throng of people. For all of her youth and timidness, Danken suspected T'riel was much more than a normal child.

After around a half a glass, they reached the colorful booth Danken had been seeking. An elderly man in bright-colored clothes was sitting in a rocking chair. Laid out on his table was an impressive arrangement of fabrics, each dyed and expertly woven.

"Well boy, what've ye come t'buy this day? An more'n 'portantly, what've ye t'trade fer it?" the old man asked in a gravelly, well-worn voice.

"I've got these antlers, skins and furs to trade. I need ten yards of white Norspointian wool, ten yards of blue Volhakian cotton and five yards of Kasani satin," Danken stated plainly in the business-like manner he had learned from his lifetime of market experience. Early on, people had thought him foolish and had tried to cheat him. This they quickly learned not to do. One man, after having stupidly reached out to steal the reins of Danken's cart, had found the boy's dagger protruding from his hand. Another had thought to give him a third of the agreed bargaining price. A mysterious shard of blue energy released into his throat had reversed fortunes and Danken had ridden off with three times what he needed. The old man here knew well of these tales and always bargained fairly.

Until today.

Out of the corner of his eye, Danken caught the old man give a slight but commanding nod as he gathered up the requested fabrics. Turning back to Bolt, Danken peered out from under his cowl. His glowing eyes quickly picked out three black cloaked men in wide-brimmed hats warily approaching from opposite angles. Danken knew that these were no common street toughs. He noticed the telltale bulges at their waists, poorly hidden beneath their cloaks. Long swords, or he was a Drissian's teething ring.

Pretending to busy himself with the straps of Bolt's harness, Danken carefully slipped his shortsword from its sheath. He tucked it under the satin. The men were getting close enough that Danken would have been able to see their eyes had they not been hidden in the shadow of their hats. His heart raced; his breath sounded like thunder in his ears. The old man tried to grab him from behind, but Danken struggled free. Springing into motion, he undid the last strap tying Bolt to the cart and leaped bareback astride the stallion. He spurred the horse on with a hard smack to the flank.

Startled, the three men converged quickly, drawing their blades. People scattered in all directions, trying to avoid the commotion. One of the attackers grabbed Danken's leg. Before he could be pulled off, Danken lashed out with his shortsword. He felt it strike his assailant's arm. The man cried out and fell away. The other two attackers were only steps behind. The crowd was still too thick to get Bolt to much more than a fast trot. Danken knew they would overtake him if he didn't do something soon.

"T'riel!" he called. The Pixie came out of his pocket alertly. "I need you to fly ahead. Pick out the least-crowded, safest route for me. Can you do that?"

"Of course this Pixie can." T'riel scoffed. The Pixie rocketed up above the crowd, a golden blur in the afternoon sun.

Following her exaggerated gestures, Danken urged Bolt on. The stallion began snapping at people too slow to get out of the way. Slowly a path cleared. Danken glanced ahead and saw a contingent of city guards in their burnished armor making their way towards him. Their long broadspears parted the crowd easily. Danken felt relief. They would help him. He looked backwards, expecting to see the attackers beating a hasty retreat. Instead, they appeared to see this as helpful.

Danken looked back in time to see the guards lowering their spears towards Bolt's chest. They were going to kill his horse to stop him!

Panicked, Danken threw his free hand out in an instinctive warding gesture, trying to rein Bolt in with his knees. As if a massive wind had sprung up, the entire contingent of guards flew backwards into the vending carts lining the street. Danken knew that somehow he had caused it. He tried to remember how, but T'riel had found a winding alley void of traffic and the chase resumed again.

He chanced another look back. The attackers were nowhere to be found. Still, Danken felt uneasy, and gave Bolt his head. The stallion seemed to glide over the narrow alley's uneven cobblestones, almost as if his hooves never touched the ground. The buildings blurred by so quickly that they were indistinguishable from one another. Not for the first time, Danken found himself wondering if Bolt weren't much more than he appeared.

The blinding pain at the base of his skull struck again. Danken nearly fell as they emerged onto a major street. He gritted his teeth as the pain receded, leaving his hair standing on end. His assailants would find him again, of that he was certain. They must work for whoever was tracking him. Danken continued to follow T'riel, hoping she could find a way out of the city.

A crossbow bolt whirred past, inches from his ear. Danken ducked low over Bolt's neck. A second arrow grazed his shoulder, slamming into an old merchant's chest. Danken was trapped on this street. T'riel could find no alternate route for at least another two hundred yards. He held his breath in grim anticipation of the next bolt. Bolt made an unexpected lunge to the side, knocking several people down. Another pair of arrows whizzed by, killing more innocent bystanders.

He was about to scream out when a woman's whisper inside of his head silenced him.

"Follow my voice to safety," she said, Danken pulled Bolt up.

"Who are you?" he asked.

"Follow my voice," she repeated. Danken obediently followed the phantom trail of her voice and found himself staring up at the fortified, imposing grey stone of Dvarin Keep.

Danken urged Bolt through the beautiful hedged gardens that surrounded the thirty-foot-high wrought iron bar gate. Townsfolk out for a leisurely stroll scattered as he barreled past and another contingent of guards moved to block his entrance. A crossbow bolt slammed into Bolt's flank, and a second into Danken's hip. He cried out in pain as a third arrow took one of the guards in the shoulder. Bolt blew past the guards, knocking them aside like lawn pins. Through his pain-filled vision, Danken saw the spiraled, pearl horn emerge from Bolt's forehead. Suddenly they were simply on the other side of the gate.

"There is no way out of this place!" T'riel buzzed in front of Danken's face.

"There is!" Danken grunted.

"Boy is not thinking straight," she scolded, fluttering about his hip.

"Inside," beckoned the phantom voice.

"I can't!" Danken shouted. T'riel cocked an eyebrow at him, probably thinking him delusional.

"Safety lies within."

"Why should I trust you?" Danken looked behind him and saw the guards in hot pursuit, trapping him between them and the inner wall.

"Because you must."

The inner wall was forty feet high surrounded by a wide moat. Danken was about to rein in when Bolt simply skimmed over the water and pushed through solid stone eight feet thick, leaving no trace of their passage.

Sure they had died, Danken was shocked when he opened his eyes and found Bolt standing calmly inside a dark armory within Dvarain Keep, his horn once again only a memory. Danken painfully dismounted. He hobbled over and cracked the door to see if anyone had seen them enter. He returned to check on Bolt, wincing with every step. T'riel perched on his shoulder, arms crossed in consternation.

"This Pixie *told* Boy there was no way out of this place."

"Aye, maybe not. But something is here. Something I need."

"What?"

Danken shrugged. "I don't know, but whatever it is, it hates who-ever is after me something fierce, and that means it might know how to help me." He rubbed Bolt's flanks fondly as he worked the cross-bow bolt out. The stallion didn't make a sound. "T'riel, is Bolt a—"

"Pearly Horn," she pronounced.

"A Unicorn?"

"Of course, silly. Are Boy's eyes not working like his brain now?"

"Very funny," Danken groaned as he pulled the crossbow bolt out of his own hip. His eyes flared in the dim light as he looked at where the length of folded satin had absorbed the worst of the dam-age. The flesh wound was painful, but nothing to panic over. Danken released a tendril of blue energy into the wound, cutting off a yelp as it was cauterized, before doing the same for Bolt.

"If Boy was fast like this Pixie, he would have been able to get out of the way," T'riel informed him, performing a quick duck and dodge in the air.

"Aye, and if I was small like you, that arrow would have cut me in half."

"Hmmph." She stomped her foot on his shoulder indignantly.

Danken felt the beckoning pull at him again. He patted Bolt on the muzzle.

"Stay put until I return, my friend."

The hallways were well lit, with rich tapestries along the walls and a plush blue carpet atop the polished stone floor. Aware that he was far from in the clear, he hurried as fast as his hip would allow. The beckoning grew stronger as he descended down a steep spiral staircase to the underground levels of the Keep. Finally, he came to a narrow stone pathway leading to a doorway at the far end. On either side of the pathway was pure darkness stretching down into oblivion. He kicked a loose stone down into the abyss and waited to hear it hit bottom. It didn't.

Danken wanted to turn back. By the Gods, why had he ever come down here in the first place? He could feel the gloom trying to seep into his very bones.

"This is not *dwei*," he muttered.

"This Pixie feels it as well," T'riel agreed.

Swallowing his fear lest he choke on it, Danken cautiously edged out onto the walkway. He thought he felt it move. He took another step, then another. This time it *definitely* moved. He felt as if he were standing atop a needle resting on its point.

"Boy should hurry. He cannot fly like this Pixie."

"That's bloody helpful. Thanks for the reminder," Danken tried to gain his center of balance. When he was sure he'd found it, he sprang forward. Almost to the floating door, his foot slipped and he tumbled off the edge. Danken caught the rough edge with his hand. The rock cut into his skin. T'riel squeaked and flew below, trying to push him up by his rear. Danken would have found such an effort comical were he not about to die. He swung back and forth slightly until his momentum allowed him to grab ahold of the walkway. Summoning all of his strength, Danken heaved himself back up.

He lay there face down gasping, clutching the stone tightly until T'riel began jumping up and down on his head.

"The longer Boy stays in this place, the closer it comes."

"What?" Danken tried to stand amid the swaying walkway.

"What makes this Pixie's ears itch," she answered cryptically before buzzing over to the door. "Now come on, Boy."

"Easy for you to say," he muttered darkly.

This time Danken was able to keep his footing and literally fell through the door. He found himself in a comfortable-looking, softly-lit room with plush white carpet and several velvet chairs around a marble fireplace. A beautiful oak bookcase was flanked on either side by a life-size marble statue of a partially clothed woman Danken recognized as a Disir—guardian spirits. He peeked into an adjoining room and found it to be a heated bath with polished tiles depicting Dragons and other amazing creatures. A third room was completely empty. Only a large, pure sapphire five-pointed knot-work star inside a silver circle was inlaid into the white marble floor.

Danken felt as if he were walking up a flat wall and the circle was the ground. He gave in to the beckoning. As he stood in the center of the star, a wave of euphoria engulfed him. He closed his eyes and drank it in. Power, unfathomable to him not a tick before was his for the taking. All he had to do—

"Take a wrong turn at the kitchen?" a woman's sensual voice asked in a Lundgarder accent.

"Gods!" Danken started from his trance and stepped out of the circle. He found himself unable to speak as he faced the woman. She was barely five feet tall and her raven hair hung in a braid to her ankles tied in yellow bows. Her slender, shapely body was hardly hidden beneath a loose-fitting transparent yellow silk blouse that ended just below her breasts. Her golden pierced navel was exposed. She wore her yellow silk pants well below her hips. Her shiny, olive skin was complimented beautifully by dark, almond-shaped eyes and dozens of golden piercings in her ears, nose, eyebrows and lips. The golden bracelets around her bare arms jangled faintly as she stepped towards him.

"What? Cat got your tongue?" she asked as a large black panther slunk into the room.

"No, I—I wasn't aware this was a residence. I'm sorry if I—" Danken shut his mouth, aware that he was babbling. He wasn't sure whether to look at the beautiful woman or the rather dangerous-looking cat. T'riel fluttered onto his shoulder and examined the pair from afar.

"I assume you have some explanation, then? I am quite forgiving of ignorance, but Makuma here is less so," the strange woman patted the panther's head.

"Explanation. Right. Aye. I'm an expletive. I mean, I have an explanation."

"Do you have a face as well?"

"A face? Oh, aye. Forgive my manners," Danken pushed back his cowl, his blue eyes flaring. The woman gasped.

"Blessed Gefjon. Can it be?" She invoked her Matron Goddess. She reached up to touch Danken's face with her soft hands. After a long while she stepped back with a smile. "Your explanation is satisfactory, Danken Sariksen."

"But I didn't even tell you—"

"You do not need to."

"Are you the one that called me here?" Danken asked then.

"No. I am Tok'Neth Urishendotir, the gypsy advisor to the Council of Elders and Senator Faldri. This is my home."

"Then who?"

"In time, child," Tok'Neth then greeted T'riel in the rapid Pixian tongue. "Greetings T'riel, daughter of F'ran Spellbreaker. Your people are, as always, welcome in my abode."

"Greetings Glass Walker, our forests are ever open to you." T'riel answered formally. Danken noticed the hint of sadness that passed through her at the mention of her father.

"Come now, there will be plenty of time for questions later. You have had a hard day, no?"

"Aye."

"*Dwei,* then I will send for food. Afterwards we can talk," Tok'Neth lead Danken into a smaller room with black marble floors and black velvet curtains. In the center was a black crystal ball on a marble stand. At the far wall was a black glass mirror lined with gold. Another wall held an apothecary shelf with several sinister and magical items. The opposite wall was hung with dozens of ancient-looking weapons of all styles and metals. "Wait here, please." Tok'Neth walked directly into the mirror.

At a loss, Danken instead turned a questioning eye on T'riel. "You know her."

"Aye. All Pixies are known to Glass Walker, and she to us."

"How?"

"Glass Walker visits often. She is a friend to the trees."

"Why do you call her Glass Walker?"

T'riel shrugged. "Why does this Pixie call Boy, Boy?"

Danken arched a brow. "I'm still trying to figure that out myself."

T'riel flew off to explore. Danken found his attention inexorably drawn back to the star. Abruptly, Tok'Neth reappeared through the mirror followed by two housekarls in livery. One pushed a wheeled cart filled with steaming hot plates of food and the other carried black satin down bedding. They quickly set the table and made the cot before standing at the ready for further orders.

"Thank you," Tok'Neth entered a dining room with rich paintings and fine silver. "Shall we?"

"Aye," Danken uncomfortably took the seat the housekarl held out for him. T'riel zoomed in and plunged into the small porcelain dish of milk, honey and jasmine, slurping loudly. Danken laughed at her lack of manners but put his own on display, conscious of his every move. The honey-glazed pork was exquisite, as were the vegetables. He was shocked to find his goblet filled with mead, for this was a drink only bestowed when the host believed the drinker to be a man capable of bearing arms and children. He hid his surprise well, not letting on that it was his first drink. He silently thanked her for bestowing upon him this honor as his father could not and his mother was loathe to do.

"I have sent your steed to the Senator's private stables to be taken care of by the best groom in the Keep," Tok'Neth told him then.

"Thank you," Danken hid his surprise, wondering how she had known about Bolt. He refrained from asking if the guards were still after him. Somehow he knew all was well here.

After the servants cleared the table, Tok'Neth held her hand on the mirror in the next room, allowing both men to leave. "Send in the bathing attendants if you will." Moments later two plump older women entered carrying towels and vials of some sort. Tok'Neth beckoned Danken to follow her to the bathing chamber, where one of the attendants hustled him behind a changing curtain painted with Dragons and flowers. Soon he was naked but for a towel and lying face down on a padded table beside Tok'Neth on a table of her own. When the gypsy saw his uncomfortable look, she laughed. "Relax, it is only a massage to work out the stress of the road before washing off the dirt and sweat. You will enjoy it."

"Boy is as red as cherry blossoms in bloom," T'riel commented, standing an inch from his face. Danken exhaled sharply when he felt the attendant's strong hands on his rear. The gust of air blew T'riel off the table. She flew off in a fit.

"How long until she is full grown?" he asked.

"Pixies grow very fast. I would guess two or three years, by the time she's eight, but she won't be sexually mature for quite some time." Danken heard a furious harrumph from the other room. "They also have *very* good hearing."

"Aye," Danken nodded, then fell silent, enjoying the massage. He began formulating the long list of questions he wanted to ask, but held quiet until the massage was finished.

"You look just like him, you know," Tok'Neth told him. Danken looked up to find her already in the pool, the steam obscuring her features. He hadn't even heard her move.

"Like who?" The attendant wrapped a towel around his waist and indicated he should join Tok'Neth in the bath.

"Your father."

Danken dropped his towel in shock. "You knew my father?"

"Of course. Now, get in," she glanced down pointedly. "Lest you catch a cold."

Danken looked down, turned red and then hurried into the pool. "Forgive me, but you can't be more than five years older than I am. My father went to fight in the Great War before I was born. How is it you remember him?"

Tok'Neth laughed, wading over to him so that he could just make out her outline in the dark water.

"Thank you for your flattery, Danken, but in truth, I am two-hundred-fifty-seven years old. I knew your father only because he fought beside mine in the war. As for details, regretfully, I have none."

"But how—?"

"Magic can do strange and wonderful things, Danken. You know this." She brushed one of the silver strands of his hair away from his glowing eyes to emphasize her point.

Danken felt warmth rush through his body. He gulped loudly. Tok'Neth seemed to enjoy his shyness. He had no idea what that meant. Danken had had little experience with such things due to his appearance. Most girls knew him of mixed Faerie blood and didn't want their children to be outcasts like him, like all half-breeds. Aside from his imaginings of Tersandi, no woman had ever even shown any signs of friendship to him, let alone anything more. He sought to ask one of the many questions he had thought up to alleviate his nervousness, but found them all washed away by Tok'Neth's closeness.

"What of my clothes?" he asked instead.

"They are being washed and repaired as we speak," she ran a finger down his chest slowly.

"Am I to stay here tonight?"

"Of course. Perhaps you thought I would simply set you out in what you are wearing now?"

"No, I just—"

"Worry not, young Danken." Tok'Neth patted his face lightly before stepping out of the bath. Danken thought to look away but found his eyes riveted by the water dripping off her. The attendant wrapped her in a long white towel and began drying her off. Tok'Neth turned to regard him with a coy smile. "You are no doubt tired. We will speak more tomorrow. I hope you find your accommodations to your liking."

"Aye, thank you," Danken watched her go, confused by the exotic gypsy. Her panther gave him one last glance and then followed after her mistress. Danken dunked his head under the water to clear his mind. After a moment he got out as well, taking the towel from the attendant with embarrassed politeness, following her to his bed in the next room before she excused herself.

T'riel was on his shoulder in an instant, mocking him.

"Can this Pixie get Boy a golden pillow?"

"You're gold, and a little soft around the middle," Danken lightly poked T'riel's bare midriff with a finger. "Why don't I just use you for a pillow."

"Because Boy's dreams of Glass Walker will keep this Pixie up all night."

"Ee, but she is beautiful. I can't think straight around her," Danken confessed.

"Pfwah!" T'riel scoffed before fluttering up to the top of the bookshelf and nestling herself in a palm-sized bed, for like all her race, she loved heights. "Goodnight Boy."

"Aye, goodnight, T'riel," Danken got into bed and blew out the candles.

"Boy?"

"Aye?"

"This Pixie would be in stupid Root Twisters' greedy stomachs this night if Boy had not been there. This Pixie is grateful. Owes Boy One's life."

"You don't owe me anything, T'riel. I'm sure you would have gnawed your way out of their stomachs," Danken smiled.

"This is true," T'riel giggled.

"Sleep well."

There was to be no sleep for him, though.

"Come to me," the voice called. Danken sat up, his eyes bathing the darkness in a blue light. He felt the pull of the star stronger than ever. Careful not to wake T'riel, he made his way to the empty chamber. Rather than simply stand in the star this time, he began walking the lines, leaving a glowing blue trail of fire in his wake. Repeatedly he traced the star, feeling its power growing. *"Come to me,"* the woman whispered.

Suddenly, the circle began to spin. Danken began to walk faster to keep pace. The blue fire was like liquid running through a canal. The star seemed to suck it in like life-giving water to the desert. A rush of air filled the chamber, followed by smooth stone rolling against smooth stone. The circle became a platform, descending into the darkness below like a screw into wood. And then it was still. Silence prevailed.

Danken stopped abruptly and took stock of his surroundings. He was in a massive chamber fully two hundred yards from wall to wall and fifty feet from floor to ceiling. Massive stone pillars ran the length of the cavern in orderly rows. All was bathed in a faint blue light emanating from a massive blue block at the far end.

Danken slowly approached the block. He saw that it was a perfectly-cut sapphire, big enough for a man to lie down on. Inside was a narrow, curved sword with a single edge and an ivory hilt carved into an eagle's talon. It was a katana, an Elven Master's blade and widely regarded as being the finest sword ever forged. Three Elven runes were engraved along the base, though he couldn't decipher their meaning.

As Danken reached out to touch the sapphire, two gigantic forms emerged from the shadows only a few feet away. They were Gargoyles. Mythical beings with lion's heads, human bodies and bat's wings made of living stone. Danken's feet were rooted to the ground even as he tried to run. Gargoyles were guardians, and they did *not* take kindly to being plundered, however inadvertently.

"He seeks the sword," one rumbled, vibrating the ground.

"Like the others," the second Gargoyle's face was only inches away from Danken's own.

"Is he the one?"

"Or is he merely one of many?"

"Let us see."

"Indeed." The Gargoyle froze Danken with its glare. "Why do you seek the sword, Sendar?"

"I don't seek it. It called me. *She* called me," Danken choked out.

"Can it be?"

"Or does his mind play tricks on him?"

"Let us see."

"Indeed. What is your claim, Sendar?"

"My claim?" Danken asked.

"Birthright or deed, Sendar?"

"I don't know. I just know I was drawn here, that's all."

"Can it be that he is unaware?" The first Gargoyle asked the other.

"Or does he have no claim?"

"Let us see."

"Indeed," both Gargoyles stepped back slowly. "You have but one chance."

"One and only one."

"If the sword does not accept you..."

"...You will not live to see the sunrise."

"If you still wish to take the sword, do so now."

"If not, leave this place and never return," the second Gargoyle finished.

Danken looked at both creatures warily, sweat beaded on his forehead. He waited for the sword to give him some sort of sign, but there was nothing.

"Little help here," he muttered under his breath. "Seriously, now. Come on then." Still nothing. "Now you want to be silent. That's *dwei*. That's bloody *dwei*."

"Time grows short, Sendar," the first Gargoyle rumbled.

"Your choice must be made."

"Is he thinking?"

"Or is he frozen with fear?"

"Let us see."

"Indeed."

"All right." Danken rubbed his hands together and blew on them for luck. Saying a silent prayer to Odin for his safety, he placed his hands on the sapphire block.

Nothing happened. Danken's stomach shot up into his throat. He darted a look at the Gargoyles. Gods, he was about to die! No! It couldn't end like this! The sword had called him. *Him!* He hadn't called *it!* Suddenly, a blue flash erupted from his hands and his arms sunk into the solid sapphire. Buried to his shoulders in what felt like liquid fire, Danken began to panic. He grasped about for any sort of purchase. Then his hands grasped onto something solid. He tried to push himself out of the stone or pull himself through it.

Abruptly, he was standing beside the sapphire once more. In his hands was the magnificent katana. A pain like a million needles stabbing into his body dropped him to his knees. A blue storm of fire so bright it illuminated the entire chamber erupted from the blade. Blinking back the pain, Danken brought the sword to his forearm unbidden, pressing it there though it burned him like molten iron. Biting his tongue to keep his scream inside, Danken pulled the blade away to reveal the perfectly healed rune "5" branded into his arm. He looked to the blade for the corresponding rune but found it disturbingly absent.

Danken tried to drop the blade as the pain and light died away, but found himself unable. Instead, he hefted the magnificent sword, feeling its near weightlessness and balance. It seemed to have been made for his grasp alone, contoured to his hand. So sharp was it, that when he ran it along his palm, he saw the blood before he felt the pain. It was part of him and he of it.

Memories flashed through his mind. Places he had never seen, cities that were long since ground to dust and Elves who had returned to the forest centuries before. Danken remembered endless turns of the glass every day for decades practicing with every weapon he could imagine. *Mak'Rist,* the Fifth Render. He saw the blade being forged from an unbreakable metal called asterite fallen from the sky. He saw the beautiful Duah Mystic who had forged it, the woman whose memories were now cascading through his brain. She was *in* the sword and now she was inside him.

The Gargoyles bowed low. The block of sapphire had disappeared. In its place, was a beautiful, ornately sculpted sapphire and silver scabbard. The first Gargoyle held it out to him. Danken accepted it gravely, sliding *Mak'Rist* into it.

"Only when in the scabbard will you be able to give it rest, Sendar."

"Only when in your hands will it be swung."

"Will he be worthy?"

"Or will he fail?"

"Let us see."

"Indeed."

"Get up, lazy Boy." T'riel was perched on Danken's nose, her foot tapping impatiently.

"Oww," Danken winced, his body a mass of aches. The events of the previous night came crashing back to him. He felt the strangely comforting feel of *Mak'Rist* at his side. T'riel shook her fist at him.

"Boy scared this Pixie last night. He should *not* have gone alone."

"Aye, I know. I'm sorry, T'riel."

"This is true," She fluttered down to observe the sword as Danken slid it from its scabbard. "This is Boy's now?"

"Aye. It bonded to me last night, though I'm still not sure why."

"Bonded?" She cocked her head to the side. Danken showed her the rune branded into his forearm.

"Aye, we are as one now."

"Ah," T'riel nodded in comprehension.

"I knew you were the one she had been waiting for from the first moment that I laid eyes on you, Danken Sariksen." Tok'Neth entered the room wearing a transparent white silk morning gown. Danken struggled to maintain eye contact. She stroked his hair gently. "How do you feel?"

"Better than I did when I thought those Gargoyles were going to kill me."

"Aye, I am sure you do." Tok'Neth stood on her toes to kiss him on the cheek. "But all is well now. Come, I'll have breakfast brought down."

As they ate, Danken noticed that T'riel was wearing a brand new golden satin dress that cut off just below her hips, a pair of golden, pointy-tipped shoes and a golden cloak.

"Oh, I hope you do not mind, Danken," Tok'Neth said when she saw his confused look. "The satin you bought was ruined by the arrow you took, so, seeing as T'riel had no wardrobe, I had one made for her from the undamaged pieces."

"Four other pairs, this Pixie has," T'riel twirled around so Danken could get a better look. "And a sleeping roll, too," she added proudly.

"Dwei," Danken smiled. "Thank you, Tok'Neth."

"I didn't forget you either," Tok'Neth signaled for one of the servers to fetch Danken's clothes. Danken was shocked by the change. His freshly-cleaned baggy deerskin pants looked as if the animal still wore them, the white spots and golden-browns contrasting beautifully. The tight, forest-green woolen shirt that had been threadbare was now a richly woven royal blue and turtle-necked. His leather gloves, belt, sword and bow straps were oiled and his bow was polished and re-stained. Most impressive of all was the cloak Tersandi had given him. It was back to its original pristine blue. The inside was lined with silver satin sewn around a fresh layer of down and the cowl was starched. Danken dressed, reveling in the feel of his new satin underclothes and the burnished look of his worn attire.

"Tok'Neth, I don't know what to say."

"Say nothing. We cannot have the bearer of *Mak'Rist,* the son of Sarik Blanesen, looking like he is a simple forester, now can we?"

"But, I *am* a simple forester."

"Not anymore, Danken."

"Are you even real?" Danken asked after a moment of digestion.

"Of course I am," Tok'Neth laughed. "Why would you think otherwise?'

"Because you've done so much for me. You've been nothing but nice to me even though you don't know me. And, the only other woman I've ever met who was as beautiful as you was a Valkyrie."

"How flattering. Aye, I am real, Danken Sariksen, and when you get older and wiser in the ways of the world, you can come back and I will prove it to you." Tok'Neth planted a long soft kiss on his lips, winking mischievously when she finished. Danken blushed. T'riel paused from noisily finishing off her dish to roll her eyes.

"Silly Boy," she said in Pixian.

"Silly yourself," he glared at her before turning back to Tok'Neth, who was feeding the leftover bacon to Makula. "We should be going now if we want to reach the forest edge by dark."

"Aye," Tok'Neth nodded. "I will make sure your mount is ready."

Danken smiled and began making his way towards the door, steeling himself for the perilous crossing once more.

"Danken," Tok'Neth shook her head. "That way is only for unwanted visitors. My guests come and go through the mirror."

"Oh, aye," Danken nodded, chagrined, coming to stand by the black glass mirror, which Tok'Neth opened by pressing her hand on it. Danken hugged her. "Goodbye, Tok'Neth. Thank you for everything. I will make it up to you, I promise."

"Goodbye, Danken. And if you want to make it up to me, when you see him, tell my father that I will be expecting him for Yule Tithe this year and no excuses. I have a feeling you two will meet soon."

"Aye," Danken agreed, hiding his confusion.

T'riel performed her best hug on Tok'Neth's ear, spouting some Pixian farewell, which the gypsy returned in kind.

"I will send my friend Arn Brynsen to take care of anymore of those assassins that might want to target you. Gods be with you."

"And you," Danken said as he stepped through the mirror and into Bolt's stables. Immediately he felt the prying eyes searching for him, but *Mak'Rist* banished them as quickly as they had come. Danken knew then that he was a part of something much bigger than he was. Only time would tell if he was big enough to face it.

CHAPTER 4
A SHADOWY PLAN

elin'Bak's portal opened in the middle of the only tavern in the small village of Lok Tryst. Five hard, farm-raised men rose in shock at his arrival, their chairs skidding back loudly. He observed them with red eyes he kept from glowing set into a middle aged Sendar face, topped with long grey-tinged brown hair. A pointy nose and a jagged scar across his lips were the only noticeable features on the sun-browned skin.

Five tiny trickles of red fire seeped unnoticed along the creaking wooden floor into the men, making them more susceptible to his every command. With a youthful voice, he addressed the stunned group in flawless Sendar, though with an unplaceable accent.

"My friends, there is an evil amongst the people of your village, tainting the very air you breathe, poisoning the water you drink. Perhaps you have felt it?"

"Aye." One man spoke up, a suspicious glint in his eyes. "I believe I may have."

"Ah," Kelin'Bak nodded, lulling them further into his deception with his seeming honesty. "So you have felt it as well, penetrating your bones at night. Perhaps you have seen the one who does its bidding?"

The men looked at each other, thinking hard on who it could be. They shook their heads.

"He is hiding behind the façade of a hardworking family boy." Kelin'Bak said, melting their intense gazes with the intensity of his own. "What if I were to tell you that as we speak, he is busy subverting your sons, daughters and wives to his malevolent cause?"

"The bastard!" one man shouted.

"Aye! He'll not get away with it!" another shouted. "By the Gods he won't."

"Tell us his name and we'll take ye to him!"

Kelin'Bak smiled inwardly. "His name cannot be spoken aloud. It is far too violent for the tongues of honest men. I shall describe him to you and you will take me to him."

Kelin'Bak followed the men past the town hall, where most of the village's people were assembled or shopping. Seeing their drawn swords, the constable stopped their angry procession with a wave.

"Where're you headed to in such an anger?"

"To kill the Demonspawn and his protectors!" Torvald rattled his sword.

"Aye!" the rest of the group yelled.

"The stead hidden by the two dead oaks?" the constable asked.

"Aye," Torvald nodded, Kelin'Bak remaining inconspicuously in the background.

"I've had my suspicions about that one for awhile now. Go on then. You'll have no trouble from me." The constable stepped aside.

The group marched off towards the secluded stead. With the Sorcerer's red fire driving them on, even the branches scratching their faces and arms could only hold them back for so long. Towards mid-day, they finally found what they were looking for. With a great roar, they charged the stead.

A worn, but still attractive woman looked up from milking the stead's cow. Seeing the drawn swords and vicious looks on the men, she bolted for the relative safety of the small grey house. Once inside, she hurriedly locked the door and grabbed a long pitchfork.

Kelin'Bak stormed around, screaming at the men.

"She is harboring him! Will you let her go unpunished?"

"Never!" Torvald shouted.

"Kill the Demonspawn!"

"She cannot be allowed to live!" Kelin'Bak's eyes blazed.

"Stay away from him!" the woman shouted.

"Burn it," Kelin'Bak ordered.

One of the men sparked a clutch of the hay, and the rest set about lighting the house on fire. The woman screamed at them to leave but

Kelin'Bak only laughed, killing all of the livestock with his sparkling blade.

"Harboring Demonspawn is the same as being one, witch!" Torvald declared.

As the house burned, Kelin'Bak whirled on the five men, eyes boring into them. In his glee, his concentration slipped and his disguise faded away. His true appearance left the men in silent shock.

He was but a boy, with spiked black hair and lips with burning red eyes. His features were unmistakably Mai'Lang as was his clothing. Long black robes with red trimming ended in high, expensive boots. His red palms raised and he leveled a devastating blast of red fire into the burning stead, bringing the roof down with a loud crash.

"There is no place in this village for Demonspawn," he told the now terrified men. "Else all your children will turn against you to serve him." At the edge of the clearing, some of the townsfolk had gathered. With an evil smile, he bowed. "You may thank me when your village returns to the way it was before the Demonspawn corrupted you."

Knowing that his enemies would be able to detect his magic use on the Northern continent, the Sorcerer opened his portal and disappeared through it. The five men left, the townspeople following quietly behind, none daring to look back, none daring to help.

Jet watched his father leading the angry group through the village with suspicion. He had seen that look on his father's face often enough to know it meant something terrible was in store for someone. Jet didn't recognize the dark haired man attempting to blend into the group. Still, what his father did or didn't do mattered little to him as long as it kept him away from their home. The man was insane and had never displayed anything that might even hint at a conscience. The less Jet was around or involved with him, the better. The safer, anyway.

Since he had been a boy, Jet had watched his father beat his mother every night and then turn on him and his sisters. His mother was now but a pale shadow of her former beauty and brilliance, as if her desire to live had fled her. Jet felt anger welling up inside him laced with fear so strong it was near panic. He shook himself and wiped the cold sweat from his forehead. Cursing himself for his weakness, Jet fled into the woods. At first he thought to head to his cottage, but a strange tingling on the back of his neck made him decide to head east. The forest was unnaturally quiet. Keeping his eyes open for any hint of danger, he pulled out a hatchet from either side of his waist. Each had a polished steel head as long as his palm with a razor sharp edge. Varnished redwood handles curved sinuously to come flush with his forearms as if they had grown out from them.

A raven's call startled him. Jet turned to locate it. Instead of remaining perched, or flying away from sure danger, the raven glided to the ground not ten feet in front of him. It cocked its head at him, as if expecting an answer to some unasked question. Jet furrowed his brows at the bird, then looked all around him for any other signs of life. When he looked back, a stunning black-haired woman dressed in skintight black leather and an ankle-length black cloak stood in the raven's place. Her eyes were completely white and her features slightly more angular than any he'd seen before. More stunning was her red palms and black lips.

Though Jet had never seen one before he knew this woman was Mai'Lang. She smiled enticingly at him, her copper skin seeming to catch every tiny ray of sun that made it through the thick forest canopy. His knuckles were white on his hatchets, yet he could do nothing but stare. Finally she spoke in a slight staccato accent.

"My, my Norseman," Hrafna flashed a sultry smile. "The High One told me you were pretty but even I am taken aback. Such a pity to waste such a gift on the meager residents of this village. Where I come from, one such as yourself would be privileged to be a noble lady's consort. Perhaps even to serve the Empress herself."

"I serve *no one,* Mai'Lang," Jet retorted angrily at her audacity.

"A temper as well?" she fanned her face with a razor-edged black fan. "This is too good to be true."

"What are you doing here? You know your kind aren't allowed on the Northern continent."

"I go where I please, Sendar. None can stop me."

"We will see."

"You would kill me for being in your forest?" she asked, arching a thin eyebrow at him. The smile never left her face even as a second deadly metal fan appeared in the other hand.

"Aye. As would you if you caught me wandering through yours," he replied coldly.

"But would you do it without first hearing what I have to say?" She took a few graceful steps towards him. He could just feel her breath on his neck. "Besides, there are many things one such as I could do for you, Jetrian Torvaldsen," she spoke his name huskily. Jet swallowed nervously. How did she know his name?

"What kind of things?" he asked unsteadily, trying to get himself back under control.

"Many things," Hrafna repeated, running a finger along his jaw.

"What is it you want?"

"You."

"Why me?"

"You have been noticed."

"Noticed? Woman, what nonsense do you speak? Stop talking in veiled terms and tell me why you are here. You aren't scared of me, else you would have just flown off, which by the way I'll soon be finding out how you did. So, what is your purpose?"

"Right to the point, and resistant to my charm. I like this."

"You are pushing your luck, Mai'Lang," His grip tightened around the hatchets.

"Very well. What do you know of Loki?"

"The God?"

"What other is there?" she nodded.

"He's the Trickster, the Bringer of Chaos." Jet answered like a schoolboy. Too much so for his liking.

"Not Chaos, Sendar, *change*. He is the Balance between Chaos and Order."

"Lies."

"Not so, ignorant woodsman. Let me give you an example you should be familiar with. When a forest fire wipes out an old forest, what is left?"

"The old, hard trees that have grown resistant."

"Very good. In this case, pretend those old trees are the foundations upon which Midgarthe is built. Unshakable, indestructible. Now what good comes from a forest fire? All the seeds and baby plants that were blocked from the sun are allowed to grow and the forest begins anew, stronger than if was before."

"That's all well and good but—"

"But nothing. Since the Great War, Order has grown stronger. The Balance must be maintained. New trees must be allowed to grow."

"Fine. But what does this have to do with me?"

"You attract his attention, just as I did. And I have been well rewarded for my services."

"And what did you get?" Jet asked, hating himself for his curiosity.

"You've seen one of my gifts already."

"The raven?" he asked.

"Aye," Hrafna answered, assessing him as he would a deer through the sights of his bow.

"And what are the others?" He despised having to drag information from her and hated himself even more for wanting to do so.

"Unlike you, I was not born with the gift of beauty and seduction. Now I have both and I'll never grow old so long as I maintain my usefulness. Think of it as what your heart has always wanted, handed to you in exchange for your devotion to the continued existence of the world. Is that such a bad thing?"

"What would I have to do to 'maintain my usefulness'?" Jet asked. Dangers and possibilities swirled around uncontrollably inside of his head.

"Attach yourself to the Sariksen. So long as he lives, you will have whatever you wish. Steer him in the direction change necessitates."

"Danken? Why would I waste my time with him?"

"It may surprise you to know that he will one day be a very important man on this continent, possibly the entire world. Managed properly, he will be a great asset to the High One. You will be his agent."

"Danken doesn't even like me and knows the feeling is *more* than reciprocated. What makes you think he will accept my sudden companionship? Besides, what am I supposed to do, twiddle my thumbs while he plows fields and milks cows?" Jet laughed, sure now this woman was nothing more than some lunatic wanderer. Pretty, though, he could always...

"It will be taken care of." Hrafna brushed her black lips against his neck. She fixed him with a stare that made him feel as if she were towering over him though he was far taller. "As for the methods, those will come. A situation will soon arise in which you will have the opportunity to kill two birds with one stone. Whether you act upon it is purely up to you, pretty one."

"You're telling me I'm just going to know what to do and when to do it?" Jet asked skeptically.

"Enough questions, pretty one. Do you agree to the terms?"

Jet inhaled sharply, feeling his stomach clench. What she said interested him more than he cared to admit, but was it real? He knew he could not trust her. He trusted no one. Not even his own blood. Trust was weakness. He had learned that long ago. Did the Trickster God really feel a kinship with him? More importantly, what would happen to him if he refused? Gods, immortality? To assume the careless ease of a bird? No, he could not turn the offer down. Besides, if she betrayed him, he could always kill her.

"Agreed," he said hoarsely.

"Excellent, my little Jetrian. Take this." Hrafna handed him a silver amulet with a single black ruby at its center. "There are only two in the entire world and I wear the other. It is what gives you the power of the High One."

Unbidden, Jet placed the amulet against his chest where his skin seemed to swallow it. His knees gave out unexpectedly and his head spun out of control. The whole world became a sickening blur as he felt nausea overtake him. The forest melted into a grotesque menagerie of mismatched colors. He tried to scream, but no sound escaped the twisted rictus of his lips. Without warning, he began vomiting so violently that he couldn't draw breath. It seemed to last forever. Dimly, he became aware of a pink slime of some sort covering him from head to toe. What was happening to him? he thought frantically.

Just when he was sure he had died, clean, cool, blessed air filled his burning lungs. He gasped for several ticks before shakily rising. Looking to where he had retched, he was shocked to see that there was nothing there. The forest was as it had been. He was no longer covered in the slick substance he could so vividly remember. The woman stood unmoving, not an eyelash out of place.

"Wh-what just happened?" he sputtered.

"You were reborn and invested with what you had wished for."

"But I never—"

"One cannot keep secrets from our God, Jetrian."

He scowled. "Stop calling me that. My name is Jet."

"As you wish, Jet. You may call me Hrafna."

"The raven?" Jet arched an eyebrow. "That's bloody original."

"You will know my true name when you are ready, Sendar. Until then, Hrafna will do. Now, look for yourself. See what our God has given you."

Jet rested his hands on his hatchets as was his habit, but they felt odd to him and he jerked them out. Each was covered in solid asterite so shiny he could see his reflection in them from edge to edge. He found that his throwing knives—all eighteen of them—were similarly coated, yet still perfectly balanced. Hatchets and knife handles alike were tightly wrapped in a black, patterned leather of fine make and firm grip.

"Our God wishes you to be well armed, for your struggles ahead are many. Also, your weapons must be the equal of the Sariksen's if you are to accompany him as such."

"I feel no different inside. Should I?" In response, Hrafna ripped a deep gash in his face with a metallic thumbnail. Jet drew back to kill her for marring his flawless features, but in the reflection of his hatchets, he saw the wound heal right in front of his eyes, leaving no scar. *"Dwei,"* Jet laughed.

"Once you are ready," she continued, unfazed. "You will be able to fly like me." She hooked her arm within his as if they were old friends. "Come pretty one, I have much to teach you before your work begins tomorrow. Let me tell you about the Oracles of Fyrdn…"

CHAPTER 5
ORPHANS

elin'Bak stepped out of his portal into a red-torch lit room. Dak'Verkat looked up from the scrying crystal in front of him. His feet rested comfortably on the corpse of the Sendar man who had been the home's owner. The Sorcerer touched the tip of his feather-pen to his black lips in contemplation. Kelin'Bak waited patiently for his mentor to acknowledge his presence as the portal snapped shut. Dak'Verkat motioned with his finger and a chair scooted across the floor. Kelin'Bak took it and summoned a cup of tea as he sat.

"The boy was not there, as you suspected."

"The boy has no reason to stay in the village now, I trust?"

"He does not." Kelin'Bak smiled wickedly.

"I would have preferred to use her as a bargaining tool, but, no matter. He will be forced to leave at any rate. The Oracles call him now," Dak'Verkat mused.

"And his sister?"

"Still hidden from me."

"Can we be sure she still possesses the Jade Oracle?"

"Hrafna placed it on the girl's person herself. The Oracle's magic will not allow the girl to discard except under threat or death. Still, we will be able to find it even if she has lost it."

"And the other two?"

"I cannot see those who possess them, but their magic will lead the boy where we need even if all other plans fail. Speaking of which…" Dak'Verkat peered into the black glass of the scrying crystal, revealing a Pixie fluttering around an empty space.

"It must be he," Kelin'Bak breathed. "And he has not yet changed."

"And as such we cannot see him."

"How will you deal with him if you can neither see nor feel him?"

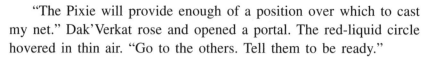

"The Pixie will provide enough of a position over which to cast my net." Dak'Verkat rose and opened a portal. The red-liquid circle hovered in thin air. "Go to the others. Tell them to be ready."

"It will be so."

Danken pushed Bolt to his limits. The unicorn raced across the gently rolling hills like a streak of white lightning. The black-robed men had been waiting for him outside the city's gates. Bolt had easily outdistanced their smaller black steeds, but Danken could feel the unseen eyes on him and he knew it was only a matter of time. They would be able to track him now. He had to get to his stead and get his mother. They would have to leave the Pixian Forest. It was no longer safe for them here.

By late afternoon, he had reached the edge of the forest. T'riel shot up into the sky to search for signs of ambush or pursuit. Danken dismounted to give Bolt a chance to rest and to stretch his legs. He pulled *Mak'Rist* free of its scabbard as he warily scanned the forest ahead. The skill with which he held the blade was so obviously not his own that he felt like a different person when he held it. Danken laughed nervously at the feeling. He swung the blade experimentally, reveling in the feeling of air splitting around it.

Danken felt a burning sensation on his arm and knew without looking it was the rune glowing excitedly in concert with the blade. At first, he thought it just a natural reaction to the blade but T'riel's shriek in his ear told him differently. He followed her tiny finger to a figure emerging from the forest. His eyes flared brightly in order to get a better look.

At first glance, it appeared to be a small child wearing a filthy cloak. The hunched figure slowly raised up to his full height. His cowl fell away as he did so, to reveal an ancient man with thin, wispy white hair matted to his small head. A crooked, liver-spotted nose stuck out from his gaunt face. But most disturbing of all were his eyes. Set deep in the sockets, they burned an unholy red. When he spoke, his voice sent shivers up Danken's spine.

"So, this is the boy from the Foretelling. The one who will bring back the Gods." Long, bony fingers reached out towards Danken's face, but his eyes kept searching, as if he were blind. A bolt of gold fire singed them, causing the ancient to hastily withdraw it. T'riel buzzed angrily over Danken's shoulder.

Danken sensed a tremendous surge of energy forming inside the red-eyed man and an anger directed more than just at the Pixie. The Sigil on Danken 's arm began to burn furiously, causing him to raise his sword in response.

"Your deceptions will not work here, Dark Tithe. Only death will you find." Danken's voice flew unbidden from his mouth and he knew *Mak'Rist* had spoken through him.

The ancient let out a hair-raising cackle. "Who's to harm me? The Pixie? Certainly not you, *boy*." Danken could feel him preparing to lash out with all of his furious energies, as if he were preparing to lay a trap or throw some type of magical net. Still, the old man couldn't seem to focus on him, and that was Danken's advantage.

Unthinkingly, Danken brought *Mak'Rist* down in a deadly arc. The ancient seemed unaware of the attack, or else was caught unprepared by it. He was unable to recall the energies he had begun to unleash. In the moment *Mak'Rist* struck the ancient's wrist, the foul red fire was deflected back through him ten-fold. His severed hand dropped to the ground while the rest of him shot backward as if fired from a ballistae.

"The Fifth Render! It cannot be!" The old man screeched in reference to *Mak'Rist*. "This is not the end, boy!"

Danken watched astounded as the ancient turned into a huge black owl in mid-air and took flight. Danken noticed one of the wings was missing its tip. The second hand was still wriggling. Danken raised his blade to strike it, but it exploded into hundreds of black and red spiders, which scattered all directions.

"Gods!" Danken yelped. He hated spiders. Fortunately, they had no interest in him and he soon lost sight of them.

The Sigil had stopped burning, reassuring him that the threat of danger was passed. T'riel landed on his shoulder with a sigh, breathing heavily.

"Are you all right?" he asked.

"Aye, tired. Gold spark takes much out of One."

"I didn't know you could do that. I guess I still have a lot to learn about your kind."

"This is true," she agreed haughtily. Danken rolled his eyes.

If Danken had expected the journey through the forest to be quiet and uneventful, he was in for a surprise. Apparently, the murder of T'riel's parents and her subsequent kidnapping had sparked a full scale war between the Pixies and the Gnomes. Bolts of gold fire shot through the canopy at swarms of fiendish, gnarled targets, eliciting screams of agony. Likewise, root monsters snaked along the ground and through the branches of trees, clutches of poisonous barbs poised to rain death upon the hated Pixies.

Bolt stamped angrily at the ground and Danken had to release tiny currents of blue energy into him to calm him, urging him to make all speed through the forest. The battle had left the path in disrepair, making the going difficult and slow. T'riel flew ahead, zapping anything that moved.

After close to eight turns of the glass of nonstop running, Danken knew that Bolt would have to stop. They were only halfway through the forest and Danken had to face the fact that they would have to set up camp. He slowed Bolt's pace to a trot that soon found them at a stream. Danken allowed Bolt to drink and found some flat ground to pitch a tent. T'riel helped by gathering a sizeable amount of dry kindling, while Danken gathered deadwood and set about arranging it into a circle which he bordered with stones, placing a *Warding* rune in the middle.

He hadn't seen any signs of Pixies or Gnomes for close to half a glass, but he was taking no chances. He kept his sword drawn. T'riel buzzed about for a few moments before giving him an all clear. Danken sparked the fire and soon was roasting a beef and vegetable stew. He set out a generous portion of oats and tack for Bolt and gave T'riel the dish of milk and honey she thrived on. By the time he had finished eating, T'riel had scouted again and was sleeping in his pocket.

Danken unrolled his bedroll and lay down, determined to sleep through the eerily silent night, trusting the Sigil to wake him in case of danger. He had scarcely closed his eyes when he felt the familiar burning. He found himself standing with *Mak'Rist* at the ready. T'riel peeked out of his pocket. "Root Twisters come."

"Aye." Danken's eyes flared.

Suddenly, as if materialized from the shadow of the humid night, they were surrounded by a dozen ugly, gnarled faces. The knee-high Gnomes brandished wicked-looking blades. T'riel shot out of concealment and began raining some sort of golden powder on the Gnomes. The Gnomes fell about scratching themselves furiously. Itching powder. Danken kicked a prone Gnome so hard it flew out of the clearing. It landed with a distinctive crack that heralded a broken neck.

The Gnomes quickly regrouped. Despite the fierce itching, the largest of the group had gained control and was barking orders in his gravelly voice. T'riel had marked him long before now and released a shattering bolt of gold fire that hit him squarely in the face. The Gnome dropped dead where he stood. The others stared dumbly at him for a fatal instant before they realized Danken was among them cutting through their ranks like butter. The Gnomes had the presence of mind to raise their root monsters. Giant, deformed limbs of long dead trees quickly sprouted out of the ground, firing their poisonous needles. Danken dodged the volley and managed to cut the roots out of the air, leaving them writhing violently on the ground, green ooze spilling out onto the forest floor.

A Gnome snuck in behind Danken and slashed the back of his thigh, nearly hamstringing him. Danken let out a howl of pain and pitched forward. He knew he was dead where he lay. The Gnome would slit his throat any moment. And anyway, he thought with despair, their blades were coated with poison, which would finish him off slowly and painfully even if the Gnome did not. Danken gritted his teeth in anticipation of the blow. It never came.

He risked a look backward. The Gnome was dead, a smoking hole in his chest. Just beyond him was a full-grown Pixie (though he was only two inches taller than T'riel) with a golden arrow aimed at Danken's head.

T'riel's voice gave the Pixie pause. "No, Boy is this Pixie's friend."

"What would Little Pixie know of friends? He is Sendar. They know no loyalties." The Pixie and a dozen others had him in their sights. To his left, he saw that one of the Gnomes was still wriggling on the ground. A bolt of golden fire from one of the Pixies ended his misery.

"Wait," Danken spoke in the Pixian tongue. "I am not your enemy. T'riel is my friend."

The Pixie looked shocked. "T'riel? Daughter of F'ran?"

"Aye, Boy saved this Pixie from Root Twisters and killed one." T'riel drew her finger along her neck like a knife.

The other Pixies fixed Danken with their fiery golden gazes. They swarmed over him like fireflies, perching on his leg and examining the wound. They spoke under their voices in their fast tongue, pointing and nodding. Then, they broke into some sort of healing chant, one after the other unleashing a burning golden tendril of energy into his leg, killing the poison and healing it in less than a quarter-glass. The lead Pixie walked in front of him, standing eye to eye with Danken, who was still prone.

"This Pixie's name is Z'nair. One offers Sendar his sincerest thanks for saving T'riel. Sendar will be given safe passage to wherever it is he chooses to go."

"Thank you," was all Danken could muster.

"T'riel," Z'nair turned to T'riel, "This Pixie offers his humble home. One has two sprouts Young Pixie's age. Young Pixie can stay with One's sprouts until she has grown."

"This Pixie thanks Z'nair, but One wishes to stay with clumsy Boy. Bonded to him, this Pixie is." T'riel sounded like an elder statesman more than a young Pixie.

"Bonded?" Z'nair sounded shocked. "But how?"

"Look in Boy's eyes," An older female Pixie flew forward. "What is this child's full name?" she asked of Danken. He found it odd to be called child by a being the size of his hand.

"Danken Sariksen." The Pixies exploded into a hushed but very excited conversation. He heard them call T'riel 'Guiding One' and something about someone called Darkperil. Finally, the Pixies turned to him. The older female spoke.

"Darkperil bears the Gift. How odd that it should pass from Tree to Sprout."

"Gift? Did you know my father?"

"All Pixies know of Silent Step. All Faerie races must. Silent Step led Blue Fires in the Great War between Light and Dark eighteen leaf falls ago. Does Darkperil not know of him or the Great War?" Danken shook his head.

"D'Sane, that is enough for now. One cannot interfere with Darkperil. These Pixies must move quickly." Z'nair cut in. The Pixies looked once more to T'riel who nodded, then disappeared through the trees.

Something was wrong.

"Forest Eater," T'riel whispered. Danken urged Bolt to a gallop.

When they crested the last forested hill before the stead and witnessed the utter destruction, Danken nearly fainted. The black plume of smoke he had seen from a distance was now cascading from the remnants of his blackened stead, like a beacon of death and misery.

"No!" he yelled, urging Bolt to an all out sprint.

By the time they reached the stead, the fire was already burnt out, smoke emanating from the smoldering ruins. Around the other side Danken caught sight of a blackened fabric on the ground. He ran toward it and saw that it was the apron his mother wore when she cooked.

And she was wearing it. Danken dropped heavily to his knees beside her, dizzy with fear. Her eyes were closed but Danken could hear her breathing. He shook her.

"Ma! Ma, please get up! Please!" She stirred, her eyes fluttering open.

"Danken?" she asked weakly, her blackened face etched with pain.

"Aye, it's me, I'm back. What happened?"

"A red-eyed man came by with some people from town. He said you were a demon." She coughed again. "They burned the house down with me inside. I barely made it out." She finished with another hacking cough. Her wheezing grew louder. Danken had to fight to retain control of himself long enough to help her.

"Ma, why would he say I'm a demon?" he squeezed her hand fiercely.

"Because you're different, Danken. Your destiny is the destiny of the world. You will understand someday, my Little Sapphire. A man your father knew named Bryn Varinsen will find you. He will," she coughed again so harshly Danken feared she wouldn't be able to breath. When she recovered, her voice was scarcely a whisper. "He will teach you of your destiny." She smiled up at him and gave his hand one last squeeze before her eyes glazed over. He heard her last earthly breath escape from her parched lips.

"No, Ma." Danken begged. "Please, don't go," but he knew she was already gone. He felt T'riel on his shoulder. She released a ten-dril of gold energy into him, making some of the ache go away and letting him know she was sorry.

"One is sorry she could not help her. This Pixie's healing skill has not fully developed yet," she told him.

"It's all right, T'riel," Danken sniffed, letting his tears flow freely. "I just don't understand why. She never harmed any of them. But I will."

CHAPTER 6
VENGEANCE

oy has death in his eyes," T'riel remarked as they rode away from the smoldering funeral pyre, leaving the cart, the stead and Danken's life behind.

"Aye."

"Will Boy kill those responsible?"

"Aye." To this, T'riel merely nodded. She too had felt this, and Danken had killed one of those responsible for her parents' death as well. Danken looked at her.

"T'riel," he asked tentatively, "do you think a person is evil if he seeks vengeance?" T'riel considered the question.

"No, this Pixie understands. Sometimes it is necessary. Though Boy should be careful not to become that which he seeks vengeance upon."

"T'riel, the more I talk to you, the more I begin to doubt your infancy. You speak like someone much older."

"Pixies mature quickly," was her evasive response. The rest of the ride passed silently as Danken contemplated his course. In the end, he chose to go with what the situation demanded, for all the planning in the world wouldn't prepare him for what was to come. The cold morning air exhaled from his lungs in clouds of vapor. The sky was grey, as if in mourning.

The tiny village of Lok Tryst sat in a valley created by the lake it was named after. Danken rode into town slowly. The streets were empty. He remembered it was the day of the Thing. The Thing was a weekly town meeting. Only men were allowed to speak. The women were *supposed* to stay at home, finishing their chores and tending to the young ones. In truth, they often held their own Thing, right alongside the men.

When Danken reached the Thingstead, his knees felt weak. He questioned his resolve. He had never killed another Sendar before. Out of the corner of his eye, he caught a flash of silver—a piece of the satin he had bought to make his mother a dress. His jaw steeled and his eyes flashed a dangerous blue.

The constable of Lok Tryst was a fat, unfriendly man who had never shown Danken or his mother the least bit of respect. His greasy hair was matted to his balding head and his beady eyes were permanently squinted against the weight of his brow. As Danken approached the Thingstead, the constable moved to intercept him. Danken dismounted. He strode toward the man impassively, ignoring the hate on his fat face.

"Where do ye think ye're goin, Demonspawn?" The constable sprayed brown spittle. Without breaking stride, Danken drew *Mak'Rist* and decapitated him. The warm spray of blood hit him in the face. He blasted open the doors to the Thingstead with his blue fire, striding inside. He pointed *Mak'Rist* at Bjorn.

"Who is to blame for my mother's death?" Danken shot a bolt of blue fire into the stunned man's mouth. "Do not lie." The hall was silent as Bjorn pointed to a group of men. Their eyes grew wide with anger.

"We were just deciding the matter, Danken. I am terribly sorry for your loss. I did not witness the act, nor do I condone it, but from what I am told, it was these five who were lead by the one with the red eyes. I know not where he went after."

"The rest of you will leave now," Danken ordered.

"Hold on one damned second," called a storeowner, shaking his finger at Danken. "You have no right." *Mak'Rist* moved so quickly that he was left staring at the bloody stump of his finger.

"There will be no negotiations. Those five or all of you." The remaining dozen or so men filed past him, some with hate in their eyes, some with understanding, some with fear. Danken faced the murderers. They drew their blades and circled him. The Sigil burned his arm. Danken, his thoughts with *Mak'Rist,* in response. It was like becoming a living weapon. Instinctively, he knew the positions of all five and their plan of attack. He could feel the sword's angry pulse. He could feel Fyrdn's wrath.

The biggest man lunged as a short man cut low. Danken jumped and deflected the big man's sword thrust. He placed *Mak'Rist* behind his head and deflected a third, fat attacker's strike, while spinning around to disembowel the big man. He brought the sword back up to parry two attacks before once again taking the offensive. He ran another murderer through, in the process using him to block two more attacks.

Danken wrenched *Mak'Rist* free and leaped backward over a bench, forcing the three remaining attackers to spread out. Once he was satisfied with their separation, he leapt back over the bench and crossed swords with his nearest opponent. Pushing his blade down, Danken brought *Mak'Rist* around and cut the man from waist to throat.

Realizing that they were going to die, the two remaining men made for the door. Danken was quicker. He cut the slower of the two down from behind, filleting him like a fish at market.

Torvald burst through the Thingstead's tall double doors. He looked for someone to help him. Danken moved steadily, inexorably forward, his flaming blue eyes promising death. Gratefully, Torvald saw his son running up the steps, wicked looking hatchets in hand. His eyes went from panicked to malicious at the sight of his well trained offspring. Danken's eyes narrowed dangerously.

"Jetrian!" Torvald called out. "I knew you wouldn't leave your old man to die!" His smile was maniacal. "Come! Together we will kill the Demonspawn!"

As Jet neared, he glanced at Danken. The pain in the youth's bloodshot grey eyes mirrored his own.

"He is not the Demonspawn, Torvald," Jet said in a quiet, deadly voice. *"You* are. This is for my mother and my sisters," Jet buried a hatchet deep in his father's chest. Torvald gurgled, blood trickling from his mouth. His dark eyes stared confusedly at Jet's enraged face. "And this is for me!" The second hatchet took his father in the neck, the lifeless body tumbled down the wooden steps. "They will be safe now. And happier without you!"

Jet collapsed then, still clutching the bloody hatchets as if they were his only link to his sanity. Sobs racked his body so violently that Danken had to hold him to keep him from seriously injuring himself. Kierna rushed up the steps, burying her face in Jet's chest. It was a long while before Danken rose uncertainly. He cleaned *Mak'Rist* with a scrap of cloth before sheathing it. The people of Lok Tryst stared silently at the grisly scene.

"I'm sorry Jet. For all of this," Danken whispered, "but I must go. This place is no longer my home."

"Where will you go?" Kierna asked, unsuccessfully trying to hide her tearstained face. She was a hard woman and in her eyes, emotions were a sign of weakness.

"South. I can't put a name to it, but I know the way. Gods be with you both," Danken retreated towards Bolt. The crowd parted before him. Jet caught his sleeve, bringing him up short.

"Where you go, Sariksen, I go."

"The Blood Debt is paid, Jet. You carried it out yourself. You owe me nothing."

"I go."

"As you wish," Danken sighed. "But I leave now, with the clothes on my back and little else."

"I am ready."

As the two headed for their horses, Danken saw Kierna having a bitter argument with Bjorn and her mother. Kierna stalked off in mid-conversation, mounting her brown mare hastily.

"What are you waiting for? We should go if we hope to find shelter before dark," Kierna said, guiding her horse to Danken's side. She adjusted the long bow on her back as if the matter was settled.

"Kierna, I—"

"Don't try to dissuade me, Danken. I can take care of myself."

"But why?"

"My reasons are my own," she snapped. "Must we have this conversation again?"

"I don't really think it's such a good—"

"How much coin do you have?"

"Enough," Danken answered defensively, wondering how she had pulled anger from the recent sadness.

"Enough to see you to what? The next village?" She shook a leather pouch apparently filled with gold.

"Fine, if it will get me out of here before sundown, you can come."

"Danken," Bjorn called. "Do you plan to return?"

"No."

"Then take this," Bjorn handed him a sack of gold coins that matched Kierna's.

"I can't accept this from you. I've done nothing to deserve it."

"For your farmland. I realize this is less than it's worth but it's all I have at the moment. And for a debt to you I've left too long unpaid."

"Very well." Danken bowed his head.

"Please look after my daughter. The world is a far bigger and more dangerous place than the three of you realize."

"I will protect her with my life if I must."

Somewhere high above the village, a lone raven cawed.

That night found the unlikely trio camped under the meager shelter of a copse of pine trees staring disconsolately at the flickering fire. Each sat as far apart from the rest as possible while staying within range of the fire's warmth, lost in their own private thoughts. T'riel peeked out from Danken's cloak and observed him haughtily, obviously unimpressed with his somber mood.

Danken tried to wrap his mind around the events of the past few days. They overlapped one another in a chaotic swirl that threatened to drive him insane. Why did the Gods hate him so? They had said they would keep him safe and yet they had taken everyone around him away. First his father, then Wytchyn and now his mother. What was the point of being safe when everyone you loved was in constant danger?

And now he had killed five men. Killed them like a rabbit for the night's dinner. Who was he? Who had he become? What destiny could be so important as to warrant all this pain? He just wished it all would end. He could go back to his simple life with his parents and Wytchyn and someone else could take the weight of Midgarthe on their bloody shoulders.

T'riel pinched his ear hard.

"Boy must stop his sulking. He is the leader. Others follow."

"I am no leader, T'riel."

"This Pixie thinks different. Why else would Star Blades, Ice Eyes and even this Pixie follow Boy if not? Boy does not follow *us.*"

T'riel's disdain for all names not Pixian still made him laugh, but he couldn't refute her logic. He jabbed a finger lightly into her tiny abdomen.

"Maybe you're right. I shouldn't be sulking."

"Who are you talking to, Sariksen?" Jet asked irritably.

"Tomorrow we'll head for the Duah Forest," Danken answered, ignoring Jet's question. "It should take us no more than two days to reach it."

"Why the Duah Forest?" Kierna asked.

"Because that's the way to where I need to be."

"I don't know about this." She looked in the direction of the Duah Elven Nation as if she could spot it from where she sat.

"You're free to leave should you choose to."

"I never said that!" Kierna snapped.

"What are you afraid of?" Jet asked, fixing her with steel gaze. She returned stare for stare until he was forced to look away from her icy eyes.

"I am afraid of nothing." Danken suddenly realized that her concern was not for herself, but for someone else in the small group. By the Gods! Kierna was in love with Jet! Of course, it all made sense now.

"They're Elves, not bloody Goblins," Jet snorted, warming to the subject with his familiar infuriatingly smug smile. Inexplicably, eight knives appeared in the air in a perfect circle. Jet juggled them without paying any apparent attention. Though they had seen him do tricks of this nature before, Danken and Kierna couldn't help but smile at his antics as he began a fantastically exaggerated tale of the 'Elf King and the Three Goblin Maids.' Soon even T'riel's stern exterior was worn down and her tiny giggles could be heard muffled by Danken's cloak.

The group fell asleep with smiles on their young faces for the first time that day. Scarred by their past and unsure of their future, they nevertheless faced the world with bright-eyed fascination and stoic resolve.

As they broke camp the next day, their resolve was immediately put to the test. The soft click of horse's hooves in the distance pushed all thoughts of saddling their own horses out of mind. Danken drew *Mak'Rist* and Jet had his hatchets resting easily in his palms. Kierna nocked an arrow smoothly.

"Jet, crouch behind that bush there and don't show yourself until they pass your position," Danken whispered. "Kierna, take your shot from that tree about ten paces behind you. I will draw their attention."

At first, he thought the townspeople had decided to attack them. The Sigil told him differently. Whoever was stalking them meant them harm, but they were far more dangerous than simple farm folk. Danken's heart raced as his superior vision picked out several black-cloaked figures. It was the same men from Savhagen and then some. They were in the process of laying in ambush. Their lookout, a young, slim girl, caught Danken's look and knew they had been discovered. She gave the word. With a roar preceding them, the black cloaks attacked.

"Kierna!" Danken shouted. "Take out their archers! Jet, take down their flankers! I'll take the van!"

Kierna's bow twanged in lightning succession, taking two archers in the face and a third through the chest. Four crossbow bolts slammed into the tree she was perching in. As soon as the last bolt struck, she fired again. Her accuracy was as deadly as her smile. Two more crossbow-men went down before they could get their next volley off. T'riel burned a smoking hole into the trigger fingers of two more. Kierna finished the deed.

With the archers distracted from the easy target he made, Danken was free to ride high in Bolt's saddle. *Mak'Rist* flashed wildly. Danken heard the blade speaking to him. He heard an ancient Elven battle hymn he couldn't understand. Danken swung his blade at anything that moved as Bolt crashed into a clutch of black cloaks. The unicorn impaled a man on his materialized pearl horn, then began bucking so none could get a clear shot at Danken. Danken held precariously on with his knees as he lashed out with his blade.

Two men came from the side, long swords raised high. Danken knew that he couldn't counter or kill both without being killed himself. Leaking a tendril of blue fire into Bolt, he communicated his plans. With blinding speed, the unicorn whirled and kicked out with both back hooves. Both black cloaks were dead before they hit the ground. Danken used Bolt's turning momentum to catch a black cloak off-guard and strike his head from his shoulders. A bolt of blue fire stalled three more long enough for Bolt to turn and put Danken in position to deal with them.

"Bloody glory hound," Jet muttered as he slipped out from the bush he had been hiding behind. Drawing four knives from his wide sleeves, he flung two into the throats of a pair trying to flank Danken. A third flanker raised her two shortswords in challenge. Jet saw that it was the girl who had spotted Danken. Her large brown eyes were empty but for pure hate under her cowl. Jet shook his head and made a soft clicking sound.

"You think you know about hate, girl?" he asked a his hatchets whirled into motion. She had skill, Jet saw, but he had more. He deflected her furious attacks without batting an eye. With a dazzling display of twirls, Jet hooked her blades in the crook of his hatchets and forced her arms down to her sides. "Hate is looking in the mirror and seeing a coward looking back at you." He dodged the knee she aimed at his groin, bending her arms behind her and placing a hatchet at her neck. "Hate is knowing that your whole life is nothing more than a charade." Jet kicked her down to her knees and put his face to hers. "You don't know a bloody thing about hate, girl. Because if you did, you would have run when you saw that I am he." Jet hit her in the temple with the butt of his hatchet and dragged her behind the bush so that none would see he had spared her. Couldn't have Danken thinking he had gone soft.

More black cloaks appeared from the woods. More than they could kill. Already Kierna was down to her last two arrows and Danken had been thrown from Bolt's back. Jet was occupied with the lookout girl and all three were tiring quickly. Not for the first time Danken wished he had denied them permission to accompany. Now their deaths, like his mother's and perhaps his sister's would be on his head. Danken fought doggedly on, letting *Mak'Rist* lead him through battle steps he didn't even know existed.

And then came a sight Danken would never forget. A bear of a man in knee-length shining chain mail under a blue and gold tunic charged into the fray on a massive black fully-armored Volhakian warhorse. He swung his four-foot broadsword as if it was a rapier into two black cloaked men and then down upon another. Beneath his shiny, open-faced helm with its large blue plume, Danken saw the man's fierce green eyes flash. They were not glowing with magic like his own, but savage battle lust as he headed straight for Danken. The rider hacked through two more black cloaks. Danken thought the man meant to kill him when he drew a throwing axe from his waist with his left hand, but the rider flung it into the back of a fleeing black cloak.

The rider leaped off his steed into the middle of four black cloaks. Danken saw three more in the treetops aiming arrows at him. Once again, he called forth the unknown wind to his aid. Without the hint of a breeze as a warning, a devastating gust of wind ripped through the pines, sending all three black cloaks plummeting dozens of feet to the ground. T'riel shot over to ensure their deaths. The rider had already killed one man and now swung his sword in a wide arc that took one black cloak through the middle and shattered the blade of another. The rider roared like a wild bear. He stepped inside a diagonal chop, impaled the black cloak and used him like a club to batter his unarmed companion to death. The rider looked around for more black cloaks to kill, almost gleefully, Danken thought. However, seeing none, the rider simply shrugged and wiped off his blade on one of the dead men's cloaks before sheathing it. His horse waited patiently for him and the rider patted it on the nose with a mailed hand.

Kierna's mouth was open in shock and she nearly fell from the tree for lack of concentration. Jet was cleaning his hatchets just as he had seen the rider do before doing the same with his knives. Danken was trying to keep Bolt from challenging the rider's steed to a fight.

The rider took off his helm to reveal a tangle of short black hair. His weathered, scarred face was nothing short of ugly, yet somehow charming. He took a long swig of mead from a water-skin, wiping off the excess that spilled onto his beard with the back of his hand.

"That was some mess you left in that village back there, Danken Sariksen," the rider said in a baritone that went well with his impressive size. He had an accent like that of Falgwyn or Southport. "Quite proud of yourself, are you?" He eyed Danken sternly, before nodding to Kierna and Jet. Kierna finally began collecting her arrows. Jet nodded back noncommittally.

"How do you know my name?" Danken asked. The man heaved a mock sigh.

"Doesn't everyone for miles now? The boy who killed twenty armed men to avenge his mother?"

"It was five. Don't mock me. Who are you?"

"All business, aren't you? Well, I guess I would be as well in your shoes." He became serious. "I knew your mother well. Marga was a wonderful woman. I'm sorry for your loss."

"How did you know my mother?" Danken asked heatedly.

"Calm down, boy. My name is Arn Brynsen. Per..."

"Bryn?" Danken cut him off. "He was your father?"

"Aye. Did she tell you of him?"

"Aye. She said he would teach me my destiny."

"Did she now?" Arn laughed. "Well, my father is in Valhalla, so I'll have to do my best then won't I? We'll start that at Mist Peak. It's as good as any for the destiny teaching and all. I must admit I'm surprised to have found you before the Sorcerer. We didn't even know Sarik had a child."

"The Sorcerer?" Danken asked. "Is he the one who sent them?" Danken pointed to the dead.

"Them?" Arn snorted. "No. These ones are Minions of the Lost."

"What in Hela's Grasp is that?" Jet asked.

"You woods folk call them Shaders."

"Shaders!" Kierna exclaimed.

"The Minions of the Lost answer only to Hrafna," Arn said.

"Who is that?" Jet asked to cover his shock.

"A very powerful gypsy. She gives them what they want, and in return she takes their will."

"I don't understand," Kierna said.

"Perhaps they wanted power, or a noble woman, or relief from a debt. Whatever it is, she gives it to them, and once they have it, she steals their very will. They are her slaves until they die."

"But why is she after us?" Jet asked.

"She's not. She was after that." Arn pointed to *Mak'Rist*. "I think she sensed it calling to you and tried to stop you from obtaining it."

"Why?" Danken fingered the hilt.

"The Fifth Render is the one thing in all of Midgarthe that Dak'Verkat fears. Hrafna is his agent. These ones here may not cause any more trouble, but there will be more where they came from sure as the leaves will fall."

"Let them," Kierna growled.

Danken's brow furrowed. "Are you all right, Kierna?"

"Why wouldn't I be?" she mounted her horse. "It was them or me."

"Even so. Killing is not something to be taken lightly," Arn offered quietly.

"Does it ever get easier?" Jet asked after a moment.

"Killing another Sendar? I'd like to say it does, but I'd be lying. There are ways to make yourself forget, but they are only learned with time. For now though, we'd best be riding."

As they started off, Danken suddenly asked, "Do you know of a man with red eyes?"

"Why do you ask?" Arn turned to regard him.

"He's the one who led those men to kill my mother."

"Aye, though I'll explain later. We'd best be making time."

"Why?" Danken asked.

"Ask the Pixie in your pocket." Arn spurred his horse on. Danken looked down at T'riel who was blushing.

"It's going to rain," she said sullenly. Danken caught up to Arn.

"Could you sense her, too?"

Arn laughed. "No. She stuck her head out to get a glimpse of me. Give her my apologies."

"T'riel, come out. He says he's sorry." She popped her head out slowly. "Why are you sorry?" he asked Arn.

"Pixies hate being seen when they're trying not to be." T'riel stuck her tongue out at him, but remained in sight. She wrinkled her nose.

"T'riel, quit it," Danken admonished.

"He has smell of Sprite on him," she said.

"What? How could he..."

"She's right, Danken. There's no use keeping the little terror a secret any longer. Looks like T'riel is as perceptive as I. Come on out, K'airn. He's a little nervous around strangers."

Slowly, a tiny silver head appeared out of Arn's pocket. K'airn was a full-grown Sprite, two inches taller than T'riel and all silver to her gold. He wore only a glittering white toga. K'airn buzzed around Arn's head for a moment before venturing over to Danken and T'riel. He and T'riel greeted each other in Pixian, he shyly, she excitedly, for Sprites were notoriously introspective. This introduction turned into a full blown conversation that Danken could barely follow. He turned to Arn, as did Kierna and Jet, just as shocked by T'riel, whom they hadn't known was with Danken.

"How did you come to be companions with a Sprite?" Danken asked.

"Well, when I was in the Mai'Lang Empire four years ago, I came across a slave trader selling Sprites. They're kept as pets there. Anyway, I killed him and let them all go, along with a few Sendar and a Troll."

"You let a Troll go?" Kierna exclaimed. Jet mumbled something about how such a flarin' ugly man must feel some kinship with bloody Trolls.

"Of course, girl, don't tell me you believe all of the wives' tales about how evil Trolls are?" Arn laughed.

"Well..." she stammered.

"Rubbish. When the Great Wars were fought, Trolls fought alongside Sendar and Elves. Anyway, K'airn here was the only Sprite who chose to stay with me. Since then, we've been inseparable, until now, I suppose," he indicated T'riel.

"How far is Mist Peak?"

"Five weeks, give or take."

"That far?" Danken asked.

"Well, we'll have to travel through the Duah, Dwarven and Vull'Kra Kingdoms. It takes awhile in each. And there are many dangers we must avoid. Aye, many dangers indeed."

CHAPTER 7
WHO WE ARE

n the shores of Lok Brae just before crossing into the Duah Elven Nation, Arn called a halt at a small village called Altae's Birth, named after three large, smooth black stones that rose up out of the water. It was said they were the three skulls of a petrified hydra killed by the legendary Elven hero, Kree'Altae before he had united the Duah against the Goblin invaders. When the races of Sendar and Mai'Lang had been in their infancy, the pacifist Duah had nearly been wiped out by the warlike Trolls, Goblins and Driss, as well as the other Elven Races, who warred with each other for supremacy. Kree'Altae and his magical sword *Paterra* had driven them all out and been named King of the first Duah Nation, stretching from what was now Wendall to an inland lake which was now the coastal port of Sancor.

The company stopped at a small, lively inn in the center of the quiet town. It was filled with raucous, drunk Sendar. Two women were doing a comedic dance to a merry song on the fiddle and a flute played by two grey-bearded Sendar men. The women kept doing odd kicks and jumps that seemed designed to expose as much of their legs as possible without having their *very* low-bust-lined, flamboyantly colored dresses come over their heads altogether. Though Danken was slightly tentative and Kierna was downright offended, Jet had them downing hard ale, clapping and laughing before Arn had even finished securing their rooms. The big soldier was about to inform the trio of their arrangements, when two tall, attractive blond women hooked his arms and dragged him out onto the dance floor. Though he was a poor dancer, Arn took it all in good fun.

Arn's rough face cracked in a grin when he took a seat at their table. A plump but pretty red-haired barmaid brought him his mead and took their orders, giving him a sly wink. The three youths were struggling to keep the astonishment from their faces. Jet shook his head with a small laugh and resumed watching the dancing girls. Danken sneaked a look at Kierna, who was still scrutinizing Arn's face trying to figure out what any woman could possibly see in it. Danken kicked her under the table and she started. Arn smiled knowingly at the two chagrined youths.

Not long after, their food arrived. Danken ate his steak quickly while at the same time trying to savor its taste, washing it down with ale. By the meal's end, he was quite full and not a little drunk. His eyes always had a slight blue glow inside them and he could keep them from flaring noticeably during the day or in well-lit buildings such as this, but the ale dimmed his control. Twice they flared up momentarily and he had to shut his eyes tightly to stop the sudden painful influx of too-bright lantern light.

Finally Arn got up, declaring himself ready for bed. He glanced over at the barmaid who giggled.

"I was only able to secure two rooms, one bed apiece. So Kierna can have one and we three will take the other. Floor is as comfortable as the ground and a lot warmer, which suits me just fine."

"I will *not* take a room by myself just because I am a woman. I won't have you treating me any differently," Kierna said forcefully.

"Dwei, fine by me," Arn said. "I'll take the single room. Yours is the third door on the left. See you three at dawn."

Kierna opened her mouth to insist that she still did not want the single room, but Arn and the barmaid were already heading for the stairs. Jet burst out laughing and Danken joined in. Kierna scowled at them until the laughter subsided. Jet put a hand placatingly on her shoulder.

"I'm sorry Kierna, but I call the bed in our room, as well." He narrowly dodged a closed fist aimed for his mouth.

"I hope you drown in the River of Swords, Jetrian," she spat. "And you, Danken, what do you think is so funny? I hope your Faerie eyes can keep you warm this night, because I'll be sleeping on all of your blankets and if you try to take them back, Freyja help me I'll send you into the Elven Forest wearing naught but what you were born in and a good helping of bruises!" With that she stormed upstairs.

"I think she likes you," Jet remarked.

"Aye, like a fox likes a rabbit."

"… I'll tell ye," a gruff, older man was telling three others around a card table, "ye've seen the way them flarin' Pixies an' Gnomes've been goin' at it of late. I'm knowin' who's the cause of it."

"Took three of ol' man Truc's cattle jus' the other morn, so the bloody buggers did," another put in. "Flarin' Root Monsters oozin' outta the ground like a nest o'bloody vipers."

"Pixies even raided the orphanage over at Dell's Creek. Only one lil' girl there they says and that'un disappeared! Stealin' babies, by Frigga. It jus' ain't right."

"Hold on, hold on!" the first man growled. "I do be tellin' this 'ere tale, not the flarin' lot o' ye. Now listen yerselves up close now, cos' my ol' voice ain't near on as powerful as it once were."

T'riel, Danken and Jet did just that, heads cocked to hear every word. The Pixie's golden eyes flashed from Danken's cloak pocket as the man noisily cleared his throat.

"Now as ye all well know, 'tis dangerous fer a Sendar to interfere wit' anything tha' happens in these woods. Ye've all bloody seen wha' 'appens to lumberjacks what cut down too many trees. Both of the bloody creatures'll stop their own killin' long enough to kill some poor fool tryin' to cut down their flarin' forest. Still though, ye know as well as I that passin' through leads to no problems.

"Well now, twas no more'n a few days back as I hear tell when someone the Forest Folk all call Darkperil rode the border 'tween the Pixian and Gnomish Forests on a white horse they say be a unicorn in diskize. Somehow or ought, they didn't recognize 'im until many 'ad died tryin' to bloody kill 'im and he was already long gone. Anyhow, 'e ended up takin' one of the Pixies fer a 'ostage 'er someought, and 'e did kill many a Gnome too flarin' stupid to know better. Now the rotters war again' each other in earnest, claimin' the other did something to make this 'ere Darkperil angry.

"Seems both sides 'ave themselves a myth about 'im. Says them tha' long ago, the Age of Dragons, some say, the Gnomes did come to the forest from afar and seek to test a new weapon out in the Pixian realm. Realizin' they was outnumbered, the Pixies used some sorta old magic to bind the Gnomes t' the bloody forest so tha' if'n they destroyed it, they'd destroy themselves. The rotters've been fightin' ever since. Well now, seems them Gnomes were 'parently the greatest inventors the world had ever known, but the bond took their flarin' wills and made 'em savages. They do believe that Darkperil will free 'em of their bond somehow and the Pixies do believe 'e will give them their forest back. They be runnin' amok cos' they both think the other made 'im leave."

"Wot's this 'ere Darkperil feller look like, I'm fer wonderin'?" one man asked.

"Well that's the thing of it now." The first man took a large swig of ale, much of it remaining on his bushy grey moustache. "They say 'e's righ' on ten feet tall with a flamin' blue sword as tall as a you'r I. 'Is eyes are the purest of fire, I hear, with 'air streaked like a fresh fallen snow. Now this I haven't 'ad confirmed ye un'erstand, but I've heard rumor that'e even talks to a Valkyrie from time to time. Say she protects 'im when 'e do battle Goblins an' such."

"Flamin' blue eyes do ye say? Sounds like one of them what live at the Peak," another man stated.

"A Mage, ye think? Bah! What'd one of them be botherin' with a lot of bloody Forest Folk fer? They've got enough t'do, what with the restlessness on the Southern continent and all them flarin' pirates and raiders terrorizin' the coasts and oceans. Not to mention the bloody Sorcerers. Should be comin' around again soon, I'm thinkin'."

"Why d'ye wanna go an talk about bloody bad business like that?"

The older man began talking about other unimportant things. Jet regarded Danken with a curious, mischievous look in his eyes.

"Ten feet tall, eh? Sword of blue fire?"

"Shut up, Jet," Danken muttered darkly.

"Darkperil. I like the sound of that. Much more fearsome than Danken."

"My name isn't Darkperil," Danken hissed, looking to see if anyone had heard.

"Ahem," T'riel cleared her tiny throat until both men looked at her.

"Do you have something to add?" Jet asked slyly.

"Boy is Darkperil," she stated, then disappeared into his cloak.

"Avenger of Wrongs, Righter of Nations. Darkperil." Jet smiled, improvising a mocking ballad, but Danken turned the tables.

"And what of you, Jet? Odd that one day you carry average weapons, and the next they are made in the same metal as my blade. Odd that you should consider yourself so normal."

"I had them made," Jet said defensively.

"We are both of us killers, Jet, with stormy pasts and futures that may be too great for us to live up to. I don't even know who I'm supposed to be while everyone else around me seems to. I don't even want to be whatever the blazes I'm supposed to be and damn it, it scares me to Hel's Gate and back. I wish I knew my father, or that my mother was still alive and I could milk flarin' cows the rest of my life, but I can't. I am who I am and like it or not, so are you," Danken said somberly as he got up. "Think on that and tell me when your bloody hatchets become too heavy for you to carry."

Without a look back, Danken negotiated his way to the stairs. T'riel stuck her head out and looked at him consideringly.

"You knew," Danken accused. "They are at war for me?"

"Boy's head becomes too big. War had begun before Boy saved this Pixie. Now that Gnomes and Pixies know Boy is Darkperil, they use him for a reason to keep fighting."

"And all this about me saving your forests and freeing them?"

"Boy will do what he will do. It is not for this Pixie to tell him what must be."

"Wonderful. That helps so much, thank you."

"Boy's head is too big anyway. If he thinks this Pixie is his hostage, One will shrink his head for him. Boy should not believe everything he hears."

"Your people knew about me before I left the forest," Danken said suddenly as the thought came to him. "Why didn't they ask me to help them?"

"Boy is not listening!" T'riel sighed. "He must do what he does unforced. None dare guide him. None can tell him his fate. Boy must find out on his own. That is why secrets are kept from him."

"All right, all right, I won't ask any more questions. I just don't like the idea of people fighting because of me."

"They do not fight only for Boy," T'riel said softly. "They fight for this Pixie."

T'riel disappeared as Danken reached their room, leaving him with more questions than answers, as always. The room was dark enough that his eyes began glowing blue unbidden. He picked out Kierna's sleeping form on the floor in the corner with none of the blankets she had promised to steal. He padded silently over and gently lifted her, carrying her over to the bed where he tucked her snugly in.

"Danken," she murmured, eyes still closed. "I must leave you but one day I will return and give to you the life I owe you to serve as you see fit."

"Kierna," he whispered and she started awake. "Are you all right?"

"Of course, why wouldn't I be?" She pushed her blond hair from her eyes.

"You told me you were going to leave me but that you would return and that you would owe me your life."

"I said no such thing," she said too quickly and turned away from him.

As always, more questions than answers.

Who in Hela's Bone Closet did Danken think he bloody was? 'Hatches too heavy.' Bloody fool. Jet *knew* who *he* was *and* what he wanted. He just wasn't sure he liked the person he had to become to get to that point. Shaking the thoughts away with a deep swig of mead, he made his way to the corner booth where the four men were playing cards. They invited him to join in. They were playing Hierarchy, a game Jet knew well. He joined willingly, steering their conversation subtly and skillfully in the direction he wanted. After a score or so hands, when Jet was comfortably up, one of the men began talking.

"Been hearin' tell of a pile of strange happenin's at Lok Tryst. Farms destroyed, livestock killed, women murdered by mobs. A crazy man with eyes like a Sorcerers and two boys killin' half the Thingstead outta revenge fer the lot of it."

"These two boys," Jet asked as he dealt, "what did they look like?"

"Well, come to think of it, they say one 'ad 'imself some flamin' blue eyes an' white streaks in his hair and a flarin' blue sword. Mayhaps he's Darkperil, or so the Forest Folk call'im if'n I'm not mistaken 'im. An' the other's said to be purtyer'n an Elf with two silver hatchets er some such. Dangerous creatures of the Faerie I'm thinkin'."

"Aye, that's fer sure," the man to Jet's left agreed. "Speakin' o' which, ye're kinda purty yerself, boy!" he laughed loudly.

"Purty for a bloody cheater!" the man across from him roared, throwing his chair back.

"Aye, there sure'n ain't six Kings in no deck I'm aware of!" the man to his right agreed, pushing his chair back as he stood. The others rose quickly, fingering their sword or axe hilts nervously. Jet eyed them calmly from his seat.

"Now gentlemen, you should be aware at your advanced ages that it isn't polite to call a man a cheater. Especially one who can kill you all where you stand."

"Make your move ye flarin' rotter." The music and talking in the inn ceased abruptly.

"I think you're making a mistake, old man. The ale is doing your talking for you."

" 'E said make yer move, purty boy!"

With blinding speed, two knives fled Jet's hands, pinning the speaker by his ears to the wall. The man to his left, the rumor man, had his sword out fastest and a knife pinned his wrist to the table. His sword dropped harmlessly to the floor. Jet kicked a chair into the nearest man before drawing his hatchets and clubbing the man twice in the head with the blunt ends. The last card player's sword stroke was caught in the crook of Jet's hatchet. Before his sword hit the ground, Jet had beaten the man to a bloody unconscious heap.

Ignoring the screams, Jet yanked his blades out of the cheat-caller's ears none too nicely before smashing his face against the table edge until he was silent. The rumor man pulled the knife from his wrist just as Jet turned to him. He held the knife awkwardly in his left hand. Without breaking stride, Jet took the knife and cut the man across the face once under each eye. The man dropped to his knees, begging for mercy. Slowly, deliberately, Jet took all the money on the table, then cleaned his blades on the man's shirt.

"Listen closely rumor man," Jet said in a voice cold enough to freeze stone. "My name is Jet Bloodhatchet." He crossed the silver hatchets in front of the man's face. "If you are here when I wake in the morn, I will cut out your tongue for your exaggerated lies. And my friend Darkperil is not half as nice. Do you understand?"

"Aye sor. I'm sorry I called ye a cheat. You're right. It must'n a been the ale talkin', sure enough."

"Dwei." Jet put his hatchets away, "and for the record, it wasn't half the town council, it was only six men. Now get your friends and your worthless self out of here and to a healer before you catch the fever." Jet flipped the man two coins.

Once the men had gone, the music started back up. The few remaining in the common room eyed him nervously as he fastidiously placed the table and chairs exactly as they had been. He paid the fat innkeeper for the minor damages before two dark-haired, attractive young serving maids appeared at his side. Saying he must be too tired to climb the stairs and sleep on the hard floor, they led him to their personal chambers with promises of baths, massages and a warm bed. Wise in the ways of women from a young age (so he thought), Jet knew he might be getting more than he bargained for. Still, he was not one to argue with two pretty women.

"Where're the Nymphs?" Kierna suddenly wondered, taken with the tiny Pixie and Sprite. She was clearly uncomfortable on this, their first day in the Elven Forest.

"Above us on the tree branch. You know their affection for heights." Danken glanced up at the two tiny beacons. He was happy T'riel had found another Nymph to talk to.

"T'riel!" he called. "Are you two going to eat?" He was answered by the familiar feeling of two feet on his shoulders and a high pitched chattering in his ear. He handed her a honey cake.

She shook her finger at him. "Impatient Boy."

"So how are you and K'airn getting along?"

"Dwei. He is older, though," she answered thoughtfully.

"How much older?"

"Fifty leaf falls."

"Fifty?!" Danken exclaimed.

"Aye, but this is nothing. To a Pixie, it is but the blink of an eye. One lives to be as old as the tree that gave One life," she said matter-of-factly.

"I guess I always figured you wouldn't even live as long as me."

"The Pixie won't if what D'Sane says is true," she said cryptically.

"What do you mean?" Danken asked quickly, she merely shrugged her shoulders.

"Goodnight Boy." She took off back into the canopy. Danken shook his head.

"Seems everyone knows more about me than I do."

"You will learn soon," Arn told him.

"If..." he began, but Arn silenced him with a wave.

"Aye, Sariksen," Jet grumbled, "shut your bloody mead hole and let the rest of us get some flarin' sleep. Garm baying before Ragnarok couldn't compete with you." He rolled over irritably. Kierna shook her head and did likewise. Arn smiled wryly.

"Soon. Not now. Get some sleep, we have a long day ahead of us," he said, laying back down by the low burning fire. Danken mumbled and cursed under his breath as he too got into his bedroll.

The Duah Forest was an old-growth forest with trees that one couldn't see the top of. Lush green vines, shrubs and ferns sprouted up from the soft floor of dead leaves and peat moss. It smelled of life and the aftermath of rain, which Danken loved.

After the initial excitement of being out on the road, they settled into a comfortable pace. Arn was a mysterious man, Danken had decided. Huge, yet soft spoken, intimidating, yet always quick with a joke or a smile. Danken reasoned that any man so big, who moved with the effortless ease of a skilled warrior, had little reason to raise his voice, but rather spoke through actions. All three youths had unconsciously begun to act in much the same way.

So it was that many miles through the Duah Forest were passed in silence, each finding solace in the peacefulness of the woods. Kierna refrained from conversation or eye contact altogether while Jet muttered darkly sarcastic comments at every turn. The Nymphs, on the other hand, chattered constantly, seemingly oblivious to all around them. When Danken commented on this, Arn shook his head.

"It's their way, Danken. But don't let it fool you. If danger arises, they'll likely know before us."

When night drew near, they set up camp about two days out from the Duah capital of Wendall. Danken busied himself with Bolt, brushing his coat while the horse contentedly munched on sweetened oats. A unicorn, he corrected. He rode a flarin' unicorn!

T'riel and K'airn meanwhile had gone off in search of fresh fruit. Winter was fast approaching and soon all of the fruit would be gone. Arn built a fire. It was imperative that a stone circle was built around it, with the rune of *Warding* carved into the center stone. Then the fire was built around that stone. To do otherwise was to invite trouble. If an Elf, no matter what size or station, were to catch an improperly laid fire, he would immediately whistle for the *Verna'ren,* known by Sendar as Duah Rangers. To do this, an Elf simply blew into a tiny bone whistle that only Duah would hear. The Rangers would appear quickly and arrest the perpetrators. Not altogether a fun prospect.

Though it may have seemed harsh to the unwitting, all on the Northern continent knew it was for good reason. A forest fire would not only kill thousands who lived in symbiosis with the trees, it would leave the Duah Nation defenseless, for the forests were its fortification. From there, it would wreak similar havoc on the Vull'Kra. For this reason, both Nations had made a pact—one of the few things Elves and Trolls had ever agreed upon.

Danken sat by the fire and looked Arn straight in the eye. An eighteen year old boy could hold his tongue only for so long. Arn saw the look and knew the boy would not be denied any longer. So he took a seat and made himself comfortable. Jet groaned loudly, plugging his ears.

"Where to start, where to start..." Arn began.

CHAPTER 8
REVELATION

arik was the greatest, most powerful and generous man I've ever met. He started out a simple farmer, married to your mother and content with his lot in life. One day a man named Bryn Varinsen changed all of that." Arn smiled. "He came on bidding from the Magi. The Magi are the force of Good in Sendar society. The Sorcerers are the force of Evil found in the Mai'Lang. Where other races have inherent magic, humans funnel all of their magic into the Magi and Sorcerers. There are only five of each so they are immensely powerful, and they are immortal.

"From all the despair in the Mai'Lang race, the Sorcerers gain their power; from all of the hope in the Sendar, the Magi gain theirs. Each group is like a circle. Four on the outer ring, one in the center. He is called the Fifth, the most powerful of them all.

"A Mage or Sorcerer can only be killed if his heart is ripped out or if his *Brag'Karn* is taken from his lifeless body before it repairs itself."

"What is a *Brag'Karn*?" Danken asked.

"It's a tiny pearl at the base of the skull that appears once a child is chosen. To kill a Sorcerer you have to remove it."

"What happens when one removes it?" Danken touched the back of his neck where the pain of the watchers had been.

"Both the Sorcerer and *Brag'Karn*'s energies disperse to the next born. You see, long ago before the land bridge connecting the Northern and Southern continents with the Lost Continents was swept away, there were two best friends. One was a Mai'Lang named Fun'Te and the other was a Sendar named Gellar. One evening they stopped at a cave to spend the night. Inside they found an ancient box containing ten identical pearls. Not knowing what they were, the two friends each took one to examine it.

"For a moment, nothing happened but then the pearls began glowing white hot and burned into the two friends' bodies, coming to rest at the base of their skulls. The remaining eight disappeared to be dispersed among the newborns of the lands. Soon the two friends began to notice strange and exciting new powers at their disposal. The power changed them though, bringing out their true nature.

"Fun'Te wanted to use their powers to gain domination over the world. Gellar believed they should help people. After long months spent arguing, the two came to blows. Their power lit the sky with fury and thus the two became mortal enemies. This is how the rift between the Sorcerers and Magi began."

"What happened to them?" Danken asked.

"They killed each other at the First Cataclysm nearly one thousand years later. Afterwards was when the first group's of fractured peoples began forming into small nations and is also how the Fifth of Sorcerers Dak'Verkat was born. After that, the two sides remained passive, only occasionally exchanging deaths if one or the other was caught unaware. For the most part, each side is equal and won't attack unless it has the upper hand. This rarely happens, though lately that trend has been starting to reverse.

"Anyway, one of the Magi—Gellar's successor—had apparently lost his love for life and removed his own *Brag'Karn*. At the moment of the Mage's death, your father was born. His heart was pure and honest, prompting the Norns to choose him. The Magi managed to keep the death of their fellow Mage a secret for nearly twenty-five years, as the people of Mist Peak are bound by a *Silence* spell, but somehow the Sorcerers found out and began planning an attack. At the same time, the Magi discovered Sarik. You see, a Mage cannot become a Mage until he uses his powers to save another person. A Sorcerer can only become a Sorcerer when he uses his power to kill. For this reason, Sorcerers are usually younger when they make the transformation.

"Once a Mage or Sorcerer is transformed, he will retain that age and appearance forever. Your father used his powers to save her," he pointed to Kierna, who scowled and looked away. Jet raised his brows. "Until then, he was just a man with brown hair and blue eyes like any other, undetectable to all. You're the first I've seen whose eyes glow *before* the transformation."

"Is that why you said you owe me?" Danken asked Kierna. "Because of my father?"

" I said nothing of the sort," she retorted. "Let him finish so we can go to sleep."

"Just so," Arn agreed. "Anyway, the Fifth of the Sorcerers, Dak'Verkat, mobilized the Dark forces of the two continents against those of the Light. At that time, the races of the world were spread out in every direction. Elves, Trolls, Goblins, Pixies and Gnomes could all be found in the same woods. Giants and Dwarves inhabited the same mountain ranges. Sendar and Mai'Lang lived in the same cities. Orcans and Shrakens, the same islands and coasts.

"When Dak'Verkat recruited his army, he chose his races carefully. He wanted those with the penchant for Evil, even if they were not at the time. In the end, he chose the Mai'Lang as his people. The Magi, realizing the imminent threat also began to recruit, while sending my father to get yours.

"When my father met Sarik, you were still in the womb. He was resistant to come at first but eventually yielded when he realized there was no one else who could do what he could. He kissed your mother goodbye and left."

"Did he know of me?" Danken asked.

"I think so. He left a shortsword with your mother and said to give it to the next man to call the stead home. At the time, she thought him crazy, but I've a feeling he knew that you would be that man.

"Though Sembalo had held the post for thirteen hundred years, he knew that Sarik was the Fifth. When you become a Mage, a rune will brand itself on your arm, proclaiming your rank. If one more powerful than yourself is born, the rune on your arm will change accordingly." Danken showed him the rune on his arm. Jet nearly choked on his dinner and even Kierna showed surprise. Arn just laughed. "Anyway, once that was complete, the recruitment of the races began in earnest. In the end, the forces were equal, more or less. The Sorcerers had recruited the Mai'Lang, the Giants, the Goblins, the Driss and the Shrakens. The Magi recruited the Sendar, the Elves, the Trolls, the Dwarves and the Orcans."

"Ahem," came two tiny voices. Danken turned to see T'riel and K'airn standing on a tree stump. Arn smiled.

"And let's not forget the Nymphs. They could only muster a small force, as the Gnomes, who were bonded to the trees they are born in, would attack," Arn amended. T'riel smirked and gave a snort under her breath.

"Anyhow, the Sorcerers and their forces attacked quickly, believing the Magi at a disadvantage with no Fifth. The first battle was fought at Kasan, a city in southern Sendar. Both sides took heavy casualties. The Forces of Darkness were pushed farther south to Lundgarde. The battle there was short and fierce and both sides retreated to lick their wounds. The Forces of Darkness went to Bang'Lau.

"The final battle was fought at Faust. It raged on for seven days with neither side gaining advantage; the entire city was destroyed. The Sorcerers decided it was time to attack and staged an ambush at Martusian's Hill. They were more than a little surprised to find Sarik standing with Sembalo and the other three Magi. By the time the Sorcerers found out that their ambush had turned against them, it was too late to run. Red and blue fire streaked across the sky from every angle. Swords came out and the battle became all or nothing. Through it all, Sarik and Dak'Verkat had eyes only for each other. They met in single combat and neither could find a chink in the other's armor. Sarik had the talent, but Dak'Verkat had the experience. After all, he is nearly two thousand years old, though he looks barely old enough to drink mead.

"They fought for nearly two days until one of the Sorcerers was killed. Desperately, another Sorcerer named Dagash, who was outmatched and close to death, fired a *Life Charge* at Sarik."

"What is a *Life Charge*?" Danken asked.

"A Sorcerer or a Mage can send his Life Force out of his body and into a charge of energy, leaving only enough strength to keep the heart beating, generally resulting in a coma. Dagash fired his *Life Charge* at Sarik, who knew it would kill him. Sarik was forced to put all of his energy into a *Deflection* spell. The *Life Charge* hit Sarik, but dissipated. But Dak'Verkat used the distraction to kill him," Arn finished sadly.

"So, he's dead then?" Danken asked, though deep in his heart he'd known it to be true all his life. Kierna put a hand comfortingly on his shoulder. Jet studied his hatchets, doubtless remembering his own father.

"Aye, I'm sorry, Danken."

"What happened then?" Danken asked, hiding his emotion.

"Well, Dagash was killed immediately after by Penn and the other two were killed soon after, but Dak'Verkat transmorphed into his owl form and escaped."

"Owl?" Danken's eyes widened, recalling the ancient outside the forest.

"Aye. That's the traditional *Avian* form of the Sorcerers. The Magi prefer falcons."

"So," Danken started, "I'm a Mage because my father died at the exact moment of my birth?"

"Aye, and from what the other Magi tell me, it means that you will be the most powerful Mage yet. That's the reason you look like them already. Most Magi retain their normal looks until the moment of transformation. Somehow, you've already taken on their characteristics. It explains the Sigil, at least."

"But, I'm not a Mage yet?"

"No. Not until you have saved a life with your powers."

"What happened in the war?" Danken asked, cataloging information in his brain.

"The Sorcerers' forces, with no one to lead them, retreated to Bang'Lau for the last time. The Magi constructed Faust's Wall and sealed off Sendar from Mai'Lang. Then, it is said that Odin colored the entire race of Mai'Lang's palms red, symbolizing the blood they had spilled and the Evil they had followed. To this day, Mai'Lang's palms are completely red.

"Afterwards, the races became Nations unto themselves. The Great Nations they came to be called. The Orcans, having attained a victory over the hated Shrakens, returned to their Western Isles, while the Shrakens, who had also lived on the Western Isles, were forced to relocate to the Hingeblade Isles. The races of the Dark own the Southern continents now just as we control the Northern."

"Have the Sorcerers got new additions like me?" Danken asked.

"Four of them, though we know not where or who yet. All exactly your age also, I might add. I would assume it's one of them who led the townspeople to your house."

"Well," Danken began but found he had nothing left to ask. "I'm going to go to sleep then. Thanks." He got up to his feet slowly and shuffled off toward his bedroll. The other two youths did likewise. Suddenly, Arn's hand grabbed him by the collar.

"You're not immortal yet, boy. Watch your step." Danken looked down to find his foot not two inches from a craftily hidden snare.

"What is it?" he asked, moving his foot slowly back towards safety.

"Snare," Arn said. "Elves use them to catch unwelcome trespassers. Trolls and Sendar like us mostly. The Elves know where they all are and they're rigged to set off silent magical alarms. It's kind of like an early warning system to let them know if they're being attacked."

"What if I would have been caught in it?"

"You would have been questioned, then released," came a melodic voice just outside the firelight. Arn and Danken had their swords drawn in a flash and Danken caught a glimpse of T'riel and K'airn making to flank the intruder. Kierna had her bow nocked and aimed while Jet twirled his hatchets in anticipation of the fight to come, a gleam in his grey eyes. Gods, the man loved a challenge.

"Who's there?" Arn called. "Show yourself if your intentions are honorable. If not, let's get to killing."

"If I'd wanted you dead, you'd be dead. I'm simply passing by and happened to catch the tail end of your conversation," came the reply, this time Danken's starlight vision caught sight of a tree-obscured silhouette with two burning green eyes.

"Do you intend to speak from afar or step into the light?" Jet mocked. Danken saw two twinkles of light on the shadow's shoulders followed by a sharp intake of breath.

The man complied. "Seeing as these two little terrors have discovered me, I don't see the harm in it." Danken caught his breath. Standing before them was the first Elf he had ever seen. He was tall for a Duah at nearly six feet. A single edged, curved sword known as a dao made from a black metal called myrkanium hung from his slender shoulders. The Elf's skin was a flawless porcelain cream. His lips were a glittering green and his eyes were green balls of flame. He had the natural graceful beauty of his race mixed with a rough edge that hinted of a hard life, but the creases in his youthful face were of one who had laughed often. The Elf wore a dark grey tunic under lacquered bull-hide armor and similar shin and boot guards over his tight grey buckskin pants. A forest green cloak hung about his shoulders. He removed the cowl to reveal long hair the color of straw flecked with green strands and the telltale pointed ears of his kind. Four silver rings hung from each ear and five silver balls from each eyebrow.

Danken had heard that in the Elven language, called Duah, the actual word "Duah" meant "Peaceful Ones." Looking at this Elf, he could scarcely see the resemblance. Duah Elves most may have been, but this man was a warrior born.

"An Elf," he whispered, sheathing *Mak'Rist*. The rest did likewise, Jet reluctantly, Danken noticed.

"Dwei," Kierna breathed in awe.

"Aye, an Elf. You were expecting a Troll?"

"No, it's just, I've never seen one of your race before," Danken said.

"Well, you're no ordinary sight yourself, young Magus. Or is it old? I can never tell with your lot, what?"

"Not a Mage, yet," Danken replied, reaching out his hand to the Duah. "I'm Danken Sariksen and this is Arn Brynsen, Kierna Bjorndotir and—"

"Jet Bloodhatchet," Jet cut in, drawing quick stares from the rest.

"Well met," the Elf said clasping their wrists. "My name is Taelun Fallenbower. You can call me Tae. Who are these two?" he asked, indicating the Nymphs still perched on his shoulder, eyeing him suspiciously.

Danken introduced them. "T'riel and K'airn."

"So, Tae, are you *Seath'ren?"* Arn asked, using the Duah word for Trap Minders.

"No, actually, I'm a *Verna'ren.*"

"I've never seen a Ranger without a bow," Arn remarked.

"Aye, usually, but I prefer this," Tae pushed aside his cloak to reveal a three foot long dark green blow gun. "It's carved out of a Giant bone. His leg actually. Must have been nineteen years back I killed him."

"You fought in the Great War then?"

"Unless it was the lesser-known not-so-Great War," he smiled. "Joke, of course, mate."

"And a funny one, too," Arn said sarcastically, to which T'riel and K'airn sniggered. He offered to share their dinner then. "It's probably gone cold but it's good. No meat in it either," he added when the Duah looked slightly hesitant, for Elves only ate meat cooked with proper ritual and were mostly vegetarians. Meat cooked the way Sendar ate it would make an Elf physically sick. It required *Elffire* and the Treecleansing to be edible.

"Aye, I'll take you up on that offer," Tae replied, helping himself to a bowl of stew and a chunk of bread. He looked over at Danken. "Did you say you're name was Sariksen, lad?" he asked with a full mouth. He certainly did not have the manners the Duah were supposed to have. He seemed more like a pirate, which was evident when Jet began to take an interest in him. And Jet only took interest in three things: women, profit and danger.

"Aye."

"As in son of Sarik the Fifth?"

"The same."

"So it's true then," Tae whispered, staring for the first time at *Mak'Rist* as if he knew it.

"What is true?"

"Nothing that won't wait until morning, lad."

"Right. Well, if that's all, I'm tired so I'll be going off to bed now," Danken said sleepily, moving over to his bedroll. "Any more traps I should know about, Tae?"

"None other than the one your boots' in."

"What?" Danken looked around before he heard Tae laughing, and Jet too for that bloody matter.

"Joke," Tae said putting his hands up. "Sorry, it's been awhile since I've been around people, even if they are Sendar. One gets tired of joking with himself."

"Well, see you on the morrow then," Danken yawned. When he, Kierna and Jet had left to their bedrolls, Tae turned to Arn. He took a big bite of the stew.

"I sense a power about that boy I've felt in no other, Arn, including his father," he said around a mouthful of bread.

"You knew him?"

"Not well. I met him at a strategy meeting as a Commander in the Navy in the war at Faust. When that boy becomes a full grown Mage, Dak'Verkat had better hope he can find a hole deep enough to hide his filthy self in."

"You seem quite knowledgeable in the ways of the world, Tae."

"I make it my business to know. In the two hundred years I've been alive, I've watched the world go from chaotic maelstrom, to war, to a peaceful—for the most part—place where all are not constantly on guard and wary of strangers. My peoples' most hated enemy, the Trolls became our ally. I never felt like all of this was real until the war ended and the rebuilding began. And ironically, I lost my sense of purpose at the same time. The Navy was my father's love, not so much mine. Being a Ranger is fine, but I need to feel like I'm doing something important." he paused.

"Tell me, Arn, have you need of a skilled veteran of war at your Mist Peak? A hundred and fifty years fighting on the briny and fifty more in the forests as a *Verna'ren* is all I have to claim, mate, but I want to be on the front lines. I haven't had to write a new Death Poem for years."

"We would be glad you have you. I'm sure there are pots that need scrubbing, floors that need waxing, food that..."

"Oh, you're a funny one, Master Arn."

"Aye, so I've been told. Another true weapon's master is always needed for the ranks of Mistgarde. The invitation is yours if you wish it, but as you well know, those who fail the testing often do not survive."

At this, Tae's eyes widened. In all of Midgarthe, there was no finer fighting force than the Mistgarde. The finest warriors from all over the Northern continent trained their whole lives to be elected as one of its members. It was created to be the protector of the realm and most of all the Magi. Out of millions, only eight thousand were chosen for the Army and half of that again for the Navy. To be included was an honor above all others.

"Even though you've never seen me fight? We've only just met."

"Your name struck a memory for me. They called you Giant Killer in the war, did they not? You killed nine of them in one glass."

Tae smiled. "Aye. Stupid buggers wouldn't bloody learn."

"You are worthy, Tae. Besides, I've been waiting for an opportunity to test something out anyway. You'll get your chance on the morrow."

"Against whom?" Tae asked.

"The boy, of course."

CHAPTER 9
A FIGHT THIS DAY

he mountain loomed majestically in the distance, a beautiful shroud of fog cloaking it in mystery. Flocks of birds floated carelessly on the warm thermals that surrounded it, singing their praise of the glorious morning. The purple sky overhead blended serenely into the fiery orange and red of the sunrise.

Shonai slicked her wet black hair back as she emerged from the cold mountain river. The two identical white marks around her purple eyes made her shiny grey skin look all the more beautiful.

She smelled the sweetness of flowers' nectar on the gentle breeze that dried her. Feeling once again refreshed, she continued her journey toward the mountain. Shonai had been traveling toward it for as long as she could remember and now it was finally within her reach. The soft grass beneath her feet felt good to her bare feet. She was content to walk at a slow, leisurely pace. After such an unimaginably long journey, an extra day wouldn't hurt her.

Shonai could feel a power emanating from the mountain, strange and mysterious, yet undeniably welcome. It was as if it was calling to her. She couldn't remember how her journey had started, or even *why* it had started. She knew only that she had to reach the mountain. What would it be like? she wondered. What exotic and adventurous sort of people called it home, and for that matter called her to be with them? She suspected the anticipation was almost as good as the reality would be.

Abruptly she was pulled back from her perfect dream.

"Your Highness," came a familiar soft voice behind her. Shonai ignored her, continuing to stare into the sky. "Your father will be displeased if you are not there to attend the ball on time."

"Why?" Shonai turned to face the speaker, an older woman who still retained an undeniable elegance. Her white hair was ornately put up, and her grey skin still gleamed in the sun. She was Shonai's childhood nursemaid.

"You know very well why, Highness. There will be many important dignitaries there; your appearance is necessary, to say the least."

"Fine, I will make myself up to sit unmoving on a throne whilst others conduct the affairs of state," Shonai sulked.

"The responsibilities of the Royal Princess of Orcana are few, Highness, but this is one of them. I will send for your servant to attend you." At this, Shonai sighed and dove into the sparkling pool, her dolphin-like skin shimmering like a pearl as she descended into the depths, the passageway opening out into the sea. Her meeting with her servant was brief and soon she was back in the open ocean.

She let her webbed feet propel her, keeping her arms at her sides. An Orcan Princess did not use her equally webbed hands for swimming unless she was in danger. It would be undignified. Shonai seamlessly made the transition from lung to gill, filtering the oxygen from the water as a Sendar would the air. The smooth, low fins on her forearms and back subtly moved, taking her drifting off slowly to her left. By now the sun was beginning to fade above the surface, making her raven hair appear to be ink. Her purple eyes took on an iridescent glow, allowing her to see in the increasing darkness.

A school of small blue fish scattered at her presence. Though the Orcans were now omnivores, much as Sendar, they still retained the markings of the cunning predators they had evolved from. The well-manicured claws on her hands and feet could rip through the tough skin of a full-grown shark with little effort, though, of course, the Princess had no need for such measures.

Shonai caught a glimpse of her bodyguards shadowing her. They were well-trained to be unobtrusive yet effective and ruthless when necessary. Though they seemed too far away to protect her, they could be at her side in a blink.

A dim glow from far below illuminated the water. As she neared it, the uniform purple began to separate into blue and red lights as well. From this view Shonai could see the city sprawled out on the ocean floor, nearly as big as the largest of surface world cities. Over two million Orcans called Sha'na home. The capital city had stood for well over one thousand years through massive tidal waves, jellyfish plagues and an ongoing war with the hated Shrakens, the Orcans' ancient enemy.

Huge marlin were used as Sendar used horses. Gigantic whale sharks were used as cargo transporters, with marlin escorts. Each was heavily guarded, for Shraken attacks were common, if not expected, especially since the attacks had been picking up again lately.

The Royal palace loomed large in Shonai's vision. It was made of lava-glass, a rare, clear metallic substance found at subterranean lava vents. It was as hard as a diamond and just as beautiful. The neon lights were actually not lights at all but deep sea fish who produced the odd gases that combined to make light. The Orcans bred them specifically for this purpose.

There was a smaller version of this palace on the surface Isle for Sendar, Duah, Vull'Kra and Dwarven emissaries, though this was the true seat of power.

Shonai entered the palace grounds with a nonchalance that had become her natural attitude towards her monotonous existence. Her bodyguards came in closer, nearly touching her. Their javelins' wickedly curved tips and serrated edges glinted in the iridescent glow. People recognized the entourage and hastily swam aside. To be caught too near the Princess would entail a javelin in the gut.

Decades of Shraken attacks and assassination attempts had left the Orcans a fierce and wary people.

When, at the end of the Great War, the Orcans had invaded the Shraken capital of Sawtooth, they had let out all of their frustrations on the city's inhabitants. They had killed every Shraken male of fighting age with no remorse. They had leveled the city with their devastating *Sonarblast* attacks, enhanced by their rage. What Shraken males had escaped returned to a ruined city and a defeated populace with almost no chance of reproducing a new generation until the young the Orcans had spared had grown.

This led to a matriarchal Shraken society, where before females hadn't even been allowed to fight, much less rule. The females began rebuilding the city, though to do this, they needed funds. There the Shrakens had turned to large scale piracy. They quickly supplanted themselves as the pre-eminent pirate force in the world. They took over the petty guilds of Goblin and Driss pirates, formed an alliance with the Mai'Lang guilds and began patrolling the shipping lanes of Sendar.

It was this that an Orcan diplomat was discussing with her father when Shonai entered the Great Hall. The discussion stopped and her father appraised her. She had changed quickly into a simple purple sealskin outfit that fit her like a glove. Out of necessity, Orcan clothing fit tight and was slick and aerodynamic.

King Hai'ten rose up and swam slowly to greet his only child and heir to the Orcan throne. His white beard contrasted starkly with his dark purple eyes. He was heavily muscled, still fit and had the imposing air of one who bore authority naturally. A jade and platinum crown encrusted with amethysts sat atop his head as if he had been born with it, which Shonai suspected he had. Her mother, the Queen was a quiet, graceful woman who preferred to listen rather than speak. Shonai rarely heard her utter a word in public, yet at home she was as open as the sea. She had the air of one who knew something no one else did, which she usually did.

"My daughter," Hai'ten smiled. "It pleases me that you have deigned to grace us with your presence." His voice resonated around the chamber as Orcans used sonar to speak underwater. He arched an eyebrow at her.

"Thank you father for your gracious acceptance of my arrival." She moved to the seat of the heir, once held by her brother. He had been slain by Shrakens before Shonai had been born. This accounted for the killing of fighting-age males in the destruction of Sawtooth and to a lesser extent, the other Shraken cities.

The council meeting took place shortly after this and Shonai resorted to her favorite pastime: daydreaming of far off places, exploring the continent and taking risks and challenges that were unavailable to her as a glorified porcelain doll made for others' amusement and viewing pleasure.

The average Orcan could expect to live more than four hundred years, but the Royal Family could expect to leave Sha'na less than a dozen times during that span. Though old enough to reproduce, Shonai was still a baby by Orcan standards, only twenty-one. Custom said she must be over fifty. Not that she was dying for the affection of one of the cookie cutter diplomats or pompous noble brats that vied for her attention. She stared off into space, keeping her face a mask of serenity, while her father discussed important matters with the self-important council members.

When the meeting was over, Shonai exchanged meaningless small talk with Orcan nobles and dignitaries and deftly deflected offers of courtship. She left as soon as she was able and swam back to the solitary confinement of her garden. She passed a squad of border soldiers on their marlins. This gave her an idea. Perhaps she would go for another tour of the reef, her real garden. Shonai smiled wickedly, veering course. She began swimming at a fast pace toward the outskirts of the palace grounds.

A disturbance in the water told her that her bodyguards had materialized beside her to inquire as to her destination.

"Majesty, to where do you travel?" asked Trinon, a young, strong and deceptively intelligent Orcan.

"The stables," she announced, giving an extra burst of speed, exhilarating in the rush of the cold water. She was a sleek, strong swimmer trained in the nuances of wave science from a young age. The bodyguards were hard pressed to keep up, though they didn't show it. By the time they arrived at their destination, all were winded.

The Royal Marlin stables were a vast network of gates and locks enclosing the Royal Family's purebred steeds. The head groom witnessed Shonai approach. He hastily signaled for a servant to get her steed, Drift. The saddled marlin was led out of the gates to her.

"Your steed, Majesty," the groom bowed. Drift eyed the man patiently until Shonai had mounted him. Her bodyguards, too, mounted steeds—though none could compare with Drift. At more than three times as long as an Orcan, he was the biggest, fastest and most perilous marlin in the sea. His sword was half again as long as his body and sharp enough to pierce a stone wall.

Shonai cooed softly to him, her sonar sending him instructions on where to go. He responded, immediately setting a pace that an ordinary Orcan could never match. Her six bodyguards dispersed, forming a perimeter around her like a wall of steel.

As they entered more shallow water, they slackened their pace, shifting their eyes from the starlight spectrum back to normal light intake. The reef loomed large, a massive collage of multicolored beauty. Giant schools of fish swirled to the surface and back. Brightly colored fish darted in and out of anemones, while some peeked out of holes in the reef to inspect the new visitors, most retreating immediately at the sight of so many large predators. Shonai could never get used to the unmatched natural beauty of the reef. She often spent hours here in a dream, exploring for new animals, plants or artifacts lost when one of the clumsy surface ships sank.

Once, when she was little, she had found an untarnished golden gauntlet in a Duah Elven vessel, around the arm of a long-dead Elf. She had playfully put it on her wrist. Unexpectedly, it had magically molded itself to her arm where it had stayed ever since. Though Shonai never told anyone, she suspected the gauntlet had given her magically enhanced abilities, for she could do things that no one else could. She sensed when danger was near and could out swim any threat in the sea. On land, where most of her kind took sometimes entire turns of the glass to readjust their bodies to walking instead of swimming, she could do it in mere moments.

When her father had first learned about the gauntlet, he had tried unsuccessfully to have it removed by both physical and magical means. In time it had earned her a title among her people. They now referred to her as Princess Shonai Golden Gauntlet, much as they caller her father King Hai'ten Shrakensbane. He had been given this name when Shonai was three at the end of the Great Wars.

She saw an odd red eel poke its head through a small crack and swam over to investigate. The eel sensed she was no threat and ventured out to touch her outstretched palm in which she held a small piece of fish. The eel could have taken off her hand with its long, powerful jaws, yet it gently took the fish from her. She knew this eel and had named it S'al, which meant 'shocker' in Orcan, for this was an oceanic electric eel. It, like so many other animals in the reef, knew Shonai and looked forward to her visits like a flower looks forward to the sun's warming rays.

A gentle nudge on Shonai's shoulder startled S'al back into his crevice. Shonai was relieved to see Daan, the matriarch of a dolphin pod. Shonai playfully swatted the dolphin on the snout.

"Where are the rest of your pod?" Shonai asked in Cetacean, the tongue of whales and dolphins.

"Feeding, playing," Daan answered, batting Drift on the snout to say hello. Though he couldn't speak, the marlin could understand rudimentary words and actions and gave a flourish of his massive tail to return the greeting. A few of the other dolphins could be seen now, poking their snouts into crevices and harassing a school of sardines.

This was where Shonai was happiest, among the creatures of the reef. It was often said that when she was Queen, she would move the palace to the reef. She wished she could, but the traffic caused by dignitaries and such would...

Suddenly she felt a familiar tingle that told her danger was near. She quickly scanned the area for an immediate threat. Seeing none, she called out to Trinon.

"Trinon! Be alert! Danger!"

"Where Highness?" Trinon called all the guards to her.

"I don't know." She spotted several dark shapes materializing out of the deep. "Daan, group your pod, I think we're in trouble." Her pod of sixteen adult dolphins surrounded the four younger ones.

"Highness!" Trinon called. "We must leave at once!" But it was too late. The shapes materializing from the front were also coming from behind. In these shallow waters, depth could not be used as an escape route. With a sinking feeling of dread, Shonai recognized the invaders.

"Shrakens!"

The Shrakens grew clearer as they rushed the reef. Ten came from each direction, riding blue sharks as the Orcans rode marlins. They carried deadly battle hooks and weighted nets. Their dull blue skin and orange glowing eyes outlined a mouth full of sharp, serrated teeth in a jaw that could crush bone. Their heads were shaped like hammers, eyes on the corners, letting them see in any direction. Body piercings everywhere gave them the appearance of metal and ripping teeth. It was said they appeared as if from a nightmare but left their victim's eyes open in terror as they ripped out their throat.

Having nowhere to go, Shonai was forced to wait for a hole to open in a battle line to escape from the Shrakens. While the young dolphins had a chance when they had made their break, the Orcan Princess did not, for she was obviously the target. The Shrakens used paralyzing clouds called *Stunspore* as they neared the Orcan line. This was a chemical that would severely dampen an opponents reflexes if taken into the gills. The Orcans knew well this trick and countered it with a *Cleansing* spell in their gills. Shraken *Stunspore* attacks only worked when used with the advantage of surprise.

The Orcans then used their *Sonarblast* in concert, killing three Shrakens and four of their blue shark mounts. The Orcans used distance to their advantage. They were open water killers, with *Sonarblast* and *Cleansing* spells, far greater sight and unmatched speed. A relatively small group of Orcans could destroy a larger group of Shrakens in open water.

Shrakens, by contrast, were ambush killers, geared for close combat. Their lethal jaws, strength and paralyzing clouds could end a close encounter fight in moments. To add to this, they had *Bloodfear,* a spell which helped them smell weakness, be it blood, fear or old age, from immense distances. They preyed on the weak, defenseless and especially the unaware.

This day, however, the Shraken raiding party found to its fatal dismay that these Orcans were neither weak, defenseless nor unaware. The Orcan battle line had caught the Shrakens by surprise. Something, the Shrakens knew, had warned the Orcans. Likely it had been the dolphins. When the Shraken lines wavered in the face of this unexpected onslaught, the Orcans leveled *Sonarblast* at their enemies once more and charged. Together, they and the dolphins circled under the Shrakens and used massive *Bubblewrath* attacks to confuse and corral the disoriented attackers.

The blue sharks, unpredictable and hard to control at the best of times, lost all sense of calm when the huge marlins charged among them, impaling two blues on their first pass. Three more Shrakens were dispatched with the Orcans wicked javelins. The dolphins played a different but just as deadly game with the blues, ramming their snouts into the confused sharks' gills repeatedly, effectively suffocating them.

The Shrakens, however, were seasoned warriors and recovered with a regrouping effort that caused Shonai to double-take. She froze, but only for an instant. The close-quarters fighting now favored the

Shrakens, though they were only half as many as when the battle had started.

An Orcan and two dolphins were the first to die, leaving Trinon and two dolphins on one side of Shonai to fend for themselves. The Shrakens ripping claws and teeth began to wear on the Orcans. Shonai decided that today would not be her day to die, nor to run away. This was her reef and she would defend it as such.

She turned to one of her bodyguards.

"Aye Highness?" the Orcan asked, frantically seeking an escape route for her.

"Today we will fight. Go assist the rear. I will help Trinon."

"But Majesty…"

"That is a Royal order, Do it!"

"Aye, my Princess, Baal protect you."

"And you!" Shonai streaked into the fray. Drift impaled a Shraken from behind. Another Orcan and her marlin killed a dismounted Shraken.

This unexpected attack from reinforcements set the Shrakens on their heels, killing two more in the fierce cloud of bubbles. Shrakens, though, were notorious for their tenacity and fierceness in battle. Instead, they intensified their efforts. Two more Orcans fell, as did all but three dolphins.

Shonai communicated to the remaining few to retreat until the two separate battle lines were one. This they did and slowly merged the lines. Shonai and Trinon worked the ends. The remnants of the dolphins swam crazily to and fro causing havoc among the blue sharks.

Drift was having a grand time of it. Wherever he went, the Shrakens were forced to scatter. Shonai was his equal, the javelin she had taken from a fallen comrade lashed back and forth, dealing death wherever it struck. As the battle progressed, she lost herself in a haze. The red, cloudy water made seeing farther than ten feet in any direction impossible. It seemed she had killed an army and yet more still came to face her.

Shonai lost sight of the rest. Only two Shrakens occupied her vision now, one mountless and his companion on a wounded blue.

Drift instinctively attacked the wounded blue. Its rider used the shark as a shield and drove his hook through Drift's head.

Shonai cried out in rage, releasing a *Sonarblast* that crushed every bone in the Shraken's body. She turned to face the mountless Shraken but he had disappeared. She looked all around and above her. A searing pain in her abdomen told her she had forgotten to look below her. A Shraken battlehook was plunged into her belly. She drove her javelin through the offending Shraken's head before he could rip his hook out.

The pain was unbelievable. Shonai had heard that gut wounds hurt but she had never imagined it could be this bad. She looked frantically for one of her bodyguards but saw nothing but red. Then, she saw only blackness.

CHAPTER 10
CAPTIVE

honai awoke and immediately shut her eyes again. She opened her eyes slowly, letting them adjust to the light. She was in an empty domed chamber with what appeared to be pearl coating on the walls. She was on a floating bed and she was still breathing through her gills. Phosphorous lamps lit the walls with a soft yellow light.

Shonai sat up until a sharp pain in her stomach caused her to collapse back onto the pillow. The battle came back in blinding flashes. What had happened to the rest of her bodyguards? Or to Daan? It was all a haze. She slowly moved her hand to her stomach. Only a small, smooth scar remained where once the hook had been.

"Lay back child, you need rest. You are not completely healed yet." Shonai followed the voice to a woman, with light blue skin and bright green hair. Her large eyes appeared to be black pearls. She was naked from the waist up but from the waist down, she was clothed in what looked like a bright green dress with a tail on the end. Shonai quickly amended this assessment. It *was* a tail, much like a dolphin's.

This was one of the fabled Mer'khan, or as the surface dwellers called them; Mermaids. Even Orcans and Shrakens knew little about them. They were rumored to live deep in the caverns of the sea.

"My name is Keran," she said in her enchanting voice. Only then did Shonai realize that she had spoken directly into her mind.

"I am Shonai, Royal Princess of Orcana," she said, using sonar.

"We know, child. Your family are well known to my people."

"How? I've never even seen one of your kind."

"Have you not?" Keran transformed her body into that of a brightly colored fish, then into a marlin, and lastly into an Orcan. "We walk among you occasionally. We swim the reef in search of artifacts, same as you." She indicated the golden gauntlet Shonai wore.

"How did I get here?" Shonai asked, unsure if she was still dreaming.

"A group of our hunters came across you sinking to the bottom. At first, they thought you dead, but they rushed you back anyway. When they brought you in, I wasn't optimistic about your chances for survival. Until I learned about your gauntlet."

"What do you mean?"

"It kept you alive and when we used a healing spell on you, it flared and added its own power to ours. I was thankful."

"It is I who should be thankful to you. Now, if you'll just help me up, I'll be on my way. I have to find out what happened to my body-guards." As she raised up, the water around her thickened, forcing her to remain prone. Keran had molded the water into a hand that held her flat.

"Child, if you move again, you will rip the stitches holding your shredded organs together. You must stay still. We have sent scouts out to determine the extent of the battle. You will be appraised of the situation when we are. In the meantime, rest." She waved her hand. Shonai fell into a deep slumber.

It was not a dreamless sleep. Shonai saw herself walking on land, surrounded by lush greenery and a clear, cool stream in the shadow of the majestic mountain. She bent down to take a sip. She caught her reflection, but it was that of an Elven girl. Behind her was a large blob of putrid green. She whirled to confront the blob and found it to be many blobs. All were faceless, but their intents were deadly. She pulled a wicked, beautifully curved javelin from her gauntlet like liquid gold.

The green blobs attacked. Shonai dove into the stream only to find it too shallow. She looked furiously for a place to run but found nothing. She had to turn and fight. The green blobs were upon her.

She fought endlessly, hitting them as they came until she stood on a pile of their dead that blocked the river and dyed it red. Yet, still they came. She couldn't win; she had to escape.

Shonai awoke with a stifled scream to find three Mer'khan females, all standing in a semi-circle around her. The youngest Mer'khan female swam forward, placing her hands, which were accented by ornate golden shells on either side of Shonai's head. Shonai felt a powerful surge of warmth and a sense of euphoria flood through her.

"Awake little Sister, come among us as you were born to be born again," the Mer'khan said in a soft voice. The other two drifted slowly over and lifted Shonai out of the floating bed. They began to undress her. The youngest one adorned Shonai's wrists with the golden shells, imbuing her with a sense of community, of Sisterhood. A silver dust began to float down on her. When it touched her, it sent shivers through her entire body. The three Mer'khan rubbed the silver into her skin methodically, without regard for her Orcan sense of modesty.

She felt she should shy away or blush profusely. Instead she encouraged them, letting her inhibitions go. The euphoria of the moment was all that mattered. A warm light pulsed at the core of her being, making her begin to glow brighter and brighter purple.

It was all becoming a blur. The warm caresses of the Mer'khan, the hypnotic silver dust, the swaying of the water until the purple glow came to a crescendo and burst. The light was so bright that it blinded her, and when she could finally see again, the Mer'khan were once again formed in a semi-circle around her. She wanted them to come to her again, to feel them all through her but they remained immobile. Come to think of it, so was she!

She stared at her body, jaw hanging open. She was pure, reflective silver, the metal reflecting her glowing purple eyes. She looked to the Mer'khan for answers.

"Break the mold," they whispered.

"But, how, it's metal!"

"You must break the mold."

"Great," Shonai muttered under her breath. She began trying to move frantically, but it was useless. Next she tried to focus all of her strength in a small area. This also was doomed to failure.

She took a deep breath to calm herself. She focused on her core, where the purple glow had originated. Next, she carefully coaxed it into growing, letting it expand with her mounting energies. She concentrated on her stomach wound, figuring it to be the weakest point in the shell. When the energy had built up to just beneath her skin, she forced it all to the scar. At first, nothing appeared but a tiny crack. She redoubled her efforts, exhausting her waning strength. The crack began to spider web. All at once, the shell exploded outward from her, once again cloaking the room in a blinding flash of energy. Shonai looked down at herself again, warily. This time she was back to her normal form, albeit with a slight gleam. A golden seashell was on each of her wrists.

"What happened just now?" she asked the smiling Mer'khan.

"Think of an intelligent sea-dwelling animal; any animal."

"Aye." Shonai quirked an eyebrow.

"Now, go to your core and concentrate on *being* that animal."

"But I can't."

"You can do many things now that you couldn't before, child. Now concentrate like I instructed you." Shonai shrugged her shoulders, once again calming herself. She reached her core quickly now. She wanted most to be a dolphin and so she concentrated on that.

She began to feel her body stretch. At first she thought the Mer'khan were pulling her toward them. Then a brief wave of nausea came and went, forcing her to drop to one knee. Only it wasn't a knee anymore, but a long, gray tail. She held out her arm to investigate and was amazed to find that it was a flipper. She spun experimentally in the water, strangely excited by this new form. She noticed that the gauntlet morphed with her.

"This is so amazing," she smiled. "Is it real?" the Mer'Khan women nodded.

After a few more moments of frolicking, she morphed back into her Orcan form. She bubbled with questions but she was suddenly too tired to ask them. She slowly laid herself down in the bed. She was immeasurably grateful to the Mer'khan for saving her and giving her these wonderful new powers, yet something seemed wrong about them. Their intentions seemed something less than altruistic.

There was another thing. She could not for the life of her figure out where she could be. The Orcans had mapped out every nitch and crevice within two hundred leagues of Sha'na. She could feel no pressure, oddly enough. So her depth readings were off. She tried to remain conscious but failed and drifted off into an uneasy sleep.

"Come child, your training begins this day." Keran gently nudged Shonai out of bed. She had been sleeping almost constantly since her transformation. Keran said it was natural. Her body had to heal and reenergize itself from its traumatic ordeal two weeks past.

"Never take these off," Keran said, indicating the golden-etched seashells. "Without them morphing is impossible." Shonai studied them for a moment after getting dressed.

"Keran, what am I training for?"

"Have patience, child," Keran smiled. "All will be revealed in time. For now, I will show you around the city so that you don't become lost."

"Keran, no offense intended, but I *am* from Sha'na."

"Nevertheless child." Keran smiled and waved her hand to open the door of the pearl-coated room. They drifted into a bright passageway lit only by phosphorus. Shonai glanced back at her room. It was the shell of a giant clam. All along the corridor were identical clams, some bigger than hers, some artfully attached to others to form extra rooms.

They seemed to be drifting upwards to a summit of some sort, though Shonai couldn't feel the change in elevation. As they crested the hill, her breath caught in her throat.

They were inside a monstrous cavern large enough to fit three Sha'nas inside. The bright phosphorus lights reflected off tens of thousands of pearly buildings. Giant seahorses drifted lazily along carrying their Mer'khan passengers to unknown destinations throughout the vast city. A soft glow pervaded the city, making it seem almost dreamlike.

Spires hundreds of feet tall dotted the landscape, reflecting the light in a billion directions. Massive domes as big as towns sprawled everywhere. Perfectly parallel and intersecting streets criss-crossed huge buildings and continued off into hundreds of corridors similar to the one she was in.

"How many people are here?" Shonai asked.

"Millions."

"How do my people not know of it?"

"We are almost a whole mile beneath the surface. Your people rarely swim this far down. Also, the cavern you see is inside a mountain and the entrance is hardly big enough for three Mer'khans to swim abreast through. Once, a group of your people came here."

"Where did they go? Why did we never hear from them?"

"We could not allow them to leave once they had found us." Keran said sadly. "We are an isolated people now as we were before your race had even come into existence. Contact with your people would expose us and drag us into war. We, too, know of the Shrakens. We have infiltrated them for centuries. Our people fear the outside world knowing of us, yet we walk among them in disguise. It is not as I wish it were, but the High, like his forbears, keeps us sealed off from the world."

"Are you saying that you *killed* my people to avoid exposure?!" Shonai rounded on her.

"No child. We merely refused their departure. We performed the same spell as we did on you, allowing you to morph, partly in compensation for freedom. Now they may live life among us as equals. They are not the only ones here. We have rescued many such as you, to heal here. In time, with reproduction, your people have become quite populous. You will not be alone. We used to rescue Shrakens, Barakans and Pir'Noh, but they are evil creatures and anyway, your people killed all the survivors immediately upon arrival."

"Are you refusing my departure?" Shonai demanded.

"I'm sorry child, it is our way." Keran reached her hand to rest on Shonai's shoulder. Shonai slapped it away.

"I am *not* your child! I am your prisoner! I am Princess Shonai Golden Gauntlet of Orcana! By holding me hostage, you declare war between our people, healing or not. You should have let me die! Do you knowingly plunge your precious city into death? For I can assure you that we have refined the art of warfare far beyond what any of your pathetic isolationists have even dreamt of. I will destroy this entire mountain and all in it and it will be you who are to blame for your peoples' destruction!"

"Shonai, you know not of what you speak. You are angry, I can understand. In time you will come to see it is for the best. For what it is worth…"

"It is worth *nothing* to me, slave-master Keran. Take me to my people that I may inquire as to what punishments you have so kindly inflicted on them."

"Very well, if that is your wish."

"It is."

"You must morph into a Mer'khan form to pass on the streets, else you draw unnecessary attention. The first lesson of a Mer'khan is to remain inconspicuous."

"I will not."

"But, Shonai, you must!"

"I will die before I accept the form of my kidnappers. You would have been better off leaving us to die than to imprison us."

"But…" Keran was cut off by a blast of sonar that left her deaf for a few dreadful moments. When she could hear again, Shonai whispered softly into her ear.

"Next time you will feel your heart explode in your coward's chest. Take me to my people. Now. Otherwise kill me and have done with it."

"As you wish," Keran whispered. For all their age and technological prowess, the Mer'khan had been too long without war. They had grown weak. In their eyes, Shonai's people were inferior, to be shown the light and live as a Mer'khan. Anything else was barbaric. They wished to remake her race in their image. They believed they were saving her as well as their way of life.

Keran embarrassedly led Shonai down the beautiful streets. Mer'khan openly stared and cursed her audacity. Shonai held her head high, making eye contact with all. A narrow alley led her to a huge, beautifully sculpted golden gate. Two huge Mer'khan men carrying tridents guarded it.

Keran instructed Shonai to remain where she was, telepathically speaking to the guards. They glanced menacingly at Shonai, then opened the gate to let her in.

"You new home, Shonai. He will show you to your quarters."

"Fine. Lead the way," Shonai answered telepathically, showing Keran that she had heard her instructions to the guards. Keran paled. "We *will* meet again." She swam past and into the Orcan section of the city.

The 'Orcan Sector' was a long corridor cut out of the cavern. Nearly half a league in, it opened into another cavern, displaying the layout of the settlement. Clam houses were in neat rows with a large complex at the center.

The Mer'Khan led her silently to her quarters and then left without a word.

"Well," Shonai sighed, "no time like the present to get started."

Her quarters were actually quite nice. As all homes appeared to be in Merkhandin, hers was a giant shell. A cozy bedroom opened into a kitchen/dining room with a small living room opening off of that. There were books encased in water proofing spells on the shelf above her bed, all from well-known Sendar, Vull'Kra and Duah authors. That these people could read surface languages struck her as either ridiculous or disturbing.

On the one hand, the Mer'khans' disdain for races other than themselves would prevent their learning of an 'inferior' language. On the other, perhaps their telepathy enabled them to steal the language directly from another mind. Granted this civilization had become weak with complacency, but should such a large, intelligent and powerful species direct their considerable resources towards conquest, there was no telling how far they could go.

Shonai knew better than to think that the Mer'khan would just leave her here and forget about her. They would watch her every move. Nor did she think she could make her way out without her people accompanying her. She decided to investigate before making her bid for leadership. If these people had adopted the Mer'khan code of ethics, it was unlikely that she, Princess or not, could take the role of leader without force, though she would try.

When she left her dwelling, she was confronted with the grim possibility that she could be here for a long time. She headed for a tavern she had seen on her way in.

The number of Orcans was astounding. There were upwards of two hundred milling in and around the tavern and its surrounding shops. It appeared to be the closest thing the Orcans had to a city here. There had to be hundreds more elsewhere in the settlement. Yet, all were in their Mer'khan forms. This angered her.

Her eyes flared. All thoughts of a gradual, graceful assimilation fled her mind. She shot like a lavender arrow into the tavern, bowling two men out of the way. All conversation—telepathic she noted disgustedly—abruptly stopped. All eyes focused on her.

"Excuse me!" the bartender exclaimed. "Just what in Nu's Bowels do you…" he never got to finish. Shonai morphed into an animal she knew well: An electric eel. She let forth a tremendous surge of electricity, incapacitating everyone in the room. She morphed back quickly, the gauntlet restoring her energy immediately. She spoke in loud Orcan.

"You will be in your true Orcan form when you address me, slaves, or not at all. I speak only to free people. You have let petty conveniences lull you from your true, proud Orcan heritage." She glared around the room, her anger palpable. One Orcan, a male not much older than herself, morphed to his Orcan form.

"Who are you?"

"My name is Shonai Golden Gauntlet, daughter of King Hai'ten, Crown Princess of Orcana, heir to the throne of Sha'na." A few of the oldest among them quickly morphed to Orcan form before bowing their heads. The rest, seeing this, did likewise. Shonai picked out the young Orcan who had morphed. "What is your name?"

"Zoltaure, Majesty,"

"When and how did you come to be here, Zoltaure?"

"My mother was wounded in a Shraken attack before I was born. I have never been anywhere else."

"You," Shonai pointed to an older, wise-looking Orcan woman. "Why are you still here? Surely you remember Sha'na?"

"Aye Majesty, but the Mer'khan have a magical force field geared only to their physiology. We tried to escape long ago but were stopped short. They didn't kill us, just apologized and led us back here. No

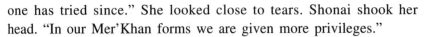

one has tried since." She looked close to tears. Shonai shook her head. "In our Mer'Khan forms we are given more privileges."

"Who is the leader here?"

"Gamarin," Zoltaure informed her.

"Where can I find him?"

"At his house just down the way. I will take you if you'll permit it."

"Very well." Shonai let a smile creep onto her face. "The rest of you, I tell you not as your Princess, but as a fellow Orcan. To be an Orcan is the finest feeling in all the realms. Can you not feel the glory of Baal flowing through your every movement? The rush of water in your gills, the beautiful sound of a sonar reflection, the thrill of the hunt. Don't hide these things. Revel in them. Do not hide behind this façade of the Mer'khan. You're held captive in body, not in spirit." With that, she left, Zoltaure following her.

"What is you opinion of Gamarin?" Shonai asked as they reached the household.

"He is a capable leader, well educated, patient and cunning."

"How does he interact with the Mer'khan" she asked, watching him with a piercing eye.

"He regards them with a very well hidden distrust. He bows to their wishes only when they suit us. They don't seem to care as long as we don't threaten their precious isolation," he said with contempt. Shonai looked at him curiously.

"Do many here feel as you do about the Mer'khan?"

"Aye, Majesty. All but the most shallow, those easily swept aside with the promise of permanent welfare. They have saved most of our lives but only to imprison us."

"Then why do you do nothing? Why do you stay?"

"Because, Majesty, we have been shut down on every attempt. We have all but given up hope."

"I will not. You may draw your hope from me, for I will never give up."

"Aye Majesty, we may have to."

"Thank you for your help, Zoltaure. It will not be forgotten."

"Aye Majesty. If you need anything else, I live behind the tavern."

Shonai steeled herself as she knocked on the outside of the clam. A rush of water revealed the hatch. An Orcan male in natural form drifted out. He was of barely legal reproductive age in Sha'na with long, straight black hair that bordered a scarred face.

"May I be of some assistance?" He spoke in Orcan. Apparently only in public did the Orcans assume Mer'Khan form.

"Aye, I am looking for Gamarin. I was told I could find him here."

"I am he."

"You? I mean, I thought you would be older," she blushed.

"Aha. Do you have a name? I don't recognize you, though you do look familiar."

She introduced herself. Gamarin's jaw dropped. He looked as if he had seen a ghost. When he recovered, he quickly bowed his head. She called him back up.

"That certainly explains why you looked familiar. I was your brother's bodyguard, rest his soul." He removed his shirt to reveal a network of horrific scars. "I was 'killed' defending him. I awoke here. I was informed later he had died. I am disgraced, Your Highness. I lead here only in the hopes of redeeming myself to my people."

Shonai hid her shock. "You did all you could, and now I ask you to help me free *our* people from this place."

"Anything Majesty. We have been waiting for someone like you to bring the spark back into our existence. You have my loyalty and all who are loyal to me as well."

"Good. Together we will find a way out."

Shonai instructed him to distribute several false stories to identify suspected spies. Next she learned of Merkhandin politics and decided to use them in her favor.

While Gamarin was busy organizing the spy catching operation, Shonai was honing her considerable skills of telepathy. The Mer'khan were careful not to invest equal telepathic powers into the Orcans. This way they could always subtly control them while the Orcans fancied themselves immune to telepathic and telekinetic attacks.

However, the Mer'khan were somewhat closed-minded in their morphing. They would not change into one of their seahorses or another barely sentient being. Shonai held no such qualms and her gauntlet had given her a higher level of telepathic and telekinetic abilities than even the highest Mer'khan.

She assumed the form of a Mer'khan merchant she had seen in the tavern (though it made her feel dirty). She approached the two guards nonchalantly, blocking her mind so that only her assumed identity's thoughts were readable. The guards asked no questions, merely let her through the gate.

Once on the streets, she swam quickly to her destination. The avenues were crowded with Mer'khan. All kept their thoughts shielded, rarely probing any others. A few soldiers along the way gave her passing probes but quickly moved onto other passersby.

She reached a rather large residence soon after. Four guards manned the gate while a transparent bubble surrounded the house, preventing any from sneaking in from another depth or direction.

A small stable rested just inside the perimeter. She caught sight of a majestic-looking seahorse. She hid herself in the shadows of a bed of sponges, which used phosphorescence instead of sunlight for photosynthesis, as did all of the plants in the Mer'khan realm. Carefully morphing back to her Orcan form, she let out a high-pitched frequency of sonar that only the animal could hear.

It raised its head at her voice. She beckoned to it come to her, which it did, passing right through the shield. As she had suspected, it only prevented objects from going in, not leaving. When it reached her, Shonai sent it off the other direction.

She had counted on the guards seeing this, which they did. Two came swimming after the seahorse. Shonai quickly morphed into the animal and wandered back out.

They led her back into the stables, tying her there this time for good measure. She maintained this guise until they had stopped checking on her. Then, morphing into a small, thin sea snake, she squirmed her way out of the knot and quickly swam to a small vent in the side of the house that cycled fresh water in and out. She slipped into the tiny opening, wriggling her way around until she was inside the complex.

Seeing no one, she morphed back into her Orcan form, swimming along a narrow, glassy corridor until she heard voices. They were coming closer. She shot up to the ceiling and became one with it.

Two Mer'khan swam slowly by, talking animatedly. One, a large, older male with silver streaks in his green hair, the other, a slight male with a rat-like face and a shaved head.

"But Tomar," Rat face was saying, "you can't truly believe that we've anything to gain from contact with other races! What else do we need. We are the pinnacle of civilization!"

"Aye D'onair," Tomar replied. "I do believe we have much to gain. We have let the world pass us by. Think of the trade we could do! We would flourish. Think of the newly learned secrets we could explore!"

"Why? We can steal them whenever we like."

"Aye, as we've done for centuries. Tell me D'onair, if we are the pinnacle of civilization, why do *we* have to steal secrets from *them*?" At this, D'onair paused, looking reflective.

"A good point you make. But what of war? That is the main question. By opening ourselves to the world, we open ourselves up to war."

"True, yet why not? We have become weak with stagnation. But with allies such as the Orcans, the Sendar and the Elves, we could grow strong again. All would know us and respect us."

"Another good point, Tomar. We will speak again," D'onair opened the hatch that was the front door.

"I look forward to it, D'onair." Tomar closed the hatch. Shonai returned to her natural form dropping silently down behind him. She decided to speak in telepathy to him to keep him calm.

"Did you mean that?" Tomar jumped, nearly banging his head on the ceiling. "Calm down, I mean you no harm."

"Who are you? And what are you doing in my house?" he asked quietly, showing her his calm.

"My name is Shonai Golden Gauntlet, daughter of King Hai'ten, Princess of Orcana." She was tired of introducing herself, she thought in passing.

"Ah of course. The one they brought in nearly dead a few weeks ago. An honor to meet you, Your Highness. Now how did you get in my house?" She tapped her head. "Ah," he nodded.

"Did you mean what you said to D'onair or were you merely postulating?" she asked.

"Aye. I meant it. I am tired of being cooped up, hiding my presence from the world. I see an enormous upside and a very inconsequential downside."

"And what of war?"

"It is the way of the world. I fear no other race. We will make allies, just as you have and many will vie for that title. We have lived too long in our isolated bubble. It is time for us to come out."

"And how do your fellow Council members think?"

"Some for, most against," he replied sadly.

"And the High?"

"Hah! Only if it were forced upon him."

"And if it was?"

"Well, then I guess he wouldn't have a choice."

"What if I could make that happen?"

"And just how would you go about that?"

"To escape and tell my people, of course."

"Do you think it's that easy? Your people have tried more than once and failed."

"Aye, or no, Tomar."

"Aye," he said after a moment.

"Good. Tomorrow, same time, can you arrange a meeting with D'onair again?"

"Aye."

"Good. I will become him, instruct your guards to let me in without question. I will get your plan."

"Very well. Don't let me down."

"You are not the only person taking a risk, you know," she informed him. "You could turn me in at any moment."

"True enough. Until tomorrow night, Princess," he said.

She left the same way she had entered, as a drifting sea snake. When she was safely away, she morphed to the Mer'Khan merchant's form and called the seahorse back to its original owner.

That night she wandered about, trying desperately to think of a way out. She was swimming the perimeter of the Orcans' cavern when a dark shape rushed by, causing her to stop in alarm. The shape returned. She prepared to unleash *Sonarblast,* when it morphed, becoming a small, brightly colored deep sea fish with long, clear teeth and flashing neon lights. She recognized it as one the Orcans bred for light.

Shonai regarded the fish, amused as it now went through a cycle of morphs, a dolphin, a seahorse, a sponge and finally back to a young, sleek Orcan male with spiky black hair and light purple eyes. She smiled when she recognized him as Zoltaure.

"Zoltaure, you nearly scared me out of my fins!"

"Sorry Majesty. But after you gave that speech at the tavern, some of us, well, almost all of us got together and began concentrating on our morphing. We went past the boundaries the Mer'khan had set for us. We shifted into anything we could think of. It was hard work, but now we are better able to defend ourselves!" He spoke quickly, excitedly.

"I am proud of you all, Zoltaure," she nodded.

"Word of your presence has spread like sand in the waves among our people, Majesty. We have hope again."

"Excellent. Tell me, who thought of the sponge?" she asked anxiously.

"Gamarin, Majesty," he answered, averting his eyes.

"He was there?"

"It was at his household."

"And what did you make up, Zoltaure? I know you well enough to know you were one of the inventors." She goaded him gently.

"I have not perfected it yet, Majesty. It would not be worth your time."

"Nonsense. Let me see."

"Aye, but don't laugh, Highness," he warned shyly.

"I promise."

"All right." He closed his eyes, concentrating. He shimmered and for a second she thought he had disappeared, but then she caught a thin outline in the light. He was transparent.

"Zoltaure," she whispered. He morphed back quickly, eyes downcast.

"I know, you could still see me but..."

"Zoltaure, it's perfect! How did you come up with it?"

"Well," he flushed, "I just saw the deep sea fish and how they were clear except for their lights. So I morphed to one, turned my lights off and then shifted back to Orcan without changing my color, which I can do more quickly," he added with a hint of pride.

"Can you show me?" she asked excitedly.

"Of course, Majesty." He proceeded to take her through it step by step until she had mastered it.

"This is perfect!" she exclaimed, hugging Zoltaure. He seemed shocked, yet he hugged her back.

"Majesty, I..." he began. She put a finger to his lips.

"When we are alone, call me Shonai," she whispered softly.

"Aye, Maj—I mean Shonai." They continued their embrace, lost in each other's gaze until Zoltaure broke slowly, reluctantly away.

"Zoltaure?"

"Aye?" he answered.

"Get with Gamarin and teach him your morph. Then instruct him to train a dozen trusted Orcans you both can agree on. Can you do that for me?"

"Aye, Shonai. It will be done." He smiled and took off towards Gamarin's household. When he had disappeared from sight, she resumed swimming the perimeter again. She had solved the problem of their morph, now she had to worry about the shield. She knew from reliable reports that it was impenetrable. Only the combined efforts of a hundred Mer'khan expert water movers and a password from the High would lift it.

She emitted a *Sonarblast* in frustration at the wall, watching off-handedly as a small group of stones cascaded down the cavern wall. She continued swimming, thinking hard. Suddenly she stopped, backpedaling a few strokes. She stared slack-jawed at the cavern wall. She unleashed another *Sonarblast* in the same spot. More rocks tumbled off, creating a crevice in the wall.

"That's it! That's how we'll get out of here!" She mentally calculated where the city was, guessing it to be at the center of the mountain. Using these coordinates, she found a spot on the wall that she hoped was closest to the outside.

She mentally marked the spot, then swam quickly back to her quarters. Tomorrow would be a long day.

CHAPTER 11
ESCAPE

trust you have a plan?" Tomar asked, offering her a slice of *taoi*, or giant squid. Shonai ate it slowly, savoring its taste. It was cooked lightly with phosphorous fire. She finished chewing before speaking, even though it was telepathically. Old habits died hard.

"Aye. I'm not sure of its time frame but it shouldn't take longer than a week."

"Really? A week? That is quite an accomplishment. What exactly is it that you intend to do?"

"I intend to blast our way out. I will use sonar to carve a tunnel out of the cavern. Then we will use a special morph to elude any pursuers."

"A special morph?"

"Aye."

"And what is it you require of me?" he asked, not just a little curious. "I'll admit you've piqued my interest, but what will my people have to do to ensure your success?"

"I will need three things. First, I will need you to keep this a secret until the day before we go. Second, I will need a large diversion of some sort. And lastly, I'll need that list. This is too important to have it compromised by a self-serving Orcan informer."

"The list I have now," he said, opening a small drawer in his desk. He handed her a waterproofed parchment list of eleven names on it. She didn't recognize any of them.

"This is all of them?"

"That is any Orcan who has ever given us information regarding the actions of your people."

"Good. Thank you. Have you any ideas on the diversion?"

"I am mulling over a few as we speak. Now, as for my part, I want to make sure I am still being taken care of."

"Such as?" she asked.

"Such as financially. While I am a fairly well placed man in Mer'khan society, I wish more. Much more. You are Princess of Orcana. After your successful escape, should you mention to your father, the King, that I was a trustworthy ally, he might be persuaded to offer me the position of trade advisor to my people?" He smiled innocently.

"I think something like that could be worked out, aye."

"Not that I don't want to help your people. I just feel it's right to be rewarded for my risk, no?"

"Of course." She smiled back, playing along, politics bred into her from birth.

"Excellent. Meet me here six days from now at the same time and we'll make the final preparation. I will inform you of any goings-on that may aid you."

"Thank you. Six days from today it is then," she said, rising. Afterwards, she morphed back to the form of D'onair and made her exit.

"Through the wall? Are you sure it can be done?" Gamarin asked incredulously. Shonai nodded, looking around his sparsely furnished living room.

"Aye. I will need the dozen Orcans Zoltaure taught the special morph. Six will be on duty at a time. Three blasting, two dispersing the rubble away and one keeping watch. Next, I will need two more trustworthy, accomplished shifters to imitate the cavern wall, alternating when they tire. This will provide any curious onlookers with nothing more than a rock face to look at."

"I can't believe we never thought about this. This could actually work!"

"Aye." She handed him the list. He perused it slowly, nodding at some of the names and raising his eyebrows at others. He went to a filing cabinet and pulled out a similar document, handing it to her.

"This is what my people compiled."

"These people must be kept in the dark."

"Aye. But what will we do with them when the time comes to leave?"

"Dispose of them however you see fit," she said coldly.

"Majesty, I didn't think you had it in you," he said approvingly.

"Where my peoples' freedom and lives are concerned, the lives of traitors pale in comparison."

"I couldn't agree with you more, your Highness. I'll get the plan set in motion immediately."

"Very well, thank you."

"It is my pleasure, Majesty." Gamarin said, showing her to the door. He dispatched an aide to collect the necessary Orcans for the job. As Shonai was leaving, Gamarin called out. "What will you do until we are ready?" She turned and regarded him thoughtfully.

"I think I'll go and pay a visit to an old friend."

After dressing, she morphed into an unknown Orcan form. She then headed to the tavern to await her ride.

Her "ride" was an old Mer'khan merchant who had found a niche selling spirits to the Orcans for their Mer'khan-subsidized welfare. He carried a large basket behind him filled with spirits and *Lukarn*, a deep sea anemone that produced hallucinations.

Shonai crept up behind him. As she placed her hand on the basket, she morphed herself into a large black sponge, much like the ones used to make the spirits. He carried a few of these in his basket as well. The Mer'khan did not drink spirits as they were a wholly underwater species. The Orcans, however, had solved the problem of spirits by creating a vacuum-like instrument that fit into the bottle. When they wanted a drink, they would filter all the water from their lungs and shut their gills before drinking.

As she made the final transformation, the Mer'khan grunted.

"Damn baskets' gettin' heavier every damn day!" he complained, still swimming slowly onward. The guards at the gate gave him little more than a cursory glance. When they had reached a main intersection, Shonai carefully shifted to a young Mer'khan girl before gliding out of the basket. The old man noticed the change in weight and whirled around thinking he was being robbed.

"Why ye damned, dirty thieves, I'll..." he stopped abruptly, seeing the little Mer'khan girl ready to cry. "Wah? Oh, I uh. Well, aye, get on with ye now young'un," he stammered. Shonai shot off as if launched from a catapult, up wide, populated avenues, negotiating the traffic with ease.

Finally she reached an avenue she knew well. It sloped upwards, to be swallowed by a well-lit corridor lined with clam shells. She swam quickly until she came to the one she had been searching for. She stared at it for a long time before heading for the hatch. Though a simple wave of the hand accompanied by a water-moving spell would open the door, Shonai had no doubt that a more complex spell was attached to set off a magical alarm if not dispelled.

Timing it just right, she opened the hatch, while performing a series of deceptively simple water-moving gestures with her hand, opening the hatch's magical gate to her. To the unwary observer, these hand signals would have made little sense, yet she had seen this hatch opened many times and had studied the proper spell.

Shonai stepped inside casually, as if she lived there. Closing the hatch behind her automatically reset the spell. Shifting back to her true form, she gave the residence a short perusal. By her calculations, she still had a turn of the glass before she would have company. She began going through the drawers and closets.

Finally she found what she was looking for—a golden shell, about the size of her palm, a larger version of the ones she wore about her wrists. She tucked it and six tiny shells into a pouch at her waist.

Her reverie was broken as the hatch to the residence opened, revealing the person Shonai had come to see. She waited until the hatch closed before telepathically speaking.

"Hello Keran," she said mildly, scaring the Mer'khan woman so badly that she nearly fainted.

"Shonai?"

"Sorry I scared you," Shonai smiled apologetically.

"You—what are—how?" Keran stammered.

"I thought we might have a talk." Shonai indicated the adjacent seat. "Have a seat, won't you? You must be exhausted after a long day of maintaining isolation." Keran remained floating.

"You have no right to be in my home!" she said menacingly, her composure regained.

"No *right?* No *right?* Who are *you* to tell *me* about rights?" Shonai scoffed.

"I'm getting the guard and..." Shonai cut her off, shaking her head.

"The hatch is locked and I've put a sound block over the entire residence. It's just you and me having a discussion about what was it? Oh that's it, rights. I believe you were telling me that you have the right to hold my people hostage for fear of exposure?"

"If you think that isolation is *my* idea or that *I* am the one keeping you here, then you aren't as intelligent as I gave you credit for." The Mer'khan said vehemently.

"I don't." Shonai replied calmly.

"What?"

"I don't. That's why you still breathe. The fact that your people have saved a number of mine from death is why I will not use violence when I leave your 'city of the past' behind."

"You still plan to leave?" Keran sat down.

"Of course," Shonai laughed. "Did you think I would bow before your welfare and wisdom, abandoning my life? Perhaps become a shell collector? Or a *taoi* chef, maybe?"

"No. I just meant that there is no way out *short of killing* many Mer'khan."

"There is, and I will use it, though if any try to stop me, their lives will become forfeit. I have no choice. I will not remain a prisoner, well-treated or not."

"And what of when you escape?"

"What of it?"

"Will you return with your armies?"

"I will tell you a story, Keran. It is an old Orcan story about a young man out on a hunt for tuna. He had been out for three days with only his marlin for company and still had not found a school. As night drew near, he saw the silhouette of a surface ship above. A net was hanging down and he saw that a dolphin had become trapped in it. He knew that where there were dolphins, there were bound to be tuna.

He reasoned that if he cut the dolphin loose it would lead him to the tuna with which he could return home and feed his people for weeks. However, he also knew that should he cut the nets, he would make an enemy of the surface ships' crew.

Now, while the dolphin was no match for the surface crew should it have come to a fight, he weighed the good of his people against the good of himself. Thus, he cut the dolphin loose and the dolphin led him to a large school of tuna. The surface crew, seeing their torn net, tried to spear him but the dolphin led him to safety, taking a spear in its fin. And still it led him to the tuna, which he caught by the dozen. He felt bad for the dolphin, yet it was happy because it had returned the favor.

He and the dolphin returned home to a great welcome in recognition of the harvest they had brought to feed the hungry people. That is how the Orcans and dolphins became allies." Shonai looked steadily at Keran who wore a thoughtful expression. "You see Keran, that is what an ally is. A friend who looks out for you because you look out for them. If they are hurt in the process, they are not angry because they know you would have done the same for them.

"It is this that has made my people strong. We choose strong, loyal allies and protect them as they protect us. Your people, for all their obvious wisdom are out of touch with the world. You have no concept of allies. You take but you do not give back. In the world there is no neutral. You are either with us or against us. When you have decided where you stand, you will have your answer. Your people alone will make the choice as to your future." Shonai finished, standing and opened the hatch without another word.

"Shonai." Keran called.

"Aye?"

"I didn't tell you before because I didn't want to upset you, but..."

"But what?"

"Our scouts returned from the scene of the battle a little over a week ago. It was quite a scene. I'm sorry, but we found six Orcan corpses as well as over a dozen dolphins."

"They're all dead?" Shonai's voice nearly broke.

"Aye." Keran rose and swam over to her. "But we discovered something amazing there also."

"What?" Shonai asked, her voice giving up and breaking, telepathy shed for sonar.

"We also found the corpses of thirty-two Shrakens and a like number of blue sharks."

"How many?"

"Thirty-two. But that's not all. The last eight were alive after the last of your bodyguards had fallen."

"What are you getting at?"

"You, Shonai. You killed all eight of them yourself."

"No, that can't be right."

"We did a magical resonance check. Your signature was on all of them, and seven others as well. I don't know where you learned to fight like that being a Princess, but I fear we may be in for a painful awakening should you choose to attack us."

"Thank you for telling me," Shonai said, her emotions back under control. She stepped out the hatch. Turning, she snared Keran in her gaze. "Maybe the next time we meet, it will be on the same side of the battlefield."

"Careful now," Shonai instructed. She was standing inside the tunnel the Orcans had blasted over the past six days. "When we break through the last barrier, the pressure in the entire cavern will change, alerting the Mer'khan to a disturbance. As soon as we open it, we must leave."

"I can hear the sea outside, Majesty," An Orcan female told her.

"Good, stop blasting. Now, all of you have a greater task. You must go and teach every Orcan in the city the new morph. We have until this time tomorrow." She turned to Gamarin. "It's time to take care of our spy problem."

"Aye, Majesty, it will be done. When I return to the tavern to help in the morphing lessons, you will know it has been completed."

"Thank you," Shonai said with a pained expression on her face.

"Majesty, I know it's hard for you to give this order, but it is the right thing to do. The freedom of our people outweighs the lives of those who would enslave them."

"You are right, as always. See to it."

"Aye, Majesty." He left shortly after the others, leaving only the two Orcans imitating the cavern wall. She swam past them, checking and rechecking every detail of the tunnel. She made her way to the tavern and assumed her usual disguise before once more making her way to Tomar's residence.

As usual the guards let D'onair pass without question and as usual, Tomar met him at the hatch. Once safely inside the residence, D'onair morphed back to Shonai taking a seat across from the Mer'khan.

"It still amuses me that you're able to imitate him so perfectly, your Highness."

"Thank you." Shonai acknowledged the compliment.

"How is it progressing?"

"We are ready. Tomorrow at just after the midday break. The spies are being dealt with as we speak. Should the guards somehow make it to the chamber before the escape is finished, I will do everything I can to prevent their deaths, though I can make no guarantees."

"I understand. It goes with the territory."

"What about the diversion?" Shonai asked him.

"That has been taken care of. It will happen exactly after the midday break."

"I trust it will be adequate?"

"*More* than adequate," he replied confidently. "Actually something I've wanted to do since I was a child."

"Excellent. The next time I see you, you just may be trade advisor for our new Mer'khan relation's committee."

"I'll look forward to it."

"Until then." Shonai smiled nervously, standing to bid him farewell.

"Aegir be with you," he said.

"And you, Tomar," Shonai said, returning to D'onair's form.

The following day found the Orcan Sector quiet with anticipation. Shonai continued to supervise all aspects of the proceedings. When mid-day break arrived, she journeyed into the corridor leading to the gate. At the last turn before the gate was visible, she stopped, taking the six tiny shells she had taken from Keran out of her pouch.

She proceeded to place them in a six-pointed star on the ceiling, ground and walls of the corridor, locking them into place. Next, she removed the large shell from her pouch and held it at the direct center of the star. Then, she began to weave the most complex water spell she had ever undertaken, placing the code words and trap doors randomly.

When the spell was temporarily set, she took a strand of Mer'khan hair from her pouch and placed it inside the shell. She wove another spell into the shield, using the hair as a basis, preventing any Mer'khan from passing through the newly-formed force field.

When the pressure in the city changed and the Mer'khan stormed the Orcan Sector to find out why, they would come up short at the shield. It would take them close to half a turn of the glass to get through it and when they did it would be too late. She swam back to the tavern, letting no one pass her the other way, which no one tried. When she reached the tavern, she nodded to Gamarin. He gave a hand signal to a group of Orcans. Immediately they disappeared.

They began to round up any Mer'khan in the Sector, bringing them to the tavern with a minimum of force. Once inside, the Mer'khan were put under another water shield which prevented them from communicating or moving, except to breathe.

When they had all been secured, Shonai entered the tavern. There were just over a score of the Mer'khan captives. She double counted to make sure none were missing. When she was sure, she spoke to them in sonar, as telepathy would not penetrate the shield.

"First off, I am sorry for the inconvenience of the shield. You are not going to be hurt so ease your minds. When your people come to your rescue, tell them that I, Princess Shonai of Orcana, thank them for saving some of my people. However, it is time for your isolation to end," She said, and they drifted out.

"Majesty." Zoltaure beckoned her. "It is nearly the end of the mid-day break."

"Good. Begin the preparations."

"Aye, Majesty." He turned and gave an order. "All Orcans, report to your designated positions in line. When you receive the signal, you will leave in an orderly fashion. We have no room for error. Switch to your designated morph *after* you enter the tunnel. From there you will follow the Princess. I will guide the exit from the tunnel. Gamarin will provide the rear guard.

"Remember, the pressure change will be dramatic, so as soon as the wall is blown, flood your depth sacs. Once you have exited, do *not* deviate from the course the Princess sets. To do so could result in your capture or the mission's failure. Do all here understand?"

"Aye!" came the chorus of hundreds of anxious Orcans.

"Good. Let's get set." Zoltaure looked to the Princess. "You should take your place, Majesty."

"Good luck, Zoltaure." She hugged him quickly before heading to the front of the line. She didn't exactly want to be here but none would hear of her performing rear guard duties. Plus, she had the most recent memory of Sha'na's location.

She took her place at the front of the line, just behind the three Orcans who would do the final blast. She greeted them and bid them a safe journey as they erected a small water shield to fall back behind when the barrier broke. The torrent of water would be quite strong initially after the blast.

Moments seemed like turns of the glass in the tense silence, each lost in their own thoughts. Some thought of the home they had known so long ago. Others, who had been born here, tried to imagine all of the strange, new and wonderful creations that lay outside of the barrier. Shonai thought only of a giant mountain she had seen before in her dreams. Its irresistible pull, calling to her. She had no idea how she knew of it, for she had never even set foot on the continent. Somehow she knew that she must go there, to Mist Peak.

A sudden, deep rumble caused all to turn in the direction of the city. Tomar, true to his word, brought down two huge dome-shaped buildings on the outskirts of the city. None would be populated, he had said, just extremely loud. He had used magnesium fuses to ignite a huge water spell at the supports of each dome. When they exploded, the domes collapsed, sending deafening ripples of aftershock in all directions, effectively drawing the attention of the Mer'khan away from the Orcan Sector.

By the time they got around to sending an emissary to inform the Orcans of the occurrence, they would be gone. Shonai gave the order to blow the wall. The three Orcans drew their energies to them and blasted the wall with a rush of sonar that exploded it out into the sea.

They retreated behind the water shield, letting it take the brunt of the impact of the sea water and giving all the Orcans precious time to flood their depth sacs.

"Begin evacuation!" Shonai called.

"Aye!" came Zoltaure's voice back.

"Let's go," she said to the three sonar blasters. They took down the shield and began swimming. The outside sea water was colder than the cavern and created a fairly strong current down the tunnel, but the Orcans were stronger swimmers and cut through the water easily. The water was pitch black causing hundreds of purple flares to appear in the inky water.

There were small children following directly after Shonai, followed by elderly Orcans and finally the adults. It took close to half a turn of the glass to complete the evacuation, a steady stream of transparent shapes heading towards the surface.

The stress of anticipation was high, at any moment Shonai expected a horde of Mer'khan to leap out from hiding to take them back, yet nothing happened. The diversion had worked better than expected and her shield had kept them out if they had even come looking. A few Mer'khan passed but the purple eyes disappeared and they swam past, unaware.

The water became lighter finally, and Shonai felt, for the first time in ages, the joy of being alive. Further up, she found a rock formation she recognized, called Sagets' Sword for a spire that ended in a sharp point. It was one hundred leagues south of Sha'na.

She wanted to see her parents but the pull of the mountain was too strong. She had to go to it. She couldn't explain it, she just knew its importance. She stopped in her tracks and let the entire procession catch up. Zoltaure came by her side.

"Majesty, why do you stop?"

"I must. Gamarin!" she called.

"Your Majesty?" he asked, floating in front of her.

"This is Sagets' Sword. Do you recognize it?"

"Aye."

"Then you know Sha'na is about one hundred leagues in that direction," she said, pointing.

"Aye Majesty, but…"

"Attention!" she called, bringing silence. "My people, you have broken the shackles that bound you. You are free. From here, you may go where you please."

"We will go with you, Majesty!" a voice shouted.

"No," she shook her head, smiling. "I must take a different path alone. Gamarin is going to lead those who wish to go to Sha'na. You can be there by tomorrow night if you swim hard. I recommend this for Sha'na and the Western Isles are the only truly safe place for Orcans in the sea.

"It has been my privilege to serve you. Now you may return the favor to my parents. Baal be with you. I will be back to Sha'na in the near future, as soon as my task is complete. Fare well my friends," she called.

"Fare thee well, your Highness." Gamarin bid her goodbye. "I will not let you down."

"You have redeemed yourself to your people, Gamarin. Here." She took a small gold ring from her finger and gave it to him. "Give this to my parents. Tell them I love them and that I will return soon. Tell them the Peak calls me."

"Aye, Majesty." He bowed and assembled the people to continue their voyage. By now, all had resumed their Orcan forms. She didn't see Zoltaure anywhere.

"Gamarin!" She called, looking around.

"Aye?" he turned back to her.

"Where is Zoltaure?"

"Probably leading the pack, Majesty."

"Tell him goodbye for me."

"It will be done, Majesty."

"Thank you."

"Good luck," he said, turning back. She began swimming towards the beckon of the Peak. Perhaps it was for the best that she didn't see him. It was not fitting to have such a close relationship with a common man. Still, as she continued swimming, she thought of him. Every time she caught herself, she would try to think of something else but her thoughts always drifted back to him.

Still she rationalized, it kept her mind off of the Peak.

Gamarin watched the Princess go sadly. He turned to the transparent shape on his right.

"You know it is violating a Royal Order to do so?" he asked.

"Aye."

"And you still wish to pursue this course of action?"

"Aye."

"Very well, you are a free man and I cannot stop you."

"Thank you."

"I will forget to tell the King."

"Thank you, Gamarin," the transparent shape began to swim away.

"Orcan?" he called.

"Aye?"

"Guard her with your life."

"Aye." The transparent form agreed, shooting off into the depths.

Shonai had been swimming nearly as fast as she could all day, pushing herself to her limits. She didn't want any of the group to follow her, it was too dangerous where she was headed. She was very hungry but had seen relatively little to eat.

As she came within a few leagues of the shore, she caught sight of a huge kelp forest. Sea Otters frolicked and played, chasing each other, as well as fish. The beauty of it caused her heart to ache for her reef at home and the unwelcome memory of the carnage she had left there.

Her hunger drove her into the kelp. She had followed a small grouper with her eyes and lunged for it, catching its gill with one of her claws. She devoured it quickly, throwing the bones away carelessly. She was so entranced with hunger, that she didn't feel the gauntlet warning her of danger until she saw a huge set of jaws lined with triangular teeth opening to swallow her whole.

She tucked her feet instinctively, preparing to kick off on the great white shark's nose, but suddenly it lost its momentum. She used this to her advantage and drew back to rip its throat out with her razor-sharp claws. However, someone had already beat her to the punch. The shark was already dead, its guts spilled out into the sea water, like some sickly den of sea snakes.

She looked hastily around for the perpetrator but found nothing. She sensed no danger which confused her all the more. A voice from behind her caused her to whirl in fright, her claws almost ripping the voice out of its owner's throat.

"Whoa!" it said. "That was close."

"Zoltaure?" Shonai exclaimed.

"What, you thought I'd let you leave without saying goodbye?" he asked, smiling.

"Oh, you never could take directions well." She replied, hugging him fiercely, then kissing him spontaneously. He seemed not to mind at all.

"Shonai, I..."

"Shh..." she laughed. "It will be our little secret.

"Aye, that it will."

"Now, let's not let that shark go to waste. I'm starving."

"As am I, Majesty, er, Shonai." He corrected himself. "Amazing creature. I'm almost sorry I had to kill it." He marveled at the huge creature.

"I forgot that you have never seen any of this before."

"No. I've just heard stories."

"Well here, eat this part." She handed him a chunk of tail. They ate for awhile, curious seals daring to come close enough to touch, stealing bites when they thought the Orcans weren't looking.

"Can I ask where we're going?" Zoltaure asked when they had finished.

"Come on, and I'll show you," she said, taking his hand. They swam to the shore. A thick forest started as soon as the beach ended.

"Where?" Zoltaure asked, shifting uneasily from his gilled form.

"Wait," she said. "You have to get adjusted to land first."

"I've never breathed air before. It's uncomfortable and I can barely stand up."

"Calm down, just stand there and concentrate on breathing," Shonai told him.

"O.K." He did so, and after a long time he began to take small steps around the beach. The sun was rising in the east, bright orange.

"You've got it!" Shonai told him, smiling.

"Aye, I think I do." He walked perfectly over to her.

"Now the next challenge." She ran over to a tree taller than most and began to climb, giving Zoltaure hints on how to do so as she went. He was still having trouble learning that he couldn't float in air as he could in water.

At last they reached the top of the tree about the time the sun began its daily ascent into the sky.

"There." She pointed to a purple smudge on the horizon. "Just to the right of that really tall one, it's the one that stands all by itself."

"How far is it?"

"About three weeks' walk, maybe more."

"It's beautiful," he said, awed.

"That it is. Come on, let's get started."

"Aren't you tired? We've been up all day and night!" Zoltaure asked, not complaining.

"Of course I'm tired but we have to travel during daylight."

"Why, if we can see in the dark?"

"Because it's too dangerous at night on land."

"There are beings more deadly than great whites here?" he asked, wide-eyed.

"Of course."

"Like what?"

"Mai'Lang, Goblins, Driss, Gnomes, Giants and worst of all, Dragons as big as a whale with teeth as long as your leg that breathe fire with every breath."

"I still have a lot to learn, I guess," he said, wide-eyed.

"In time," she called as she descended the tree, Zoltaure following, ever more graceful.

"Shonai?"

"Aye?"

"Why are we going to this Mist Peak?"

"Why, Zoltaure! To save the world, of course."

CHAPTER 12
A TEST

anken awoke to a rough shake. He looked up to find Arn holding his finger to his lips. Tae was crouched next to him scanning the darkness.

"Quiet," Arn whispered.

"What is it?"

"Sabercat," Tae replied, "and he's hunting." Danken looked in the direction Tae was facing and saw a huge cat nearly the size of Kierna's horse.

"Can you see it?" Arn whispered. Danken nodded, realizing only he and Tae could see in the starlight spectrum.

Tae loaded his blowgun soundlessly.

"Wait." Danken placed a hand on his arm. "Let me try something."

"No way!" Arn shook his head.

"Aye don't be stupid. You aren't invincible, I don't care what he told you," Kierna hissed.

"I'll be careful. Besides, Tae will cover me."

"Aye mate. The beast'll not lay a claw on him."

"It's about bloody time we see some action," Jet muttered.

"Very well," Arn conceded. "But, don't do anything stupid; you're too important to risk your life needlessly."

Danken nodded and slowly, deliberately made his way downwind of the sabercat. The animal was resting on its haunches with its ears perked and its nose raised to test the air. When Danken had crept to within a few feet, he paused to observe the magnificent creature.

It was white with black stripes over a sleekly muscled frame. Two huge dagger-like teeth as long as his forearm protruded from its upper jaw. Like a bear trap. The eyes resembled golden orbs with tiny black slits in them.

The horses shifted nervously back at the campsite. The cat immediately turned toward the sound. Danken used this distraction to spring forth and clamp both hands around the beast's head and let forth a singe of blue energy, instantly pacifying the cat while communicating their peaceful intentions. Then he asked if the cat needed help, which it did.

"Danken!"

"Be calm, Arn," Danken told him. "He is still wary of us. He's starving. He left his mother's den awhile back and hasn't really learned to hunt on his own yet."

"By the sword of Unflinching Frey," Tae whispered.

"Aye," Arn agreed.

"His name is Shard and I told him we'd feed him." Arn's eyebrows raised. "Well, I will," Danken said quickly. "You all can go back to sleep."

"Not bloody likely with that great lump about," Arn shook his head as he started back toward the camp.

"You're something else, lad. I wouldn't have believed it if I hadn't seen it with my own eyes," Tae marveled.

"He didn't want to hurt us. Though he was looking rather fondly at our horses," Danken said, petting the cat's huge head. He was startled by the loud purring that came from Shard. Kierna took a step back, eyes wide until she realized the cat was purring from pleasure.

"Apparently, he likes to have his ears scratched. Will he mind if I...?" Tae asked.

"Not at all. As a matter of fact, I'm sure he would rather enjoy it." Tae reached over and tentatively scratched Shard's ears, eliciting more deafening purring.

"Quite an audible fella, isn't he?" he remarked, still a little nervous, for even with their connection to the forest and all in it, Elves could still be on a large predator's menu.

Danken rose. "I'm going to go get him something to eat," Shard rose with him. Danken looked quizzically at him but shrugged and made his way to the cart. Shard followed and stopped when Danken stopped.

"Looks like you've got a new shadow, mate," Tae laughed.

"It appears so," Danken said, smiling. T'riel landed on his shoulder and stood poised with her chin in her hand.

"This Great Stupid Cat; he is Boy's friend now?" she asked.

"Looks like it," Danken agreed.

"Then he is this Pixie's friend, also," she declared, flying over to Shard and landing between his ears. She released her tendrils of gold into him and soon they were having an animated, if slightly one-sided telepathic conversation, to which K'airn soon joined in. Danken and Jet pulled a heavy sack of cured meat from the cart.

"Wonder what the Magi will say when their Fifth comes marching in with an Elf, two Nymphs and a sabercat?" Tae remarked.

"Probably admonish me for my youthful naiveté and set me to raking leaves for the winter," Danken and Jet poured the sack of salted venison in front of Shard. The cat looked up at Danken with undisguised longing. Danken nodded that it was all for him and the cat tore hungrily into the meat. Over one hundred pounds became a pile of bones in less than a quarter glass.

Bolt eyed the great cat fearlessly, but the other horses pranced about nervously at the sight of the giant carnivore. Danken released tendrils of blue into them to reassure them and to let them know that Shard would be accompanying them. Still slightly unconvinced, they nevertheless went back to grazing.

Danken released a strand of energy into Shard making sure he understood that these animals were not for food. Shard understood and added that he would not need to eat again for a week anyway, though, on a full stomach, he could concentrate on hunting better.

Danken awoke well after dawn to find his leg numb.

"Ach, you great beast, move your head," Danken mumbled to the cat, who rose and stood staring at him. Danken shook his leg to get the feeling back and stood slowly, wincing at the pins and needles in his foot.

"Danken," Arn called. He turned to see Arn beckoning him to a pot of oatmeal. He took a bowl and sat down next to the fire.

"Where's the rest?" he asked.

"Preparing," Arn replied.

"For what?"

"To be tested. I have invited Tae to become one of the Mistgarde. He will be given three tests. The second one will be defeating you in armed combat."

"Me?" Danken exclaimed. "But I'm just a novice. He'll bloody kill me!"

"Novices don't kill five armed men at once. Besides, your weapons will be given a *Dulling* spell that will spare either of you bodily harm, save a few cuts and bruises. When you are done eating, you too, should prepare," Arn said as he rose and walked off into the woods. Danken looked at Shard.

"Well, there's a great way to spend my day." Shard yawned lazily in agreement. Danken drew *Mak'Rist* and began testing it, drawing lines of blue fire in the air as he swung. He merged his consciousness with the sword again and felt the feelings of power return. With this blade he was invincible, none could challenge him, he thought, the blade singing with battle lust.

He parried imaginary foes back and forth, eyes closed. He moved with a fluid grace, as if it were a dance, which is how Danken came to think of it. He was a living weapon. Shard watched him silently, along with a discreet Kierna, who hastily left again when he saw her.

"Danken!" came Arn's voice. Danken followed until he came to a clearing circled in stones. Tae sat at one end meditating. Arn stood at the other over a small fire, heating a metal brand. Kierna and Jet had taken up positions to watch the events. While Kierna looked pensive, Jet appeared to be thoroughly enjoying the prospect of a duel.

"Danken sit here," Arn motioned to another smaller circle of rocks. Danken sat down. "Observe in silence." Arn walked over to where Tae sat with eyes closed. He drew a single-edged shortsword much like the one Danken carried.

"Are you ready to be tested?" Arn asked.

"Aye," Tae responded. Without hesitation, Arn swung for Tae's exposed neck. Danken's eyes widened but he kept silent. Tae's hand shot like lightning and caught the blade between his thumb and two fingers, without ever opening his eyes. Performing this several more times, Arn fired off question after question about military tactics, sword counters and an assortment of other difficult subjects. Tae never faltered, leaving Danken's mouth agape in awe. Even Jet's snide grin had disappeared.

"How is it possible?" Kierna wondered.

"I've heard it said that one who is one with the blade can see it without ever really seeing it, like it projects a constant picture of itself in their mind," Jet guessed quietly. "They can go so deep into their subconscious that their mind is actually what stops the sword from touching them.

"Congratulations," Arn said. "You have passed the first test." Tae rose to his feet.

"Thank you," he handed Arn his blade.

"Danken, set your blade in the circle," Arn said, indicating a circle drawn in blood. Danken set *Mak'Rist*—sheathed—in the circle. Arn showed a cut in his wrist. "This circle is drawn in my blood. Each of you must draw the rune of *Protection*, within the circle, in your own blood." He then cut both Danken and Tae's left wrists with a small dagger. Both men drew the *Protection* rune inside the circle. "Now, draw the rune of *Dulling* on the flat of your blades," Arn instructed. Both men did so and coated the edges of each blade with blood.

"Are you both satisfied with your runes?" Arn asked.

"Aye," both answered.

"If your runes are incorrectly drawn, the spell will be void and one of you will die. Are you still certain of your runes?" Arn asked again.

"Aye," came the response.

"Are you both satisfied with each other's runes?"

"Aye," they replied in unison.

"Very well. You have been given three chances to recant. The spell is set. Tie these around your wrists," Arn said handing each an enchanted Elven healing scarf. Each would heal a minor wound instantly by wrapping it around the affected area. Both tied the scarves about their wrists.

"Very well. Draw your blades," Arn stood back outside the circle. "The first to score a fatal hit will be the winner." Both fighters took their stances, each eyeing the other. This was serious business and neither would take it lightly. Both would put their friendship aside until one had fallen. "Fight!" Arn called and both warriors began circling. Danken merged once again with *Mak'Rist*. He began to search out holes in Tae's defense. To Tae's credit, none were readily apparent, but Danken would continue probing.

Tae launched his Elven blade, *Rivertwain*, into his first attack. Danken parried easily, though he was caught off guard by the other's speed. Their blades met again in the center, each gauging the other's strength. Danken let Tae push him backward before executing a spin move that should have separated the Elf from his legs. But Tae had expected it and turned Danken's blade aside, leaving the boy open for attack.

Danken kicked him in the chest and rolled away. Tae did not let up and soon was banging away on Danken's defenses, forcing him backwards. Danken parried furiously before getting inside Tae and head-butting him, turning once again to the offensive. Blood ran freely from Tae's nose as he backpedaled, looking to gain the advantage once again.

He feigned an injury to his ankle and dropped down to one knee. Danken, thinking victory at hand, raised his sword for the killing thrust only to find Tae's sword driving for his belly. Only the Sigil saved him. He used the killing stroke to instead deflect Tae's thrust, which earned him a kick in the chest that knocked the wind out of him.

Danken was once again being driven back and was looking desperately for something to aid him. He found it as Tae overextended on a thrust. He grabbed Tae's sword wrist with his left hand and pushed it downward, bringing *Mak'Rist* up just above it. Somehow, Tae managed to get *Rivertwain* into his left hand and deflect Danken's blow, sending both careening to opposite sides of the circle to re-evaluate their opponent. Each stood for several moments catching their breath. Tae wiped his nose on his sleeve.

Tae was the first to start moving again and Danken quickly followed suit. He thought he had had the other man twice and both times, he had nearly been killed. He was too confident, he decided. While Tae didn't have *Mak'Rist* guiding him, he did have two hundred years of experience behind him.

So it went for some time. Each darting in for an attack, waiting for the other to make a mistake, sometimes attacking, sometimes defending. Both sported bloodied noses and fat lips. Tae was favoring his sword arm from Danken nearly breaking it. Danken was breathing shallowly from bruised ribs. Each man was pouring sweat and was stripped to the waist, green and blue eyes flared at each miniscule movement.

Finally, Danken grew bold and went to an all out offensive stance. Tae was driven back to the edge, barely parrying Danken's furious blows, each one eliciting a wince. Danken battled down Tae's blade and stepped inside, driving his blade upwards, toward Tae's chin. Only, when it reached the desired destination, it merely grazed by, leaving Tae's face cut but Danken's side exposed. Danken looked down to find Tae's blade touching the front of his stomach, a tiny trickle of blood running down to his waist. He was dead. Kierna gasped quietly.

"Good fight, Danken," Arn clapped, bringing both him and Tae back to reality. For a brief while, this battle had become the only thing in the world. Jet wore a respectful but still condescending grin on his smooth features.

"I lost," Danken said disappointedly.

"Aye, but you fought better than any man I've ever battled in my lifetime. And that is saying something. In no time you will undoubtedly be my better," Tae told him matter-of-factly.

"Congratulations, Tae," Arn said. "You have passed the second test." He turned to the brand he had left in the fire, then held it aloft. "Do you wish to take the final test?"

"Aye," Tae answered solemnly.

"Hold out your right forearm," Arn instructed and Tae did as he was bidden.

"This is the mark of the Mistgarde. Only the correct brand imbued with the proper charm can leave this sigil on your arm. You

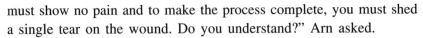

must show no pain and to make the process complete, you must shed a single tear on the wound. Do you understand?" Arn asked.

"Aye."

"Very well." Arn pushed the red hot brand into Tae's exposed flesh, making a sizzling sound. Tae's face remained impassive but a single tear rolled down his cheek. Arn pulled the brand away just as the tear fell into the still-smoking sigil. When it hit, the sigil exploded into multicolored fire so bright, Danken had to shield his eyes. When the fire died down, Tae was still in the same position, staring at the now completely healed sigil.

"Congratulations, Taelun Fallenbower. You have now joined the ranks of Mistgarde," Arn said, clasping Tae's wrist and for the first time, Danken realized that Arn had the same mark on his forearm.

CHAPTER 13
FEELINGS NEVER FELT

he sun was just cresting the horizon as the odd procession entered Wendall, the Duah capital. Danken had never seen a city so beautiful. Glittering white marble walls soared forty feet high and were as thick as a man was tall. From one corner of the wall, one could not see the other. On top of each parapet stood an immobile guard dressed in shiny red lacquer armor and crimson cloaks lined with gold trim designs. Two huge guard towers stood on either side of the main gate, through which hundreds of arrow slits had been cunningly carved. The whole wall appeared to have been grown from the surrounding forest.

As they neared the gate, two sentries came out to meet them. When they were within whispering distance, Arn and the rest lowered their cowls to expose their faces. Both Elves stood a little straighter.

"Arn Brynsen. You honor us with your presence," the sentry spoke in Sendar. Most Duah could speak both. In the Northern continent, Sendar was the language of trade and had been for centuries. It was as close to common tongue as there was and even most of the races of the Southern continent could speak a little of it.

"Thank you," Arn returned their bows.

"Who are your companions, if I may ask?" the first Elf asked. "We are acquainted with Taelun Fallenbower but..." he let the statement hang, looking at Danken. Arn made introductions. "If I may be so bold, why is the sabercat following you?" The Elves looked nervous. Tae smiled knowingly.

"His name is Shard," Danken told them. "And he is my companion. He will cause no harm to any in your city."

"Forgive me, but I will have to get permission from the Captain of the Watch to let him enter."

"By all means," Arn said. The two Elves bowed and sprinted back into the city. Moments later, an older Duah approached. When he reached them, he placed his hands flat across his chest with his thumbs hooked and they returned with slight bows.

The Captain of the Guard came out and gave his permission for Shard to enter. Arn informed him that he wished to speak with King Llethion and it was arranged shortly.

And with that, the unusual procession marched into the city. Tae broke off soon after to speak with his commander about his transfer. Danken was instructed to sell all they had for a new horse for Tae and only to keep as much food as they could carry in their saddlebags. Arn went off to speak with the King. They agreed to meet at the Palace gates at dusk.

Danken found Wendall to be the most beautiful city he had ever seen. Where as Sendar cities were built for convenience, Duah cities were built for beauty. White-marbled buildings were artfully woven with living trees as if from a dream. Every street was lined with brightly colored flowers which sang tunes in the breeze like wind chimes. The white-blossomed trees that grew on every corner gave off sweet scents that wafted throughout the whole city. Elven children played in them or sucked on their sweet nectar.

Such was one tree that the trio passed with Shard in tow. The children had never seen a sabercat before and now flooded around it. They dismounted their horses and smiled at the young Duah. Most could stand erect underneath Shard's belly. Danken feared Shard might have squashed the children if they hadn't been preoccupied with him. They had never seen glowing *blue* eyes. All of them had green. One touched his hand and he looked down to find a little girl staring at him. Her clothes were ragged and her face was dirty. Danken felt a stab of sorrow. He had been blinded by the beauty of the city and had thought that all in it were well-to-do and happy. He picked her up and set her on Bolt's back, releasing blue energy into her.

"Can you show me where your family is?" he asked quietly in Duah, his spark of blue teaching him the rudiments of the language in moments as only a Mage could do. She shook her head shyly. Kierna stroked the girl's hair gently, cooing unintelligibly to her.

"Do you have a family?" Danken asked. Again, she shook her head. "Where do you live?" She pointed to an alley in between two meticulous shops.

"On the street?" she nodded. He closed his eyes. "When was the last time you ate?" he continued the stream of questions. She shrugged her shoulders. Danken reached into his pack for a loaf of bread and gave it to her. She ate it quickly, never taking her beautiful green eyes off of him. Jet busied himself cleaning his knives, but he was undoubtedly taken with the child, sneaking disapproving looks at her dirty clothing and face.

"Well, does she want to bloody come with us, or not?" he asked. Danken translated with a small smile at Jet's seeming indifference. The girl nodded hopefully and Danken motioned for her to stay on Bolt's back. He walked back to where Shard was standing with T'riel and K'airn on his head. A group of parents had shooed the children away. Danken patted Shard on his nose.

"Good job, boy. Thanks you two," he said to the Nymphs.

"What does Mage have on Pearly Horn's back?" K'airn asked. T'riel fluttered over to Bolt to get a look and then landed on Danken's shoulder.

"Boy has rescued Little Elf Girl like he did this Pixie?" she asked.

"I guess so," Danken looked embarrassed. He turned to find Tae approaching.

"If this keeps up, we'll have a small army by the time we reach Mist Peak," he laughed, guessing the situation immediately. But Danken thought he detected something else in the Elf's eyes. Recognition of some sort, or else... "And does our new warrior have a name?" Tae was back to his carefree self.

"She can't speak," Danken answered. Tae looked at the child.

"Maybe not in Sendar."

"No, not at all. I tried Duah too." Danken answered. "But she can understand it." He added.

"Do you not have a name?" Tae asked her in Duah. She shook her head. "Well, that's never going to do. What shall we call her, Danken, mate?"

"Well," Danken looked at the child's face. It was perfect, like all Elven features except for a little green mole right above her green lips. Tae wore a suspicious smirk.

"How about, Princess Fleaslayer or Queen Frogsquasher, eh?" he tickled the child and she laughed hysterically, like a chorus of windchimes.

"How about Dot Windsong?" Kierna put forth.

"This Pixie likes," T'riel chirped landing on the child's shoulder, releasing her golden energy into her to introduce herself. K'airn did likewise.

"Well then, Dot Windsong, it is. Now first things first, Danken," Tae said. "There's a market over there where we can sell the supplies for a fine horse for yours truly and some clothes for young Dot here. Plus some finery for you farm boys, I'm thinking. Aye? After that, we'll have to hurry back to make the Palace gates by dusk."

By dusk, they had traded nearly all of their supplies for a young chestnut stallion and an entire wardrobe for Dot. Tae had quickly become quite the doting father figure. They arrived at the Palace gates with Dot sleeping on Tae's lap, wrapped in a woolen blanket like a cocoon, and Shard still attracting children by the dozen. Most touched him and ran off screaming in delight, but one or two of the braver ones would try to hold onto his swishing tail until T'riel zapped them in the bottom with a bolt of fire. The palace was all gold and white marble with spires that rose hundreds of feet intertwined with living trees. Giant archways dominated the architecture along with red marble and gold pillars. It was breathtaking. Unmoving guards in crimson-lacquered helms and armor over white silk trimmed with red and gold stood at full attention.

Arn was there waiting for them. When he saw Dot, he didn't seem surprised at all.

"It must run in the blood. Your father managed to rescue three baby Trolls from a Goblin raiding party, even though he and Bryn were riding day and night to reach Mist Peak before the Sorcerers found them!" He smiled. "Anyway, I was speaking to the King about the matter of the Shrakens."

"What?" Danken asked.

"The Shrakens have been raiding Elven merchant vessels again and I promised to set Mistgarde's Orcan division on the lookout."

"Mistgarde has an Orcan division too?" Danken exclaimed.

"Of course. Who do you think keeps the seas safe?" Arn asked. "Anyway, the King has offered us quarters to stay in and stables for our horses."

"What about Shard?"

"As long as he doesn't fight with the King's hounds. Now come on, we must get ready for the banquet."

Jet and Danken held their robes tightly around them as they entered the Royal Baths. A cedar planked walkway divided six small rooms walled in frosted glass. The first two the uncomfortable Sendar checked were occupied with no less than half a dozen naked Elven women each in a steamy square shaped bath of white tiles. They apologized profusely, thinking there must be a separate bathhouse for men but the next two rooms were full to the brim with Elven men *and* women. The Duah women paid them scant attention.

"Little uncomfortable here," Jet grumbled out of the side of his mouth.

"What're you waiting for mates?" Tae asked as he entered the bathhouse, clapping them on their shoulders. "It's not everyday a lad has the opportunity to bathe in the Royal Baths, now is it?" he dragged the two into the last room.

Inside were four Elven women laughing at something as they reclined in the spacious bath. The steam did nothing to hide their nakedness, nor the two Sendar's averted eyes and red faces. Tae greeted the women casually but not by name, as it was forbidden in the baths, as he stripped off his robe and lowered himself into the tub. Danken and Jet stood stock still, eyes furiously studying the floor.

"Do you plan to let the steam wash you then?" one of the women asked, her accent quite different from Tae's. Flowing, sing-song and distinctly upperclass.

"Maybe," Jet growled. "Just give us a bloody moment will you?"

Taking a deep breath, Jet stripped off his robe, followed reluctantly by Danken. The water was very hot but felt unbelievably good to their travel-weary bones.

"For a people that live so short of lives, it has always astounded me how afraid Sendar are of the opposite sex," another woman remarked offhandedly to the others.

"We're not afraid, my *Lady,* I believe we call it decency," Jet retorted. "Perhaps you're familiar with it? It can't be *that* foreign of a concept to you."

"Shut up," Danken hissed. "It's not *dwei* to speak to nobles like that."

"Still, they manage to have so many offspring in such a short time," one woman commented as if Jet not Danken had spoken.

"Are we animals to have our breeding habits discussed as if we were too stupid to understand them then?" Jet growled. Tae shook his head in despair for the embarrassment soon to fall about the boy.

One of the women glided over to him slowly, a scented bar of talcum in her hand. Jet was trapped by the attractive Duah. With little effort, she turned him around and was scrubbing his tightly tensed back. His protests were ignored and Danken was about to laugh when he was similarly manhandled.

"An Elf knows that promiscuity is not a detraction from one's character. It is an extension of the Moon Dance, a more personal form. It is not to be hidden, but celebrated," she told the black-haired youth calmly.

"Aye, well it's a wonder there aren't Elves flowing like water down the streets if that's the case," Jet said, somehow finding himself washing her back, albeit with a shaky hand.

Tae laughed aloud. "Elves do not conceive in that manner."

"Then how—?" Danken asked, forcefully pressed into service himself, and very uncomfortable with the subject matter.

"An Elf and his or her partner must ask the Treemother for permission. Once given, they will be bound as one identity with the tree until the child is born of the tree."

"They probably aren't familiar with the art of *Shulaset* either I'm assuming," one woman commented to the others and they tittered. Jet snorted as if to say, 'of course we do.' The Elves raised skeptical eyebrows and launched into another conversation amongst themselves. Jet waited a moment before leaning over to Danken discreetly.

"What in Hel's Rivers is *Shulaset?*" he asked out of the corner of his mouth.

"I've no bloody clue," Danken answered likewise.

"Do we want to?"

"I'm thinking no."

"Good to know we're on the same page there, no?" Jet coughed to cover his considerable embarrassment. He was well experienced with women but there was just a certain way to do things and this was certainly *not* it. "Flarin' Duah," he muttered.

Any further conversation between the two was cut abruptly short when Kierna entered, disrobing easily and stepping into the bath without a look at any of them. Danken and Jet hastily averted their eyes.

"Did you just see anything out of the ordinary?" Jet hissed to Danken, both even more embarrassed.

"No. I saw nothing. You?"

"Nope, *Dwei*. So..."

"I'm going to leave then," Danken said under his breath, quickly jumping out of the bath and grabbing his robe, followed closely by Jet. Tae and the other Duah laughed heartily at the two boys' fleeing forms.

"Sendar and their odd notions of modesty," one of the women said and the others agreed, shaking their heads.

Not long afterwards, Danken, Jet, Kierna, T'riel and Shard entered the banquet, clean and finely dressed. Shard had been painstakingly bathed after a long chase and growling confrontation. He even had a blue scarf around his neck and a bow on the tip of his tail, T'riel's idea. The guests at the table all thought it irresistibly cute. Danken had to remind the giant cat not to eat them when they laughed.

Tae was already seated in his finest white silk with his hair pulled tightly behind his head in a lavish braid. Dot sat next to him in a green silk dress that made her positively glow. An older lady—approximately nine hundred thirty years older—fussed with Dot's hair, which was naturally curly and shining. Very odd since Elves had straight, fine hair.

Arn was the biggest surprise, however. His thick, black beard had been shaved into a trim goatee and his unruly hair was slicked back with oil. Kierna was resplendent in an ankle length silver satin gown with a very low, laced neckline and her hair put up stylishly. Jet sent the Duah women to swooning with his pure black flowing attire and his hatchets that fit easily at his waist. His hair hung straight and lustrous to his shoulders, catching every nuance of the torch light.

All of this came to naught when Danken entered the room in blue silk, trimmed in white. His bangs flowed magnificently down the sides of his face like strands of silver that reflected the blue flames of his eyes. *Mak'Rist* hung regally at his side, its ornate scabbard polished to a shine. The hubbub of the banquet abruptly ceased when he entered. Many present had known his father and all knew a Mage when they saw one. Elves could sense magic, and Magi—even those not yet immortal—had it in abundance.

"Danken Sariksen!" the troubadour announced.

"Danken, over here!" Tae called to break the silence. Danken hastened over to him. The crowd began to converse again and Tae whispered in his ear. "Good thing you didn't say anything, you're voice might have shattered their faces. I imagine you'll have no shortage of offers to dance."

"Boy looks good," T'riel commented from his shoulder.

"How about your new boyfriend." Danken gibed, pointing at K'airn, who was wearing a red coverall, sitting in the special place prepared for himself and T'riel, a miniature table and chairs with small glass dinnerware.

"He is *not* this Pixie's treefriend!" she exclaimed embarrassed, but nevertheless, she went to sit by him and in no time they were complimenting each other's dress. He knew that K'airn was like a big brother to her but he enjoyed jibing her. Danken sat in between Arn and Dot, with Kierna and Jet on either side.

"Danken," Arn told him, "the King wishes to speak with you."

"Lead the way," Danken replied, shocked. He gave a deep bow and a wink to Dot, and she winked back, giggling.

The King was a middle-aged Elf, which put him in the range of five hundred or so. He had short, carefully brushed and styled blond and green flecked hair with the flawless pointed, porcelain cream features which marked his race. He wore crimson and gold, the Royal family's colors, and carried his ruby-encrusted crown on his head like it weighed nothing. The Queen was a stunning woman with snow white skin in a red silk gown beaded with gold, and her crown was a thin gold circlet with a single ruby.

"Your Majesties," Arn began. "This is Danken Sariksen." Danken bowed.

"An honor to meet you, your Majesties."

"I should say the same, Sariksen. Your father saved the realm and united the four Duah Kingdoms under my family. Without him there might not be a Duah Nation. From what my old friend, Arn, tells me, you are no different, though let's hope you do not have to face the horrors Sarik did."

"Thank you, your Majesty."

"Arn tells me you're quite the swordsman."

"I think my friend Arn gives me too much credit," Danken said modestly, shooting Arn a warning look.

"He says you killed six armed men, a dozen Gnomes and fought a member of Mistgarde to a standstill. Not terribly shabby for a lad of barely mead drinking age."

"Well, your Majesty, to be fair, I killed four men because they killed my mother, the fifth was just trying to prevent me from doing so. Jet killed the sixth. As for the Gnomes, it was only eight. The Pixies killed the rest when I was lying wounded on the ground. And as for the member of Mistgarde, he beat me."

"Nevertheless," the King said wryly, "I would still like to see an exhibition tonight if your modesty will permit it."

"He would be glad to, your highness," Arn answered for him, turning to the crowd, his voice booming out over the crowded hall and Danken's objections. "Ladies and Lords, if I may have your attention for a moment, please. In approximately one turn of the glass, my esteemed colleague will disarm three Moon Watch Guards of your choosing all by himself. Please place your bets now. Thank you," Arn finished. The assembled guests began immediately wagering on the upcoming contest.

"Aye, thank you, Arn," Danken grumbled. Few things were loved more in Wendall than a contest, and three deadly-looking Moon Watch

Guards, all reputably the best swordsmen in Wendall, were set up in the middle of the dance floor. Jet placed everything he had on Danken, while Kierna pretended not to pay attention as she played with Dot.

"All right lads, do your best to kill him!" Arn yelled. Danken looked at him wide-eyed.

"What in Hela's Bed Chamber do you mean 'kill him'?"

"Don't worry. Just keep your head about you and disarm them as quickly as possible without hurting them," Arn patted him on the back. Danken looked over to see Tae smiling at him. Was there something he didn't know?

"All contestants!" the King shouted. "Begin!" The three guards began circling him. Danken looked once more at Tae.

"Close your eyes," Tae mouthed, "trust me."

"Trust you," Danken sighed. "Always my first instinct when people are trying to dismember me." Nevertheless, he closed his eyes and merged with *Mak'Rist*. Both he and the blade began to glow blue. At first, he felt helpless without sight and almost gave up and opened his eyes. But then a strange clarity came to him. He could *feel* the other men and he knew beyond a doubt what each would do. He had their first moves before they tried them and dealt with each accordingly. It was as if he were reliving a battle Fyrdn had fought long ago.

The guards attacked as one, but Danken had already sidestepped their thrusts and brought himself up behind one attacker, twisting his wrist so hard the Elf dropped his blade. The other two had to come in from the side to avoid killing the first. Danken had already moved into position and swung his blade upward to push the second Elf's arm up. Then he stepped in and punched the Duah in his exposed armpit, forcing him to reflexively curl. With a simple flick of the wrist, the second Duah was disarmed. The third Duah had used this time to move in closer and swung what should have been the killing thrust, only Danken had shifted imperceptibly to the right. The Elf's blade shot harmlessly by his side. Danken clamped down on it with his elbow, twisting so fast that the Elf was left staring at his hand.

Danken opened his eyes to thunderous applause. All of the Elves clasped his hands in wonder.

"Bravo! Bravo! I've never seen anything like it! You disarmed my personal palace guards in two bloody ticks. Marvelous! Though I shall have to train them much harder now," the King remarked to the smiling Queen.

"Well done, Danken," Arn congratulated him as Jet collected a bounty from a rueful Duah Lord.

"How did Tae know that I could do that?"

"He noticed it when you fought him. Twice he attacked you when your eyes were closed and both times you nearly defeated him. The glowing blue part was something unforeseen."

"Excuse me," came a melodic female voice. Danken turned around to find a devastatingly beautiful Elven girl in a crimson and gold dress looking at him. He recognized her as one of the women from the bath. She had been watching him all night.

"Aye, milady?" Danken answered awkwardly in court fashion as well as he knew it; which was to say not at all.

"The music is starting and I have decided that we should dance. Do you not agree?" She sounded shy, yet confident. He raised her delicate hand to his lips.

"Of course," Danken answered. She led him out onto the dance floor. The Elven harps played a slow song. "I'm afraid, milady, that I am not schooled in the ways of Elven dancing. You will have to lead, else I'm likely to send us both tumbling."

"I would be glad to," she answered, leading him slowly until he picked it up. "May I call you Danken?" Her fiery green eyes stared up at him from a porcelain white face so perfect he feared it would shatter.

"Aye, if you'll tell me your name as well."

"Forgive me," she laughed. "I forgot you are not Duah and wouldn't know. I am Amaria Sonatala," Danken nearly lost his step.

"The Royal Princess?"

"Aye, is that a problem?" she asked coyly with an arched blond eyebrow, her green lips sparkling and pursed.

"Not at all," Danken assured her. "I just never pictured someone as important and beautiful as yourself asking me to dance, nor bathing with..."

"Elven class is different than that of Sendar, even a Senatorial society such as yours. When not acting in an official capacity, an Elven Noble—even myself—is no different than the average citizen."

"You are anything but average," Danken told her.

"You are sweet." She rested her head on his shoulder. The warmth of her body sent icy hot chills running down his spine. No woman had ever touched him this way before. He looked at the other women in the room. Many were looking at him as if he were spoiled meat. The men, the younger ones, that is, were looking at him with undisguised jealousy.

"Amaria, why do all of these people look at me this way?" he asked, somewhat hurt. She laughed.

"Two reasons, mainly. The first is simple: You are a Sendar who dances with Elven royalty. You rival them in every way, and Elves are not used to being outclassed by anyone. Secondly, they are aristocrats, used to getting everything they want. The women despise me because now that I have danced with you, they cannot. It would violate court protocol. The men despise you because you have demonstrated yourself to be the most powerful and enigmatic man in the room. Nothing they can do now will draw the women's attention away from you. They also despise you because they want to dance with me and they can see by looking into my eyes that I will only dance with you."

This last statement caught Danken off guard. He felt as if they were floating and soon as if no one else was around. They locked eyes, and in that moment, Danken could find no other reason for living but her. She filled the void of his empty childhood, the void left when his twin Wytchyn had disappeared. She filled the void of his mother's loss and for the first time in a long time, he felt complete.

"You seem far away," Amaria commented, touching his cheek.

"It's just that this all seems so unreal to me. My sister Wytchyn was the only person who ever truly understood me. We were born on the same day and did everything together from then on."

"Yevn'daialanthe," Amaria smiled, using the Elven word for twins, which Elves found fascinating since there was no such thing among them.

"Aye," Danken smiled, but his eyes were pained. "But when she was lost, I never recovered. I never made another friend. I was alone."

"I am sorry."

"It wasn't so bad. I learned the language of the forest and the animals within. I was at peace there to some extent."

"Many Duah say that the people of the Pixian Forest and the closest thing to the Faerie Races that a Sendar can be."

"Don't let them hear you say that."

"You were an outcast because of your gifts."

"Aye. Wytchyn was like me, but no one else was." Danken paused. "I was no one. No one cared. I had just grown accustomed to my lot in life, when my mother was killed by a Sorcerer, and my destiny was forced upon me. Now I am the enemy of one people and the savior of another. Overnight my lot changed. Suddenly, I matter," Danken's eyes were wet with unshed tears. He felt sure she would turn away from him in disgust at his weakness. He hadn't wanted to tell her any of it, and yet something about her seemed to invite his confidence. Amaria lightly brushed his face with her soft fingertips.

"And now?" she prompted.

"And now, with you, I don't feel alone anymore."

"Nor I."

"But we've only just met. How can I feel this way?"

"Sometimes people meet for a reason, their destinies intertwined long before they were born." Amaria spoke barely above a musical whisper. "Sometimes we have felt something our whole lives but we haven't been able to describe it until we meet one another. And sometimes when we have lost so much, we appreciate what we gain so much more, and hold on to what we have."

"But why me?" Danken asked softly. "Why me when you have all of this? Your life is so safe and comfortable. Why would the Norns set you on the same path as me?" His eyes took on a haunted look. "Those who follow my path find only death."

"Because you will not allow anyone to walk it beside you. I cannot explain why I feel the way I do. I only know that I do. From the moment our eyes met in the bathhouse, I knew. I did not have to hear you speak from your pure heart. I did not have to see you wield a

Duah blade with the grace only an Elven Master could attain. And I did not have to feel the warmth of your breath on my neck or the strength of your arms around me." Amaria cupped his chin in her hands. "I just know. All the questions and doubts in the world will not change it. I have been waiting for you my entire life. Frey has given me his blessing and I will honor him."

"By the Gods, if that is to be the way, then I cannot imagine better."

"Come," Amaria took him by the hand with a suddenly mischievous smile. "I want to show you something." She led him to where Arn and her father were discussing the matters of the realms.

"Father, may I show Danken the garden?" she asked in her best pouting voice, batting her eyelashes at him.

"Feverian tith," he smiled. "Why must you look at me like that? You know I cannot refuse you." He turned to Danken, "No funny business, young Sariksen, Mage or no," he told him sternly, a flat stare in his glowing green eyes. He was very protective of her, Danken saw immediately. She was both the Royal Princess *and* his daughter, which made for a volatile mix. But he knew what it was like to be young and it didn't last forever, even for Elves.

"No, your Majesty. No funny business," Danken agreed.

The Royal Gardens of Wendall Palace was more like a forest of flowers. White marble paths wound their way with symmetric perfection through countless fragrant plants and ornately carved statues. Three Moon Watch Guards trailed at a discreet distance behind them. Amaria seemed to be unaware of their existence as she led him along.

"This is my favorite place in the castle," Amaria told him, holding his hand. "I come here to get away and to be at peace."

"I can't imagine a better place for it."

"When I was little, I used to play out here everyday. I would pretend I was a *Verna'ren*. I would patrol the forests and fight Goblins and Trolls with my sword. I imagined I could walk through a village and not have a single Elf bow to me. They respected me because of my deeds, not because of my birthright. It sounds strange, I know. Most little girls dream of being a Princess. But I just wanted to earn my own reputation instead of having it handed to me."

"It isn't so strange," Danken said. "That's a tremendous amount of pressure to lay on the shoulders of a child. People don't often factor that into their fantasies. But I have heard it said that a good ruler is one who doesn't want the job."

"And did you pick up such wisdom in the forest?" Amaria jabbed him lightly with her elbow.

"My mother told me once that Arn's father had said the same thing to my father. I always thought it—" Danken cut off when Amaria leaned up and kissed him. She pulled slowly away and they stared into each other's eyes. "I would kiss you back if I didn't think it fell into the 'funny business' category," he smiled.

"Who says it has to be funny?" She began to kiss him again, but he pulled back reluctantly, for these things took time where he was from. Though he had developed instant feelings for her, it was all still strange to him.

"What of the guards?"

"They are mine, not my father's. Their concern is only for my safety, not my personal life or who I choose to involve in it."

"Do you speak from experience?" he asked, feeling a stab of jealously.

"No," her eyes glinted. "But I will after tonight."

"But—"

"Shut up. And *that* is a Royal Command."

Danken fell silent as Amaria leaned up and kissed him once more. Softly, at first, and then with more fervor as he let go of his inhibitions and questions and each gave in to their passion. Amaria took off his cloak and unbuttoned his shirt slowly, never letting her lips lose contact with his, as if by doing so would shatter the moment. Danken pulled off the shoulder straps that held her dress up, marveling at her perfection. She shivered as the night breeze touched her bare skin. He couldn't believe this was happening so soon. They hardly knew each other, yet somehow, she wanted nothing more in the world and as for him, he *was* a teenage boy.

She led him behind a bush to a patch of soft grass underneath one of the sweet-smelling white-blossomed trees. Danken laid her down atop his cloak, her skin as smooth as the satin lining. His pants and boots were tossed carelessly aside. From there they joined and be-came one. The curious observer would have been surprised to find an odd blue-green aura emanating from a seemingly normal tree.

CHAPTER 14
N'FAMAR

here have those two gone off to?" King Llethion wondered aloud. "Andren," he called to the Prince, a boy of about twelve. "Go find your sister out by the garden. Tell her the banquet is ending."

The Prince bobbed his unruly blond-haired head, his green eyes flashed mischievously.

"Aye father," he said in a voice not-yet-broken.

"And Andren," the King called as the boy ran off, "don't sneak up on her, she may be...preoccupied."

"Aye father," and with that, the boy was gone, three more Moon Watch Guards in his wake.

"You seem to believe young Sariksen is up to, funny business, as you call it?" Arn smiled at his old friend.

"Aye. I'd be a fool not to see it. The way my Amaria looked at him, I knew. He is her *N'famar*. No self. So powerful it can never be broken, no matter the pain. There can be no other when an Elf experiences *N'famar*. *Very* rare and even more so with a Sendar. The Norns have a cruel sense of humor sometimes. I only hope the boy knows what he is in store for. That girl has been kept under lock and key for seventeen years. And no matter how much he wants to, he can never love her as she loves him, for she is not his *N'famar*. He will move on and she will be left alone."

"I have a feeling he'll be fine," Arn said. The King knew of Danken's childhood; similar indeed, if only in relative terms. The boy was responsible and would do what was right.

"The scary thing is I don't hate the young man. I know it is not the boy's fault, but a father is supposed to hate all who compete for his daughter's hand, no?" the King said exasperatedly.

Arn laughed. "I have yet to find a sentient being Danken couldn't win over in under a quarter glass. It's the mark of a powerful Mage, your Highness."

"The daft girl. A bloody Sendar, of all she could have fallen in love with. Magi or not, marriage to him would prevent her from assuming the throne when I have gone."

"This is true. But do not stress yourself. You're an Elf in his prime. You still have over five hundred years left in you, and things can change in five hundred years, you know as well as I. I will live for perhaps eighty more and harbor no doubts that the world will be a different place in that time."

Kierna had been so completely engrossed with staring daggers at Danken's back, that she didn't even notice the finely dressed Elven Lord at her elbow until he gently touched her. She started, catching her breath before she let slip an unladylike curse. She nearly lost herself in his green eyes and flawless features. He spoke in sing-song Sendar that she found comical.

"I am Lord Walinhytha," he bowed. "I would be honored if you would dance with me."

"Of course," she flashed one of her rare smiles and he led her onto the dance floor. Like Danken, she was unfamiliar with the strange elegance and grace of Duah dance, so her first few attempts were clumsy and left her face flushed.

Soon she got the hang of it and even managed to add her own style to complement Walinhytha's. She thanked him graciously when he praised her aptitude and beauty, unused to such comments. She had a type of rugged beauty and hard features that were not readily apparent and more often than not overlooked. Still, the Elves, with their pointed features and perfect proportions found the combination to be quite attractive, and she ended up dancing with quite a few young Duah Lords—or old, she could never tell.

Though her numerous conversations were usually stimulating, she still found enough time in between to glare at Danken. He seemed unaware, however, lost in the eyes of the Duah Princess. When he left to accompany the Princess to the garden, Kierna was so taken aback that she tripped over her dancing partner and would have fallen had a lightning fast Jet not caught her in his arms.

Those Elves nearby looked at them askance and Kierna affected a fainting spell, much to her disgust. With apologies, Jet led her over to their dinner table and sat down with her. Jet was instantly set upon by a small swarm of Elven Nobles' children, begging him to perform. He flourished several brightly colored silks seemingly from nowhere. One moment they were separate, the next knotted into one long multicolored line that he waved around, making impossible designs in the air. While the children were occupied, he leaned over to the chagrined Kierna who was dabbing furiously at eyes that certainly were *not* crying. She simply had a speck of dust in them, that was all.

"Do you want to talk about it?" he asked, making the silks a figure eight hanging suspended in midair.

"No. I mean, what is there that I could possibly want to talk about?"

"I don't know, perhaps the fact that you're in love with him."

"Who?" she asked defensively.

"Don't play stupid, Kierna. I've known you for half of my life. You know very well I'm talking about Danken."

She opened her mouth to protest but shut it abruptly as she realized it would only make her look more guilty. Instead she raised her chin and looked down her nose at him to retain what little dignity she could of the situation.

"Who I am in love or am not in love with is none of your concern, Jetrian Torvaldsen. Understand?"

"Absolutely, Kierna Bjorndotir," he emphasized her last name to show her his disdain for his own. "I wouldn't dream of making your personal life my concern."

"*Dwei,*" she sniffed, glancing around the ballroom as if to show him he was of no further importance to her. Jet continued to entertain the children, now with card tricks, though she could feel the grin on his face burning a hole in her back.

Finally, a dazzlingly beautiful young Duah Lady got up the courage to ask Jet to dance. He accepted with his own heart-stopping grin, kissing her hand softly. The children groaned and ran off to play with Dot and Shard. Jet leaned down, putting his mouth just behind Kierna's ear.

"Just for the record," he whispered, "you're in love with him."

Danken and Amaria lay side by side in silence, each contemplating the most recent change in their young lives. Each was lost in their own communal, yet still private thoughts, though their hands remained clasped. Danken felt as if he were floating. He never wanted this to end, though he knew it must. He also did not want to hurt Amaria.

"Amaria," Danken whispered, "you know I must leave for Mist Peak on the morrow, right?" he gave her delicate hand a light squeeze.

"Aye," she leaned over and kissed him. "But what we have shared can never go away. Part of you lives inside me now. Besides, you will visit often until I am old enough to leave, will you not?"

"Absolutely my Princess," he said softly, returning her kiss. Neither spoke of what would happen then. Danken felt what could be the beginning of love but he was still young and unsure of his future. Political complications aside, Amaria would see them together forever, one way or another, he knew it just as surely as he knew the sun would rise. Still, it was not such a bad thing.

The sound of small footsteps on the pathway awoke them from their revelry. Amaria giggled as they both struggled to dress quickly.

"It is my brother," she held a finger to her lips. As they finished getting dressed, Andren spotted them.

"Father says the guests are leaving and you are to go greet them." Andren looked at Danken's face, which was covered in the glitter Amaria wore as lipstick. He gasped, "Eww! You kissed him!" Andren shouted and made to run back to the Palace. "You kissed him!" He was cut off as an opaque globe settled about his head, effectively silencing him. Green sparks of energy lanced from Amaria's fingertips into Andren's backside, causing him to leap to a stop. Amaria turned to Danken and gently wiped the glitter off of his face.

"One of the benefits of being Duah. I can scale flat walls too," she smiled at Danken. "*Dwei*, no?" she asked, the Sendar slang sounding odd in her upper class accent.

"Aye, and what of him?" Danken asked, indicating the conspicuously silent Prince.

"The globe will wear off in a few ticks. Long enough for me to see the guests off," she said coyly. They held hands all the way back to the Palace, where she entered first, and he a moment later, to maintain at least the pretense of dignity.

"Amaria!" her father called. "There you are. Come see our guests off." She curtsied.

"Aye father."

"And Amaria?"

"Aye father?" she turned. He reached into her hair and pulled a small leaf from it. She blushed a furious green, fearing he would be angry at her.

"Now go," he said smiling.

"Aye father," she leaned up and kissed him on the cheek. "Thank you," and now it was his turn to blush. She made her way to the door and began thanking people for coming.

When all the guests had left, only Amaria and Danken remained, with two silent guards who neither saw, nor heard anything, they were so well trained.

"One last dance?" Danken asked her.

"Aye. I would like that." And together they moved in silence, this time Danken led the way, demonstrating his new found techniques.

When the dance was over, they discreetly kissed goodnight before going their separate ways to their chambers, each feeling the pain of separation.

Amaria retired to her suite in a dreamy haze, her heart feeling as if it might leap out of her chest. She ran her hands down her face and along her satin red gown, caressing softly as he had, remembering his touch and replaying every last instant of it in her mind again and again. She closed her eyes and breathed deeply, as if to breathe in this moment and never exhale. She clung desperately to this feeling of perfection, of contentment beyond all boundaries, afraid that it would never come again, for she knew at her core, that Danken would never feel the same way about her. He was Sendar, how could he? They could never feel *N'famar.*

She calmed herself and quelled the panic she began to feel when she thought of never being with him again. What would she do? She gracefully disrobed and slipped on a green silk nightgown. She pulled her hair back and clipped it with a golden hair clip set with a perfect jade ball in the center. The cool night breeze caused her to shiver slightly as she stepped out onto her sweeping veranda on the top level of the palace, fully three hundred fifty feet above Wendall.

Amaria gazed out over the sleeping city as she leaned against the rail. The stars lit up her glowing green eyes like candles. A muted disturbance in the calm night caught her attention. Before her eyes a huge raven morphed into a stunning Mai'Lang woman in a very low cut black gown. The two black, razor-edged fans in her hands were instantly in motion, one at Amaria's throat and the other cutting off her escape route.

"Two men are in your brother's room as we speak, Princess. They have orders not to disturb him unless you scream or do not cooperate with me in any way. Do you understand?" Hrafna said in soft, staccato Duah.

"Aye," Amaria swallowed weakly.

"Good, because I do so hate having the lives of children on my conscience, even if they are filthy tree-born Duah."

"I will do as you say. Please, just don't hurt Andren."

"I'm so glad we've got that nasty piece of business straightened out *Princess.* Now give me what I want and this can all go away. You can go back to your garden, or whatever you useless Duah do all day."

"What is it you want? Please, just take what you want and leave." Amaria dared not move, as her throat would have been forfeit.

"Oh, believe me, I will. I did not waste the last eighteen years planning to control the Sapphire Son just so some stupid Duah could wreck it all. Now tell me where the Oracle is."

"Oracle?" Amaria asked meekly, not caring about this Sapphire Son, only her brother's life.

"Do *not* test my patience, child. The jade ball the King's divers found while pearl diving off the coast of Mai'Lang mainland eight years ago. It does not belong to you. I cannot allow Sariksen to obtain it. I hope you understand," Hrafna said, seemingly reasonable. What did it matter what she told the girl? She planned to kill her anyway.

Amaria's docile mind suddenly clicked and began racing furiously at the mention of Danken. She no longer feared for her safety or even her brother's. Nothing. There was nothing but him. This woman meant to harm Danken with the Oracle, or whatever she had called it. None of this showed in Amaria's almond-shaped eyes though, as she nodded her head meekly. A plan rapidly formed in her mind.

"You will get it for me now, no?" the Mai'Lang asked solicitously.

"Aye. It is in the dresser next to my bed."

"Then go and get it. And remember, your brother's life is at stake as well as your own. Make no sudden moves."

"Aye." Amaria walked quickly, keeping her head turned towards the woman so that the clip in her hair was not visible. As she reached the double doors to her suite that opened out onto the veranda, she used one hand to swing one of the doors at the woman and the other to undo the hair clip. She threw it out over the balcony railing before the Mai'Lang could stop her, yelling *"Doaak'noa twoi!"* as she did so, a Duah curse that meant 'May your cursed soul never be reborn.'

Before Hrafna could retaliate or go after the golden hair clip, two large, angry Moon Watch Guards with swords drawn kicked in the door and rushed into the room. More shouts multiplied throughout the palace in the next moment. As she ran towards the balcony, Hrafna shot an icy look at Amaria and yelled over her shoulder.

"You will die for this, Princess, do not doubt it!" and then she was the raven once again, winging into the night.

Six floors below them, a soft, enchanting song like wind through the leaves of a tree filled the air with power. Unnoticed by the Elves rushing about was the golden hair clip floating up out of the courtyard and into a small, outstretched hand. As it did so the wind ceased with the song and the Oracle was hidden from view by a green cloak. Its owner shut the terrace door and retired to bed.

Danken rushed into Amaria's room followed closely by Arn and Tae. The King, Queen and several soldiers were surrounding her and Andren. After it had been determined the two were all right, two extra guards were placed outside their doors as well as three more on the veranda. Many were dispatched to search for her hair clip. The King reluctantly left to talk to Arn and Tae and the Queen went to Andren's room with him, leaving Amaria and Danken quite alone. She rushed into his arms and buried her head in his chest, letting forth a torrent of tears.

Afterwards she told him all that happened, more than she had told her father or the Captain of the Guard. The mention of the woman with the black fans made Danken's blood run cold. The woman who had separated him and Wytchyn had been here and he hadn't even known it!

"Amaria, why didn't you just give her this Oracle, or whatever it was? She really could have killed you or Andren."

"I could not. She wanted to use it against you."

"So what? I can take care of myself, you know," he brushed a hand gently through her hair and she leaned her face into his caress.

"I had to do what I did, Danken. If you are dead, nothing in my life is worth saving."

"How can you say that? We've only just met. I'm hardly more important than your family," he took her by the shoulders and pushed her chin up so she had to look in his flaming blue eyes.

"You can never understand what it is to be *N'famar,* Danken. You are my every thought, my every wish. I cannot control it anymore than you can control the sunrise. If you asked me to jump off a cliff for you, I would do it gladly just to make you happy."

"Don't talk like that."

"I speak only the truth."

"You are not a slave. You have your own free will. I am not worthy of such dedication. I am nothing but a woodlander who happened to be born to a Mage."

"And I am nothing but a woodlander who happened to be born to a King," she retorted. "You are correct. I do have free will. In every matter except those pertaining to you. I must always do what is best for you even if you don't even know it yourself yet."

"I would never ask you to do anything that would harm your family or you. Even if it meant my own death," he took her soft, trembling hands in his own, strong and rough from years of hard work. " I care for *your* safety and happiness. That's what is best for me, my perfect Princess."

"Do you, I mean, I know that you can never feel for me what I feel for you, but do you think you could come to love me? To love me and no other?" Amaria asked, tears welling up in her green eyes again.

"I have already begun to. It will take time but—"

"Say no more, please," she said softly, kissing him.

Danken never made it back to his own room.

The next day loomed bright on the horizon as Danken and the rest saddled their horses. All were back to their riding leathers, but each felt rejuvenated. Danken hated to leave Amaria but he also had a duty to his own people. The King and Queen were there to see them off. Amaria stood to her father's left, unsuccessfully trying to hold back tears. Danken and she locked eyes, before she looked away towards the gate. Danken caught the King looking at him. Llethion gave an almost imperceptible nod towards Amaria. Danken needed no second bidding. He took her face in his hands, wiping away her tears with his thumbs, and then he kissed her.

"I will return."

"I will be waiting," she smiled. "Always will I wait for you."

"Your Majesties." Danken bowed.

"Be safe, Sariksen," the King told him and with that they mounted up. Dot rode on Shard's back as they had become inseparable. T'riel landed on his shoulder.

"Now who is in love, silly Boy?" she teased him with her tongue out. He laughed.

"Why must you insist on calling me Boy?"

"Boy will always be Boy to this Pixie!" she told him matter of factly.

"Bloody *dwei.*" Danken said sarcastically.

CHAPTER 15
TO NOWHERE

ou come back real soon now, honey." the once-pretty Sendar woman said, her stringy, brown hair unkempt as her scant clothing, which did little to hide her sagging breasts. She pocketed the two copper pieces the man had given her for her company the night before and retreated to her room to prepare for her next client.

The man who had enjoyed her services pushed his long, greasy black hair behind his ears and tried to pry the sleep from his eyes. He scratched his thick, black beard idly as he bellied up to the bar. His mouth tasted foul and he ordered a glass of Elven spirits to wash it away. The Sendar bartender raised his eyebrows.

"A little early for spirits, isn't it?" he asked, indicating the rising sun through the grimy window.

"Just do it," the man rasped.

"All right," the bartender said, shaking his head and pouring the glass. The man slammed it back with a grimace.

"Keep it comin'," he said, laying a copper on the counter. As the bartender refilled his glass, two burly, haggard-looking men made their appearance at the bar after similar exploits the night before. The older of the two slapped the man at the bar on the back.

"Diedrik, lad, already at th' bar?"

"Aye, you great slob, Rork. Now get your paws offa me."

"Tha's no way t'talk to me brother, mate." The younger twin laughed and ordered a round of spirits. "Yer bein' far too nice if'n y'ask me."

"Shut it, Veg, it's too early for your antics," Diedrik said as he threw back another shot.

"So where to t'day, Diedrik?" Rork asked.

"I'm thinkin' Brayl. I've heard talk of a few inns that need guardin'."

"Tha's two bloody weeks away. We'll need a bit more supplies'n we got," Veg noted. "Leas' more booze. Got t' have tha' at leas'."

"We'll have to make do," Diedrik said, staggering to his feet. The three left the inn and saddled up. The cool wind blowing in off Lok Brae was a dull wakeup call to their heavily drunken senses.

The three had been best friends since childhood, growing up in the Sendar trading city of Keyre. Rork and Veg were a year apart, but for all intents and purposes, were the same in every way. Their dark hair and eyes matched well with their tan skin.

They had been fishermen up until a year ago, well to do and happy with their lot in life. All had been well liked and respected, and Diedrik had been a prized bachelor for his chiseled good looks and youthful appearance. At the time, he had been the best sword in a city known for its weapons-prowess.

Then, a year ago, Diedrik's bride-to-be had died of the wasting disease, and he had turned to drinking. He'd lost his boat and money to the battle against sobriety and one night he'd just left. His mother had always been distant so he didn't speak to her much and hadn't even told her he was leaving; his father had written the book on drunkenness.

A few days out, Diedrik had passed out on the plains north of Volhak. He'd woken to find a fire burning and two men staring intently at him. It had been Rork and Veg. They had left shortly after him in pretense to watch after him but in reality because of an incident with a city councilman's daughters.

The three had been wandering ever since, selling their swords for food and lodging, in desperate times even resorting to burglary. Once such acts would have gone against Diedrik's honor code, but he was more concerned now with his next drink.

They rode at a brisk pace towards the Duah Elven Nation and their next temporary job. As they did so, a well-built blond-haired man came down the stairs of the inn they had left. His cowl was up, but even so his glowing green eyes were clearly visible.

He stopped at the bar and watched the three men departing before turning back to the bartender.

"Coffee and a sweet roll," he said softly, his well-worn black cloak swaying with each graceful movement. The handle of a slender, long sword could be seen at his waist and a polished bow and quiver hung easily over his shoulder.

The bartender asked how he had slept, as well as some other idle questions while the green-eyed man ate quickly. The black-cowled man answered simply and politely, constantly looking around the room and out the window. His pointed ears picked up the slightest sounds and he had the bearing of a natural warrior.

The bartender noticed this right away and treated the man with a little added respect. He knew that such men talked little and kept to themselves but it was his nature and job to ask questions.

"You a Ranger?" he asked, washing out a glass.

"Something like that," the man answered into his coffee mug.

"We get quite a few of you in here since we're on the border and all."

"Aye."

"You after the three that just left here?"

"Something like that." The man rose and paid for the food. "Good day," he said as he walked out the door. Myrisan Deathsong mounted his white horse and followed the three Sendar into the Duah Forest.

As night fell on the woods, Diedrik, Rork and Veg began looking for a suitable shelter, for the nights had begun to grow chilly. To top that off, it had rained for three days straight and even in their drunken stupor the clamminess of their skin bothered them. Not one of the three had a single stitch of dry clothing to wear. Rork and Veg made a game of complaining loudly but Diedrik, by far the most experienced and best trained with a blade, remained stoically silent. Even drunk, his senses were still alert for the possibility of danger. The two brothers noticed nothing.

"Why, I bet even a bloody sal'mander be's mis'ble 'n this weather!" Rork said, wiping a grimy thumb across his thick eyebrow to brush away the rain.

"Aye, tha' do be true. Lookit, even the birds're too wet an' mis'ble to sing an' fly an' such," Veg agreed.

"Slimy snails an' the like don't be needin' t' make none slime fer theirselves, I'm guessin'. They just crawl 'long all mis'ble like. Overslimed, they is."

"Overslimed, ye say? Does that be a word?"

"Course it do!" Rork punched Veg square in the mouth.

"I knew it did be!" Veg tackled his brother into a tree trunk.

"Tha's what I said!" Rork growled between a mouthful of Veg's arm.

"No 't'aint ye great liar!" They rolled around, kicking, punching and biting until Diedrik kicked them both apart roughly. The two brothers got to their feet sullenly, complaining about their bruised bodies.

"I do believe ye broked my spleen, mate," Veg groaned, holding his shoulder. Rork nodded fervently, looking cross eyed at his nose.

"Aye an' my nose's broke fer sure. Lookit 'ow crookit it be! I do feel mis'ble indeed now."

"Aye, mis'ble and broked! Also don't ye ferget soaked. Hey! I rhymed!"

"Look, you bloody idiots!" Diedrik growled. "Your nose ain't broke anymore than it was when that Dwarf girl smacked you in it with the flat of 'er axe when you called 'er the only beardless man you'd ever seen!"

"Ha! That was a good one. She sure did wallop ye a—" Veg slapped his knee before Diedrik smacked him in the face.

"And just what in Nifleheim 're you laughin' at? You don't even know what a spleen is you flarin' ox! And fer the last bloody time, the word is miserable. Not mis'ble."

"Aye, mis'ble. Ain't tha' wha' we said, mate?"

"Aye, mis'ble. Ain't tha' hard t' say," Veg grumbled. "Bloody schoolmarm ifn' ye ask me."

"He do 'ave a mighty temper tonight," Rork commented. Diedrik shook his head, taking deep breaths to steady himself. Their mother must have been drinking Drissian spirits when she'd been pregnant.

"Morons," he addressed them. "Do you see the moon in the sky?"

"Aye. Course. What're we stupid?"

"Never that," Diedrik gritted his teeth. "So, it's flarin' night out, we're in the middle of the bloody Duah Forest and there's the ruins of a bloody Drissian city right over there. In *which one* of those three instances are you *not* registern' danger enough to shut your bloody gobs so as to not attract attention to ourselves?"

"Uh, can ye say tha' las' part again?" Veg wrinkled his brow.

Before Diedrik could punch him, however, the sound of a bow-string snapping rapidly came from the forest around them, followed by the screams and curses of more than a few Goblins. They could see the dozens of yellow flames of Goblins' eyes now as well as a single pair of green in their midst. Diedrik's practiced ears quickly figured out that it was one fighting many. Knowing glowing green eyes were the mark of Elves, he knew that he was definitely not with the Goblins and so must be the one fighting them. He also saw a *terykt* plummet from the dark sky, two Elven arrows through its huge leather wings. The Goblin Rider on its hairy back clung on with a frozen rictus of fear on his ugly features. Diedrik shivered involuntarily.

He was about to come to the Elf's aid when five Goblins burst into the narrow path he and the brothers were on. Though far from alert, Rork and Veg were not cowards and in fact practiced fighters. Their swords rang out at the same time as Diedrik's and they formed into a three-pointed fighting group. Adrenaline washed drunkenness away in the span of an instant.

The first two Goblins met Diedrik's broadsword with their own but their strength couldn't hold up and their fate was quick. The remaining three Goblins, no longer with the advantage, tried to run, but Rork took one through the chest and Veg cut the other two down from behind. As quickly as it had started, it was over. Diedrik searched the surrounding forest, finding only eight Goblin corpses and three dead fear hounds. There was no sign of the Elf. Bloody Duah were like plankton in a fisherman's net, jumping moon rays and disappearing into the night.

"I thought ye said 'twas a *Driss* city over yonder. I did hear no tell a flarin' Goblins 'er the flarin' like." Veg accused, taking a deep swig of spirits from a half empty bottle. Rork shoved him roughly as he snatched the bottle away. They had practically forgotten the fight already.

"Aye, a'*bandoned* city ye did say too. Flarin' Yelloweyes're after our spirits I may s'pose."

"Maybe it'll teach you to shut your bloody gobs when I tell you to then won't it?"

"We's bein' mighty quiet. Only a bit a talkin'."

"A mite, really."

"A word 'er so."

"Aye, ain't nothin' wrong wit a smatter of talkin'."

"Shut up. Come on." Diedrik took a healthy swig from his own bottle and headed out towards the ruined Drissian city of Nerriss, long abandoned and plundered after the Great War. "Naught but shadows and shades now."

"Hold up. Ain't this the way t'that Driss place?" Rork asked.

"You don't go lookin' fer trouble, mate. Ain't we had 'nuff fer tonight?" his brother asked.

"We need a place to sleep and one we can defend if necessary. I, for one, have never seen *Greedfire* cut through stone."

"Aye, tha's a *dwei* plan, mate."

"Aye, 'tis. But I do tell ye, if'n a great flarin' ugly Driss thing does jump out at us, I'm sendin' 'im yer way first, mate. D'ye hear?" Veg hiccupped.

"Aye, first dibs ye'll 'ave. Make a good show of it too. Wouldn't want me'er my brother 'ere t'get all the glory would ye?" Rork added with a slur.

"Considering you two bloody oxen will more'n likely be in a muddled stupor, I don't suppose they'll have any cause to worry about your flarin' carcasses anyway, what with your worthless throats slit and all."

"Oy mate, tha's no thing fer ye t'wish 'pon yer mates!" Rork smacked himself in the forehead.

"Aye, 'tis'nt. An' if'n it do come true, I'll bloody haunt ye as a right scary ghost fer the resta yer life!" Veg chortled, warming instantly to the subject. "A big un, ye un'erstan', with poison claws an' gnashin' yellowed teeth an' the like."

"Aye, an' a pair a empty sockets what fer eyes."

"Wait up a tick now, I do need one eye fer I can see 'im t'haunt 'im an all," Veg considered.

"Aye, that's right, mate. But only a flamin' red 'un per'aps. Jus' one now, though."

"Aye, red does be rather evil lookin' all right," Veg conceded.

"Aye, tha's the bloody reason I did say it!"

"What? *I* said it! Ye idea snatchin' Goblin kisser!"

"Goblin kisser?" Rork punched Veg in the gut and they began to fight again. Diedrik didn't even bother to pull them apart.

Myrisan waited until the three Sendar had finally nodded off before trotting back to his captive. On the way, he carefully avoided a dead fear hound, rapidly turning into an acidic steaming black sludge. It was no use trying to retrieve his arrow from its corpse as it was already dissolving. Filthy abominations, he growled. Made with Goblin magic by merging a Goblin slave with a rabid hound so that they became one tormented creature with only one desire: to kill. He was also concerned with the appearance of the *terykt,* which were created the same vile way. They should not be on the Northern continent. It was a bad omen. And where were the Duah Gryffyn Riders? *Terykt* shouldn't have been able to cross the border without being intercepted. A bloody bad omen indeed.

He eyed the pitifully whining, hogtied Goblin hanging from a tree branch with disdain. It was tied with *Everhold,* a magical Elven vine that prevented Goblins from wriggling free, for they could squeeze through a woodpecker's hole with enough time and effort. He slapped the whimpering creature to get its attention and then twice more for good measure. Myrisan took the bloody gag from its mouth, being none too careful with its obviously broken teeth.

"Why did you attack those three Sendar?" he asked in the guttural simplistic Goblin tongue.

"Theysa in our ways," It whimpered.

"Where were you going?"

"Whersa mistress tells us's to a goes."

"Where?" the black-cowled man asked carefully, knowing that the Goblin would be prevented from revealing his mistress' name by a *Silence* spell.

"Whereversa Sapphire Son goesa," the Goblin began to smile, confident that the more it said, the better its chances of getting out of this alive were.

Myrisan's eyes flared dangerously with the intensity of his question. "What do you know of the Sapphire Son, Goblin?" He grabbed the suddenly very frightened Goblin by its thin neck.

"I's only knows thatsa mys mistress hasa finded him."

"Where is he? What do you Darkspawn know of the Foretelling?"

"I's not knows!" it choked out, struggling to breathe.

"Tell me filthy Goblin scum!"

"I's not know! I's not know!"

"Then you are worthless to me." He stuffed the filthy gag back in its mouth. Myrisan gave it a shove and the Goblin spun around helplessly as it dangled from the branch. Let the Rangers find the cursed thing and deal with it, the man thought. After a quick meal, he once again pushed the whining Goblin and began surveiling the three men, their leader in particular.

Diedrik and the two brothers had found work at a decent inn just outside of the Duah city of Brayl. Veg and Rork as laborers to fix the roof and Diedrik as a hired sword to keep the place from being robbed or trashed by drunken brawlers.

He watched as the innkeeper's daughter, an Elven girl named Hosanal, fetched water from the stream. The heavy forest around the inn made for good shade and a pleasant atmosphere. A ray of sunlight struck the girl's green-streaked hair and pale skin at just the right angle to make her appear to glow.

Diedrik continued to watch her until she went back inside, unaware of his intent gaze. He'd been around whores and riff-raff so often of late, he'd forgotten how much he missed proper women. He felt a pang of sadness at the memory of his beloved Ana. His eyes hardened and he took a drink from his hidden flask.

Two travelers were approaching on foot down the grassy, unforested slope on the other side of the inn and Diedrik figured he'd better go put in an appearance. As he walked off to inspect them, he thought he saw movement deeper into the woods. He stopped and stared unblinkingly at the spot, but when nothing moved, he continued on.

Behind him, Myrisan slipped out of the woods and towards the inn. He kept his cowl up when he entered, scanning the sparsely populated dining room. When he found no threats, he approached the innkeeper.

"I need a room for a few days. I don't know how many." He spoke in melodic Duah. The innkeeper, an older Elf, nodded, replying in the same.

"You can pay for a week and collect what you don't use when you leave."

Myrisan payed the innkeeper two silver coins and received a key.

Myrisan walked up the steps slowly, testing each for creaks. He did the same in the hallway, noting where each one was in his mind. This would help him move silently if he had to and also to tell later if he was being snuck up on. Myrisan heard voices outside and entered his room to look out the window to where the man he was following was coiled like a spring, the scent of his anger only masked by alcohol.

The two Elves Diedrik had gone to talk to were speaking to each other in Duah, much to his consternation for he could only speak it rudimentally. The men exploded in laughter and continued riding towards the inn. Diedrik took a deep breath to calm himself. He was here to keep the place running smoothly, not to kill its customers. His knuckles were white around his sword handle and he had to concentrate hard to loosen his grip. Bloody Duah, thinking they were better than everyone else. No better than flarin' Goblins, he thought bitterly.

Diedrik looked up at Rork and Veg hammering—and jabbering—away on the roof and shook his head. They were as dumb and as clueless as the nails they were hammering. No fewer than three times he saw them miss and hit their thumbs, yelping painfully as they blamed each other or the hammer. Diedrik went back to the front door of the inn to resume his post.

Myrisan stepped away from the window and began checking his room for hiding places and escape routes. The time was near, he could feel it. For what, he knew not but he was ready all the same.

As he went back down to the dining room to order lunch, Myrisan noticed the Elven girl and pulled his cowl a little tighter. For he was a Hafalf, his father Sendar and his mother Duah. He had learned long ago that most Elven women shied away from him for fear of their child being part Sendar, an outcast, like him. Only true, rare and undying love could make someone overlook race and their children's future. It was just the way of the world. Myrisan didn't hold it against them.

So when Hosanal approached him, he didn't make eye contact. He ordered in Duah, looking down at the table. She smiled slightly.

"You don't have to wear your cowl around here, you know," Hosanal said. The Hafalf looked up sharply.

"You wouldn't say that if you knew who I am," Myrisan said softly.

"You mean a Hafalf?"

"How—?"

"You'd have to lose about four inches, forty pounds and shave more often if you wanted to go undetected around here. Nearly half of the Rangers in the Duah Forest are Hafalves."

"And that doesn't bother you?" he asked.

"Why should it?"

"I'm impure," he mocked.

"Please." She laughed and Myrisan laughed with her. They talked on through the day and by nightfall were fast becoming close friends, something Myrisan had none of. It helped take his mind off the task at hand.

CHAPTER 16
BITTER BETRAYAL

et heard the raven's caw just as he had settled down to keep the first watch. He had nearly forgotten about her. He glanced nervously back at the still forms snoring softly around the fire. Once he was sure they slept, he snuck off into the surrounding forest. Hrafna materialized from the shadows in front of him radiating danger. He felt the irresistible lure of her, her intoxicating scent filling his head close to bursting, leaving him a babbling mess. Her black lips parted seductively.

Angrily he shook his head to clear it of her overpowering influence. As if his resistance to her power seemed to make him more desirable to her, she seized him by the back of his neck and kissed him hard on the mouth. He pulled away, reluctantly but forcefully.

"We must make this quick. They will notice my absence," he whispered.

"Relax, pretty one. We are safe here, they will not wake. I am sure of it," she purred confidently. "But first, I have instructions for you. Do you remember the Oracles I told you about? The High One does not have the same plans for them as the one who created them. We must insure that events happen as the High One wishes, not their creator, for his gain would destroy the Balance."

"Aye," Jet nodded warily. "I am aware of the situation."

"Someone in your company came into possession of one at the palace in Wendall."

"How?" Jet asked worriedly, for he'd known it had been her who had attacked Amaria.

"I gave the first Oracle to the Mage's twin sister eight years ago. I don't know how, but she managed to lose it. I think she may have drowned."

"Danken has a sister?" Jet nearly shouted.

"Had. Keep your voice down unless you wish us to be caught."

"Who has the Oracle now?" he whispered.

"I don't know, but they keep it so close it cannot be retrieved without their untimely demise. The Mage was supposed to be led to his sister once we were ready. If he finds the Oracle without it being attached to his twin, or someone he *believes* is, it could ruin everything. It must be returned at all costs. This one will lead him to the others. I must have it."

"You never said anything about killing innocent people, Hrafna." Jet's jaw clenched.

"You will not have to. There is an inn just to the north of Brayl. Make sure your companions stay there tomorrow night. I have a surprise in store."

"What kind of surprise?"

"Take this," Hrafna handed him a tiny black vial. "Drink this before you sleep tomorrow."

"What is it?"

"Do it if you wish to live," she told him coldly.

"Do you intend to go after Danken?"

"No. He does not have it. If he did, he would know something was wrong."

"Very well, it will be as you say."

"Good. Now come to me. I have missed you."

As Jet returned to camp, he became aware of another presence in the dark woods. He drew his hatchets. Danken stepped out from behind an oak tree only a few feet away. His eyes lit the night as he glared at Jet.

"Where did you go?" Danken asked softly. "You were supposed to be on watch."

"I had to relieve myself. Or did I need your permission for that?"

"Awfully long time to relieve yourself. Did you need some help, maybe?"

"I drank a lot. Now mind your own business, Danken."

"Well, see, I would. It's just that you make it so damn hard."

"Try harder."

"I shouldn't have to."

"Too bad."

"Aye, it is."

Jet's voice grew cold. "What I do, or who I do it with is no concern of yours."

"Except that it is. It's you who travels with me, not the other way around. So I'd like some answers."

"I don't respond well to interrogations."

Danken shrugged. "Then let's have a chat, you and I."

"About what? I have nothing to 'chat' with you about."

"Don't you? How about those hatchets?"

"What about them?" Jet gripped them tightly.

"Where did they come from?"

"Around."

"Around where?"

"I could ask you the same question." Jet nodded towards the drawn *Mak'Rist*.

"Aye, you could. But you didn't. Because you already knew. How is that, I wonder? How is it that you just happened upon the identical hatchets to those you once held, except now..." Danken flicked his blade, "they're made of the same metal as my sword? How is that you happened to have your saddlebags packed before we left Lok Tryst? How did you come by such fine clothes?" Danken suddenly lashed out with his sword, just nicking Jet on the cheek. "And how come that cut won't be there by the time we're done 'chatting'?"

Jet fumed. "You ask questions that you don't want to know the answers to, Danken."

"Maybe, but I'll have them nonetheless."

"Not from me you won't."

"No?" Danken flicked Jet's hatchets in taunt.

"What are you going to do? Beat it out of me? Please. We both know that's not going to happen." Jet twirled his hatchets. "Not when I hold these. You might be destined to be some big, important Mage, but you're not yet. And even when you are, you still won't be able to beat me. This isn't some stupid staff tournament. This is the real thing. And I don't think you can handle it." Jet's hatchets blurred as he hooked Danken's blade. "But you're welcome to try." After several tense moments, Jet put away his hatchets and laughed as he pushed past Danken. "That's what I thought."

As the procession neared Brayl, night began to overtake them and at Jet's suggestion they decided to stop at an inn for the night. It was a busy affair, tucked in an alcove not far from the path. It was formed out of a huge stand of pine trees caressed by the Elves into a giant hollow.

A pleasant din could be heard coming from inside, the sounds of glasses clinking, shouts and music. Horses were stabled outside and the company moved that way. T'riel and K'airn took Shard out around back where they had found an unoccupied willow tree for him to sleep under and for them to sleep in. They weren't fond of crowded spaces and Shard wasn't welcome inside. Danken was torn about leaving them outside but their travel gear needed washing and repairing and a cold night without gear was close to unbearable.

So Danken, Tae, Arn, Kierna, Jet and a reluctant Dot stabled their horses and entered the inn. Their cowls were drawn close around their faces to avoid any unnecessary attention. Inns were notorious breeding grounds for informants and other undesirables who would sell their identities to the Sorcerers for a shaved copper if the opportunity presented itself.

Though the pipes and flutes kept playing, most, if not all conversation stopped as they entered. The four large cloaked men with long, well-used blades, the cowled woman with the longbow and the likewise cloaked little girl were an odd, yet wholly imposing sight. Arn surveyed the room like a wolf surveying sheep. It was mostly Duah and Sendar but there were a few Dwarves as well. Most looked like traders and ruffians, but there were a few respectable looking men. Even though the Northern continent fought for the forces of Light, there were more than enough undesirables among them to go around.

Danken, however, was unconcerned as he walked directly to an open table in the corner. The rest followed his lead, taking up positions that gave them a wide view of the establishment. An Elven girl not much older than Danken came by and took their orders. She was slim and had large, green eyes with short hair that hung over them.

Her eyes lingered on Danken for a moment, perhaps catching the glint of blue in his eyes. He smiled at her and she stopped to ask Dot what she wanted.

"What can I get for you cutie?" she asked sweetly in Sendar. Danken released a small tendril of energy into her and got her answer.

"She'll have the stew and a cherry pie, please," he told the girl in Duah. She seemed not to have heard him though, as she stared at Danken's hands where the energy had come from. "Miss?" he asked.

"I'm sorry. Stew and cherry pie," she answered quickly. Jet winked at her and Kierna rolled her eyes.

"Happens all the time," Danken answered her as she hurried off to get their order. Arn left the table to go get rooms for them.

"Wager the whole establishment knows about you in a moment," Tae commented, eyeing the crowd.

"And that'll be excellent fun for us, I'm sure," Kierna said. Jet seemed to recoil at the thought, odd since he was normally so apt for a fight.

"Aye, lots of sleep we'll be gettin' with this lot peeking in our windows all night. Well Dot, it looks like you'll be pulling guard duty tonight," Tae said with a raised eyebrow. Dot gave a resolute nod and her best scowl. Danken laughed, Kierna ruffling the girl's hair affectionately.

"Well I don't think any bands of Goblins will attempt to get past that!"

"Here's your order," the waitress said, laying out the steaming stew and mugs of ale, doing her best to avoid eye contact with Danken. She seemed even less inclined to look at Jet's breathtaking handsomeness.

"Thank you kindly miss…" Tae said, giving her a reprieve from his disconcertingly powerful Sendar friends. For such a rough and tumble sailor, he was surprisingly smooth when he wished to be.

"Hosanal," she smiled shyly.

"Taelun Fallenbower," he said rising to give her the traditional Elven greeting of hands crossed in front of his chest. She responded likewise.

"And this here is Dot Windsong, Kierna Bjorndotir, Jet Bloodhatchet and my matey, Danken. The big ugly bloke at the bar is Arn. Does your family own this inn?"

"Aye, for four generations. That's my father, Tumbledo and my mother, Berylin at the bar."

"Hey! Waitress! We been waitin' fer half a glass! Move it!" came a Sendar voice from across the room. Danken started to rise but Tae's hand on his shoulder stopped him.

"Not now, laddie."

"I'd better get going," Hosanal said as she walked towards the voice.

"Why did you stop me?" Danken asked.

"It's the way people here are. You can't teach them manners with a blade without starting a free-for-all in here." Jet seemed to think otherwise but once again oddly decided to follow Tae's lead. The one time Danken wanted the bloody man to fight and he didn't!

"Aye," Danken said, tasting his soup, vegetarian he noted, wishing for some red meat.

"I've gotten us four rooms for the night," Arn said as he returned to the table. "We'd best be eating quickly. We've got an early day tomorrow." He looked over at Dot, whose entire face was covered in cherry pie. "I see that won't be a problem for *some* of us."

"I'm going to go outside and check on the Nymphs and Shard," Danken told them, taking a few cherries and a big piece of mutton out of the inn. A beefy hand slapped on his chest nearly knocked him flat.

"Where de ye think y'ere goin' boy?" Rork said in the heavily drunken voice Danken recognized from across the room. "Ye ain't paid fer that yet. I'm thinking yer a t'ief." The bearded, dark-haired man wobbled unsteadily.

"Really?" Danken asked smiling. "Because I was just thinking about stealing your filthy hand from your wrist." Another man stood up behind the first. Both were large, dark-haired, unshaven and unkempt, and Danken marked them as brothers.

"Ye din't answer th' question boy. Where de ye think y'ere goin' wi' that wi'out payin' fer it?" Veg spat. "We do be the peacekeepers an such round 'ere."

"Well, I was thinking about heading over to your mother's house for a *dwei* time. What do you boys think of that?" Danken smiled. Both brothers' eyes grew wide but before they could react, Danken punched Rork squarely in the nose and kicked Veg in the groin.

Rork swung an ale mug at his head but Danken sidestepped it. He kicked the man in the side of the knee and when he dropped, Danken followed up with a punch to the side of his greasy head. Danken turned to Veg, who was still bent over holding his groin. Just for good measure, Danken kicked him in the head. Both men lay squirming on the ground.

A larger, more clean-cut man with dark, hard eyes stood up slowly, eyeing the two men on the floor. He looked at Danken steadily. He smelled of alcohol but held it well.

"Now, I know you didn't steal that stuff," Diedrik pointed at the mutton and cherries on a nearby table, "but those were my friends and on top of that, it's my job to keep people in line here."

"Well, I can under..." Danken started, but was cut off by the man's fist in his jaw. Diedrik rushed him and threw him on the table. He smashed Danken's head into the table, making him see stars. Danken grabbed the man on either side of his head and head-butted him twice. The man cried out and stumbled back. Danken hit him twice more and Diedrik went down.

He looked around the silent room. Tae and Arn were holding back a Hafalven man in a dark cloak who was looking at him with a mixture of anger and awe. Kierna wore a scolding look while Jet looked hurt he hadn't been included. Danken felt for his cowl and realized it had fallen. He put it quickly back up, took the mutton and cherries and stepped wordlessly out into the night.

He saw his breath freeze and walked quickly over to the willow where his trio of friends were sleeping. He felt T'riel's tiny feet on his shoulders before he saw Shard materialize in front of him.

"Good to see you all are remaining vigilant," he said, scratching Shard's ears to the sound of loud purring. "Where's K'airn?"

"Patrolling," T'riel answered simply. "Boy has been in a fight."

"Aye," Danken laughed, wincing as he remembered his head hitting the table. "Just a scuffle. I've had far worse growing up, believe me."

"Hmmph."

"I brought you and K'airn some cherries," he said, as T'riel excitedly took them to the tree tops to eat, chattering something in his ear as she did so. "And I got a little snack for you too, fuzz ball," he said, handing the mutton to the huge cat. Shard licked it a few times before swallowing it whole.

Just then a high-pitched squeal materialized into two tiny blurs streaking towards him.

"Goblins!" T'riel squeaked as the Sigil began to burn.

"K'airn!" Danken said quickly. "Alert Arn. Go!" The Sprite shot off like an arrow towards the inn. "T'riel how far away are they?" he asked as they sped towards the inn.

"Not far!" she shrieked back, rising into the sky.

"How many?"

"Fifty! More come from the other side!"

"Damn!" Danken cursed as he heard the war cries of the Goblins surrounding the inn, closing on him. As he reached the other side of the inn, he saw most of its patrons flooding out with weapons drawn. Arn called Danken over to him.

"There's no escape! We're surrounded! Looks like a fight!" he yelled over the clamor of voices. The voices stopped suddenly as the Goblin horde emerged from the forest—some astride fear hounds—into the clearing nearly two hundred strong. Two *terykts* glided overhead out of arrow range, their Goblin Riders surveying the scene. Jet's heart stopped when he saw Hrafna's raven circling overhead. It wasn't supposed to be like this. Hastily he drank the vile-tasting black liquid, feeling terribly guilty. He had caused this. No one was supposed to die. He had to be able to ensure his immortality some other way than this. He had known he couldn't trust Hrafna. Trust was pain. The residents of the inn numbered barely fifty. However, these were not simple peasants. They were traders and brigands who knew their way around a blade.

The contingent of the inn stared grimly at the huge Goblin host, cackling in guttural screeches while banging their poisoned blades on small, round bone shields. Their slanted, flaming yellow eyes were indistinguishable from the tips of lit arrows they carried. As Tae and the other Elves were hastily scrawling their Death Poems or reading from one they had already prepared, Arn began to recite an ancient Sendar battle refrain called, "The Battle Hymn of the Valkyrie" in his baritone voice that carried clear across the field. Soon the rest of the inn's patrons had joined in, gaining confidence as the volume grew to a crescendo. Their thunderous voices silenced the suddenly confused Goblins, who milled about nervously, for the Sendar were actually smiling, battle lust in their fierce eyes.

Atop the slain a Valkyrie

Her flaming sword she points at me

Through the mist of battle clear

Absent of pain, absent of fear

Open the Gates, for I am near

Open the Gates, for I am near

Valhalla calls me

And I am not afraid.

The refrain ended in a great roar, Sendar and Duah charging. Some unseen force spurring them on, the Goblins gave out a chilling cry and charged, sending sparks of yellow fire at the inn patrons. The Elves fired their own green energy back and the few Sendar with bows used them to great effect, Kierna greatest among them.

The battle was met with a resounding crash. Metal on metal, cries of pain and the smell of brimstone pervaded. It began to rain heavily soon after, thunder and lightning adding to the drama. The Goblins, hardly four feet tall, were a hard foe to fight because they were fearful and cowardly and at turns also viscous and cunning.

Danken had left Dot and the few other non-battle prone women and children with Shard, Kierna and the Nymphs, as well as a few older men so he could devote his all to the battle. He, Arn and Tae formed an unstoppable triumvirate in the exact center of the battle.

Arn was something Danken had only heard about in the legends. The huge man and his likewise huge broadsword cut literal pathways through the advancing Goblins. Tae used his sword with deadly finesse, finding holes in every defense and exposing them. Once in awhile he would use his *Moonfire* or blowgun to clear an area to work in or protect someone's backside.

Danken merely closed his eyes and became a whirling blue instrument of death. The tide was turning against the Goblins but many of the inn's residents were dying. Danken saw a Goblin raise for the death strike on the third man he had fought in the bar. He leapt into the way of the blade just as it descended and blocked it with *Mak'Rist* before disemboweling the stunned Goblin. Diedrik looked stupidly at him, as the Hafalf man from earlier rushed over to aide them. Rork and Veg lay dead at his feet.

"Come on!" Danken yelled, helping Diedrik up. "It's not over!" As the man got up, a bolt of yellow fire just missed him and hit Danken in the chest, knocking him out cold. Diedrik and Myrisan killed two Goblins moving in for the kill and began to stand guard over Danken.

As the first Goblins made it through the Norsemen's lines, they were met by a volley of arrows, most of which came from Kierna's longbow. Still a good few managed to make it to the small group of children and elderly. The three old men met the charge bravely, leaving her free to pick her shots. She killed nearly a dozen before the old men fell dead one after the other to relentless Goblin blades. Drawing her belt knife, Kierna prepared to defend the old woman and four scared children. With her life.

Before she could do so however, a glancing bolt of *Greedfire* erupted at her feet, sending her flying. She landed heavily but adrenaline dulled her pain. Kierna pushed an Elven corpse out of the way along with the pile of Goblins that surrounded it, when two bloody blades drew her attention from beneath the body. Pushing the Duah further aside, she grasped the hilts of the blades, staring in wonder at their finely crafted long, thin double edges of Elven beauty and design.

A roar from Shard brought her back to reality. The sabercat had killed over a dozen Goblins but he had suffered many wounds from being forced to fight defensively. The Nymph's energies were nearly expended as well. Kierna leapt into the fray with a savage growl that stopped the Goblins cold. Before they could recover she was among them, twin blades working in deadly harmony. Even Shard was forced to retreat from her fury. He placed his back to the corner containing the refugees and let Kierna go about her work. Though she had never once touched a sword, it was as if she had been born with them in her hands.

Jet was a black ball of rage, his hatchets' twin blurs leaving red mist trailing in their angry wake. He vented his frustrations on the hapless Goblins mercilessly and soon they were pushing against each other in their frantic efforts to scramble away from him. It did them no good. Before, he had taken the name Bloodhatchet as reminder of his ill deed. Now, his silhouette atop a literal pile of corpses with hatchets dripping foul Goblin blood gave the title a real, chilling meaning. After the battle, those who had survived had his name on their awed lips more than any other, for he had saved a dozen lives while himself bleeding freely from a score of surely fatal wounds about his torso. Still more intriguing was his refusal of all medical help. Tae had seen the wounds and the aftermath in which they had simply disappeared, but remained silent.

A flash of lightning illuminated the battlefield, showing a few dozen remaining Goblins retreating into the woods. Suddenly, dozens of bolts of green fire came out of the woods into the fleeing Goblins, followed by a hail of arrows. The survivors were met by a score of *Verna'ren* who cut them down easily then ran to secure the battlefield. The huge silhouette of a Gryffyn Rider above could be seen killing the two *terykts* as the Rangers worked. They and the unharmed residents helped carry off the wounded. All kept a wary eye on the woman with the two swords, as she still looked as if she might kill anyone in range. Her vicious glare sent chills down even the most hardened soldier's spine.

The rain washed away the blood from clothes and faces as if it was consoling those who had lived to see another day. Its earthy smell cleansed the ground of the smell of blood and death. Though nothing could wash away the looks of pain and sadness and loss etched on the faces of the few who had survived.

Arn and Tae searched frantically among the fallen for Danken. They saw the man Danken had fought earlier that night standing on a pile of Goblin corpses with his sword still drawn. He peered through

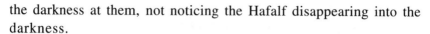

the darkness at them, not noticing the Hafalf disappearing into the darkness.

"Is it over?" Diedrik asked.

"Aye," Arn replied, eyeing the departing Hafalf.

"He saved my life, you know, I figured it was only fair to do the same," Diedrik sheathed his sword and hoisted the unconscious Danken over his shoulders. *"Greedfire* knocked him clean out."

"Thank you. You can't imagine the service you've done to the realm." Arn motioned to two Rangers with a stretcher.

"My father's dead!" Hosanal sobbed. "I can't go in." The inn smoldered behind her.

Arn put an arm around her. "I know, I'm sorry. But he died fighting for your future so don't make it in vain. You'll get through this." He smiled sadly before going to check on Danken inside. A group of people surrounded the boy. The *Greedfire* had acted like a club and its energy had put him into shock. It should have killed him but Tae said he detected a faint resonance of a fire shield Danken had unconsciously used. Judging by the dryness of his clothes, it had kept even the rain from touching the boy, let alone weapons. He was shaking and his skin was a pale blue. The room's sparse furniture and dim lighting seemed somehow appropriate.

"There's nothing more that we can do for him right now," said one of the Rangers. "We have to see to other patients." Tae nodded and the two moved on.

"I'm going to go check on Dot," he said weakly, turning away.

"Aye," Arn said.

"Help me get his clothes off," came Hosanal's voice from the door. Arn turned to find her holding a bucketful of warm water and a towel. Arn hid his surprise and did as she asked. "You might as well get some sleep, you can't do anything else for him right now. He can be saved. I'll take care of him," she said as she wrung the towel, letting the drops hit Danken's lips to help his parched throat. Arn took one last look and left the room. One did not question Duah intuition, especially not a woman's.

Jet silently watched the Elven girl tending to Danken and felt sick to his stomach. All of this had been his doing, and they hadn't even retrieved the Oracle. They had hurt Danken, the one person they could *not* hurt if the plan was to succeed. Idiots! All those lives wasted for what? His ambition? His desire to live forever? The scary thing was that he was so far into it now that he wasn't sure he could get out, even if he wanted to. Did he want to? Would he give it all up? This couldn't be what keeping the Balance entailed.

Feeling the overwhelming urge to bathe and breathe fresh air, Jet backed soundlessly out of the room. He avoided the battlefield by exiting through the burned-out back exit. He continued on into the forest until he came to a small pond lit only by a thin streak of moonlight forcing its way through the thick clouds. Tiny ripples caused by raindrops soothed his restless thoughts and he shed his problems as he shed his bloody clothes, one at a time.

The water was cold but he barely noticed, scrubbing himself fiercely as if he could wash away the death on his hands, the blood on his soul. Somewhere in between his anger at himself and his sorrow for those lost, he reached a compromise with himself. Nowhere had it been stated that he must follow orders. He was to ensure change as *he* saw fit. No one else unless it came from Loki himself. Hrafna had been given an initial directive, but her methods and actions were her own.

Feeling a little better about things, Jet pulled himself out of the pond, shivering in his nakedness but uncaring, his mind on the future. He supposed he could tell Danken and the rest what he had done but that could be dangerous. Besides, that would require trust, and Jet Bloodhatchet had never trusted anyone. Trust got people hurt. Trust was pain.

The wind dried him as much as the drizzle would allow. Heedless, he pulled on his spare underpants and socks. Considering it a small price to pay for peace of mind, he threw his bloody shirt into the pond as he laced his knee high boots, their shiny steel toe the only part exposed outside the wide bottoms of his black buckskin breeches. As he bent to retrieve his hatchets and holstered daggers, a broken twig heralded a visitor.

"You were right," Kierna emerged from the shadows, leading her saddled horse. Going about his business as if he had not nearly whipped a knife into her chest, Jet responded calmly.

"About what?" he asked, raising an eyebrow at the twin sword hilts crossed behind her back.

"I do love him. So much so that I lose my breath when I even think about him, which is all the time," she confessed in a flat voice. "Ever since I was old enough to know."

"What do you intend to do?" Jet asked softly, shaking the excess water from his hair.

"Nothing. It is not reciprocated."

"How would you know? You've acted as if he were little better than a Troll our whole lives. You've spited him nearly as much as I have. He thinks you hate him."

"I thought—I hoped it would fade but it never did. It only got worse the older I got." She closed her eyes as if wishing the memory away.

"It's not too late, you know. We are young."

"It *is* too late." She tossed her blond ponytail over her shoulder in irritation or frustration, Jet couldn't tell which. Maybe both. "I had hoped that I would be safe from my calling in his love, that his power would be enough to keep me away. All my life I have avoided touching a sword¾any sword, thinking that as long as I did not, I could avoid my fate. The Norns decreed differently though, for in the battle my hand was forced. These two are too long, but they will do for now," she indicated the twin blades crossed at her back. "Only Danken's love could have kept me from my calling."

"What are you saying?"

"I am a Spirit Blade. I go now to the Sacred Falls of Thor to declare my allegiance to the Sisterhood."

"Spirit Blade?! Are you bloody insane?"

"Please don't tell Danken about any of this," she begged. "Give me your oath on it, Jet. Please. I must do as I must."

"I think you're making a mistake, Kierna."

"Jet," she pleaded.

"Aye, fine. In Loki's name I swear it. My *Fylgia* desert me should I break it,"

"A solemn Binding Oath to Loki?" Kierna asked.

"You must do what you must. As must I. We all have our secrets, Kierna. Some darker than others. Yours is safe with me."

"Keep him safe, Jet. Tell him my destiny called me elsewhere and I wish him luck in his."

"Gods be with you, Kierna Bjorndotir."

"And you, Jetrian," Kierna spurred her impatient mare off into the dark forest. "With luck we will never meet again," she called back to him, her old hardened self once more.

Shirtless, Jet headed back to the inn. The rain washed his old life away. From this point on he would do as he chose, not as others dictated. If he had the power to alter the Balance, he would reshape it in *his* image. No more needless deaths would be caused by his actions. Hrafna would be in for a rude surprise when she realized he was a true trickster, a twister of fate. Loki had not chosen him for nothing.

Now if he could only resist her charm long enough to work his own.

The first thing Danken saw was the pretty, shorthaired Elven girl from the inn. She was touching him and he felt warmth wherever her touch was. He felt strangely good though he had the distinct feeling that something bad had happened.

Before he could ponder the subject, the Sigil began to burn, not of danger, but of something far more primitive. The temperature in the room dropped noticeably. Danken's breath froze in front of his face. He noticed that time seemed to have stopped. Water droplets from Hosanal's sponge hung unmoving above his chest and she was still as a stone. A blue-grey tint filled the room.

Danken found that he could move but before he found the strength to try, an unimaginably powerful presence overwhelmed him. He caught a movement out of the corner of his eye and followed it until it stood directly in front of him. It was a huge man in a black cloak and a cowl that shadowed his face. Danken made out dark red hair and a long grey streaked beard with one eye covered by a patch.

"Who are you?" Danken whispered, unable to muster a strong voice against this being who inexplicably impaled him with fear and awe.

"I am known by many names amongst men," he said in a perfect baritone voice that threatened to steal Danken's breath away. "But Sanngetal will do for now as you seem to be somewhat lost."

"What do you want with me?" Danken eyed the huge spear the being carried.

"You think you have found your destiny, do you? Becoming a Mage, fighting the forces of Darkness across the realms? Battling Sorcerers in glorious mortal combat? Aye, that is but a small part of it, though. Your path is a far greater one but one fraught with danger. You must use your head, not just your emotions to save Midgarthe as we know it."

"Why do you wish to help *me*? Could you not achieve such goals easily on your own?"

"Would that I could, young Magus, but my time on this plane has long since passed. Remember what I said. Fulfill your potential." Just as suddenly as he had appeared, the being vanished, setting time in motion once again. With it, the previous night came back to Danken and he remembered seeing the yellow fire plunging into his chest. And now he was here. But where were his friends? He tried to sit up, startling Hosanal and catching a glimpse of his naked body in the process.

"You're awake!" Hosanal exclaimed in Duah.

"Aye. Water please."

She held a glass to his lips. He drank greedily, spilling some down his chin. "How are you feeling?" she switched to Sendar.

"Weak, but fine. What happened in the battle?"

"We won. A company of *Verna'ren* showed up and killed the Goblins who were left."

"My friends..."

"They are safe." She indicated T'riel and K'airn, curled up in a ball on top of a chandelier above his head. He smiled.

"You helped save me?"

"Aye," she blushed, "but it was mostly them."

"I think you helped more than you think," he said, sitting up all the way. "Huh, I really am naked. I thought it was just a dream."

"I'm sorry, but I had to because..."

"You don't need to apologize. Actually I'm kind of used to it by now," he said, smiling as he maneuvered himself to dangle his legs off the side. Hosanal helped him as he stood, shakily at first but soon he got the hang of it. Next, she helped him dress which was an awkward, yet intimate moment.

"Thank you for helping me get back to health," Danken told her, hugging her tightly before she retired to her bed. He walked quietly down to the kitchen and made himself some tea and honeyed bread. He tried to block out the searing, throbbing pain that permeated every bone in his body.

After he had finished, he hauled himself to his feet and trudged off to see to the wounded of the battle in the back room of the inn. Surprisingly, there were only eight and none of them life threatening. Goblin blades were rusty, jagged and usually coated with poison so if a man was hit in any meaningful way with one, it was usually fatal. These men and Elves were recovering from the poison and *Greedfire* as he himself had been.

Satisfied that he could do nothing here, he headed towards Dot's room where he was not surprised to find Shard at her feet, like the scariest watchdog in history. Danken smiled and kissed her on her forehead before pulling the blanket up to her chin when he felt her tiny arms go around his neck.

"Hey there," he whispered. "I'm glad to see you're all right too." She set her arms back down and fell promptly back asleep. Danken moved quietly out of the room and found himself wandering aimlessly through the halls of the inn. Eventually he came outside to survey the battlefield, which by now was empty but for a smoldering pyre of Goblin dead and the ashes of the thirty-one dead from the inn.

The rain had stopped and so the ground was no longer soggy. Most of the blood on the ground had been washed away, but Danken could still feel it in the air. He stood in the rising sun's first rays and closed his eyes, taking in the sights, smells and sounds and realizing that although he was horrified at the mayhem he could cause with his blade, he realized he felt complete only in battle. The prospect made him shudder.

"It's what you were born for, you know." Arn's voice came from behind him, causing him to start.

"*What* is what I was born for?" Danken asked, turning around to regard him.

"Battle," Arn said simply.

"Battle," Danken repeated skeptically.

"Aye. It's why you're so good at it, it's why you feel like you're whole when you do it. You like it but you also fear it, am I right?"

"Aye. How did you know?"

"I've lived with Magi my whole life. I've learned a thing or two. Trust me, you're all like that."

"That's what I was afraid of."

CHAPTER 17
A WINDOW TO THE PAST

he didn't tell you where she was going?" Danken demanded as they left the inn. Jet shook his head, answering for the tenth time.

"No, Danken. She said she had her own bloody destiny. Once she has fulfilled it, she'll flarin' come back. I cannot tell you more so stop flarin' asking for the God's sake."

"I have to go after her, to see if she's all right."

"Why? So she can rebuke you and chastise you for putting the flarin' world at risk simply to check on her? You should know better than that by now."

"Maybe it was something I did," Danken fretted.

"It's not what you *did,* it's what you *didn't* do. What you couldn't do even had you wanted to. By Thor's Goats, Danken! You worry like an old maid."

"What are you talking about? What didn't I do?"

"You don't bloody listen for starters!" Jet bellowed. "I can't flarin' tell you so shut your mead hole!"

"She shouldn't be alone," Danken sulked.

"Seriously. Do you honestly think that Kierna, who beat you unconscious with a staff and kicked you when you tried to rise, needs *you* or *me* to protect her? That *Greedfire* must have knocked something loose in that flarin' Faerie head of yours. Now, I've sworn my oath and not even you can make me break it. So whether or not you think *she* should be alone, please leave *me* alone!" Jet grated and spurned his horse further ahead to where Tae was leading them.

"This Pixie hates to admit it," T'riel said as she landed on Danken's shoulder, "but Silver Blades is right. Ice Eyes would skin Boy alive if he did not make it to the Peak."

"Aye. But that doesn't mean I have to like it."

"Good." She nodded importantly. "Then Boy will please shut up. This Pixie's head hurts from healing him."

"Your support and compassion are like embers on my funeral pyre," Danken told her sarcastically.

The rest of the journey through the Duah Kingdom passed uneventfully, and after five days they had reached the river Cam. This was the boundary between the Duah and Vull'Kra Kingdoms.

From here one could see the fortified Vull'Kra city of D'ran, which stared across the river at the fortified Duah city of Brayl. Both cities had been built in a past era when wars between the two races were commonplace. It was now a gigantic trading post. Dwarven barges would sail down from Greyore with iron tools, weapons and raw ore. The Elves and Trolls sent back lumber and manufactured goods as well as rare objects obtained from the coastal trade routes. The Dwarves did not have a port and besides that, hated anything they couldn't see the bottom of, except for mines laced with ore, that is.

The Duah and Vull'Kra Nations had competed in the oceans for millennia and built some of the finest vessels afloat. Both built their vessels for trading as well as war, for even with each other as tentative allies, they still had regular fights with the Goblins, Driss and Mai'Lang ships that traded in the South, not to mention from the pirate crews of Shraken raiders that had been prowling the coasts since the end of the Great War.

The Vull'Kra city of D'ran was an imposing place. The walls were all of granite and the buildings inside appeared to be the same. However, Arn told them they would not be staying in the Vull'Kra Nation this time around. They had stayed in Wendall only to sell goods and so he could speak with the King.

But expecting to cut through the Vull'Kra Nation without meeting any Trolls was naive. By their second day, the companions encountered a large band of *zandbirjadn*. The band had sung the wood from a sizable section of forest. All were dressed in the purple and bronze of the Royal Family so Arn knew they were the King's men. *Zandbirjadn* never cut down a tree, they instead asked it to give them a piece of itself, called *zandbir* wood. It was highly prized throughout the realm.

The sight of the Trolls took Danken's breath away. Here were the most fearsome fighters in all of the Northern continent. Dark green skin covered massively built bodies up to a head and shoulder taller than Danken. Bone blades protruded from elbows as thick as Danken's leg. Razor-like talons extended from their four-fingered hands. A thin braid of seaweed or red colored hair grew from an otherwise cleanly shaven, ridged head. Their faces were cut as if from stone, square nose and chin with a protruding brow and deep-set glowing dark amber eyes the color of pine sap.

There were a few female Trolls among them. They were taller than Danken and about the same build. Their heads were also shaved but for a square on the crown of their skull, which was grown nearly to their waists. They were not unattractive as he had been led to believe, merely different. But they were undeniably intimidating.

The leader of the group, the largest stepped forward and spoke in thickly accented Sendar.

"What is your business?" His impossibly low baritone vibrated on Danken's bones.

"We are passing through. Looking for a worthy opponent for my friend," Arn stated in an equally authoritative tone. The lead Troll burst out laughing, a sound like tympani drums in Danken's ear.

"Opponent? You wish Challenge then?" the Troll asked. "With all that accompanies it, indentured servitude and all? The Way of *M'Racht?*" In Vull'Kra, all Trolls followed a strict honor code called *M'Racht,* which meant 'The Hand' in honor of the sacrifice Tyr had made so the Gods could bind the Fenrir Wolf. Sacrifice and Courage were valued higher than any other attribute. It was also physically impossible for a Troll to tell a lie. If a Troll swore to serve someone, he would never stop. Generally, when a Troll won a duel, he would allow the loser to continue as before, only calling in the eternal marker when necessary.

"If you wish a Challenge, we will oblige," Arn said calmly. The Trolls gathered to conference. "All conditions of *M'Racht* met."

"What is going on?" Danken asked.

"They will send a challenger to meet one of us, you. It is their way. Vull'Kra society is hierarchal. Each must know his place. They are established. They must know where we fit in. Try not to kill him."

Arn once again sought to test him and had baited the Trolls into accepting.

"One of *them? I* should be worried about getting killed!" Danken exclaimed. Arn merely shook his head.

"Remember to keep your eyes closed. That will impress them."

"Why do I care about impressions?"

"Because you're building a legend. By the time we reach Mist Peak, all in Sendar will know of the Sariksen. This gives them hope, which is the source of your strength, and puts them on a personal level with you. If we have to fight another war, all will join to fight alongside you. That is why I spread your deeds to all who will listen," Arn said with all seriousness. "A Mage does not sit about relaxing, a Mage fights. That is what you were born to do. It is your destiny. The better you are with that blade, the longer you will live when the Sorcerers come calling, and they will."

The Trolls broke conference and sent their challenger out. It was a slightly smaller Troll, but nearly as large as the leader.

He carried his gigantic battle axe with ease and swung it experimentally faster than Danken thought possible. However, whereas Elves were the essence of speed, Trolls were strength and power incarnate. Danken stepped forward, drawing *Mak'Rist.* Clearly the Vull'Kra had expected someone else to take up the challenge. The leader merely nodded knowingly. He knew, Danken saw.

"My name is Valshk. I am Sixth of Clan Nok." The Troll spoke in thickly accented Sendar. Placing his left fist against the bridge of his nose between the prominent brows. "By *M'Racht,* my honor is my axe."

"My name is Danken Sariksen," he rolled up his sleeve to expose the Sigil. At this, Valshk's eyes widened. Contrary to popular belief, Trolls were far from stupid. They knew who the boy would be. His appearance alone hinted at his future to most. Faerie Races generally knew more of magic and its denizens than the average superstitious Sendar. "I accept Challenge," Danken said raising *Mak'Rist.*

"Then let us begin," Valshk said, raising his battle axe fearlessly. Danken closed his eyes, merging with *Mak'Rist*. Once again the familiar feeling of calm settled him. He knew where Valshk was and what he planned, yet it still would have knocked the blade from his hands had such a thing been possible when he countered the Troll's opening swing. He recovered quickly, though, and the Troll's second cut found nothing but thin air. Valshk tried to regain his advantage, but Danken was already behind him. He swung *Mak'Rist* so hard at the handle of Valshk's axe that it severed the shaft.

Valshk looked dumbly at the axe head on the ground, then at the magnificent blade Danken wielded at his throat.

"Well fought, Danken Sariksen. I am your servant. What is your wish?" Valshk lowered his head. Danken looked at Arn who offered no help.

"You have fought bravely this day, Valshk. I will not make you a slave."

"You must!" the leading Troll shouted. "Honor demands it!"

"I decide what is demanded of me!" Danken's eyes flared. "And I decide that he is free. I live not by your rules."

"Aye, maybe not. But you *fought* by our rules. You must give him a standing order, else he will be exiled. A rogue with no Clan. He will be in your debt for life, to do with as you please, regardless of whether or not you accept him. If you make him your servant, he retains his position of honor within the Clan. *M'Racht* says it shall be so."

"Very well then. As my first order as your Master, I order you to go free." Danken fixed the head Troll with a stare. "Now he is free. No longer a slave. Will you accept him back into the Clan?"

"I..." the Troll looked at the others. "I do not know what this situations demands. It has never happened before."

One of the other Trolls said something in the Vull'Kra tongue. Valshk looked at him questioningly.

"He says," Valshk began, "if he gives me his axe, can I accompany you on your journey as a representative of the Vull'Kra Nation's interest in the safety of the Magus?" Valshk looked straight ahead, proud even in defeat.

"Aye. And send word to your King that I owe him my gratitude."

"It will be as you say." The lead Troll tipped his head. Valshk took the axe from the younger Troll, thanking him in Vull'Kra. He touched his left fist to his forehead in salute to the lead Troll, who returned it.

"Do you have a horse?" Danken asked.

"Trolls do not ride horses. It is beneath us. Besides," he added with surprising humor, "no horse can carry a Troll for more than a day. I would have to carry *it* the rest of the journey. I will make due on these," he patted the tree trunks he called legs.

"Very well," Danken agreed. Tae came forward to face the Troll. Valshk looked him in the eye. Better to get any unpleasantness out of the way before the journey. Tae surprised them all by offering his hand which the Troll clasped. Introductions were made.

"I have the feeling that I would have lost no matter who you sent forward, including the Nymphs I saw flanking the *zandbirjadn,*" Valshk grinned. The Nymphs, however, were in a tantrum, cursing under their breath. Danken laughed as they set out on their way.

It wasn't long before Danken realized why Trolls didn't need horses. Valshk was leading their horses at quite a clip through the hidden shortcuts in the Vull'Kra Forest. He seemed to walk faster the longer they traveled.

In the early morning light, Danken saw through his freezing breath a crumbling stone wall in the distance. He pushed past a bush and felt the icy dew spray his face. His attention was transfixed on the growing number of walls. He noticed then that most of the ancient trees surrounding the walls were twisted and gnarled.

"Tol'Rok." Valshk said.

"What is it?" Danken asked.

"Goblin city abandoned after we destroyed it during the Great War."

"It seems so unreal," Danken said as they rode over the crumbling walls and into the twisted ruins of the desolate city. Most of the stones from the walls had been pilfered and taken to other cities and the trees twisted into crude houses were either dead or dying.

New trees and plants grew abundantly, as if the forest was waging its own war against the Goblin ruins. An ethereal mist hung just above the ground like a blanket and the group had to step carefully. An eerie silence pervaded, as if even the birds had abandoned this forsaken ground. Jet grumbled something about a nice big fire doing the trick, earning him a baleful look from Valshk as well as Tae. Dot tried her best to imitate them but was reduced to giggles when Jet began tickling her.

As the day progressed, the sun warmed the land, and they left the Goblin ruins behind. The group breathed a collective sigh of relief as the sounds of the forest once again filled their ears. "Bloody Goblins sure to know how to ruin a perfectly good hunting ground," Jet complained. "What I wouldn't give for a nice slab of venison right about now. Aye, black on the outside, red inside..." Tae looked ready to vomit.

"Is it the only one?" Danken asked, ignoring him.

"No," Tae answered. "There is one near Myr and another east of Wescove. The Driss had two on Lok Brae as well as one near B'rak. You forget, the world did not used to have the unified nations. The Goblin port of M'Kom was a Duah city and the Drissian city of Ssithk was once Vull'Kra. Volhak and Kasan were Mai'Lang cities as are the ruins near Breakwater. Bokat and Kang were Sendar cities. The world has changed, Danken." They continued to walk in retrospective quiet through the Vull'Kra Forest.

So it was a days later, they had reached the river Tor on the border of the Dwarven Kingdom. Across the great river, they could see the majestic peak of Kildarine's Spire, the highest mountain in the greatest mountain range in Midgarthe, the Axorines. The Dwarves who called these mountains their home were regarded as the finest craftsmen in the world. Their steel mills had produced the weapons that had won the Great War.

From here they would travel to Silverstaff at the base of Kildarine's Spire and from there through the passes to Mist Peak. Arn needed to speak to Aurvang Ripplewake, the master smith about the forging of several new long pikes for Mistgarde. Also, he wanted to let Danken enhance his reputation further by wounding the fierce Dwarven pride of a few unlucky challengers. The thing about the Northern continent was that honor was tantamount to all the races. There would never be a shortage of proud warriors to do battle with.

And all would go to building Danken's reputation as the best swordsman in the realm as well as the most kindhearted. Thus, he would be
a great leader, if only he could live that long.

As night fell, Arn (along with an intent, gleeful Dot and a scolding
T'riel) began to prepare dinner while Valshk and a grumbling Jet
went off in search of dead wood for the fire. Danken noticed Tae
squatting over something further into the forest and, detecting an air
of confusion, or perhaps the dawn of realization in his friend's manner, he went over to investigate. Though the Ranger almost certainly
detected his presence, the Elf didn't give any indication that he had.
He simply stared at the polished silver arrowhead he was caressing
as if it would disappear if he took his eyes off of it for even one moment. For a few long grains of sand, Danken stood silently off to the
side, figuring Tae would speak when he was ready. This theory was in
danger of being disproven, when the Elf abruptly began.

"Eight years ago I had just been promoted from *Seath'ren*—
Trapminder—to *Verna'ren*. My father was a sailor, and his father
and his father before him. I never would have guessed that after one-
hundred-fifty years of fighting on the briny that I'd don the green
cloak of a Ranger, but I did, and I was bloody proud of it, too." He
smiled at the memory. "I was on my patrol one day when I came
across the most beautiful woman I've ever seen in my life, to this very
day. She had long, curly red hair like the hottest of flames and the
brightest green eyes of any Elf you ever flarin' saw. She was a three-
quarter Elf but by Blessed Frey, I couldn't have cared less if she
were a bloody Troll.

"There she was, wading in one of the sacred, hidden healing
springs, and with so many arrow holes and sword cuts in her, and the
water so green with her blood and magic it was impossible to even
comprehend how she could still be alive, and yet, she was. The thing
I remember most is how she acted as if it were an everyday occurrence, like that sort of thing just bloody well happened sometimes,"
he scoffed at the notion. "I would have been screaming like a hungry
babe on a cold night, and I don't mind saying I wouldn't have been a
flarin' bit embarrassed about it, either. And when she looked at me
for the first time," Tae whistled as he shook his head. "It was all I

could do not to trip and taste the bloody soil, mate. Imagine that, will you? Me, a veteran of a thousand ports and more women than was my rightful share, rendered half-dumb like a flarin' Goblin drunk on his own bloody ale by a mere slip of a girl! She was barely *your* age!

"And by the Gods she was tough, mate. Hard as my myrkanium blade and twice as sharp. So finally, I get my voice back and tell her that I'm going to call for an *Atha'ren* to come and heal her, and do you know what she bloody tells me? She says, as calm as can be, 'If I needed a Healer, I'd have called one myself, now get in here and hold this shut while I stitch it up, if you please.' If you bloody please, lad! As if she's asking for a cup of tea!" Tae snorted. "So I stayed with her in the healing spring for two straight days, and then spent another two weeks on the bank while she was nigh-on catatonic, taking care of her like a bloody nursemaid. And do you know what thanks I get when she's finally well enough to stand? She tells me that my flarin' cooking nearly killed her as surely as the flarin' arrows! My cooking is bloody great! All my mates aboard ship thought so. I could cook a rock and make it worth your gold, so I bloody well could.

"So anyways, the next day, I go out in search of more herbs to redress her wounds with, and when I return, she's bloody gone. After all of that, she didn't even say goodbye. I tracked her, of course, or at least I tried to, but that girl twisted her trail into knots so flarin' complex I ended up tracking my flarin' self. So I finally gave up and went back out on patrol. My Commander was ready to chew a hole in my arse for disappearing like I had anyway, but for some reason I couldn't think about anything but her. I didn't even know her name or where she was from, and then I started seeing her *everywhere.* In other Elves' faces, behind a tree or just over the next hill. And then one day, she *was* there. Not an illusion, not a memory. It was her.

"At first I didn't even recognize her. She wasn't much but tattered rags and a network of scars the last time I'd seen her so I was in for a bloody shock. If I had thought she was beautiful before, this time I *was* left speechless, mate. Everything she wore was blood red leather and silver lace that showed off every curve of her perfect body and her glitter and lips were a shiny silver I've never seen before. She carried a bow trimmed in pure silver with silver fletched and bladed arrows and two swords like mine but glowing blue like your eyes. All the scars were gone and the way she moved, so confident and elegant and downright dangerous, I knew that she wasn't feeling even the slightest bit worse for the wear. I've never seen even the sacred healing springs heal someone like that." Tae paused, twirling the arrowhead slowly in contemplation.

"It's funny, but I realized then that she never had to tell me her name, or where she came from, or even what she did. Because in that moment, I knew, and it both exhilarated and disgusted me. You see, anyone around the Duah Nation or the northern parts of Sendar where you were born knew her, by reputation if nothing else."

"Coldblade the Assassin," Danken whispered and Tae nodded.

"Ariel Starvayne. The woman of my dreams was Ariel Starvayne. She'd been the most feared woman on half the Northern continent ever since she was not much more than a babe, when Zorrid, the Dragon Leader of the Fearless first found her. She'd probably killed more people in her eighteen years then I had in my first half a century or more. And there I was, face to face with a woman none but the Fearless came face to face with and lived to tell.

"At first, I figured she had come back to tie up her loose ends—namely yours truly, don't you know. So, I drew steel and so did she, smiling all the bloody while, she was. Now, I fancy myself pretty good with a blade, mate. There hasn't been a soul I'd come across in all my days I couldn't beat hands down in a fair fight, and I didn't plan on starting with a mere girl, regardless of who she was. But then things don't always go as we plan, do they? Aye, I gave her a fight, likely the best of any she'd ever had, but in the end, she beat me." Tae grew quiet for a moment, shaking his head ruefully. "Now, as you can plainly see, mate, I'm still alive and unharmed, save for my bruised little ego.

"See, she just wanted to show me that she could, is all. Oh, aye, when I felt that blade against my neck, I thought for sure it was over and I recited my Death Poem as quick as I could. And those bloody magical swords she carries left me shivering like a Dwarf over water for a bloody turn of the glass or more."

"Is that why they call her Coldblade?" Danken asked.

"Oh, I'm sure it has a might to with it, don't you doubt it, but I say it's because she likes to toy with her victims, like a cat with a mouse."

"How do you mean?"

"She cuts them so many times in so many places that they start shivering from loss of blood and shock before she finishes them. That or because it just sounds scary as Hela's Cold Embrace," Tae added with a short laugh. "So anyway, she laughed at me for far too flarin' long and then she just sat down next to where I was kneeling and pulled out two homemade *cla'thes*—special Duah cakes—and hands me one with a little girl's grin. By the Gods, mate, it was the best thing I'd ever tasted in all my days. Mostly because it was bloody delicious, but also a little bit because I was still alive to eat it. She told me then that *that* was what real Elven cooking tastes like." He smiled at the memory.

"Turns out she had had a little run-in with Zorrid and the Fearless. Apparently she had taken a liking to a young orphaned Sendar girl she had met on one of her exploits and decided to train her as an apprentice. But when Zorrid saw the girl, he recognized her as the one some very powerful people were after and had put a significant bounty on, so he threw her in the dungeon until the exchange could be made. Ariel wasn't having any of it though, and started a war with the whole bloody syndicate over it. She helped the girl escape but it seems she had a few too many shadows within to go with the child and so she stayed to fight, thinking it would be her last day of life.

"Ariel said she couldn't remember what happened next, except for bright red fire and then a terrible explosion. That was when I found her and when she left, she had gone in search of Zorrid to kill him but he was either dead or gone. I knew she hadn't turned over a new leaf, but I didn't care. I just wanted to be near her and I guess she felt the same. For the next six months we were practically inseparable. I asked her to perform the Treejoining with me—"

"Treejoining?" Danken cut in.

"Aye. You Sendar would call it marriage, but when Elves do it, it is physically binding," Tae explained, then continued. "She said aye, and it was the happiest day of my life, mate. But the day before it was to take place, she disappeared again, and this time she never came back."

"I'm sorry, Tae," Danken put his hand on the Elf's shoulder. Tae shrugged before turning to stare at Dot.

"I didn't hear of her for a little over a year and a half—exactly the time it takes for a Treebirth—and then I heard of a merchant being killed by her in Wendall. That was six years ago."

"You believe she gave birth?"

"Aye. She had such beautiful curly hair, Danken. And a little green mole just above her lips," Tae said with a sigh, and Danken slowly turned to stare at Dot as she played with Shard.

"You don't think—"

"No, mate, I don't think. I *know,*" Tae said seriously.

"But why would—"

"Ariel was too young, by Elven standards, at least. And she is a wandering spirit. I think she may have been too proud to ask for my help, but too humble to believe she could raise the child on her own, so she gave her to the Treemother to protect. I don't know how Dot ended up on the streets of Wendall, though. Elven orphans are always well taken care of by the forest."

"The Norns have woven your paths back together," Danken said simply. "Yours is not to question why, but to be grateful."

"You sound like a Gothi, mate," Tae smiled, referring to the keepers and teachers of the Holy Edda.

"Will you tell her?"

"About me? Aye, when she's ready. But not of her mother. No child deserves to bear the weight of being unwanted, for any reason."

"I understand." Danken thought of his own father. And just then something Tae had said earlier clicked in his head. "Tae, do you remember anything else about the girl that Coldblade trained?" His heart began beating so rapidly he feared it would burst.

"The girl? Let's see, come to think of it, aye. Ariel said she had purple eyes that glowed like an Orcans, and—" he looked sharply at Danken. "—white streaks in her hair."

"What was her name, please," Danken begged, barely above a whisper as his throat closed with hope and fear, realization nearly drowning him.

"Gods, mate, it's been awhile, hold on a moment and let me think." Tae tried to calm his friend's urgency, but only made it worse. It was all Danken could do to keep from shaking him violently. "It was such an odd name." Tae looked at the arrowhead again, then brightened. "Wytchyn. It was Wytchyn, I'm sure of it."

Danken's knees gave out and tears burst forth from his eyes. Tae knelt over him and patted his back reassuringly, realizing who the girl must have been.

"Don't be sad, mate. She escaped. The Mai'Lang didn't find her, just like they didn't find you. She's probably thinking about you right this very moment."

It took many moments for Danken to regain his composure and nod in agreement. Tae flashed him a trademark grin, his numerous piercings jingling faintly, reflecting his bright green eyes and the moonlight to give him a slightly scary but strangely reassuring look.

"A pair of sad souls we are, eh? Me finding out I have a daughter by a bloody Assassin and too scared to tell her, and you finding out your lost sister was the reason we even met in the first place." He clapped Danken on the back. "Look at it this way, mate. If Wytchyn hadn't come into Ariel's life, Dot wouldn't be here."

"Aye," Danken smiled. "You're right."

"Take you own advice, Danken. The Norns weave our fates. It is for us to make of them what we will and be glad of the opportunity to do so. All the worrying in the world won't a whit change the path Odin has chosen for you, so eat, drink and enjoy it while it lasts," Tae told him with another pat on the back before they returned to camp to eat. He ruffled Dot's hair fondly as she hugged him and knew that things would work themselves out in the end.

CHAPTER 18
A KILLER, A SAVIOR

he Axoriens were normally fair weathered but with the Winter season fast approaching, they were beginning to get chilly. All had donned their wool cloaks and knit caps. About four days into the mountains, Arn brought them to a halt.

"We must be extremely careful here. T'riel, you and K'airn scout ahead, look for any footprints and report back to me any movements in the area surrounding the path." The Nymphs acknowledged and shot off down the path.

"What is it?" Danken asked.

"Just taking precautions. This is a dangerous stretch of mountain," Arn answered, but Danken sensed he was holding something back. The Nymphs were gone for quite awhile and Danken began to worry. Then, just before dusk, he felt the familiar tickle of two tiny feet on his shoulder.

"What took you so long?" She nodded to Arn who had received the report from K'airn.

"Myicine," Arn said, "Snow Goblins. K'airn says they found over sixty tracks ahead. That means a tribe."

"What are they?" Danken asked.

"Imagine a smaller version of a Goblin. Now imagine it twice as dumb, and territorial to a suicidal fault. The Dwarves have been trying to get rid of them for years but every time they think they've killed them all, another, larger group appears."

"*Dwei.*" Jet's eyes gleamed excitedly, as he gripped his hatchets. "Snow Rats."

"That's not the worst part," Arn said. "T'riel says she saw some huge tracks leading up to the peak of that mountain," Arn pointed. At the top was a huge cave.

"So what does that mean? Giants?" Danken asked.

"I wish," Arn shook his head. "No, that can only be one thing: Isahagilaz, the Diamond Dragon. From what T'riel described, I think he has a mate."

"These mountains will be scoured of life before the Draglet leaves," Tae said.

"Aye, and if we wish to avoid that fate, we'd best get a move on it," Arn said. "T'riel, you and K'airn get some food and scout ahead. The Myicine will undoubtedly have an ambush set up for us. The rest of you, we'll have to hurry to find shelter before dark. This is one night I do not wish to be caught in the open." Arn began preparing to ride on.

By dark they had found a large, unoccupied cave just off the path. Just recently unoccupied, Danken thought. There were the scant remains of a large bear carcass towards the back. T'riel and K'airn had come back with news of the Myicine ambush not far ahead. Arn elected to bed down for the night, keeping someone on watch at all times. The fire burned bright into the night, keeping them warm, but Danken couldn't sleep. He quietly dressed and looked at Shard. Danken tapped him on the head lightly. The sabercat rose silently and followed him out of the cave. Valshk, who was on watch, saw them but said nothing. Danken nodded his thanks. After a few feet, he had to strain to see the Troll, whose innate *Shimmer* spell allowed him to blend into his surroundings, making him all but invisible.

For some unknown reason, Danken was being drawn toward the cave he knew Isahagilaz to inhabit. What did the Dragon want with him? Or was there something else up there? Suddenly, Danken remembered the Myicine. He was nearly to the spot where T'riel had found the ambush. Thinking quickly, Danken sent Shard around to a rocky outcrop above the main concentration of the ambush. He closed his eyes and could see every attacker along the path. While the Myicine may have thought their ambush crafty, Danken knew otherwise. He stood at a bottleneck in the path. Giant boulders lined the path for several feet in either direction. Here, however, there was only room for two men to stand abreast.

Danken pawed the dirt with his boot. Soft, yet nothing he would slip on. He drew *Mak'Rist* and merged with it as he had so often of late. He saw Shard perched nonchalantly above a group of unsuspecting Myicine. They were playing an unfamiliar, violent game of some sort, expecting his party to come along after first light.

Danken drew his power to a center within him, concentrating on each and every attacker. He then sent forth a tendril of blue to act as a beacon to him. Dozens of tiny currents lanced into each hidden Myicine, effectively illuminating them.

This had the desired effect of startling the unwary creatures into abandoning their hiding places. They poured out pell mell into the path only to inadvertently press the unlucky front runners into Danken's fell blade. Their crudely-fashioned stone weapons were no match for the unbreakable asterite of *Mak'Rist* and they fell before him like wheat before a scythe.

"Reap ye the benefits of your wickedness!" came the unbidden voice from his mouth, spewing blinding blue fire in all directions. Fyrdn was speaking through him again as if alive. He was untouchable, a whirlwind of death. He cut through defenses as if they were made of parchment. None got even remotely close enough to strike him.

Finally, Shard decided it was time to enter the fray. He leapt off of his perch, crushing four of the albino creatures as he landed.

"Dash'to'lai! Dash'to'lai!" the Myicine shouted hysterically, apparently, their word for sabercat. But the appearance of this hated foe seemed to drive them to even more of a suicidal frenzy.

They rushed Danken by the dozen, climbing over their own dead to reach him. He cut them down as well. Danken felt nothing, heard nothing as he waded among the ranks of swarming white bodies. He was one with the primal need for battle in his soul. It was as Arn had said, *"A Mage is born to fight."* Danken realized that it was so during battle and he felt as if he were at peace, as odd as it seemed.

Shard seemed to be genuinely enjoying himself. He pounced like a playful kitten, batting heedless Myicine into rocks hard enough to crush every bone in their bodies. His saber teeth tore limbs from bodies with careless ease.

All was lost in a blue haze as they methodically went about the grim business. Within half a glass, Danken and Shard stood atop over five dozen dead Myicine, breathing heavily. Danken opened his eyes and looked at Shard, who was licking a small scrape on his paw.

"Well, I guess that takes care of our bloody ambush problem, huh?" Not so long ago, one of these creatures would have posed a significant threat to him. Now sixty were of no consequence.

Danken looked away as Shard began feasting on the Myicine. He knew it was natural, and also helpful. They didn't have even a portion of the meat required to feed him anyway. But the Myicine had been sentient beings and Danken couldn't watch them be devoured. When the cat was finished, Danken turned to head back to camp. He was too tired to make the hike to the Diamond Dragon's lair this night.

Before he had taken two steps though, the Sigil on his arm began burning, warning him of danger. At the same time, Shard let out a low warning growl of his own. The sound of a rock being crushed drew Danken's attention to the shadows at the other side of the path.

All of the stories of giant, fire-breathing Dragons could not have prepared Danken for the sight of Isahagilaz and his mate.

Isahagilaz was pure, sparkling white with purple horns, wings and talons. Fiery, crystal-clear eyes with large black slits peered at him, nearly freezing him in place. His mate was a Silver Dragon with a body like a living mirror with quartz-like horns, wings and talons and reflective silver eyes. Each stood three times the height of a man at the shoulder with half that height again to the head. Fangs the length of Danken's leg protruded from a mouth that could swallow him whole. Two sets of razor sharp bony plates of identical color to their horns ran down the length of their backs to end in four spikes at the end of the tail. They were easily seventy feet long from tail to head if not more. Isahagilaz had what looked like a white moustache that hung down four feet from each side of his long snout as well as a thick strand from his spiked chin. His white eyebrows curved up wickedly from his ridged brow like lightning bolts.

As they strode onto the path, the ground shook so that Danken feared he would lose his balance. He had the feeling that should he take his mightiest swing at one of these beasts, it would leave barely a scratch. He felt fear for the first time since he had been cut down by the Gnome in the forest. Pure, primal fear.

Then he saw something that made his heart skip. A Draglet emerged from behind its parents. It was hardly the size of its parents' foot, yet still bigger than Danken. It was a Silver, like its mother. He noticed that the young Draglet had a steel trap around its foot and could tell the wound was infected. For some reason, though he was in mortal danger, he ached to help the beast.

The Dragons eyed the carnage left in the path. Isahagilaz looked down at him and in his eyes, Danken could see a great intelligence. What came next nearly floored him. The Dragon spoke. All the stories he'd ever heard had all Dragons as savage man eating beasts. He soon learned different.

"Is this the handiwork of thee and thine feline?" the Diamond Dragon spoke in perfectly accented Sendar, each baritone syllable eliciting a puff of smoke from its nostrils. Danken was unversed in Dragon lore and was not aware that all Dragons could speak not to mention that the Gem Dragons were actually good and fought the evil Painted Dragons. But to most Dragons of either set, the Mortal Races might as well not even have existed. They only cared about treasure, power and food. But even through their vanity, they could see that some mortals could benefit them or even harm them so they occasionally took interest. Danken was one such mortal. He sputtered an answer.

"Aye. They planned an ambush and they failed. I am sorry if they were friends of yours, but..." A great fiery laugh exploded from Isahagilaz's throat, sending white flames as high as a redwood into the sky.

"Friends? Hah! I merely inquired as to thine intentions pertaining to the disposal of yonder fiends. Doest thou intend to engorge upon thine slain enemies?"

"Engorge? Me? Oh. Oh no. No. The cat has had his fill. Pardon my inference. I meant no disrespect. You are free to do with them as you wish. Not that I could stop you if I wanted to," Danken added, under his breath.

"Ah, modest thou art, young Magus. Tell me, doth Sembalo still reside at Mist Peak?"

"As far as I know. Do you know him?" Danken asked, surprised.

"Had he not free'th me from the trap of a roguish band of Giants thirteen hundred years past, I surely would have been turned to a mantelpiece. Imagine," the Great Dragon pondered, "the famous Isahagilaz as a trophy!"

"I would not want to," Danken told him sincerely.

"Thou dost not bear the fear that one such as I often encounters. Dost thou not wish to run?" Isahagilaz asked, a toothy grin making Danken gulp loudly. Good or not, a predator was a predator.

"In truth, I did. But when I witnessed the trap on your young one's foot, I could not."

"Ah," Isahagilaz breathed, "compassion as well as bravery. The Norns have chosen well with thee, young Magus."

"Thank you," Danken replied, embarrassed. "May I look at the young one's foot?"

"Mislogagner," the female Dragon Sellatauris spoke for the first time, her voice like a winter wind. "The Draglet's name be Mislogagner."

"Thank you," Danken accepted the Dragon's unspoken permission. He approached the Draglet slowly, letting out tiny tendrils of blue to reassure it of his disposition. The baby snapped its jaws at him, letting out a scared whimper. His mother cuffed him about the head and said something in Dragon speech to it.

Danken moved to touch it and the Draglet did not shy away. He softly stroked its head spikes, gaining its confidence and bidding it to let him examine the trap. It was a fairly new Dwarven trap with sharp steel teeth meant to sever a Myicine's leg, though it merely bit deeply into Mislogagner's.

Danken touched the infected leg, prompting the young one to let out a hiss. Next, he placed *Mak'Rist* between an opening in the teeth of the trap. He put his foot at the base to steady it, then pushed with all his might. The trap gave a small whine before opening slowly.

When it was far enough, he bade the Draglet to pull its foot slowly out. This it did and when Danken was sure the foot was clear, he let the trap close with a snap.

For all their might, Dragons were too big to open such a small trap.

"You may want to cauterize that before it closes," Danken told them. Isahagilaz bent his gigantic head down and released an amazingly small stream of flame into the infected leg. Mislogagner hissed in pain but remained in place until the flame had cauterized the wound.

"How can we repay thee?"

"Nothing is needed."

"Ah, I have just the thing. Wilt thou wait here?"

"Of course, but…" Danken was cut off by the beating of massive wings. A windstorm arose beneath them and he struggled to keep his footing. When the tempest subsided, he looked up to see Isahagilaz flying towards the cave at the summit of the peak. It was a breathtaking sight to see something so large float majestically through the sky.

Within moments, the Diamond Dragon had returned carrying a metallic instrument of some sort in his huge clawed hand. At first glance it appeared to be a double-edged axe. However, on closer examination, it was revealed to be much more than that. Two curved blades ringed the axe head with scarcely a thumb's width separating them. The handle of the blade was actually a clasp that fit on the forearm with an actual handle underneath the blades. Danken looked at the glistening weapon with awe.

"This I gleaned from a brave but unskilled Dragon-Slayer eight hundred years ago. He used it as an axe but did not see its true use, as I'm confident thou wilt." He handed the weapon to Danken, who clasped it onto his left forearm. He scarcely felt it for all its impressive size and obvious craftsmanship. The gleam from the finely polished metal was substantial, especially for this time of night, as if every star in the sky ached to add its reflection to the blade.

"Does it have a name?" Danken asked.

"That is for thou to decide. Give Sembalo my greetings when thou seest him. I shall take my leave now, young Magus." Isahagilaz bowed his massive head. He nodded to his mate and the young Draglet. They collected all of the Myicine corpses before winging off into the night.

"I must still be dreaming," Danken said to Shard, who yawned in response. The two set off, back to the cave to catch up on what small amount of sleep they could before the sun once again beckoned them onward.

Jet was on guard duty when they returned. He had his hatchets cocked to throw before realizing it was Danken and Shard. He looked curiously at Danken's bloodstained clothes and face. Shard's normally pristine white face was stained red and heavily matted with blood as well.

"You have met with foe?" Jet asked quietly. "And you didn't tell me?" He was hurt. "Not *dwei,* Danken. Not *dwei* at all," he sighed. "Are they all dead?"

"Aye. I don't think watch duty will be necessary any longer."

"What of the Myicine and the Diamond Dragon?" Jet pressed.

"They are no longer a threat. Get some sleep. I will relate the tale to you in the morn."

"Aye," Jet acquiesced sullenly and went off to find his cot. Danken stripped off his soiled clothing. He heated a vat of water over the fire, then poured it over his head to wash the stink of battle away. He was donning a fresh set of clothes when he caught a gold sparkle out of the corner of his eye.

"Boy should have told One about leaving," she scolded. "Boy is *very* stupid for not doing so."

"I'm sorry, T'riel. You're right I should have. I didn't wish to involve you in this though. It was dangerous."

"Pfft," she scoffed.

"I know, I know, you laugh in the face of danger. I just didn't think about it. It was like I was being drawn to battle." He nodded to Shard who was meticulously cleaning his paws and face. "For some reason I knew he should be there."

"Next time," T'riel shook her finger at him. "Boy had better bring this Pixie along."

"Aye," Danken laughed. "Next time it is, then."

The next morning came far too soon for Danken and the questions of the night before came not long after. Danken patiently told them all that had happened. When he finished, he was greeted with looks of disbelief. As they saddled the horses, the conversation continued.

"The Dragon spoke Sendar?" Jet asked, highbrowed. "I always thought they had their own language."

"Aye, both he and his mate."

"Are you bloody daft?" Arn yelled. "Why in the Nine Worlds didn't you wake me?"

"I'm sorry, Arn. It didn't ask for you," Danken replied calmly.

"It?"

"The feeling I get that tells me what I need to do. This time it said I only needed Shard."

"We'd best be going," Tae said in the silence that followed.

When they'd reached the place Danken had battled the Myicine the night before, Jet turned to him disgustedly.

"Sixty?"

"Aye," Danken nodded.

"Ach. I'll wager the Dragon and his kin ate well last night."

"And for many nights to come," Tae put in.

"How far to Silverstaff?" Danken asked Arn.

"Not long. We'll be at the base of the Spire in three days," Arn told him.

The base of Kildarine's Spire was a gigantic valley filled with the massive stone city of Silverstaff. Impressively enough, the largest part of the city was underground. Built out of the rock, Silverstaff was as imposing as it was breathtaking, but black plumes of smoke rising from all quarters of the city told Danken something was seriously amiss.

"Blessed Gods," Arn said softly. The Sigil on Danken's arm began to burn. He drew *Mak'Rist* and the rest did likewise. Danken looked at Dot who was clutching onto the scruff of Shard's neck.

"Protect her, Shard," he told the cat, who narrowed his eyes. Danken's heart pounded in his chest. He caught movement from behind a large boulder. Suddenly, a score of hardened, scrunched faces appeared from all around them. Each carried a pick or axe as tall as his body, which would have come up to Danken's elbow, though they

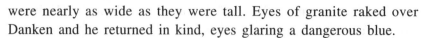

were nearly as wide as they were tall. Eyes of granite raked over Danken and he returned in kind, eyes glaring a dangerous blue.

"Put down ee weapons 'er boi moighty Motsognir ee'll be slain where ee stand."

"Not likely," Arn said, removing his cowl. The rest did likewise. A hush fell over the ambushers at the sight of the Captain of the Mistgarde.

"Arn Brynsen?" came a gravelly voice from a stout black-bearded creature who stepped out from behind his chosen rock. It was a Dwarf in full chain mail and a patterned kilt.

"Aye Jairn Nimbleaxe. It has been too long, old friend."

"Old eeself. Ee weren't no but a wee bairn when I met ee Da." He clapped Arn on the back. "How are ee?"

"Well, under the circumstances. What has happened here?" Arn asked. A great anger surfaced in the Dwarf's eyes.

"Etinkin. An no a few o'yon bastards either."

"Giants? How could they get here without being detected?" Arn exclaimed.

"We dinnae ken, but they did an caught us boi surprise. We did be nearly overtaken but fer one ee do ken well."

"Skafeth Ninescar."

"Aye, that's yon one. Single-handedly killt four of 'em. Gave us enough time ta counterattack. Gave 'is life for yon city. An I'll tell ee this, he'll no be goin' unavenged." Nimbleaxe added fiercely.

"How many Giants?" Arn asked, deeply saddened at the news of his lost friend.

"Five score, 'bout. But none lived, save one. We still got 'im."

"Oath! How many of you were lost?"

"Five hunnert, an a ton o'buildings, too."

"Can I talk to this prisoner?" Arn asked.

"Aye. But yon Etin ain't sayed a word to any o'us." By this time the rest of the Dwarves had come out and were eyeing the company. "Who's this ee got with ee, Brynsen?"

Arn made introductions.

"Tell me, Nimbleaxe, is Ripplewake still alive?" Arn asked afterwards.

"Aye. Yonder 'un fought loike a sabercat," he glanced at Shard who was looking at him curiously. "Compliment, o' course. Anyhow, he killt 'is share an' then went back ta gather yon council. I'll take ee to 'im."

As the company walked through the city, Danken was amazed at the number of Dwarves who were helping out with the cleanup.

"How long ago was the attack?" Danken asked.

"Yesterday," one of the Dwarves beside him answered. Danken's jaw nearly dropped. The city was almost back to normal. Any Sendar city would still be in shock. But then he remembered that these were Dwarves, the hardest workers in the realms. It was said that they could work for a week straight with no sleep. Instead of horror and defeat on the faces of the Dwarves, he saw grim determination.

They arrived shortly at a two-story grey stone building with freshly painted sides. The sign over the door proclaimed it to be a tavern but the lack of music told Danken otherwise. Nimbleaxe pushed open the door to reveal a dimly-lit room with twelve Dwarves seated in a semi-circle around a large oak table. All wore beards to their waists, all shot through with grey, denoting they were a council of elders. The youngest Dwarf was probably not younger than five hundred years old. What soft amount of noise they had been making came abruptly to a halt when the company entered.

"Honored Elders," Nimbleaxe began. "I bring ee Arn Brynsen an' 'is company."

"Ach, I ken who he be, Nimbleaxe," spoke a black-bearded Dwarf. "Me'an that 'un have battled together afore."

"Good to see you again, Borin Ripplewake, though I wish the circumstances were better," Arn said.

"Aye," the council chimed in.

"What do you know of the Giants' appearance?" Arn asked, cutting straight to the point. Ripplewake nodded. Dwarves were not much for ceremony or small talk.

"Well, most o'yon oi witnesses were killt afore they could tell, but one, a youngster by yon name Omarko Swifteye o' Clan Splitgem saw 'em." He turned to another Dwarf. "Fellar, would ee get 'im fer me?"

"Aye." Fellar Stonesight of Clan Stonesight nodded and stepped out of the room. A few ticks later he appeared with a wiry Dwarf with a pale complexion and silver, pupil-less eyes. He wore a long sleeved chain mail shirt with his spiky, shiny bluish-silver hair gleaming just as brightly. He had on the blue, silver and yellow kilt of his Clan with soft, knee-high blue leather boots.

"This be yon youth." Ripplewake nudged the Dwarf over toward Arn. "He dinnae be speakin' very often. Only a few o'us 'as e'er e'en heard 'im. But he tol' Stonesight here he saw 'em. He won't say anythin' else though. He be an odd one t'be sure. Got talents I ne'er seen in a Dwarf."

"Is he blind?" Arn whispered into Ripplewake's ear. In response, Ripplewake drew his mace and swung it at Swifteye's head.

Before any could stop him, a blur of silver motion stripped the mace from Ripplewake's hand and stood behind him, grinning from ear to ear. It was Swifteye.

"This one sees in a different way. He feels vibrations through yon ground. Senses movements in yon very air, he does. We call 'im Swifteye 'cause no one can see him move. Ee can bet yon flarin' Giants din't either. He killt eight o' 'em."

"Amazing," Arn whispered. "Tell me, would it be all right if we took him to Mist Peak to have Sembalo talk with him?"

"Well, seein' as he's an orphan, I guess it'd be up to 'im." He turned to Swifteye. "Well, what'doee say, boy?" Swifteye paused to stare with his cloudy silver eyes at Danken for a moment, then disappeared. Before anyone could ask where he went, he was back with a fully packed satchel.

"Bloody circus," Jet grumbled.

"I guess that means he's coming!"

"Nimbleaxe wi' yon Captain o' Mistgarde an' a pair a Sendar ta see yon prisoner!" The Dwarf shouted to the guard, who nodded before opening the thick iron gate for them.

"Las' cell on ee roight." The guard told them.

"Aye." Nimbleaxe replied, walking past him.

"Oh, an' Nimbleaxe?" the guard called after him.

"Eh?"

"That'ns in one helluva a foul mood. Tha's yon thing 'bout Etins. Big as all Hel wi'a wee tolerance fer pain." He laughed cruelly as he walked to the Giant's cell, keys jingling.

"Pain?" Danken asked.

"Aye," Nimbleaxe replied, keeping his eyes forward. "An a lot of it if Ripplewake's already been here."

"Dwei." Jet cracked his knuckles in anticipation.

The cell was a large one with huge cement blocks on three walls and an iron door close to a foot thick. The guard opened the door slowly, his axe drawn just in case. The cell was dark and musty with an overpowering smell of fecal matter. Danken's eyes glowed, picking out the Giant in the far corner, huddled and whimpering. If he didn't know better, Danken would have felt sorry for the monstrosity cowering before him.

"Don't let 'im fool ee. He ain't scared o'ee," the guard warned.

"Thank you. We'll take it from here." Arn told him.

"Are ee sure?"

"Aye."

"Alroi' then," the guard said, closing the door behind them. Danken felt the Sigil tingling and drew *Mak'Rist* just as the Giant lunged at them. It was surprisingly quick for something so big, nearly twice as tall and five times the weight of himself, so he took no chances. The Giant swung a huge fist at Arn's head, manacles as thick as Danken's leg carried effortlessly. Danken was quicker though and severed the Giant's massively muscled arm above the elbow. Jet's hatchets hacked four lightning gashes into its torso just as smoothly.

The Etin howled out in pain and lashed out with its remaining arm. Danken and Jet easily dodged while Arn recovered quickly and hamstrung the fiend. The Giant writhed in pain on the floor, cursing them in its own crude language.

"I must be getting slower. You saved me a huge headache, young Sariksen. I owe you," Arn said breathlessly. "You as well, Jet."

"No problem." Jet grinned wickedly at the howling beast.

"Aye," was all Danken could manage, breathing more heavily with relief then fatigue. He looked to the copious amounts of blood pouring from the Giant and cauterized them none-to-gently with his blue fire. This elicited another howl of pain until Danken filled its mouth with crackling energy, singeing its vocal chords.

"From what city do you hail?" Arn asked the now silent Giant. Danken began to squeeze its airway, suffocating it, while releasing its vocal chords.

"I tok! I tok!" The Giant spat out in terrible Sendar.

"Then do so," Danken threatened.

"I fum Din."

"What is your name?" Arn asked.

"Doog."

"How did you get here?"

"Red suckle. Wok trough. Den dere, now here. Start killin' puny Dwarves," it spat.

"Who made the red circle?" Arn asked carefully. At this, however, the Giant began thrashing and kicking. A white foam bubbled from its lips. Doog gave one final thrash before dying. Danken was shocked. Even Jet looked slightly repulsed.

"What happened?" Danken asked.

"A bloody rabid dog, he was," Jet commented darkly.

"*Silence* spell." Arn answered, sheathing his sword. "Sorcerers use them to keep their agents from revealing secrets, though I doubt that any of the new ones could have worked it yet."

"So, that leaves..." Danken started.

"Dak'Verkat. There will be another war soon." Arn finished ominously.

PART II

EMERALD RANSOM

PART II:
EMERALD RANSOM

he perception of amassed power is often the basis for an ultimatum, yet the pivotal act of decreeing it will surely be the catalyst that allows power to dissolve. Such actions are the calling card of a Despot who by any other name is a coward.

The owner of a dull mind will never advance because he lacks the capacity to deceive, for deceit denotes intelligence, necessary for survival or at the very least, prosperity. But to have the capacity and yet refrain from using it denotes something else entirely: Honor.

One with such a rare quality as this has confronted his greatest enemy, himself and accepted his flaws but not his inability to correct them. His goals, no matter how lofty and impossible they may seem are worth whatever price that accompanies them. For courage is not the absence of fear, but the ability to harness it and forge it into a fell weapon at one's disposal.

Such is the mark of a true leader of men, but one not readily apparent to the naked eye. Nor is it visible to a Despot, where sight is clouded by jealousy and denial. A leader is felt more than he is seen or heard. If the eyes are windows to the soul, in a true leader's, one would see not only his future, but theirs as well.

–Archives Magus Gellar
This sacred year, 87
Age of Mystery

CHAPTER 19
AN INDENTURED SWORD

he white rapids of the fork that split the River Tor stretched almost as far as the eye could see, the opposite bank a faint blue smudge on the horizon. Kierna had made good time to get here but dared not cross the mighty river on any but the sturdiest of barges. The journey through the Vull'Kra Forest had been uneventful, as most of its imposing residents had left her to her own. In her present state of mind that was just as well for them as for her. Her swords had elicited sideways looks but thankfully no Challenges.

The large town of Tor Forks was one of the few places in all of Midgarthe that more than one race called home without the accompanying threat of war. Stout green-skinned Trolls worked pulley lines side by side with Sendar as half a dozen barges made their way back and forth across the rushing current. Ruing her hasty departure from the Elven inn and her subsequent forgetfulness concerning all of her coins, she ignored her growling stomach. She'd had to live off what she could bring down with her bow along with scant fruits and nuts so she hardly had any money for a crossing.

Her grey riding leathers and green wool cloak were brown from travel's dust and her blond hair wasn't nearly as shiny as she would have liked after several nights sleeping on hard ground. Thus, the first ship's captain she approached eyed her as if she were a street urchin. He was a large man with a thick red beard and a stained white shirt opened at the chest and the look on his bulbous face was not one she generally ascribed to generosity.

"Excuse me, Captain," she started sweetly, but he stopped her with a grubby hand.

"'S two silvers, unshaved."

"That's bloody extortion!" Kierna snapped.

"Swim across if y'like," he laughed. "'Course, has been a long time since I've been with a wench…"

"Look in the mirror and you're likely to spot the reason for that, Etinspawn," she spat angrily as she stalked off, leaving the man grinning nastily in her wake.

Two other ships yielded similar results, so Kierna decided to try a different approach. Her temper was hot enough now that negotiations and a sweet voice would do her little good in any case. She headed for a large, boxy barge with smooth, polished wooden sides and a white rail. The barge was crewed entirely by Trolls and she soon pegged the Captain by the subtle nuances of Vull'Kra etiquette. He was huge, like all Trolls, with a grey-tinged green braid hanging to his belt. Oil-slicked brown leather split-side skirts ended at the ankle held up by a wide black, gold and blue sash that denoted his Clan flowing diagonally over a bare, rippled chest. With his massive arms planted on his hips and his bare feet planted easily on the swinging deck, he was an imposing figure.

Kierna scaled the barge's ladder before the big, but slow bosun could intercept her and dodged her way to the Captain, who barely raised a grey eyebrow in response. He towered over her but she fixed him with her hardest stare, giving him no advantage, besides the many he already obviously enjoyed over her.

"Who are your two best fighters aboard?" she demanded, voice like cold steel. He cocked his head at her before beckoning two younger Trolls nearly as big as himself, and dressed likewise.

"Aside from me," he rumbled, "these two are my finest fighters. Why does a pretty Sendar girl such as yourself want to know? There are none in the market for a wife so far as I know," he grinned broadly.

"I wish to propose a deal."

"My crew is not for sale, girl."

"You mistake my intentions, Captain," Kierna said smoothly. "I wish to Challenge these two in accordance with *M'Racht* in exchange for passage across the river."

The Captain smiled slightly, rubbing the bone spikes protruding from his elbows behind his back, considering. He glanced at her twin blades and then at the bow strapped to the saddle of her horse on shore, assessing her danger. Before he could respond she added another provision, a very dangerous one, but one that would certainly

ensure her passage should she live. That and many stories that would
be told of her, greatly exaggerated over ale that night.

"Also, I will do so unarmed."

"Do you have a death wish, girl?" the Captain bellowed. "This
may not be *Jafa'aht,* but people still die occasionally in Challenge."

"The consequences of my actions are not important so long as I
reach my destination. If I lose, should I not die, I will be your indentured servant until you release my bond."

"Your destination sounds like a place I know well, and you fit the
description of one who seeks her fate there. Very well, you have a
deal." The Captain took a step back, saluting her formally to display
his intention to hold to the agreement. The Troll introduced himself
as Terashtei, Third of Clan Sorjei. The other two Trolls introduced
themselves as Belek, Eighth of Clan Sorjei, with a long green braid
and two even scars across his bare chest; and Welgran, Twelfth of
Clan Sorjei, with a black braid and narrow, cunning eyes. Each carried a long double bladed battleaxe, hefted easily in their big, clawed
hands.

"My honor is my axe," Belek intoned solemnly.

"I will try to spare your face, Kierna Bjorndotir," Welgran told
her as he began circling. "It would be a shame to mar your beauty,
even for a Sendar."

Kierna ignored his sly remarks, meant to draw her into an un-
planned attack. She stood on her toes but motionless as the two Trolls
warily circled. Without warning, Belek swung at waist level but though
quick, his axe caught only air as she leapt high, her knees at her
chin. She managed two quick, solid kicks to his exposed jaw before
landing in a roll, dodging by a hair a diagonal chop from Welgran. As
she came up, she kicked him in the side of the knee and danced behind him to avoid Belek's back swing.

She grabbed Welgran's braid, using it to swing herself around to
land a two-footed blow to Belek's midsection while forcing Welgran
to whip himself around to avoid breaking his neck. Kierna smashed a
knee into Belek's lowered face, using the reverse momentum to kick
Welgran in the groin, sending him stumbling. She twisted Belek's wrist
so severely he dropped his axe. Instead of reversing the twist to flip

him, she used it to propel him over the barge's rail. He landed with a groaning splash.

She dove to the side as Welgran's axe took a chunk from the rail where she had been standing. As he tried to dislodge his blade, she planted six well placed shots to his neck followed by a knee to his abdomen as the axe came free. He swung wildly, having trouble breathing and she easily dodged, stepping inside to jam her elbow under his square jaw. She used his momentary stunning to her full advantage, once again slipping behind him. When he whirled with a vicious, seemingly careless swipe of the axe, she somehow came in behind it, landing three successive kicks to the side of his head. She had thought they would drop him, but he had accepted the kicks in order to get his axe in position. Kierna felt its blade against her neck and Welgran's clawed hand clamped on her shoulder.

She couldn't believe she had lost.

The Trolls cheered loudly for her skills but were obviously peeved at their Clansmen for not making a better show. It should not have taken two Trolls to defeat her. She was only a Sendar, and a woman at that. Terashtei shook his head before ordering Kierna's horse aboard and Belek rescued from his precarious perch on the dock ladder. The lines were untied and the Trolls put their considerable strength into pulling the thick pulley mounted lines to drag the barge across the unstoppable flow of the river. Kierna stood sullenly be the port rail. She was indentured to the Vull'Kra until they released her, and even then should Terashtei recall her. She could feel the pull of the Swords like a giant hand with her in its grip. What would she do now?

A turn of the glass later, they reached the opposite shore, with each Troll glancing sideways at Kierna as if expecting her to jump. All Vull'Kra knew Sendar were not to be trusted to adhere to *M'Racht*. They had no honor. Terashtei watched her calmly as she eyed them all defiantly, wondering what to do with her, for she would be no good to him except as a servant, and Trolls did not keep servants, believing it made one soft. He faced her with the stern expression of a conflicted man, his hard, square features making the image even more stark. The dark amber glowing eyes seemed to go from anxious to disapproving and back again.

"I have decided what your indenture is to be, Kierna Bjorndotir," he growled, turning to the young, slim Vull'Kra girl beside him. She was taller than Kierna but not nearly as big as the other Troll women aboard. Her eyes seemed a lighter amber than the others and her features had a softness and beauty not found in Trolls. Her ears were pointed and her long braid was green flecked blond, like spun gold. Two sword hilts stuck up from behind her shoulders.

"By The Hand, I am yours to command, Terashtei." Kierna bowed imperceptibly, trying to hide her anger and her shame.

"You will allow my niece to accompany you. You will be her teacher and guide. Until she wears white, you are indentured."

"Where I go—" Kierna began.

"You go where I *allow* you to go, Sendar," he rumbled. "She is a quarter-Duah and thus not allowed in the cities nor in the honored places among the Clan. Yet, this ship is not the life for her nor is there anything left I can teach her. Look," he lifted one sword half-way out of the scabbard at the girl's back, then let it drop back with a snort. "It is just not right," he muttered under his breath, something about a good battleaxe snapping shoddily forged, worthless swords in two.

"Still," he continued, "where you go, you and others like you can teach her and give her what she needs. I cannot pretend to approve but it is out of my hands now. These are the terms of your indenture. By *M'Racht* I declare it to be so."

"Aye," Kierna nodded. "But I make no promises once my destination is reached. I cannot force the Spirit Blades to accept her. She must prove that she is worthy on her own, as I must. By The Hand I will see her safely there, my word."

"Agreed. Clan Sorjei honors your debt, Kierna Bjorndotir." He said something to the girl in Vull'Kra. She scurried off and soon appeared with a travel bag. She said her goodbyes to her Clan, then saluted Kierna. She wore a forest green, very short toga that hardly covered her curving hips and leaving her broad shoulders bare but for the Clan sash with knee-high brown boots laced with leather straps all the way up her legs.

"I am Corsha," the girl said in well-spoken Sendar. The two women clasped wrists and stepped off the barge. At a horse stable just beyond the dock, Corsha purchased a large white and brown draft horse and saddled it as expertly as any Sendar. As they left the river bank, Kierna eyed her out of the corner of her eye.

"I had always though that Trolls did not ride horses."

"Most Trolls do not simply because they say horses are too small to carry their weight and are useless in our thick forests. We may not lie but we surely exaggerate and sidestep, do not doubt. The real reason is that they are afraid to have their feet off the ground," Corsha answered factually, but humorously with a broad wink at the Sendar woman.

"You do not feel the same?"

"I am part Elven. Heights are as comfortable to me as the ground, and horseback is hardly high," she laughed.

"No, I don't suppose it is," Kierna smiled.

Four days later, Kierna and Corsha reached the mountains that separated the River Tor from the River Mist. The sky was overcast and a slight drizzle that had persisted for the last two days made their skin clammy and cold. A large village could be seen through the fog at the base of the mountain and they headed for it. They talked longingly of taking a long hot bath and eating a real meal for the first time since they had set out. The two women had grown quite fond of each other during their brief travels. Kierna found herself smiling more lately than she had since she had been a little girl.

The smell of burning wood reached their nostrils and they soon discovered the source. The smoking black remains of a farmhouse sizzled as the light rain touched them. They ran over and searched the surrounding area but found no traces of anyone, dead or alive. Corsha smelled the ashes and examined the ground while Kierna searched for prints but the rain had obscured them.

"Looks like something big was here not long ago. But the tracks are too big for anything I know," Kierna told her. "All I know is that it is very recent."

"I do not like the smell of this ash," Corsha growled. "It is fouled somehow."

They kept on towards the village, coming across several more abandoned, burned farms. As night fell, they came within sight of the village. The silence added to their unease. Only the faint creaking of a doused lantern swinging from its hook in the icy breeze gave any indication that they hadn't gone deaf. The numerous shops and inns were either burnt or leveled with the mist lending the scene the surreal quality of a dream. The town's small Temple had been burnt and Corsha said urinated on, enraging both women.

They dismounted their tired horses and tied them to a charred stake in a narrow alley between two blackened husks of buildings. Corsha became a shimmering blur, a distortion of the surroundings and Kierna heard the two long swords on the Troll's back being drawn. She herself drew her twin blades and drew her cowl tight around her face as they slowly advanced through the eerie streets, curious and not wanting to leave if there was anyone left alive to rescue. She saw the mine entrance at the other end of the village but before she could comment, Corsha yanked her unceremoniously to the soggy ground.

"Be still," the Troll whispered. "There are six Drissian soldiers standing guard at the mine's entrance. Another patrol of six is just now entering the village's Western quarter and a third group of six will turn the corner of the street we are on shortly."

"How—?" Kierna began, trying to focus on the shimmering Troll.

"My Elven talents are good for something."

"Very well. You take the group at the entrance and hold it until I get there."

"Where do you go?" Corsha asked.

"I will deal with the rest. Now go," Kierna ordered and watched the Troll disappear ahead. Taking up a position beside a partially razed building, she waited until she heard the rhythmic footsteps of the Drissian patrol. She snuck a peek to get an idea of their positions and assess their readiness.

Their scaled brown faces rimmed with shiny blue scales around the ridged brow would have done any pit viper proud, with slitted yellow eyes and a flickering black tongue atop tall, well-muscled bodies. Each thumb claw carried enough poison to kill a man as did the barbs on the end of their long, muscular tails. They wore tight, formfitting black scaled armor from chin to clawed toe. A blue cotton sash over each shoulder was tied with a black rope at the waist before it trailed down in front in one wide piece just past the knee. It was split in back over the base of the tail. Each carried a long black metal blowgun with a serrated knife hanging from the black rope at their waist.

She felt her blood rushing through her veins as if seeking some means of escape from her rising temper. As the patrol neared her intersection, she placed her twin blades in front of her face and closed her eyes. The sound of their hissing language gave her the exact moment to attack and she took full advantage of it. Without a sound, she was in their midst.

She took the heads of the first two before they even saw her coming and the next two as they struggled to draw their knives or swing their powerful tails. She ducked the tail of one of the remaining two, cutting off his leg at the knee with her left sword and blocking the other Driss' dagger thrust with her right. The unharmed Driss followed warily as she rolled away, heedless of his companion's hissing groans. Kierna caught an imperceptible movement at the injured Driss' waist. He was raising his blowgun slow enough that he hoped it would be to his lips before she noticed it.

Using his tactics against him, Kierna edged over further so that the uninjured Driss was nearly blocking his companions shot. Kierna lunged directly at the uninjured Driss, one sword deflecting his tail and the other his blowgun just as the hurt Driss fired. As the uninjured Driss moved to block her, he stepped into the dart's path. With a muffled grunt, he dropped dead and Kierna ran the injured Driss through unceremoniously.

She could hear the nearby shouts of the other patrol closing in on her position and ran to grab her bow from her horse's back. Picking an awkward, heavily-leaning awning as her cover, she was afforded a view of the entire main street and the major intersections the approaching Driss would have to use. Drawing her bow back, Kierna silently hoped that their horses would not make enough noise to draw the Drissians' attention to her prematurely, if at all. One could hope, could she not?

Kierna let loose just as the first Driss appeared and had another arrow nocked before her shot took him in the neck. Her second shot she fired low as the next Driss ducked when he saw his comrade fall. Had he remained upright, it would have taken him in the leg instead of his head. The other Driss crouched low behind the scant remnants of buildings, trying to discern the number of attackers. Kierna's keen vision picked out one through a tiny knothole in the wooden planks of the charred, overturned hay cart he was hiding behind. Praying to Thor for a calm breeze, she loosed her third shot, catching the stunned Driss off guard as it punched through the armor into the side of his ribcage.

The remaining Driss shrieked and charged her position, firing their poisonous darts, one of which missed her eye by less than an inch. The three Driss suddenly became six as they used their *Illusion* to make a mirror image of themselves, though it was not physically real. Kierna had to hope she could distinguish between them, for a mistake would cost her her life. She shot a last arrow, thudding into the closest Driss' stomach. He was real and his *Illusion* winked out as he dropped to the ground. Realizing she could not get off another, she picked up her blades and charged the two remaining Driss, throwing off their timing for their next blowgun attack. The darts whizzed harmlessly by. She ducked an illusory dart and, therefore, barely managed to avoid a deadly tail swipe that grazed her hair. The closest whipped his barbed tail at her, only instead of ducking it this time, Kierna brought both swords down like scissors and cut the tail off cleanly near the base. Without his tail, so integral for balance, the Driss stumbled and he could not stop the sword that impaled him.

Kierna deflected two furious attacks from the other Driss as she killed the first, trying to get her sword out of the body's chest. Grunting, she kicked the limp form off her blade and into his companion, only the corpse fell right through the illusion. She had misjudged which one was real. Desperately she flung herself at the real Driss, inside his claws with both swords like the tip of a spear that was her body. Thanking the Gods she had avoided his poison, she yanked both blades unceremoniously from his corpse. The third Driss, with her arrow still in his stomach, lurched for her unsteadily. She almost felt bad for slitting his murderous throat. Then again, not so much.

Corsha had snuck up so quietly on the detail guarding the entrance to the mine that she had killed the first three before the first body hit the ground. The next three stood just as little of a chance, not having time to focus on the shimmering mass before they met their fates. Drissian eyes could see Vull'Kra even when using *Shimmer* if they lowered a filmy lens that was normally used to keep out water over their eyes. These Driss' lenses were still tucked away in their scaly eyelids. They were helpless. Corsha let out a deep breath, not having had the opportunity to fight with her swords before now and strangely exhilarated by the feeling, though it had not required much skill.

Corsha did not have long to relish it, however, as she heard hissing voices coming from deeper into the mine. The flickering torch light hurt her glowing eyes until they adjusted from the amber-tinted darkness outside as she made her way down the narrow passageway. Three Driss rounded the corner not thirty feet away. Corsha stepped behind a high wall torch, hoping her shimmering shape would be dismissed as fumes and heat waves. The Driss in the middle was taller than the other two. His gold-laced sashes and polished armor marked him as an officer as surely as the way the other two tiptoed around him.

As they came within range, Corsha balled her fist and punched the officer so hard he was out before he hit the ground. With the other two so close, she couldn't swing her swords, but neither could they use their tails. Still, their thumb claws were just as deadly should she get hit more than a few times. In her *Shimmer* form, Drissian poison had little effect on her as long as she kept moving to work it out of her. Corsha put her elbow spike through one's eye and caught the other under the chin with her sword hilt, giving her room to run him through with her blade, his armor unable to withstand the force.

She threw the unconscious officer over her shoulder and dragged the two bodies out of the mine entrance. As Corsha hid the bodies behind a large boulder, Kierna made her appearance. Both women's clothes were bloody, and Corsha's toga was ripped diagonally from her breast to well past her waist so that if she didn't hold it together it would fall off. Like all Trolls though, she had no modesty and continuing the fight wearing nothing but her Clan sash did not seem to bother her in the least. While she talked, Kierna busied herself tying the toga back together. It looked odd but at least she wouldn't be naked. Had bloody Trolls never heard of underclothes?

"What have you seen?"

"The shafts go very deep and I believe there are many more Driss down there. Also, the same smell from the farms is stronger here. Whatever beast caused all of this is down there somewhere," Corsha kept a sharp eye on the entrance.

"We have to find out what's going on here," Kierna said vehemently.

"Aye, but do we do so at the cost of our lives? We can warn no one if we are dead."

"I know you're right. We'll just go far enough to get a—"

"I have a better plan!" Corsha smiled. Taking our a tiny vial of smelling salts, she woke the Drissian officer. Next, she forced a thick black liquid down his throat. He attempted to cry out but her strong hand closed his mouth smartly. "You will tell us what we want to know, aye?" she smiled evilly at the wide-eyed Driss. He nodded frantically as he felt Corsha's blade pressed against his throat, his slitted eyes glazed over like frosted glass.

"How many of you are in the mines?" Kierna asked.

"Ssoussandss," he hissed, in barely intelligible accented Sendar.

"Why?"

"Ssa Ancientss vishh ssiss ssoft land for sseir breeding groundss. I and my Brosserss of ssa Blue Sscaless have come viss ssem to sshare in sseir glory."

"What is he talking about?" Kierna demanded.

"The Driss are all male except for their Queen. The strongest and best male is selected every year to fertilize the thousands of eggs she will bear. The Driss believe themselves descended from Dragons and more specifically each one believes he is descended from a certain Color of Dragon. So all of the warriors join their particular Color

Sept upon reaching maturity, competing to have one from their Color mate with the Queen. To prove themselves, they pick out the strongest Dragon of their Color and do great deeds and sacrifices to strengthen their Color in the Dragon's name," Corsha explained, surprising Kierna with her knowledge.

"What, so you're saying there's a Blue Dragon down there with thousands of bloody Driss to boot?"

"Not one," Corsha shook her head. "Two."

"Two?"

"Ssa mighty Darandoross hass taken a mate," the officer laughed, his glazed eyes blinking rapidly with their filmy, opaque lenses.

"Two Wyrms. How could no one notice this?" Kierna shook her head.

"What does Darandoross plan to do?" Corsha asked.

"Add to hiss tressure after he sscourss ssiss mountain range clean of ssa veak rassess ssuch ass yoursselvess."

"Mighty ambitious of him," Kierna scorned.

"No osser Ancient hass claim here. Not even von of ssa veak Diamondss, Ssilverss, Bronzzess or Goldss. Who can sstop him?" he laughed, a grating hiss.

"We must go," Corsha declared, preparing to kill the Driss.

"Wait," Kierna stayed the Troll's hand. Quickly she stripped the babbling Driss naked.

"You can't possibly want to—to *touch* him in *that* way, can you?"

"What?" Kierna nearly screamed. "No! Uggh! I can't believe you would even *think* that!"

"Well what then?"

"Shh. Just keep watch for me."

Using the blade of her sword, she cut off the Driss' thumb claws, tail barb and fangs. Next she tied his hands behind his back with his waist rope and kicked him in the opposite direction from the mine, telling him he could not stop walking until they told him so, and that they would be following him every step of the way.

"You are too soft-hearted," Corsha growled as they ran back to their horses and galloping out of the ruined village.

"One of my rare moments. Don't get used to it. What was that you gave him anyway?" Kierna asked.

"Streshalt."

"Why do you carry that with you?"

"Trolls may have many partners before they marry but never a child. A Vull'Kra woman cannot get pregnant by accident. If she wishes to do so, she must force the man to submit. *Streshalt* in his evening ale makes it easier for us and less painful for them." Corsha grinned at Kierna's shocked expression.

"But—"

"Trolls require much space to live and the world is only so big. We live too long to go about things as you Sendar do, breeding like rabbits. The forests will not last forever."

"It just seems so…" Kierna shook her head, disbelieving.

"Violent? As I said before, Kierna Bjorndotir, you are too soft-hearted."

"How do you know so much about Driss?" Kierna asked later. Corsha took on a lecturing tone.

"The Elven Races were not our only enemies long ago. The Driss, like the Orcans and Shrakens came into being after the Gods left the world at the dawn of the Age of Dragons. They and a few races from the Lost Continents even worship different Gods than you or I do. They are more in line with the animalistic side of nature, called the Ennead. Sorry to get off track," she grinned. "Anyway, though they came into being after the Vull'Kra, we lived in such close proximity for so many millennia, that both races began evolving to combat the other."

"That's why they have that lens to see you and their poison doesn't affect you when you use *Shimmer?*"

"Aye."

"Why not the Duah? You race surely fought them longer than the Driss."

"The Moon Dancers? They were not always so adept at fighting, and even when they were, they were usually too occupied fighting the other Elven Races to do much but try to keep us out of their forest. The Jin and the Kel were the dangerous ones then anyway. The land bridge is gone now though and only the Duah remained on this continent. We have learned to co-exist now."

"I had no idea you were a scholar, Corsha."

"Not all Vull'Kra are so obsessed with *M'Racht* that they forego knowledge, Kierna Bjorndotir."

"Not all Sendar will violate their obligations to *M'Racht* either, so you better use that knowledge to pass the Tests, so I don't have to nanny you until I'm old and grey." Kierna scolded jokingly. Corsha scoffed. The White would be hers.

CHAPTER 20
A NEW HOME

s the sun rose in the east, the immensity of Mist Peak made its full impression on all. An ancient volcano, it rose up out of the fertile Fal Valley. A perpetual mist hung about the base, but Danken could clearly see the path to the top blasted into the side.

"Welcome to Mist Peak," Arn said joyously. He led them to the base of the mountain. A huge moat surrounded it with only one bridge spanning it. Two behemoth pearly white towers stood on either side of it. Arrow notches lined the towers from the bottom up and two catapults sat at the tops. A full garrison was housed on the other side of the moat.

A low thunder seemed to be coming from the mountain, which Danken soon recognized as hoof beats. A score of fully-armored knights charged over the bridge to stop within hailing distance.

"Name yourselves and declare your business at..." the thunderous baritone of the soldier cut off as Arn removed his hood. At once, all of the knights dismounted and saluted, right fist to left shoulder. Arn saluted back. "Captain, welcome back to Mist Peak. Password?"

"Gellar's Falls," Arn replied easily. "Lieutenant. Be so kind as to dispatch two of your men on the fastest horses to tell Sembalo to prepare for the coming of the Fifth." The Lieutenant's eyes widened momentarily as he scanned the company, but discipline kicked in and he did as ordered.

"Aye, sir." Two soldiers barked before racing back to the barracks to saddle their mounts.

"Gentlemen, this is Danken Sariksen, the Fifth," Arn said as Danken removed his hood. As one, the detachment saluted again.

"Hail!"

"Also, I would like to introduce you to the rest of the company." Introductions were made all around. The soldiers then formed a protective formation around them and escorted them up the peak.

By noon, they had reached the summit and the sight left the company speechless. The vast crater that was the extinct volcano teemed with life. A huge lake fed a beautiful waterfall that became the River Mist. A Majestic, sparkling white-spired castle rose up into the clouds, crowned by a rainbow from the waterfall. An entire city stretched out from there like flowing white satin.

Most impressive of all were the entire legions of Mistgarde arrayed in blue and white in parade formation. Each division made up its own race, Troll, Dwarven, Elven, Sendar and Orcan. The population of the city was out in force cheering. Four blue-robed figures stood at the head of the assembly. All looked to be in their early twenties, but their white hair marked them as Magi. One, an average-sized man with long flowing hair and a beard to his waist, held up his arms. The entire city went quiet. He turned to the company who were now standing beside them.

"Arn, my good friend," Sembalo turned to him, "you have succeeded. We will discuss the problems of the land after you get some rest. But first, let the people see their new Fifth. They have been waiting for over eighteen years, you know." His face crinkled into a smile perfected over a thousand years. "Now then," he turned to Danken, "you must be the Sariksen. By the Gods, how you look like him. In a moment you will meet your people, but first, introductions."

"My people?" Danken asked.

"Of course, you are the Fifth, you are a Mage. All of the Sendarian magic is given to you, to us. We are their protector against all threats. These are the other Magi." He turned to indicate the remaining three. They greeted him in order of rank. A tall, lean man with long hair and a clean-shaven, angular face clasped his wrist first.

"My name is Penn, I am the Third," he said in a distinctly upperclass Sendarian accent, and then stepped back. The next man was short and stocky with sunbrowned skin and short, spiky hair. His lilting accent marked his as either a Kasani or a Lundgarder.

"I am Urishen, Second of Magi," he said in a quiet baritone. Danken recognized him immediately as Tok'Neth's father.

A tall, wiry man with shoulder length hair and a long goatee came forward. His accent was that of the Eastern coastal cities.

"My name is Kai, the First. You have your father's eyes," he said. All the other Magi laughed, their blue eyes flaring. Danken nervously joined in. The bearded man smiled.

"I guess that leaves me, Sembalo, Fourth of Magi. That's twice your family have knocked me down the totem pole," he remarked. He spoke in the same accent as Danken, though perhaps farther north, maybe even Norsepoint.

Danken smiled.

"So," Penn said in a lighthearted tone. "Are you ready to have the weight of Sendar placed on your shoulders?"

"I hope so," Danken replied.

"Excellent." Sembalo patted him on the back. "Now, who are your companions, if I may ask?" Danken turned and made introductions. When he had finished, Sembalo shook his head. "It never ceases to amaze me the companions a Mage accumulates in a journey. It has been like that since we have existed, yet no two are ever the same. Just so. Come now, we have plenty of time for conversation later. It is time to meet the people of Mist Peak."

As they negotiated the crowded streets, waves of smiling, anxious people called out to Danken, or reached out to touch him. Danken was a bit taken aback but his questioning mind was never dormant for long.

"You think they will approve of the blood on my hands?" he asked Sembalo.

"I will tell you what Arch-Mage Gellar, the first of our kind told me. The difference between Good and Evil is simple. We kill because we have to, they kill because they want to. We are all killers; there are no innocents among us." He indicated the other Magi. "We do what we must to protect the world from Evil. I know it is hard to accept but it is the way of the world. We merely fulfill our end of the bargain."

"I guess I never thought of it that way. I always felt guilty."

"It's only natural. As long as you keep feeling that, you'll know you are doing the right thing. Now, come on, I'll show you all to your quarters." He led them to White Castle. It was a long walk, but none minded as it was so beautiful, so pristine. Everything was built for beauty and warmth, though all held an underlying quality of strength.

Long, wide streets paved with white brick meandered through huge gardens dotted with massive oak trees. People on the streets waved to them as they walked by.

"Is it always like this?" Danken asked.

"No, just when a new Mage comes, which is quite rare," Sembalo answered. They reached the castle soon after. Danken thought that surely over a thousand people must call it home it was so huge. A drawbridge was raised over another smaller moat. Sembalo lowered it with a wave of his hand. As they entered, Danken asked Sembalo.

"How many people live here?"

"A dozen, maybe, not including the servants and such. They live off the grounds. Basically, it is us and a few gypsies. No one else can pass the barrier that you just walked through," he pointed overhead to a huge arch made of white stone, "without one of us to accompany them. It would be too much of an ordeal."

"Why the barrier?" Danken asked as they entered the main hall, a gigantic room with an oak table able to seat one hundred people with five larger chairs at the end.

"Because inside this castle are so many magical artifacts, books, mirrors, potions, cloaks and the like, that we can't let anyone in without a Mage accompanying them. It's just too risky." They exited the Main Hall and arrived at a wide spiral staircase that ascended higher than Danken could see. Sembalo took the stairs two at a time.

After what seemed to most a climb to the sky, Sembalo bade them to follow him to the guest rooms. Here he unlocked separate rooms for Jet, Valshk, Swifteye and Dot. Each went in to inspect it and set it up for themselves. Tae followed Dot in, along with Shard. He would stay with her until permanent quarters were set up for him near the Mistgarde Elven garrison.

Arn, Danken and Sembalo then climbed another three flights of stairs to reach another hallway, this one long, brightly lit and lined with large portraits of every Mage who had ever lived.

"Yours will be up there soon."

"Soon?" Danken asked.

"Aye, our painter is skilled, you will see," Sembalo replied. Danken stopped at a painting at the end of the hallway. The inscription beneath it read: *Sarik Blanesen, Fifth. He was an average man who became the greatest we had ever known. Died the way we all wish to, battling Evil.* "Your father was mourned for a long time. The people loved him more than any I've ever witnessed, myself included. I sense it will be no different with you."

"Ah," Sembalo said, stopping at two huge double doors made of solid oak. "Here is your new home, Danken, welcome." The doors opened slowly to reveal a large window-lit room big enough to fit a hundred Giants in, with room to spare. Oversized, comfortable white leather sofas were arranged artfully around stout-looking mahogany tables, a fireplace and a steaming pool. The thick blue carpet was so intricately woven with amazing designs and gold and silver thread that Danken almost feared to step on it.

Another room opened off of this one revealing a mammoth four poster bed covered in blue and silver satin sheets. A canopy of similar design hung regally down over it. Drapes of the same color were unpulled beside each window. The floor was a polished white marble with several plush rugs.

"This is mine?" Danken whistled softly. *"Dwei."*

"Of course. You are free to redecorate as you see fit. You will be here for awhile. Oh, and out there," he nodded to a balcony overlooking the entire crater, "is your garden. It also doubles as a launch pad when you have chosen your *Avian* form.

"Now, I hate to dampen your welcome, but there are instabilities in the land that need to be dealt with immediately. We'll meet the other Magi in the war room." Sembalo then led Danken back down a flight of stairs and into a huge, dark room lit only by blue fire torches in the walls.

There was a round table in the middle of the otherwise empty room. The three other Magi were situated around it along with three unfamiliar men as well as two women.

"Danken, this is Kinma, she is commander of Mistgarde's Elven garrison," Sembalo said. An attractive Elven woman with short, blond hair bowed her head. "And this is Gran Treblecore, commander of our Dwarven division," he continued, as a barrel-chested Dwarf with a grey beard roughly saluted.

"These are Rowan and Hilta, commanders of our Troll and Sendar legions, respectively." The former, a giant of a Troll with a long red braid and a braided mustache that reached his chest, winked at him while the latter rose and bobbed her head, causing her waist-length black hair to cascade in front of her sparkling green eyes and a scar that ran from her left eye to her chin. "And this is S'at, commander of the Orcan division," Sembalo finished as a short, powerfully built Orcan nodded his raven-haired head.

"Well met." Danken greeted them, taking a seat beside Arn, the leader of them all.

"Very well," Sembalo said. "Arn, tell me the news of your journey."

"The Elves report heavy Shraken activity on their trading routes. The Sendar near Savhagen have reported numerous Goblin sightings. The Pixies and the Gnomes have gone to a full scale war over the Pixie, T'riel, who is now present, and a band of Goblins attacked us at an inn near Brayl. I'll get to that more in a moment. The more pressing matter is that of the Giants.

"Ripplewake told me war will be declared by tomorrow or the next day and I don't disagree. The young Dwarf, Swifteye, saw a portal open. The Giant Danken and I questioned said the same after Danken severed a few limbs." This garnered a few askance looks at Danken who only shrugged.

"Don't waste no time wi' yon blade do ee?" Treblecore asked, grinning.

"Aye." Arn nodded. "Anyway, when we got into who had sent them, he keeled over and died on the spot. I recognized it as a *Silence* spell."

"So, we are headed for another war," Sembalo said. "The Orcans have declared war on the Shrakens for an attack on the Princess Shonai, who was nearly killed. It seems she was rescued by an unknown race called the Mer'khan, who are apparently what we call Mermaids. They are a huge civilization who has been in hiding for thousands of years.

"It remains to be determined who they'll side with, if anybody, in the upcoming struggle. The Princess meanwhile is rumored to be here on the surface. I've sent our best scouts out to locate her and bring her here. To add to that, two relatively unknown underwater races, the Barakans and the Pir'Noh seem to have surfaced and allied with the Shrakens."

"What of the Mai'Lang?" Arn asked.

"Their pirates, along with the Driss and Goblins, have been attacking our ships for a few years now. It seems likely that they will follow. Besides that, Dak'Verkat will be wanting to test out his new Sorcerers. He will know of Danken soon, if he doesn't already."

"I think I may know the answer to that," Danken said. He told them of the old man on the road back from Savhagen.

"It sounds like Dak'Verkat," Sembalo said thoughtfully. "He may have taken the form of the old man to lull you into thinking yourself superior in strength."

"But surely I could not have defeated him so easily," Danken protested.

"You are not a Mage yet. Therefore, you are invisible to him, he can't even see you. We are the same with those who are not yet Sorcerers. He probably just sensed your presence attached to the Pixie. He was preparing to lash out in hopes of hitting you but underestimated you. He didn't know of *Mak'Rist*. It was forged with the specific purpose to kill him. He was most likely shocked and retreated before you went for his head."

"Will his hand grow back?"

"Aye, certainly has."

"And then there was the red-eyed man who convinced the people of my town to kill my mother. What of him?"

"Probably one of his new Sorcerers. They must have learned your identity when we did and came looking for you as Arn did. Either way, you, like your father, are about to receive a crash course in the art of Magery."

"But can I learn before I have saved with my powers?"

"Of course. There are only two things that come with being a full-blown Mage: Immortality and your *Transport* spell. Everything else is a spell you are capable of enacting right at this moment. Kai will be your first teacher. Go to your room and get some sleep, you're going to need it. You start at sunrise tomorrow."

CHAPTER 21
A FAST LEARNER

embalo was as good as his word. At the first hint of light, Kai was at Danken's door with a smile. He directed the sleepy teenager to a walk-in closet in which there were a massive array of robes, cloaks, pants, shirts, hats and shoes all perfectly fitted to him. Kai told him to pick out a light-weight white robe and some cotton pants.

"You're going to work up a sweat today, young Danken."

"Aye, I have no doubt of it," Danken mumbled, getting dressed. When he had finished, Kai herded him down to the kitchen. T'riel remained fast asleep.

"First lesson, Danken. Moving objects with your mind."

"Can't I eat first?"

"Of course. After you bring all you want to eat over here and cook it with your mind," Kai told him. "Now, see that box of eggs right over there on that counter?" he pointed.

"Aye."

"*Dwei.* Now, concentrate on it until it's all you can see. When you've done that, try to make the air beneath it like a cloud, soft and buoyant. Then just move it slowly towards you by redirecting the air currents in the room. It's going to take awhile, but it will be worth it."

"All right." Danken took a deep breath to steady himself, remembering the wind he had called forth on prior occasions, then did as Kai had instructed him. He isolated the egg carton and then lifted it a small distance before dropping it. "Damn!" he cursed, as a few broken eggs leaked their contents onto the countertop.

"Try again and remember, you have to maintain the cloud when you summon the breeze. Remember, your spells are dependent on the will of the Gods. You must achieve a higher relationship with them than normal people. The closer you are to the Gods, the more powerful you'll be."

Danken's eyebrows came together and he once again went through the process. This time he kept the eggs aloft while manipulating the air current, bringing the eggs to him and setting them down. He then repeated the process with the bacon, bread and oats, placing them in pots and pans over the fire until he had cooked his own breakfast, using only his mind. It took seemingly ages, but as Kai had said, it was worth it.

"Wow," Kai whistled. "Do you know how long it took me to master the spells you just used? *Airlift* and *Breezesummon?*"

"No, how long?" Danken asked around a mouthful of eggs.

"A month," Kai answered, ruefully.

"A month? How did *I* get it so quick?"

"I don't know, but it does work to your advantage. The faster you learn all of your spells, the less of a chance Dak'Verkat has to out duel you. You may have begun learning at an earlier age than the rest of us. You are special."

"So, what's next?"

"*Magesight,*" Kai said, leading him to a walk-in pantry. He extinguished all of the torches using *Breezesummon.* The room was nearly pitch black but for a tiny crack under the door. Kai faced away from him. "Now, I want you to concentrate very hard on seeing me. I know it…"

"Kai?" Danken said in a small voice. Kai turned around to see Danken's eyes already burning blue. "I'm sorry, but is this what you wanted me to do?"

"How did…?" Kai stammered, knowing that his earlier conjecture had been correct.

"I learned when I was ten."

"Ha! I tell you what, Sariksen," Kai laughed, opening the door to the pantry. "I want you to tell me everything you *can* do that normal Sendar can't and we'll go from there."

"All right," Danken thought, then sent out a bolt of blue fire into an egg on the counter, causing it to explode. He looked to Kai for approval.

"That's called *Magefire.* Anything else?"

"Aye. Can you call a servant in here?"

"Aye" Kai raised an eyebrow.

"Oh, and tell them to bring an animal with them."

"Any kind?"

Danken nodded. Kai left and returned briefly with an older, very dignified looking Elven woman in servant's livery carrying a small dog.

"This is Mistress Palthyna, head of the Castle's servants and her dog, Lady," Kai told him.

"Thank you. If you would be so kind as to set your dog down," Danken bade her. She did so looking at him askance. Palthyna was not one for constant bowing, for which he was thankful. He placed his hands near the dog's head and let a small tendril of blue energy into it. He then stood up and pointed towards a window at the end of the kitchen. The dog ran over to it. Danken waved his hand back towards a cabinet at the other side of the kitchen and the dog ran to it as well.

Next, he pulled his hand to his chest and the dog came running back to him. He raised his hand and it jumped, he lowered it and it sat. Finally, he nodded at Palthyna and the dog leapt into her arms. She curtsied with a giggle that seemed to surprise her. Soon she was all calm dignity once more.

"Thank you, Mistress. One more thing, please. Think of a number, a word, a color and a place." He waited for a second and then asked if she had them. She nodded yes. He let a blue tendril snake into her. "Thirty-seven, bath towel, green, the ocean."

"How did...? Well, I guess that's why you're a Mage." She answered her own question, adding a hasty, "Master Danken" on the end.

"Aye. Thank you for your time, Mistress." Danken smiled.

"The pleasure was all mine, Master Danken." She curtsied again. "Wait until I tell the others," Palthyna laughed as she left the kitchen, struggling to maintain proper manners and hurry all at once.

"*Obeyance* and *Mindscan*. Impressive," Kai said approvingly.

"Also, I have a danger warning. Is that a spell?"

"Aye, it's called *Dangersense*. Anything else in your repertoire?"

"I think that's about it, well, except I can make someone be silent by freezing their vocal chords. Is that normal?" Danken asked. Kai laughed aloud.

"By the Gods, Danken, I would hate to be Dak'Verkat when you meet him! And in answer to your question, aye, what you did is called *Speechless*. Do the opposite and see what happens to your own voice."

"All right," Danken nodded slowly, thinking.

"That's called *Amplify*. Can you do that?

"I'll try." He concentrated on his vocal chords, remembering the spell he used on others and inverting it. It was time consuming, but not very difficult. Then he spoke, nearly knocking Kai off of his feet. "Like this?"

"Dwei," Kai said, holding his ears. "Next time, control your volume."

"Sorry," Danken whispered.

"It's *dwei*. Come on, let's go to the castle's garden. We'll have plenty to work on there," Kai led Danken to a magnificent garden set inside the castle walls. There were plants and trees of every variety giving off sweet smells and birds chirping to greet the sun.

Kai began picking up pinecones and setting them in a straight line.

"I want you to walk across there without making a sound."

"How?"

"You'll figure it out," Kai answered him. Danken stepped on the first pinecone, causing it to crack loudly. Instead of cursing, he closed his eyes, listening for the sound waves. Stepping on another, he found them. As he stepped on a third pinecone, he bent the sound waves back in on themselves, canceling out the sound. He tried the same on a bed of loose rocks, trying to find their waves.

Soon he didn't have to find the waves of anything, he could just bend the waves back on his first try.

"Danken, you're an astounding young man. You just learned *Stealth* in half a turn of the glass."

"I don't know how I'm doing all this."

"You're the Fifth. This is what you do best. Now, one more spell and we'll be done for the day. I want you to make those trees right there hold hands."

"What?"

"It's simple really. Merely take a branch of *this* tree and wrap it around a branch of *this* tree," Kai explained, a mischievous glint in his flaring blue eyes. Danken found it hard to believe that this man who looked no older than himself was probably old when his great-great-great grandpa had been young.

Danken let forth two tendrils of blue into the bases of both trees. Inside he was shocked to learn that trees were vast and complex entities. He felt himself washed away in one of the countless tributaries carrying nutrients to and from place to place. It was a massive network of areas working symbiotically.

After an eternity, he finally found his way around inside and moved to the branches of both trees. He then sent energy signals to the nerve centers of both trees telling them what he needed them to do. They resisted at first but the constant pressure of persistent persuasion eventually coaxed them to obey.

Thanking the trees for their cooperation, he let his consciousness flow back into his body. He opened his eyes to find the sun setting in the west and Kai asleep on the ground. A young Sendar woman was waiting for him with a tray of food. She curtsied immediately.

"How long have you been standing here?" He asked her.

"Since noon," she replied with a shaky voice.

"Noon?" he exclaimed. "Waiting for me?"

"Aye. Is that all right?" she asked, afraid that she had done something wrong.

"Gods," he said, as he took the tray from her. "Sit down, please. You must be tired."

"I really must be getting back, Master Danken. I..."

"I'll take care of it. Sit, please," he bade her quietly. She curtsied before sitting down cross-legged across from him. "Eat with me, won't you?" he asked. She blushed furiously.

"I couldn't." She fretted with her apron strings.

"It's really all right. I want you to," he said, picking up a pastry and taking a large bite. She did as he had bade her and ate. Only then did he realize her true age. Her long, brown hair and amber eyes were set in a face a few years younger than his own. How long had she been working? he wondered.

"What's your name?" he asked.

"Maple, Master Danken."

"Please, just call me Danken," he said lightly. "How long have you been at the castle, Maple?"

"Since I can remember. My mother is Head of the Kitchens."

"Do you attend school?"

"Aye. I work when my lessons are finished to earn my wages and retain our rooms in the Servant's quarters. Mother has been ill recently."

"It sounds like you're a smart girl, Maple," Danken commented. "Tell me, how do you like children?"

"I like them Danken, but I hardly know any. I'm not far past a child myself."

"Aye, but I'm talking about a young girl. She's an Elf and she has no one to talk to but myself, Tae and her sabercat, Shard."

"Are you talking about the little girl that came here with you yesterday? Dot?" she asked, then blushed again as she realized her forwardness. "Forgive me, I—"

"Aye, that's the one." Danken cut her off gently. "I wonder, would you like to be her nursemaid? She needs a woman to teach her and neither Tae nor I fit the bill. You can still go to school and I'll triple whatever you're making now aside from your room and board."

"You would do that?" Maple asked, tears coming to her eyes.

"Aye."

"Of course I will do it. Thank you, I won't let you down, I promise."

"I know, come on, I'll introduce you to her." Danken smiled, leading her back to the chambers where Dot was living.

"What about Master Kai?" Maple asked, eyeing the sleeping Mage.

"He'll be fine. I'm sure he's tired of watching me all day anyway."

They reached Dot's room shortly after and Danken opened the door, using his newly learned *Airlift* spell. Dot was inside with Shard painting a picture. When she saw Danken, she flung her paintbrush aside heedlessly and ran to him, hugging him as he picked her up off of the ground. Shard came padding over next and nuzzled his big head against Danken's chest, begging for pets. Danken obliged him, letting a blue spark into the huge cat, telling it that Maple was a friend for Dot.

"Dot, this is Maple. She's going to be staying with you from now on, *dwei?*" Danken ruffled her curly hair. She focused her large green eyes on Maple as if searching her soul. She nodded, satisfied.

Danken watched the two of them together for awhile, petting Shard. He had mastered the spells easily enough but it had still taken quite a bit out of him. After awhile he rose to his feet.

"Maple, does your mother have anyone taking care of her?"

"Oh aye, I'm usually never home so we have one of the ladies from the kitchen check on her often."

"Do you need anything?"

"No thank you, I'm fine."

"If you do, the servants have been given instructions to treat you as they treat Dot."

"Thank you Danken, for everything." Maple said, rising and hugging him tightly. Her hair smelled of flowers and honey, he thought, hugging her back. She really was quite pretty. When she let go, she appeared embarrassed and he saw tears in her eyes again. "I'm sorry, I think I cried on your robe."

"It's fine, I'm sure," Danken assured her, embarrassed himself. He leaned over and kissed Dot on the top of her head. "Be good little Windsong," he said, as he left the room. He knew he should go talk to Sembalo but he decided against it and instead retired to his room.

He stepped out onto the terrace that overlooked the crater. Breathing in the cool night air, he thought of his mother. He wondered if she was up there in the sky somewhere, watching over him, or if she was with his father, living the life now that they hadn't been able to then.

Did she know of the things he had done since her death? Of the things he had done to her killers? Would she approve of his victories? He hoped so. He went back inside to his bag and unpacked the silver satin he had bought for her in Savhagen. He unfolded it gently and hung it in his closet.

When that was done, he snuffed out the candles and went to sleep.

"It's the most amazing thing I've ever seen," Kai told the other Magi. "It was like everything it took us so long to learn, he either already knew, or he learned in a day. I assigned him *Faunagrow* because I figured it would slow him down, maybe take him a couple of days to learn. I laid down and took a nap after I called a servant girl to wait with food when he got tired and gave up. When I woke up, he and the girl were gone."

"A man after my own heart." Penn laughed.

"No," Kai was shaking his head. "He heard that her mother, the Head of the Kitchen, was ill so he offered the girl a job babysitting the little Elven girl Dot for three times her ordinary wage. But that's not even the odd part."

"Oh?" Sembalo asked, eyebrows raised.

"No, he didn't even tie the branches on the trees."

"Well, he only had a few turns of the glass, man. He is only a young Sendar." Urishen commented.

"No, no," Kai laughed, as if unbelieving. "He, uh, he didn't tie the branches, he *fused* them. He connected every root in the trees, all around them. Now, instead of six huge old trees, there is only one, ten times the size of a Dragon. You can see it from the outside of the bloody castle."

"You're joking," Penn said, eyes wide.

"No, I'm afraid not."

"Well," Sembalo mused. "What did we expect? He is the son of a Mage. All the power that was his fathers was given to him tenfold through their common bloodline. Urishen, tomorrow you will teach him the next set of spells. At the rate he's going, he'll be fully trained in a week!"

"Aye, it seems that way," Penn agreed.

The next morning found Danken dressed and ready when Urishen knocked on his door.

"You're up early."

"I'd like to get a quick start today," Danken replied.

"All the better. Today we'll go to the lake."

"*Dwei,* I've been wanting to go there since we arrived," Danken said excitedly, following Urishen out of the castle.

The trip to the lake was peaceful as most of the residents of Mist Peak had not awakened yet. As they neared the great waterfall that the lake fed, the sun crested the horizon, creating rainbows in the mist. The smell of dew reminded Danken of home, making him smile. They reached the edge of the lake and Urishen turned to him.

"Today we will work on six spells. *Levitation, Magefreeze, Stonespeak, Shimmer, Everwarm* and *Waterbreath*. We'll start with the easiest. You already know *Airlift*. To enact *Levitation*, you must instead place the cloud under yourself."

"Should I try it?"

"Aye, whenever you're ready. But here's the catch! You'll be doing it over water, so get your concentration down now," Urishen told him, smiling. Danken nodded and began to concentrate as Urishen untied a rowboat at the edge of the lake and had Danken get in it. Next, he rowed out to the middle of the lake. "If you can *Levitate* out of the water, air will be easy!" And with that, he promptly pushed Danken into the water.

"Gods!" Danken gasped when he came to the surface. "It's freezing!"

"Well, then you'd better hurry up and get out of there. You see, I like to teach under pressure. It adds a feature of reality to it, don't you think? Your father thought so."

"Uggh! Now I know where Tok'Neth gets if from." Danken shivered, but he closed his eyes, concentrating on the air around his head.

He performed the *Airlift* spell, but instead used it to part the water. He filled the vacuum with more air and slowly began to rise up out of the water. Urishen raised his eyebrows.

"Ha! Well, I'll be a Dragon's chew toy," Urishen said, picking up the oars. "See you on shore, Sariksen!" he called as he rowed off. Danken was so astonished at this turn of events that he lost his concentration and fell back into the lake with a large splash.

After performing the spell again and using *Breezesummon* to take him to shore, Danken collapsed in a disheveled heap.

"Ah. Glad to see you made it. Cold, are you ?"

"W-w-w-what do you thhhink?" Danken shivered.

"Good! No better time to learn *Everwarm* than when you're freezing, now is there?"

"E-e-e-everwarm?"

"Of course. It's really a simple concept. You just take your *Magefire* and turn it inwards. Carefully, mind you. Don't want to disintegrate yourself. Just do it slowly. Feel it flowing through your veins like blood. Go on now, hurry before your freeze to death," Urishen urged him. Danken, though he could hardly think straight, did as he was told. Somehow he felt his *Magefire* at the tip of his fingers.

Instead of releasing it, he turned a small bit inward feeling it go into his hand.

"It burns!" he yelled.

"Good, that means you're doing it right. Now push it through your body quickly and it will go away," Urishen instructed. Danken did and he found himself warm all over. "Are you warm now?"

"Aye."

"Then discharge it into the ground."

"The fire?" Danken asked.

"Aye, unless you'd rather cook your organs like a pot of haggis!" Urishen replied. Danken discharged the *Magefire* into the ground, singing the grass, but he was amazingly warm.

"Did I do it?"

"Aye. Two down, four to go. Next, since you seem to have your *Magefire* so adeptly under control, we will use its opposite, *Magefreeze*. Every cell in your body has water in it. Therefore, you can use that water for your own purposes, as well as the water in the air and land around you.

"Imagine how you use *Magefire*, burning stored up energy. To use *Magefreeze*, you just do the opposite." Urishen showed him a long icicle protruding from his fingers. Danken thought hard for a long while, isolating the water in his system.

When he had it, he concentrated on dropping the temperature as it flowed through him towards his hands. By the time it reached them, he unleashed it towards a flower, sucking the excess heat from the water as it passed through his fingertips. The flower was instantly encased in ice.

"Excellent." Urishen applauded. "Remember though, using such spells depletes your reserves. When you use *Magefire* you get hungry, right?"

"Aye." Danken answered reflectively.

"That's because you are burning up your body's resources to do it. The same goes with *Magefreeze*. You *must* drink water after using it or you'll become dehydrated," he said forcefully. "If you use too much power without replenishing your reserves, your *Brag'Karn* will desert you and leave you as nothing but a pile of blue dust." Danken, feeling his parched mouth, ran over to the lake and started gulping. Just in case.

When his thirst was quenched, Urishen led him to a large grey rock sticking out of the green grassy ground like a tombstone. Danken had heard that was what Mai'Lang marked their graves with. He shuddered. To be buried instead of burned? Aye, they were definitely a cruel people.

"Place your hands on it," Urishen ordered.

"Like this?" Danken asked, his palms on the smooth face of the rock.

"Aye. Now, remember how to use *Faunagrow?*"

"Aye."

"Good. This is remarkably similar as are most of the spells I'm teaching you today. They are secondary to the primary spells you learned yesterday. This one is called *Stonespeak*. By letting your energy into the stone, you can speak to it. You can learn many things from it.

"There are two main plates underneath us. One under the Southern continent, Mai'Lang, and one under the Northern continent, Sendar. By putting your energy into this rock *here*, you can reach the plate down *there*. From the plate, you can see anywhere above it just by asking it to take you there."

"You mean it will let my consciousness see through it?"

"Aye. Now, there are some places that are warded against it, such as Isle Sin, the home of the Sorcerers, here at Mist Peak and at the Towers of the Cardinal Points."

"The what?"

"The Towers of the Cardinal Points. Each of the Four Magi has a Tower in one of the cities in Sendar. Kai's is in Eastbank, Sembalo's is in Norspoint, Penn's is in Wescove and mine is in Southport. A Tower is an extension of a Mage's power. The more powerful he is, the bigger and more complex the Tower. When he dies, it disappears with him. The Sorcerers have the same in Mai'Lang."

"What about mine?"

"You are the Fifth, your Tower is wherever you place it. We'll get into it more later. For now, think of a place that you'd like to see, then ask the stone to take you there."

Asking the stone proved a little harder than Urishen had made it seem. He milled about endlessly, asking the stone questions and receiving no answers. Finally, at his wit's end, he decided to give it one last try. He thought of Amaria and conveyed that thought to the stone.

In a deafening groan, he felt the stone's language pounding into his head and suddenly he could speak to it. He told the stone he wished to go to the Royal Palace in Wendall. With the sound of molten ore, Danken felt himself caught in a tidal wave of rushing stone. At first he panicked but the stone strangely reassured him, as if a child.

In no time, he found himself staring at the garden he had first kissed her in. There, sitting on a small slab of redrock, was Amaria. She kicked her feet idly, singing a Duah song of some sort. She smiled as a warm breeze touched her hair. Danken watched her for a few more precious moments before reluctantly tearing himself away to return to his studies. After he had been trained, he could be with her again. It was a powerful incentive to finish his training quickly.

He came out of the rock with a rush, sending him face first into the ground and he rose slowly, rubbing his nose. Urishen was nowhere to be seen. The sun was at its zenith, telling him he'd probably been gone for quite awhile. Urishen had probably gotten tired of waiting and gone off to do whatever it was Magi did during their free time.

A shimmering shape in front of him caused Danken to go for *Mak'Rist*. The shape quickly materialized into Urishen. Danken put the blade away, shaking his head.

"You scared the Ice of Hel out of me!"

"As was intended," Urishen replied. "You came here with a Troll, correct?"

"Aye."

"And did you ever see him disappear?"

"Aye, once."

"Good, then now that you've seen it twice, it should be easy to accomplish. Stand against the stone facing me." Danken moved over to the stone. "Now, imagine that you yourself are this same, grey, smooth rock."

"If you say so."

"Now let *Magefire* surround you like a shield," Urishen told him. Danken did and a crackling blue layer of electricity surrounded him like a cocoon. "Good. Now form that shield into what you're imagining."

Danken slowly formed the shield of energy into the stone he was imagining. Soon, he became nearly indistinguishable with the rock, a slight distortion, nothing more. Urishen congratulated him. Thus, he had performed *Shimmer*.

"The same works with any object on the face of the planet. If you wish to become it, you will. Now then, time for the last lesson of the day. It's going to make you *so* happy to know that you get to go back into the water."

"What?" Danken groaned.

"What did you think? That you could learn *Waterbreath* on land?"

"Great," Danken mumbled.

"I know. Off you go now." Urishen dove into the lake. "Remember, use *Everwarm*," Urishen reminded him. Danken dove into the water, using *Everwarm* to keep him from freezing. "Now, this is going to be hard. You have to swallow a lungful of water. You'll feel like you're drowning but if you are calm, you'll find that it's just like breathing air. Your body will take the oxygen right out of the water. You see, it's not really a spell so much as something you've always been able to do, just were too scared to."

"I'm not scared," Danken protested.

"Of course you aren't, that's why you haven't let your head go beneath the surface once."

"I was..."

"I don't want to hear it, come on," Urishen said, disappearing under the water. Danken followed his example and watched as the Mage sucked in a deep breath of water. Not only did he not choke, he breathed out bubbles. As Danken's breath was getting harder to hold, he gave in and inhaled.

At first he felt sure Urishen had played a trick on him. He began to thrash wildly. Only Urishen's hand on his shoulder calmed him enough to exhale. He inhaled unconsciously before he could stop himself and found that he was breathing. He smiled and did a few experimental flips in the water, blowing bubbles at random. Urishen beckoned him back up to the surface.

"I did it!" Danken said, as he coughed up a lungful of water.

"Aye, you did. Come, let's get dried off and head back to the castle," Urishen suggested and Danken was in no mood to disagree.

They returned home around dusk with a jovial air and Danken headed straight for Dot's room. Inside he found Tae, Maple and Dot playing *Towar*, an Elven card game while Shard was busy sunning himself on the balcony.

"Danken!" Tae shouted. "How are you, my record-breaking friend?"

"Record-breaking?" Danken asked.

"Of course. Word around the crater is that you've learned more than half of your spells in two days. Arn tells me it took Sembalo almost half a year."

"Maybe I already knew them," Danken answered modestly, taking a seat between Maple and Dot.

"Aye, maybe," Tae conceded, though the look in his eye told Danken he didn't buy it for a moment.

"So what have you three been up to all day?"

"Well," Tae replied, "Dot here was just lecturing us on the finer aspects of how to eat a Giant without waking him up," Dot giggled hysterically.

"Wouldn't you know it?" Danken said mock serious. "I'm never here to learn the really important things in life!" He picked her up and tickled her until she had tears in her eyes. When he set her down, he looked at Maple, who was radiant in a light green dress with her hair put up in an artful bun. "And how are you today, Maple?"

"Couldn't be better."

"Ha!" Tae scoffed. "She nearly knocked my head off when I came to see young Princess Dot here. I had to have Dot prove I was Taelun Fallenbower, dashing savior of the Duah before she'd let me in the door. She had a club, I tell you, ready to bludgeon me to a pulp!"

"Oh you great liar!" Maple declared, smacking his arm.

"See?" Tae appealed to Danken, who merely laughed. "Nearly two centuries her senior and brow beaten like a wee babe. It's not right, mate. You see?"

"I see all right, and quite right she was, too."

"Ahh! Outnumbered, two to one." Tae flung his arm across his eyes and held out his hand to Dot. "You'll help me, won't you Dot?" She giggled again, taking his hand and sitting on his lap. "Excellent. Oh, Danken," Tae said seriously, "Valshk and Swifteye are looking for you."

"Oh Muspleheim's Ashes!" Danken slapped his forehead. "I forgot. I'll be back later tonight if I can."

"Aye." Tae bid him goodbye and Dot and Maple waved. He strode quickly down the hall and down the flights of stairs until he reached Valshk and Swifteye's rooms. They were both in Valshk's, playing a game of tables. They rose when he entered.

"Sorry guys, I almost forgot. Are you ready to go?" he asked.

Both were ready and he led them out of the castle. They traveled down a well lit street until they reached a blacksmith's shop. Inside a roaring fire crackled behind a short silhouetted form. He called out in a gruff voice without turning around. Dwarves could feel vibration in the ground like a Sendar could feel a punch in the face.

"What is it?"

"Shirver Rambatter, its me, Danken Sariksen. We spoke two days ago, when I arrived?"

"Aye. I crafted a mace fer yon bairn' o'a Dwarf an' I welded yon Greenskins' battleaxe to a steel-shaped handle." The gruff Dwarf said, fetching the two weapons and handing them to their new owners.

"Was the sum I paid sufficient for the work?" Danken asked the Dwarf.

"Aye, more'n sufficient."

"Thank you for crafting them so fast."

"It's what ee paid fer, it's what ee get."

"Thank you sir," Valshk said in his baritone voice. "And this one here says the same," he indicated Swifteye who was busy inspecting his new, shiny mace with spikes as long as his stubby fingers on a heavy steel ball attached by a short chain to a long steel handle.

"Aye. Now be gone with ee, I got work t'do," the Dwarf said, turning back to his forge. Danken and the other two made their way back out to the street.

"Danken," Valshk asked, "I have been meaning to ask you, where did you get the money to pay for this?"

"When we got here, Sembalo told me that should I need anything, I just had to go to the storeroom and sign it out from the clerk. So I remembered that you two needed weapons and Arn told me that Rambatter was the best smith in the crater. So I just went and ordered them made."

"But how did you obtain my axe without my knowing?" Valshk asked.

"I just took it when you were sleeping. It wasn't that hard."

"Errr," Valshk growled. "This comfortable castle is dulling my senses."

"No, I could have stolen it from you anytime. Even if you were awake."

"How?" Swifteye kicked him in the ankle and waved, smiling like a mischievous toddler. "You?" Valshk groaned. "I should have known," he said as they entered the castle.

"Aye," Danken agreed. "I have to get back now. Enjoy yourselves."

"Aye, we will, thank you, Sariksen," Valshk called.

"No problem," Danken called back, heading up the stairs. He opened Dot's door quietly. Dot was fast asleep on Tae's chest. Maple was silently cleaning. She looked up as Danken entered and a smile lit her face.

"Looks like those two had a long night," he whispered.

"Aye, he's great with her. He'll make a good father for her," she whispered back. They walked out onto the balcony where Shard was sleeping. He cocked an eye at them and then went back to sleep. The moon was nearly full and lit the land like a giant candle.

"How do you like it here?" Maple asked him.

"I like it. It's my new home, though sometimes I miss my old one."

"I've never been outside the crater," she confessed.

"Never?"

"No, what is it like?" she asked, gazing at the stars.

"It can be beautiful, but also ugly. It is dangerous and one must always be on guard. There are many who are kind and decent and for the most part, that's who you meet. But at any given time, you may be attacked by pirates, bandits or just plain evil creatures. As odd as it sounds, I love it."

"Will you leave?"

"Eventually, but for now I am happy here."

"Some say war is coming," Maple commented.

"Aye. If so, I will leave to go fight in it," Danken said, matter-of-factly.

"Are you scared?"

"No. It's what I was born for. It's what I'm good at."

"I think you are good at more than just that, Danken," she said, softly, looking into his eyes. He met her gaze and looked away.

"So, how is your mother?" he asked, changing the subject.

"Better." Maple smiled. "The healer says she'll be back to work in no time."

"I'm glad to hear that."

"Aye," she replied. They continued to stare out at the landscape for some time before Danken bade her goodnight and made his way to the nightly briefing.

As they left the briefing, Danken and Arn discussed mundane things and Danken's progress with his spells. The Mistgarde Captain was in a jovial mood. Danken didn't know whether it was the upcoming war or possibly a new flame? He decided to keep his thoughts to himself.

"I saw the weapons you had made for Valshk and Swifteye."

"Ah, well I figured they deserved—"

"I think they are well deserving. Rambatter of Clan Nimbleaxe is the best. Even M'Zour the Pixian smith couldn't have wrought more delicate work like the inscriptions on the handles," Arn commented approvingly.

"Pixian smith?" Danken asked, perplexed. "What good would a Pixie be as a blacksmith?"

"You don't think a Dwarf could forge the tools the Forest Folk use, do you?"

"I didn't even know they used tools," Danken admitted. "Do they use weapons?"

"Aye, of course. Some very powerful ones also."

"Like what?" Danken asked, only then remembering the bows the Pixies had pointed at him.

"Same as us. Bows, swords, spears. They use their magic to enhance them. Not often deadly but damn painful."

"Where can I find this M'Zour?" Danken asked, an idea's light flaring in his blue eyes.

CHAPTER 22
TINY DISCOVERIES

fter the first three days, Zoltaure had lost the ability to morph along with this telepathy. The seashells lost their magic if they were away from Merkhandin for too long. Shonai had retained hers because of the gauntlet. The journey through the forest was long and slow going. Zoltaure had become adept at nearly everything on land and was genuinely enjoying himself. He climbed trees, smelled flowers and chased flying insects with a child's grin on his face. Though her mission to Mist Peak was probably fairly serious, Shonai couldn't bring herself to stop him. She laughed with him instead.

"Smell!" he exclaimed more than once.

"What?"

"Smell! I've never smelled so many wonderful fragrances. I can't even separate them. Underwater, all I could ever smell was blood, death or phosphorous."

"Aye. The land is a place of great beauty but also of great danger. It's not the large predators so much, it's the small ones you have to worry about," she told him matter-of-factly. He nodded his head, catching a bright pink flower out of the corner of his eye. He bent down to smell it.

"Ahh!" he screamed, standing bolt upright, holding his nose.

"What happened?" Shonai asked, trying to pry his hand away from his face.

"Ah, it burns!" he jumped up and down, his eyes watering.

"Zoltaure! Calm down and tell me what..." she stopped as she moved his hands from his nose. "Was there a little yellow and black thing in the flower you smelled?"

"Uh huh," he whimpered.

"That's called a bee. When you threaten them, they sting you. Here." She reached for his nose quickly, before he could stop her and yanked the stinger out. He yelled but quickly took one look at the stinger and laughed.

"That's it?" he shook his head ruefully.

"That's it. See that brownish ball hanging from that branch over there?" she asked.

"Aye."

"That's where they live. Its called a hive. There are thousands of them in there. If you irritate them, they will all attack you. So don't irritate them. Leave them alone and they'll leave you alone. That's the way the surface works. Take that for example." She pointed to a shimmering, silky web span between the trunk of two trees.

"Oh, it's beautiful." He began walking towards it before Shonai grabbed his arm, shaking her head.

"Stop. See that little black thing in the center?"

"Aye."

"That's a spider. If it bites you, you'll probably die within a day, so leave it alone."

"But how?"

"Poison, just like a blowfish or a sea snake. They have those too, you know."

"Blowfish?"

"Snakes, Zoltaure, snakes. They live in holes in the ground. Avoid them as well."

"I'm sorry, Shonai, I must seem terribly dumb to you, but I always thought that the surface was a myth. I never even thought it could be real. Be patient with me. Tell me what I need to know so I can help you."

"I know, Zoltaure, and I will. Just, as we go. I have to get to the Peak as soon as possible."

"Fair enough, Majesty."

"I thought I told you not to..." she was cut off as he kissed her long and softly, his arms holding her tightly to him.

"Sometimes I just have to remind myself who you are," he said with a smile.

"You are a dangerous young man, Master Zoltaure."

"Aye, Princess, that I am."

"Well then, Captain daring, see if you can find us some dry firewood to make a fire with. Like this." She showed him a small piece of dead wood. "I'm going to find a place to set up camp."

She perked her ears and heard the sound of a stream nearby. She headed that way quickly, for she was starving. They hadn't eaten since the rabbit that morning. They had taken a little of the shark with them, but raw meat did not last long on land.

She reached the stream soon after and was delighted to find a pond not much further away. She dove in without hesitation and saw an abundance of fish scatter. She swam deeper, as she knew that was where the big catfish were. By the time they reacted to her presence, it was too late and she caught two big ones easily.

She was getting ready to head back up when a gleam caught her eye. Further investigation revealed a small golden ball buried in the sand. She pulled on it and pulled on it until at last it came free along with the rest of a long javelin in an emerald encrusted golden handle.

This was the weapon from her dreams. She stared at it for a long time before she picked it up. It flared a green so bright she thought she'd stared directly at the sun. At the same time, her gauntlet seemed to burn her arm like fire. She cried out in pain so fierce she feared she would lose consciousness.

Abruptly, the light and the pain vanished, leaving her floating half conscious in the current, still gripping the javelin like a vice. An otter, sensing her pain, swam close to her, inspecting her for any signs that she might wake up and eat him. She already had her food, it figured, seeing the two catfish with her claws in their gills.

Although not able to talk, most mammals could communicate emotion to a receptive being. The otter placed its nose on hers.

—All right?— it asked. Shonai's eyes fluttered.

"Help," she thought back. The otter swam underneath her and began pushing her slowly to the surface. She paddled her arms weakly and flooded her depth sac to raise her buoyancy.

Before she knew it, she was on the shore with the otter licking her face like a dog. She laughed, gaining her strength back surprisingly quickly.

"You deserve a reward," she said telepathically, gently as the otter's mind was not big enough to accommodate her thoughts easily. She took out one of the catfish and gave it to him. He looked at it tentatively before she nodded, smiling at him. He took the fish in his amazingly dexterous claws before eating it quite politely, offering her some after every bite.

"Fire," she said, projecting the image of Zoltaure and her cooking the fish around a fire.

—Friend?—the otter asked.

"Aye, friend," she answered. A loud cracking in the forest told her that her "friend" was here. No other creature in the forest would be that loud.

"Shonai, there you are. You wouldn't believe what happened. I was out looking for wood like you said when I came across a whole dead tree on the ground. I started breaking it up when this little furry ball jumped out, with lots of little spikes, and started squeaking at me. I remembered what you said about all the small killers but he looked so cute I just kept doing what I was doing. Then the little guy bloody shot me with his spikes. So I took what wood I had and went to look for yoooooooou." He let the word continue when he spotted the otter.

"This is an otter, he saved my life just now," Shonai told him. The otter looked up from his dinner long enough to sniff Zoltaure, then went back to eating.

"And what does he do? Does he use that tail to impale people? Does he have poison claws?"

"No, none of that. He just swims around looking for fish."

"Ahah, I see. So he's one of the few good ones."

"There are lots of 'good ones,' you're just running into the bad ones. And for the record, the thing that shot you was a porcupine. You were using his home for firewood. I would have shot you too."

"And what of this one?" he indicated the otter. "How did he save your life?"

"Well," she said, putting the firewood in a stack and drawing the *Warding* rune in the middle. "I was fishing for us when I saw a golden ball in the sand. I pulled it out and it was the haft of a javelin. The gauntlet started burning so bad I almost blacked out. The otter here pushed me to the surface."

"Wow. So where's the javelin?" Zoltaure asked.

"It's right..." she stopped, looking all around her. "Where did it go?"

"Shonai? Are you all right?"

"I'm fine, but I lost the javelin!" she said exasperated. "Maybe I left it in..." she looked at the otter, it was touching her gauntlet.

—Hiding—

"The javelin?"

—Hiding—

"In my gauntlet," she whispered, holding her arm up in the air. "Come out, *Salindrist*," she called, the strange name coming from nowhere. A bright green flash and the smell of brimstone preceded liquid gold flowing down her wrist and forming into the golden shafted javelin she had found. The blade molted into steel so sharp she could cut air.

"Amazing," Zoltaure breathed.

"You," she said to the otter, "are one surprise after the other." She picked him up in her empty hand and kissed him on his nose. "Thank you." Zoltaure mock glared at the otter.

"Careful mate..." he shook his finger at the otter, who stuck out his tongue. "I like him," he laughed.

"Me too," Shonai agreed, setting the otter down to finish her dinner. The javelin melted back into her gauntlet. She took out a phosphorous chunk and used it to light the fire. "We'll have to get flint and tinder soon from one of the people we meet tomorrow."

"Tomorrow?"

"Aye, we'll enter the Duah city of Brayl tomorrow. We'll fish all day before we get there so we'll have something to trade for some horses and a weapon for you." She put the fish on a spit and placed it over the fire.

"Well, I guess I better brush up on my people skills then, huh?"

"You'll be fine. Here, have some." She passed half of the cooked fish to him. He ate it quickly.

"Hey, this is good. I've never had it cooked before." He was about to offer the otter some when he saw it resting on its back with its fat belly sticking up. "Well, I guess *you* don't need any more."

When they had finished, Shonai began piling leaves into a long pile, and Zoltaure followed her example, making his pile next to hers so they touched. She set two more logs on the fire and then laid down in the pile. Zoltaure did likewise, marveling at how comfortable it was. The otter ran over and snuggled in a ball right between them.

"Attention stealer," Zoltaure mumbled. Shonai laughed and grabbed his hand, holding it tight. "Shonai?"

"Aye?"

"What is it that's at Mist Peak? Aside from our destiny of world-saving, I mean."

"Well, it's the home of the Mistgarde, an elite group of Elves, Trolls, Sendar, Dwarves and Orcans. All the best warriors from every race there to defend the Magi."

"Who are the Magi?"

"They're the Sendar with all the magic of the whole race. They're only five of them so they're immensely powerful."

"Then why do they have to be defended?"

"From the Sorcerers, the Mai'Lang counterparts to the Sendar's Magi. If the Evil races attack, the Mistgarde are the first to go into battle."

"What does it look like?" Zoltaure wanted to know.

"I've never been there but I've heard it's the most beautiful place in all the world."

"I would love to see it."

"You will."

"Aye. Goodnight Princess."

"Goodnight, my Prince," she sighed happily. The two fell asleep, hands still clasped tightly. Shonai's mind tried to decipher her feelings for the irrepressible Orcan at the same time as it tried to puzzle out the reasons she was being drawn to the Peak. When the Magi had need, even subconscious, they rarely, if ever consulted you beforehand. You were drawn as if attached to a rope with a whale pulling you along.

Sunrise found them still deep asleep. The past few days had been strenuous and they had done without a moment's rest. The otter was the first to wake and he wasted no time diving into the pond in search of breakfast. He returned with two fat trout and set them by the fire.

Next, he nudged Shonai's foot. When she didn't respond, he moved up to her face where he promptly sneezed in her ear. This had the desired effect of causing her and Zoltaure to jump up out of their leaf bed.

"Oh, you bloody waterdog!" Shonai exclaimed, mouth agape.

"Well, he does have a way of making up for it," Zoltaure commented, putting the fish on the spit. He put the last two logs on the dwindling fire.

"Aye, I suppose he does," she nodded, patting the otter on the head. When the fish were finished, Zoltaure divided them up into three equal portions. The otter seemed to enjoy cooked fish as much as he did.

"Shall I put out the fire?"

"Aye, we have a long day ahead of us. First, we must reach the river Cam, fish until nearly dusk and then sell all our efforts."

"Sounds like chock-full of fun."

"Aye, well, that's the way you travel on land. Everyone else has weapons so you must as well. Not only must you have them, you must be skilled with them. And the way you get anywhere on land is on horseback."

"What exactly does a horse look like?"

"Have no doubt, you'll see soon enough."

"Well, are we ready to leave?"

"Aye," Shonai agreed. She looked down at the otter, who was pawing at her ankle.

—GO?—

"Aye, we must." She thought back to him, showing him the Elven city.

—I GO?—

"You want to go? But this is your home."

—LONELY—

"It's a far journey to a big mountain."

—I GO—

"Well, in that case, I guess you'll be needing a name. Do you have one?"

—NO—

"Hmmm..." Shonai thought. "How about Rip?"

—RIP—

"Do you like it?"

—LIKE—

"Well then, Rip, it's time to go," she said aloud.

"Rip? Is that his name?"

"It is now." She watched as the otter bounded off, standing on its haunches to wait for them.

"What's he doing?" Zoltaure asked.

"Leading the way."

"Well, we'd best not keep him waiting," he said as they marched off to the River Cam.

They arrived at the huge river by early afternoon and preceded to fish until their makeshift net was full to the brim. Rip contributed significantly to their numbers, finding mollusks and medicinal plants by the pawful.

"Have you ever seen an Elf?" Shonai asked around dusk.

"Just in books," Zoltaure answered, drying himself in the late day sun.

"I'll be able to sell more as an Elf so I suppose I'll have to morph here." She morphed into a beautiful Duah maiden. Rip was somewhat taken aback by her new appearance. Only her familiar smell kept him from bolting.

—YOU?—

"Aye, it's me. Climb onto my shoulders and don't come down until we leave the city.

Rip leapt onto her shoulders.

"Let's go, the city's just around that bend." They each grabbed the heavy canvas full of fish and walked it to the gate of Brayl. Directly across from the river was the Vull'Kra city of D'ran. A plethora of ships sailed in and out of the harbors, trading everything under the sun.

Shonai and Zoltaure walked to the fish market on the docks. Thousands of Duah were out and about. Shonai pulled the Duah language, most of which she already knew, from the minds of every Elf passing her by. She could only read surface thoughts so it took her awhile. She instructed Zoltaure to be on his guard and follow her lead, for he had never been around surface people before.

She had never had to buy anything before so she stole bargaining skills from a few of the most successful merchants.

They stopped at a large merchant's cart.

"Sir, would you be interested in buying our catch?" she asked.

"That all depends on what's in it, when you caught it and what you're selling it for."

"I believe I have satisfactory answers for all of the above," Shonai said, smiling prettily.

After an intense half a glass of bargaining, Shonai had gained enough to buy two fine horses *and* an expensive weapon for Zoltaure, due largely to the medicinal plants Rip had found. They left the fish market and entered the walled city.

They arrived at the market proper around sunset. Shonai wasted no time buying two stout mares, black in color and shiny of mane. Next, they stopped at a small shop called 'Naritems.' Naritem was a famous weapons' maker, an older Elven woman with white hair but still attractive. On her walls hung a number of blades and bows.

Zoltaure studied them with interest, sometimes lifting them to feel their balance. Naritem watched him thoughtfully before going into a backroom. A few moments later, she emerged with a long, green box. She opened it to reveal two beautifully crafted steel tsai.

The tsai were as long as Zoltaure's arm and had two shorter blades forming the hilt to make a trident-like sword. Zoltaure lifted them reverently. There was nothing greater in all the realms than hefting a weapon that was made for only one.

"They're perfect," he breathed.

"Aye," Naritem agreed, "your kind have always preferred the tsai when on land. Javelins are too unwieldy in close quarters. Not for you though," she said to Shonai. "You still prefer the javelin."

"Aye." Zoltaure agreed, without thinking.

"Wait," Shonai leaned forward, "you said *our* kind. *My* kind is *your* kind."

"Ha!" Naritem laughed. "Not unless Elves can breathe underwater, your Highness!"

"What?" Shonai checked her disguise. No, she still wore the Elf form, the seashells absorbed into her gauntlet.

"No need to check yourself, your disguise is just fine. Though, I am curious how you managed to morph. I didn't think Orcans could accomplish that.

"But how...?" Shonai started to ask.

"I noticed something odd about you when you entered, a feeling of familiarity. It took me a few moments to place it. You see, I was only twelve the last time I felt it. I was with my father, Joomus, who was also a weapons' maker. He had just finished his *Lokn'Shaita*, or life piece. His was a golden gauntlet with a matching golden shafted javelin. He inscribed them with the *Unity* Rune, letting both pieces mold into one, though they were separate until the owner wore the gauntlet.

"After it was completed, he set out for the Western Isles, but he was ambushed by a band of Driss. During his subsequent capture, he managed to put the gauntlet on his arm but it would not accept the javelin into it as he was not its predestined owner. So, sadly he was forced to throw it into a lake, though we never knew which one.

"The Driss took him, along with a few score of others onto their ship to be sold into slavery. In those days, it was commonplace. Somehow, their ship never reached its destination. When I heard that you had been named Shonai Golden Gauntlet, I knew."

"But how, if I hadn't even been born yet, could I be its rightful owner?" Shonai asked.

"You aren't."

"But it bonded itself to me. It won't come off."

"There must be enough similarities in your blood to make it work."

"Similarities to who?"

"Your father. It was meant to be given to him at birth. Tell me, you haven't by any chance found the javelin, have you?" Naritem asked. In answer, Shonai shifted back to her natural Orcan form and let the javelin leak sinuously from the gauntlet, forming perfectly in her hand.

"I found it in a pond not thirty miles from here."

"Amazing. The gauntlet led you to its counterpart."

"I highly doubt it, Naritem. I'm actually off on a calling of a higher sort. To Mist Peak."

"Ah, but make no mistake, young lady, it was the gauntlet drawing you. Perhaps the Peak is just where you are destined to go with it."

"Perhaps." Shonai said, uncomfortable with this strange Duah's insight. Bloody Elves were always showing off their vaunted intuition. It was very disconcerting since they were almost always right.

"I see great things in your future, Princess. I am not a seer, if that's what you were wondering. I merely sense powerful auras such as yours. You have a presence I have not felt in one since the Great War."

Shonai stammered her thoughts. "What do we owe you for the tsai? I'm not sure if we have enough. Horses are nearly as expensive as a marlin once autumn draws to a close."

"It was worth it to see my father's *Lokn'Shaita* again."

"Naritem, I don't think I could—"

Zoltaure interrupted. "You're a Princess. You can pay her a thousand times over for them when you return to Sha'na. Just accept the offer and thank her, Your Majesty," he added as a hasty afterthought.

"Aye, you're right. I'm sorry Naritem, thank you for your help and thank you to your father's spirit for the gauntlet. I will thank him personally when I return home. His grave is not far from there."

"Princess?" Naritem asked hesitantly, suddenly timid. "When you return to Sha'na, could you have my father's remains sent to me for a proper Elven Treegiving?"

"I will."

CHAPTER 23
IMMORTAL

he next day started out much the same had the previous two, with Penn at the door at sunrise. Danken was up as usual and T'riel had decided to drag herself out of bed to accompany him today. She buzzed excitedly in his ear, spouting nonsensical Pixian songs as Penn led them out of the castle. They arrived at a huge meadow in the center of the crater, lush green punctuated by symmetrical patches of yellow daisies.

"As insane as it sounds, you have completed the most difficult stages of your training in two days. Today, you will learn War Spells. Once you have mastered one, you will be able to master the rest quickly. They are all based on weather, which you can already manipulate. The spell names are simple, elements and such.

"As you have already learned *Breezesummon, Gale* will be the easiest to master, so we'll start with it. This is simple spells on a greater level, thus, requiring more power, so if you feel drained, do not hesitate to stop and eat or drink. Any questions?" Penn finished.

"No, I'm ready," Danken answered.

"Splendid, let's begin." Penn raised his hands in front of him. "To summon *Gale*, you must begin as you would with *Breezesummon*. Once you have that, you must concentrate on bringing hot air from above down and cold air from below up until they meet. This will cause the air to begin to funnel. Instead of allowing it to do so, however, you must direct it towards a certain point. Thus, creating a highly focused gust of wind." As Penn talked, Danken acted. He focused on a small sapling a few hundred yards in the distance.

With a howling that threatened to deafen them, the wind uprooted the tree and whipped it into the horizon.

"Astounding, Sariksen. I wasn't even done explaining. It seems that you don't need instruction so much as the knowledge that what you are attempting is possible. I fear if I were to tell you that you could touch the sun you would lasso it in and burn us all up in the process. So, thinking along these lines, I will simply *tell* you your next spell."

"Boy's head is getting too big," T'riel chirped in his ear. "Soon he will fall over from its weight."

"It's not my fault. Would you rather me play dumb?" Danken retorted.

"Would *rather* have Boy stop talking and start spellcasting. No more wasting this Pixie's time! Hurry, Great Stupid Cat needs bath tonight and One must help Little Elf Girl."

"You're infuriating," Danken said, pinching the bridge of his nose.

"Shh, Mage speaks."

"Ah, just so," Penn said with a raised eyebrow, having heard only Danken's side of the conversation. "Right. As I was saying, the next spell is *Stormcell*. Lightning, thunder, rain, hail, the whole package." He clapped his hands once. "Let's see it."

Danken pushed up his sleeves and raised them towards the cloudless sky. He used *Breezesummon* to push the nearest storm clouds towards him, though this took awhile. Next, he began pulling the moisture from the ground surrounding him. This, combined with the storm clouds rolling in over the rim of the peak, made a hard black, ominous cloud form directly above him. He charged it with as much electricity as he could, causing a huge thunderclap to sound as a dozen bolts of lightning lit up the already bright sky.

Soon after, hail the size of marbles began falling all around them, though none landed within a small radius of them. As soon as it started, the storm subsided, once again returning to a cloudless blue sky. Penn was shaking his head.

"It took me over a hundred years to create a *Stormcell* spell as powerful as that."

"See?" T'riel pinched Danken's ear.

"Good," Penn said. "Next, you have learned *Magefire* and *Magefreeze* using your body's resources. Now, use the resources of the land around you. Create a wall of ice around us and a wall of fire around that. These are appropriately called *Firewall* and *Icewall*." Danken nodded, but first gorged himself on a few sandwiches and a pint of water.

He concentrated on the spells a few moments before enacting them. First, he put up a shaky, misshapen *Icewall*, which he quickly reinforced. Then he created the *Firewall* around that, using his innate blue *Magefire* to ignite the suddenly dry and brittle grass around it. When the fire had burned the ice, he snuffed it, leaving a perfect circle of burned grass in an otherwise serene landscape.

Penn used *Faunagrow* to reseed and regrow the grass and the displaced sapling, leaving no visible trace of the trauma the landscape had endured.

"Excellent. Last, but not least, we will learn *Elementals*. There are four, *Earth, Air, Fire* and *Water*. These are the most powerful spells at our command, and the hardest to control."

"*Elementals?* Are they alive?" Danken asked.

"In a sense. They are primal beings. You have already mastered their environs. Now you must speak to them, ask them to form at your command." Penn replied. Danken did so and spent the better part of the afternoon communicating with the elements. Penn watched patiently, his eyes never leaving Danken. T'riel had gone off to help Dot give Shard his bath, a task which would take nearly as much effort as Danken himself was spending.

Finally, Danken stood back to inspect his efforts. In front of him was a huge, bipedal creature constructed of boulders and soil with fingers the size of Danken's forearm. Next to it were a dozen firedrakes, roughly the size of his palm each and a liquid form of a female Sendar. Last was a shimmering creature of the same form hovering in the air.

Danken dismissed them with this thanks and turned to face Penn, who was smiling broadly.

"That is all for today, Danken. You have once again surprised your teacher with your power. There is still plenty of daylight left for you to enjoy."

"Thank you, Penn." Danken nodded and walked off toward the city. When he came to the edge, he realized he had no desire for company and set our towards Gellar's Falls.

When he reached them, he found himself on the edge of the craters' walls staring out at the vastness of Sendar. From here, he could see the statue of Thor that rose into the sky above the falls of Falgwyn, though they were over eight days on horseback away. He continued to stare out over the land until the sun began its descent below the horizon.

He let his mind wander and predictably it drifted towards thoughts of Wytchyn. He remembered her bright purple eyes that could discern his most hidden thoughts. She had always been able to read people like an open book. He smiled as he recalled the time they had been chased through the forest by an old steader they had stolen blackberries from. They had eaten most and then begun laughingly smearing them in each other's faces. So many other memories flashing through his thoughts.

He sometimes felt as if he could feel her in the back of his mind. Sometimes happy, sometimes sad but always so determined. Though he could not explain it, he knew her to be alive and well, though where only the Gods truly knew. Part of being a twin, he guessed. He replayed the day she had been lost like a constant whip against his bare back, mercilessly thrashing him time and time again. He would find her, he vowed for the millionth time, once again realizing that his fists were balled tightly, making his knuckles white and his teeth clenched together painfully. He tried to calm down.

That thought process eventually brought him to Amaria. So perfect, so in love with him. Did he deserve her? She had not thought twice about throwing her life and that of her only sibling away just to save him from a *possible* problem in the future. It was bloody insane. What had he gotten her into? He was danger incarnate and she was planted firmly in front of him, determined to save him from the world. She was perfect, everything he had always wished for and now that he had her he questioned himself. Who did he think he was? He was bloody lucky to have her and he would not throw her love aside like a weaker man would have done in his place. He couldn't protect everybody from everything.

And yet, how could he tell her that he had been and always would be head over heels in love with Tersandi, the beautiful Valkyrie who had saved his life and watched over Wytchyn. His love would never be reciprocated, but could he love two women? How ironic that the one woman who loved him beyond measure he was unsure of and the other did not even remember him, yet she was what had filled his thoughts since he had been a boy. He sighed, having made no decision.

His legs grew tired and he decided to sit. He took the weapon Isahagilaz had given to him and laid it on the ground, recalling the great Dragon's words. The weapon's true use had not been discovered, nor had its name. Unthinkingly, he shot a probing bolt of blue into it. Instantly, it flared and a concentrated bolt of blue fire formed on top of the weapon.

Danken picked up the weapon so that it rested parallel with his wrist. In this position, it resembled nothing so much as an axe-shaped crossbow. Danken leveled it and aimed it at a slab of rock rising from the water. Somehow it focused his *Magefire* and fired it into the rock, which blew apart as if a Giant had hit it with a sledgehammer.

As if the weapon had spoken to him, he knew its name. *F'laare*, a psionic crossbow. He aimed for another rock twice as far away and once again disintegrated it with uncanny accuracy. He marveled at its potential power as he trekked back to the castle. He arrived long after dark and retired immediately to his bed.

"Today I will teach you the only other thing you can learn without becoming a Mage proper." Sembalo told him as they surveyed the landscape from the parapets of the castle.

"Only one spell?"

"Aye, though it is the hardest and most time consuming. It is the spell *Avian*. You will find a suitable candidate and draw it to you. Once you have accomplished this, you must map out its every inner and outer feature. After you have done this, you will morph yourself into this creature, becoming one with it. Your thoughts and memories will combine and you must assert your will over that of the raptor.

"Most Magi choose the falcon as it is the swiftest raptor, yet one of the fiercest as well. Sorcerers choose black owls for their craftiness, ferocity and color. Your choice will be your own. Choose wisely though, for it can never be revoked." Sembalo instructed before he turned and disappeared back into the castle, leaving Danken alone.

There he waited throughout the day, eyes fixed on the sky. He spotted a few ravens and a single falcon but none called to him. He didn't grow discouraged, however, merely sat and watched. As night fell, his eyes grew weary and he decided to call it a day. Danken returned to his room with a sense of failure, yet he knew that there was nothing he could have done.

Tired as he was, sleep did not come and he laid awake with his restless thoughts. Around dawn, he heard a screech that jolted him from his quasi-rest. Danken ran out onto the balcony and peered up at the sky. There, a tiny dot on the multicolored background was what he'd been waiting for. He grabbed *F'laare* and focused before letting a harmless net of energy soar off into space. It would ensnare the bird and he would reel it in.

After a tense quarter-glass, Danken saw the bird in all its glory as it landed majestically on the rail of the balcony. It was a proud, defiant and utterly gargantuan bald eagle, the king of the skies. Its fiery golden eyes bored into him as he increased his energies inside of it.

He mapped the eagle's features for the entire morning before he felt comfortable enough to begin the morph. As he did, something unexpected happened. The eagle began radiating and slowly dissipated into his hands. He could feel it merging with him. At last there was nothing there. Danken quickly wrested the control from the proud raptor and felt his physical features begin to melt into that of the eagle's. He leapt from the balcony to survey the land in his new form.

Shonai and Zoltaure exited the mountains around midmorning. Mist Peak rose up before them like a wall of hope, though it was still half a day's travel away. The sunlight of the open grasslands was a welcome change from the shade of the heavily forested mountains. The season was turning and all additional warmth was appreciated. Zoltaure had mastered horseback surprisingly quickly, Shonai thought.

They made little conversation throughout their journey. Shonai's feeling, drawing her toward the mountain grew stronger. Zoltaure had become paranoid, often stopping to survey their surroundings. His humor and childish wonder at the surface and all of its inhabitants seemed to have disappeared. He remained mum when she asked him of it, though she could tell he suspected something. Rip, however, was unconcerned and playful as always, often romping off into a small pond or stream to frolic. Shonai forced a smile at his antics. Their mounts seemed uneasy, taking their cues from their increasingly nervous riders.

Towards the end of the day, they stopped at a stream. Zoltaure searched the high brush around them for signs of danger. Something was wrong. The air seemed to thicken. Suddenly he drew his tsai. Their ring filled the meadow. Shonai caught a green reflection in the water exactly like that of the dream she had had in Keran's household. She whirled around. Two score Goblins surrounded them. Zoltaure was already fearlessly moving into position.

The gauntlet released the javelin which Shonai twirled with skill. The Goblins released a volley of arrows. Shonai and Zoltaure cut many of them out of the sky as another volley took its place, this time made of yellow fire. Some found their mark. The Goblins closed for battle, their serrated blades gleaming dully in the afternoon sun.

Shonai glanced at Zoltaure who recklessly charged the oncoming horde. He had not learned the proper techniques of the tsai yet but adapted quickly. The sounds of metal on metal rang out as the battle was met. Zoltaure roared a defiant growl into the air. The number of Goblins was just too many and Zoltaure's tsai became sluggish as exhaustion and numerous cuts and burns took their toll. Shonai battled to protect him, though an arrow in her chest sapped her strength.

Just as she felt herself fading away, a piercing screech tore through the meadow and a giant bald eagle swooped down. Its razor sharp talons ripped the heads off of the two nearest Goblins. As it landed, it became a white-robed Sendar, his long black hair and silver bangs twirling as he swung a great shining blade about effortlessly. His metal crossbow fired off two quick bolts of flaming blue, disintegrating an untold number of Goblins.

The Sendar's blue eyes flared with rage as his magnificent sword sundered heads from torsos left and right. A flaming wall of fire engulfed one group of Goblins while another was frozen by a thick wall of ice, which he pulverized with another bolt from his crossbow.

In bare moments, he stood alone over the meadow littered with Goblin corpses. Glancing at Zoltaure, he called forth a shimmering creature that floated on thin air. Rather, that *was* air.

"Take him to the castle as fast as possible," the Sendar commanded. Zoltaure was immediately swept away at a tremendous speed towards the peak. Next the Sendar focused his burning eyes on Shonai. Her vision was clouded with pain, yet she saw his face clearly. The feeling pulling her toward the mountain dissipated as she locked eyes with him.

He placed his hands on her chest and concentrated on pulling the arrow out without causing further damage. Once he had completed this, he began fusing the wounds together by creating new cells with his energy. He repeated this process on the many other wounds and burns she had suffered, trying his best to leave no scars. All the while, Shonai's purple eyes never left his ruggedly-handsome face. She could tell he felt every twinge of her pain acutely within him and that it was almost too much to bear. Doggedly the Sendar pushed on until neither was sure what was her and what was him.

When Shonai was healed, she fell into a restful sleep, the night sky watching over her. Danken felt like he hadn't eaten in a month. He was just about to pick the sleeping Orcan woman up when a huge flame of blue fire hit him from the erupting ground like a stone wall. He felt his whole body go rigid as more strands of fire engulfed him, filling him with untold amounts of power. Trees cracked and fell and huge chunks of dirt and rock spewed from the ground hundreds of feet into the sky.

With a scream that would curdle the blood of a Giant, Danken dropped to his knees, the fire conspicuously gone. He panted like he had just come up from the depths of the sea. Spots chased each other in his vision as he struggled to retain consciousness. An otter hesitantly made its way out of the river and looked into the Orcan woman's face. It turned its attention to Danken next, touching his hand with its nose.

–FRIEND?–

"Aye," Danken nodded, confused by the creature. It nodded its head towards Shonai.

–MY FRIEND–

"She is your friend?" Danken asked. "I'm guessing you'll be wanting to come with her then when I take her to the peak?"

–SLEEP–

"What? Sleep?" Danken asked. "I'm not going to sleep. I'm taking her to..." he passed out in mid-sentence, coming to a none too gentle landing beside the Orcan. The otter stood on its haunches and watched for danger while the two slumbered.

Danken awoke slowly, searching for the Orcan next to him, only to find the smiling faces of Dot and Maple. A wet sandpaper tongue licked his face, showing him that Shard, too, was there. A golden blur and the light touch on the tip of his nose revealed T'riel, who had her hands on her hips.

"Boy is pushing his luck. Always getting into trouble when One is not there to protect him," she sniffed indignantly.

"It's nice to see you too, T'riel." Dot leapt in the bed and planted a wet kiss on Danken's cheek. "And you as well, mistress Windsong. Perhaps you, too, would like to have battled the evil Goblins with me?" She nodded, pretending to swordfight with Shard, who nearly knocked her over with his tongue.

"We missed you, Danken," Maple said softly, a tear in her eye. "We weren't sure what had happened when they brought you in."

"Who?"

"The Mistgarde. They saw the fire and heard a battle. When they arrived, you were sleeping next to the Orcan Princess."

"Princess?" Danken asked, wide eyed.

"Aye, of Orcana. She is Shonai Golden Gauntlet."

"Well, I know how to pick 'em, don't I?" he laughed.

"Aye," Maple answered. She rose and kissed him softly on the forehead.

Danken grinned. "I'm going to have to get knocked unconscious more often."

"Hmm," T'riel scoffed. "Next time, this Pixie will knock boy unconscious for fighting without One."

"Aye, I'm sure you will." Danken laughed. Maple left to gather the other Magi. She returned soon after with them along with Jet, Arn, Tae, Valshk and Swifteye.

"Good to see you awake, Sariksen," Sembalo said for them all.

"Thank you. How is she?"

"Doing well, thanks to you," Urishen answered.

"And the other one, the Orcan man?"

"Not as well, I'm afraid. He was poisoned." Penn answered. "By the time the *Elemental* got him here, it was nearly too late. I did the best I could but he's still in a coma. No magic but his own can bring him out of that."

"I wasn't even sure if he was alive when I found him," Danken said. "I sent him to you because somehow I knew I could only heal one of them and she looked like she had the best chance."

"Aye, and a good choice, too," Kai piped in. "So, how does it feel to be immortal?"

"I honestly don't feel any different," Danken mused thoughtfully.

"I'm sure that'll change when you decide to go into battle again by yourself against forty Goblins and one stabs you," Kai joked. "You can watch it heal in front of your eyes, though it hurts like Hela's Freezing Sword, I must say."

"I'll keep that in mind," Danken grimaced. "Speaking of hurting, I never thought healing someone would hurt so much."

"Serves you right," Jet grumbled. "Always stealing all of the flarin' action."

"Aye," Tae seconded.

"That's because you are taking their wounds into your body," Sembalo said, helping Danken as he rolled out of bed. "So, I hear you chose the form of a bald eagle."

"Aye. It seemed the right choice. When can I see the Princess?"

"How are you feeling?"

"Good, like I just woke up from a long nap."

"You can see her now, she's already awake, though not feeling nearly as well as you." Sembalo ushered him out of his room and down the staircase to a room adjacent to Swifteye's. There, propped up on a pillow, was Shonai. She had been bathed and garbed in clean clothes. Her coal black hair shone and her purple eyes had a radiant glow to them he hadn't noticed before. She was startlingly beautiful and Danken had to try hard to keep from staring.

He failed miserably when she looked up at him. Both stared at each other until Sembalo cleared his throat loudly.

"Danken, this is Shonai Golden Gauntlet, Princess of Orcana. Princess, this is Danken Sariksen, Fifth of Magi," he introduced them.

"Your hair," Shonai commented, and only then did Danken realize that it was all sparkling white.

"It comes with the territory, I'm told," he said. "I'm glad to see that you are all right, Princess."

"You saved my life, Danken Sariksen. Without you we would have been left for the Goblins to dispose of."

"You seemed to have had the fight pretty well in hand when I arrived. I merely gave you a breather," Danken replied, avoiding her gaze.

"Ha! You killed over *half* of them in mere moments! Not to mention saving both of our lives!"

"You are a Princess, you cannot be expected to be trained in battle as I have been. Though, the javelin that is part of your gauntlet graces you quite well. You companion wields his tsai admirably. You could hardly have done better than to kill over a dozen before I arrived."

"Zoltaure," she sighed, "Sembalo tells me he is in a coma, had it not been for you, he would be dead. Tell me, what was it you called to carry him away to safety?"

"An *Elemental*."

"It was like an Autumn breeze come to whisk him away to safety."

"If the two of you young warriors will excuse me, I have a prior engagement. It is good to see the two of you in health." Sembalo made his excuses as he retreated out the door.

"He sure has refined the dignified exit over a thousand years, hasn't he?" Danken smiled. Shonai laughed, a beautiful sound.

"When I saw you morph from the eagle and decimate the Goblins, I felt sure you were Fate come to collect my soul after one battle too many. I have cheated Death twice now, and I have come to realize that you *are* Fate. My fate. I was drawn here from the sea by some unknown force. When I saw you, when you touched me, I knew that you were the one who had called me."

"I'm sorry, I don't know what..." Danken started.

"Not called me consciously. Your presence drew me to you."

"Well, I hope it was worth getting ambushed by a rogue band of Goblins," Danken quipped, with a raised eyebrow.

"Aye," she said, locking eyes with him again. "I believe it was." They spent the rest of the day talking like old friends until Shonai couldn't keep her eyes open any longer. Danken tucked her in and quietly let himself out. He found Sembalo in the hallway observing a painting next to Sarik's. When he reached him, his jaw dropped.

"Quite accurate, don't you think?" Sembalo mused, never taking his eyes off of the painting. Danken didn't either, for he was staring into a perfect likeness of himself.

"When did this get here?"

"The instant you became a Mage by saving the Princess."

"But how?"

"Magic. How else?" Sembalo chuckled. He beckoned Danken to follow him. Heading out of the castle, Danken followed him to a clearing on the edge of the crater. Sembalo stopped suddenly, the moonlight glimmering off of his hair.

"What are we doing out here?" Danken asked.

"Think of someplace you wish to go that you've seen before."

"All right," Danken said hesitantly.

"Now imagine yourself there."

"All right."

"What are you doing there?"

"I am paying my respects to my mother's final resting place."

"Now imagine the distance between here and there as a length of rope."

"All right," Danken said, eyes squinted in concentration.

"Now make the rope touch, here and there," Sembalo instructed. As he did so, a circular blue disk like a thin sheet of water tall enough for a man to walk through appeared in front of him. Unthinkingly, he walked through it only to find himself in the field outside of his old stead. He had expected to find himself wet but was not, and turned to find the portal gone. In its place stood two young Sendar, a man and a woman, one of whom Danken recognized as Henrik Bjornsen, Kierna's younger brother, his unruly red hair flailing about in the light breeze.

"Magus." Both bowed low. Danken realized that Bjorn had given Danken's stead to his son.

"Henrik?" Danken asked. "Why do you bow to me?"

"Danken? It *is* you." Henrik spoke quietly, reverently. The young woman remained silent, staring wide-eyed at him.

"Aye," Danken answered, confused.

"You are a Mage. Your position demands our subservience."

"Subservience?" Danken scoffed. "I am the same man who left this village two months ago. I don't even look any different. Save for a few strands of hair, maybe," he amended.

"Aye, but now you have the power that bonds us to you. We can feel you when you are near, like a beacon of hope. Your exploits have spread like wildfire throughout the realms. All in the land know of your vengeance and righteousness. All in this town have been sacrificing to the Gods daily for your forgiveness. They feel ashamed for the way you and your family were treated. We just couldn't believe you were a Mage."

"You knew of my father. Why did none feel ashamed eighteen years ago?"

"None believed it could have been your father. We are but peasants, please, forgive us. We were blind to what was right in front of us."

"Your humbleness does not do you justice. If you wish forgiveness, you must atone for your actions. Not to me or my family, but to yourselves and to the Gods. When comes the time to fight, remember who it is that leads you into battle. You must forgive yourselves. To be tricked by a Sorcerer, is to fail in your duty to your people. There are no excuses. Your will cannot be broken if you pride yourself on it and take care to strengthen it," Danken finished. With a prayer to the Gods to watch after his mother's soul, he made to open the portal again but the Sigil stopped him.

The familiar feeling of temperature rapidly dropping and the frozen looks on Henrik and his wife's faces preceded the staggering power of Sanngetal's arrival. Danken turned slowly around and found himself staring at a barrel chest. He wasn't surprised to find that Sanngetal stood nearly a head and shoulders higher than him, nor was he to see two behemoth ravens glaring at him, one from either shoulder.

"A valiant speech you gave just now. I'm impressed, I expected spite," the breathtaking voice said.

"Ignorance isn't well combated with ignorance. Or the edge of a blade, for that matter," Danken said quietly, finding it hard to keep eye contact with the being. So much knowledge and power was stored there that it threatened to draw him in and never let him go.

"Spoken like a true leader. You learn quickly, I am pleased." Sanngetal observed him with his all-knowing one eye for several moments, then continued as if he had never stopped speaking. "Aye, very pleased. But a great decision looms ever nearer for you, young Magus, and one you will never be able to recant.

"Choose one way and you may feel gratification but it will ultimately prove wrong. Choose the other and you will pay a heavy price but it will be worth it in the end."

"You speak in riddles of the future, why not just tell me which is correct?"

"Would you have your choices dictated to you? Would it matter? Your emotions are your power, Magus, but they are also your weakness. You must learn to control them or they will control you." The being disappeared without warning and time started.

"Wait!" Danken yelled, reaching his hand out vainly and looking frantically around. He saw Henrik and his wife looking at him oddly.

"Magus? Are you all right?" Henrik asked.

"Aye, I'm fine. Just having a conversation with someone is all," Danken said distractedly. "Tell your father that Kierna was well when I last saw her but that she chose to go her own way awhile back. I know not where she went after."

"Can we get you anything?" Henrik's wife asked.

"No, thank you, I have to go," Danken said. Putting Sanngetal out of his head, he opened the portal and stepped through with haste, leaving the two Sendar in shocked silence.

CHAPTER 24
THE BURDEN OF POWER

anaia blew a thin layer of dust from a heavy leather-bound book. The tiny motes created a spectrum in the magical green candlelight. Using a fine-tipped brush, she carefully finished dusting it, before using a special oil to return the binding back to its original luster. Once a year she repeated this process with the over four thousand volumes in Mist Peak's library, and she had been here for a week before completing it. It was the largest in the realms, composed of everything from ancient spells to cooking recipes to histories.

She tucked her long, pale blond and green flecked hair behind her pointed ears. Her green eyes radiated like those of all her race as did her finely sculpted features. She was a young adult, one hundred eighty three and carried her attractiveness modestly, unlike most Elves.

She had risen quickly to head librarian with her wits, organizational skills and love for books. Most Duah preferred the moonlit forest, but she was at home in the catacombs among her books. She had read each one cover to cover twice or more. There was virtually nothing she didn't know about any of them.

She dusted the last book and placed it back on the shelf. Lanaia retraced her steps through the narrow, shelf-walled corridors. She reached the exit, snuffing the candles with a thought on her way out.

As always upon leaving the dim library, protected by its numerous preservation spells, the sunlight caused her to squint though it was nearly dusk. The fresh air assailed her nostrils, forcing a thousand new smells into her brain. Lanaia made her way along the sparsely populated streets of the city until she reached her cozy residence at the end of a well-lit street. The sun radiated a purple and orange against the sky as it descended behind the wall of the crater.

Her house, like most Elven houses, was made out of the magically-shaped roots of a giant Baobab tree. Only her presence could entice the living tree to open its hidden entrance.

Or so she had thought.

Hrafna emerged from the shadows as Lanaia entered and locked her elbow around the Elf's neck. Lanaia struggled feebly, but Hrafna's vicious grip never loosened. The blood began to drain from Lanaia's face, leaving her pale. Her kicking faded slowly, then ceased altogether. Hrafna laid the unconscious Elf out on the floor. The Mai'Lang woman pulled a black crystal out of her dress, dangling it from a golden chain in front of the Elf's face. Prying open one of Lanaia's eyes, Hrafna began to rhythmically swing the crystal white she chanted in a hypnotic cadence.

When she was sure all was as it should have been, Hrafna placed an ancient-looking scroll in Lanaia's limp grasp. The Mai'Lang sprinkled a black powder over both hand and scroll. A puff of red smoke followed by the smell of sulphur rose up. Hrafna knew her time was up. She leaned in until her black lips grazed Lanaia's pointed ear and whispered softly into it in Duah.

"You know what you should be doing. Why are you sitting around here? Find him. You must warn him."

With that, Hrafna rose to leave. She looked back to where two white wolves were bound on the floor beside their mistress. With a wave of her hand, the ropes began to dissolve. Hrafna morphed into her raven form before winging off into the sky. Perhaps she would see what her pretty Jet was doing.

Lanaia woke, her wolves licking her face. Her head felt as if it were about to split as she sat up. She must have hit her head on something when she had entered. She couldn't remember. Her wolves seemed agitated, so Lanaia released a spark of green into both to see what was wrong. She got back only distortion. It was odd, she thought, but she attributed it to their being cooped up alone for the past five days. She stood then, setting a scroll down on a table. She must have taken it from the library on accident, she thought.

Her wolves darted about restlessly. Lanaia decided to take them for a run around the crater as soon as they were fed. As they left the edges of the city and reached the crater wall, Lanaia felt a strong wave of power rush over her. She looked around immediately for the source and her eyes locked in on two sets of bright blue eyes flaring in the dark, not a hundred yards away. Her keen Elven starlight vision quickly picked out the forms of two white-robed young men she recognized instantly as Magi.

She had seen Magi before but the tall, well-built one with the long white hair looked unfamiliar.

"Good evening," spoke the slimmer Mage, whom she instantly recognized as Sembalo.

"Good evening," she replied, transfixed. "Forgive my intrusion into your studies."

"It's *dwei,* we were done for the day anyway," spoke the one she hadn't recognized.

"Forgive me, but I do not recognize you," Lanaia said to the Mage petting her wolves. He rose and held out his hand. It was surprisingly calloused, she noticed, and strong as iron.

"I am Danken Sariksen, Fifth of Magi," he answered easily. She stared at him, slack jawed.

"The son?"

"Excuse me?" Danken cocked his head.

"Of Sarik! You're the son of Sarik!" she exclaimed.

"Have you been living in a cave?" Sembalo asked, perplexed.

"Something like that. I am head librarian. I've been doing my yearly book restoring," she replied, still staring at Danken.

"Ah, of course!" Sembalo slapped his forehead. "Lanaia, isn't it?"

"Uh, aye, it is."

"Are you all right?" Danken asked.

"Oh, aye, I'm fine. It's just that seeing you just made something click in my head, I've been trying to figure out for years."

"And that is...?" Danken prompted.

"A scroll. Do you think I could stop at the castle to meet with you in a few turns of the glass?"

"Me?" Danken asked, looking at Sembalo, who shrugged.

"Aye. I just have to go back and retrieve the scroll."

"I don't see why not," Danken answered.

"Thank you. It will be worth your time, I promise." Lanaia bobbed her head before calling her wolves and sprinting off towards the library.

"Is she serious?" Danken asked.

"I would assume so," Sembalo mused. "She is the head librarian of Mist Peak for a reason. Perhaps she has information on your father."

Jet had explored every inch of the wondrous castle not warded with magical shields since his arrival. He had found a few items of interest, including one that had set his mind to furious calculation. It was a small asterite key inscribed with three lightning bolts formed into a triangle. He had found it among hundreds of other keys in a dusty glass case in some forgotten room. Jet rubbed it between his fingers constantly, feeling its familiar shape and texture. He knew this key and ironically it had unlocked his memory. A memory he had thought never to recover.

When Jet had been a very young boy, he and his parents had lived in the Myrkwood, a forest south of Dark Depth in Mai'Lang. Sunlight never penetrated its canopy and a constant fog made seeing past one's hand impossible. Their village had been built in the tree-tops, with walkways spanning between homes hundreds of feet in the air. This had been the home of the Stormdogs, a thieves' guild backed by a mercenary army. Outcasts from every nation and of every skill called this foreboding place home. Jet's father had been a soldier and his mother a healer.

For some reason Jet hadn't been able to figure out, they fled the Stormdogs one night. They had secured passage aboard a small skiff on the Mal River and landed on the Northern continent more than a month after leaving. Torvald had told Jet that the Stormdogs had betrayed them so he had taken the Key of Fog from them in retaliation. He had put the key around Jet's mother's neck, but something had gone wrong. Jet's eyes began to water at the painful memory.

A violent storm had kicked up as they attempted to cross the River Mist. Jet could still see his mother's face as she fell in, swept away by the raging current. Her black lips parted in terror, her white eyes wide and her red-palmed hand reaching out to Torvald for help, but it was too late. Jet started from the painful memory, sweat beaded on his forehead. He rushed into his room to stand in front of his mirror, flinging aside two porcelain flower vases that obscured his view. He didn't even register their loud shattering.

His long, raven black hair shined almost blue in the sunlight streaming through his window. His pale grey eyes scanned his perfect facial features, horrified at finding the high cheekbones and sharp jaw of a Mai'Lang mixed with the high brows and angular nose of a Sendar. His mother had been Mai'Lang. The Sendar woman he had called mother his whole life in Lok Tryst was his father's second wife. All of his brothers and sisters, blond-haired and blue-eyed, were only half related to him. Jet wanted to scream. As the memory flooded back to him, his knees buckled. He curled into a ball on the floor, sobs racking his body. His whole life had been a lie.

Awhile later Jet had regained control of himself and steeled his emotions once again. His course was determined. Danken would live or die no matter what he did and Hrafna's plans, well, he would deal with her when the time came. Packing a small bag, he made his way down to the treasury room. Two Mistgarde soldiers, one an Elf and the other a Sendar, guarded the vault. An old, wispy white haired man sat at a paper strewn desk, spectacles at the tip of his bulbous nose.

"May I help you, young man?" the old man asked.

"Aye. I require four hundred golds, unshaved please."

"On what authorization?"

"Danken's—Excuse me. Magus Sariksen's."

"You have his signature?"

"I will sign for it," Jet said calmly. The man eyed his hatchets.

"You are the one they call Bloodhatchet," he stated.

"Aye, I am."

"And you arrived with the Magus?"

"I did."

"Very well. On your oath, then."

"You have it," Jet lied.

The old man beckoned the two soldiers to stand aside and opened the thick round steel vault door. He returned with a bag and counted the gold into it. Jet signed for it and thanked the man before leaving.

He left the castle and headed for Gellar's Falls. After making sure no one was around, he turned into a giant raven and took to the air.

Danken found T'riel napping on the top of one of his bed posts when he returned. She woke sleepily but flew to perch on his shoulder nonetheless.

"Boy has been back to Pixian Forest!" she accused, her sharp sense of smell making her tiny nose twitch furiously.

"Only Lok Tryst," Danken smiled at her scowl.

"Without this Pixie?" she stamped her foot.

"Only for a moment."

"Boy has—" she gasped. "Boy has been talking to another Pixie!" she squealed angrily, a possessive look on her golden face.

"Aye but for good reason." Danken sought to reassure her but she would have none of it.

"This Pixie is not good enough for Boy any longer?"

"T'riel, I wouldn't do that," he laughed.

"Hmmph," she sniffed, turning her back on him, though still on his shoulder with her arms crossed tightly. Danken reached into his pocket and pulled out a miniature velvet box the size of the first knuckle of his thumb. He place it in front of her.

"What is this?" she asked haughtily, trying to keep the sudden excitement from her voice.

"Open it and find out," he told her.

She did so, at first as if she didn't care, but soon excitedly. Inside was a small golden bow with two quivers of twenty-seven golden arrows each.

"This is for this Pixie?" she asked, wide-eyed, awestruck.

"Aye, made by M'Zour, the best Pixian smith in the crater."

"Boy *does* love this Pixie!" she exclaimed, fiercely hugging his ear before lapsing into nonsensical Pixian gibberish that made his eardrums hurt.

"Aye. Now I must get ready to meet someone. Don't shoot anyone with that."

"Boy should talk," she said as she zoomed out of the room.

The red fire of the magically-lit torches cast their sinister glow over the vast interior of the harem. Its black walls and ceilings seemed to suck all hope from its forced occupants. Two black pillars rose from the cold floor to the ceiling six stories above, their sides studded with thick iron rings. On each of the rings were attached three chains ending in a neck shackle. Each shackle contained the neck of a naked woman, her mind obviously destroyed along with her freedom. All in all there were five dozen, some from every race, sitting on black and red silk pillows, their lifeless eyes dull and despairing.

A score of heavily-armed and capable Driss of the Red Scales observed them from the far side of the chamber, their slitted eyes dilating in the flickering red light. They were held in check only by the threat of the one who had called them here. The man with the power to destroy minds and lives if he wished to do so, which he often did. The Driss commander, a dangerous man of three hundred years, had witnessed the Sorcerer's power on more than one occasion and did not wish to be on the receiving end of it. Death was preferable.

The door behind them opened slowly, the air thickening around it to push it along its track. Four black cloaked figures glided in, their feet never touching the ground. Each looked barely old enough to drink mead, with raven hair and fiery red eyes. They sat down in a four-pointed circle just in front of the terrified Driss, their glowing eyes closing in concentration. A fifth cloaked figure entered soon after and sat down in the exact center of the circle.

His long black hair hung elegantly down to the middle of his back, its glossy texture reflecting red light. His high cheekbones and sharp eyebrows were set above thin, tight black lips with a red streak through the middle. His red eyes emanated an evil so vile, even the malevolent Driss were taken aback. The magnificent, magical sword he carried at his waist pulsed an angry red at the thought of so much innocent blood to be had this night. Dak'Verkat held his arms out, red palms up and called out to Surt in Langjian.

"Mighty God of the Fiery World, lend us your strength as we seek to unleash Chaos on those that defy you. We implore you to show us favor and block the Aesir from interfering as we destroy those that serve them." He turned to the other four Sorcerers in succession, checking their *Stadhas* and concentration.

One of the Driss let out a muffled sneeze, breaking the Sorcerer's concentration. He reached to his belt, lined with nine black and red fletched darts. They were magically enhanced weapons called *Prakras.* They could pick out a chosen target a mile or more away. When he threw them, they were charged with his *Serfire,* to disintegrate what they touched upon impact. Once dispatched, they would reappear in his belt by magical reclamation, along with the energies of the one they had destroyed.

So, with breathtaking speed, Dak'Verkat drew one and hurled it at the offending Driss. The snakeman had no time to move and pawed at the dart buried in his chest just before it dissipated him into red dust. The other Driss flinched but made no move to fight or flee. They stood transfixed as the Sorcerer raked them over with his fiery glare.

"I apologizze for sse sstupid oness lack of mannerss, Dak'Verkat," the Drissian Commander hissed, bowing low.

"Do not let it happen again."

"It vill not, Sser."

Dak'Verkat repeated his prayer and the other four joined in.

"Mighty Surt, lend us your fire to shroud these agents of Chaos in unbreakable cloth and skin. Aid them in their effort to further your cause and bring disorder to the Races of Light." They chorused in unison three times, their voices coming to crescendo upon the last deafening note.

The air in the room thickened, the pressure like a pair of giant hands crushing their unlucky victims. The whirling red light that came from the torches suddenly ceased, covering the room in oppressive darkness. Red crackling energy leapt from the fingertips of all five

Sorcerers to the center of the circle above Dak'Verkat. There it rose in a thin pillar to the ceiling before arching at its zenith. It came down in nineteen separate bands and collided with the frightened Driss.

A bright red flash temporarily illuminated the huge room, filling it with the heavy smell of brimstone and fear. In the ensuing silence, several of the enslaved women whimpered. One by one the torches sprang to life, once again lighting the room with their unholy light. The Driss looked around themselves shakily, unsure of what had happened, if they were still alive, which one was not, leaving eighteen.

"The weakest always die," Regan'Shune said, repeating a lesson Dak'Verkat had taught the young Sorcerer not long ago.

"Aye," Dak'Verkat agreed, pleased with his apprentice, Fourth of Sorcerers. "The spell will only allow a number divisible by three."

The Driss looked uneasily at their charred comrade.

"You know your mission," Dak'Verkat told them. "Serve me well and your rewards will be great. Fail me and you will wish you had died at the hands of the Northern weaklings."

"Ve undersstand, Sser," the commander said with another low bow.

"Good that you do."

"Any final instructions?" Regan'Shune asked.

"I have confidence in you."

The Sorcerers combined their magics once again and a red liquid portal sprung up in front of the now *Serfire*-shielded Driss. One by one they ran through it, blow guns at the ready. Their poison-tipped tails swung wildly just before they disappeared, giving them an added burst of speed. Regan'Shune followed behind them to ensure their success.

When they had all gone, Dak'Verkat instructed the other three to keep the portal open for their return. He walked past the cowering slaves as if they did not exist, sweeping out onto a beautiful black stone balcony. The full moon shone down on the dark forest that covered Isle Sin and the glassy black surface of Dark Depth. Dak'Verkat felt giddy with the plans he had worked on so long finally beginning to come to fruition. He flexed his newly regrown hand in excited anger.

With a laugh that would stir goose bumps from the hardest of men, Dak'Verkat silenced the chorus of insects on his dark island. The sound of sword play followed by the groans of the dying broke his reverie. He cocked his ear and was rewarded by the sound of a woman's bloodcurdling scream and the portal closing behind her. He returned to the harem to see his new guest. She was struggling with the six Driss that had made it back.

"Welcome to Isle Sin," he snarled at her just before Regan'Shune knocked her unconscious. "We've been expecting you."

Lanaia arrived later that night as Danken was getting dressed after his bath. She carried a scroll with her, yellowed parchment wrapped around two wooden rollers.

"Are you decent?" she asked, seeing Danken with no shirt on in the next room.

"Aye, I'll be out in a moment," he called.

"Where should I set my things?" she asked.

"Wherever you'd like, I'm not particular."

"Very well," she said to herself, setting the scroll on a long glass table. Danken came out shortly after, his damp hair hanging loosely over a thin white shirt. He looked tired but felt awake as ever after Lanaia's frantic imploring to meet him.

"So, you said something about a scroll?"

"Aye. This one in particular. I never understood it until I saw you. I believe it to be a prophecy of the future related to the Foretelling and I think you are its subject."

"Me? What makes you think so?"

"I'll show you." She opened the scroll and carefully laid it out on the table. Danken bent forward to read it.

Ere will come the time when darkness will flow like blood over the land, erasing new found peace. Through great tragedy, the Son of Sapphire will rise from the ashes of a loved one's death to lead the forces of Good against the overwhelming tide of Evil.

A band of great power and diversity will surround him: one who dodges the wind and one who vanishes with it. One who fights with gold and one who glows with it. One who heeds the call of destiny and one who discovers it.

A quest will they undertake in search of Emerald Ransom to be paid in the blood of its captor. The three Oracles of Fyrdn will guide them. They are Courage, Power and Wisdom, uncovered in the Hand of Silence, the Grasp of Ashen Gold and the Serpent's Maw.

In the process will he who has been chosen uncover his destiny as well as the truth about himself. He will come face to face with the Emerald betrayer, yet know it not. Will he stand alone against a palm stained horde and turn them to ash, after Quintets do battle?

"This is you," Lanaia whispered. "The rest has changed numerous times by magic, but you have remained."

"Aye, so it would seem, though there are many unanswered questions. Also it's twice now I've been called the Sapphire Son. I can't seem to remember where the other time was though. I don't even know what it means."

"I haven't figured it all out yet as most of it is in the future, but the Sapphire Son is the one who is supposed to bring the Gods back to the world. The Foretelling says it will be so. I believe you are he."

"Who are these people who should accompany me? And where is it I'm supposed to go?" Danken asked, wondering if it was all some sort of hoax. Surely he could not bring the Gods back to Midgarthe if they could not themselves...

"I know little more than that I am one of them."

"You?"

"Aye. I am 'the one who discovers destiny.'"

"That makes sense," Danken said, searching her pristine features and realizing how much she looked like his Amaria with her pale hair and skin, and her emerald green eyes—he caught his breath, his heart sinking to his feet. "No," he whispered. "The Sapphire Son."

"Danken, what is it? What's wrong?" Lanaia asked, concerned.

"Wait here, don't go *anywhere*." Danken ordered. He called up a portal and quickly stepped through it.

He appeared on the other side in the court of King Llethion in Wendall. It was in chaos, advisors, aides, soldiers and nobles ran to and fro. Most, if not all, stopped to gape at him as he closed the gate. The smell of Sorcerers magic and brimstone assailed his nostrils. Drissian and Elven bodies were scattered everywhere.

"What has happened here?" he asked a nobleman.

"Driss, Magus. They were everywhere. Everywhere and then nowhere."

"Where is the King?"

"I am here, Sariksen," a familiar voice called from behind him. Danken turned to see the King, dark circles under his puffy eyes. Andren lay on the floor, two Duah healers working furiously to stem the flow of blood from a bad gash on his leg. The Queen hovered over him fretting, her face blotchy red from crying.

"Where is Amaria?" Danken asked, on the verge of panic.

"She is gone, Danken. They took her. Somehow they appeared right in our midst and stole her, my beloved daughter." The King's voice broke. He absently scanned the bodies of Elven and Drissian dead.

"Where? Where did they go?"

"I don't know. They left a note behind, saying that if I ever wanted to see her again, I had to keep my forces out of the war. And now my dear Andren lies poisoned as well." The King broke into tears. Danken felt a cold stab of agony deep within himself. Amaria, who had loved him beyond all reasonable expectations, had put herself at odds with those who would harm him, without a thought for her own safety. He felt the guilt flooding through his veins like the most vile poison imaginable. And now those people had taken her to get at him. She was hurting because of him!

Pushing back the surge of bile in his throat, he forced himself to uncurl his fists, which had been balled so tightly that his nails had drawn blood in his palms. He tried to keep the growl out of his voice but it still came out, startling those within hearing distance.

"I will get her back, you have my word on it," he barked, pushing the healers aside and placing his hands on Andren's leg. With a flash of blinding blue, he forced his energies into the Prince, seeking out the poison the Drissian weapons had filled him with. He cried out at the tremendous pain he found there, but kept searching.

He found it making its way through the bloodstream towards the young Elf's heart. Evil looking black daggers destroyed the healthy, round red cells as they flowed past. Danken became a million wicked looking blue cells and began battling with the black daggers, destroying them mercilessly. They sought to avoid him in the mazelike capillaries but he relentlessly pursued them, disintegrating their weak defenses.

When the poison was no more, Danken healed the deep gash in the Prince's leg. He took the wound into himself, swooning at the burning agony. The fever that accompanied it was only narrowly countered by an internal blast of *Magefreeze*. He fell heavily on his rear, head spinning from the effort. The wound healed on his leg, itching fiercely, and the Prince sat up slowly as Danken stood.

The King thanked him and the Queen hugged him but their temporary joy was tempered by Amaria's kidnapping. Danken set his jaw and tried to rein in his maelstrom of emotions. Dak'Verkat had violated a pact between the Magi and Sorcerers older even than him. Ruling families of all Nations and peoples were to be left alone, thus minimizing the need for the two groups to battle.

A dedicated army of Elves or Goblins could kill a Sorcerer or Mage if they were willing to sustain hundreds, if not thousands of losses, but a Royal family had no chance. The effects would be catastrophic in an event such as this. The Sorcerers and Magi would surely come to blows. Danken checked his mounting rage. He opened a portal and turned to the King.

"Prepare your forces for war."

CHAPTER 25
THE BLADES CALLING

iding hard and sleeping little, Kierna and Corsha had reached the outskirts of Falgwyn in record time. The city's massive grey riverstone walls stretched for miles around the northern edge of Lok Fal, all the way up the canyon walls that bordered the thousand foot drop of Thor's Sacred Falls. In effect there were two cities, one below the falls and one on the mesa above, both dominated by the seven hundred foot tall marble statue of Thor, his mighty hammer, Mjolnir raised in triumph, lightning bolts arcing off in every direction as he straddled both huge rivers.

The Lower City gates were accentuated by two towers fully one hundred feet taller than the impressive battlements carved into large arches. Soldiers in shiny mail with purple, red and silver finery and well wrought but simple swords observed the midday throng of traffic. Kierna and Corsha elicited several sideways looks in their battered, bloody clothes with the two swords crossed on their backs atop horses that had seen far better days. The smooth riverstone streets were lined with houses of the same rock painted lively purples and reds on their tiled roofs and window shutters.

The people were working class and dressed in common wool or cotton threads cut for work, not show. The low rumble of the falls was at first distracting but soon became indistinguishable from the other sounds of the huge city. Shops with brightly colored awnings and multitudes of goods featured men and women in aprons shouting out their wares. The two women were so exhausted that they could not find a smile even for the street performers on nearly every corner. Their eyes were only on the magnificent cascade of the falls.

Wide paths had been blasted into the side of the sheer rock face to allow travel between the Upper and Lower Cities. A long arched walkway crossed the northern tip of the lake, its stone rails carved with intricate knot work and Dragons. At its middle, a stairway descended to a stone path that seemed to float on the water's surface and disappeared into the white-watered falls. A transparent archway left a perfect gateway in the falls, darkness visible beyond, into the very rock behind. This was the Spirit Hold, the home of the Spirit Blades.

At either side of the arched walkway stood two women wearing white blouses tight in the torso and very wide in the sleeves and white pants similarly tight in the hips and wider than their white leather boots at the ankle, cutting off less than an inch from the ground. The material was some shiny, sturdy substance neither had ever seen. At the center of their breasts was a blue *Valknut,* three triangles knotted together, the symbol of Odin. Each woman wore her hair with four braids on either side of her head with an impossibly detailed larger braid in the back. Two identical swords were crossed on each woman's back, a white cowl tucked between the hilts.

They stood silent, immobile, eyes forward with their hands clasped behind them, though Kierna doubted they missed anything. She and Corsha dismounted as they reached the walkway and came to stand before the two women. One of the women, an Elf, stepped forward and eyed the bedraggled women with hard, intelligent eyes.

"What do you seek, Sisters?" she asked.

"We seek our destiny," Kierna replied.

"Do you seek to know the Gods as you know yourself?"

"We do."

"You may enter, Sisters," she snapped her fingers and instantly two small girls with their hair in a single braid, wearing plain brown robes appeared and led their horses away. Another Sendar woman in a *gi,* as the white uniforms were called, appeared from the falls and led them in.

The sound of the water was deafening as they passed through the opaque archway into a gigantic entryway, its ceiling over five hundred feet above them. Walkways had been carved out of solid rock every fifteen feet all the way up, with numerous passageways shooting off further into the stone. Two spiral staircases, one on each side of the cavern wound their way to the top. The scene was bathed in the iridescent green shimmering light of sunrays filtering through the falls and torches shrouded in pale green frosted glass. Dozens of white garbed women bustled about as well as hundreds of young, brown robed girls.

They took one of the spiral staircases all the way to the top, their legs burning by the end. The Spirit Blade led them into a long, wide arched passageway that sloped gently upwards. At its end was another large circular cavern with smooth stone sides and a pale green pool in its exact center. Twelve impressive stone throne-like chairs ringed the far edge of the pool, each with a gold *Valknut* inlaid into the headrest. They were bade to wait. While they waited, a brown-robed girl brought them a filling but tasteless porridge and two steaming cups of tea which they consumed quickly.

A short while later, twelve older women of varied races wearing *gi's* but with gold stripes down each arm and leg took their places in the empty seats. The swords at their backs were identical. The women fixed their disconcertingly hard gazes on the weary Kierna and Corsha. A white-haired Sendar woman was the first to speak.

"You have news for us, do you not, children?"

"Aye," Kierna said, hiding her surprise and proceeded to tell them of the Blue Scales.

The women nodded and continued to gaze at them impassively, eliciting every scrap of information without uttering a single word. When she had finished, the women turned their gazes on Corsha who added her own perceptions.

"It seems," said a Vull'Kra woman with a grey-tinged green braid, "that we may have a serious problem on our hands should the Dragons turn their gazes towards Falgwyn."

"Scouts?" pondered a woman who appeared to be a Lanalf—or half Mai'Lang, half Elf. Her features were Duah but her lips and hair were black and her glowing green eyes had no pupil or iris.

"Aye, scouts should be dispatched this day," an ancient Duah agreed.

"And the Mistgarde notified as well," remarked a Haftroll with the features of a Sendar woman and the size, coloring and amber eyes of a Troll.

"Agreed we are then," the first Sendar woman declared. With a snap, two young women in *gi's* appeared from behind Kierna and

Corsha. The Sendar gave each their instructions before they were dismissed. The women turned their gazes back.

"You have the desire to become Spirit Blades?" an ancient Orcan asked.

"Aye."

"From what do you run?" another Elf asked.

"I run from nothing," Kierna replied quickly, checking her rising temper.

"We all run from something, child," the Lanalf said.

"I run from my heritage," Corsha said softly.

"Ah, a Bancrae you are," a dark haired Sendar commented, the word used to describe half Troll and half Elven people, literally meaning 'banished.'

"And you, child?" another white haired Orcan asked of Kierna.

"Love," Kierna whispered.

"The most powerful of reasons," the Vull'Kra said admiringly.

"The only one that can break the pull of the swords," a Sendar commented.

"Know this," the first Sendar said. "If you agree to the Testing, you must pass else you will die. Do you still wish to become Spirit Blades?"

"Aye," they chorused.

"Your hearts must be true to the Gods. If not, they will cease beating in your chests. To be a Spirit Blade requires dedicating your every waking moment to devotion. To be half sure will split you in two. Literally."

"We understand."

"Strip off your soiled clothes," the Sendar commanded and the two women quickly did so leaving even their swords on the ground. "When you are ready, dive in the pool." Kierna looked questioningly at Corsha who wore a grim look. Taking her hand, Kierna pulled the reluctant Troll into the pool.

The water was so cold Kierna couldn't understand how it was not frozen. She looked for Corsha but the Troll was nowhere to be seen. The surface was no longer there either, somehow covered in solid, smooth rock. The water seemed far darker than she remembered and soon only a tiny light far below her was visible. She checked her panic with a monumental effort. There was no way she could hold her breath long enough to reach the light but it seemed her only choice. The harder she swam, the further away the light got.

Her muscles burned with lack of oxygen and felt numb from the cold at the same time. She never gave up even as she exhaled in a cloud of bubbles. She breathed in what should have been icy water but instead found herself in a dimly lit, dry cavern breathing in stale air that smelled of manure. There was a tall metal grate at one end of the large circular room but aside from it, the walls were bare. She noticed several crevices in the wall, as wide as her palm and just as deep. This drew her attention to the ceiling thirty feet above, where several iron chains hung down, each with a ring on their end.

Her time to contemplate these matters was cut short when the grate opened noisily. She began to inch her way towards it when a loud snort from the darkness within stopped her cold. A low, throaty growl like that of a sabercat came from beyond the gate, followed by a narrowed pair of burning red eyes. These quickly materialized into a creature fully twice her height and five feet wide at the rippling shoulder. It had the head of a lion but pitch black on top of a Giant's body, armored with inch thick bone scales. Shaggy, black-haired legs ended in two-toed clawed feet as long as her arm. It was naked and its phallus erect. The creature was filthy beyond belief. Arms as big around as Kierna's waist ended in three-fingered hands with claws as long as her fingers, four spikes around each wrist and one protruding from each elbow and shoulder blade.

Eyes wide with fear, Kierna backed up until her naked back hit the cool stone. The smell of the creature was so overpowering she almost chose not to breathe. Its red eyes seemed to bore into her and she could feel their heat like a flame to her skin. One of her hands brushed a crevice in the wall. She pried her eyes from the beast long enough to survey the other crevices, and then she was using them as handholds, scrambling up the sheer wall.

The creature lunged for her but she had just gotten high enough to elude its grasp. The vibrations it caused when it slammed the wall caused one of her hands to slip. Kierna hung there precariously for a moment before getting her grip again and going higher up. The beast roared as it smashed into the wall repeatedly and the echo was enough to make Kierna wish she'd gone deaf. She reached the top and grabbed hold of one of the iron rings, swinging from one to the next like an acrobat. Adrenaline and fear gave her strength she had never had before. Her mind was sharp as a razor.

When Kierna had positioned herself directly over the leaping, flailing and roaring creature, she shimmied up the chain so she could touch the ceiling, where it was connected by a sharp iron hook. Using all her strength, she somehow wrenched the hook loose from its moorings. When it came loose, it and she plummeted to the waiting beast below. As she fell, Kierna grabbed the chain in one hand and the hook in the other. Just as the beast thought it had her, she drove the hook into its massive head, at the same time wrapping the chain around its thick, hairy neck, choking off its roar of pain.

The beast staggered but did not fall, clawing violently at the strangling chain while a steady stream of blood poured from the hook wound. Finally it wedged a claw behind the chain and with impossible strength, flung her across the chamber, chain and all. She groaned as she landed, a tangle of bruised limbs. The beast wasted no time.

Before she knew what was happening, both of her arms were pinned in one of its hands above her head. She felt its crushing weight on top of her and its rank scent filled her with a revulsion she had not thought existed. She tried to scream, but its black tongue filled her mouth. She tried to kick out but her legs were pinned as well. The pain of the beast's movements was unbearable. The rough, cold stone floor scraped her back mercilessly as the creature slammed into her. *You will survive this,* she forcefully told herself over and over and then suddenly Kierna was pounding her fists against a strong chest covered in soft blue wool, her sobs filling the chamber as fully as the beast had. The pain of the beast inside her was abruptly gone, replaced with an all consuming euphoria.

"Kierna. It's all right. It's me. Everything's going to be all right now," said the soft, soothing voice she knew so well.

"Danken?" she asked, seeing him in all his beauty through her teary eyes. His blue robes were of expensive cut, his silver hair reflected the dim lights of the chamber back a thousand fold and his blue eyes flared with a warmth that filled her soul. Kierna felt his breath like a warm blanket.

"I'm here, it's all right," he assured her, burying her head in his chest as he wrapped his strong arms around her. In that moment she wanted nothing else in all of Midgarthe. She had never wanted anything else. Only him. And now he was here. She didn't care why. She didn't. Except that she did.

"How are you here?" Kierna asked quietly.

"I followed you after you ran away at the inn. Jet told me everything. Why didn't you tell me how you felt?"

"I couldn't. My path runs opposite yours. Freyja help me, I love you so much but it can't be!" she cried.

"You're right," he said coldly, pushing her away from him. "It can't." He drew *Mak'Rist,* his eyes hot with blazing hate.

"Danken?" Kierna's voice broke pitifully.

"Don't make this harder than it has to be, Kierna," he taunted as a score of jet black, completely featureless men strode in, each with a sword ready in his hand.

They attacked as one entity, working off each others' moves and reactions. She bent at angles she hadn't known she could and jumped higher than she was tall to avoid the slashing swords, her feet and fists flailing. She managed to get the swords from two of the faceless soldiers, cutting them down as she did so. Instead of falling, they dissipated, turning to thin air. All the while Danken watched calmly, his eyes forcing hers away at every turn.

Long and hard she battled, parrying and thrusting her twin blades. Kierna whirled around, leaping in all directions and screaming like a madwoman. She sundered one faceless head from its body, turning to face the next but there was none. Only Danken, clapping his palm against his blade's startling gleam. She glanced at her two blades, the same the white-clothed women carried and not a drop of blood on them. Her body, on the other hand, was a different story altogether, with so many bad gashes bleeding freely, she wondered how she was still standing. Danken walked into the dark corridor through the open gate, calling back to her as he did so.

"Follow if you will into the darkness. But do you dare? For it is only I that keep the creature at bay. He may not be so gentle a lover the next time," he laughed cruelly and then was gone, swallowed up by the darkness. Steeling her quivering jaw, Kierna followed.

The darkness was oppressive, like a living thing threatening to engulf her. Squeaks and skittering sounds around her set her already taught nerves to fraying. Rough, cold hands reached out to caress her, drawing back as she swung her swords at them. Suddenly the floor wasn't there and she tumbled into the cold darkness. On and on she fell, willing herself to stop to no avail. At last she positioned herself cross-legged with her swords across her lap and her eyes closed. The cold, the rush of air all died away. She sat in a trance, blocking the illusion out.

The feel of cold tile on her bottom opened her eyes and Kierna rose slowly to find herself in an empty stone cavern but for a single gold-edged mirror in the exact center. She paced around it cautiously, amazed to find it always pointed in her direction. Approaching it slowly, she studied her reflection. Her disheveled hair was as dirty as her body which was covered in dozens of nasty cuts and bruises. Her face looked worn and her ice blue eyes had lost their luster, like the film that came with death.

Her reflection began looking her up and down as well, disdain on her face. Kierna blinked rapidly as if to ensure herself she was not seeing things.

"What?" her reflection barked. "You think I'm happy with this, this *thing* you've stuck me with?" She looked disgustedly at her body.

"Stuck *you* with? I've been fighting for my life!" Kierna shouted.

"Is that your pathetic excuse then?" the reflection asked mockingly, suddenly wearing a slinky red gown, her blond hair shiny and her skin golden and creamy. Her crystal-clear blue eyes stared at Kierna angrily. "Look at this then? Is it any better?"

"Of course," Kierna stammered.

"Wrong, stupid girl. This is the best you have to offer and it still isn't worth more than a whore's shaved copper. No wonder no man will have you. You disgust me. Don't even look at me anymore you ugly—"

Kierna screamed, swinging one of her swords at the reflection. Instead of shattering glass though, she fell through the mirror. Breathing shallowly and feeling close to breaking, she struggled to her hands and knees. From the corner of her eye she caught the shimmering of the pool and the smiling old faces of the Sprit Blade Council of Twelve. Kierna stood shakily, amazed to find herself whole and uninjured, surprisingly clean feeling. Yet in each hand, she still carried the swords she had taken in the mirror. She breathed a choked sigh of relief. Each woman then repeated a ritual greeting.

"Congratulations, Sister Kierna. Welcome. May my swords be your comfort and strength."

"Thank you, Sisters."

A small brown-robed Elven girl brought her another bowl of the bland porridge and hot tea, which she gratefully accepted.

"Sisters, has Corsha made it back yet?" Kierna asked.

"No, Sister," A Mai'Lang told her.

"You made it through faster than any tested since have sat on this Council," said one of the Duah.

"Aye, she could be entire turns of the glass, or even days coming," an Alfin told her, her Orcan and Elven features creased into a permanent glare.

"You should get rest, Sister. You may do nothing for her here," the first Sendar woman told her.

Kierna went to pick up her soiled clothes but they were no longer there. She flashed the woman a questioning look. The Sendar woman snapped her fingers and once again a small brown-robed girl entered the chamber, this time carrying a folded set of white clothes and under garments. Kierna thanked the silent Orcan girl, who retreated as soon as Kierna had taken the clothes. She put them on hastily, amazed at their perfect fit and comfort. She could feel every pebble on the floor through her sturdy yet soft-soled white leather boots laced to her knees.

A third girl came in bearing two simple yet expensive scabbards, each with the *Valknut* at their base. Kierna strapped them to her back and slid her swords smoothly in. A Spirit Blade came in and escorted Kierna out of the cavern. She was a Duah woman older than Kierna with her hair in the same braided fashion as all the rest, four on each side and one in the back. Her hands and feet were invisible beneath the wide sleeves and pants, as were Kiernas, she realized.

"My name is Phaeryn. May my swords be your comfort," the Elf said, taking her down the long passageway.

"I am Kierna. May I be the edge of your blade," she said as they stepped out into the main chamber, the sunlight no longer streaming through the thundering falls. Phaeryn led her a separate way from the way she had come in, down winding passages that seemed to go for miles. Other Spirit Blades passed by with cordial but brief nods, always seeming to be on important business.

"I have heard that you are the fastest to pass the Test since any can remember."

"So I'm told. Though it didn't seem fast to me when I was in that cursed place." Kierna remarked, shivering at the memory.

"It is like that for each of us." Phaeryn nodded sagely.

"Does it go away?"

"Eventually. For some it takes days, other years."

"Dwei," Kierna scoffed sarcastically to which Phaeryn laughed softly.

They arrived at a long corridor lined with doors every fifteen feet. After passing close to one hundred of them, Phaeryn stopped at a nondescript door and opened it. Inside was a wooden desk and chair, a small wooden bed and a wash basin. A large *Valknut* was inlaid into the smooth stone floor. An ironing board was folded against the wall next to two folded sets of *gi* and a thick white cloak. A polished, pearly white bow hung above the bed along with a quiver packed with white-fletched arrows. Spirit Blades apparently liked white, Kierna observed.

"These are your quarters, Kierna. You may decorate them as you see fit. Breakfast is at sunrise. Afterwards I will show you the baths, the practice yard, the library, the Temples and the gardens. Please sit," she indicated the desk chair. Without further ado, she began braiding Kierna's hair. "Pay attention, for you will have to do this for your fellow Sisters often."

"Who are the little girls in the brown robes?" Kierna asked.

"Orphans, mostly and half-breeds disowned by their families. They find a home here and learn our ways. When they are old enough, they are given the choice to take the Test or leave with money enough to start a new life."

"Do many leave?"

"Some. But most hear the Blades calling."

"Did you come here as a child?"

"Aye."

"Do you ever leave?" Kierna asked.

"Aye, when I am chosen for duty. Mostly just to the Temples, though. That is our main job, besides studying. To maintain and protect the Temples."

"How many Sisters are here?"

"Five hundred at any time with at least two thousand out in the lands on Temple business."

"Gods. I never knew there were so many."

"We are few compared to our enemies."

"Aye," Kierna agreed solemnly.

They talked for a turn of the glass more until Phaeryn was finished with her hair and then bade her a good night. Kierna blew out her candle and fell quickly into a deep, dreamless sleep.

On the western side of the cliffs, just to the left of the falls and suitably removed from the rest of the city were the Temples. Carved into the solid riverstone, with a life-sized replica of their respective God or Goddess in a circular fountain in front, they were all cunningly modeled to reflect their Patron's personality. Twin stone pillars lined with golden runes bordered each entrance flush with the cliffside, the torch-lit insides solemn and sacred. Each had rows of benches facing a stone altar with a large space in the center of the chamber for Circle to be held.

There were twenty-four altogether in a perfect line down the cliff base with breathtakingly beautiful gardens spanning the length. There was more gold and silver inlaid in these Temples than in any other place but the Royal Palaces of the Nations. Hundreds of common folk milled about, paying respect to their Patron Gods or Matron

Goddesses or just all of them in general. Dozens of Sprit Blades could be seen tending their chosen Temple or helping the people that came to pay their homage.

"You have chosen your Patron?" Phaeryn asked as she and Kierna strode the promenade early the next morning.

"Aye. I have chosen Freyja."

"That is a rare choice for a Sister with our solitary lifestyle."

"Aye," Kierna nodded.

"You have not chosen her as a fertility Goddess then?"

"No."

"You wish to be a Valkyrie?"

"If I am worthy. And you?" Kierna asked.

"I chose Balder."

"You are a Soldier of the Light."

"Aye," Phaeryn answered as they passed by the Temple of Thor which had by far the most Sisters attending it.

They reached the walkway arching over the lake where two Sisters stood immobile guard.

"Sisters, may our swords be your comfort," Phaeryn greeted them.

"May we be the edge of your blades, Sisters," they replied as Kierna and Phaeryn passed by.

"Have you heard any word yet on Corsha?" Kierna tried to keep the worry out of her voice.

"I have not. Fear not Kierna. She has until this afternoon before you must worry. It usually takes from midday until midday to complete the Testing.

"So what do we do now that I've chosen my Matron and visited the Temples?"

"Now we report to the Practice Yard. Then to the baths and then to the library for study."

"We do this everyday?"

"Of course. Your swords have not yet reached their full potential. Weapons Master Tonis will hone your skills. Your mind is not yet filled. High Scholar Vynal will teach you. Also, your name will be added to the rotation of your Patron's Temple. When it is your allotted time, you will report to the Senior Sister of your Temple for instructions."

"Lead on Sister," Kierna was eager to start her training.

The Practice Yard was a massive cavern stretching for hundreds of feet with a ceiling over forty feet above them. Over one hundred Sisters, young and old, were paying rapt attention to an older Duah Sister who was lecturing them on the finer details of the swords. Kierna and Phaeryn took their places towards the back and watched, awed by her knowledge.

Tonis was grace incarnate, working her swords so beautifully that it was an art form all its own. The silver stripes down her sleeves and pants flashed elegantly as her body moved fluidly. After a turn of the glass, she split them into pairs, where each Sister was given two rattan sticks of like weight and size to their actual blades. As they sparred, Tonis stalked around, criticizing or praising at equal turns. This went on for two turns of the glass until Kierna's limbs were on fire and she was drenched in sweat. She and Phaeryn made their way to the baths along with the other Sisters.

Far below the surface of Lok Fal were several huge, naturally carved hot springs spread out among massive stalactites. The Sisters filed in, excitedly talking about their lessons, Kierna surprised to learn she was doing the same. The water was so hot that they had to ease their way slowly in but once they had done so it felt marvelous. She felt her knotted muscles slowly unwind from the ordeals of the past weeks.

While they were drying off, a young Sendar girl in brown robes approached.

"Sister Kierna?" she asked.

"Aye?"

"I am asked to tell you that Sister Corsha is sleeping in her quarters and that you may see her later tonight."

"Thank you child," Kierna breathed a sigh of relief.

They made their rejuvenated way down many more snaking corridors until at last they reached the four massive chambers that were the library. Stone shelves were carved out of every wall, lined with huge leather-bound books, odd artifacts and ancient yellowed scrolls. Girls in brown robes darted to and fro, constantly cleaning or straightening. High scholar Vynal was a tiny, square shouldered Hafrok—or half-Sendar, half-Dwarf. She wore two shortswords across her back. Her gray hair and silver eyes were buried in a massive volume bound in what appeared to be Dragon scales. She, too, had silver stripes on her *gi*.

Other Sisters filed, heading straight for the items they wished to study or to Vynal to inquire about where they could find what they wanted. Vynal was gruff and to the point as she showed Kierna and Phaeryn the books they wanted, bustling off before they even had a chance to thank her. Kierna was astounded at how much she did not know and anxious to learn it all that day. Two turns of the glass later showed her that years would be more of her time scale.

A brown-robed Alfin girl curtsied with a slight cough to let Kierna know she was there. Kierna and Phaeryn reluctantly looked up from their studies, eyes red with concentration.

"What is it child?"

"Pardon, Sisters. But I am instructed to tell you both that the Council of Twelve wishes to speak with you immediately."

Kierna glanced questioningly at Phaeryn, who shrugged, a pensive expression on her perfect features.

"We had better hurry," Phaeryn said, "it is uncommon to be called by the Council of Twelve unless we were on Escort duty or in…"

"Or what?" Kierna asked as they carefully placed their study materials back on the shelves.

"Unless we are to be sent on Temple business."

CHAPTER 26
A BECKON

aptain Jarl Tamlinsen leaned over the rail of the *MGS Windstrike*, a breeze blowing through his tied back long, blond hair. The sun glinted off of the water, causing him to squint his eyes against the glare. He was a tall, muscular man and his sun-bronzed skin highlighted his dark hazel eyes.

He wore the traditional garb of a sea captains in the service of Mistgarde. Black, baggy pants tucked into spit shined black boots one could see his refection in. A thin, white shirt with golden buttons was collared loosely at the neck. Blue epaulettes adorned the shoulders. In full dress, he wore a large, black triangular hat and a blue jacket, as well.

The *Windstrike* cut through the water like a hot knife through butter, her sails full with wind. She was a huge, three-masted vessel made of polished red wood. Her crew of two hundred thirty were the best of the best and Tamlinsen kept them that way. Where the *Windstrike* went, it was master of all it surveyed.

Tamlinsen glanced for'ard. Two ships on the horizon would soon find this to be true. The chase had been on since midmorning and *Windstrike* had steadily gained on the two. They were Goblin pirates, probably captained and escorted by Shrakens.

As on all Mistgarde ships, his crew was made up of Sendar, Dwarves, Elves, Trolls and Orcans, so Tamlinsen held no worries of Shrakens. They had no element of surprise and as such were no match for the highly trained Orcans, who swam beneath the ship in shifts.

The Elves found their skills best suited to the rigging and their excellent sight made them ideal for the crow's-nest. The Trolls preferred the hard labor to this and were generally used as craftsmen, bosuns and steersmen. The Dwarves, notorious for their hatred of the sea, had nevertheless found their calling in the kitchens. They were superb cooks who rarely ventured on top deck. Their tireless work ethic also made them a perfect fit for the pumps. They were so afraid of sinking that they would pump psychotically until there wasn't a drop left.

While the Orcans lived underwater, they found the surface ships ill-suited to their sense of gravity. They preferred to stay in the water unless they were sleeping or drinking spirits. Eating and everything else could be accomplished away from the nauseating sway of the ship.

The Sendar, however, were the premier sailors. They were as at home on the sea as they were on land. They were highly adaptable to any situation and could readily plug a hole in any portion of the ship. They were well-known to have an uncanny sense of navigation that was rumored to center around the core of the world. Rarely were officers in Mistgarde's Navy anything but Sendar.

Tamlinsen turned to his Senior Lieutenant. "Port side one notch."

"Port side one notch!" Senior Lieutenant Ragnarsen shouted to the Troll at the helm.

"Port side one notch, aye sir!" the Troll shouted.

"We should catch them by mid-afternoon, sir," Ragnarsen commented.

"Hopefully, if the winds hold. I wonder if there are Shrakens in those ships. They are handled well."

"Aye. Do you think they will split when we catch them?"

"They would have done so already. No, they will turn and fight, hoping to out match us."

"Not likely, sir."

"No, not likely at all, yet overconfidence does not become us. Every dog has its day."

"Aye sir. Should I call changing of the watch?"

"Aye."

"Change the watch!" Ragnarsen called to the master at arms, a huge Sendar with a goatee to his chest.

"Aye sir, change the watch!" he called, blowing a small whistle. Immediately, men began orderly descending from their perches, or from swabbing the decks to trade places with the next watch.

"I'll be in my cabin. Alert me when we are closing in." Tamlinsen informed Ragnarsen.

"Aye sir."

"You have the command, Lieutenant." Tamlinsen said, descending below decks to his cabin. It was a small affair, as were all things aboard a ship of war, though it was spacious compared to the crews' quarters, which were little more than cots stacked high in a large sleeping area.

They had been on cruise for close to a month now and would be for another two before returning to their home port of Southport. Already they had overtaken six ships, mostly Goblin though the last had been Driss. He shuddered involuntarily at the thought.

Though they had been slaughtered to a man, the Driss had put up a vicious fight that had left seven of Tamlinsen's crew dead. He had had to sink their ship rather than man it with a skeleton prize crew as he had done with the Goblins!

The Shrakens sent small escorts with each pirate to "protect" them, but in actuality it was to make sure that all profits were split in the right proportion. The Shrakens aboard or beneath the ships they were chasing probably numbered less than a dozen, no match for the score of Mistgarde Orcans sailing with the *Windstrike*. He put his mind to rest.

He decided to nap so he would be refreshed for the battle. Laying down in his hammock, he let the gently rolling of the ship lull him into the welcoming embrace of sleep.

A knock on his cabin door woke him.

"Enter," he called. The door opened to reveal a Junior Lieutenant.

"Sir, Lieutenant Ragnarsen sends his respects and the watch reports the ships we are pursuing are less than half a league away."

"Very good. That will be all."

"Aye sir," he said, shutting the door. Tamlinsen got his boots on quickly before ascending to the top deck.

"Captain on the deck!" An Elf in the rigging called. All saluted. Tamlinsen saluted back.

"Lieutenant, report."

"Aye sir." Ragnarsen stood to attention. "Winds blowing southeast, approximately thirteen knots. Crow's-nest reports one Shraken on each deck. He estimates each crew at one hundred ninety-five, sir."

"Very well." Tamlinsen stared at the two ships, clearly visible now. "Be prepared, on my mark, bring her into the wind. They will try to split soon so that they may board us from both sides."

"Aye sir," Ragnarsen said. He was a seasoned sailor, expert in the ways of the seas. He had sailed with Tamlinsen since they had been midshipmen all those years ago. He was a few years Tamlinsen's junior but a patch over his left eye and a few days' stubble gave him the appearance of a far older man.

"Sir! Ships are splitting!" came an Elven voice from the crow's-nest.

"Very good. Bring her into the wind."

"Aye sir." Ragnarsen acknowledged. "Bring her into the wind."

"Bring her into the wind, aye sir!" the steerman called.

"Take in those sails!"

"Aye sir, taking sails in!" came voices from the rigging.

The *Windstrike* came smartly into the wind, causing the two Goblin ships to veer out to avoid hitting her.

"Deploy the Orcans! Eight to each vessel! Four to stay under our hull!"

"Aye sir!" An Orcan officer saluted before diving into the water.

"All sailors, prepare to latch on and engage for boarding!" Tamlinsen bellowed. Only the steersman remained in place. The rest of the crew shot down from the rigging or up from below decks and lined the sides.

Ropes were tied from the masts to swing across from ship to ship. In a matter of moments, both Goblin ships had come alongside. Grabbing their ropes, the Goblins sought to board the *Windstrike*. They were more than a little surprised to find sailors from the *Windstrike* already swinging to board *them*.

All three ships came together with a resounding crash, timbers groaning under the impact. A thunderous roar arose from both sides as the battle was met.

Green Elven and yellow Goblin fire leaped across, burning holes in all unlucky enough to be caught in their path. The Trolls, fully twice the size of the Goblins, became chameleons when they boarded, a shimmering mass taking on the properties of its surroundings. Only their burning eyes were visible. While the Goblins could *see* the mass, they couldn't get a fix on the weapon it carried, denying them a chance to parry an attack.

The Goblins struggled to use *Greedfire* to burn holes where they thought the weapons to be, tiny yellow flames that dissipated the illusion of the shimmering weapon. This did little good, as a Goblin blade alone was no match for a Dwarven-made battleaxe in the hands of a nearly invisible Vull'Kra warrior.

The Sendar boarded the Goblin ships with wicked grins on their faces, swords gleaming in the afternoon sun. The battle lust in their eyes was a magic in itself, putting a dagger of fear directly into an enemies' heart. All, including Captain Tamlinsen boarded the Goblin ships for they had no need to guard the *Windstrike*. Any fool Goblin that boarded it ran into a small army of psychotic Dwarves, carrying butchering knives and spiked hammers.

The Orcans beneath the ship wreaked havoc on the small group of Shrakens guarding each Goblin ship. *Bubblewrath* and *Sonarblast* attacks set them into a confused and battered state while the Orcans systematically darted in and killed with their deadly claws.

This underwater battle raged fiercely, a maelstrom of bubbles, claws and teeth set in a red haze. The Orcans managed to corral the two groups of Shrakens into one. This was a favorite Orcan battle tactic accomplished by using *Sonarblast* and *Bubblewrath* to slowly coerce the Shrakens closer and closer together. While on dry land, having an enemy spread out was preferable in battle; underwater, a massed enemy could be killed with a single sonar blast. After accomplishing their feat, the Orcans circled the Shrakens, who, realizing their predicament, made one last, furious effort at attack. They would not surrender. The hatred between these two races was unassailable. They would kill each other on sight without regard to numbers.

The Orcans released a torrent of powerful *Sonarblast,* turning the charging Shrakens into little more than jelly.

Two Shrakens above, the Captains of each Goblin vessel were screaming orders to their Goblin allies. They emitted waves of *Stunspore* on groups of tightly concentrated Elven and Sendar sailors, slowing their reflexes by half. As this started to take effect, the Elves shot *Silence Globes* around each Shrakens' head, stilling their commands. Their fire could not penetrate the shield of *Greedfire* around each, though.

Captain Tamlinsen, with Ragnarsen beside him, waded through the battle towards the Shraken Captain of one ship. Three Goblins who had just killed a Troll together, rushed them. Tamlinsen's saber took the nearest through the chest and swung its limp body around to act as a shield against the remaining two. Ragnarsen took full advantage of his superior reach and decapitated the one closest to him.

The last Goblin's final sight was the battle-crazed Lieutenant's eyes before it was cut in half.

"Right then, Lieutenant, let's kill that damn Shraken before he paralyzes us too."

"Spoken like a true aristocrat, sir!" Ragnarsen said, kicking a wounded Goblin over the side of the ship.

The Shraken was still madly screaming orders, unaware that no one could hear him due to the *Silence Globe* and neither could he hear them, though he didn't know why. He remained unaware of the two Sendar officers as he continued his tirade. The Goblin fire shield would protect him from the *Moonfire,* but it would not protect him from cold steel.

As Tamlinsen snuck up, the Shraken saw a Goblin pointing frantically behind him. He turned in time to raise his arm in defense before Tamlinsen's sword took both the limb and its owner's head off.

"Let's go get the other one," he declared, his sword dripping blood.

"Won't be necessary, sir," Ragnarsen responded, pointing with his sword at the other ship. A group of Orcans were scaling the sides of the ship. He watched grimly as they ripped the Shraken Captain apart, limb from limb. The two Sendar turned their attention to the battles aboard the ship they were on.

The green and yellow fire was less frequent in these close quarters and the din of battle was deafening. Elves, with their long, thin blades, kept the Goblins at bay while the Sendar waded in and hacked them apart. Shimmering Trolls could be seen standing on a pile of bodies, occupying as many as four Goblins at once, never taking a step in retreat.

Since the Mistgarde Council had declared no mercy for pirates, there were no prisoners taken. The few Goblins remaining as the battle began to wane leapt over the sides of the ship only to be dragged under by waiting Orcans.

"Get a cleanup underway if you will, Lieutenant," Tamlinsen ordered.

"Aye sir." Ragnarsen left the observation deck to supervise the cleanup. Goblin corpses were discarded into the ocean and soon the decks were being flooded to wash away the blood.

"Sir!" The Junior Lieutenant who had alerted him of battle, saluted.

"Aye, what is it?"

"I have a report of our dead and wounded, sir. Do you wish to hear it now?"

"Aye, I might as well." Tamlinsen braced himself for the inevitable survivors' guilt to come.

"Sir, we have eleven dead. Four Sendar, two Trolls, three Elves and two Orcans. We also have numerous wounded but most if not all are expected to live."

"Very well, Lieutenant."

"Sir. About the four Sendar, sir. I am sorry to report that Second Lieutenant Velsen was among the casualties, sir."

"Damn." Tamlinsen shook his head. "Well, I guess you just got a promotion to Second Lieutenant then."

"Aye sir. Thank you, sir," he saluted.

"I know it's not how you wish to be promoted, Lieutenant Zukesen, but it is the way we live. We are men of war. Sometimes we die, even the best of us. Keep a level, cautious head about you and be perilous in battle. You will be fine."

"Aye sir. I will return to my duties now then, sir."

"Very well," Tamlinsen said. He swung over to *Windstrike* to check in on the wounded.

He watched the surgeons work for over an hour before Ragnarsen tapped him on the shoulder.

"Sir, shall I assign prize crews to the ships?"

"Aye, but they'll be traveling with us."

"Sir?"

"We're going back to port. I have the strangest feeling we are needed there. A feeling like the Magi send."

"Better we adhere to it then, sir."

"Aye. I'm thinking so myself. Besides, if nothing else, we can pick up our last six prize crews and a score of new sailors to make up for the ones we lost. I'd like to get back to our full complement of two hundred thirty. We're thin enough right now that we barely have enough for three watches."

"That would be good, sir. On the subject, we will need a Junior Lieutenant."

"Do you have any suggestions?" Tamlinsen asked, knowing the answer. Ragnarsen took a great deal of pride and interest into the junior officers. He was like a grizzled father to them.

"I was thinking about Midshipman Daserdotir," Ragnarsen put forth, idly scratching his beard.

"A seemingly wise choice. Make it so."

"Aye sir. The prize crews will be set to sail within the turn of a glass, sir."

"Very well." He stayed and watched the surgeons for a little while longer until he was sure all his sailors were all right. He was a deeply caring Captain and the crew loved him for it.

He left sick bay and headed to the top deck. He found the Orcan Commander Kamotal leaning over the aft rail watching the sun set. The Orcans had their own command structure as they were not actually sailors. They only took orders from Tamlinsen.

"Ever since I was a boy, I've loved watching the sunset," Tamlinsen remarked, taking a place beside the Orcan on the rail.

"As have I, Captain. I remember sitting on the beach in the Western Isles watching it fall beneath the waves marking a path for the stars to come out."

"Perhaps it is this way with all the races, even the Evil ones. To give thanks to Sol and Delling for the day's warmth and to welcome Mani and Nott and ask for a peaceful slumber."

"It is hard for me to imagine," Kamotal said thoughtfully, "a Shraken or a Giant giving thanks for anything but death or power, but I suppose all must bow before the might of the Gods."

"Agreed." Tamlinsen said simply. The two of them continued to watch the sun set in silence until at last it dipped beneath the waves.

"Captain?" Ragnarsen called.

"Aye?"

"Prize crews are ready, sir."

"Very well. Set heading for north by northeast. Open only auxiliary sails."

"North by northeast, aye sir!" The steersman called back.

"Aye sir, auxiliary sails only," the rigging officer echoed.

"Are we returning to port, Captain?" Kamotal asked, watching as the three ships turned simultaneously in one fluid motion, white sails reflected the pale early moonlight.

"Aye."

"So soon?"

"Aye. I am bidden."

"Ah, I see." Kamotal nodded in understanding. A splash in the water roused their interest and made them lean even further over the rail. A pod of humpback whales swam beside them.

"Beautiful." Tamlinsen remarked, as the whales called out in cetacean.

"Aye. Forgive my abrupt departure Captain, but they have crucial scouting information I must hear."

"Understood. Let me know what you find."

"Aye," the Orcan acknowledged, diving into the water without so much as a ripple. Tamlinsen continued to stare out at the ocean, lost in his own thoughts of the Magi's call to him. Why did they need him? Who knew? He admonished himself for speculating, which he hated with a passion. No amount of thinking was likely to change the outcome of the future. Only action could do that and right now he was content to let his actions take him into port.

Another ripple in the water heralded the reemergence of Kamotal, shining wet in the moonlight.

"Sister Zokaan says the way to the continent is clear except for the Sea Dragon, Solokintrelies, but he's sleeping. She said to keep our noisy ships quiet, she could hear you from two leagues away."

"These ships are quiet as they come!" Tamlinsen protested.

"Not to a sea creature. Don't worry, Dragons can sleep through anything. Except someone stealing their treasure. If he hears no gold or jewelry worth taking, he won't bother us even if he wakes."

"Perhaps you didn't see the holds of those ships we took today."

"Full?"

"Nearly. Enough to fill Mistgarde's coffers for awhile. I think these are the ones that hit one of our treasure ships last week, though that's only half of what they took. There must be two more ships out there."

"Or down there." Kamotal indicated the murky depths.

"Aye. Say, would you like a drink?" Tamlinsen asked as he pulled a small flask out of his breast pocket.

"Does a Shraken have teeth?" the Orcan answered, accepting the flask. He drank deeply, wiping his mouth when he had finished.

"To the sunset." Tamlinsen toasted.

"To the sunset."

Danken stepped through the portal like a thundercloud. Lanaia looked alarmed at him.

"Danken, what is it?" she asked. He fixed her with a glare like ice.

"The Emerald Ransom you mentioned, she is Amaria."

"The Duah Princess? *That* Amaria?"

"Aye, the same. She was captured by Driss just this evening. I must go after her."

"And what of your companions? The ones it says will accompany you?"

"If it is destined, they will come of their own accord."

When he finished packing, he headed down the stairs towards Dot and Maple's room. In the hallway, he found Valshk and Swifteye practicing with their weapons. They stopped immediately at the sight of his bag.

"To where do you go?"

"To rescue Amaria," he replied simply.

"When do you leave," the Troll asked.

"As soon as I have spoken to Maple," Danken said, entering the room. He found Shard with one eye open and went to pet him. "I need you to watch over things here for me while I'm gone." He patted the giant cat once more before walking silently over to where Maple slept. He lightly brushed her hair with his fingers until she woke. She smiled sleepily at him, the dawn sun reflecting off of her skin.

"Hi," she said.

"Hi."

"What's going on?" she asked, seeing in his eyes something amiss.

"I have to leave. I'll be gone for awhile. Please watch after Dot and keep her safe. The job is yours forever, even if I never return." She grabbed his shirt and brought him close to her where she whispered in his ear.

"I know not where you go, but you *will* return. I will not lose you so soon after knowing you and coming to…"

"Maple, I…"

"I know, but it is how I feel, all the same."

"Aye," he acknowledged as she let him go. He turned to find Dot standing in her nightgown behind him. In her hand was a jade ball, a little bigger than a shooting marble. She handed it to him. He felt the power surging through it like a tempest. "Dot, what is this?" not expecting an answer.

"Courage," Dot announced in a small but clear voice that was more like the song of wind then anything. Danken and Maple stared at her aghast.

"Dot, you spoke!" Maple exclaimed, picking her up and hugging her.

"The Hand of Silence," Danken whispered to himself, putting the Oracle in a small pouch at his waist. He put his arms around them both, hugging them tightly, kissing Dot on the head and Maple on the cheek.

"Be safe Sariksen," Maple bade him.

"Goodbye," Danken said as he left the room. In the hallway he found Valshk, Swifteye and Shonai all wearing bags. He stared at her.

"Did you honestly think I would travel all the way here to see you just to have you disappear?" Shonai asked.

"Apparently not."

"I told her of your departure and she insisted on coming," Valshk said.

"Seems to be contagious," came Lanaia's voice from down the hall. Danken introduced her to all, her two wolves instantly becoming favorites. Danken was loathe to leave Bolt behind but knew that he could not go where they went. He nearly laughed aloud when he thought of how angry Jet would be to miss out on this action.

"I guess that's about it," Danken said, then caught himself, "excepting T'riel. Does anyone know where she is?" A familiar sting on his ear gave him his answer.

"Where she's supposed to be. Watching after reckless Boy," T'riel stated. "Elven King is scared. He is counting on Boy."

"I thought I felt an extra passenger when I ported," Danken said, placing his hands against the stone. He used *Stonespeak* to view the area in and around Southport, the closest city to the Driss Kingdom on the Sendarian continent. Once he had seen it, he returned and opened a portal.

"So as you can see," Sembalo was saying, "the Dwarves are amassing at Bluestone. The Orcans are on the move as we speak, and the High Councilor of Sendar is putting out a call to arms. He has informed us that we are to make ready for war."

"I suspect the Duah and Trolls will begin the same preparations soon?" Penn asked as an aide burst in the room.

"Excuse me please, but I bear urgent news from Wendall."

"Out with it then," Kai said.

"Princess Amaria Sonatala has been kidnapped with the instructions that the Duah must refrain from entering the war lest she be killed."

"No." Sembalo's head drooped.

"Who told you this?" Penn demanded.

"Why, Danken Sariksen, sir." The aide trembled.

"Well, where is *he?*" Sembalo asked.

"Gone," Arn said quietly.

"What? How do you know?"

"He is her *N'famar,* but she is not his and his guilt will not let him. He will not sit idly by while we decide what to do. He will have already left to do it. Trust me, I know him," Arn answered, leading the group to the stairway. On the floor, Dot, Swifteye and Valshk lived on, a smell of brimstone wafted down to them.

"He's ported," Urishen announced.

"Aye," Arn agreed, entering the hallway. On the ground was an ancient looking scroll. He picked it up and read it aloud.

"Lanaia," Sembalo said.

"Who?" Kai asked.

"After I trained him to use *Transport*, the Head Librarian, an Elven woman named Lanaia told him she had read a prophecy about him. This is it, I suspect, and she was dead on the money, too, by the looks of it. He will have to go it alone, for we are needed here to protect the land from Sorcerers. Gods be with him. Gods protect the Sapphire Son."

"Ahoy the ship!" Danken called.

"Ahoy the land!" Lieutenant Zukesen called back.

"Is Captain Tamlinsen aboard?"

"Aye, who wants to know?"

"Danken Sariksen."

"*The* Danken Sariksen?"

"Aye."

"Sorry sir, I'll lower the..."

"Not necessary," Danken called, using *Airlift* to float them aboard.

"Sir!" Zukesen snapped to attention. "Welcome aboard sir."

"Thank you, Lieutenant."

"Attention on deck!" the Bosun bellowed. All present saluted, which Danken returned.

"Fetch the Orcan Commander as well." Moments later, Captain Tamlinsen came topside. He saluted Danken, who returned smartly, presenting orders. Tamlinsen read them quickly. When he finished, he looked up at Danken.

"When do we leave, sir?"

"As soon as you can make it so," Danken replied. He turned at a dripping sound on the deck. Commander Kamotal stood there, wringing his hair of water. He scanned the deck for Tamlinsen but his attention was captured by Danken. He bowed.

"You have need of me, Magus?"

"Not I. But perhaps she could think of something," Danken said, stepping out of the way to reveal Shonai. Kamotal's eyes grew large and he dropped to his knees, as did the few other Orcans on deck.

"Princess! You are alive!"

"Aye, Commander. Perhaps you could pick out two-score Orcans to add to our current complement."

"At once, Highness." Kamotal dove seamlessly into the water. Captain Tamlinsen gave orders for special quarters to be set up for them while they waited.

Every Orcan in Southport had turned out to see the Princess, who stood on the bow of *Windstrike*, waving. Even in her traveling clothes she cut a regal figure against the sky. Kamotal returned in the midst of all of this with his handpicked additions to the Orcan complement. They leapt out of the water in a synchronized salute to Shonai.

Spirits were high as *Windstrike* untied and slowly, gallantly sailed out of Southport harbor. A dangerous journey awaited them all, yet none could find a reason to do anything but smile.

CHAPTER 27
PROTECTOR

s the Hafalf made his way through the rocky terrain of the Dwarven mountains, his strong frame and lithe muscles tensed. Myrisan sensed something ahead and dismounted his horse to investigate. He eyed the hard packed earth for signs of an ambush.

Eleven days ago, after the battle at the inn, he had taken his belongings secretly from his room after the Elf and Sendar man had come to collect the fallen Mage. He had seen Hosanal taking care of him and told her to keep the money he had paid for the rooms and that he was very sorry about her father.

With one last longing look at her beautiful face, he had ridden off into the woods. There he had waited for Diedrik to say goodbye to his friends. Once the Sendar was done, he had set off into the mountains and the Hafalf had been one step ahead of him ever since.

Myrisan looked around him now at the densely forested, rocky surroundings for the source of his ill feeling. Seeing a tiny movement out of the corner of his eye, he drew his bow and had an arrow notched in moments. When the movement happened again, his excellent vision pegged it as a Sendar loading his own bow.

Myrisan detected several similar movements around him and knew he was being ambushed, probably by the bandits that abounded in these passes. Without warning, he let his arrow fly. It went straight and true, killing the Sendar he had seen first.

Five more bounded out of their hiding places, weapons drawn. He narrowly avoided an arrow and quickly had another one of his own notched. The leader of the group, at whom the arrow was pointed, held up his hands and called off his men. "Hold on there, friend," he said, his ugly, bearded face showing no emotion. "No need for anymore killin'.

"I'm not your friend, and it was you who ambushed me," the Hafalf said icily.

"No, we were just lookin' to see who ye were is all," the man said, turning to the rest of this bank. "I'nt that right boys?"

"Aye," they said gruffly, ready to attack at the drop of a hat.

"Now, what do ye want here?" the man asked.

"I heard there was good money to be made in these mountains protecting passes," Myrisan said, thinking quickly.

"Did ye now? Well why din't ye jus' say so?" The leader laughed, sheathing his sword and holding out his dirty hand. "We're doin' jus' that. An seein' as how we're one short now," he indicated the dead man, "I guess tha' makes room fer ye. What d'ye say?"

"All right," the Hafalf said with a feigned smile.

The rest of the group put their weapons cautiously away and Myrisan did the same. The leader introduced his fellow bandits and then himself.

"Th' name's Yorok, leader 'o this 'ere group."

"Aye, I can see that," the Hafalf said, taking the offered dirty hand.

"Well, ye got a name, don't ye?"

"Oh, aye, you can call me Deathsong. Myrisan Deathsong."

"Deathsong, eh? Tha's a pretty good name fer a bandit, I wager."

"Aye."

"Well, come on then, we'd best set up our watch on the passes again then. Don't want to miss out on a good autumn caravan, now do we, boys!"

Diedrik Fanarsen was in trouble. He had taken Malta, his paint warhorse he'd bought before he'd left home into the heart of the Dwarven mountains on his way back to Keyre. Unfortunately, he had let his mind wander and now found himself face to face with six hard looking and heavily armed Sendar. He mentally reminded himself to quit drinking. This would make it twice in two weeks he'd have to fight half-drunk.

While these mountains were Dwarven territory, as with all nations, they had their share of bandits from all races. These bandits were not amateurs, nor were they all Sendar, Diedrik noticed. A young-looking man at the rear was obviously a Hafalf, his size and blond facial hair marked him as Sendar, but his green eyes, lips and sculpted features were distinctly Elven, though like all half-breeds, he lacked most of the innate talents of either race.

Half-breeds were outcasts throughout the realms, most living in their own societies like the Elven village of Suun, or becoming high-waymen. Some had managed to carve out respectable lives for themselves in the cities, using their mixed talents as craftsmen or most commonly, fighters.

"What can I help you with?" he asked in a loud voice, his hand gripping his broadsword tightly.

"That all depends on what you're carrying through the pass," the leader, a bear of a man, said quietly, falsely jovial.

"I carry nothing but food and bedding."

"That will do then."

"I'm sorry, but I cannot part with any of my possessions if I want to make it through these mountains alive," Diedrik told the man firmly.

"I'm sorry as well because now you won't even make it out of this pass."

"We'll see," Diedrik said through clenched teeth, drawing his sword. The six men broke into action, moving to flank him, but Malta reared up on his hind legs and kicked the nearest man in the head, knocking him to the ground. Unbeknownst to Diedrik, as the man was getting up, the Hafalf discreetly killed him. Diedrik hacked away at another man as Malta whirled around, severing the man's arm at the shoulder. Once again, Myrisan dispatched the wounded man unseen by all.

Malta galloped back down the path, negotiating the narrow, rock-strewn terrain easily. At a large outcropping, Diedrik reined in the thundering warhorse and turned to face the charging bandits. He drew his crossbow and fired off a bolt. He had been aiming for the Hafalf, who gracefully sidestepped it and, when it hit the man beside him in the neck, finished him off.

Diedrik, however, was too busy reloading his crossbow to notice. He clicked the bolt home just in time to fire into the Troll-like face of the leader. He narrowly blocked the remaining Sendar's sword with his own as Malta swung around, knocking the man back.

The horse, though, took it one step further and used its razor-sharp incisors to bit a large chunk out of the attacker's face. His agonizing scream was cut short when the horse's back hooves struck him squarely in the chest, knocking him into an outcropping of rocks. He fell to the ground, writhing in pain and gasping for breath before the Hafalf's sword plunged into his chest.

Diedrik stared unblinking as the Hafalf cleaned his sword on the dead man's tunic before sheathing it. With a look of disappointment, Myrisan shook his head at Diedrik.

"Idiot," he said quietly, taking the money from the dead men's pockets.

"Excuse me?" Diedrik asked, confused and surprised he was still alive.

"I said you're an idiot," the Hafalf repeated. He clicked his tongue twice and his horse came out from hiding in a nearby cave. "You're one of the smartest men I've ever known, yet you drink yourself into a stupor at every chance you get."

"Who are you?" Diedrik asked as Myrisan mounted his white horse.

"Does it matter? You'll be too drunk tomorrow to remember any of this and eventually I'll have to save your deadweight arse for the fourth time in two months."

"The inn," Diedrik breathed, finally recognizing the man. In response, Myrisan put his cowl up and rode back the way he had come from.

Diedrik scanned the rocky terrain around him for any sign of a threat. When none were apparent, he urged the now calm Malta slowly along the path. He noticed that nearly all of the dead bandits bore fatal sword wounds that he had not administered.

As the adrenaline flooded out of his system, it thankfully took the drunkenness with it, leaving him sober for the first time in a long time. His mind was sharpening and soon the Hafalf's face was all he could see. Ever since he could remember, the Hafalf had been there on the outskirts of his life, though for some reason he had never noticed.

For nearly thirty years, Diedrik hadn't noticed his constant companion. Thirty years old he thought, and he didn't look a day over eighteen. The Hafalf, too, looked far too young to have been there the whole time, but he knew it was so.

Diedrik had left Brayl without his two now deceased friends. He hadn't been sober since and the Hafalf had probably gotten him out of more jams than he was letting on. He took the Dwarven spirits out of his saddlebag and threw it against the rock face with an angry yell.

As the sun made its descent in the cloudy mountain sky, Diedrik set about looking for a place to set up camp. It had been four days after he had quit drinking and he was still in a foul mood about it. He was about to turn a sharp corner cut into the corridor made by two steep rock faces on either side of him when he heard two voices arguing. He halted abruptly and listened intently. Not that he could have *not* heard their thunderous, rock crushing voices if he'd wanted to.

They were arguing loudly about who got something, he didn't know what. He heard their words faintly, a guttural, crude mixture of Sendar and something else. From the smell of cooked meat in the air, he deduced they were arguing about who got the last piece of it. Diedrik thanked the Gods he had stopped drinking. It was the first time he hadn't cursed them for exactly the same reason.

Slowly, silently, Diedrik dismounted and peeked around the corner for a better look. He nearly dropped his sword at the sight. Two full-grown Giants were seated around a roaring fire with meat spitted over it. As they sloppily ate, they yelled at each other around mouthfuls. They looked as if they had just come from a battle, with bad cuts and bruises all over, their bald heads lumpy and swollen.

Holding his breath, Diedrik slowly backtracked to where he had left Malta. His heel kicked a loose rock and the Giants' voices stopped. He froze, fear flooding through him, knotting up his stomach and sucking the moisture out of his mouth. Cautiously he began walking again back to his horse, who was thankfully silent.

Reaching Malta, he closed his eyes in relief and quietly saddled up. As he did so, the horse snorted loudly. Diedrik cringed and this time the Giants got up to investigate. He saw their massive shadows flickering in the firelight against the rock face.

"Not good," he said under his breath, turning Malta slowly around in the tight corridor. The sound of the nervous horse's hooves on the cold-packed earth spurred the Giants on. They rounded the corner just as Malta made the final turn and Diedrik spurred the horse on mightily. He turned and fired a crossbow bolt that hit the larger of the two in the chest.

The Giant screamed immeasurably loud before breaking the shaft off and following his cohort. The Giants' immense size and weight worked against them in the narrow rock corridor, and Malta's nifty footwork left them far behind. He turned left at a fork in the path to further confuse them.

Just when Diedrik thought he had lost them, he ran smack into a dead end where the path drove steeply upwards to the top of the rock face. He knew he probably couldn't make it up on foot which meant Malta had no chance. He knew that if the Giants pursued him down this path, he was finished but he would not leave the horse that had saved his life behind. Bloody Etins would be feasting on his sword before he'd let them eat his horse.

He solemnly loaded his crossbow and drew his sword after he dismounted. Patting the horse on the neck, he walked back the way he had come, hoping to catch the Giants by surprise. Besides, Giants could not be fought on horseback unless rider and horse were fully armored and armed with a lance. He took up position about ten feet up the rock face on a ledge with a view that would allow him to fire two, possibly three crossbow bolts before he would have to engage the Giants in hand to hand combat.

"*Dwei,*" he muttered. "Just flarin' *dwei.*"

He would have liked to climb higher out of their reach, but Giants were notorious rock throwers and he would no doubt be crushed or knocked from the ledge. Diedrik heard the rumbling footsteps and his last vestiges of hope evaporated. They rounded the corner cautiously, which for Giants meant refraining from yelling. At least not too loudly.

As the first came into sight, Diedrik let fly his first bolt, hitting the Etin in its thick neck. The Giants stopped in surprise at the unexpected attack, giving Diedrik extra time to reload. His second shot hit the same Giant directly in its cheek, causing it to stagger. The second Giant, whom he'd shot earlier in the chest, charged and Diedrik shot him in an already bad looking wound in the stomach he must have received in his earlier fight.

The Giant's charge slowed as it roared in pain. Just then a longer, thicker arrow appeared in the Etin's right eye as if by magic, followed by a cloaked figure who leapt from the top of the ridge to land with his sword buried in the Giant's heart. The Etin fell silently face first like a felled tree, the cloaked figure scurrying under its legs to face the second.

Diedrik broke his trance and fired a third bolt into the charging Giant, this time hitting it just below the collarbone. He leapt from the ledge and rushed to aide the cloaked figure against the enraged monster, who was now unsuccessfully trying to smash its agile opponent.

Diedrik took advantage of the Giant's preoccupation by hamstringing it with his broadsword. It arched its back in pain, leaving its belly open to the cloaked figure, who plunged his sword into the hilt. As the Etin's leg gave out, Diedrik jumped and took a mighty swing at its neck, cutting deeply.

The cloaked figure sliced off the Giant's club hand and then finished Diedrik's neck cut from the other side. The Etin tumbled to the ground with a ground shaking thud. In the throes of *Etinrage* though, it took a long time to die and both men stood well clear. The two men stood breathing heavily in silence. Diedrik saw the green eyes under the cowl and knew it was the mysterious Hafalf. Bloody smug look on his face too, Diedrik groaned inwardly.

"I guess I owe you more thank yous than I know," Diedrik said.

"Aye," the Hafalf said, calling his amazingly agile horse down from the ridge as Malta, too wandered onto the scene. The Hafalf's white steed negotiated the steep slope as easily as its rider.

"You've been with me since I was a kid and I don't even know your name."

"It's not important," the Hafalf said, saddling his patient mount.

"It is to me," Diedrik said fervently, mounting his wary steed.

"Myrisan," he said simply, riding off towards the Giant camp. Diedrik followed.

They came upon the camp where the argued-over meat was still cooking on the low burning fire. While Myrisan checked the Giants' belongings, Diedrik took the skewer off the fire. It didn't smell half-bad. Even Etin's couldn't mess up a simple flarin' piece of meat, he thought.

"It's a little burned, but no sense letting good meat go to waste," he said, taking a bite and offering some to the Hafalf who looked at it with obvious distaste. Myrisan just laid down his bedroll as if nothing had happened at all that night.

"That's Dwarf you're eating," he said as he sorted through some stolen jewelry. Diedrik immediately spit out the meat and continued to do so for sometime afterwards, brushing his tongue with a handkerchief.

"How did you know?" he asked finally.

"Can't you smell it?" Myrisan asked. "Anyway, these bones around here are obviously Dwarven as are most of the stolen valuables."

"Damnit!" Diedrik yelled. "This taste is never going to go away!"

"Since the camp's already made, we might as well stay here tonight. Keep your ears open, though. A Dragon'll be coming to get those corpses soon, I'll wager. We don't want to be dessert. Diamond Dragons or not, with a Draglet, one never knows."

"Aye," Diedrik nodded, a disgusted look still on his face as he laid out his bedroll. Malta and Myrisan's horse, Stell, grazed unconcerned on some nearby shrubs, so he figured they were relatively safe for now. He offered Myrisan some jerky and crystallized fruit which was accepted.

"So," he said when they had become at least partially comfortably situated. "Tell me why you've been watching over me for thirty years."

"You don't need to know."

"I think I'll be the judge of that."

"Isn't it enough to know I'm there?" Myrisan asked.

"Not anymore. Tell me why," Diedrik said, fixing him with his dark-eyed gaze.

"Fine, but don't say I never warned you," he paused. "Have you noticed how young you look compared to other people your age?"

"Lately, why?"

"When was the last time you were sick?" Myrisan asked. Diedrik thought for a moment.

"I don't remember."

"Never. You've never been sick. Do you know what gypsies are?" he continued.

"Of course. They're magic. Half-breeds of some sort, no offense," he added hastily.

"None taken. Aye, they are half-breeds of some sort. Only their fathers are Magi. That's why they live as long as Elves without ever getting sick. They aren't magic, as you say, they're just sensitive to it, and they can use magical artifacts."

"What's the point of all this? I know who my father was," Diedrik protested weakly, though his mind was in turmoil.

"When I was fifteen, the Mage Penn approached me about a mission. He knew my father well as he was a commander in Mistgarde. As I was a Hafalf, I was looked down upon by most, but the Magus, he saw something in me. He told me that he had a son by a woman he was in love with and he wanted him discreetly watched over.

"However, the Mage did not marry her as his family would have been put in danger by his status. So he was forced to send the child and the woman to live with the son of an old friend who had agreed to marry the girl and adopt the boy. I was charged with protecting the boy in order to give my life purpose and to become a member of Mistgarde." He showed Diedrik the scar worn by all members of Mistgarde.

"Are you saying that I am the son of a Mage?" Diedrik felt suddenly very weak.

"Aye. Aside from a bloody idiot, that is. I'm sorry you were never told, but look at it this way, you've got a good nine or ten hundred years left in you to get over it."

Diedrik and Myrisan left the forested slopes of the Dwarven mountains late in the day and welcomed the warmer, lowland air. The grassy hills were studded with multicolored Autumn flowers and seemed to roll on endlessly. The sky was a cloudless blue so deep it looked as if they could swim in it.

Myrisan had shaved his beard and wore his cloak at all times to hide his well muscled body. This way he would appear to be fully Elven to the casual observer. Diedrik had shaved off his beard as well but for his bushy black goatee. His long, black hair was now shoulder length all in preparation for their return to Sendar-controlled territory.

They spotted a large, four-story inn on the horizon that was well known to both, for they had stayed there many times. Diedrik, of course, hadn't known Myrisan was there, though. Memories of their last stay at an inn were still fresh more than a month later as they approached.

The courtyard of the inn was full of people coming and going. Retailers peddling their wares to the weary travelers, stable boys, barmaids and patrons went about their business quickly before darkness set in. Diedrik and Myrisan felt relief at the normalness of it all as they paid a stable boy to quarter their well-worked steeds.

They entered the inn relatively unnoticed. Myrisan found them a seat while Diedrik got them rooms.

Diedrik then took the two steaming plates of food and the mugs of ale precariously over to the table where Myrisan was still warily eyeing the room.

"Thanks," he said, taking a plate and a mug for himself.

"Why're you looking so intense?" Diedrik asked. "Something amiss?"

"Just force of habit, I guess."

"Aye, I suppose it would be. Tell me something, Myrisan, what about *your* life?"

"What do you mean?" the Hafalf asked, not looking Diedrik in the eye.

"You know, what about what *you* want in life? Women, family, money, doesn't it bother you that you spend all your time watching over me?"

"All I ever wanted was to be a member of Mistgarde. This assignment is my reward for fifteen years of never-ending training to reach that goal. This *is* my life and I am happy with it. I have risen higher than any Hafalf in the realms but for my fellow Protectors. And for the record, I have had more than my share of women and money during your life and I'm only forty-six. I've got eight hundred years left to start a family."

"Aye, well, after thirty years of service, don't you deserve more recognition?" Diedrik asked, "Within Mistgarde, I mean?"

"Mistgarde isn't about recognition. It's about service to the Northern Peoples. Anyway, I'm a Hafalf, this is my station in life."

"I don't believe that. Not one bit."

"Be that as it may, Diedrik, that is the way of the world. I am actually rather fortunate," Myrisan said.

"How do you figure?"

"Think about it. A Haftroll usually kills its mother in childbirth and thus is an orphan. A Bancrae cannot even *live* in an Elven or Troll city, much less gain acceptance. A Hobgoblin of any race is usually the result of rape and killed at birth and we *know* the result of Half-Giants. A half-Orcan or Shraken can't even breath underwater. Landar are blind most of the time, and I've never even *seen* a Hafrok.

"As a Hafalf, I still have the relative lifespan of an Elf. I can still scale flat walls and see in the dark. I don't have the *Elffire* or the *Silence* spells but I am bigger and stronger than an Elf. I'm as comfortable in the mountains, plains or on the sea as I am in the forest, and I am a member of the most elite fighting force in the realms. I am doing the bidding of the Magi and in that I am content."

"I guess I never looked at it that way," Diedrik conceded.

"Aye. We should get to sleep soon. It's a long way to reach Keyre by nightfall the day after tomorrow."

Diedrik rose well before dawn the next day only to find Myrisan already up and dressed. He rolled out of bed and got ready quickly, and joined the Hafalf downstairs for breakfast. They unstabled their horses quietly and set in brisk pace towards Keyre to the sound of birds waking and singing their first songs of the day.

Towards midday, they reached the shores of Lok Keyre and stopped to eat. They made idle chatter for awhile, watching the fishing fleets troll the great Lok's surface in search of their livelihood. The light, Autumn breeze helped to fill their sails as they jockeyed for position.

Diedrik looked around, suddenly uneasy. A feeling in his gut he had felt before but couldn't identify was telling him something.

"Do you feel that?" he asked the Myrisan, who came instantly on guard.

"No. What is it?"

"I don't know," Diedrik answered, getting up. The source seemed to be coming from the other side of the Lok. He promised himself he would investigate after he had informed Rork and Veg's family of their passing and take care of a few small matters in Keyre. "No matter, we'd best be getting on though."

"Aye," Myrisan agreed, still looking around. They mounted up and continued on towards Keyre.

CHAPTER 28
NIGHTVEIL

et kept his cowl low over his face as he walked the nearly empty streets of Maka. The night was warm and the torches of the streets dim, but he took no chances, for he did not look like a Mai'Lang to any but the most casual observer. The black face paint he used on his lips only distracted any observer's gaze from his steel gray eyes for so long. He kept his hands on his hatchet hilts at all times both to be ready for ever-present danger and to hide his conspicuously un-red palms.

He could not remember ever speaking Langjian but had found upon his arrival that he could understand it. Tentatively he had tried speaking to a busy merchant and had been aghast to learn that he spoke it fluently. He rubbed the Key of Fog between his fingers, the memory of his mother speaking to him, singing lullabies, all in Langjian. Shaking his head, Jet focused on the task at hand. He stopped in front of a large, three story inn where it was rumored that any information in the city could be bought, sold or coerced.

He entered into a cloud of smoke and the sounds of drunken men and the odd-keyed pipes the Mai'Lang loved to listen to. Jet liked them, too, he realized. There were easily a hundred people in the common room, with dozens of scantily-clad women being harassed at every turn. Jet had no doubt they were slaves. Bloody Mai'Lang loved their flarin' slaves. He spotted the inn keeper, a white haired, fat man with a hawkish face beneath his double chins. He ordered a glass of Goblin spirits, keeping his cowl low, and his eyes on the crowd.

"You don't look to be a man interested in drinking," the inn keeper commented.

"It all depends on what's for sale otherwise," Jet said, feeling the spirit's cold burn trickle down to his empty stomach. The two and a half days it had taken him to fly here had taken much out of him. He wouldn't be able to turn back into the raven, much less fly for days. He set a gold piece on the countertop. The inn keeper eyed it greedily, for it was more than four people would have to pay if they drank all night.

"Mayhaps I can be of assistance."

"I'm in need of someone with knowledge of the riverfront area. Someone who won't tell those on the riverfront who I'm looking for as soon as I leave," Jet told him.

"That one," the inn keeper pointed to a giant of a man with a long waxed moustache and a bald head dressed in longshoreman's garb. He was the center of attention in a loud conversation with four other equally-tough looking men, though he never said a word. Jet left the gold piece on the counter which the inn keeper quickly snatched up.

Jet tapped the man on the shoulder—nearly level with his eyes—and the man turned around to glare down at him with his white eyes. The man had to be seven feet tall and almost twice Jet's weight. The other four men took a step back, expecting a fight. Calmly, Jet placed two gold pieces into the man's beefy, calloused palm. The man's bushy eyebrows shot up in surprise, then searched the dark recesses of Jet's cowl.

"I wonder if I might speak to you in private. Outside, if you please."

"Aye, I suppose," the man rumbled in a low baritone like a Troll's.

They stepped into the quiet street, taking up positions facing each other far enough apart to draw their weapons if need be. Jet eyed the huge broadsword the man carried and wondered idly if he himself could even lift it. He stated his deal.

"There's another two golds waiting for you if you take me where I want to go. Before you accept, there're two things you need to know. First," Jet pushed back his hood. "I am Landar." The man inhaled at the half Sendar features but nodded. "Second, if you tell anyone of me, I will kill you and them without hesitation." The bald man looked doubtful but agreed anyway.

"Where is it you wish me to take you?"

"There is an old man who lives by the riverfront. I need you to take me to him. His name is Duarta'Rhan." Before the word was even fully out of his mouth, the bald man slammed Jet against the side of the inn, holding him by the neck with one massive arm a foot off the ground. Jet had two knives at the man's throat just as quickly.

"What do you want of Duarta?" the man demanded, heedless of the knives.

"No harm," Jet said tightly.

The man eyed him a moment longer before dropping him. Jet took several deep breaths, both to calm himself and because his windpipe had nearly been crushed. He put his cowl back up.

"Tell me why you wish to see Duarta'Rhan."

"He is my grandfather," Jet said, the word still sounding odd in his head even though his memories confirmed that the man was his mother's father and that he had helped them escape from the Stormdogs.

"Do you speak the truth?"

"What reason do I have to lie? I've already showed you my face," Jet said.

"My name is Katir'Tua. If you're blood of Duarta, then I am your man."

"I am Jet Bloodhatchet." They clasped wrists, Jet's dwarfed by the man's massive hands.

"Follow me, Bloodhatchet. And wipe off that lipstick. It convinces no one and makes you look like a woman. Besides, no one will trouble you when you walk with me." Jet scowled but did as the man said.

The riverfront was a never ending series of docks, shops and warehouses pressed right up against the Mal River, the largest river on the two continents. Katir took Jet to a well-kept, three-story residence built in the Mai'Lang style of roofs that curved up at the corner on every level. Three well made cargo crafts were docked out on the shore tended by two men who didn't even look up when Jet and Katir passed by. A hard looking woman with a black head scarf and a tattooed face barked orders at them. Katir knocked twice on the door and stood back as a thin wiry man opened the door. He wore the traditional brown smock of Mai'Lang servants. Slaves, Jet corrected himself. Bloody slaves.

"Ah, Master Katir'Tua. How are you this night?"

"I am well, Hui'han. I wish to speak to Duarta'Rhan. I bring a guest he may wish to see."

"Ah," Hui'han nodded, eyeing Jet's black cloak and cowled face. "Please come in, I will inform Master Duarta'Rhan. May I inquire as to your identity, Master?" he asked Jet.

"You may not. And don't call me Master again," Jet answered icily. Hui'han looked helplessly at Katir, who nodded with a twinge of a smile.

"Right away." Hui'han disappeared into a back room. The struggle to refrain from saying Master was evident on his tortured features.

The sitting room was sparsely but elegantly decorated with low slung furniture and pillows of multicolored silks and satins. They knelt on the pillows, Katir with his hands on his lap, Jet's on his hatchets. The wait was not long before Hui'han appeared carrying a silver tray with two cups of a dark, almost black tea, handing one to Jet and the other to Katir'Tua. Jet took a sip and found its bitter taste actually quite good. He was lost in thought when a low voice brought him back.

Jet had always been taller than most people and looking at the tall, lithe frame of the gray haired Mai'Lang in front of him, he could see where it came from. Though the man had to be pushing one hundred, he was still healthy and strong with sharp white eyes. He wore a long black silk shirt buttoned down the right side in Mai'Lang fashion with matching pants. Katir greeted him warmly, though Duarta's eyes never left Jet.

"Well, then, who are you?" he cut straight to the point. Jet glanced at Hui'han and pointed towards the door. After a nod from Duarta'Rhan, he fled. Jet pulled back his cowl, fixing the older man with his gray eyes. Duarta inhaled at this but said nothing.

"My name is Jet Bloodhatchet. You may know me as Jetrian Torvaldsen."

"By Hod's Eyes. Jetrian? My daughter Plentis' baby boy?" the man's eyes became watery. He grabbed Jet's hand, searching his face once more.

"Aye. Though I regret to inform you that both she and Torvald are no longer in this world."

"Aye," Duarta nodded sadly. "I feared as much."

"I remember you helped us escape from the Stormdogs."

"Aye, though I'm surprised you remember that. You were but an infant at the time." Duarta continued staring at him for a moment. "Bloodhatchet. That name I heard just the other day. Something about a man who took on a Goblin horde and stood atop a mountain of corpses twenty times dead and still fighting."

"Aye. It's a bit exaggerated though. I had help," Jet shrugged.

"Is that where you got the name from?" Katir asked.

"No. My father's blood coats these blades."

"Torvald." Duarta nodded. "I do not mean to speak ill of the dead, but he was a truly evil man. I never knew what my Plentis saw in him. She was headstrong like her mother," Jet snorted and both men looked hard at him.

"I'm sorry, it's just weird for me to hear a Mai'Lang call someone evil."

"I assume it would be." Duarta smiled. "But not all Mai'Lang are evil just as not all Sendar are good. You should know that better than most."

"Aye," Jet agreed quietly.

Before Jet could answer, the back door swung open and a woman in skintight black leathers that came to her chin along with a long black cloak that grazed the floor strode in. A thin silver chain was threaded through her lustrous black, waist length hair connected to a black veil, except for two long stands of white that hung in front of her beautiful face. Startling, glowing purple eyes peered out from small, intricate purple tattoos around her brows and temples. Her lips were tattooed purple as well. She was by far the most beautiful woman Jet had ever seen, making Hrafna seem a toad by comparison.

Upon making eye contact, the girl pushed the black veil down over her face and drew a long double-bladed spear from its place at her back. He noticed that her palms were not red but tattooed with detailed purple designs all the way up to the knuckles on the tops of her hands as well. Without saying a word, Jet could tell she was *very* upset with him for having seen her face. She was Sendar sure as his own sisters.

His hatchets were out so quickly that he did not appear to even have moved. He wasn't sure by the look on Katir'Tua or

Duarta'Rhan's face whether he should put away his weapons or fight, but either way it was evident they expected him to lose. He would bloody show them. No one had ever defeated him when he carried the hatchets, though he suspected Danken might have had a chance. Not some Sendar girl scared to show him her face.

"What is the situation, Duarta?" he asked, never taking his eyes from her, not that he could have even if he'd wanted to. She did the same.

"Situation?" Duarta'Rhan asked innocently, sipping his tea unconcerned.

"Who is this?" he demanded, wondering how a Sendar could have survived this long in Mai'Lang.

"You will address me when you speak, Sendar or you will do so from your knees," the girl snapped. "And you will treat Duarta'Rhan with the respect he deserves!"

"Please sit, both of you," Duarta'Rhan said quietly. Jet hesitated but followed suit when the girl did so immediately. "That's much better. Now, Wytchyn Nightveil, please meet my grandson, Jet Bloodhatchet."

"A flarin' pleasure," Jet smiled wryly at the girl's hanging jaw which she quickly snapped shut.

"Wytchyn was one of my first students, Jet," Duarta'Rhan said with a fond pat on her arm. "She is the fastest learner I've ever taught."

"Congratulations," Jet scowled.

"You may raise your veil, Wytchyn," Duarta said to the girl. "He has seen your face and anyway, he is Landar. You have nothing to fear. He will not inform the Emperors Legion."

"Informing is for cowards and honorless thugs," Jet said coldly.

"All is well then? Excellent, pour yourselves some more tea."

"What of Hui'han?" Wytchyn asked as she did so.

"It seems Jet does not like slaves," Katir'Tua rumbled.

"Better to bloody die," Jet grumbled.

"It seems you two have much in common," Duarta clucked and both young Sendar bristled. "So why have you come back, Jetrian?" Duarta'Rhan asked finally.

"To claim what is mine," Jet showed them the Key of Fog.

"You seek to be a Stormdog?" he was disapproving. Wytchyn laughed out loud into her tea. Jet ignored her, though it was very hard, for she had such a wonderful laugh.

"No. I seek to lead the Stormdogs," the other men's eyebrows shot up.

"Lead them? Are you serious, boy?" Duarta exclaimed.

"I can defeat *any* two men in single combat, I'm a better leader than any they have if the rumors I hear are true, and I have the Key of Fog," Jet declared.

"That may be but—"

"There are more than two of them, Landar," Wytchyn scoffed.

"I will kill every last one of them and build from the ground up if I have to. With or without your help. Preferably with, I *will* lead the Stormdogs."

"May I see?" Duarta asked calmly.

"See what?"

"The skills with which you intend to take over the most powerful mercenary army in the world." Before Duarta was even through speaking, all eighteen of Jet's knives successively formed a silhouette of him on the wall. The old man never once blinked. At the same time, Katir attacked, thinking Duarta dead. His massive blade rung out loudly, but Jet was ready for him this time. His hatchets redirected the powerful swing and twice hit the giant man in the head with the blunt side. Wytchyn seemingly didn't budge, eyeing him critically, but he would have drunk a vial of Drissian poison if she hadn't disappeared and then reappeared. He felt a tiny drop of blood at the back of his neck and saw to his disbelief a miniscule drop at the tip of her blade. The woman could have killed him!

Duarta calmly turned and observed the perfect precision of Jet's throws. Katir was smiling broadly, shaking his head ruefully, unfazed. Jet swallowed his pride. The man was invincible.

"Should have known he was of your blood, old man," Katir grumbled, sitting down heavily and rubbing a knot on the side of his skull. Jet only had eyes for the girl and she him. He ached to talk to her but knew somehow that a woman like her spoke when *she* felt like

it. And for all of his legendary talents with women, he had no clue
how to handle this one. Bloody women.

"Aye. I haven't seen anyone throw knives like that since your
mother," Duarta agreed. Eyeing Wytchyn with a fatherly smile, he
pulled the knives from the wall and handed them back to Jet, who
profusely apologized for acting so rashly. "No need to apologize, boy.
I asked you to show me and you did. Granted, I expected Katir to
beat you senseless. You have given me much to think on. Hui'han will
show you to a guest room and bring you something to eat. Tomorrow,
we will discuss what you plan and how I can help."

With his baggy, wide-ankled and wristed black riding leathers
freshly pressed and scrubbed, it was impossible to tell Jet's real size,
nor how many knives he carried. He kept his face clean-shaven and
repainted his lips, along with a special red dye Duarta gave him for
his palms. In the heat of the Mai'Lang day, he would not be able to
wear his cowl so he brushed his silky black hair close around his pale
gray eyes. Besides, it wasn't as if Landar were unheard of, it was just
that they were usually blind. That gave him an idea.

Taking a strip of thin black silk, he wrapped it around his head,
covering his eyes with his hair over the rest of the fabric to at least
maintain a small piece of his considerable vanity. He could see just
fine yet couldn't see his eyes in the mirror and it was better than his
hair cutting off his peripheral vision. He hung the tail of his leather
shirt over his hatchets so they weren't readily apparent and unbuttoned the front past his chest to gain some relief from the heat.

He was putting the finishing touches on his disguise when he saw
a cowled Wytchyn in the mirror. Jet whirled only to find no one there.
He pulled off the black silk eye wrap and looked again in the mirror.
There she stood, impassive and carrying that wicked shornstave. He
checked the room again but found it empty. With a determined look
in his eyes, he watched the mirror while he reached out for her. Just
as he was about to touch her, she slapped his hand away roughly.

"What the bloody—?"

"Watch where your hands go, Landar. This is not a slave market," she said haughtily. "And watch your language as well."

"How are you doing what you're doing?" he asked, and in response she pulled back her cowl, rendering her visible once more. She seemed to be reading his thoughts. He could almost *feel* her in his head.

"You are not all powerful and you are in a foreign land. There is much you do not know that can hurt you."

"I suppose you're going to tell me not to go then?"

"Why would I care?" Wytchyn scoffed, though he really was handsome, she thought, fighting down a blush behind her veil. And he hid his secrets so much better than most. Interesting. She would need more time to discern them, which should prove to be fun.

"I'm missing your point then."

"*I* don't care, but Duarta'Rhan does."

"And therefore..." Jet prodded irritably.

"And therefore I will be accompanying you to the Myrkwood."

"The flarin' wheels of Freyja's Chariot you are!"

"Your choice Landar. My help or no help."

"Loki help me," Jet said under his breath. "Bloody fine. Let's go. We don't have all bloody day."

"Glad that you see things my way Landar." Why couldn't women call him by his flarin' name? "And watch your language. This isn't the North."

"My name is Jet Bloodhatchet. Jet flarin' Bloodhatchet! *Not* Landar."

"Very well, Landar." She became invisible again. Jet gritted his teeth. The woman had seen right bloody through him! And why was his flarin' heart beating so fast? He was certainly not afraid. He was— Damn the woman! Why could he not get her face out of his head? Or the smell of her perfume, like a spring breeze...

He slapped himself hard, shaking his head vigorously. He was Jet Bloodhatchet, and no one made it past his defenses. She had tried but he was stronger. He would not allow himself to trust. Never again. He had sworn it to himself all those years ago. Trust was pain. Trust was pain.

Duarta'Rhan and Katir'Tua were very impressed by his disguise. Jet took off the blindfold with a smile as Hui'han served them breakfast. Fish eggs and sweet rice cakes. Jet repressed an urge to fling the plate away from his palate and instead washed every bite down with sweetened black tea. Duarta began speaking as if they had not had half a day's break in between conversation.

"The Stormdogs are led by a Shraklan named Blackclaw."

"A Shraklan?" Jet winced, for any Mai'Lang wishing to be intimate with a sandpaper-skinned Shraken would either have to be very careful or else resistant to the pain of having delicate parts cut open. "Ouch."

"Aye," Duarta sighed. "As I was saying, his *Stunspore* magic is somehow mutated so that instead of paralyzation, it actually enthralls his victims."

"Enthralls as in makes them obey?" Jet asked.

"What other kind of 'enthralls' is there?" Wytchyn asked but Duarta'Rhan merely continued talking.

"Aye, and he's a deadly fighter with two hooks. His Lieutenant is one of the most, if not the most, deadly assassins in all Midgarthe. A Shraken named Ureshk. He uses two daggers, churiken, poison, you name it, he's an expert at it."

"But I have the Fog."

"Aye and it's your greatest ally, too. Without the Fog to hide their hidden city, the Stormdogs have had to fight two Goblin hordes and an entire contingent of Driss. The Stormdogs won't hesitate to steal that Key just because you wear it. They'll take it along with your head if you're not careful."

Jet nodded, taking the Key from around his neck and off of its chain. He took one of Duarta's sharp table knives and cut a very deep gash in the underside of his left forearm. The two Mai'Lang eyed him as if he was crazy. Wytchyn gasped loudly. Calmly, he pushed the key into the wound and held it closed. A few ticks later, he wiped the blood away to reveal his arm perfectly healed over the impression of the key's shape.

"How is that possible?" Duarta gasped. "A Healing Scarf? But no, that wound was too great. What then?"

"As I said before, I can defeat *any* two men in armed combat, assassin or not."

"By the Blind God, boy you may just have a chance!" Duarta laughed. "Come, I will prepare you for your journey and inform you of all else pertaining to the Stormdogs as we go. Katir, you as well my friend."

"You will help me then?" Jet asked.

"Three times I have sought to dissuade you, or prove you incapable. Three times you have thrown my doubts back in my old face. Aye, boy, I will help you."

Duarta'Rhan gave him any helpful information his old mind could think of, which was considerable. Jet's saddlebags were stuffed full as he mounted a large, sleek black stallion with a fiery temper. Katir rode up, also dressed in black riding leathers for the road on a massive dark brown Clydesdale with a white tail, mane and fetlocks. Wytchyn was saddled up as well, her cloak tied behind her and her shornstave across the pommel.

"Duarta'Rhan, I thought—" Jet began.

"I wish I was still young enough to ride with you, grandson, but alas, these old bones are too fragile to travel any farther than into town. Katir will go with you."

"But—" Jet sputtered.

"He will be your sword when you sleep, Jetrian." Duarta'Rhan turned to the huge, bald Mai'Lang with a pat on his leg as he sat astride his horse. "My old friend. Your debt to me has been erased long since. If you still truly wish to protect me, then protect all I have left of family in this world. Besides, there are plenty of people to watch over this old man."

"I will serve your blood as I served you, Duarta'Rhan. Though you misjudge me if you think I believe you need protection," Katir'Tua scoffed. Wytchyn did also as she and the old man said their goodbyes. She could not hide her tears behind the veil though.

"Goodbye, grandfather," Jet said as his horse began its trot. "Thank you for your help. Once things are settled, I will return and hear more of your crazy stories."

"Aye, I've no doubt of it. Good luck!" Duarta'Rhan called and they were on their way to the Myrkwood.

CHAPTER 29
DEAD WOODS

A day out of harbor found *Windstrike* sailing south at a fast clip. Danken, Shonai, Lanaia, Swifteye, Valshk and T'riel were in their communal cabin.

"Why didn't we just port all the way to Isthok?" Lanaia asked.

"Because I've never been there, nor have I the ability to use *Stonespeak* to see it until we reach the Mai'Lang continent," Danken explained.

"I've seen you use an eagle shape before," Shonai commented, "why not just fly there?"

"I can only hold the form for so long before I'm drained. I'll need all the energy I can get when we arrive in Isthok."

"Are you so sure she's even *in* Isthok?" Lanaia asked.

"No, not until I can use *Stonespeak* to find her. I know only that she is no longer on the Sendarian continent. If Driss took her, it stands to reason that they still have her."

"Aye," Valshk agreed.

"And what of Captain Tamlinsen?" Lanaia put in, "What does he know of this mission?"

"Nothing save our destination," Danken said. "He claims he wasn't due in port for another two months. He said he returned because he received an unconscious beckoning, much like Shonai apparently. How did he put it? He 'did as destiny bid him.'" Danken told them.

"It's him!" Lanaia announced. Danken spun around but there was no one there.

"It's who?" he asked.

"In the prophecy. He is the one who heeds the call of destiny!"

"I suppose so. Yet, I very much doubt the good Captain will abandon his ship to tramp through the heart of the Evil continent."

"The prophecy says he will, he will," she said resolutely.

"Aye, if you say so."

"Sail Ho!" came a booming voice from above. They scrambled on deck to see for themselves.

"What is it?" Tamlinsen bellowed.

"Four sails, sir! West by southwest!" The crow's-nest shouted back.

"Can you identify them?"

"Aye sir. They appear to be Shrakens, sir."

"*All* of them?" Tamlinsen's eyes widened.

"Aye sir, all four."

"Damn." Tamlinsen turned to Ragnarsen. "Put on full sail, east by southeast."

"Aye sir."

"Belay that." Danken's voice echoed into the silence of the ship.

"Excuse me?" Tamlinsen whirled.

"I said belay that. If the Shrakens want a fight, we'll give them one."

"Perhaps you are unaware of situations at sea, Magus. Four Goblin vessels will give us a run for our money. Four Shraken vessels will cut us to shreds."

"Perhaps *you* are unaware, Captain, of whom it is you are addressing. I will, however, forgive your inexperience as you have never seen a Mage do battle. Sail directly for them. You and your crew needn't worry about the defense of *Windstrike*. My companions and I will handle the Shrakens on deck. The Orcans will deal with whatever resistance is below. Is that acceptable to you, Princess Shonai?"

"Absolutely. I've been looking forward to this."

"*Dwei,*" Danken said. "Here is the plan."

As the Shrakens closed on *Windstrike*, they thought they had happened on a plague ship. Only Danken was visible to them, though he wore his cowl tight over his face to prevent recognition. The four ships began to close in.

Suddenly Danken invoked *Firewall* on all four ships, setting the dry timber and rigging alight. Shrakens screamed as their carefully thought out plan of attack crumbled and panic set in. They ran about, passing baskets to try and put out the perpetual fire. Danken used *Breezesummon* to keep the flames from touching *Windstrike* as the colossal ships crashed together.

Most of the Shrakens who had been under the ships swam to the surface to witness the fiery tombs their ships had become. As they did so, the Orcans, led by Shonai, shot out from their concealed spot behind the ship. They unleashed powerful *Sonarblasts* that caught the preoccupied Shrakens completely by surprise, devastating their superior numbers. The Orcans were among them instantly, cutting their hated enemies down with Dwarven javelins.

Up above, Danken used *Airlift* to move Valshk and Swifteye to one ship while he himself boarded another. The crew of *Windstrike* divided and rushed the two remaining ships. Next, he used *Magefire* to kill all four Shraken Captains simultaneously.

Valshk and Swifteye were a fearsome tandem. The Shrakens, unaware of their presence aboard, were systematically cut down. Valshk was an invisible monster, swinging his mighty battleaxe with precision, while Swifteye slew any who drew too near with his spiked mace. A blur of silver surrounding a shimmering specter of death.

Danken went about his battle in a far more straightforward way. He began by killing the nearest Shrakens with *Magefire*, fired from *F'laare*, punching through their ranks. Those who avoided this fate were met with a flashing blade wielded by a lunatic who radiated blue. Danken lost track of the day as he slew Shrakens by the dozens. Those with half a mind chose to dive over the side. There they believed they would be safe. Instead they encountered the deadly trap the Orcans had set for them.

The *Windstrike* crew were the best in the realms and it showed. They fought with unmatched ferocity and cunning. One of the major reasons Mistgarde ships were so powerful was that the races that comprised them worked in perfect harmony. The Elves led with *Moonfire* and long, slender blades. The Trolls cut shimmering swaths through enemy forces and the Sendar filled the holes, welcoming all comers.

Once Danken had cleared his ship (with help from T'riel, of course) he moved to Valshk and Swifteye's. The Shrakens had regrouped and made a concerted attack only to be mercilessly cut down.

Danken fired a few bolts of fire at the remaining Shrakens to end the fight.

Next, they boarded one of the ships the crew was fighting aboard. Though the Mistgarde sailors had the battle well in hand, Danken and his two companions helped mop up. The battle ended soon after with not a single Shraken survivor, as was the law of the sea.

An uncommonly long silence pervaded long after the last sword had been sheathed. Only the crackling of the smoldering flames and softly flowing waves broke the illusion of deafness. Even the wounded remained quiet as they witnessed the awesome spectacle around them.

One crew of Mistgarde sailors had completely wiped out four fully crewed Shraken vessels loaded with treasures. Most turned to stare at Danken, Valshk and Swifteye. Danken bid them silently to return to *Windstrike*, as the Shraken vessels were near to capsizing. The Orcans, too, filed on deck. Princess Shonai presented a casualty report, as did Captain Tamlinsen. Danken read it grimly. Seven Orcans, four Elves, five Trolls and six Sendar.

"These men and women died for something important," Danken said softly, though all present could hear him. "Not just the margin of Shrakens dead to ours, but the message that a time for change has come for us all. No longer will the proud races of the North cower in the face of piracy or robbery. No, we will rise against it as we did eighteen years ago.

"No longer will we tolerate senseless and unprovoked attacks on our people. We are as one and we will fight as such. You more than any understand this, for it is you who embody this concept. You have fought bravely this day, condemning to the deep hundreds of enemies who have doubtless killed a dozen times their number and would have continued to do so. You have helped to secure this ocean for the foreseeable future though the fight is far from over. Well fought, my friends, well fought."

"Aye!" Tamlinsen yelled, thrusting his blade into the air. Soon everyone was doing likewise, a thunderous roar in the face of Evil.

"You are something else, Danken Sariksen." Shonai told him as they once again set sail for Mai'Lang.

"You are no pushover yourself, Shonai Golden Gauntlet."

The dawn found the *Windstrike* sailing on stormy, wind-chopped seas. The violent rocking of the ship made sleep impossible though Danken hardly noticed. He had spent the majority of the night helping, if not outright healing the previous day's wounded. He swung carelessly in his hammock, oblivious to the turbulent sea.

While the crew went about the days work as usual, the Orcans below kept a vigilant watch over the surrounding seas. Shonai and Kamotal swam in the center of the large formation discussing life back home in Sha'na. Kamotal was originally from Cona, an Orcan city in the channel of the Western Isles. He had only ventured to Sha'na when he had enlisted in the Royal Guard. From there, he had become a distinguished warrior, subsequently drafted by Mistgarde.

He had risen through the ranks quickly to become Orcan Commander of the most famous War Ship in the Navy. He was over two hundred fifty years old and the grey streaks were starting to appear in his black hair. This, however, was not a mark of the elderly among Orcans, but a sign of wisdom.

Thus, it was that a tiny speck in the distance aroused his danger senses at the same time as the lead scout called back urgently. Instantly, he broke into action. A messenger was sent to inform Tamlinsen as the Orcan squadron assembled into battle formations.

Shonai's gauntlet began to burn furiously. Her keen vision picked up two gigantic forms approaching them at a fast clip.

"Sea Dragons," Kamotal said quietly. "Two of them. Probably making their way north to breed at Sea Dragon Isle."

"Will they attack?" Shonai asked.

"If they're hungry. Or bored. Or angry. Or..."

"I've got it. So what do we do?"

"Hit them with all we've got before they get close enough to use their *Hypnosis* or *Whirlpool* attacks on us and wreck the ship."

"You mean we will fight them?"

"If they continue heading toward us," Kamotal replied calmly.

"And can we win?"

"Doubtful. You should leave while you can, Majesty. I'll assign you a guard."

"Not likely, Commander." Shonai shot him an icy glare.

"I thought as much. In that case, don't *ever* look them in the eye. Go for their throat or ear holes." Kamotal told her as a splash above them heralded a sight that took both by surprise. Danken was swimming towards them gracefully, as if he had been born underwater. Shonai beamed sonar at him.

"What are you doing down here?"

"Helping," he said simply, letting his energy trickle into the two Orcans to communicate. His eyes burned blue as he peered through the depths at the rapidly approaching Sea Dragons. "Wait here. Make no move unless I am harmed."

"But they'll kill you!" Shonai exclaimed.

"Unlikely." Danken winked as he swam towards the giant creatures. He nearly forgot to breathe as he neared them. They were impressive, light blue with white undersides. They had heads that resembled a common Dragon's, but were more sleek and aerodynamic. Their horns were swept back nearly horizontal, running along slender, vertically flat bodies that were quite similar to a snakes, except they were over six times the length of a man. Their wings were now giant fins. Female Sea Dragons were much smaller than their male counterparts and nearly five times as numerous. They were not nearly as dangerous and most were unknown even by Dragon chasers. Still, they only migrated to breed every three hundred six years so they were not to be taken lightly.

Danken shielded his eyes from the glowing yellow slits that threatened to overtake his will. Sending out powerful tendrils of blue to each, he made his presence clear and powerful. The two stopped in their tracks as his energy reached them.

"A Mage underwater." One of the Dragons, a large female, scoffed. "In eight hundred years, I thought I'd seen it all, but a swimming Mage takes all."

"A preposterous notion, to be sure," the smaller female Dragon replied.

"You speak nothing like Isahagilaz or any of his kind," Danken remarked.

"Ah! A world renowned expert on Dragons!"

"It's because they're of the old breed. We Sea Dragons have evolved."

"Relics, if you will."

"I see," Danken said warily, aware of their attempts to hypnotize him.

"Good that you do. Tell me, do you have a death wish, young Magus?"

"Not particularly."

"Then help me to understand your motives for stopping a *pair* of Sea Dragons in mid-migration." The larger female narrowed her eyes.

"Forgive me. It's just that you're swimming directly for my companions, most of which are quite nervous at your appearance. There seems to be the small matter of you eating them they are wary of. Interestingly enough, I was going to ask the same question of you."

"What question would that be?" the small female asked.

"If *you* had a 'death wish,' as you so eloquently put it. Grand and deadly as you may be, eighty Mistgarde Orcans may prove your downfall."

"Frightful," the large female hissed dangerously.

"Indeed," the small one agreed. "And if we were to snatch you up and hold you for some future pleasure?"

"You would undoubtedly find it most unpleasant as I melted your insides together before freezing your lungs. Quite hard to breathe that way, I'm told, with the lungs frozen and all."

"A war of words then is it?"

"Far from it. I merely wish to save us all a lot of trouble. We both have prior engagements, no need for either of us to miss them. Unless, of course, your engagement is with death. Better, I think, to pass as though unnoticed, wouldn't you say?"

"Aye, a valid point," the large one said slowly.

"Perhaps it is best we spare the poor wretches. Not much of a meal anyway, what with their gaminess and all."

"Precisely."

"I'm sure a boatload of Shrakens or Goblins would suit your distinguished palates much nicer." Danken smiled as the two leviathans began to swim away. The small one turned slowly.

"You play a dangerous game quite well, Magus, yet you seem unable to see all of the pieces on the board. Two dead Sea Dragons are better than two vengeful Dragons with long memories. You would do well to heed that if your so-called immortality is to last."

Danken said nothing, merely watched them slowly fade away into the murk. His energy was nearly gone, using *Waterbreath, Everwarm* and *Obeyance* simultaneously. He rose to the surface and climbed aboard *Windstrike* slowly, leaving a squadron full of Orcans slack jawed and giddy with relief.

The crew of *Windstrike* cheered him wildly as he dried off before returning to his cabin and falling instantly to sleep.

"Land Ho!" The crow's-nest called, jolting Danken awake. He dressed hurriedly before climbing to top deck. Most of the crew had assembled along the starboard side to catch a glimpse of the Mai'Lang mainland. It appeared as a small grey patch on the grey sky, rendering it somewhat invisible. As they neared, it grew larger until it was clearly distinguishable.

Keeping their eyes peeled for any sign of danger, *Windstrike* sailed into a cove at the edge of the land. Dropping down a shore boat, Tamlinsen sent a scouting party to secure the landing place. They rowed silently before coming aground. Once they had done so, they fanned out into a wide formation, weapons at the ready.

After what seemed like forever, they finally rowed back to *Windstrike* to make their report.

"No danger we can see, Captain, but the Dead Wood gives me the creeps." The Bosun's mate, a Sendar named Salk, said.

"Are you sure this is where you wish to land, Magus?" Tamlinsen asked Danken.

"Aye. It will do, You and your crew are needed elsewhere, I'm sure."

"Not likely, Magus. I will be sending a guard detachment along for your journey, accompanied by myself."

"I'm afraid I cannot permit that, Captain," Danken said, shaking his head.

"I'm afraid I have no choice. The Elven Princess has been captured, you go to her rescue."

"How do you know of this?" Danken asked heatedly.

"A carrier pigeon landed on deck carrying message of her kidnapping by Driss. I simply made the deduction and you confirmed it. Either way, it matters not now, for I will have a mutiny on my hands if I don't send an Elven guard to help find her, an Orcan guard to protect the Princess and a Sendar guard to protect *you*. Or perhaps, I am supposed to sail back through what we just faced with half of a crew. I can hide the ship in the cove and leave a half crew to guard it."

"Eighteen only." Danken pointed at Tamlinsen. "Including yourself. I don't care how you pick them, but we leave now."

The entire crew volunteered and Tamlinsen picked them quickly. He left all of the races respective commanders on board and Lieutenant Ragnarsen in charge.

"Captain, I'm not..." Ragnarsen started to say.

"You've been ready for this as long as I have. You'd be Captain on any other ship in the Navy if you didn't insist on watching my back. You'll be fine. Wait here for one month. If we don't return by then, take her back to Southport."

"Aye sir." Ragnarsen saluted. Tamlinsen saluted back.

"Be careful my friend."

"Aye sir." Ragnarsen smiled.

Supplies were loaded onto the shore boats quickly as were the chosen soldiers. Three Trolls, three Dwarves, three Sendar, four Orcans and four Elves, all the best of the best. Fully armed and eager, the group set out for the mainland.

As they landed on shore, the escort fanned out much as the previous group had done, aiming their bows into the dark, eerie woods. All of the trees were petrified. Nothing living grew anywhere. A dread silence pervaded. Only the light drizzle of rain made any noise.

As Danken set foot on the ground, a peculiar sense of draining set in upon him, causing him to stagger. All but the Sendar apparently felt the same. A Duah named Nelkin approached him.

"Magus, these are the Dead Woods. I was here during the Great War. There is no magic here, no life. Your powers are useless as are all of ours. There are many rumors of these woods. We should proceed with extreme caution."

"Aye. Thank you."

"Does that mean we won't be porting to Isthok?" Shonai asked.

"Aye. It seems that way."

"You couldn't anyway," Lanaia told him. "Without the Oracles, she will be invisible to your *Stonespeak* spell. You must find all three first."

"I have one. The Jade one, Courage." Danken showed her. Lanaia's eyes widened. Her two wolves sniffed the air constantly for any signs of life and found none.

"The Hand of Silence, where was it?"

"In the castle." Danken didn't elaborate. "Shonai."

"What is it?"

"Come with me into the ocean for a moment," Danken bade her, wading in. Curiously, she followed. Danken felt his magic return the instant he submerged beneath the waves. "Your javelin," he told her. "Draw it now or you'll be without it for the remainder of the journey through the Dead Woods." He drew *Mak'Rist* from its magic scabbard as Shonai did likewise.

They emerged from the water, weapons drawn. Most looked at them oddly but said nothing. Walking slowly, the group entered the Dead Woods. T'riel rested on Danken's shoulder, her normally frantic buzzing conspicuously absent.

"What's wrong?" Danken asked.

"No magic makes flying very hard. One can only do it for a short time," the Pixie answered.

"We'll be out of here soon," Danken reassured her.

"Not for awhile," T'riel responded grimly. "Two days to pass through this treedeath, no less."

"Well, we'd better get a move on it then."

The woods were dark. Huge petrified trees rose up hundreds of feet to the grey sky blocking what little sun there was. Starlight vision was of no use to any as it was a product of magic. A smoky fog further impeded their vision, surrounding them like a cloak of foreboding.

They traveled in a tight, battle-ready formation as they negotiated their way though the tightly woven trees. Often a peripheral movement caused one person to stop and stare into the gloom, in effect making the entire group stop. Danken, too, caught shadowy glimpses out of the corner of his eye.

So it went until dusk when they had to find an acceptable place for camp. A clearing between four gargantuan trees provided the perfect spot and they went about making camp. Petrified wood was easy to find and a large fire that burned bright and very slowly was set in the center of the clearing. They pitched their rations in and the Dwarves set about preparing dinner.

After they had finished cooking, the Dwarves dished out a delicious stew to everyone, along with rolls and flasks of ale. It was the only ale they carried and it was heavy so the group drank it now.

The respective races broke up into small groups to speak their native tongues. Valshk sat with the three Vull'Kra sharing war stories to determine their rank. Swifteye sat with the Dwarves, who questioned him endlessly about the Giant attack and his role in their demise.

Lanaia sat with the Elves. She told them of many historic events in Duah lore, while they taught her the rudiments of archery.

Shonai sat with the Orcans, who were in awe of her. She had a special knack for making them relax though and soon they were laughing and telling stories like the best of companions. The two females asked her what Zoltaure was like. She told them of his sad childhood and his travels with her though she made no mention of their intimate relationship. The two males sat in avid silence as she recounted their ambush by Goblins and Danken's subsequent rescue.

Tamlinsen and the three Sendar men recounted their exploits in the Shraken battle and speculated on their destination. They alone were unaffected by the absence of magic in these woods as they had none to speak of anyway. All heartily congratulated Tamlinsen on his recent engagement, throwing in joking warnings of his lost freedom.

Danken and T'riel sat alone, staring into the fire. They more than any of the others felt the loss of magic acutely.

"What is Boy thinking?" she asked.

"That I won't find her in time," Danken replied candidly.

"Boy will. Two more Oracles and he can port right to Elf Princess."

"Do you think I made the right decision landing in this forsaken place instead of taking my chances in Shun'ka?"

"Aye. Oracle Boy has is leading him to others, Boy must follow it."

"How do you know so much about it?" Danken asked.

"One held it when Little Elf Girl was sleeping. It pulled this Pixie, too."

"You knew of it? Why didn't you tell me?"

"Boy wouldn't have understood then. Now he does."

"Ah," Danken said. They sat in silence for awhile until T'riel spoke.

"Does Boy ever think about his parents?"

"Of course, all of the time."

"Sometimes One does also," T'riel said quietly. "But sometimes this Pixie can't remember them."

"What I do when I have trouble remembering," Danken said, "is think about the best times we ever had and picture her face while she's doing whatever it is. Whether it's making dinner for us, teaching me to read or tucking me in at night, I remember her face."

"Boy is not always dumb," T'riel said, pinching his ear before flying into the treetops to sleep.

"Thank you, T'riel," Danken said sarcastically into the fire. Lanaia and Shonai were sitting together now as everyone drifted off to sleep or took their watch.

"What do you think it is about him that makes you feel as if he's the only man in the world?" Lanaia asked, staring at Danken as he warmed his hands by the fire on the other side of camp.

"I don't really know," Shonai answered. "But I felt it as soon as I saw him, even with an arrow in my chest."

"Perhaps it's the fact that he doesn't even seem to care. His heart belongs to another."

"Ironic, is it not, that the only man in the world who could have his pick of women wants only one?"

"Though I sense you are pledged to another as well. Zoltaure, is it?"

"What makes you think that?" Shonai asked.

"The way you looked when you spoke of him to the others. These pointy ears aren't just for show, you know."

"I suppose you're right, though it can never be. He isn't a Royal or even a Noble."

"Cannot the ruler make the rules?"

"Not in Orcana."

"Shame. Perhaps a *special* advisor's job?" Lanaia laughed and Shonai joined in.

The wolves' bark broke the light mood of the camp. All who had been sleeping rose bearing arms. The watch called a silent warning. Something was moving in the darkness. A few somethings.

Danken immediately took eight sticks alight with fire and flung them into the woods in all directions, lighting up the surrounding woods. The shadows recoiled, but not before they were revealed. They were Mai'Lang, with red palms and milky white eyes. They wore long black cloaks that masked their size, which was amazingly small. They appeared to be children, but the rusted blades they carried betrayed their age. They were Pygmies.

They encircled the camp quickly, yet none made a move. Danken tried speaking to them in Sendar but they seemed not to understand.

"Meli'kou van moulang lin ju mai?" Tamlinsen said suddenly. All of the group turned to stare at him.

"Keli mai? Monla gola." A Pygmi larger than the rest replied in a high-pitched voice.

"What are they saying?" Danken asked.

"They want to trade one of their women for ours," Tamlinsen replied.

"No."

"Obviously," the Captain rolled his eyes.

"Tell them that it's against our religion and to do so would condemn us to Nifleheim, or whatever they fear in the next life," Danken told him.

Tamlinsen told them. The gathered Mai'Lang gasped. Tamlinsen nodded gravely. They continued speaking for several moments.

"What now?" Danken asked.

"An exchange of gifts. I asked them to show us the fastest way out of these woods tomorrow and they want us to teach them how to make fire."

"They don't *know*?" Danken asked incredulously.

"These are not typical Mai'Lang, Magus. They are primitive people who've probably lived in these Dead Woods for centuries. Their Langjian is rudimentary at best, a child speaks it better."

"Tell them it's a deal."

"Aye." Tamlinsen turned back to the Pygmies. *"Soon da. Hol Gin. Kuma set tu ma?"*

"Ah, ah!" The Pygmies jumped up and down, dispersing into the forest.

"What just happened?" Danken was looking around.

"I offered them the mugs we drank ale out of in exchange for them keeping watch for us tonight. We won't need them again anyway. We can use our flasks."

"Whoi dowe no jus' chop em up inta foire wood an have it done?" A Dwarf named Panir asked, slapping his axe against his palm.

"Are we to trust them?" Danken asked the Captain, who was glaring at the unperturbed Dwarf.

"Aye. They're excited to help. We're in their territory and they would have attacked had a deal not been made, but now that it has, they will adhere to it like a command from the Gods."

"Well, let's get some sleep then," Danken told the group.

The next morning came far too quickly for most, and the light drizzle didn't help creaking joints. Tamlinsen was already up, teaching the Pygmies how to use flint and tinder and how to find more of it. Danken approached while the others were still waking. T'riel was on his shoulder again. Tamlinsen greeted them.

"I've been talking to these people all morning, Danken, and they're really quite bright. They fish in the ocean at night. Apparently there's some type of fish that swims close to shore that glows at night. They also catch crabs that seem to be nocturnal and they say inside these trees is a special rock that's gold but that when they soak it in fresh water, it becomes sweet. Amazing."

"Definitely a curious people," Danken agreed. Once the Pygmies had mastered the flint and tinder, they formed a troupe and led the group through the forest, clashing their new mugs together often.

So it went for the rest of the day until well after dusk. The Pygmies stopped abruptly, milling and chanting. They pointed south and then began to melt back into the woods. As simple as that, they were gone.

"They say the forests of Mai'Lang are that way," Tamlinsen informed them. The group set out through the woods and into a large clearing that separated the two forests by about five hundred feet. They set up camp quickly in the clearing and as they did so, their magic started to return.

Watches were set after dinner and the group quickly fell asleep. Danken took the last watch with Valshk and Swifteye. They stared out into the grassy plain between the forests, like a green river flowing between the land of the dead and the land of the living. Danken's eyes again burned a fierce blue as Valshk's glowed dark amber and Swifteye's silver like beacons in the night.

Danken sent his *Stonespeak* into the ground first to all of the Drissian cities and then into the Mai'Lang's. Finding nothing, he moved on to the Goblin and Giant cities and finally the Shrakens. Still he found no trace of Amaria. Without the remaining Oracles, it was useless.

The Jade Oracle's pull was undoubtedly guiding him towards the Driss Nation though he knew not what for. Was it Amaria or the second Oracle? He knew only that if he used *Teleport*, he would some-how go too far or not far enough and porting that many people back and forth was a strain on his energy he could ill afford to waste. Not to mention that physical magic would alert the Sorcerers to his pres-ence, should they choose to look for it.

"Horsemen," Valshk stood.

"Aye and quite a few of them," Danken agreed. Swifteye had al-ready woken everyone up and most had their weapons drawn. "Put out the fire," Danken ordered. Sand was thrown on it quickly.

"Our presence cannot be detected in these lands," Lanaia said urgently. The sun was rising. If they were to make a run for the for-est, it had to be now.

"They have horses, though," Nelkin, the Elf, pointed out. "It would make our journey far faster. We *are* at war," he reminded them.

"Aye," Danken said, thinking. "The rest of you hide in the for-est. Swifteye, you and Shonai stay with me. If they attack Swifteye, we attack. If not, they can continue on, understood? When I attack, the rest of you come out from the woods, using *no* attack magic, only passive magic. The Sorcerers will be able to detect our attack magic."

The group ran to the nearby woods. Danken gave quick orders to the two and then used *Shimmer* to become an extension of a dead log. Shonai used her morph to become a grazing sheep, as her morphs would only allow her to be something alive. Swifteye stood by the now-smoking fire as if making sure the campsite was secured. The riders approached soon after and found the young Dwarf with the short patchy bluish-silver beard seemingly unconcerned by the two score riders in Mai'Lang armor.

"Hey you," the commander said in Langjian. Swifteye didn't seem to hear. The commander ordered three of his men to dismount and take the Dwarf into custody. They would sell him on the slave market in Mai, he told them. Danken shook his proverbial head at their sealed fates.

The soldiers dismounted and approached the Dwarf. As they did so, an explosion of silver killed all three. The sheep and the log turned to Shonai and Danken who began dealing death with their magical weapons before the Mai'Lang even knew what was happening. They started to retreat but found their way blocked by a band of deadly Mistgarde warriors.

The milling and confused Mai'Lang proved no match for the group, who sustained not one casualty. The horses were rounded up quickly. Those that weren't used were sent off into the Dead Woods. The group, silent after the slaughter, rode quickly into the Southern forest.

CHAPTER 30
A HARD DECISION

hree days out from Falgwyn, Kierna, Corsha and Phaeryn stopped in a small village where the River Mist split called Braggi's Delta, for the poetry the land surrounding it inspired. A stable boy took their white horses away as they reached the village's only inn, a quaint two story affair with fresh blue painted sides. The inn keeper was an old plump woman with rosy cheeks and a no-nonsense manner. She brought them three vegetable stews as they took their seats in a corner table, eyeing their white outfits and swords respectfully, for all in the Northern continent knew of the Spirit Blades and their service to the Gods.

The men of the inn cast them sideways looks, vacating the tables nearest the trio. Three dangerous Spirit Blades, known for the fierceness and short tempers were best avoided as far as they were concerned. The three women paid no attention to any of this though, as if nothing but they themselves existed. They were aware, however, of every tiny action around them, though if it did not register as a threat or as suspicious, it was quickly discarded.

The meeting with the Council of Twelve had been brief and quite shocking. Two of the three scouts dispatched had been killed and the third had been in a bad way upon returning, bringing information on the same lines of what they had expected. Four thousand Blue Scales and two Blue Dragons intent on conquest. All two thousand Spirit Blades abroad had been ordered back to Falgwyn with specific orders to avoid the Driss-held territory. Kierna and Corsha, being the only ones remaining with first hand knowledge, had been dispatched along with Phaeryn, who had flatly refused to be left behind being as she was the two women's Initiation Sister. The Council had given in, ordering the three to meet the Mistgarde regiment in this village to represent Temple interests and provide information.

Two turns of the glass after arriving and well into the evening, two Sendar Mistgarde soldiers in battle dress entered the inn and all conversation ceased. Both were hard, dangerous looking men and their predators' gazes raked the room until they fell on the now standing Spirit Blades, who approached confidently. The higher ranking officer nodded curtly to the three women.

"You are the Spirit Blade escort, I presume?"

"Aye," Phaeryn nodded back. "Please take us to your commanding officer."

"Follow me if you will."

The soldiers led them to a colossal encampment just outside the village where a large group of townsfolk were watching fifteen hundred blue, white and silver armored Mistgarde soldiers setting up camp. Elves, Dwarves, Trolls, Sendar and even a few Orcans worked efficiently and quietly, ever vigilant. Nearly a score of transport ships were docked off of the river's bank, their crews swabbing decks and checking lines. A large blue tent in the center was where they headed, past two imposing sentries.

Inside a huge Vull'Kra with white streaks in his green braid was pouring over a tattered map. He straightened to his impressive height, over seven feet tall, at their entrance. He eyed them scrupulously with his wise, battle-hardened amber eyes before speaking in his rumbling baritone.

"Spirit Blades. I am Regiment Commander Rekfoll." Kierna, Corsha and Phaeryn introduced themselves and their purposes for being there. "Well met. Tell me, which of you are the ones that have seen inside the mine shaft?" he asked.

"Corsha and I have seen only inside the entrance, no further," Kierna told him.

"Very well, tell me what you know," he ordered and they did so. Afterwards, he sat in concentration for several moments before speaking again. "My scouts will return by tomorrow night with updated information. If the Driss truly do intend on conquest, it makes sense that they will soon spread to other locations if they have not already. We must be absolutely certain of their locations and intents before we move."

"That could be days!" Kierna exclaimed. "How many more people will be dead by then?"

"How many will die if my forces are outflanked by a force three times as large?" he asked heatedly. "You may be good with those blades, girl, but you know nothing of military strategy."

Kierna's blades were out in a flash at Rekfoll's throat, who had his battleaxe drawn and a deadly expression on his square face. Phaeryn and Corsha had their blades pointed at the two Sendar that had escorted them as well as the two armed sentries who came bursting in.

"My name is *Sister* Kierna Bjorndotir of the Spirit Blades. You may address me with any combination of the aforementioned, but you will *not* call me girl again, Commander. That goes for my Sisters as well." Without waiting for a response, she sheathed her swords, Corsha and Phaeryn doing likewise. The Mistgarde did so after an angry nod from Rekfoll.

"Take the Sisters to their tents, Corporal," he told one of the escorts in a low growl.

"One tent," Phaeryn said, putting a warning hand on Kierna's shoulder.

"Excuse me?"

"One tent is all we require, Commander."

"As you wish. Make it so, Corporal. We will keep you up on all new occurrences." Rekfoll exhaled slowly to calm himself, his clawed hand still tight around his axe hilt.

"Thank you, Commander. We appreciate your hospitality," Phaeryn nodded. "Until tomorrow then." They turned to leave.

"*Sister* Kierna." Rekfoll called quietly, dangerously stressing her title.

"Aye, Commander?" Kierna turned.

"After I have disposed of the Drissian threat, I will request temporary leave from my duties in order to seek you out. Know that by *M'Racht* I intend to challenge you to *Jafa'aht.*" Corsha gasped quietly, for *Jafa'aht* was a duel to the death.

"I look forward to it," was all Kierna said before ducking out of the tent.

When they were alone in their tent, Phaeryn whirled on her furiously, her eyes flaming with anger.

"What in the freezing pits of Nifleheim were you thinking?"

"He should not—" Kieran sputtered, caught off guard.

"So what? You draw steel on a Commander of the bloody Mistgarde? Are you flarin' insane?"

"Now listen—"

"No, *you* listen, *girl!* Our mission objectives are the Driss and two, repeat *two* angry, hungry and very powerful Blue Dragons! Not your foolish pride! Do you understand me?"

"Who are you to tell me what *our* objectives are?" Kierna snapped. Without warning, Phaeryn slapped her twice, so hard her teeth vibrated. The Elf's pale skin was flushed a deep green with anger.

"I am your superior, that is who." Phaeryn pointed to the two blue rings around each of her shirt's wrists, then to the single ring around Kierna's and Corsha's. "Remember that the next time your temper inflates your pride. Now, it is late," she declared, ending the argument by laying down with her back to the other two. Kierna fumed silently before she too lay down.

She woke before dawn, bothered by her argument with Phaeryn and uneasy about the length of time the Driss would be able to kill with impunity. She slipped out of the tent and wandered through the still camp, her cloak pulled tightly about her to ward off the night chill. The sentries at one edge of the camp paid her little more than a passing glance as she entered the village. The stables were unmanned when she entered, so she retrieved her saddlebags and saddled her restless white mare herself.

Only when she had mounted up did she realize what she was doing, running away from her duty, directly disobeying the Council's orders. No, she reasoned, they said to look after the Temple's interests. That meant saving lives and making sure more Temples weren't desecrated. As she rode off, she wondered how she was going to stop four thousand Driss. She put her head against the horse's strong neck, letting the landscape blur by as she tried to think.

Towards midday, she stopped at a small pond to give her lathered horse a rest and a drink. As she ate a quick meal of crystallized oats and cheese, approaching riders put her on alert. She had an arrow nocked, eyes scanning the low-lying shrubs and thin aspen groves for signs of pursuit. The flash of silver and blue-lacquered bullhide armor was the only thing that kept her from releasing. The sight of the blowgun at the rider's waist nearly changed her mind until she saw two white-cloaked women behind him. She cursed silently.

The rider dismounted, pulling his helm off to reveal scowling green eyes. The two women did likewise, tongue lashings at the ready. The rider quieted them with a stiffened leather-gloved hand. He scratched his short, green flecked blond hair. The piercings on his face and ears glinted in the sun.

"You've got yourself a bad habit of running away," Taelun Fallenbower said irritably. "And of picking fights with people you couldn't kill on your best day."

"Tae?" Kierna was in shock. "What are you doing here?"

"As you may or may not have noticed, that was a Mistgarde Regiment back there of which I'm hoping you're beginning to remember I'm a part of. Coming back to you now a little or..."

"I meant *here.*"

"He's the one who alerted us to your little endeavor," Phaeryn growled.

"*Dwei.* And I suppose you're here to take me back and lecture me again? Save it. I'm too tired and honestly, I don't think I can refrain from drawing my swords right now. You're not in violation of your orders yet so if you return now you probably won't be missed. Do us both a favor and leave. This is not your affair. You too Corsha." Kierna turned away and began fussing with her horse as she prepared to saddle up.

"If you weren't so thick-headed and so bloody hot-tempered, you'd know that we are not part of the Commander's plan and that neither is the Council of Twelve;" Therein said. "But no, you had to waggle your entirely-too-loose tongue and force me to step up the timetable."

"What are you talking about?" Kierna asked.

"Do you really think the Council of Twelve would allow the desecration of a Temple or the deaths of two Sisters to go unavenged?

Our objective was to give the Mistgarde our information and then I was to take you to our advanced guard to direct our forces."

"I believe what the lady is trying to say is that you dropped the proverbial ball," Tae offered helpfully.

Kierna ignored him. "Advanced guard?"

"Aye, there are over three hundred Spirit Blades less than ten miles from here, with dozens more trickling in everyday from the cities since they have been recalled."

"Then what are you doing here?" Kierna asked Tae again.

"Isn't it obvious? I'm protecting Mistgarde interests. Also, you're going to need all the help you can get to accomplish what you need to," Tae said, taking a bite of an orange.

"What is it we're supposed to accomplish?"

"We're leaving the Driss to the Mistgarde. The Council asked their permission to give us exclusive rights to the Dragons," Phaeryn answered.

"Oh, is that all then?"

Corsha mounted her horse. "We'd best be moving if we want to make it there by dark."

"After you, fearless leader."

Kierna didn't receive the reprimand she had thought inevitable upon entering the Spirit Blade's camp. Weapons Master Tonis, who was the Senior Sister, simply gave her a look that suggested she had done what the wise old woman had suspected. Kierna was uneasy about this but made no comment as she made her way towards her tent. On the outskirts of the camp, Tae was pitching his own Mistgarde tent, an extremely uncomfortable look on his normally smiling face. She changed course and went to talk to him.

"What's the matter, Tae? I thought you'd be ecstatic to be the only man among three hundred women."

"Hah! Women, you say? Dangerous women I'm all for. Strong willed, temperamental women too sometimes. I'm not particular, most Duah aren't as long as both find each other attractive. But Spirit Blades are promised to the Gods and I don't know about you, but

I'm guessing the Gods don't take kindly to, how shall I say it, exploits with those promised to them. Call me old fashioned."

"You aren't here because of orders are you, Tae?" she asked.

"Aye, I am. Just not from the person you thought." He flashed a small, tightly folded parchment. "I even wrote my Death Poem before coming."

"What?"

"You know Danken and Jet almost came to blows because Jet wouldn't tell him where you went? Danken was so sure you'd be in bloody danger because of him that he was threatening everyone and attempting to go chasing after you. It took all Arn and I had to get him to see flarin' reason. I know the call of the swords is strong but couldn't you have at least said goodbye to him and saved us all a mess of trouble?"

"I could not face him again once I had touched the swords. It would be like having two Dragons pulling me in opposite directions. Besides, he was still unconscious when I made my decision."

"Ah, even better. Leaving a man on what might have been his deathbed. Where, pray tell, did you acquire such admirable qualities?" Tae said archly.

"Shut up," Kierna rolled her ice blue eyes, the hint of a smile tugging at the corner of her mouth. "So, how is he?"

"Gone."

"Gone? Where?"

"No one knows. Cursed Drissian oathbreakers," he spat onto the ground, anger flashing his flaming eyes. "Kidnapped the Princess Amaria and nearly killed Prince Andren but for Danken saving him. He went chasing after her, without a word to anyone."

"Is Jet with him?"

"No. He disappeared that very morning. Stole four hundred gold too, the bugger."

"So he's all alone?"

"No. Valshk, the Troll, Swifteye, the blind Dwarf, Lanaia, the librarian and Shonai, the Princess of Orcana are with him. Some army. Chasing after Driss and Sorcerers. The bloody Mage is as thoughtless as yourself."

"It seems we three are meant to walk our own paths," Kierna sighed.

"Aye, or drive those of us around you flarin' insane, one or the bloody other."

"You're doing a *dwei* job of that on your own, Elf."

"So, Dragons," he changed the subject. "Have you ever laid eyes on one before?"

"No."

"Well then, this'll be a good learning experience for you."

"Aye. I always enjoy observing the nuances and beauties of flarin" Dragons while I'm trying to kill them," Kierna said sarcastically.

"Take advantage of the opportunities that present themselves as they come, my old Captain used to say. Good saying, don't you agree?"

"Indeed, 'tis," she said absently. Tae arched an eyebrow.

"Did you just say 'indeed 'tis'?"

"What?" she snorted. "No."

"Aye, you did. You said 'indeed 'tis'," he guffawed.

"I did not you great liar!" she punched him in the shoulder.

"Alas, what type of cruel world do we now inhabit in which perilous, swearing, sword swinging, swashbuckling women muster up the aristocratic dignity to utter the words, 'indeed 'tis'?" He laughed out loud, holding his sides.

"Oh go dance around a flarin' tree, Pointy Ears, or whatever it is you bloody Elves do," Kierna sulked, getting up and stalking towards her tent, muttering darkly about Elves mating with rotten logs and wanting to shove a piece of uncooked meat down his bird-chirping throat. Tae's laughter could still be heard long after she had laid down to sleep.

The camp had been asleep for a few turns of the glass when the alarm sounded. A large Mai'Lang slave ship was slowly negotiating the river. The fire obviously caught their attention as the boat abruptly came to a halt.

A raiding crew consisted of around sixty men. About half of these disembarked and headed cautiously toward the camp. Danken and the group evacuated the campsite and hid in the shadows, barely getting the horses out in time. The raiding party entered the campsite with its still smoldering fire and immediately sent their forces out into the surrounding forest, calling the remaining crew out from the boat.

"They are experienced and well-armed slave traders, Danken," Nelkin informed him. "They search for unwary travelers and capture them. In Mai'Lang, you travel the main roads or not at all. They search for outlaw groups, Goblins, mainly, looking for women but for hard laborers as well. They may not know who we are, but they know we're out here."

"Aye," Danken said. "We can't run from them, we'll have to fight them with stealth, but we can't use our magic yet. If the Sorcerers happen to come across it, they'll know my mission and kill Amaria. We'll have to fight the hard way. Shadow them on the outskirts of their formations. When the opportunity presents itself, take them out silently," Danken told the group. They fanned out on the fringe of the slowly advancing slave traders. Lanaia led the horses as far away as she could, her wolves in tow.

Danken took the most dangerous spot, right in between the two groups. He moved silently, closing his eyes to see where every Mai'Lang was. He stopped suddenly, becoming one with a tree as two men came slowly by him, their weapons drawn and at the ready. Only magic that left no trace was available to him. It didn't matter.

He materialized behind them and in one smooth stroke decapitated them both.

The Trolls operated in much the same way as Danken, appearing out of thin air and quickly dispatching an unsuspecting raider. The Elves chose a different route. They used their superb climbing skills to ascend the trees and shoot arrows down on their opponents from above.

Swifteye predictably was the most effective, his silver trail whisking from one soon-to-be slain opponent to the next. The other Dwarves used their rock moving talents to create pitfalls in the ground. They lined the bottoms with hastily sharpened stakes to impale the unlucky raider who happened upon the seemingly grassy ground. Quick work for a people who could rebuild a city in days.

The Orcans set about disposing of the watch aboard the slave boat. They would emerge from the black water and pull the stunned raiders into it with them on the wrong side of a hooked pike. Once the watch was disposed of, they boarded the boat.

Shonai led them down the hatch into a dark, foul-smelling galley where close to fifty slaves sat over rows of oars. They were mostly Mai'Lang women, but she found a few Goblins and two Elven boys who appeared to be twins, though their faces were so dirty she could hardly tell.

The Orcans undid the chains of all the slaves but took only the Elven children to the top deck. As they prepared to leap overboard, Shonai saw something that made her stomach clinch. There was another slave ship docked not three hundred yards down the river.

"Ambush!" Shonai yelled out at the top of her lungs as the others embarked for the second slave ship. Shonai bid the two Elven boys to climb the highest tree they could find and wait for her. She crashed through the forest in pursuit of her friends.

Shonai's call came as the terrible sound of dozens of loosed arrows filled the air. Danken was the target of many of them and *Mak'Rist* only cut down half. At least ten thudded into his body, throwing him back to lie in a motionless heap on the forest floor.

A fierce battle raged as the new assailants made their presence known. Most of the first ship's crew had been killed by this time. The sound of steel on steel and the hollow clicks of crossbows filled the once peaceful night.

The Mistgarde forces were hard pressed in the face of such a vastly more numerous foe. They were outnumbered four to one, but as the saying at Mist Peak went, that's just the way they liked it.

The Duah rained death upon the unwary Mai'Lang below, while the Trolls appeared in the middle of a charging group of Mai'Lang, cutting them down with their huge axes.

The Dwarves, rid of the need for silence, charged like dense balls of fury, wielding their spiked war hammers like they weighed nothing. They cleared swaths through the Mai'Lang's ill-formed lines, while Swifteye picked off the stragglers.

A fierce counteroffensive by the Mai'Lang killed two Sendar and two Dwarves. The arrow volley at the onset of the battle had killed a Troll and an Elf. This only further enraged the Mistgarde warriors, who redoubled their own attack. At first the Mai'Lang had sought to keep their prey alive but now were just trying to stay alive themselves.

The appearance of Shonai in the middle of the battleground, her purple eyes flaring and her magnificent javelin dripping blood turned the final page of the battle. In no time, not a single Mai'Lang could be found alive. Tamlinsen sent Nelkin and the other two Elves to find Lanaia and the horses. He and the rest collected the dead.

Shonai, however, began looking for Danken. He must be off healing someone, she thought. After several directions tried though, she began to worry as she headed southwest, parallel to the river. A pair of legs sticking out from a tree made her heart skip a beat. She ran over the them and found Danken propped against the tree, his chest and neck full of arrows. His eyes were closed in pain as he broke the shaft of the last arrow.

"Danken!" Shonai knelt by him. "What happened? *How* did this happen?"

"I said no magic and I meant it. I had to rely on my swordsman skills. Apparently they don't include taking twenty arrows out of the air." He winced.

"What can I do?"

"Pull the arrows out."

"But it will rip you open!"

"That's the point. My flesh is starting to heal around the shafts."

"Already?"

"Aye."

"This is going to hurt," Shonai warned.

"I'll be all right." Danken lied.

Shonai yanked an arrow out of Danken's neck. He groaned in pain. "Sorry," Shonai said as she pulled another from his gut. She

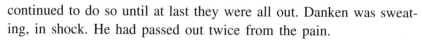

continued to do so until at last they were all out. Danken was sweating, in shock. He had passed out twice from the pain.

"F-f-food," he stammered.

"Food?" Shonai asked, not understanding.

"Food. G-g-get m-me food. Lots of it."

"Hold on," Shonai said, running back to camp and grabbing huge portions of bread, cheese and a flagon of water. She arrived with the food and fed him. He inhaled the food like a tornado, not even chewing. It was simply unreal. In moments, it was gone. She sat back amazed as she watched him heal right in front of her eyes.

He was still too weak to walk so she took off her bloody clothes and covered him with them to keep him warm until she could get help. She made sure he was all right before dressing again. She walked quickly to the river where the other four Orcans were shepherding three small Sendar girls towards camp. Shonai leapt in the river to cleanse herself of the grime of battle.

When she emerged, she remembered the Elven twins, whom she called down from the tree. As they headed back to camp, they saw the slave ships shove off, only now they were captained by the freed Mai'Lang and Goblin slaves.

"Will they disclose our location?" an Orcan asked.

"Doubtful."

The group went to bathe in the river. The freed captives, too washed, for the slave ship had been none to clean. They were given clothes from those who had died. They were too big for the children so they were hastily mended or torn to fit.

Though they were exhausted, they knew they couldn't remain here. They followed the river until they reached the marshes that were the Drissian Nation. The trees shifted from huge, coniferous to deciduous trees growing out of half an arm's depth of murky water. Somewhere not more than a few day's travel away, lay Isthok and, hopefully, Amaria.

CHAPTER 31
STORMLEADER

he journey down the mighty Mal River was proceeding nicely in the speedy river craft. Her Captain was the tattooed faced woman Jet had seen in Maka, a complex Sendar named Merid. One moment she seemed ready to murder everyone of them with her cutlass, the next a giggling girl making doe eyes at Katir'Tua and whispering conspiratorially with Wytchyn. It was more than enough to make Jet wish he'd had enough strength left to morph to his raven form and leave the bloody lot of them behind.

Wytchyn eyed Jet discreetly, for he seemed to be able to see right through her veil though that should be impossible. He often saw things long before the rest of them and could pick out the tiniest of imperfections in a blade. She had had to bite her lip and turn away to keep from laughing when he'd pointed out several such things on Merid's blade and her old friend had nearly choked with rage. The man had more secrets and hidden emotions than any ten she'd ever come across. He was so hard to read she almost gave up but for how much he intrigued her. Was it wrong that he was the first man she had ever wanted to see her face as it truly was, yet she had barely even met him?

She broke away from his perfect features reluctantly and went to talk to Merid, who was in the middle of a tirade at Katir'Tua who seemed to think it mildly amusing as he looked down at her from his gargantuan height.

"You can't be bloody serious! You said you were only going to see him safely there!" Merid grated in Langjian. "Now you tell me you plan to *stay* with him?"

"Aye," he rumbled.

"That's it? A bloody aye?"

"Aye." He brushed a lock of her dyed-black hair away from her green eyes affectionately. She attempted to slap his hand away but

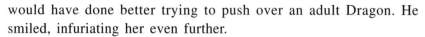

would have done better trying to push over an adult Dragon. He smiled, infuriating her even further.

"What of Duarta'Rhan?"

"The old hound will be fine, wife, just as he was when he rescued the both of us. He has a dozen more apprentices eager to learn. I am past thirty years old and you are close. It is time we went out on our own." It was the longest speech Wytchyn had heard the huge man give in a very long time.

"And what of me then?" Merid asked coolly. "Do you intend to just drag me along by the hair and throw me in a bloody kitchen?"

"By the Blind God woman, I married you on the sea. What makes you think I would try to take you off of it?"

"Then what of us?"

"You will see me when you call port as you always have. Nothing has changed but my location." He enveloped her in his tree trunk arms against her will but soon she was hugging him back. Wytchyn cleared her throat.

"Well, if it isn't my old friend, with her eyes as big as two moons over the dark water and her jaw slack as a frayed mast line," Merid said mischievously. "You must have just come from spying on the young Landar again."

"I was not!" Wytchyn blushed furiously.

"Husband, was she not?"

"Perhaps I will go inspect the crew." Katir'Tua squeezed by them hastily. "Or drink bilge water," he muttered under his breath. Merid shook her head angrily, then fondly in turn.

"Why would you think that?" Wytchyn wanted to know.

"Isn't it obvious, little sister? No one can be alone forever. Not even Wytchyn Nightveil, the invisible girl. A woman would have to be blind to miss the way you've been acting."

"That's just—"

"It's always your friends that notice first. You're the last to know. Hey!" She yelled at one of her crew in the rigging. "That bloody sail isn't made of steel, you flarin' heap of fish guts!"

Wytchyn smiled and walked back to the prow as night fell about them. She stared at the southern stars for awhile, her mind drifting into the past she could not remember before she could stop it. The only image she had was of the boy and even that was hazy. She could remember his blue eyes, his frantic shout to run. Had he survived what he had been trying to protect her from?

She felt guilty for leaving him. She was sure she had. Who was he? What had her parents been like? Her life? She wondered what—

"I never knew the stars changed when you were in a different part of the world." Jet said quietly as he leaned on the rail beside her, startling her so bad she nearly jumped out of her boots. "I'm sorry if I scared you."

"You did not scare me," she said too quickly. "And if you were not so afraid everyone will betray you and hurt you when you're not looking, you wouldn't have to sneak up on people the way you do."

"How did—I don't—" Jet was speechless, her words hitting him like a hammer in the gut. It had to be coincidence. She could not possibly know that that was *exactly* the reason he walked the way he did. "I am afraid of nothing, it's just being cautious is all."

"Oh please. You always try to cover your embarrassment with bravado."

"The bloody Ice of Nifleheim I don't!" Jet sputtered. "How would you know what I do and don't do?"

"I know, Landar, and you know I'm right. And watch your filthy tongue."

"You're right about nothing. The only thing I know for sure is that you have no bloody right even *thinking* you know anything about me. And my name is Jet Bloodhatchet!" he growled.

"You get angry when someone finds out one of your secrets," she continued, unflinching from his rising temper. "And when you're nervous you loosen your hatchets in their scabbards like you're do-ing now because when you were small, a man caught you stealing and almost killed you when your knife got stuck in its sheath." Jet's sharp intake of breath could have sucked the heat out of the warm air, but Wytchyn didn't seem to notice. "Don't worry Landar, you don't have to be nervous. You will lead the Stormdogs. They will follow you into the River of Swords if you ask them, for once they are yours, they will never be anyone else's. You are the born Stormleader and they will know it instantly upon seeing you."

"How can you know all of this?" he asked quietly.

"Trust me." There was that word again, Jet groaned inwardly, shutting his eyes tightly and when he opened them, she was gone. Bloody trust.

After disembarking from the speedy river craft three days out from Maka, Jet, Wytchyn and Katir had ridden hard to reach the Myrkwood by midday of the fourth day. They stopped so their horses could have a brief rest before pushing into the dark, eerie forest. As they walked, a thick, waist-high fog formed around them, spreading out in a straight line parallel with their every step.

"You bring the Fog, Bloodhatchet. It is a powerful ally and an even more powerful enemy," Katir said quietly, his white eyes ever wary. Jet nodded, for just killing Blackclaw would not win the Stormdogs over. He was an outsider. He just had to hope the Fog would bind them to him as if he had never left.

"Let's hope it makes what we have to do easier," Jet wiped the paint off of his lips and the dye off of his hands. Wytchyn remained uncharacteristically quiet. Jet was thankful for the silence. She made him uneasy.

He navigated solely by an old, blurring memory but by evening, they reached a place he instinctively knew to be the domain of the Stormdogs. Upon reaching it, the Fog continued to roll into the darkness, leaving the entire forest floor shrouded. Jet stared up at the tiny lights of the village hundreds of feet up in the ancient sequoia treetops. He heard a low whistle from three directions that he knew to be a sentry's warning so he announced himself loudly in a voice all within a league could hear.

"Stormdogs! My name is Jet Bloodhatchet, Bringer of the Fog, Bearer of the Key!"

Suddenly, there were scores of thick hemp ropes hanging to the ground. Not long after, hundreds of men, women and children of every race slid down expertly to eye the pair. They were hard, experienced people and not the highest paid mercenary army in the world for nothing. A cloaked Shraken stepped forward, followed by a Shraklan, his skin grey and rough with sharp teeth and orange eyes but the body of a Mai'Lang. The Shraken held a poison tipped throwing star in each hand. He was looking amazedly at the Fog, as was everyone else, though he tried not to show it.

"What is your business here?" Blackclaw growled in Langjian, though Jet detected a weakness about the man. A timidness. How could a leader be weak? Then his eyes focused on the Shraken, who the so-called Leader seemed wary around.

"To fulfill a promise. I bring the Fog as my messenger," Jet declared.

"You seek to become one of us, or do you seek to employ us?" Blackclaw's eyes darted around to the Shraken—whose eyes never left Jet's.

"Both," Jet answered, sensing Blackclaw readying to release his modified *Stunspore* to make them more susceptible to suggestion. He readied his mind for the assault. He could feel Wytchyn and Katir do the same. Surely some of Blackclaw's supporters would try to interfere. Jet's two companions would have to deal with them. He felt a moment of worry for Wytchyn, hurriedly pushing the ludicrous thought away.

"How do you propose to do both?"

"By the Right of Birth and the Right of Fog, I plan to challenge you for leadership," Jet answered. Blackclaw's eyes flared and he released his *Stunspore,* as did the Shraken assassin, Ureshk. Unthinking, Jet used the Fog to dispel both attacks. Two of his knives blossomed in the Blackclaw's throat, the Fog swallowing him up like a living thing. Jet knew then that Ureshk was the true power.

Three large Shrakens rushed forward only to be cut in half by Katir's huge blade. Wytchyn immediately engaged two more who attempted to join the fight. They did not last long. At the same time, Ureshk had flung his churiken, which Jet only barely avoided as he flung three successive knives at the Shraken. Ureshk dodged them and Katir single-handedly pushed the other Stormdogs back so the two would have room to fight.

Jet's hatchets crossed with Ureshk's two long daggers in an eerie shower of sparks. The Shraken's daggers were quicker but had a harder time deflecting Jet's heavier hatchets. Jet took two bad slashes across the arm and chest before catching Ureshk with a glancing blow to the side of his head. The two retreated, both flinging knives or churiken with blinding speed. Both were astonished at their continual failure to connect. Jet hadn't missed with a single knife, much less five since he had been a child, running the streets of Rakshoal and picking pockets.

The two charged again, their weapons colliding in a breathtaking dance of deadly skills, each seeking the advantage. From the look in the Shraken's eyes, Jet could tell that he had never before met anyone near his equal. He was a little fearful but mostly intrigued. Ureshk scored two minor slices, taking a heavy cut across the shoulder in return. He landed a solid kick to Jet's midsection before stumbling away in pain from the combined wounds on his head and shoulder.

They circled each other again, neither wasting the precious energy necessary to throw anything at the other. Ureshk felt the Fog beginning to envelope him. Seeing no other option, he sheathed his daggers, grabbed ahold of one of the many ropes with his good arm and gave it two hard yanks. Immediately he was catapulted up to the town above, Jet following on his own rope directly after.

Jet came up into a cleverly-carved trapdoor in a small but cozy wooden home. One candle was all that lit his way to the door, which opened onto a precarious swinging rope and bamboo bridge. He made his way cautiously, keeping his senses extended in hopes of detecting the Shraken before he was himself detected. He stepped lightly across the porch of another house that connected to the next bridge, the heavy silence deafening to him.

Then, out of the corner of his eye he caught Ureshk exiting a house cattycorner to him, his arm hanging limply at his side. There was no bridge leading directly to him so Jet would have to take the long way around, thereby serving the Shraken notice of his approach. Once Ureshk spotted him, a full out chase began. The huge network of bridges and buildings was like a maze to Jet, but he got the hang of it quickly, gaining ground on the Shraken.

Jet lost sight of him behind a building with four bridges extending in different directions from it. Approaching slowly, he readied himself for anything, sure the Shraken was planning a last ditch attempt at retaining the leadership of the Stormdogs. Ureshk's quiet, jagged-edged voice from somewhere he couldn't place, stopped him cold.

"Where did you find the Key?"

"My father gave it to me," Jet lied, still unable to get a fix on the direction the voice was coming from.

"Then your father is a thief."

"Was a thief. And a murderer as well I'm told."

"How is it that you heal?"

"What?" Jet asked, confused.

"The wounds you have sustained should have killed you by now. I know, for I have killed men with far less. Yet, here you stand, as if none of it had happened and you are in no pain," Ureshk accused. Jet knew the truth of it and said a silent word of thanks to Loki. He was not as skilled as the Shraken. Yet.

"I never said I was not in pain. You just assumed so because I am able to keep my emotions and feelings hidden if I choose."

"I learned to fight at the direction of a Master Assassin more than a hundred years before the Great War. In my reef just beyond what is now the Orcan city of Mana, I learned how to survive and even prosper against three, sometimes four times my number of Orcans. I have taken more lives than you have taken breaths. My people sought to use my skills to their own gain, to manipulate me. They soon learned that I serve no one but myself.

"Here I found my place. An army free of manipulations and politics, run by skill, intelligence and loyalty. With that coward Blackclaw, I could control every situation, make every outcome favorable to myself. And now you come here, barely dry from the womb with skills and powers it took me a century to accumulate." Jet could feel the Shraken's anger emanating from somewhere very close.

"What's your point?" Jet asked impatiently. "I didn't come for a bloody history lesson or a sob-story on your life. I came here to take over the Stormdogs."

"Why?"

"Because it suits my purposes."

"What purposes?"

"None of your concern, Needleskin. Now if you're quite finished talking, let's finish this. Unless you wish to surrender. I will accept your banishment from the Myrkwood with the Fog as my walls. You would be too valuable and too dangerous to let go, but you would be more dangerous if I let you stay."

"Oh, I intend to surrender. But there will come a day when you don't have the Fog to protect you. When that day comes, I, Ureshk Greytide, will end your life."

"I can live with that. Now, throw your weapons down and show yourself."

A creaking rope was all the warning Jet had as the Shraken exploded from the building, his good arm working furiously towards Jet's throat. Jet barely managed to deflect the blows even with two hatchets. He steadily retreated from the onslaught until his heel caught on a raised bamboo step. As he stumbled, Ureshk's bad arm suddenly came to life, plunging its dagger into the left side of Jet's ribs. Jet lashed out at the same time, catching Ureshk with a devastating blow to his hammer-shaped head with the butt end of one of his hatchets.

Both Jet and Ureshk toppled over the side, plummeting towards the deceptively soft-looking Fog below. Jet managed to catch a rope only thirty feet above the ground but Ureshk caught onto his pant leg. The combined weight of the Shraken and the severe rope burn on his hands caused him to let go, swinging Ureshk far away and himself crashing to the ground.

The silence was permeated only by the gurgling sound of his own blood filling his lungs and Ureshk's soft moans. The Shraken was the first to rise, blood running down the side of his head and his shinbone sticking straight out of the skin. He couldn't see Jet beneath the thick Fog, and the sight of Katir'Tua crashing through the undergrowth ended any thoughts he had of killing the Landar. Painfully, he limped off into the night.

Jet forced himself up with a sharp gasp, his vision narrowed to almost nothing. The pain was so great that upon seeing the fleeing Shraken, he passed out. He was not out long before Katir found him and propped him up against a tree. The rest of the Stormdogs and their families were beginning to arrive as Katir went about setting broken bones making Jet inhale deeply to force his shattered ribs back into position. Clucking like an old hen, Wytchyn used a wet rag to clean his rapidly-healing cuts.

She sent two children running for food and water. By the time they returned, Jet was awake and lucid, to the complete shock of the Stormdogs. Jet devoured the food quickly and soon was even smiling. He took off his ripped and bloodied shirt, noting that that was two fine shirts lost in the past month. Wytchyn somehow had another of the same cut out from the saddlebags of his horse and over Jet's head before he could protest. He caught her admiring his torso and also a hint of relief in her purple eyes, still hidden behind her black veil.

"It is cold, Stormleader. Put on your cloak as well," Katir'Tua ordered. The notion of this seven foot giant of a man acting like a fussing nursemaid made Jet burst out laughing. The Stormdogs eyed him as if realizing for the first time that their new Stormleader was in fact, insane. Nevertheless, Jet saw in their eyes that they acknowledged him as Stormleader. He thanked Loki once again. Wytchyn had been right. They followed him as if they always had. Strange, but more than welcome.

"What is funny, Stormleader?" an enormous Troll asked, apparently wanting to join in on the laughter. Jet smiled wryly at Katir.

"Two things that hurt," Jet commented. "The first is a long dagger through the ribs, followed by a three hundred foot fall."

"And the second?" Katir prompted.

"Landing on a pinecone so hard that I fear it's become a permanent fixture of my arse!" Jet grinned ruefully and the Stormdogs burst out laughing, as much in relief of tension as to demonstrate their loyalty to this strange and dangerous man who had taken the position of authority with a brashness and boyish confidence none could help but to marvel at. Katir hauled him to his feet as the laughter quieted down. Jed fixed the entire group with his steel eyes, drawing their undivided attention inexorably toward him. The Fog swirled around him like water, silhouetting him against the blackness of the night.

"I realize the events of this night have come quite suddenly to you, and may be somewhat disturbing to those of you who have known no other way than Blackclaw's. Please, allow me to put your mind at rest. For I am not just some random wandering warrior who has taken it into his head to lead the famous Stormdogs. You see, my mother and father were Stormdogs and I was born a Stormdog.

"In case you haven't realized it yet, my father was the cursed man who stole the Key of Fog from the Stormdogs in the first place. He is no longer of this world and I have made it my destiny and moreover my duty to return and set things right." Jet raised his arm, his sleeve falling away to reveal the Key illuminated by the Fog, embedded in his flesh. The Stormdogs gasped as one but quickly went silent again when he resumed speaking. "Because the Key of Fog should have never left the Myrkwood in the first place!" He declared and the Stormdogs gave off a thunderous roar.

"Bloodhatchet! Bloodhatchet!"

"Some of you older hands," Jet continued when the cheering died down, "may even remember me from when I was a babe, and now I have returned a man. I bring with me prosperity. The kind that can only come with change," he motioned for Katir to unload the sacks of gold he had taken from Mist Peak.

"Who is the Treasurer here?" he asked and an old, stooped Goblin leaning on a cane limped forward. He pushed his gold spectacles back up his long hooked green nose.

"That's would bea myself, Stormleader," he said in a rickety old voice. Throughout Midgarthe, Goblins were known for two things: their cowardess and their amazing talents with money and banking.

Jet told nodded thoughtfully. "Divide this equally among every person here."

"Aye, twilla bea dons Stormleader." He bowed and hobbled off, yelling at two younger Goblins to help him carry the heavy sacks.

"Now," Jet turned his attention back to the Stormdogs. "There's two hundred times that amount stashed away in a keep just on the outskirts of Mai. But we must leave on the morn if we wish to recover it before it is dispersed. How many ships do we have in port on Dark Depth?"

"Four, Stormleader," a grizzled Haffin—half Sendar, half Orcan—said from the back of the group. "Enough t'carry all th' fightin' men anywhere y'wish t'go."

"Who are their Captains?" Jet asked.

"Myself and these three are the Captains," the Haffin, named Ingtai indicated two Sendar men and a Mai'Lang woman.

"Very good. You four gather your crews and make the ships ready by the dawn. Can you do that?"

"Aye, Stormleader," Ingtai bowed and began barking orders to the crews and other Captains, who snapped to smartly.

"Now then, who's the Weapons Master?" Jet asked.

"Ureshk was, Stormleader," the huge Troll answered.

"Well then, who's the best with a blade in his absence?" The group laughed and several made loud boasts. When the tumult had died down, a soft, melodic voice spoke up.

"I am the best, Stormleader," a beautiful but hard, scarred young Elven woman said, pushing her way to the front. The quiet confidence in her eyes and voice lent credence to the ease with which the sword at her waist was worn.

"Do any here dispute it?" Jet asked and when none spoke up, he fixed the woman with his gaze. "What are you called?"

"Seranna, Stormleader."

"Very well, Seranna, you are now Weapons Master. See to the provisioning and arming. Everyone, this is my Second in Command, Katir'Tua. Any questions or suggestions you have, go through him. He is my voice when I am absent. Seranna, let's get a move on, we leave for Mai in a turn of the glass."

Jet turned to Wytchyn as the Stormdogs exploded into motion, hustling to get themselves ready. He sensed an anxiousness but also a very palpable eagerness about them. Even through her veil he could feel her gaze on him, searching, finding. She stared at him with that look he had become all-too-familiar with, peeling away any pretense he made at secrecy. His whole life, living on the streets, moving from town to town and even when they had finally settled in Lok Tryst he had been one to keep his secrets locked inside. No one ever got close enough to learn that inside his hard exterior was a boy who had never known safety, only fear. How many times had he let his guard down only to be betrayed? Never again. He had betrayed Danken, sure that if he did not he would be betrayed himself but had he been wrong? Could anyone be so righteous as the bloody boy seemed?

And Wytchyn knew it all. Knew it as if he'd told her himself. Gods, but she turned his calm, collected demeanor into nothing more than a pathetic façade. She was an enigma to him. So open it seemed and yet, when he probed deeper, there was suddenly nothing there. She was how he wished he could be. Flarin' *dwei. He* was the one who was supposed to make women all go a-flutter, not the other way around. It just wasn't bloody right!

Aboard the river craft that had taken them down the Mal River, he had tried to speak with her on numerous occasions to no avail. She and that bloody insane woman Merid had prattled on about Jet as if he were merely a curiosity. A foolish boy with foolish dreams, the Dark take them! Yet when she did speak to him, it was as if the sun came out from behind a wall of dark clouds. With other women, even Hrafna, with her bloody hypnotizing magic, he had merely found them pretty or exotic or momentarily interesting. But with Wytchyn, he could not even find the words to describe how he felt. That is, except for two: Bloody foolish.

"Are we to have a staring contest for the rest of the night, Landar?" She asked finally, yet he still could not look away.

"Are you all right?" he asked after a moment.

"Am *I* all right? This coming from the man who heals from fatal injuries in naught but a few ticks." She was offended, he could tell, as if he was implying that four armed men were too much for her and that she couldn't handle herself.

"Sorry for letting myself show a bit of bloody concern," he said sarcastically.

"You have found the Key of Fog. You have become Stormleader. You have fulfilled your dream. But you have not won me, so keep your concern and your filthy language to yourself Landar," she *tsked* irritably.

"Then I have not fulfilled my dream," he said, surprising himself and wishing instantly he had it back. Her features were obscured beneath the veil, but his keen raven's eyes saw her nostrils flare and her beautiful eyes widen.

"What did you say?" she asked, barely audible.

"Nothing. I'm sorry," he cleared his throat, looking away from her, "You plan to go back to Duarta'Rhan now that you've seen me here safely?"

"I think not." She recovered quickly, the haughty look back. "These Stormdogs are not well organized or disciplined. You will need to know who is loyal and who is not. And who could spy for you better than I? On those here or those out in the world."

"You would place yourself under my command?"

"For now it suits me. I sense excitement and adventure surrounding you."

"Then you will stay?" he tried not to let the hope creep into his voice and was sure he'd failed miserably.

"Aye. It is nice not to be an outcast," she indicated all the odd assortment of Stormdogs. "It is nice not to have to hide from everyone." And then she was gone before he could say another word. It was bloody disconcerting.

Though not near as disconcerting as knowing what love felt like for the first time in his life. Not by bloody half.

"Therefore, we will need all of you to win the upcoming struggle against the tide of darkness," Sembalo finished. The Council of Sendar, made up of Senators from every major City-State in the realm, was convening in the Sendarian capital of Sendaria. The High Councilor, Xand Nordsen, sat at the head of the table flanked by the four Magi. He was a middle aged Sendar with carefully placed straw-colored hair. He wore a magnificent tunic of blue, purple and silver that highlighted his dark indigo eyes. He was clean-shaven and bore the responsibility of power well, a fact that had helped him be re-elected for the past ten years.

In Sendar, the Senators from all the cities came together every two years to vote on the High Councilor just as they themselves had been elected by the Council of their respective cities. Each city was the capital of a large city-state that encompassed all of the smaller cities and towns in its borders. The councilors from each town elected the Senator of the capital. They wielded tremendous political as well as economic power, for they were all merchant lords, crop barons or retired Mistgarde officers.

However, military matters were strictly the province of the Magi. Thus, in these matters, the Senators' only purpose was to commit their cities to battle. Often city-states would battle others over territory or rights to certain business, sometimes quite bloodily. The Mistgarde were always able to quell the unrest though. They argued over minute points to establish their worth and importance but in the end, all agreed to the Magi's plan. They trusted the Magi enough to commit the bulk of their militias and fighters to war without legitimate fear of invasion by a rival city-state.

The mammoth ceiling of the Council room of Sendaria's City Palace was six stories high, featuring paintings from the realms' greatest artists on its domed surface. The blue and white marble that made up the entire structure was set aglow by artfully placed torches in its hollows. Sembalo had sat here thousands of times and still got shivers when he gazed upon it. After allowing the assorted Senators their brief says, he stood and asked them for their final votes.

"My warships are ready Magus," the Senator of Rakshoal announced. The other coastal Senators of Norspoint, Eastbank, Breakwater, Southport, Kasan and Wescove voiced their readiness as well, eager not to be outdone. The inland cities of Savhagen, Keyre, Volhak, Falgwyn and Lundgarde committed their troops to battle also, trusting in the Mistgarde and the Spirit Blades to take care of the Drissians and Dragons threatening in the mountains.

In Sendar, the only standing Army was Mistgarde. In times of war, the call to arms was sounded and all men and women who wished to heed it would meet in the nearest city. From there, they were issued regimental uniforms and weapons and then sent to the coastal cities where warships would transport them to their destinations.

The Duah had a standing Army as did the Rokn, Vull'Kra and Orcans, but at times of war, many more would volunteer. They operated on their own agendas, though they would work in concert with Sendar if it benefited them. This being the case, a threat to the Northern continent concerned all and war was declared universally.

King Llethion Sonatala of the Elves had responded to Danken's order by secretly mobilizing his forces and trickling them to Myr, where all warships were "coincidently" returning to port early. The common people had heard the secret call and many of them made the journey as well. Though the Elves were notorious for their careless and dreamy lifestyle, they were fierce and fearless fighters when the need arose. Warships were outfitted hastily at night with a strict watch to prevent spies. The armory used an underground entrance to distribute weapons and uniforms. After all was prepared, they secretly boarded the ships and set sail in the middle of the night.

The same thing was occurring in the Vull'Kra Nation. King Mashtor issued the call to arms to coincide with King Llethion's. The Trolls, however, used their *Shimmer* spells to achieve secrecy. Their ships left port on the same night as the Elves from the port city of B'rak.

The Orcans had a head start as they had begun mobilizing at the attack on Shonai. Their forces consisted of every able bodied Orcan not entirely necessary to the defense or maintenance of Orcana. They were waiting to provide the escort for the Duah and Vull'Kra Nations.

The Rokn, at the attack on their city by Giants, had marched nonstop day and night and would soon arrive in Eastbank where they would be ferried over to the Mai'Lang mainland two days after the Elves and Trolls had left port. From there they would march on the Giant Nation.

These were the advance lines. They would attack their counterparts while the Sendar conducted their famous city raids. Once they had secured these cities they would either move to the next city on the coast or move inland.

Mistgarde would stay on the Northern continent to protect it alone.

The Mai'Lang were not docile by far. Their forces were also being mobilized and they were nearly three days ahead of the Sendar. They moved their conscript Army, which consisted of every male above the age of thirteen in the land to Bang'Lau and their fleets off the coasts of Singo, Soling'Ta and Shun'ka.

The Giants had already begun their march to Lok Fong to set up their defenses against the Dwarves. King Nog appointed his son, Gern, General as was custom and every Giant able to lift a club followed him. Their defeat at the hands of the Rokn in the Great War was far from forgotten. They aimed to avenge this defeat now.

The Goblins, under King Mek'Lo, and the Driss, under Queen Issfal, met in the Drissian port of Riss to await the arrival of the Shrakens. There they would meet the hated Elves, Trolls and Orcans in open combat on the seas.

The Shrakens, under Queen Darkfin, left the Barakans around Donjna Point near Singo and then continued on towards Pir'Noh. They left forces in Mortegen to harry Sendar warships and protect their isles but the majority went to fight. War was coming and the world held its breath in anticipation of the outcome.

Jari Splitgem, Head of Clan Splitgem was in a foul mood. The grey-bearded Dwarf didn't take kindly to delays. He paced back and forth on the dock while a crew of Dwarves repaired the pulley they were using to load supplies onto the Sendar transport ships that would take them to Mai'Lang. He spat into the water and wrinkled his bushy eyebrows. The cigar he smoked was churning around as he gritted his teeth in frustration. Like all Dwarves, he had the patience of a badger and the temperament to boot.

"General?" An aide called from the next dock over.

"What is it?" Jari barked.

"Crew says yon pulley's near ready. We'll be able t'board boi noightfall as planned."

"We'd better, er I'll haf t'do yon damned thing moi self!"

"Aye."

"Where in Nifleheim is Vreker Rocksifter at?"

"Here," another grey bearded Dwarf said, walking over to the General. He was also a General, from the Rokn city of Ironforge.

"Oy, le's get our boys ready t' board, make sure they've all gone t' yon head an all that."

"Aye." Vrekr nodded and went off to organize the troops. Jari continued to scowl until that evening when the transports finally shipped off for the Mai'Lang mainland.

Sembalo was exhausted as were the other three Magi. They had been porting around for two days now, monitoring and coordinating the Sendar forces. They were now back at Mist Peak, deploying the Mistgarde forces to their battle stations. If another threat like the Driss in the mountains emerged on the continent, they would be able to mobilize to combat it immediately.

The Northern Army, meanwhile, was making excellent progress. Forces from Savhagen had made the journey to Rakshoal in seven days and were only three days behind the Duah and Troll fleets. Forces from Wescove had mobilized quickly and were shoring up the city's defenses while they waited to join the Rakshoal fleet.

Forces from Sendaria were only three days away from Kasan and Falgwyn's troops had already reached Southport. The troops from Volhak and Keyre were converging on Eastbank as was the fleet from Norspoint.

Lundgarde's forces were already beginning to probe enemy troops from Bang'Lau at Faust's Wall. Commanders there expected the battle to begin within two days or so.

"Intelligence filtering in from the Southern continent has pegged interior city troops taking up stations in coastal cities. The Mai'Lang clearly expected the coastal attacks we have planned. That the war was planned has been obvious from the beginning. They are days ahead in every aspect of the game, yet they wait in defense. It's as if they know our strategy and like their chances better on home soil." Sembalo briefed the other Magi and Mistgarde commanders.

"Should we change our plan of attack then?" Kai asked.

"Slightly. Instead of hitting *all* of their coastal cities, we will only hit three. The forces compiled in Eastbank and Norspoint will attack Son'Lau. From there, we can stage an attack on Singo, Bokat and provide assistance to the Dwarves if need be. Forces from Southport and Kasan will attack Shun'ka, putting us squarely in position for an attack on the Goblin and Driss nations. Last, forces from Wescove and Rakshoal will sail behind the Elven and Troll fleets. Once they have engaged the Goblin and Driss fleets, they will sail around and attack Soling'Ta, giving us access to Kansaka and Kang.

"This gives us a three-way pincer with which to clamp down on Mai when the time comes. As a secondary assault, forces from Breakwater will attack Kybo in two days to make the Mai'Lang believe we plan to assault every city with a separate fleet."

"A good plan Sembalo," Penn remarked. "But what of the Sorcerers?"

"What of them?" Sembalo countered. "Are they not just as busy as us?"

"Aye, but the Sorcerers have all five of their numbers. We have but four and no clue if Danken will return or if he will be back in time."

"We have no control over that Penn," Urishen interjected.

"Aye," Sembalo agreed. "But I wouldn't worry too much about Danken, he may be young but we've all seen his power. Dak'Verkat may be in for more than he bargained for."

CHAPTER 32
BLOOD OF THE CAPTORS

he horses were extremely unhappy about wading through this eerie realm but they did so anyway. They had started traveling not too long before dawn and were making decent progress. One of the Elves had lost his horse to the numerous, huge and terrifying alligators that lurked just beneath the surface. They had killed a half dozen of the scaly creatures since. The Dwarf, Panir Brokenshaft, had lost his mount to an anaconda fully thirty feet long before he had hacked it apart with his battleaxe. He did not complain, though, he was a Dwarf and didn't like horses anyway. An anaconda was good eating besides, he claimed.

"It seems as if we've been inordinately unlucky in our pursuit of remaining inconspicuous on this journey," Lanaia commented.

"That's because we travel in other creature's homes," Danken reasoned. "If a Mai'Lang group were to travel through the Duah Forest, they would be discovered as well."

"I suppose so."

"Besides, even if we hadn't been…" he stopped as a powerful wave of nausea enveloped him. In a haze, he steered his horse off of the path.

"Danken?" Lanaia asked, following him. The rest of the group stopped to see what the commotion was about. Danken kept riding until at last the nausea passed and he was able to see clearly. As his eyes drifted back into focus, he found himself staring at an ash tree. Thick yellow sap oozed out of the side like liquid gold. Encased in the petrified sap like a glass coffin was a Goblin, a surprised look on its ugly features. Danken dismounted his horse and slogged through the water to the tree. The Goblin's outstretched palm held something and the sap around it was still unhardened.

Inexplicably, Danken reached his hand into the sticky substance. He felt a small orb inside and pulled it out. It was amber, exactly the same size as the Jade Oracle. He felt its power surge through him and an even stronger urge pulling him towards the Driss capital. He dunked his hand in the water to rinse it off.

"The Grasp of Ashen Gold. It's the Power Oracle, Danken," Lanaia told him.

"Aye, and it's telling me we have to hurry. The third Oracle is in Isthok," he replied, as he mounted his horse.

They stopped to eat their lunch around midday, eating it cold as there was no place for a fire. The hot, humid marsh was making them all uncomfortable and Danken was severely tempted to use *Breezesummon* to cool them off. They ate in silence in a high up, thick tree branch, giving the horses a much needed rest.

A ripple in the placid water caught Shonai's attention. She summoned the other Orcans to keep their eyes on the water. Then, as if from nowhere, six flat-bottomed boats carrying seven Driss each converged on the horses, who bolted. In the process, one of the boats was overturned, spilling its occupants into the stale water. The rest were surprised but quickly recovered and used blow guns filled with poison darts to attack the Mistgarde forces in the tree.

Using their cloaks, Danken's group blocked most of the darts and the Elves began returning fire. The Driss were all of the Green Scales. They were merchants, however, so they carried no swords and wore no scale armor. Still, they had their blowguns, poisonous thumb claws, fangs and tails that were very effective in the marsh.

Tamlinsen and his crew were the only ones with experience fighting the Driss, and they called out orders as they dropped from the tree to do battle. The Orcans dove into the shallow water, where they could use their *Sonarblast* to great effect, disintegrating the unsuspecting Driss's ear holes. When they fell, the Orcans pounced, using their own predatory claws and teeth to dispatch them.

The Dwarf Panir, of no use in the water, used himself as catapult ammunition, having Swifteye fling him into a dense group of Driss. Whirling his battleaxe, he crashed into the Driss with enormous impact. Those that weren't killed initially, found themselves staring up at the crazed eyes of an angry Dwarf from their bed in the water.

The wolves stayed with Lanaia to protect her as she fired her crossbow to great effect on the Driss. The Trolls, as usual, wreaked havoc with their *Shimmer* and raw strength. The Green Scales' batch of poison didn't seem to work on them at all when they became transparent, a fault in the breeding that would surely result in the Green Scales disqualification from the mating selection if the Queen found out. Trolls were supposed to be resistant, not immune.

The Driss had apparently not anticipated such resistance and began to fall back. Danken, however, was too fast for them. He was a whirling, slashing dealer of death. The Driss avoided him at all costs, often running into a crossbow bolt or a Sendar sword as a result. Swifteye chased down any who tried to run, braining them with his spiked mace, after T'riel disabled them with magically charged arrows from her golden bow.

When the battle was over, the waters were dyed red. Dozens of corpses littered the area. One of them was an Orcan. The horses had bolted and were nowhere to be found so they took three of the Driss boats and prepared to leave. Shonai and the other three Orcans sang a prayer for their fallen comrade before setting him on a vacant boat and setting it aflame.

They rowed in shocked silence. They had known the mission would be dangerous, but of the two dozen who had started the mission, only seventeen remained. There were countless trails of bodies in their wake and more still to come. Danken remained stoic. They had given their lives not only for Amaria but for the entire Duah Nation's survival. He would not diminish their sacrifice by weeping. Instead he would remember them as they had lived and avenge them when he met with their enemies.

T'riel seemed to sense this and she hugged his nose. He smiled at her.

"What's that for?" he asked.

"Boy is starting to understand now," she said cryptically.

"What do you mean?"

"Nothing."

"Nothing?"

"Nothing."

"T'riel, that's what I love about you."

"What?"

"Our stimulating conversations, what would I do without them?" Danken asked sarcastically.

"Probably talk to Boy's self."

"Probably." Danken laughed as T'riel moved to her launching pad that doubled as his shoulder. She took off with a buzz to survey the surrounding area for unwelcome Driss. Their surprise had to be complete to succeed. To be tipped off would require magic to save them from certain annihilation.

Night came quickly and with it came the Driss capital of Isthok. In the eerie moonlight, the city appeared to float above the calm waters. Huge wooden walls, coated with clay, rose up in a great circle around the city. On closer inspection, the city was actually on stilts. Waterways ran like streets through countless multitudes of wooden and clay houses.

Boats ferried Driss around like horses would in a Sendar city. Torches lined the waterways with a dim glow, backlighting the numerous guards who patrolled the parapets. The Driss were quite certain, however, that none would dare cross their unforgiving marshes to attack them. This made them vulnerable, especially as most of their soldiers were in Riss.

Danken decided to take a risk. They would try subtlety and if that didn't work, they'd fight their way in. He put everyone but the Trolls, himself and Shonai under the tarps the Driss used to protect cargo from water. Next, he tied all three boats together with Shonai in the form of a high-ranking Driss merchant in the lead boat. He and the Trolls became shimmering shadows, eyes shut tight to keep their color from exposing them. As they reached the side gate to the city, the patrolling guards eyed Shonai intensely. It was slightly odd that a Driss carrying so much cargo should be alone.

She used her Mer'khan-given telepathy to speak their language as if she was really talking, then told them her crew had been ambushed by Mai'Lang slave traders. Only she had escaped. The guards shrugged their shoulders. It was just as likely she had killed the crew to alone profit from the cargo. It was a common occurrence among Driss.

They waved her through as an armada of trade boats floated in behind her. They sailed as quickly as possible through the waterways until after an eternity of searching, they found the waterway that led to the Queen's palace. Suspicious Driss in boats passed them constantly, eyeing the cargo the group carried but Shonai's dangerous looks warned them off.

Now would be the time for brute force. Danken waited until a squadron of half a dozen palace guards approached them holding poison tipped spears, wading through the waist deep water.

"Apophis bless the Queen," Shonai told them in their minds. She could only read surface thoughts with her telepathy, but it was enough to tell they weren't buying it. As they prepared to attack, she brought her javelin out from her gauntlet and disemboweled the nearest two.

Danken and the Trolls dispatched the rest while the Elves and Orcans came out with bows ready and killed the guards that still patrolled the palace gates. The Elves scaled the gates and opened Portcullis from the other side. They entered the palace, which was the only building in the entire city with water flowing *through* it.

Steps cut out of solid rock ran from either side of the light green waterway into the upper levels of the palace, creating a canal through the center. Eerie green lights lit the dim interior as if torch light would turn the Driss to dust. From there it was an ordinary, if sinuous castle layout with halls, banquet rooms, bed chambers and most importantly, a throne room.

A large detachment of Palace Guards intercepted them as they entered a large foyer. Arrows and poisoned darts filled the air as the two groups crashed together. Valshk and the other two Trolls became shimmering massive forms and led the charge, deflecting most of the darts. Shonai, Lanaia and the wolves stayed behind a huge pillar, keeping the scared children out of sight.

Nelkin and another Elf, along with two Orcans, fired deadly arrow after deadly arrow into the marauding Driss. A dart hit the Orcan in the shoulder but she shrugged it off and continued firing through the burning pain. One of the Elves took out a Driss who had snuck in behind Tamlinsen and the others. The Captain wrought devastation along with the last Sendar sailor.

Four Driss ganged up on them, whipping their tails into them in an attempt to keep them off guard. The Elf cut off one Driss' tail and waded in, his sword flashing. Tamlinsen leapt over a swinging tail and narrowly dodged a flying dagger. He swung his sword in a short arc that forced the Driss back, unwittingly into the poison tipped dagger of the tailless Driss. Wide-eyed, the tailless Driss was too stunned to deflect Tamlinsen's flashing sword. The Sendar sailor finished the remaining two.

The Dwarf Panir tried to stay close on Swifteye's heels, hacking at anything that remotely resembled a Driss with his mighty axe. Swifteye went about his usual business of picking off stragglers or those who had managed to sneak behind someone. His mace flashed viciously back and forth as he cleared swathes through the numerous Driss. Suddenly, he found himself surrounded by five of the foul creatures, with his back against a pillar.

He dodged the first wave of darts and avoided a thrown dagger, leaping up with his blinding speed and bashing one Driss with his spiked mace. Swifteye caught another on the collarbone, causing it to crumple in a moaning heap, but the thick tail of one beside him slammed him into the pillar. Luckily he hadn't been hit by its poison tip but he knew it wouldn't matter in a moment.

From nowhere, the offending Driss split completely in half at the waist. The shock of the moment was enough for two arrows to kill the other two without further incident. Panir yanked his axe out of the corpse and buried it again in the moaning Driss on the floor. His red beard was matted with blood and his scrunched up face was nearly unrecognizable until he wiped the gore off of it.

"I told ee t' slow down!" he shouted at the stunned Swifteye, as he struggled to remove his axe from the dead Driss. Swifteye dodged around him and dealt two swift blows to two approaching Driss dropping them where they stood. Another was hit by an arrow leaving them momentarily in the clear.

"Thank ee," Swifteye breathed. "I thinked I'd had it fer a bit yonder."

"Thank I when us're outta yon damned sewer!" Panir growled as a new group of Driss attacked the pair.

Giving up on dislodging his axe from the corpse, Panir merely swung the dead Driss into its charging companions, scattering them. Swifteye shot back and forth, killing three Driss as they struggled to rise. Panir clubbed one to death until his axe finally came free.

"See?" he shouted at Swifteye as he hacked at another Driss. "Tha's how ee get rid o' a sticky situation!" he laughed. "Hey! Driss can no push daisies when they doie, eh? Do ee think they push water lilies? sloimy Lizards'll soon foind out, I c'n guarantee ee that!"

Swifteye shook his head as the red-bearded Dwarf dove head first into three more Driss. Two arrows took out a like number of Driss running to enter the fray and the stubble faced, blind Dwarf did likewise. Behind him, Danken was wreaking havoc on the hapless Driss.

Mak'Rist flashed in deadly arc after deadly arc. His *Magefire* shield deflected all hits easily and soon he found that his sword was hacking into more backs than fronts. So close to his destination, the Mage no longer cared for secrecy, desired only the third Oracle and his beloved Amaria. Eight Driss launched a coordinated attack from behind him but he easily parried.

He knocked the nearest two swords aside and disemboweled the first. He cut the second from shoulder to waist with *F'laare* and deflected two more thrusts in the same movement. With deadly efficiency, he decapitated two and cut off the hand of another. He kicked the uninjured Driss in the chest, putting it right in line with Valshk's swinging axe.

The Trolls fared the best as the Drissian poison did little to them in their *Shimmer* form. They worked in fatal tandem, a coordinated twirling of their massive axes at different heights left nowhere to go for the Driss but the grave. Soon none were left to stand before them and the group stood, breathing heavily. One of the Duah was dead, and an Orcan was close.

Danken rushed to her side, where Nelkin was trying furiously to revive her. He placed his hands on her shoulder where the poisonous dart had gone in but knew instantly it was too late. She was dead. He shook his head and immolated the two women's bodies, leaving only a black scorch mark on the stone floor. Snapping back to reality, he led the group down another corridor.

Dispatching another small group of guards at every turn, they finally walked into the torch lit throne room. Danken began to gather his power. He instructed the rest to wait out of sight and protect the children. The throne room was lined with red carpet leading to a monstrous solid gold throne inlaid with rubies. On either side of it stood golden statues of cobras with rubies for eyes and behind the throne was an even more impressive pit viper, so huge that its golden fangs were as big as Danken.

Standing on either side of the red carpet were rows of high ranking soldiers and nobles. In the throne was the sickeningly obese and grotesque Drissian Queen, her bloated, stubby-limbed brown form unable to move from its present position. Several Under Queens with normal bodies took up positions in front of her immediately, weapons at the ready.

At the sight of the intruder, the Queen raised a fat, scaled arm and shouted.

"Vat iss zza meaning of zziss?" she shouted in Drissian. Danken stole the language from her head with *Mindscan*. He sheathed himself in a *Magefire* shield and walked slowly towards the throne as hundreds of poisonous darts bounced harmlessly away. He walked past the terrified Queen.

They stared at him aghast as he blew open the huge golden pit viper. Using *Airlift*, he picked up the Obsidian Oracle that was the third Oracle, Wisdom. The power suddenly surged through him and he knew, without a doubt, where Amaria was.

The Driss remained shocked that their deadly weapons continued to do him no harm. Now he faced the Queen.

"I have heard that in your religion, to be killed is an honor. However, if your eyes are removed, you won't be able to find your way to the next life, to serve Apophis. "I know not what Apophis thinks of the suffering you have caused in the world, but I do know you won't be able to find your way to him to find out," Danken said coldly. He raised his hands and let forth a hundred bolts of *Magefire*, hitting every Driss in the room. The Queen's eyes were burnt out sockets in her skull.

Shonai was the first in the room. She saw Danken standing in the middle of the room with a disturbing look in his eyes.

"What happened?" she asked, as the rest filed in. Danken showed them the three Oracles.

"You found them all!" Lanaia exclaimed, oblivious to the terrible stench of burnt flesh around her.

"Aye," Danken said, still staring into emptiness. Panir eyed the dead Queen.

"I do gotta say, with a Queen lookin' loike yon fat lizard, i's a wonder yon scaly bastards're still around. I ken I'd rather meet Moighty Motsognir in yon flesh than t'lay with that'un."

"And what of our purpose for making this expedition in the first place?" Tamlinsen asked.

"What?" Danken seemed confused.

"Princess Amaria, where is she?" Tamlinsen asked again. This seemed to break Danken's comatose behavior. He turned to regard them all, his eyes flaring their characteristic blue once again.

"Come, we have no time to waste," Danken told them as the sounds of hundreds of boots on stone reached them. The Army was here.

Danken made a portal and ushered them all into it. Behind him, he left a globe of blue energy, then stepped into the portal. The Driss entered just as the portal closed. When it did so, the globe exploded, leveling the entire throne room.

The portal opened up into a forested pathway. They stepped out into the darkness and, as one, asked Danken where they were.

"We are outside of Mai," Danken told them.

"Why?" Shonai asked.

"Because Amaria is in there."

"So we'll port in, right?" Lanaia asked.

"No, I can't see the inside of the palace, it's been shielded. I only can *feel* she's in there."

"So use the Oracles to see her," Valshk put in.

"I can't. They're more like a blood hound than a scrying glass. They tell me where she is, generally, but they don't let me see her, even with *Stonespeak*."

"Now that we're exposed from the magic fireworks in Isthok," Lanaia said, "why don't we just blast our way in then?"

"Because all Mai'Lang cities, like Sendar cities, have magical triggers that alert the Sorcerers if a Mage uses his magic in the city. They'll all port at once and I'll have to fight all five, which is a death sentence."

"What about Isthok?" Tamlinsen asked.

"They, too, have a trigger but it takes much longer, like Elven, Troll and Dwarf cities because there's no collective Sendar or Mai'Lang mind scream to speed it along."

"So what will the Sorcerers do?" Valshk asked.

"They'll know we're in Mai'Lang in a short time. It'll take them another day or so to trace my portal and then they'll be on us."

"So what do we do?"

"Go it the old fashioned way."

"How's that?"

"Like thieves."

CHAPTER 33
BALANCEKEEPER

s the ships docked off of a heavily forested and uninhabited shore just west of Mai, Wytchyn checked the position of the early dawn sun to determine the time they would have to reach the keep. Seranna was on shore directing the fighters with a calm authority Jet was pleased with. Ingtai was barking harsh orders backed with curses and threats as the ships were anchored. Jet, Wytchyn and Katir stood on the prow of the lead ship supervising the entire operation, though the Sendar girl was typically invisible, retreating into the safety and comfort of her cloak. Jet pulled his mind away from her.

"They are excited to be active again," the huge Mai'Lang announced.

"Aye. They have been too long without action. Fighting men need constant movement to keep their skills sharp," Jet agreed.

"You sound like Duarta'Rhan," Katir mumbled.

"You miss him," Jet stated.

"He was the only father I ever knew."

"I never asked, but why were you in his debt?"

"My grandmother was a Giant. My father, her son, abandoned my Mai'Lang mother not long after raping her. She died in childbirth. My birth. The people of her village wanted to kill me, but Duarta'Rhan took me instead."

"Then you knew my mother?" Jet asked, shaking his head at the big man's misfortune.

"Aye. Plentis was ten years my senior and always went her own way. She played with me sometimes when I was little, but she married your father when I was still young."

"It's a small world." Jet shook his head.

"It is that, Bloodhatchet."

Once the Stormdogs were unloaded, they donned their black cloaks emblazoned with three lightning bolts formed into a triangle.

The ship's crew put them back out of sight with orders not to sail back in to shore until Katir gave them the signal. The three hundred strong army melted into the thin woodlands with Jet and Katir at their head. Wytchyn vanished far in front of the army as she invisibly scouted their forward obstacles.

By evening, they reached the keep, only three miles out from Mai. It was a large white stucco residence with a gray roof and ten foot gray stucco walls surrounding the perimeter. Four Mai'Lang sentries guarded each of the four walls, walking in slow, deliberate rounds, carrying crossbows and swords. Wytchyn was already inside, planting traps for the unwary defenders.

Jet sent eight archers to each side, hidden by the thick scrub brush that surrounded the keep. On his signal, each archer let loose into his determined target, two arrows sprouting from each guards' chest simultaneously. At the same time, four soldiers on each side with grappling hooks had ropes ready and within moments, the entire force was over the wall. Torches were being lit in the residence as its inhabitants began to realize that something was amiss.

The Stormdogs kicked in the doors and flooded the keep. Goblins poured out from every direction and soon the hallways were filled with fighting soldiers. Katir cleared the way with his massive sword with Jet close behind, as they bounded up the wide staircase to the second floor. A dozen Goblins stumbled upon them, but between Jet's knives and Katir's sword, they didn't last long. Stopping only long enough to retrieve his blades, Jet searched every room on the floor to no avail.

As they reached the third floor, a massive oak door blocked their way. Jet reared back his hatchets to chop it down, but Katir blew them open with a shoulder tucked charge. Behind was a gigantic room spanning the entire floor with so much gold and silver finery atop shelves and priceless paintings on the wall that Jet almost hated to have to fight in it. At the room's rear, fully one hundred yards away, stood five large, armored Mai'Lang circled around Hrafna, in her finest black and red gown.

Jet surveyed them with grey eyes so cold they could have frozen fire. He drew his hatchets slowly, deliberately.

"You have gone astray, pretty one," Hrafna purred menacingly. "We could have been something more, but you threw that away. He has found the Oracles, and now instead of benefiting from them, you will suffer the same fate as he. Speechless are you? Beg me for forgiveness and I may let you live, my precious."

"I am the calm before the storm; I am the tip of Loki's spear; I am the Bringer of the Fog; I am Jet Bloodhatchet and I am a Stormdog."

"How poetic. Do you now write a Death Poem like a worthless Duah?"

"Can you take the soldiers?" Jet asked Katir, as if Hrafna did not exist, which infuriated her above all else.

"Without breaking a sweat," Katir replied easily.

"Do so. The woman is mine."

"Aye, Bloodhatchet." With a roar, Katir charged and the soldiers moved to intercept him, leaving Hrafna and Jet alone. She flipped open her deadly fans.

"When I found out you had left the Mage, I knew you had betrayed me, dear Jetrian." She lunged at him, her fans at separate angles and speeds to throw his counter off but he was undeterred. Deftly he turned them aside with his hatchets.

"You betrayed Loki," he launched an attack of his own, beating her back further and further. "You tried to make me believe I was serving him through your plans. I serve him my way."

"What would you know of him?" she sneered. "I made you what you are! I gave you all you have and *this* is how you repay me?" She darted aside and set him on the defensive, her fans a blur. One caught him slightly across the face, but he kicked her in the gut before she could follow through.

"You gave me nothing. You would have me serve Chaos and forsake Order. I serve only the Balance, Hrafna. Or should I call you Zyrnal'Verkat, the daughter of the Fifth of Sorcerers?" He attacked again, their weapons blurring so fast that only the fast-paced ring of metal on metal could distinguish when a blow had been launched or countered. Jet took two minor cuts because her speed was too great with the fans for him to deflect every shot, but he knew that all he needed was one shot from his hatchets and it would be over. Hrafna recovered from her shock at his knowledge of her identity quickly.

"The Balance?" she spat at him. "Is that what you tell yourself so you can sleep at night? Is that how you justify all the lives you have taken this night? How you justify trying to kill the woman who has given you *everything* she had to give?" She increased her furious attacks, slicing him deeply across his shoulder and landing two successive kicks to his face.

Jet stumbled back but was still more than ready for her renewed attack. Gauging her rhythm, he timed her out perfectly. In her confidence she had settled into a pattern. With a quick sidestep, he turned her fans aside, sending one skittering off across the floor. She tried desperately to parry his rain of blows but it was of no use.

"I serve the Balance," Jet repeated, his hatchet coming in for the death blow, "and you are tipping the scales, Hrafna." Inexplicably his hatchet stopped a hair's breadth from her throat. Time seemed to have stopped. He glanced to where Katir had one soldier held above his head with one arm and his sword plunged through the chest of another. The temperature in the room plummeted and he noticed a handsome blond man in wolf's skin whose edges kept shifting so that Jet couldn't focus on him. Still, Jet knew him immediately for Loki.

"I have chosen well with you, Raevyn Balancekeeper. You have served me well at every turn," the God said in a voice that seemed constantly on edge the of laughter, using the name Jet had been given in Asgard, a very rare honor.

"And Hrafna?" Jet asked, awed by the being's raw power.

"She was useful. I needed her to find you. I must admit, at first I wondered if she had chosen wisely, you seemed to be too easily lured by her own plans, but you came around better than even I expected."

"She does not serve the Balance then?" Jet asked.

"No, only one may keep the Balance, and you are he. Half Mai'Lang and half Sendar. Born of Evil, raised among Good. You were the obvious choice, with your affinity for tricks, luck and your intelligence."

"What are your wishes of me?"

"Keep the Balance, that is all. You will forever know how." Loki bent over Hrafna and placed his hand in the center of her breast. The amulet floated out of her chest and into his palm, where it disappeared. Next he removed Jet's hatchet from its precarious trajectory.

"What should I do with her?" Jet asked.

"I will take care of her. She will lose her gifts and her memories. I will allow her to retain her beauty but I will alter her appearance. She has too many enemies who know her and it would be a shame to erase beauty like hers. My only advice to you, Bloodhatchet, is to remember those who have helped you and been a friend to you. They are few and far between, even more so to one such as yourself," and then he was gone.

Hrafna was nowhere to be found and only the dying scream of the final soldier punctuated the stillness. Katir hurried over, a questioning look on his face, but Jet had no answers. They made their way back to the first level, where the battle was ended, victorious Stormdogs seeing to their wounded, and when they saw him, they gathered around. He looked to Seranna, who was covered in blood but apparently unhurt. Wytchyn had four Goblins on their knees and bearing all of the money-keeping books and accounts of the Keep. They would be priceless. She met his smile with one of her own. Very rare. With an effort he pulled his attention from her towards his Weapons Master.

"Take everything of value you can carry back to the ships, then proceed back to the Myrkwood. Leave ten men here as sentries. Have them find the servants and get this place clean. From now on, any mission we conduct in or around Mai will be run from here. Pick someone competent to oversee the operation. Katir'Tua is in charge until I return."

"Aye, Stormleader," she acknowledged.

Jet took Wytchyn off to the side gently beside a huge marble column where the rest of the Stormdogs watched expectantly. She began to protest but he put two fingers over her lips as he raised the veil from her face. Her eyes narrowed angrily but he ignored them. Ignored the way they seemed to penetrate into his very soul. Gods! Why did she make him so flarin' nervous? He spoke quietly, so that only she could hear, hoping his voice would not tremble as his insides twisted up.

"Look now, Wytchyn Nightveil. I'm tired of dancing around this and feeling like a bloody scolded child every time we talk. Gods! Every time you even look at me! I don't know how, but you know things about me I've told no one else and you haven't told anyone about any of it. Somehow or another I can't seem to make myself not trust you. So the way I see it—"

He never got the chance to finish as she pulled his head down and kissed him long and hard and when she let go, he was glad to realize that he wasn't the only one out of breath.

"You talk too much for one with so many secrets," she said with a smirk.

"Aye. I have to go now."

"Be—" she stopped herself from saying careful. "Perilous."

"Aye. And Wytchyn?" he tilted her chin up to him with his finger. "You never have to hide your face around me."

"I know, Jet Bloodhatchet." She kissed him again, his name sounding like a bird's song on her lips. When he turned around, the Stormdogs were smiling widely, beaming with happiness for their Stormleader. The surprises never stopped. He had earned the loyalty of hundreds of battle-hardened killers with his hatchets. She had won their loyalty with a kiss.

"Where do you go? I will send a bodyguard detachment," Katir said.

"I have something I must do alone. Congratulations, Stormdogs, we have begun our march towards becoming something more than we ever dreamed." Jet stepped to a window, becoming a raven and winging his way east. The Stormdogs stared amazed after him, unbelieving.

"What are you all staring at?" Katir bellowed. "You heard the Stormleader! Get this place looted!"

The capital city of Mai loomed like a gargantuan puddle of darkness as they exited the forest. It was set grandly on a huge, gradually sloping hill. Black walls rose up into the night, creating the illusion that one was merely seeing a mirage. The city was vast beyond imagination, even Sendaria paling in comparison. More people called this city home than any other on the two continents. Even at this late hour, flocks of Mai'Lang traveled to and from the city, mostly in caravans, for few dared travel the bandit-riddled roads alone.

Donning their cloaks and cowls, the group ate a hasty meal. Danken, T'riel, Valshk, Shonai, Swifteye, Tamlinsen, Alaan, Nelkin and the Orcan male, Sani would be going into the city. The rest would stay back to protect the children. Panir's growls of disapproval could be heard past the forest line.

A large caravan was making its way towards the city and Danken and his group joined up with them discreetly. Shonai had become a Mai'Lang merchant man walking beside Tamlinsen, whose red palms marked him as Mai'Lang as well, though he was careful to keep his cowl over his eyes.

Danken and the rest climbed into a big wagon underneath its cargo, mostly rice and corn. As they neared the gates, the caravan slowed as guards from the city checked the influx of merchants. The gates to the city were five times the height of a man and close to a man's height thick. A small army of soldiers gave precursory checks to people and their goods before waving them in. The leader of the caravan they were hidden in met the guards with a perfunctory nod and detailed his cargo. The guard checked under tarps, looked at the people in the caravan and asked them a few questions.

After they had passed, the caravan entered the common grounds of the city. Prisoners were beheaded here daily. Performers lined the streets doing tricks for coins and beggars occupied all of the corners, lining them with hay.

Danken and his companions parted ways with the caravan at the Merchant's Quarter. With their cowls pulled low, they made their way through the grey-stoned streets, lined with tightly-packed shops. Livestock were led bleating through the streets, combined with the immense hubbub of people to create a dull roar that drowned out anything that wasn't yelled. It only got worse as the sun rose and more people filled the streets.

As they traveled into the city, however, the better the houses became and the streets became cleaner. Merchants' calls filled the streets, each trying to out-shout the next. Time was running out though, for cowled, black robed figures stood out in the heat of the Mai'Lang day. Where Winter was setting in in Sendar, Mai'Lang was rarely cold.

The Emperor's palace was carved from black marble and obsidian. Like some imagined beast, it bestowed upon them all an undeniable feeling of dread as it made its presence known. Spires two dozen stories high rose out of all four corners. Rounded cone-like structures comprised the roof and beautiful but macabre stained glass was in every window.

Another wall surrounded the palace, but unlike the Driss, the palace guards here were vigilant. Getting in would be difficult. The two Elves and T'riel snuck off to a corner out of sight of the main gate. There the Duah used their innate talents to quickly scale the smooth walls. Once there, they attached a sturdy hook to the wall and let a long length of rope down.

T'riel, meanwhile, was busy sprinkling itching dust on the five guards who patrolled their part of the wall. Instead of walking, they dropped to their knees in agony as they scratched in vain. Getting the all clear, Danken and the rest quickly climbed the rope.

Once on the ramparts, they quickly dispatched the itching guards. From there, they rappelled into the courtyard. It was a beautiful garden surrounding a large pond in which large orange, white and gold fish swam lazily. They narrowly avoided a patrol of guards walking the grounds by taking cover under the drooping branches of a willow tree.

Taking care not to be seen by the remaining guards, they sprinted across the garden to hide behind a large bush. Valshk became invisible as he approached the heavily guarded door. He moved silently until he was right on them, swinging his axe to deadly effect. Swifteye was there in a flash and they slew the guards before they could utter a cry of warning.

The group quickly dragged the corpses inside the palace and followed Shonai, who had gleaned the location of Amaria from the guards minds just as they had entered the welcoming embrace of death. She led them down hallway after hallway until they reached the stairway where they encountered another patrol of guards.

Shonai nearly slid into them and only Nelkin and the Orcan Sani's crossbow bolts saved her from being impaled. Danken was among them then, *Mak'Rist* a blue flash spraying the black walls with red. The sound of the battle brought a dozen other guards running but their fate was similarly sealed. They ran down the stairs until they reached the lowest level of the palace. It was dark, musty and smelled of urine and stale air. Two sentries stood behind a locked gate made of iron bars. Nelkin and Sani killed both but none could reach the bodies to get the keys to the gate. T'riel triumphantly shot through the bars and retrieved the keys from the guard's belt. They were as big as she was and three times as heavy, but she managed to drag them across the floor until Valshk could grab them.

After unlocking the gate, they checked each and every cell. Most were empty as executions had taken place earlier that morning. A few held Mai'Lang but the last one held a dirty, bruised Elven woman. She lay balled up in the corner and cowered noticeably at the sounds of keys. Danken opened her cell door and stepped in.

"Amaria?" he asked gently. She looked at him questioningly before rising to her feet shakily.

"Who's there?" her voice sounded defeated and confused.

"It's me. Everything will be all right now," he said with tears in his eyes. Still she seemed not to recognize him, looking blankly at the rest of the group, her green eyes dull and unfocused.

"We must go *now*," Valshk reminded them.

"He's right. Let's go. Stay with me." Danken led her by the hand back the way they had come. They retraced their path until they heard a multitude of voices around the next corner. They were only one hallway away from the gate but the platoon of soldiers rushing them stood between them and it.

The soldiers yelled when they saw they group and rushed to attack. Danken, too, rushed to attack along with Valshk, Swifteye, Tamlinsen, Nelkin and Sani. He bade Shonai and T'riel to stay with Amaria. Crashing into the Mai'Lang lines with the force of an enraged berserker, Danken immediately set them back on their heels. He became one with *Mak'Rist*, closing his eyes and letting the ancient blade guide him.

He saw in his mind's eye the Mai'Lang and countered their every attack. He was a whirlpool of flashing metal, sucking in all who came too close and spitting them out in pieces. He used *F'laare* to deflect and catch blades *Mak'Rist* could not, yanking their owners off balance before cutting them open from shoulder to waist.

Swifteye and Valshk were a devastating tandem as well with the shimmering Troll cutting down swathes of men while the Dwarf smashed any who got too close. They worked on the opposite side of Danken so as not to get too near his rampage of destruction.

Tamlinsen used his skilled swordsmanship to defend the archery trio of Nelkin, Alaan and Sani as they decimated the Mai'Lang from afar. As many as they killed, though, more seemed to take their place. A never-ending trickle of fresh bodies for the slaughter. One group broke through and charged the trio, sustaining many casualties as arrows rained on them. They reached Tamlinsen, inciting a free-for-all broke out. Nelkin, Alaan and Sani dropped their bows and drew their blades, leaping into the fracas. The clang of steel on steel was tremendous and the screams of the dying were shattering. A Mai'Lang sword caught Sani from behind before Tamlinsen could save him and he tumbled lifeless to the ground. The fierce battle raged on and soon was being fought atop the bodies of the slain. Alaan was the next to fall, his head severed.

Danken caught two Mai'Lang running full tilt towards Shonai and cut them down from behind. In doing so, he also cleared out the group fighting Tamlinsen and Nelkin, who were on their last legs.

"Guard the Princess!" he shouted.

"We must fight!" Tamlinsen said.

"They are the *reason* we fight!" Danken yelled. "Protect them with your lives." He ran back into the battle, where the Mai'Lang numbers were dwindling. Valshk was waning and Swifteye was having trouble keeping the men off of the Troll.

Danken's resilience changed all of that. He scattered the Mai'Lang and cut his way to them.

"Protect my back!" he yelled at them. They acknowledged and formed a circle around him as he destroyed the red-palmed ranks. The Mai'Lang could not retreat inside their own castle and so threw themselves at him with savage but futile fervor.

The battle ended abruptly with Tamlinsen firing a crossbow into the last soldier, who clutched the arrow in his throat as he fell. The ensuing silence was permeated only by their heavy breathing.

Valshk was wounded in a half dozen places, as were Nelkin and Tamlinsen. After checking on Amaria, Danken led them out of the palace. The gates of the walls were closed and two guards fired arrows at the group upon their appearance. Danken deflected them while Nelkin and Tamlinsen calmly killed the two. Another patrol of a dozen was similarly dispatched along with six more wall guards before the courtyard was clear.

Nelkin scaled the walls and opened the latched gate for them. On the other side, they found a milling crowd staring at them with much speculation as to the alarm that had been sounded. Shonai quickly stepped behind Valshk and emerged as the High Chancellor of Mai'Lang, the right hand of Emperor Stanlan'Kante whom she had seen in many of their minds.

"My people!" she called into the hushed crowd. "We have suffered a grave attack on this day by rogue Giants from the mountains!" The crowd gasped. "But our one time enemies, the Northern Peoples of Sendar, came to our aid and saved us. We owe them our gratitude and thanks. Please treat them with courtesy as they leave our city and journey homeward."

The people parted in awe as the cloaked and hooded, ripped and blood-stained group passed through. They walked quickly through the city until another group of soldiers came at a dead run towards them. Dropping all heroic pretense, Danken and the rest ran into an alley and turned down another parallel street, keeping close so as not to lose anyone. They barreled through the streets, people scattering out of their way.

The companions ducked into a tavern where Shonai, in the guise of the Chancellor, ordered everyone into the backroom. The bartender followed and the group ducked behind the counter. Shonai morphed to the bartender and began washing glasses as a group of soldiers burst in.

"Norsemen!" their commander barked in Langjian. "Have they been through here?"

"No." Shonai shook her head.

"No?"

"No, I have not seen any Northerners," she replied, also in Langjian.

"People outside said they saw them enter here," he said, moving towards the backroom.

"They must be mistaken."

"I think not," he said, kicking in the door to the backroom. As he did so, Danken and the others sprang up and attacked the guards, who went down before they could even raise their blades. As fast as they could, they put the soldiers uniforms on, leaving their cloaks open but their cowls still covering their faces. They exited the building with Shonai morphed as the soldiers' commander and marched off down the street. Danken kept his clothes as there were not enough unbloodied and unripped uniforms. He was forced to act as a beggar of the soldiers.

They neared the city's gates soon after and marched confidently through without so much as a word. The companions crossed the parade ground hurriedly but in strict military form until a hail of arrows thudded into the ground around them, killing Nelkin and wounding Valshk. He fell, clutching the back of his knee. Danken and Tamlinsen helped him up and they began to run for the forest.

Upon entering it, the rest of their group hailed them and reached them at the same time as the soldiers. With the children they had no choice but to run. Valshk fell to his knees, unable to run any longer. The other two Vull'Kra stopped to stand with him.

Danken turned to regard them as the others made a fighting retreat.

"Valshk, what are you doing?" he asked exasperated.

"We will hold them back," Valshk said calmly.

"Come on, we will fight them later. We must go *now!*" Danken told him.

"Go now, Sariksen, Gods be with you. We only ask that you tell our Clans we died with honor," the Trolls became shimmering masses. "By *M'Racht!* Our honor is our axe."

"You won't die!" Danken yelled as they fought off the first wave of soldiers.

"It is what we live for! Now go!" Valshk bellowed as he and the other Trolls gave their battle cries and charged the enemy.

"Gods be with us," Danken bellowed as he turned to stand with them. He couldn't use his own portal until they were sufficiently far away from the city without alerting the Sorcerers, so it was fight now or die later.

A red flash brought him up short. It was a portal and five Sorcerers stepped out of it. Automatically, Danken created one of his own and pushed the rest of his group through with *Breezesummon*, taking one last longing look at Amaria before closing it. He knew that the Sorcerers could reopen it if it wasn't completely shut so as he shut it, he leveled a tremendous blast of *Magefire* at all five of the Sorcerers.

They easily deflected it, but it had given his friends a clean escape to *Windstrike*. Everything seemed to go in slow motion then. He saw the soldiers overcome the Trolls, killing Valshk with several sword strokes after taking severe losses themselves. The Sorcerers fired what looked like a rope made of red *Serfire* at him. He deflected it with his own shield but found it was constricting him.

"It's called *Firerope*." One of the Sorcerers said. "But I am impolite," he bowed, "I am Dak'Verkat."

"Are you my next instructor?" Danken asked sarcastically, struggling to keep the fire away with his shield. The Sorcerer laughed.

"It was a brave thing you did, sending your friends back without you, knowing we would kill you."

"It was a brave thing your mother did, bringing your carcass into the world, Ser," Danken sneered, his breathing labored and short.

"Quick-witted too, I see," the Sorcerer said darkly. "Though, apparently not quick enough to see through my trap. You see, I had information from your friend, the one called Bloodhatchet, I believe. He set up the Goblin attack at the inn in the Duah Forest as well as informing me that you and that prissy bitch the Elven Princess were close. I figured you would be reckless enough to seek her out and come valiantly to her rescue. From there I just coaxed the librarian to bring you to me. You Norsemen are so predictable. Take heart though, boy, for originally the plan was for you to find the Oracles through your sister's death. But alas, she was not very cooperative

and had to be...dealt with. It was quick, I think. Or maybe not. Nonetheless, doesn't it feel good to know that those you trusted were in
fact betraying you to me?"

"I don't believe you," Danken yelled hoarsely. It could not be
Wytchyn. She was alive. He knew it. The Sorcerer was lying. He had
to be. Lanaia would never willingly help Dak'Verkat. But Jet...? He
might. "I don't believe it! Not one word from your lying mouth!"
Danken raged.

"I don't care," Dak'Verkat laughed evilly.

"And the Elves? They had nothing to do with this, did they?"

"Pfwah!" Dak'Verkat scoffed. "Do you think I'd waste my precious time worrying about the pathetic Elves? You or I could wipe out
their whole Royal Family if we so desired. Take your massacre of the
Driss Royalty for instance."

"And I suppose you're here to punish me?"

"Hardly. I could care less about them. They are merely a swarming mass to do my bidding, it matters not who leads them. They are
puppets, one and all. No, I wanted to trap you because I wanted you
to have a slow death for the hand you cut off." He held out his recently formed right hand. The skin was still a little pink.

"I had a feeling that was you on the road. Actually," Danken
said, gritting his teeth against the pressure the *Firerope* was exerting
on him, "it was more of a stench, like a dead, rotting cattle carcass,
or possibly feces."

"Funny." Dak'Verkat shook his head. "Tell me, do you think
you're so much more righteous than I?

"Isn't it painfully obvious?" Danken retorted.

"I wonder, how many men have you killed in your short eighteen
years? Hundreds, thousands? In the name of what? Good? When does
the number of dead stop reflecting your cause and start reflecting
you?"

Danken was silent.

"In your short years, you have killed more people than these four
Sorcerers around me combined. Where is the good in that, young
Magus?"

"You and your minion forced my hand. Had you not, I never would have come to your worthless continent." Danken spat.

"Ah, so the life of one Elf is worth the lives of four hundred Mai'Lang and Driss?" Dak'Verkat said calmly.

"If you provoked it, *you* bear the responsibility of their deaths, not I."

"Rationalize it however you want, Magus, it doesn't absolve you of guilt."

"Only the Gods can absolve me of guilt, Ser."

"Are you so confident they will?"

"Of course. It is their cause I serve," Danken answered.

"And who is it you think I serve?" Dak'Verkat asked.

"Your own selfish greed."

"The same Gods as you, just in different sides of the spectrum. You see, without us, there are no Magi, we are necessary to each other's survival. So to wipe out one of our groups is to wipe out us both."

"Better that we did," Danken replied.

"My feelings on the subject exactly. However, should we win, the world will know naught but change, Chaos. Should you win, it will know only lazy, ordered, identical days where no one changes. Boring, don't you think?"

"Your voice or your story?" Danken said.

"However," Dak'Verkat continued, "to truly win the war, we must keep you Magi alive but in a catatonic state where we can keep an eye on you. Thus, we remain alive and can sculpt the world in our image."

"Thus, you're insane."

"Aye, but the greatest leader the world has ever seen, nonetheless." The other four Sorcerers laughed. Dak'Verkat turned and issued a series of orders to the gathered soldiers in Langjian.

"Telling them I'm going to kill them all, are you?" Danken asked.

"Actually more along the lines of dragging your useless body through the streets once your shield gives way. Then they'll throw you in a special cell where you'll spend eternity trapped inside your

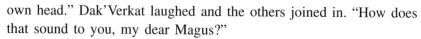

own head." Dak'Verkat laughed and the others joined in. "How does that sound to you, my dear Magus?"

"Delightful."

"I'm so glad you approve."

"Is this the part where I'm supposed to beg for my life?" Danken asked wryly, still struggling against the constricting wave of fire.

"No," Dak'Verkat smiled. "That comes when your shield breaks and you find you can't control your own bodily functions. Anyway, I was wondering how it felt to know that because of you, every Magi ever born will have to suffer an eternity and Sorcerers will rule your precious Northern realms?"

"About the same way you'll feel when you realize that you were outsmarted by an eighteen year old. That should be right about the time my blade separates your *Brag'Karn* from your cold body."

"Ah, bravado. Such violence in the youth today. Oh well, like father, like son, I guess. But I promise you this, Sapphire Son, by the time I am finished with you, you will beg me to let you use your sword for any purpose I choose. You, and the Oracles, are mine. Come, our time runs ever shorter and we have four more of these worthless Magi to kill." Dak'Verkat bid his four followers. They disappeared into a red portal and Danken was left alone with the evilly grinning soldiers. He felt his strength giving out. He had been up for two days straight, battling constantly and he hadn't much left to expend.

The soldiers kept their distance from him but their snide remarks traversed the distance with no problem. Danken knew he had to act fast. His hand was cramping from holding *Mak'Rist* so tightly. Thankfully, the spell had not made him drop it as it had *F'laare*. It had to be because it wasn't in its scabbard. Danken made a mental note to thank Tok'Neth if he got out of this alive.

He used all his strength to maneuver the tightening shield to accommodate *Mak'Rist* until it was pointing right at his chest. As his strength failed, the shield collapsed and drove *Mak'Rist* straight into his beating heart. He spasmed uncontrollably. The pain was unbelievable. His last thought was of Jet's betrayal before he dropped like a stone to the ground, unmoving, dead.

PART III

WAR

PART III:
WAR

 o much happens in the span of a moment. Great feats are achieved, great sacrifices are made. So much happiness, so much pain, so much hope, so much despair. That one tiny moment becomes immortal through the beings and forces that swim in its fathomless depths.

An emotion, a word, an action act like brands on the delicate fabric of time which is itself so closely intertwined with the threads of fate. A changed decision not only changes one's course, but the entire course of time, never to be revoked. Predetermined or not, we will never understand its mysterious ways, merely ponder how our seeming insignificance can have such a profound impact.

I choose to leave my impression with such vehemence and passion that it will achieve immortality in memory as well as time. For creation is the ultimate form of communication, a direct insight into the mind. To envision something unique, never experienced before and manifest it into reality is the only true way to leave one's mark on the world.

Thus, I now realize that my worth to this world is not judged by my birthright, my intelligence, my appearance or any combination of the aforementioned. It is what I make of my given talents that represents my contribution. In simplicity, the pride that comes from looking back and being able to claim credit.

–Archives Magus Gellar
This Sacred Year 87
Age of Mystery

CHAPTER 34
IT BEGINS

he *Firerope* spell lost its directive and dissipated into the air. Danken's hand still gripped *Mak'Rist* firmly. The soldiers gathered around him in amazement to see if he was dead. The commander gave the order to drag him back to the palace and carry out Dak'Verkat's orders. With a few vicious kicks, they obliged.

The soldiers tried to pry Danken's hand free from the blade but when they could not, they merely shrugged. The commander and his entourage were already heading back towards the city. They left Danken in the care of twelve soldiers with a gurney. Placing his unmoving body onto it, they began to carry him back to the city. The journey was bumpy and arduous but they reached the gates in decent time. They entered the city in grand procession, with spectators cheering at the subdual of a Mage. More than one piece of rotten fruit hit Danken's body on the way through the winding streets.

They reached a side street near the palace where the crowds fell off and they were alone. Jet materialized from the shadows, twelve knives finding their mark in twelve Mai'Lang throats. He rushed over and yanked *Mak'Rist* from Danken's heart, his grip still firm. With a gasp, Danken sat bolt upright. His eyes focused on Jet but he was too weak to talk. Jet carried the Mage into a nearby tavern where he threw two patrons and the bartender out of the way before ransacking the pantry.

Danken ate like a bear fresh from hibernation. The people in the bar stared aghast as he shoved whole loaves of bread into his mouth and downed flagons of water as if they were thimbles. The bartender started to shout in Langjian after the shock of watching the hole in Danken's chest seal itself had worn off. Danken irritatedly shot a bolt of blue into his throat, effectively silencing him. Jet returned from collecting his blades and menaced the crowd with his hatchets. Danken eyed him murderously.

"It was you," Danken accused.

"Aye," Jet nodded, to Danken's surprise and also anger.

"Why?"

"I was tricked. I let myself be lulled by promises and beauty and by the time I realized it, it was too late. I didn't know about their plan for Amaria, I went along with the Oracles because I thought it the only way to remain immortal."

"Give me one good reason not to kill you," Danken snarled.

"You already have it. I don't need to give you one."

"What about Kierna then? What did you do to her?"

"Nothing. Do you honestly think I'd hurt her?"

"It wouldn't surprise me. How can I trust anything you've said or done?"

"She's fine, Danken. She left to become something she couldn't be in your all-powerful presence. But I swore a binding oath and I won't break it."

"And why did you help me now?"

"My life is tied to your life. If you die, I die whether it be tomorrow or in a thousand years. At first, I did so to gain immortality, but then I started to like you. I don't like it anymore than you, but where you go now is dangerous. Therefore, I go with you. Besides, I'm dead if I stay here."

"Then I hope your cloak is warm, betrayer. And if you cross me again," his eyes flared dangerously, "I will kill you myself, if you don't die from exposure first. Just stay out of my way. There is nothing you can do to help me. We will finish this discussion once I have dealt with Dak'Verkat."

Danken was exhausted from healing and his lack of sleep, but he had to find the Sorcerers before they wiped out the other Magi. Out of the corner of his eye, he saw the patrons of the bar and its owner make a move for the door, but didn't try to stop them. It would make his job easier. He waited until he heard the rhythmic sound of running soldiers' boots outside before opening a portal and leaving his signature blue trap behind him as he and Jet stepped through it.

He hoped the Sorcerers would detect it and port back to stop him. Then they would run right into his energy trap. If not, at least it would take out as many soldiers as possible. He had to port to the only place where the Sorcerers could meet with the Magi undisturbed. Now he just had to figure out where that was.

General Feala Regerdotir was in her element. Her red and silver streaked hair was cut close to the scalp as were all of her forces'. She watched the pre-battle unfold with an eagerness only a born soldier could understand. Her forces were spread out on the grassy plains just beyond Faust's Wall. Close to forty thousand Sendar in their blue and silver uniforms stood stoically facing the red-clad Mai'Lang force of more than twice that size.

However, numbers were deceiving, Regerdotir knew. The majority of the Mai'Lang forces' numbers were men under eighteen who had been pressed into service. They were ill-equipped and ill-prepared. Still, more than eighty thousand men made for formidable opponent.

Both forces stood immobile for what seemed like an eternity before the Mai'Lang war horn blew. The infantry began advancing at a slow walk and Regerdotir gave the order to hold. As the Mai'Lang infantry began its trot, their archers let off the first volley. At this, Regerdotir gave her orders in her rough, Norspoint accent.

"Cavalry, full attack! Archers, volley one! Shields up!" Three thousand fully armored knights thundered towards the Mai'Lang infantry, as the Sendar archers let loose their opening salvo on the advancing line before taking cover from the Mai'Lang arrows.

The missiles thudded into the shields of the Sendar and they stood to find the Mai'Lang cavalry, seven thousand strong, advancing at a slow trot. The order was given on both sides to fire at will and Regerdotir sent in her infantry at a slow trot so as to let the Sendar cavalry do as much damage as possible before they were eventually overwhelmed. She ordered her archers to fire on the Mai'Lang cavalry.

The hail of arrows from both sides was as if the overcast skies had dumped lethal rain on the armies. Forces from both sides were equally devastated as the Sendar knights crashed into the Mai'Lang infantry. Armed Sendar on gigantic, fully-armored Volhakian paint warhorses swung broadswords as tall as a man in great, sweeping arcs at all in range. As they didn't have to worry about killing their own just yet, they were free to wreak havoc on the frantic foot soldiers.

The Sendar arrows could not penetrate the heavy armor of the Mai'Lang knights but the porous chain mail their steeds wore allowed the arrows to slip right through. A knight without a steed is a lumbering, cumbersome and utterly ineffective warrior as their steel armor makes them too heavy to move quickly. Their horses' numbers were cut by nearly a third and those knights who found themselves steedless, frantically struggled out of their armor, leaving them vulnerable to arrows once again.

The Mai'Lang arrows also found their mark among the Sendar infantry, killing some and wounding many others. By the time they reached the battle, most had numerous arrows sticking out of their shields and legs. They slammed into the battle at the same time as the Mai'Lang knights, forcing both sides to halt archers and change tactics.

Sendar knights began picking out targets instead of carelessly swinging and infantry used their arrow-studded shields to block swords. The Mai'Lang knights had no such qualms about choosing targets and hundreds from both sides fell before their blades.

The deafening sounds of battle were music to Regerdotir's ears. She thrived on every minute point, won or lost. As the battle raged on, she saw a large contingent of Sendar knights engaging an even larger contingent of Mai'Lang knights, leaving Sendar infantry on the left flank exposed to Mai'Lang reserves, who had just been called in.

"Damn. I had hoped to keep our reserves for a counterattack tonight."

"Aye, what shall we do?" asked General Tovairsen, Regerdotir's second in command. A younger man at forty-five, Tovairsen's wit had led him up the ranks quickly and Regerdotir valued his advice.

"Have the archers fire on the reserves until the battle is met. In the meantime, send half of our reserves. Keep two thousand back."

"Aye." Tovairsen nodded and issued the order. Sendar arrows began raining down on the quickly advancing Mai'Lang reserves, dealing destruction wherever they fell. Likewise, Mai'Lang arrows began hitting the Sendar reserves making their way at a full run towards the fray.

The Mai'Lang forces reached the front lines first, pushing the beleaguered Sendar infantry back towards the chaotic battle between the knights. As the Sendar reserves arrived and stabilized the line, Regerdotir expected the arrows to stop. But, to her dismay and shock, they continued to rain death upon Sendar as well as Mai'Lang. As there were more Mai'Lang on the field, the Sendar losses counted more heavily against them.

"Damn!" Regerdotir yelled. "Archers! Full trot! Two hundred paces forward! Switch to long-shot! Take out those archers, now!"

"Should we send in the reserves?" Tovairsen asked.

"No. Give the order, they are to keep firing until our reserves have reached the enemy archers. You will lead them around the main lines."

"Ma'am?"

"Give it!"

"Aye!" Tovairsen gave the order and then he and the reserves set out at a full run around the huge battlefield. The Sendar archers were now in position and began firing on the confused Mai'Lang archers, to spectacular effect. After two volleys, and close to two hundred casualties, the Mai'Lang archers caught on and began returning fire.

Regerdotir watched anxiously as Tovairsen led his troops on the outskirts of the battlefield. With the Mai'Lang archers so occupied with the Sendar archers, they made it past virtually unscathed but not unnoticed. A detachment of Mai'Lang knights fresh off of a victory over the smaller group of Sendar knights, moved to block them.

However, this left the remaining Sendar knights free and clear to deal death to the Mai'Lang infantry once more. The Sendar were still heavily outnumbered and hard pressed but they had gained the upper hand and were starting to take advantage of it.

The Sendar reserves, all two thousand of them, crashed into the eight thousand Mai'Lang archers at the same time as the five hundred Mai'Lang knights. The archers dropped their bows and drew their swords and now there were two battles on the same field. As the second battle was met, Regerdotir smiled.

"Archers, cease fire! Draw steel! Let's show these red-palmed bastards why we won the Great War!" She shouted, drawing her massive broadsword and closing the visor on her helmet. The archers drew their swords collectively and gave a thunderous roar. Leading them on their fully armored warhorses, Regerdotir and the few remaining officers charged full out into the fray.

Tovairsen and his troops were outnumbered two to one with no heavy cavalry, but the Mai'Lang archers were poorly trained swordsmen and presented no real trouble to the seasoned Sendar warriors. The Mai'Lang cavalry were far different. They continued their careless sword swinging, killing everyone in range.

The knights, however, were growing tired, as were their lathered steeds. Recognizing this, Tovairsen ordered his forces to retreat and spread out in a long, thin line. As the knights and the remnants of the archers pressed their attack, Tovairsen's troops spread out even further and continued their fighting retreat, forcing the knights to pick precise targets.

Horses' legs were cut out from underneath them and the knights were easily dispatched. The disoriented archers milled around aimlessly, swinging their swords at anything that moved, often one another. They were trampled by horses, accidentally killed by angry knights or easily killed by Sendar soldiers.

Regerdotir and her archers were much better trained and it showed as they helped turn the tide of the battle against the Mai'Lang. The battle began to wind down as the day did and patches of fighting were all that was left. The remaining Mai'Lang finally scattered in retreat, harried all the way by Sendar knights and archers.

Tovairsen and one hundred men were all that was left of the reserves. He led them back to the main battle sight where around four thousand infantry and two hundred cavalry were exhaustedly taking off their armor. Most were in a circle, though instead of cheering, they were somber. More than thirty thousand Sendar had died here today, and Tovairsen was horrified to realize so had General Regerdotir.

He pushed through the troops to see his fallen superior one last time. Her horse had been cut from under her and she'd been killed. Tovairsen knew that as new Commander, he was required to say something. The victorious army looked at him with tired but intent eyes.

"We have lost much this day," he began somberly, "but we have gained even more! The first victory in this war. We have created a small bastion of light in a sea of darkness." He looked to the blood-soaked grass. "I don't have much else to say, you fought bravely. Let's collect the wounded and get them taken care of before we burn the dead and go back to the Wall."

While the Mistgarde Army was busy preparing its defenses across Sendar, the Mistgarde Navy, with its huge Orcan divisions and ships of the line was relentlessly patrolling Mortegen Bay. They sailed within leagues of the Shrakens Isles and within view of Mai'Lang ports. Any enemy shipping or underwater activity was mercilessly destroyed. The Shrakens that had been left by the main war division in the bay to harry Sendar shipping were being harried themselves and many had been slain.

While all the races had their own shipping, most were merchant vessels with sailors *and* warriors. Mistgarde was the only true Navy in the realms. The Darkwatch, the Southern continents' equivalent of Mistgarde had been in the process of building a Navy but it only consisted of a few ships and they were strictly held in reserve.

Thus, with nothing but Shrakens and the occasional supply ship to occupy them, the Mistgarde Navy, eighteen ships strong, had more or less secured Mortegen Bay. Admiral Pana'Kol, the highest ranking Orcan in the Navy, was more than a little aware of this fact when he convened with four Orcan Lieutenants.

"Lieutenants Maxal, Operan, Tal'foil and Rascan, you will take forty Orcans with each of you to Kasan, Southport, Breakwater and Eastbank respectively to inform them of our limited subdual of the bay, perform reconnaissance and then report back to me. Avoid confrontation if at all possible."

"Aye sir," the four barked simultaneously.

"Good luck," Pana'Kol said, gazing at the South Coast of the Shraken Isles, as the sun set. Such a pity that such beauty was wasted on his most hated enemy. No matter, though, after their defeat at Faust's Cape, the Shrakens would have to return through the bay, where he would kill them to a man. Maybe then the Mistgarde would permit him to take the isles and wipe out the Shrakens and their worthless civilization for good, he thought.

Lieutenant Rascan eyed the Orcans assembled under his command with barely concealed glee. He would be in command of his first mission and he was determined not to fail. He remembered the icy purple eyes Pana'Kol regarded the world with and tried to imitate them. Gods, he thought, the man was the best Orcan commander in the Navy, but he was a bloodthirsty killer. Everyone knew it and perhaps that was part of his mystique. He couldn't be like that, Rascan thought; Of course, his whole family hadn't been murdered by Shraken Raiders either, as Pana'Kol's had. Maybe that incident had pushed him over the edge.

Nonetheless, the Admiral was his idol and he would do his best to make the man take notice of him. So, with his best icy glare in place, Rascan informed the Orcan crew of their mission. They had to travel to Eastbank, the farthest of any of the groups and, therefore, the most dangerous.

"Any questions?" he finished, and when none answered, he turned to a younger Orcan woman. "Drylyn, you're second in command."

"Aye, sir! Orcan crew, move out!" she yelled and the squad shot off through the water, maintaining a pace faster than a horse could run.

They passed the Dwarven barge flat preparing for its landing twenty leagues north of Bokat a little before midday the next day and continued at this breakneck pace of forty knots. It was still light out as they rounded the northern tip of Kybo Island when Drylyn called out for the group to halt. After three days of nearly nonstop swimming, the Orcan crew welcomed the breather.

"What's going on, Midshipman?" Rascan asked.

"Sir, scouts say there are between thirty and forty Shraken-like creatures on the reefs one league north of here. They say they could be the Barakans we've been hearing about lately."

"Aye, I think we've encountered them before, but they usually keep to themselves. We've had reports, though, that they've allied with the Shrakens."

"Should we attack them sir?" Drylyn asked anxiously.

"Our orders are to avoid confrontation and I don't know what these Barakans are capable of. We don't know their powers." He called the two scouts forward. "What were their demeanors?"

"It looked to me like an ambush sir," said one, a youngster named Golin.

"Aye sir. I concur," put in the second.

"All right then we attack. Form into battle positions. As soon as their position is known, team one gives a *Sonar* blast and charges. Team two waits in reserve for a second ambush if there is one. Be careful, we don't know what they're capable of."

"Aye sir," the Orcans barked before moving out cautiously. When they reached the ambush sight, they met up with the other two scouts who had been left to monitor.

"Confirm position," Rascan ordered.

"Confirmed, and we also detected movement on the other side of that coral," answered one of the scouts.

"Team one, go," Rascan said quietly. With a piercing blast of *Sonar,* the Orcans rushed the kelp, algae and anemone covered reef. At the blast, a commotion occurred behind a large chunk of coral and suddenly there were thirty shapes speeding towards them.

At first glance, they appeared to be all teeth, but as they grew closer, Rascan got their measure. They were slightly smaller than Shrakens but their jaws were nearly a third of the length of their bodies. Instead of legs, they had a tail ending in long, vertical fins. Their arms were flat and streamlined, ending in hands with two hooked fingers and a thumb. They were silver in color, with metallic blue stripes and their black eyes didn't so much give off light as swallow it. Rascan kept coming back to the jaws.

The Barakans shot a widespread *Concussion* blast from their snouts, which the Orcans barely had time to counter with another *Sonar* attack before the battle was met. Team one maneuvered deftly into its first *Bubblewrath,* confusing the Barakans and allowing Orcan javelins to dispatch seven of them.

"Team two, keep watch on that reef. I think we may have company," Rascan said, just as another *Concussion* blast came from the direction he was pointing, followed by another forty Barakans. The Orcans countered with successive *Sonar* blasts that muted the *Concussion* and then turned the aftershock back on the recklessly charging Barakans, disorienting them for a precious few fatal moments.

By the time the second group of Barakans had recovered, Rascan and team two were among them with their *Bubblewrath* and deadly javelins, cutting the Barakan's numbers nearly in half on the first pass.

The first group of Barakans were now using their *Concussion* to dispel the *Bubblewrath* and their insanely huge jaws to rip Orcans in half. Drylyn's team one, however, adjusted to this with ease and formed their famous and deadly *Circle*. Using their *Bubblewrath* to corral the vicious Barakans into a tight group before one piece of the *Circle* broke away, the Orcans unleashed their most powerful *Sonar* attack. The remaining Barakans were easily dispatched with javelins.

Rascan's squad fared better, as their initial attack had left the Barakans reeling and they had never let them recover. After the last Barakan was killed and the area was cleared, Rascan took stock of his squad.

"Casualties?" he asked.

"Aye sir," Drylyn confirmed, "seven."

"Not like fighting Shrakens, is it?"

"No sir, their *Concussion* dispelled our *Bubblewrath* and they did seem to be faster than us."

"Aye. Their lack of weapons bothers me though. Surely the Shrakens would have armed them?" Rascan wondered.

"Maybe they fight better without them, sad as *that* is," Golin piped in helpfully.

"Aye, but let's not forget, we're Mistgarde Orcans. We're used to fighting *four* to one and winning, two to one shouldn't *ever* be a problem."

"Aye sir."

"Midshipmen, move 'em out. We need to hit Eastbank by dawn."

"Aye sir," Drylyn saluted. "Orcan crew, move 'em out!"

They reached Eastbank just after dawn. Rascan marveled at the nearly five hundred ships in its huge harbor. As his crew came ashore and began their adjustment to land, he sent a young Sendar boy to fetch the Fleet Admiral and the Orcan Commander.

A thin, wiry man with an older Orcan rowed ashore from the fleet soon after. Rascan recognized the Sendar as an Admiral and knew the Orcan as well. While the fleet was made up of merchantmen ships commissioned for war and outfitted with soldiers and merchant captains, the Orcans assigned to them as well as the flagship crew were all Mistgarde.

"Sir!" Rascan came to attention as best as he could while still readjusting as did the rest of his crew. The Admiral and the Orcan Commander saluted back.

"I'm Admiral Mastersen, this is Orcan Commander Yardin. I'm from Fleet, what is your business?"

"Sir, I'm Lieutenant Rascan. This," he took out a glass encased scroll and handed it to the Admiral, "is a message from Admiral Pana'Kol. He wishes me to inform you of our limited sub-dual of Mortegen Bay. Also sir, on our way here, we were alerted to an ambush by Barakans on the North Reef of Kybo Island. It is my belief that they were part of a much larger group lying in wait for Breakwater fleet sailing to attack Kybo, sir.

"I decided it best to attack, sir. We were first alerted to a group of forty, which turned out to be eighty, sir. Our first *Sonar* attack killed ten and I sent half of my crew to finish, sir. I'll have a full report on the action as well as any observations about the Barakans on the Port Admiral's desk by tomorrow morning, sir."

"Very good. Casualties?" Mastersen asked.

"Seven sir. Sorry sir. We were a little wary fighting them because we were unfamiliar with their powers."

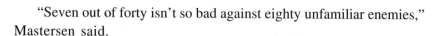

"Seven out of forty isn't so bad against eighty unfamiliar enemies," Mastersen said.

"We're Mistgarde sir. Not so bad isn't good enough for us," Rascan answered.

"You're right, it isn't." Yardin spoke for the first time. "And next time you'll do better, I'm sure."

"Aye sir." The Orcan crew responded as one.

"Quarters will be available to you at the Port Authority building. Three and a half days is a long journey. Dismissed," Mastersen told them.

"Aye sir!" Rascan saluted before leading his crew to the Port Authority building to sleep before they left for Fleet the next day.

The fleet from Norspoint sailed into Eastbank harbor at dusk. Admiral Mastersen observed their formation in the fading light before giving the order for his own fleet to shove off. Taking command of the entire squadron, the wiry grey-haired Admiral knew his was not only a responsibility to this fleet, but to all of Sendar.

He shifted his ice-blue eyes to the peninsula of Northern Mai'Lang as his flagship *Berserker* headed to the forefront of the armada. He felt a swell of pride in his chest at the sight of Sendar ships as far as the eye could see. Tens of thousands of brave men ready to deal the enemy his most resounding defeat. The rampant piracy and attacks on their homeland would not go unpunished. Growing up in Breakpoint he remembered the horror of Mai'Lang slave raids all too well.

They rounded the peninsula around dawn the next day. After the initial eagerness of the voyage had lifted, the fleet had settled into a hard, fast pace. Jokes were often made as a release to the tension of an upcoming battle, and Mastersen laughed along with the crew. It was important to let the men see your confidence and an easy smile and firm command were his trademarks.

A light southerly breeze sped them along and Mastersen had to put his jacket on to ward off the chill it brought with it. They would be nearing the port of Tau soon so he gave the order to make the fleet ready for battle. They had no intention of invading the city, but any shipping met along the way would be destroyed.

"Sail ho!" came the voice from the crow's nest.

"Identify!" said Captain Broderinsen, second in command, in his confidence laced Sendarian accent. All people from the Sendar capital spoke as if they owned the world. Being in the Mistgarde only slightly dampened their fire.

"Between forty and fifty ships, sir, in battle formation."

"Are they insane?" Broderinsen asked. "We outnumber them sixteen to one. Where is the rest of their fleet?"

"They were only expecting one fleet, not two I'd guess." Mastersen shook his head. "Still, it makes little sense. They know we have to pass here to attack any of the Eastern cities."

"Perhaps they aim to lead us into the Singo straits to equalize our numbers in such close quarters and shallow waters."

"Perhaps. But I'm thinking they have a trap set for us in Tau. Thus, if they give us the city, we take it and then our ships or men are sabotaged. I can smell it. Give the order to go to attack formation."

"Aye sir." Broderinsen turned to the signalsman. "Send the message. Attack formation."

"Attack formation. Aye sir!" the Signalsman ran up the flags to the rest of the fleet. As perfect as a school of fish, the massive fleet tacked and came on identical course in a diamond wedge with *Berserker* at its point.

As the fleets came within hailing distance, Commander Yardin shot from the water and on to the deck.

"Barakans, sir. Thousands of them just below their fleet," he said, out of breath.

"Can you deal with them?" Mastersen asked, his jaw muscles clinched.

"Maybe sir, but they outnumber us nearly eight to one. You only have one Orcan for every ship in the fleet and after this, you'll have none," Yardin said grimly as he prepared to dive back into the water.

"Commander, pull all your forces out of the water now."

"Sir? They'll tear our ships to shreds!"

"Just do it, and be ready to dive back in."

"Aye sir," Yardin acknowledged as he dove seamlessly into the water. Moments later, eight hundred and fifty Orcans jumped onto their assigned decks, anxious, confused and angry.

"Signalsman!" Mastersen yelled. "Run up this message to the fleet: As soon as your ship makes contact with Mai'Lang, drop three phosphorous bombs. One at seventy-five clicks, one at fifty and one at twenty-five!"

"Aye sir!" The Signalsman ran the flags up as fast as possible and the rest of the huge fleet acknowledged.

"Next, send this: Archers, fire at will."

"Aye sir," the Signalsman nodded. Soon there were thousands of arrows crossing from both fleets. Moments before the two fleets crashed together, the crow's nest called down urgently.

"Admiral. Three hundred sails approaching from the east and another three hundred fifty coming from the south!"

"I knew it! Damn it!" Broderinsen cursed.

"Boarding crews, ready for action!" Mastersen shouted, drawing his sword.

"Aye sir!" the Master-at-Arms called back. Mastersen stood unflinching as an arrow killed a sailor running past him.

With a bone-jarring crash, the two fleets came together and boarding crews from both sides swung to adjacent ships. Men in the crow's nest and rigging fired arrows into the crews on the decks while they moved from ship to ship in search of enemy troops.

As soon as the fleets came together, Mastersen gave the order to submerge the phosphorous bombs as he could see the Barakans' sinuous shapes under his ship. In deafening succession, twenty-four hundred explosions rocked the ships of both fleets crazily making most lose their balance and throwing more than a few unsuspecting Mai'Lang out of the rigging and crow's nest. Those that were in midswing from ship to ship, were thrown right into the water.

Phosphorous bombs, developed after the Great War by the Dwarves to help with mining, had been adopted by the Navy with a few small changes. They were put on anchor lines to hold them far enough below the ship so as not to cause damage to the hull. Whereas the Dwarves had rigged them for concentrated, one direction blasts, the Navy had filled them with aerodynamic metal pellets that exploded in all directions.

They were huge contraptions weighing nearly five times as much as a man. Their explosive power wasn't strong enough to cover more than the perimeter of a ship's hull so they were highly impractical on land, not to mention that the phosphorous only reacted to saltwater. They had only been experimented with and never been used in battle so Mastersen held his breath.

After the huge explosions, the Sendar forces having anticipated them, gained the advantage. The rest of the Mai'Lang fleet had joined the battle now and helped to even the tide. Mastersen ordered the Orcans into the water as soon as he was sure all the phosphorous bombs had gone off. Nearly nine hundred eager Orcans dove in to even out the Barakans' advantage.

The fleets now looked like one huge manmade island. Every ship was tied together so that men could swing easily from one to the next. Gradually the outer ships emptied out and the fiercest fighting could be found in the center. The battle was even on decks and as one ship was cleared of Sendar or Mai'Lang, the victors would move to another.

The fighting was the most intense aboard *Berserker* but Mastersen and the rest of his Mistgarde officers held her admirably in Sendar possession. Broderinsen had instructed the crow's nest archers to fire on the boarders and leave those Mai'Lang already on board to the officers, and the strategy worked with deadly effectiveness. Soon, less than half of the Mai'Lang that tried to cross onto *Berserker's* deck even made it, and those who did were outnumbered and outmatched.

Commander Yardin's first impression upon entering the water was that the bombs had exploded red dye into the water and not pellets, for he could hardly see it was so thick, but he could see sinuous shapes lurking within it. He gave a high frequency sonar call that drew all the Orcans to him over which distance they navigated by sound, not sight.

They arrived on the scene with looks of bafflement on their faces, because they hadn't encountered a single Barakan since submerging. All had since come to the realization that the red dye in the water was blood and the lurking shapes were shredded bodies. The cloud had started to clear somewhat, giving them a better view.

"It can't have killed them all," an Orcan remarked. "It's not possible."

"No." Yardin shook his head. "There's not eight thousand bodies here."

"Do you think they retreated?"

"Maybe, but I doubt it. Spread out, get me some readings," Yardin ordered and the rest spread out and took sonar readings. Suddenly, a massive succession of *Concussion* blasts thundered up from the bottom and some Orcans didn't react in time to keep them from being hit. Some were killed and others were knocked unconscious and left to the mercy of the battle.

"Attack formation!" Yardin shouted and the well-drilled Mistgarde forces came into position. They unleashed a devastating *Sonar* blast that dispersed the over three thousand attacking Barakans into manageable groups, which the Orcans took full advantage of. They used their *Bubblewrath* to excellent success for the first wave until the Barakans began countering it with their *Concussion* and using their greater speed to slip between the Orcan defenses and wreak havoc with their jaws.

Unexpectedly, once they were amongst the Orcans, their reflective bodies made them hard to see and resulted in more than a few accidental deaths. The Orcans regrouped to regain control of the situation and Yardin adopted a new strategy. He had noticed that the Barakans preferred to attack from below, so he grouped the Orcans into a spearhead. They then shot like an arrow down through the approaching Barakan ranks, unleashing *Sonar* to set the enemy on their heels.

Once below them, Yardin once again spread his forces out and used their coordinated *Sonar* blasts to corral the now confused Barakans, who foolishly pressed their attack downwards. The difference this time, though, was that the Barakans metallic camouflage against the surface light worked against them, making them easy targets for the Orcan *Circle* attacks.

Still, despite their clear advantage, the Orcans were severely out-numbered and the battle was long, drawn out and bloody. When it was over, nearly five hundred Barakans used their speed to escape certain death and headed south. Only three hundred Orcans were left along with another fifty who were seriously injured.

Topside the battle was equally fierce. It had now been concentrated on forty ships with *Berserker* at the exact center, but it was hardly the eye of the storm. The maelstrom of the floating battle circled chaotically, some men having switched ships over one hundred times in search of the enemy or to avoid him when he got too strong.

Broderinsen was in charge because Admiral Mastersen had been taken down to sick bay. *Berserker* was still in Sendar hands but many of her archers had been killed. The battle was in its twilight and the Mistgarde flagship had played a pivotal role in it. It was the only ship that had not changed possession at least once. Its decks had been cleared of corpses twice to make room to stand and its crew was still at three-fourths of its original compliment. In a sea of chaos, it was a lone bastion of stability.

It was long past midnight the day after leaving port when the Mai'Lang lines finally broke. They made a fighting retreat back to their ships though nearly three hundred were abandoned as there weren't sailors enough to crew them. The victorious Sendar gave valiant chase and their archers gave the Mai'Lang a deadly sendoff. Moments later, Yardin surfaced and came aboard *Berserker.*

"Where's the Admiral?" he asked Captain Broderinsen, his equal in rank.

"Critically wounded in sick bay. I'm in command. How did it go down there?"

"Bad, but it could have been worse. We lost five hundred Orcans to their seven thousand, give or take. The phosphorous bombs took out half before we even started though."

"Half?" Broderinsen exclaimed. "Gods, if they weren't trying to kill us, I'd be sick, but still..." he leaned over the rail in exhaustion and revulsion.

"They won't fall for it again. All they have to do is dive to avoid the pellets."

"Well, it won't be a problem, we only have one left on each ship. We'll only be able to use them in a surprise attack in a port from this point on anyway and they're so bloody expensive and impractical that I doubt even that will ever happen. Still, they saved us today. What are your plans now?"

"I want to sink some of their escape ships," Yardin said, indicating the retreating fleet.

"It's your call."

"Aye," Yardin said as he dove back in the water.

"Lieutenant," Broderinsen called to a young blood-stained man.

"Aye sir?"

"Load the bodies aboard the abandoned Mai'Lang ships and cast them off before setting them alight. Set skeleton crews and the wounded aboard our empty vessels and send them back to Eastbank."

"Aye sir." The Lieutenant saluted and hurried off to carry out his orders. Broderinsen watched tiredly as trailing Mai'Lang ships began to founder. He took a grim satisfaction from it, though it left him feeling empty. He knew that thousands of men had given their lives this day and he took no satisfaction in that.

Captain Tamlinsen leaned over the aft rail, staring at the midday sky in deep thought. The portal had spit them out aboard *Windstrike* with less than half of the number that had originally left on the expedition plus the Elven Princess and the five children, and minus their most important member, Danken. He remembered seeing the Mage close the portal and turn to attack. He felt helpless, angry and worried all at the same time.

Lanaia had told them that he had done it because the Sorcerers were coming out on the other side of the clearing. To leave the portal unguarded, with the energy bomb or not, would have left the portal open to them and they would have appeared aboard *Windstrike,* killing everyone, the two princesses aboard, included. Still, it was hard to justify leaving Danken and the Trolls to fight for their lives while he sat safe aboard ship.

He had given orders to wait for one day for Danken but that time would be up at sundown and he'd have to order the ship back to port. He glanced into the Dead Woods wondering what he could do. Could Danken have been taken prisoner? It didn't seem likely, but what if he had? It was Tamlinsen's duty to rescue him if he was. Besides, he would likely lose his commission when he informed the Admiralty of his woeful incompetence. But he also had a duty to the Orcan and Elven Princesses, as well, to return them safely to Sendaria.

"Damnit!" he shouted at the sea. Many of the crew paused to look at him before his icy glare caused them to scurry on about their business.

"Sir?" Ragnarsen said as he too approached the rail. "Is everything all right?"

"Would you kindly ask Princess Shonai to join me?"

"Aye sir." Ragnarsen saluted and quickly went below to fetch the Princess. Moments later, she was standing beside him, her skin-tight black clothes cutting an astounding figure against the setting sun.

"You wished to see me, Captain?"

"Aye, thank you for coming, Princess."

"I think after all we've been through you could call me Shonai, don't you think?"

"Aye. Sorry." Tamlinsen paused and informed her of his conflict of emotion and duties.

"Ah," she nodded, "I see."

"So, I'm taking the ship to the cove just above Maka. We'll reach it just before dawn tomorrow. From there myself, five Sendar and six Trolls will disembark. Lieutenant Ragnarsen and the rest of the crew will see you back to port safely."

"A dozen men into the heart of Mai again without Danken is suicide."

"Aye, but I'd rather die then be disgraced for not trying."

"Don't you think he knew what he was doing?" Shonai asked calmly, looking at him intently.

"Aye Majesty, acting selflessly to save you and Princess Amaria. But with all due respect, my duty is to the Magi."

"Very well. I understand your feelings. I, too, wish to go, but my place is with my people in battle."

"Aye Majesty." Tamlinsen turned to the steersman. "Steersman, make your course east by south-east, full sail!"

"East by south-east, full sail, aye sir!" the steersman called back.

"I just hope we're in time."

CHAPTER 35
EMERGENCE

 he snowcapped mountain towered over the clouds, creating the impression that it was the only piece of solid ground left in the world. The skies above were clear but it was far below freezing. At the base of the peak were sandy beaches lined with deadly, breeding Sea Dragons. This was the only place in the known realms where the races had never set foot. This was Mount Taeria, the lone peak of Sea Dragon Isle and the site for the most devastatingly powerful fight in the history of the realms.

After unleashing a small *Serfire* attack on Sendaria, the Sorcerers had ported here and left the trail clear. Unable to avoid it, the four Magi had followed and the battle had been joined. The five Sorcerers immediately attacked, setting the outnumbered Magi on the defensive where they were destined to stay. The Magi's only hope was that their greater experience would make up for their missing member. If not, they would soon give in.

The Magi erected a powerful shield made of *Magefire* that the Sorcerers were forced to use *Serfreeze* to attack directly, which was both time and power consuming. Attack magic cost more physically than defense and the Magi, knowing this, erected powerful defense after defense. They attacked rarely and then only to keep the Sorcerers off-guard.

Dak'Verkat guided his young apprentices with graceful but deadly expertise. They were novices but they were powerful and their numbers began to wear on the Magi.

"Where is your precious Fifth to save you this time, Sembalo?" Dak'Verkat spat. Sembalo didn't answer.

"We can't hold out much longer," Urishen said through gritted teeth. "It's been too long. We've been fighting since mid-afternoon and it's already dawn."

"The boy will show. Have faith, Urishen," Penn replied as their shield collapsed, sending them flying backwards as if carried on the wind.

Streaks of *Serfire* lanced across the void between the group which the beleaguered Magi blocked and then returned a coordinated *Gale* attack. The Sorcerers easily blocked it with their own and attacked with a *Firewall.* The Magi barely had time to block it with *Icewall* so their next erected shield was weak.

"The boy won't show, pathetic Magi," Dak growled as he and the other Sorcerers unleashed a concentrated *Icebeam* attack on the poorly constructed shield, once again strewing the four across the snowy ground.

"As if you'd know, dog!" Kai shouted.

"Oh but I would." Dak'Verkat laughed as their shield wavered. "You see, he's rotting in a Mai dungeon as we speak, helpless! Like the lot of you, sad, scared and weak!"

"Liar!" Kai shouted, but the tail part of the word was drowned out by the tremendous implosion of the Magi shield.

The backlash knocked the assembled Magi back into a huge snow-drift, exposing them for a fatal moment. The Sorcerers let fly a hail of *Stalactite,* razor sharp shards of earth which hit the snow above the Magi, causing a miniature avalanche to cascade down upon them. Momentarily frozen, the Magi were helpless and the Sorcerers Kelin'Bak and Regan'Shune decapitated Urishen and Sembalo, quickly stealing their *Brag'Karn,* their bodies dissipating into blue dust.

Kai and Penn managed to get their shields up but it was just a matter of time before it too, broke. Once it did, they would have to rely on their blades to protect them against five vicious and angry Sorcerers.

Dak'Verkat was so enraptured by his approaching victory that he failed to notice the change in power when a blue portal opened on the other side of a large rock behind him. He was so confident that all of his painstaking work had paid off that he didn't comprehend Danken's presence until it was too late. Jet shivered with the cold and crouched low, knowing that he could do no good here.

"I told you worthless Magi that the boy wouldn't come but you let your precious *hope* disillusion you and now look where it's gotten you!" Dak shouted. Danken saw the burn marks in the snow left by

Sembalo and Urishen's deaths. He felt his rage overcoming his senses and had to fight to subdue it. Steeling himself, he drew *Mak'Rist* and *F'laare* silently using *Stealth.*

As he stepped out from behind the rock, he raised five huge and very-hard-to-control *Earth Elementals,* one behind each Sorcerer. As each giant came alive, the Sorcerers' concentration broke in shock. Their defenses were down for a split second and Danken took full advantage of their overconfident egos.

Danken fired an enormously powerful bolt of *Magefire* from *F'laare* at one Sorcerer, blowing a hole though his chest. The Sorcerer's heart was torn from his body and his *Brag'Karn* evaporated into red dust. Danken let his consciousness meld with *Mak'Rist.* The Sorcerer Shuka'Mal was the only one of the remaining four who had not gotten his defenses up since the *Elementals* had appeared as Kai and Penn had unleashed a powerful *Magefire* attack in concert with Danken's appearance. *Mak'Rist* singled him out instantly and before Shuka'Mal knew what had occurred, Danken had taken his head off with one deadly stroke. He deftly flicked the *Brag'Karn* from the Sorcerer's neck with the tip of *Mak'Rist.* Red energy vaporized the surrounding snow.

Penn and Kai, energized by Danken's presence, had unleashed *Fire Drakes* to further harry the Sorcerers. It was now three on three, but Penn and Kai were spent. Danken tried unsuccessfully to cover for them. As the Sorcerers easily defeated the *Elementals,* they once again turned their focus to attack and Danken found that his energy was the only one holding up the shield.

"It's no use, Danken." Penn said tightly.

"Aye," Kai agreed. "It's time for us to give back to the Gods. I hear Odin calling. The Valkyries are here. We should not keep them waiting."

"What are you talking about?" Danken asked, though in his heart he knew.

"On the count of three," Penn told them, "I'll send my *Lifecharge* into Regan'Shune and Kai will send his into Kelin'Bak. It's useless to use it on Dak'Verkat, he'll deflect it. It's the same tactic he used to kill your father. Highly ironic, don't you think?"

"No," Danken said quietly. "There has to be another way."

"I'm afraid not. Just make sure you get their *Brag'Karn*. Dak'Verkat won't be able to stop you because he'll have to kill us. Then it will just be the two of you."

"When you kill him," Kai said, "you'll be the only one left. Use your power to protect our people and to find the next generation of Magi."

"Aye," Danken said, pumping more power into the shield. "I will make you proud."

"You already have, Danken," Penn told him. "Now, one, two, three!" he shouted and he and Kai unleashed their breathtaking energies into the two young Sorcerers, knocking all four unconscious.

Dak'Verkat stared insanely around before realizing his predicament. Danken was already moving with his shield up. If he killed the two Sorcerers before Dak'Verkat killed the two Magi, he might be able to save them.

"Damn you!" Dak cursed him as he ran to the fallen Magi. Time seemed to slow as both struggled to finish the slaughter ahead of the other to gain the advantage.

Danken cut out Kelin'Bak's *Brag'Karn* but had to go the same distance to Regan'Shune, giving Dak'Verkat time to catch up. He killed Kai and Penn at the exact moment Danken killed Regan'Shune. Both turned and released *Magefire* and *Serfire* at each other, catching both in a whirlwind and rocketing them back to land in the deep snow.

They stood then in silence, eyeing each other, neither attacking, both breathing hard. They circled each other restlessly like two primal animals. Danken watched his breath freeze and made sure he was using *Everwarm* subconsciously. He knelt down and picked up two large handfuls of snow and ate them, never taking his eyes off Dak'Verkat. Next, he took a loaf of stolen bread and a hunk of cheese from his cloak and devoured them instantaneously. He could feel the hunger emanating from Dak.

"So, you broke the *Firerope,* I see," Dak'Verkat said softly.

"Aye," Danken replied just as softly.

"Very interesting indeed. It seems I should have stayed to ensure its success, though in truth I did not see the need. It should have been impossible. But, no matter, I need you alive anyway, for who but the Sapphire Son can bring the Gods back to Midgarthe. Surt demands your servitude. Still, it would have made things so much easier had you not broken the *Firerope*. Do you mind if I ask how?"

"This." Danken tapped his head. For the first time he felt a warmth near his chest. It took him awhile to figure out what is was until he remembered the Oracles. They were lending him strength, compensating for lack of sleep and sending visions of Amaria crashing through his thoughts. He remembered Jet's involvement with the Oracles as well, knowing that he had sought to have Danken forever alive and bound so that he himself could live forever. Changing his mind and saving Danken was the only thing that had prevented him from killing Jet. He swallowed the bile in his throat. That could wait.

"You know," Dak'Verkat said smugly, "we could both just walk away to meet another day with our minions, when they have been regenerated. You don't have to die here on this beautiful day."

"We could. *Or,* we could test your experience against my power. Tell me, who do you think would win if we did that?"

"Me, of course," Dak said as if it were a foregone conclusion. "We're both nearly out of power, enough for one, maybe two attacks at best before we can only use it for defense. Then, we'll clash swords, and for all your vaunted power, two millennium of experience with a sword gives me the clear advantage."

"Well, that is an intimidating set of reasoning. But, I wonder if this elaborate plan of yours will work as well as your last one, because if it does, you may find yourself as a cloud of red dust like the rest of your brethren, Ser."

"So be it!" Dak'Verkat released *Stalactite* which Danken deflected and returned with *Gale,* throwing Dak'Verkat back to land on one knee.

"Temper, temper, Ser." Danken taunted, though he felt his strength waning, Oracles or not. The visions they conjured became more insistent and violent, forcing him to catch his breath. Dak'Verkat attacked once more but it was a weak *Serfire* attack which Danken sidestepped. He took a chance with his last attack and called forth two *Air Elementals*. If Dak'Verkat was too weak to attack, he would have trouble defeating the *Elementals* and Danken would have the upper hand. Dak'Verkat threw two of his *Prakras* which Danken destroyed with a bolt from *F'laare*. Their energy seemed to be at an end.

As it turned out, Dak'Verkat had enough left to dispel the *Elementals* but it left him exposed to Danken's opening attack with *Mak'Rist*. He reacted in time though, drawing his blade *Shirkal*. So it was that the two most powerful beings on the planet, drained of power, strength and awareness, battled mightily atop the most remote peak in the realms, each struggling to maintain *Everwarm* as they did so.

Each was such a master swordsman that the metallic rings of their blades came so quickly that they were nearly indistinguishable. They fought on pure willpower, each lost in his subconscious. They searched in vain for holes in the other's defenses, neither giving any ground.

It was an intricate dance of death that each was acutely aware of and absurdly good at. Finally, Dak'Verkat slipped on some loose rocks and his defenses fell momentarily, which was all Danken needed. He rushed in and went for the kill, but Dak was able to jump back. Nevertheless, he took a bad slash the length of his chest that would be slow to heal.

Dak backpedaled quickly to the edge of a high cliff and Danken followed warily. Suddenly, the Sorcerer morphed to his *Avian* form, a huge black owl and leapt off the edge. Following suit, Danken morphed to his eagle form and gave chase.

Dak'Verkat was in a nose dive down the side of the peak with Danken following closely and the heavy winds buffeted them dangerously near to the jagged rocks. As they entered the heavy cloud layer, both birds' eyes began glowing to navigate the murk. Danken struggled to keep Dak'Verkat in sight while avoiding the deadly obstacles in his path as electricity shocked their systems. As they exited the cloud cover, Dak'Verkat swooped up sharply. Danken did likewise, only his path was suddenly impeded by a monstrous blue head and a virtual cavern of a mouth entirely filled with dagger like teeth nearly half as long as he was tall. A thunderous roar from the head preceded a massive jet of water that Danken only just avoided.

Danken glanced down to the beach where dozens of breeding Sea Dragons were angrily looking at the two invaders. Danken gained altitude and caught sight of Dak'Verkat flying low over the water back towards the continent. He kept his eye on the owl as he rose higher for a perfect dive height. Dak'Verkat's chest wound was slowing him down and his flying was becoming erratic. He was seemingly finished, struggling to press on in vain.

Danken prepared for his dive, visualizing the point of contact. He knew that in *Avian* form was when they were the most vulnerable, because a bird's head could be pulled off relatively easily, leaving the *Brag'Karn* exposed. He readied his talons for just such an action and began his dive, careening towards the water at breakneck speed.

Dak'Verkat sensed his presence and started to fly evasively but he couldn't shake the perilous eagle and Danken was reminded of the dream he had had before his mother had died. A thousand possibilities crossed his mind in the moments before contact but none compared with what actually happened.

As Dak'Verkat dove again to the point where his wings were nearly dipping in the water with each massive beat, he didn't see the dark form below the surface raise its mammoth head out of the ocean just in front of him with its huge mouth agape. By the time Dak saw the Sea Dragon, it was too late and the deadly jaws closed on the owl just behind the wings. With a sickening crunch and toss of its head, the Sea Dragon flung the severed lower half of the owl's body in the air before devouring it as well. Without further ado, the serpent dove into the depths, disappearing beneath the freezing waves.

Danken broke his fall with two heavy wing beats, coming to a halt just above the surface and slowly rising again. He looked at the water in shock. He considered using *Waterbreath* to follow the Sea Dragon and check to see if Dak really was dead. But he had been up for three days and didn't even have the power to use *Waterbreath*, let alone battle a Sea Dragon.

If Dak'Verkat was still alive, he wouldn't have the energy to put himself back together and would be slowly digested, which Danken figured was just as good as dead. Still, he couldn't shake the feeling of doubt in the pit of his stomach. His strength gave out unexpectedly then, and he plummeted toward the freezing sea. A strong set of talons attached to a mighty raven caught him and carried him to the distant horizon.

When he reached the shore, he called up all his reserve strength and conjured up a portal. Jet helped him slowly through it and came out on the other side in the first place away from home he'd ever felt truly welcome.

The marauding Driss were indeed dispersed (as Rekfoll had predicted and to Kierna's consternation) over a broad expanse of mountain range, leaving relatively no rear guard to protect the two Dragons. Receiving word of the Mistgarde forces who had begun marching on them earlier that day, the Driss had spread out to better use their superior numbers. The small groups in the path of the Spirit Blades were taken completely unaware and summarily wiped out, for none had reported the Spirit Blades' arrival or positions. The surprise was total.

In the darkness of a moonless night, the Spirit Blades glided through the burnt out town beneath the mine, neutralizing what small resistance there was. They darted through the dimly lit mine shafts, following the growing heat. Finally, they came upon a great cavern shaped like a beehive, with narrow walkways spiraling up from the bottom more than fifteen hundred feet below. Sendar, Duah, Vull'Kra and Rokn slaves were in abundance, hauling rocks or dull shovels and all manacled to one of a hundred huge iron chains that hung in the center of the chasm. Dozens of Driss stood along the precipice, whipping any slaves in range. Wails and screams echoed throughout the humid and stifling stone chasm.

Knowing that making their way down the crowded spiraling walkways would not only alert the Dragons to their presence but also perhaps cost the slaves their lives, Tonis ordered all but fifty Spirit Blades to attach ropes to the chains and slide down. Fearlessly they did so, only halting their free fall by tightening the slipknot just before they impacted with the ground. The fifty above began systematically working their way down the spiral, killing Driss and freeing slaves as they went.

Kierna, Tae, Corsha, Phaeryn and the others reached the dark, blisteringly hot bottom of the chasm. Immediately they killed the score or so of Driss that were guarding the slaves on the main mine tunnel burrowing even deeper into the ground. A wide passageway that sloped gently downwards opposite the tunnel was the source of the sweltering heat and so they followed it, swords gripped tightly in sweaty palms. At the end of the dark corridor was a bright light, like that of a large fire. Braving the painful heat, the Spirit Blades pushed into another immense cavern. The smell of death and sulfur was nearly as overpowering as the oppressive heat.

Tonis immediately dispersed her forces around the two gargantuan sleeping Blue Dragons. Even asleep, they instilled a primal fear in even the bravest of hearts. Darandoross was over seventy feet long with a mouthful of rows of dagger-like foot-long teeth, shiny blue scales and yellow horns and wings. His mate was similarly colored, only ten or fifteen feet shorter than him and slighter than his great bulk.

Quietly, Tonis led them in the Pledge, each Sister taking heart and drawing courage from the familiar words.

Lo the pull of the swords calling me to join the dance
Lo the song of the Gods calling me to make my stand
May my swords ring true and my knell be ever raised
May my honor and faith be the edge of my blades
My life, my soul, my all, this I pledge.

"Draw bows," Tonis whispered and silently the Spirit Blades did so. "Aim for eyes and nostrils. When they wake, put your second volley in the back of their throats just as they prepare to breathe fire, then get out of the way. Use your swords where the scales overlap. It's the only place they are vulnerable. Understood?" The Spirit Blades nodded. "Make your *Cooling* Runes." Each Spirit Blade turned to another and used the tip of their arrows to slice the *Cooling* Rune into each others' forehead. It would protect them from anything but a direct blast of Dragon Fire.

When this was completed, Tonis gave the order to fire and the first one hundred fifty shafts thudded into the Dragon's eyes or nostrils. Those that didn't bounced harmlessly away off the thick scales.

Both Wyrms came awake with a deafening intake of breath, their faces like bloody pincushions. As the Dragons opened their mouths to roar, the second ranks' volley crashed into the back of their throats. The Spirit Blades dodged as the severely weakened blasts of flame heated nothing but the stone wall.

They were surrounding the behemoths then, plunging their swords into the soft spaces between the overlapping blue scales. The Dragons, blind and unable to draw another breath sufficient to breathe fire, thrashed about violently, their spiked tails knocking chunks of solid rock loose as often as killing a Spirit Blade. Kierna and Tae found themselves on top of Darandoross' back, dodging between yellow bone plates as tall as themselves. They struggled to the Dragon's head.

Two massive scales protected the Dragon's spinal column here, so, with each grabbing onto a plate, Kierna and Tae began hacking away. Darandoross thrashed his head back, his horns missing the two warriors by a hair's breadth. Before he had time to do it again, Kierna plunged both blades directly into his spinal cord, and the great Blue Dragon dropped heavily. The cloud of pulverized stone dust blinded and choked them all, and when it cleared, Kierna could see Darandoross' mate's death shudder as her hundreds of wounds finally overcame her vicious strength.

The Spirit Blades cheered then, and Kierna was astonished to realize they were chanting her and Tae's name. She and Tae leapt off the dead Dragon's back.

"Sisters, I thank you for your praise, but we all played our part today. Please, we have fifty Sisters still fighting for the slaves and we have many wounded to tend to. We can celebrate later."

The Spirit Blades immediately snapped to, carrying the wounded behind an advance guard that cleared their way. They met with the Spirit Blades who had been left behind and set up a makeshift infirmary at the bottom of the chasm. Patrols were sent out to clear the mines of any remaining Driss and a stout guard was set up at the entrance.

The Mistgarde arrived the next morning and several isolated, pitched battles ensued. The Spirit Blades not necessary for the care of the wounded also took part along with an army of emaciated, enraged former slaves carrying shovels, pickaxes or even rocks. The Driss, who had thought the Dragons' invincible, were crushed by news of their demise and their demoralized troops were no match for the highly trained Mistgarde forces. Some escaped death but as Blue Scales they were disgraced. Many later found themselves in the Myrkwood, enlisting with a famous mercenary army called the Stormdogs.

CHAPTER 36
ON THE DEFENSIVE

iedrik and Myrisan had left Keyre with a profound sense of unease. The odd feeling had been growing in Diedrik's gut more every day. He hadn't told anyone about it but Myrisan suspected something. Diedrik turned Malta around to look at the city's gates. Something about them bothered him, but he couldn't place his finger on it. Myrisan continued to scan their surroundings in silence. Diedrik decided to confide in the Hafalf.

"You say I'm a gypsy, right?" he asked. Myrisan turned to regard him.

"Aye, if you wish to call it that."

"And I'm supposed to be sensitive to magic?"

"Not supposed to be, you *are.*" Myrisan answered.

"I guess that explains it then."

"Explains what?"

"The feeling I keep getting from the eastern side of the Lok," Diedrik said, eyeing the forest line suspiciously.

"I was wondering why we were headed there. You suspect something?"

"Something wrong. Very wrong."

"Well, we'll have to remedy it then."

"Aye," Diedrik answered as they entered the thick coastal forest.

The journey was a peaceful one. The sounds of birds and insects were abundant. On several occasions, they glimpsed Dryads shooting through the canopy. These were tiny, glowing blue creatures made entirely of energy. They were born of the forest and helped maintain it, oblivious to all else. Their joyous buzzing and zinging permeated the air.

"How much further is this 'feeling' we're searching for?" Myrisan asked after they had ridden some distance into the woods.

"I don't know. It's not like I can see it. It's just there, leading me on."

"Ah," Myrisan said, calling his horse to a halt. "Should we stop for lunch now, then?"

Diedrik dismounted. "If you think that's best."

They ate their food cold, keeping a wary eye on the surrounding forest. As soon as they finished, they mounted up again and continued on.

"You don't feel anything?" Diedrik asked. "Anything at all?"

"Shh!" Myrisan stood.

"What is it?" Diedrik whispered.

"What do you hear?"

"Nothing."

"Exactly. Nothing. No birds, insects or even Dryads," Myrisan breathed.

Diedrik was loading his crossbow when the feeling hit him like a sledgehammer in the chest. He nearly fell off of his horse as he gasped for breath.

"What is it?" Myrisan hissed.

"It's here," Diedrik gasped.

"What is?"

"The feeling. It's right here."

"Where is it coming from?" Myrisan looked around alertly.

"I don't know."

"Wait!" Myrisan pointed off into the shadowy distance. "Do you see it?"

"No," Diedrik answered, straining his eyes.

"There. The shimmering. Like a Troll. Do you see it?"

"Gods," Diedrik breathed. "It's huge. What could it be?"

"Hold on," Myrisan said, firing an arrow into the shimmering mass. It struck something unseen and then with a groan, a Mai'Lang soldier fell over dead.

"What the..." Diedrik started in shock before he realized what this meant. "This is bad, I'm guessing."

"Get out of here!" Myrisan shouted. Both turned around and galloped back towards Keyre as fast as their panicked steeds would take them.

A tremendous roar came from behind them as thousands of Mai'Lang came out of their magical hiding spots, where the Sorcerers had placed them weeks ago.

"We've got to warn the town!" Diedrik shouted.

"Aye, if we make it!"

Two arrows thudded into a tree trunk a few feet in front of Diedrik. He urged his horse to even greater speeds. Fortunately for the two fleeing men, their mounts were well versed in forest riding. The Mai'Lang horses were mostly used to plains and were slowing noticeably.

They thundered into Keyre just before sunset as most of the fishing fleet was returning. The townsfolk looked at their lathered horses and panicked faces and crowded around them.

"Mai'Lang!" Diedrik yelled. "Thousands of them in the forest! They're coming this way!"

"Everyone inside the gates!" a man called from the towers. A loud foghorn blew the emergency signal out over the Lok.

As the last of the late travelers made it inside the gates, a loud rumbling came from the forest and with it, thousands of battle-ready Mai'Lang soldiers. The gates were hurriedly closed and every able-bodied person in the town lined the walls with bows, boiling pitch and anything else they could find.

Crews of children and elderly began gathering buckets of water. Diedrik and Myrisan stood on the walls with the rest, awaiting the opening salvo. Most of the fighting men had gone off to fight in the war, so the city was outnumbered and ill-equipped.

As the Mai'Lang came within range, the militia commander, ordered the archers to fire at will. Hundreds of arrows left the wall where most were blocked with shields. In return, a line of Mai'Lang lit the evening sky with fire, as hundreds of burning arrows streaked into the city.

The fire crews went immediately to work dousing blazes in houses and businesses. They were largely successful, setting up bucket lines throughout the city.

As the Mai'Lang neared, they became easier to kill. Their arrows were relatively harmless to the defenders behind their parapets, especially as they were on the move. They reached the gates with a mighty crash, throwing grappling hooks by the hundreds up the side.

The defenders tried unsuccessfully to cut the lines down. There were just too many. They poured boiling pitch on the thickest concentration to devastating effect. But the Mai'Lang reached the top of the battlements and the hand-to-hand fighting began.

Their superior numbers and weaponry gave them the advantage, but the hard, toughened people of Keyre were fighting for their homes and their families' lives. The fighting was fierce and the defenders were forced to fall back little by little until eventually they were forced completely off of the parapets.

The fire crews were evacuated to fishing vessels along with the wounded. The battle moved into the city.

As predicted, the sea battle was met near the Goblin port of Mok. The Duah Admiral Kanumus and the Vull'Kra Admiral Magha had joined with the Orcan forces under King Hai'Ten himself at Wescove. The Sendar Fleet was a day behind them.

The Commander of the lead Orcan regiment came aboard Kanumus' flagship, *Evergreen,* his grey, smooth skin glistening in the pre-dawn moonlight. Captain Dain "Lucky" Breezin was on deck to receive him, peering intently to the south-east with his green eyes glowing.

"Our scouts have encountered the lead Shraken and Pir'Noh elements fifteen leagues south-east of here. The rest of the fleet is approximately four leagues behind, just off the coast of Mok," the Orcan said in a quiet voice. Dain nodded imperceptibly.

"Aye. What do you intend to do?"

"King Hai'Ten says we will stick to the original battle plan unless the situation changes."

"Are their numbers as we predicted?"

"Aye, we are outnumbered two to one by the Shrakens and Pir'Noh, you and the Trolls are similarly outnumbered."

"These Pir'Noh, will they present a significant problem?" Dain asked, eyeing the black waters.

"Aye, they could. We have limited knowledge of them, as they have kept out of any conflicts until now. We trade with them occasionally, but their battle tactics are relatively unknown to us."

"Aye, then we'll meet sometime early this morning."

"I will keep you informed," The Orcan told him before leaping back into the water. Dain turned to the Signalsman.

"Send this message to the fleet: Battle plans unchanged. Will meet enemy early morning."

"Aye sir," the Signalsman confirmed.

"Helm, take her two points starboard."

"Aye sir, two points starboard."

"Lieutenant, send the Admiral my respects and inform him of our expected engagement early this morning and of confirmation on troop numbers."

"Aye sir." The young Lieutenant saluted and scampered below decks. Dain steadied his twitching nerves with a deep breath.

Soon after, Admiral Kanumus came on deck in his full dress red and gold uniform.

"Two to one, eh?" were his first words upon reaching Dain with a confident smile.

"Aye sir, mostly Goblins and Pir'Noh boosting their numbers," Dain answered, drawing confidence from the older Elf's demeanor.

"Aye, probably. No matter, we will overcome them, whatever the cost."

The two stared out at the ever-brightening sky in silence until the calm was broken by the crow's nest.

"Enemy fleet sir, two leagues due east."

"Aye, Signalsman, inform Admiral Magha and the rest of the fleet to prepare for battle."

"Aye sir."

"All hands on deck!" Dain shouted and soon the clatter of hundreds of feet coming onto the top deck filled the air.

"All hands, prepare for collision! Archers, fire at will!" At the command, thousands of fire arrows let fly from both fleets as they sailed directly for one another. Two hundred thousand Elves, Trolls, Goblins and Driss held their collective breaths as they waited for the deadly shafts to come raining down and claim the first lives of the battle.

Below the surface, King Hai'Ten and his Orcans were formed into an immobile battle line awaiting the oncoming swarms of Pir'Noh and Shrakens. Above them they could see the two fleets nearing one another and an ethereal orange glow that indicated many ships were already on fire. Hai'Ten raised his webbed hand calmly above his head as the enemy lines drew near. Once they were within range, the hand dropped. Eighty thousand Orcans unleashed a simultaneous *Sonarblast* attack that literally vaporized the leading lines of Pir'Noh.

The Pir'Noh were as large as Shrakens with huge, bulbous heads set atop Sendar-like torsos with two powerful arms that held long hooks. Their legs were six long tentacles lined with teeth-filled suckers. A giant, multicolored eye was placed on either side of the head, seemingly all-seeing. Their skin was nearly translucent so their numbers were hard to gauge in the early morning light.

In response to the *Sonarblast*, the Pir'Noh expelled a black, inky substance into the water, called *Confusion,* virtually blinding the Orcans, who were forced to use sonar to detect their enemies. The Shrakens, having developed a temporary counter spell to the substance were among the Orcans before they knew what hit them. The close-quarters combat heavily favored the Shrakens and they did serious damage to the Orcans and their marlins before the ink dissipated.

Once among the blind Orcans, the Shrakens used their *Stunspore* to further hinder them. In the confusion, not all of the Orcans were able to counteract with their *Cleansing* spell. Those who didn't were slaughtered quickly by the Shrakens and their blue sharks. The Pir'Noh used their Shraken hooks to deadly effect, wrapping up Orcans with their tentacles and hacking away.

On the surface, the Duah and Vull'Kra were faring much better. The Duah archers were the best in the realms and it showed in the number of burning ships and enemy dead. As the two fleets crashed together, *Moonfire* and *Greedfire* lanced across like an insane lightning storm.

Boarders began their crossing, leading the way with a bolt of fire or a shot from a bow. Driss were excellent close combat fighters, with their vast array of poisonous attributes. They used their blow guns to give them openings, then moved amongst the Elves and Trolls where they proceeded to flail wildly about, their claws and tails poisoning everyone in range.

The Goblins were not big or especially good fighters, but they had overwhelming numbers and knew well how to use them to their advantage. They specialized in surprise attacks and retreated unequivocally if the odds were less than two to one in their favor.

The Trolls also excelled in surprise attacks, appearing to be part of the ship and then lashing out with their huge battle axes. Their great size and strength made it hard to fight them even if the enemy *did* know where they were.

The Elves stuck to the tactics that had earned them the name Moon Dancers in the Great War and throughout the realms, not only for their ability to move in the moon's rays like light itself, but for their peaceful-seeming movements. It was as if they were performing in a ballet, their graceful, flowing movements as beautiful as they were deadly. Goblins had been known to stop fighting altogether to watch them in a trance only to be killed by the objects of their fixation.

The great, wooden island that was the two entwined fleets cast long shadows on the ocean as the sun made its presence known. It was later said that the clamor of the battle could be heard sixty leagues away in the Driss coastal village of Caross.

King Hai'Ten had regrouped his shocked forces and made an effective counterattack on the superior enemy troops. The devastation he had seen after the initial *Sonarblast* had confirmed his suspicions. The Pir'Noh were not adapted for distance combat. They actually turned to a jelly-like substance if hit full-on. If the Shrakens were prepared for *Sonar,* they could usually counteract it, but the Pir'Noh could not.

Thus, with his inferior numbers and the carnage he'd witnessed in close combat, he reluctantly ordered his forces into a full retreat. Most did not understand how they could leave the fleet unprotected but followed his orders anyway. But then, no one knew Shrakens like Hai'Ten Shrakensbane.

He knew the sight of retreating Orcans would excite their *Bloodfear* so much so that the fleet would be forgotten. The Pir'Noh were merely swept along by the tide of frenzied Shrakens. Hai'Ten staggered his defense lines over and under each other so that as they retreated, a steady barrage of *Sonar* would be kept up to decimate the Pir'Noh and any Shraken frenzied enough not to counteract the attack.

The Orcans continued to fall back, pursued relentlessly by the vast host of Shrakens until the fleet was no longer in sight. His only goal was to drag the Shrakens on for as long as possible while avoiding any more close-quarters skirmishes. His strategy was working excellently, as they were moving too swiftly for the Pir'Noh's *Confusion* to be effective and only the front lines were actually in hand to hand combat.

On the surface, the Elves and Trolls had turned the tide against the overwhelming odds and were now actively pursuing the retreating Goblins and Driss. They had unlatched their ships by early evening and were making a hasty retreat. Admiral Kanumus ordered his triumphant sailors to surround the scattering Driss and Goblin fleets. Admiral Magha did likewise and with a hail of fire arrows and deft maneuvering, the enemy fleet was forced into the shallow waters in the port of Mok.

Three Orcans suddenly splashed onto the deck of Admiral Magha's flagship, *Dostav'ka.* Her Captain Malkashu rushed to their side.

"What is your status?" he asked.

"We were overwhelmed. King Hai'Ten was forced to make a fighting retreat. The Shrakens and Pir'Noh believe us defeated, so they trail us doggedly and we are slowly picking away at their numbers.

King Hai'Ten says it cannot last though as they are already twenty leagues south-east of M'Kom and both sides are exhausted."

"M'Kom?" Malkashu exclaimed.

"Aye. King Hai'Ten advises you to take your forces ashore if possible in case the Shrakens come back. We will only be able to attack them sporadically."

"Aye. Thank you. Please, take as long as you need to rest and eat," Malkashu told them. All three bowed their thanks, but refused and dove back into the ocean. Admiral Magha was in his cabin and Malkashu sent a Lieutenant to fetch him.

When Magha came on deck, Malkashu informed him of their predicament. He looked introspective for a few moments before answering.

"Helm, take us alongside *Evergreen.*"

"Aye sir." The Helmsman did as ordered and soon the huge flagships were side by side. Magha crossed over and informed Kanumus. Arrows continued to fly from both sides as the two Admirals discussed their options in Kanumus' cabin.

"I believe we must attack them and the city. If the Shrakens catch us in open water, we're all dead," Magha said vehemently.

"Aye, but in the city we could be overwhelmed. You know how Goblin cities are, half underground, half in the trees, surrounding the city proper."

"I don't think we have a choice."

"Aye. Let's make plans then to invade the city."

General Jari Splitgem's grey beard fluttered in the gusting winds howling through the barren rock strewn plains where the two armies were to meet. The Rokn had dug hundreds of pitfalls and rock traps for the approaching Giant army. The Giants had set up an ambush just north of Bokat but the Dwarves had spoiled it and lured the enraged Etins to their field of choice.

The short, compact and powerful Dwarves were in full armor and carried their double headed axes and maces with ease. They hid behind several hundred large boulders to disguise their numbers from the marauding Giants, who never used scouts.

A faint rumbling in the distance preceded a cloud of dust which grew larger until the host of Etins could be seen. They numbered as many as the Dwarves, Jari noted bitterly, for the Dwarves were only a quarter of the Giants' size. All their considerable ingenuity and ferocity would be needed to carry the day here.

General Vrekr stepped forward and ordered the Stonemasters to do likewise. Feeling the ground through their feet, they judged the Giants' approach perfectly. He gave the order to attack and four thousand Stonemasters used their innate talents to fling the thousands of fist-sized stones into the oncoming horde of unsuspecting Etins. Many were bludgeoned to death before they could retaliate. The Giants slung boulders the size of a Dwarf with deadly accuracy into the Dwarven positions.

While this was happening, the Giants continued their pel-mel advance and unwittingly stepped into the Dwarven pitfalls. These were huge pits thirty feet deep and lined with sharp, jagged rocks.

Hundreds of heedless Giants fell into them never to emerge. The rest continued with their slings, never stopping their headlong rush. As the armies neared, the Dwarves used their final magic attack, *Rockform.* Huge, perfectly spherical boulders magically cut from the ground were lovingly coaxed by the Dwarves to roll at dangerous speeds into the attacking Giants, flattening any in their path.

The Giants reached the Dwarven position with nearly a fourth of their numbers already dead or seriously wounded. They were in for another surprise. The small army of Dwarves they had thought they were attacking suddenly tripled as Dwarves sprang out from their hiding places and attacked the confused Giants from behind.

However, the Giants soon turned their confusion into *Etinrage,* a condition that allowed them to fight on long after they should have been dead. They swung their stone clubs wildly around at anything that moved, including each other. Their bone chilling yells echoed across the battlefield. The Dwarves set about hacking off the Giants' feet to bring them down where they could decapitate them.

The Dwarves had to be nimble, because it was impossible for them to block an Etin's blow without being crushed. They ran from Giant to Giant, some of the colossal creatures killing each other to get at their hated enemies. For all their grit, tenacity and planning, the

Dwarves were outmatched by the powerful Giants. Vrekr looked to Jari, who gave the grudging, painful order to retreat. The Stonemasters flung their second line of rock traps at the pursuing Giants to give themselves room to retreat.

The Giants milled about angrily at the sudden end to the fighting. King Nog's son Gerd had been killed and it was some time before a clear successor was determined. It was decided they would chase the fleeing Dwarves down until there were none left to chase. Giants did not tend to their wounded, they killed them. So, as the effects of *Etinrage* wore off, more than a few badly wounded Giants sat down to nurse their severed hamstrings or missing appendages. As soon as this weakness was detected, though, the rest set upon them like a pack of feral animals, ripping the wounded Giants limb from limb to scores of vicious laughter.

After this culling of the ranks, the survivors set up camp in order to rest. The Dwarves, already eight miles east, had done likewise. They were in a foul mood. Dwarves hated losing more than dying and were none too happy about their hasty retreat. Sensing their palpable discord, Jari stood up and called for their attention, which they grudgingly gave.

"Alroight lads, now look it 'ere. I know ee all be a bit angry o'er our lil' skirmish back yonder an' I am too. But yon lot of us kilt in this worthless land ain't goin' t'do none o'us or our wee ones back home no good.

"We'll foight yon way Dwarves foight best, wi' ambushes an' traps all yon way t' Son'Lau. Yonder we'll meet wi' yon Sendar an' help 'em hol' down yon city 'gainst all comers. Deal?" he asked gruffly. An angry and fierce aye came from the assembled army and the rest followed suit.

Kanumus and Magha sat drinking Goblin spirits in the hollowed shell of a massive tree complex that had, until this day, been the palace of the Goblin Warlord. They had fought the Driss and Goblins for two days inside the winding, honeycombed city. Finally, they had defeated them in a decisive battle near the gates and the survivors had retreated into the woods.

Other than constant sniping and occasional raids, the city was relatively peaceful. The conquering Elves and Trolls allowed the Goblins to conduct their daily business, albeit under strict supervision. Word had been sent that morning to King Llethion and King Mashtor to inform them of the city's capture and to request further orders. Until they heard back, the two Generals had set about strengthening the city's defenses and quartering their soldiers.

Dain and Malkashu had been put in charge of the city and they were attacking the task with great zeal. They had subdued virtually all resistance left in the city and even convinced the local Goblins they were there to help. Off-duty soldiers solicited the numerous Goblin taverns and paid for everything they did. Goblins were thought of, in the realms, as stupid, but they were excellent merchants and they knew that if they were to rise up it would no doubt cause this steady influx of money to cease. Thus, everyone waited in relative peace for the next move.

"Lieutenant Rascan?" An Elven Lieutenant asked the anxious Orcan.

"Aye."

"The Admiral will see you now."

"Aye, thank you," Rascan said, rising to his feet and entering the Admiral's office. "You wished to speak with me, sir?"

Admiral Binir Oreshatter was a short, immensely stocky Dwarf with white hair and a matching beard to his knees. He was the only Dwarven Admiral in Mistgarde. He had a perpetual scowl on his face that intimidated even the most perilous sailors in Mistgarde's Navy. "Now then," he started, eyeing Rascan's report. "It says 'ere ee encountered eighty Barakans offa Kybo Island?" It was more of a statement than a question.

"Aye sir."

"Bonny. We've got word that a e'en bigger crew o'em was encountered at Son'Lau an that 'nother be 'spected yonder at Soling'Ta. This be a moighty danger t'yon secret Sendar fleet attackin' yonder city in some few days. Admiral Pana'Kol 'as sent 'alf o'is forces, seven hunnert Orcans t' aide in yon effort. Sposta 'roive near mid-day where ee'll be takin' command."

"Aye sir," Rascan barked. "Admiral sir. Respectfully ask if you are aware of my junior rank, sir."

"Aye, I do be aware of it," the Dwarf smiled widely, pushing two silver stars across the polished wooden desk, one for each lapel, pro-moting the stunned Orcan to Commander. Rascan put them on quickly, trying to control his surge of giddiness.

"Thank you sir. Any further orders, sir?"

"Aye. On top o'yon seven hunnert Pana'Kol be sendin', ee'll also be takin' command o'yon fifty Orcans that be in port, 'cludin ee former command. As soon as yonder be done now, ee'll haul ee slick-skinned grey arse t' Son'Lau, where our forces 'ave secured yon city. Yonder ee'll turn over command t' Commander Yardin. Ee'll then act as second in command an special 'visor t'im."

"Aye sir."

"From yonder, ee are t'kill dead any Barakans ee foind long yon way, while goin' with 'streme urgency to Soling'Ta."

"Aye sir."

"Once yonder, ee are t' defend yon Sendar fleet at all costs, un'erstood?"

"Aye sir," Rascan answered.

"Bonny. 'Ere are ee sealed orders t' be opened 'pon lettin' go a ee command t' Commander Yardin," Binir ordered, handing him a glass-encased scroll. "Dismissed."

"Aye sir." Rascan saluted before turning to leave.

"Oh an' Commander," the Admiral called after him. Rascan turned quickly back. "I did mean t'ask ee. Do ee 'ave a recommen-dation t' replace ee as Lieutenant?"

"Aye sir, Midshipman Drylyn, sir," Rascan answered without hesitation.

"Bonny then," Binir said, handing the Orcan two more stars. "Make it so."

"Aye sir." Rascan saluted again and hurried out to wait for his command. He saw Drylyn eating breakfast in the Orcan barracks and came to stand next to her. "Midshipman Drylyn," he said solemnly. She stood to attention.

"Aye sir?" she asked.

"Congratulations, Lieutenant."

CHAPTER 37
ENEMIES IN OUR MIDST

anken awoke slowly and groggily. His body hurt every-where, but he felt remarkably refreshed and good. He opened his eyes to see the dark, beautiful face of Tok'Neth. He blinked several times as if he wasn't sure if he was still dreaming.

"I'm real, Danken," she smiled, and her panther licked his face in greeting.

"I can't seem to get my mind around that can I?" Danken asked, sitting up slowly.

"Although, I must confess, I was more than a little surprised to find you passed out on my kitchen table," she laughed, her smile brightening the colorful room. Her long black hair was intricately braided and she wore a simple purple garment that hugged her ample curves.

"Sorry, it was the first place I could think of," he blushed.

Even after all of his experiences, she still had that power over him. He got up tenderly off of the cot to stretch his tense muscles, and only then did he realize that he was in a sterling white robe. The dirty, bloody, tattered one he'd been wearing was conspicuously absent.

"My cloak," he said under his breath, realizing that she had seen him naked. Again.

"Oh," Tok'Neth laughed. "It was too beat up to salvage so I threw it out. I hope you don't mind."

"No. It's...it's fine," Danken said, looking around for his weapons. He found them on the other side of the table and strapped them on. Then he remembered Jet saving him again over the ocean. Though the man had been partially responsible for everything that had happened, he had twice saved Danken's life. He didn't know how he felt about that, realizing he had at least partly hoped Jet would die in the freezing snows of Mount Taeria.

"Where's Jet?" he asked finally.

"The handsome black-haired boy?" Tok'Neth asked, a mischievous smile on her face.

"Aye."

"He left yesterday. He said he didn't want to here when you woke because he didn't like you anyway."

"Dwei. Sounds like Jet." Danken allowed himself a smile.

The events of the past few days were swirling crazily around in his head. He tried to put them in order as Tok'Neth watched him curiously. As they all fell into place, he looked into her dark eyes.

"What is it?" she asked.

"I'm the only one left."

"What do you mean?" Tok'Neth asked, her eyes wide.

"We battled on Mount Taeria and I arrived too late to save them and then I killed the others and now I'm the only one left and..."

"Danken." Tok'Neth stopped him. "You're telling me you killed all of the Sorcerers?"

"Aye."

"Even Dak'Verkat?"

"Aye."

"And what of the Magi?" she asked.

"All dead, except me," he said quietly.

Tok'Neth sat down heavily. Danken unthinkingly released a tendril of blue energy into her. He knew the pain of losing a father.

"He told me to tell you that he loved you," Danken said quietly.

"I guess I just never thought he would die. He was immortal."

"I know. But Urishen will always be with you. And so will I."

"Thank you." Tok'Neth's eyes began to water and Danken wrapped her in his arms.

"You know," she began after she had calmed down. "We had two hundred and sixty years together. That's more than most people get, right?"

"Aye," Danken agreed sadly.

"I almost forgot who I was talking to," she said quietly.

Danken was about to reply when the room froze, its temperature rapidly lowered. He recognized the sense of power as Sanngetal's calling card and turned to find the huge being staring at him with his one, all-knowing eye.

"I see you didn't heed my advice," he began.

"What?" Danken asked, on guard.

"I warned you not to act on emotion and yet you did exactly that. In doing so, you set off a chain of events that may be your undoing. Do not blame the other. You are responsible, Magus."

"I did what the prophecy said to do," Danken protested.

"Prophecy?" Sanngetal scoffed. "Didn't you think to test it?"

"Test it how?"

"The same powers you use to destroy can also be used to heal and probe. You had but to open your mind to the parchment and you would have seen it was false. Even now you know it was."

"But what of Amaria and the Oracles?"

"Think about it, Magus, who had the power to create the whole scenario? Who is powerful enough to use the Sapphire Son for his own purposes? Who kidnapped the Elf in order to make you use the Oracles?"

"Dak'Verkat," Danken sighed in dismay. "He planned it all."

"He desperately wants the Oracles, but only you could use them. He is a master at manipulation."

"You said 'is.' He's dead. I killed him," Danken said with a sinking feeling of dread.

"No, you see, you fell right into his trap. He planned it that way. Did you feel the Oracles burning when you fought him, lending you strength?"

"Aye."

"They were creating a spell around him, letting him die and be reborn as his own son," Sanngetal said darkly.

"What? How is that possible?" Danken asked.

"It's the way he created the spell. The moment of his death, his powers *and* his entire essence was transferred to a newborn somewhere in Mai'Lang. If he wasn't more powerful than you before, he will be when he grows up and I don't think that will take very long. He doesn't care about Surt's return to the world. He needed you, the Sapphire Son to use the Oracles to make *him* into a God."

"Gods. What of Amaria then?"

"She was lost to you the moment he enspelled her. She serves only him now."

"No." Danken shook his head.

"There's nothing you can do for her now."

"How can I stop Dak'Verkat?" Danken said angrily, hot tears in his flaming blue eyes.

"That is not for me to say. Your path is yours to determine," Sanngetal said in his bone-jarring baritone. "Use your head, Magus, not just your emotions. Together, they will not fail you." And with that, he was gone.

Tok'Neth rubbed her arms and shivered a little. Danken stood in stunned silence.

"Danken?" she asked. He still didn't answer for a moment, when suddenly it came to him. The Oracles would lead him to Amaria and Amaria would lead him to Dak'Verkat.

He shot his *Stonespeak* into the ground to get a quick fix on her but as he did so, he felt a great disturbance in Midgarthe. He probed the four corners of the continent and found to his horror, enemy armies attacking Northern cities, their magical trail showing him they'd been hidden by the Sorcerers.

A Mai'Lang army was inside of Keyre and looked to be winning, as did the Goblin army laying waste to Sancor, the Driss army attacking Crask and the Giant army fighting inside the rock walls of Iron Forge. So that had been Dak'Verkat's plan all along. The Sorcerer had led them to believe they were superior when the whole time he had held all the cards.

He came back to Tok'Neth to find the gypsy staring at him concernedly.

"Tok'Neth, I'm sorry, I have to go," he said, impulsively kissing her before opening a portal and stepping through.

He stepped out on the other side at the parade grounds of Mist Peak. Without hesitation, he placed the *Amplifying* spell on his voice.

"All Mistgarde," he boomed throughout the crater. "Report to the parade ground on the double!" A loud horn sounded the call to arms soon after and in less than half a glass, the entire force was assembled on the field below him.

"Members of Mistgarde," he thundered. "The time has come to put your skills to use. Sleeper forces from the Southern continent are attacking four cities. Everyone but the Home Watch will depart immediately, form up!"

"Aye!" the amassed soldiers boomed back.

Danken braced himself and opened a portal in front of the Sendar division, who ran through it fearlessly. He did the same for the Duah, Vull'Kra Dwarven divisions, sending them to their respective cities to help fight. He strained to hold the portals open long enough. He turned to the Home Watch and deployed them in battle formation around the Peak. Next, he called each division's Commanders and gave them specific instructions.

After all of this was completed, Danken sat down exhausted. He asked a steward to fetch him as much food and water as possible. He used *Stonespeak* to look for Amaria again but she wasn't on the continent. He ground his teeth as he waited for the food, knowing the next few days would determine the fate of Midgarthe. He had seen something else with his *Stonespeak* as well and as soon as he got his food, he would investigate.

Diedrik and Myrisan, along with forty other men, were the last line of defense in the city of Keyre. The staggering number of wounded were being cared for on ships sent out into the lake for safety. The remaining defenders were holed up behind a makeshift wall to negate the Mai'Lang's vastly superior numbers.

A massive surge from the Mai'Lang threatened to overtake them and Diedrik felt sure they would all die here this night. Suddenly, when all seemed lost, a deafening roar came from behind the Mai'Lang. It soon became discernable as the Battle Hymn of the

Valkyrie, sung from hundreds of throats. Diedrik strained to see its source when he heard Myrisan beside him.

"Diedrik!" he shouted. "It's the Mistgarde!"

The Mai'Lang, moments before so confident of their victory, now turned to see their defeat in fifteen hundred angry Sendar eyes. They tried to retreat but found their way blocked at every turn. They were slaughtered to a man.

Of the original Keyre defenders, only Diedrik, Myrisan and eight others escaped injury or death. The Mistgarde forces set about putting out fires, caring for the wounded and routing out the remaining Mai'Lang in hiding. Their Captain, a tall, broad shouldered ugly man with black hair and piercing green eyes wiped his sword off on a dead Mai'Lang's tunic before approaching the battered defenders.

He stopped when he saw Diedrik and Myrisan. The three stared at each other for a moment before the Captain, a Sendar named Arn Brynsen spoke.

"It seems we are destined to fight together, Diedrik Fanarsen." He smiled, then turned to the Hafalf. "I don't believe we've been introduced, though I remember you watching over the Magus as well."

"Aye, Captain Brynsen. My name is Myrisan Deathsong, of the Mistgarde Protectors division, sir." He showed Arn the scar on his forearm.

"Protector?" Arn's eyes narrowed as they slowly looked over to Diedrik. "I see. It makes sense now," he nodded. "It seems you have done well. Well Fanarsen, the offer's still on the table if you want it, though I regret to inform you that your real father is dead."

"You know my real father? He's dead?"

"Aye, if he was a Mage, he's dead. Only the Fifth, Danken Sariksen, the Mage from the inn still lives."

"What of the Sorcerers?" Myrisan asked.

"All dead from what I hear," Arn answered.

"I believe I'll take you up on your offer, sir," Diedrik said finally.

"I'm glad."

The story was similar in the Duah city of Sancor, where marauding Goblins had set fire to the surrounding woods and killed everyone caught outside the city's stone gates. King Llethion had issued orders to all *Verna'ren* to douse the fires as soon as the magical alarms had been set off.

Sancor's gates had been battered down around midday and a free-for-all had begun in the once pristine city. The Elves, heavily outnumbered and caught off guard, were dying quickly. The Rangers were forced to put out the devastating fires lest all of the Duah Nation be set aflame and so could not help the city's beleaguered inhabitants.

The Mistgarde Elven division arrived just in time to save the city. Sadly they were not able to save the city's Elflord or his family, who along with their many guards were burned alive in their residence. The cowardly Goblins found themselves at slightly better than even odds with the Elven division and retreated into the forest, which was now filled with Rangers.

The Goblins were caught in between the two armies and cut down with brutal finality.

The Vull'Kra coastal city of Crask was penetrated not by force but by stealth. The Driss had snuck in unnoticed until it was too late. They methodically made their way through the city, killing any unlucky enough to be in their path.

They met the Vull'Kra resistance in several tight cornered streets with many obstacles. The Trolls, invisible in the shadowy streets, took the conceited Driss by complete surprise. They used the tight spaces to their advantage as it inhibited the Driss's slashing claws and tails. The Trolls used their size and strength to corral the Driss into smaller spaces where they were hacked apart by Dwarven-made battleaxes.

The Trolls' natural resistance to Drissian poison also gave them the advantage but the Driss had something else up their scales. Deadly throwing knives coated with a poison they had only recently developed. The Trolls weren't immune to it and it caused amazing amounts of damage.

The Driss had routed the Vull'Kra nearly to defeat when the unmistakable Mistgarde horn blared out over the chaotic sounds of battle. The Driss fought savagely and to great devastation but they were out-classed by the Mistgarde Trolls.

The burning forest and buildings inside the city were put out quickly but most of the damage was done. Troll Commander Rowan sent a junior officer to find a Troll named Dardogh. Awhile later, a gigantic white-haired Troll covered in Drissian blood approached him.

He saluted him as a leader which Rowan returned in kind.

"I am Dardogh, First of Clan Nok."

"I am Rowan, Second of Clan T'rak, Commander of Mistgarde Troll division," Rowan answered, his braided moustache swaying in the light breeze.

"You have need of me?" Dardogh asked.

"Aye. I was instructed by Danken Sariksen, Fifth of Magi to inform you that Valshk, Sixth of Clan Nok has passed onto the next life. He and two others from Clan V'Senat died accordingly with *M'Racht* protecting the Magus and the Duah Princess from Mai'Lang soldiers."

"Thank you." Dardogh nodded proudly and stalked off to aide in the cleanup. He would add Valshk's name to The List, a group of names every member of the Clan had memorized along with their deed. Very few were honored this way. The List of *M'Racht* was an honor above all others. Rowan watched him go, then sat and waited for the First of Clan V'Senat.

The Dwarves had fared better than the others, mainly because Giants were the opposite of stealthy. Mining crews around the Rokn city of Ironforge felt the stones groan in protest at the Giants' sudden and clumsy appearance. Saddled on great razor-hoofed mountain goats, the outlying Dwarves beat the slothful Etins to the city easily.

The city, carved into the side and underneath of a mountain, was highly defensible. Even those who were not able-bodied contributed with the hasty building of rock traps and pitfalls, for they were Dwarves and none in the realms enjoyed hard work like they did.

When the Giants arrived hurling massive stones, the already well-defensed city sprung to life. Both side took heavy casualties, but the Giants were still trying to break the city walls when the Mistgarde Dwarves showed up.

The Dwarves' insane anger at the destruction of Silverstaff made short work of the remaining Giants. When it was over, the Dwarves used their innate *Stonemoving* talents to repair the significant damage to the city. When that was finished, they got drunk and recounted each and every one of their severely exaggerated exploits.

As Kierna and the rest of the Northern forces busied themselves caring for the wounded and disposing of the thousands of dead, a sound like a ripped parchment followed by a thunder halted them. Most looked to the grey Autumn sky but soon all eyes were focused on the liquid blue portal and Danken as he stepped through it. He immediately strode over to where she, Tae, Corsha and an injured Phaeryn were tending to a high ranking Mai'Lang Spirit Blade.

"Danken, mate!" Tae jumped up and grabbed him in a bear hug. "What are you doing here? And what of Princess Amaria?"

"She is in good hands now, Tae." Danken smiled, hiding his pain. "I just came to make sure everything was in hand here," he quickly related all the news, staring at Kierna, who was studiously avoiding him.

"So this is why you left us," he stated.

"Aye. Danken, I—"

"You owe me no explanations Kierna."

"I do, though," she pulled away from the rest. "Your pull on me was so strong that I hoped it could drown out the call of the swords. But it couldn't. Yet, I still owe you my life and when you claim it, I will come." She bowed her head.

"You owe me nothing," Danken snorted. "And I wouldn't claim you anyway from your destiny and what you want."

"One day you will claim my loyalty, Danken. When that day comes, so will I." Kierna repeated. They talked for a short while longer, Danken telling her about Jet, which she took in stride. The

Mai'Lang Spirit Blade they had been tending approached quietly, hiding the pain of the sword slash in her leg.

"Pardon me, Magus," she bowed.

"Aye. What service may I do for you, Spirit Blade?"

"I couldn't help but overhearing your conversation. Forgive me, but did you say Jetrian?"

Danken stepped out of the portal with a determined edge. He looked around at the stunned people around him. Finally he saw the man he'd been looking for.

"Don't you have anything better to do than search for lost Magi, Captain Tamlinsen?" he asked with a smile.

"Aye sir. I suppose I do now," Tamlinsen smiled widely, hiding his considerable surprise and relief.

"Good. Make your course for Shun'ka."

"Aye sir," Tamlinsen acknowledged unable to hide a saddened, pained look. "Helm! Make your course due south."

"Aye sir, due south," the helmsman yelled back.

"What's the problem, Captain?" Danken asked.

"I'm sorry Magus, but Princess Amaria disappeared two days ago. One moment she was in her cabin, the next, she was just gone."

"Damn. I had a feeling she wouldn't stay put."

"Sir?"

"Nothing. Where is Princess Shonai?"

"Below decks, Magus. Should I send for her?"

"Aye, and Kamotal as well."

"Aye sir," Tamlinsen said, sending Lieutenant Zukesen to carry out the orders. Soon both Orcans were standing in front of him. Shonai threw her arms around him and hugged him tightly.

"We thought you had been killed," she said happily.

"Not that easy, I'm afraid."

"What are you doing here?" she asked.

"I believe your people are in dire need of your leadership, Shonai. Kamotal, pick eight Orcans ready for combat," Danken ordered.

"Aye sir." The Orcan dove into the water, returning shortly after with eight sleek, dangerous-looking Orcans.

"Good luck, Princess Shonai," Danken said opening a portal. "Kamatol, you and the rest protect her with your lives. Your nation's future depends upon it."

"Aye sir." The eight Orcans saluted. With one last curious look back, Shonai stepped through the portal.

"Captain Tamlinsen," Danken said as the portal closed, "send for Swifteye, T'riel, the children and Lanaia if you would, please."

"Aye sir."

A few moments later, the silver blur of Swifteye appeared next to him followed shortly after by the familiar tiny feet on his shoulder of T'riel. She cursed him loudly in Pixian until Lanaia came on deck with the five children.

"Hey there," the Elf said, hugging him. Danken hid the fact that she had been used by Dak'Verkat beneath a smile. It seemed a small deal now.

"Boy should *not* have sacrificed himself for us," T'riel scolded.

"I missed you, too,"

"Valshk?" Swifteye asked quietly, silencing them all.

"I'm sorry, he didn't make it. He was trying to save us," Danken said sadly. Swifteye nodded but remained silent.

"Lanaia, I need you to take these children back to Mist Peak. Tell Dot hello for me."

"Of course," she said, as the portal opened. "Be careful." She led the hesitant children and fearless white wolves through the portal.

"Captain Tamlinsen, Shun'ka was captured by Southport and Kasani forces yesterday. They're having trouble securing the harbor, though. *Windstrike* will do that for them."

Shonai and her guard found themselves at the rear of a devastated and disorganized Orcan army. The fighting retreat had almost become an actual retreat. The armies were only fifty leagues south of the Western Isles and soon the Orcans would have to make their final stand.

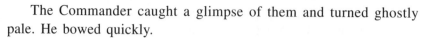

The Commander caught a glimpse of them and turned ghostly pale. He bowed quickly.

"Highness, you should not be here, it's too dangerous."

"Where is my father?" she asked in response.

"I'm sorry, Highness, he was gravely wounded and rushed back to Sha'Na," he said sadly.

"What is our status here?" she asked, steeling herself against the news of her father.

"Fighting retreat, Highness. The Pir'Noh made ink clouds we could not dispel and the Shrakens cut us to pieces. However, our *Sonarblast* is very effective against them. We estimate that only one third of their original numbers remain but the Shrakens are too numerous and we've lost nearly half of our forces."

"Half!?" Shonai exclaimed, horrified.

"Aye Majesty and soon we will have to make our final stand to protect the Isles."

"Have the cities been notified?"

"Aye Majesty." Word of Shonai's presence spread like wildfire throughout the beleaguered ranks, giving them renewed hope.

After they had reached their final battle line, Shonai gave the order to spread out as far as possible, both horizontally and vertically. She ordered all Orcans who still had marlins underneath them into a spear formation. As they prepared to receive the oncoming army, Shonai silently called *Salindrist* out of its gauntlet.

Once the enemy army was in range, Shonai gave the order for staggered *Sonarblasts* to keep them off guard. It worked better than she hoped as the Shrakens, used to blocking one and having free reign afterwards, were caught by surprise. They died almost as rapidly as the Pir'Noh before making the adjustment.

Still, their numbers weren't significantly diminished and they continued to press their attack. When the two armies were close to converging, Shonai ordered her force to charge, once again surprising the Shrakens, who had expected only defense. The Pir'Noh's *Confusion* attack overshot the new positions and the battle was joined in clear water.

Shonai and a small reserve force waited in the rear to establish weak points and remedy them as needed. She was about to lead them into the fray, when her danger sense warned her of something behind her. She turned to see the most astonishing thing her eyes had ever beheld: Thirty thousand pale blue, green-haired figures carrying golden tridents. They were Mer'khan.

She had the sinking sensation in her stomach that her Orcans would be caught in between the two armies and destroyed. The massed forces stopped not far from her and her guard detail condensed around her. Two figures swam quickly forward. Shonai recognized them as Keran and Tomar. She remained silent.

"Looks like you could use some help," Keran said telepathically.

"What?" Shonai asked.

"What, you didn't think we'd let our new allies down already, did you?" Tomar asked, grinning like a wild man. "Mer'khan, morph!" he told the assembled army. In awe, Shonai watched the amazing transformation take place. They morphed into Orcans but the tridents remained. "Attack!" he called and the huge army rushed to the Orcans' side.

"I'm in shock," Shonai said, her guard detail, having never seen the Mer'khan before, were equally shocked. "I thought you were here to attack us."

"Now that would be a violation of our treaty, Princess Shonai Golden Gauntlet," Tomar said snidely.

Shonai made to answer, but the crash of the Mer'khan into battle drowned her out. They used their *Waterspells* to herd the frantic Shrakens and Pir'Noh into groups where the Orcans used their *Sonarblast* to decimate their hated foes.

Most of the Orcans were as confused as the Shrakens at the new arrivals, but they needed all the help they could get. The battle raged on with the enemy fighting fiercely but to no avail. They were the ones who were outnumbered now and after a long, hard battle, they were forced into a full retreat.

The Orcans picked off stragglers, pressing the attack after so long on the other end of it. The Mer'khan, fresh from their first open water battle in millennia, used their *Waterspells* to create solid walls in the water, forcing the Shrakens to go around, where they were butchered.

Shonai sent a small detachment to escort the numerous wounded back to Sha'Na. Next, she sent ten messengers on the fastest marlins to warn the Elven and Troll fleets of the retreating Shrakens. Her troops were too exhausted to press the attack any further as she gave them a well deserved rest.

Tomar sent half of his fresh troops to continue the attack and the other half to remain with the battle-weary Orcans. He and Keran approached Shonai happily. They used their telepathy to talk to her so her guards wouldn't hear.

"Not bad for being three thousand years out of practice, wouldn't you agree?" Tomar asked, his white-streaked green hair flowing with the current.

"Not bad at all," Shonai smiled. "I don't know what to say."

"You don't have to say anything, child," Keran said softly.

"You said something about a treaty?" Shonai asked.

"Aye, that I did," Tomar answered. "Signed by your father's hand and mine."

Admiral Olafsen of the Wescove fleet watched the dark shapes underneath his vessel with growing unease. The Sendar fleet from Rakshoal and Wescove was only two-thirds the size of the other two Sendar fleets and had no Orcans protecting it. Their mission was stealth as Soling'Ta wasn't expecting an attack and as such had no sizeable fleet protecting it.

He could see Soling'Ta's harbor on the horizon but he was beginning to doubt if he'd ever get there. He watched as over two hundred Mai'Lang vessels approached his fleet of five hundred. He narrowed his eyes when the lookout confirmed his suspicions that the nine vessels in front were not just ordinary Mai'Lang. They were Darkwatch, crewed with the best of all the races from the Southern Continent.

His flagship, *Ravager* was the only Mistgarde vessel in his fleet. Still, the numbers wouldn't present a difficulty if it weren't for the Shrakens under the water's surface. The carrier pigeon yesterday had sent word of another threat to his fleet, as if one or two weren't enough. It mentioned something about a race called Barakans.

The dark shapes he saw under his ships seemed to fit the description the Port Admiral of Eastbank had sent to him. He made a quick decision he hoped would save his fleet and salvage the mission.

"Signalsman. Send this message: All ships, full sail into harbor. Repel all boarders, do not engage."

"Aye sir," the Signalsman acknowledged.

As one the fleet tacked and came on line with the harbor. The Mai'Lang fleet was caught off guard by this change in tactics. They struggled to come on course with the Sendar fleet, but it was too late to intersect them. They exchanged arrows but never came in contact.

The Sendar fleet made it into the large harbor just as their ships began to be ripped apart by the Shrakens and Barakans, who had belatedly realized there were no Orcans guarding this fleet. Many of the ships crashed onto the shore where their crews quickly disembarked. The rest of the ships latched onto these before their crews came ashore as well.

The trailing ships were set afire just as the Mai'Lang fleet secured their lines. This started fires among their whole fleet which were put out only after a long battle. The Sendar used this distraction to their advantage by finding a defensible position on the shore to hold their lines.

The city guard of Soling'Ta didn't even attempt to engage the Sendar forces. They skirted the Sendar lines and joined with the Mai'Lang coming ashore along with the one thousand Darkwatch sailors. However, the Mai'Lang had only a little over half of the Sendar forces and were hesitant to attack. Their whole battle plan had been based around the Barakans, who were milling about uselessly in the bay.

Olafsen knew that Darkwatch forces could be here in four days from Isle Sin so it was important to fortify the city as quickly as possible. The forces of Mai'Lang had been caught off guard by the Sendar's strategy of attacking only three mainland cities and their troops were now moving to counteract this. Kybo had been taken with heavy casualties on both sides by forces from Breakwater as a diversion and it had worked perfectly.

Shun'ka had fallen easily but its nearness to the Shraken Isles had made its harbor a constant war zone. Son'Lau had fallen soon after the battle at Singo Bay but the Giant army, as well as forces from Bokat, Singo and Kang were converging to take it back. Forces from Maka were en route to Shun'ka and rumor was that after their victory at Bang'Lau, Sendar forces had encountered a second army and had been forced all the way back to Faust's Wall, which was in danger of falling into Mai'Lang hands.

With forces from Kansaka and the Darkwatch almost certainly coming to retake the city and no possible way out by sea due to the Barakans, Olafsen knew he had to completely annihilate the Mai'Lang here. It would be no easy task with the Darkwatch Navy forces adding their weight, but he had no choice.

He ordered a full attack directly on the waterfront. The Sendar forces charged out of the city and onto the beach. The Darkwatch stood at the center of the lines to anchor them, and their presence lent the Mai'Lang strength.

The initial contact was bone jarring, the sand making footing hard. The Darkwatch performed amazingly, as their Mistgarde counterparts so often did, but their numbers were too few. The Sendar knew that their lives depended on the fortification of this city and the Mai'Lang were in the way. They slowly pushed the Mai'Lang towards the water line, the tide stained red.

Olafsen could see the Barakans milling in the shallow water and he ordered his archers to fire into them. Once they had dispersed into deeper water, Olafsen sealed his fate to the city. He ordered his archers to fire both unguarded fleets. The wooden armada quickly took to burning, the rigging and rails the first to disintegrate.

By the time the Mai'Lang were backed into the crashing waves, most of both fleets were sinking, cutting off their retreat. They realized this and made one last desperate charge at the Sendar but they were repelled. Those that weren't killed retreated into the water only to disappear beneath the blood red waves.

The Sendar forces, wounded but intact, moved to secure the city. They encountered pockets of violent resistance but by nightfall, they were in full control of the city. Scouts were already reporting increased activity in Kansaka so Olafsen knew they would have another, more deadly battle on their hands soon. He reinforced the impressive city walls and left every man on constant vigil for the attack they knew would come.

Captain Luca Broderinsen stood atop Son'Lau's ramparts with a scowl on his normally smiling face. The Dwarven army had entered the city after a long and quite successful guerilla campaign against the Giants, which were only half a day out.

Forces from Kang and Bokat were also a half-day out and the combined remaining forces of Singo and Tau had landed on the prominitory to the northeast of the city that morning. Broderinsen had arranged all his forces along the stone walls of the port in anticipation of the coming struggle.

The Orcans had left to battle the Barakans at Soling'Ta, leaving him stranded in the city should it be retaken. From carrier pigeon reports he had received that morning, he guessed this to be the case in every city they had taken. He pinched the bridge of his nose with a deep sigh to calm his nerves.

"Sir," a young Lieutenant saluted. "Scouts report the Mai'Lang and Giant armies will be in sight soon. They are attacking as one army, sir."

"Dwei." Broderinsen said sarcastically. "Call all men to battle stations. Lock the city down."

"Aye sir," the Lieutenant said, rushing off to see to the arrangements.

After what seemed like an eternity, the enemy army finally appeared on the gray horizon. They came into focus shortly after and Broderinsen felt his stomach knot. There were over twice as many Mai'Lang as there were Sendar, as well as Giants in full battle mode.

Broderinsen turned and observed his battle-experienced forces along the ramparts starring dispassionately at the approaching army. The sight made him smile and strengthened his resolve to carry the city. He turned to Jari, the Dwarven General and nodded. The Dwarf gave the order to attack to his Stonemasters. The Dwarves used their well-practiced rock traps to great effect on the charging army. The front lines were virtually destroyed and those behind ran directly into thousands of Sendar arrows.

The walls of Son'Lau were too tall and well defended to climb up so the Mai'Lang had brought a huge battering ram. When the army reached the wall, they began exchanging arrows while six huge Etins rushed forward with the battering ram as if it weighed nothing. The rest slung their huge stones at the defenders, crying out to their God Hrym for victory.

Boiling pitch was poured over them as they hit the gates with ground shattering force. When one died, another ran to take his place. They were Giant pincushions hammering at the gates relentlessly. However, these gates had been built to withstand just such an attack and did not give in to the immense pressure being placed on them.

Soon there was a hill of Giants in front of the gates. The gates had cracked though and would be breached by nightfall, Broderinsen thought, watching the rapidly descending sun. He ordered his reserve forces to the gate to meet the first charge when it came.

As he had predicted, the gates fell that night. The charge was insane but tempered by the final hail of arrows from the defenders. The clash in the narrow confines of the gate was chaotic. Arrow slits in the walls let the defenders control the pace of the battle but soon it moved into the city and became hectic and disorganized.

It raged in hundreds of streets, buildings and houses with no rhyme or reason. Luckily for the defenders, the Giants were relatively few after their protracted battle with the Dwarves and their troubles with the gate. The Dwarves used the cobblestones of the street as projectiles before ferociously launching themselves at the attackers.

The Sendar battled valiantly and intelligently, their various pockets struggling to optimize their superior archers. Most of the Mai'Lang's advantage had been negated by their attack on the fortified walls but the Sendar were still outnumbered. Broderinsen used his tactical fall-back options to their advantage, with ordered retreats to more defensible positions, leaving the Mai'Lang momentarily vulnerable at every point.

The turning point of the battle was when the Sendar retreated behind a previously constructed barricade. Once secure, the Dwarves had utilized a well-crafted pitfall that had utterly crushed the invaders. Over one fourth of all the remaining attackers perished instantly and nearly the same number died from arrow wounds in the following ambush.

The Mai'Lang retreated hastily, pursued doggedly by the weary defenders. They were forced out of the ruined gate not long after, where many more were picked off by archers on the ramparts. The defenders gave a rousing cheer at their hard-won victory. They had lost almost half of their numbers but had retained the vital city of Son'Lau for good.

General Vrekr had been killed along with the majority of the Dwarven forces. Jari Splitgem led the survivors over to the gate, which they wasted no time in repairing. Broderinsen tiredly walked to the Warlord's mansion which he had turned into his command center. He entered the building to cheers and heavy slaps on the back.

Admiral Mastersen was propped up on a bed, his normally tan, leathery skin pale white. His smile remained, though, and Broderinsen marveled at the man's strength.

"Sir, how are you?" he asked, taking off his bloodstained jacket.

"Never better, Luca," Mastersen said through clenched teeth. "Seems you led our forces admirably, Captain."

"Aye sir. If so it's because I learned from the best."

"Ha!" Mastersen laughed, ending in a racking cough Broderinsen feared would tear the man's chest apart. When he had recovered, Broderinsen handed him a glass of water. The Admiral was too proud to let others feed him. "You never needed me, Luca, you had it in here," he pointed to his heart, "to be the leader you are."

"Sir, I think you're being too modest, but thank you, just the same."

"Aye. Anyway, I'm sure you've heard of Admirals' Right?"

"Aye sir."

"Well, I'm using mine on you," Mastersen told him, pointing to two silver stars on the nightstand. Broderinsen glanced at the Admiral's now empty shoulders. He steeled his eyes and snapped to attention giving a crisp, final salute to the man who had been his Commander since he was a midshipman. The Admiral gave a weak salute back.

He smiled as Broderinsen put the epaulettes on. Broderinsen continued to sit with the Admiral until that morning when his eyes glossed over, his face still creased in a smile.

CHAPTER 38
A BITTERSWEET ENDING

eneral Tovairsen watched as the Mai'Lang approached Faust's Wall for the second time that day. They had been repelled once and apparently had gathered even more forces for their return. The wall could be defended by a small number of men, which was good because he only had twenty-six hundred left, including reinforcements from Lundgarde. They had been defeated easily by the large Mai'Lang force after their costly victory at Bang'Lau and it looked now as if they would be again.

Tovairsen cringed at the thought of twenty thousand Mai'Lang forces sweeping into Lundgarde. He and his men would all be dead before that happened, though, he had vowed. With less than one-tenth of his forces from Bang'Lau left under his command, he had to set them in two shifts instead of three so most were operating on little or no sleep after that morning's battle.

"Colonel," he called softly, eyes never leaving the approaching army.

"Aye sir?" the brawny blond man answered.

"Call to arms, please."

"Aye sir. Call to arms! All soldiers take your positions! Archers, stand by!" he called in a loud, clear voice.

The soldiers around the wall sprung into action, every one of them carrying a long-bow. The Mai'Lang were still far out of range but the reverberations in the ground could be felt even on top of the massive structure that was Faust's Wall.

It had been built at the end of the Great War as a way to protect the Northern continent from the only land connecting it with its Southern neighbor. It was made of solid gray stone the color of the overcast sky that perpetually hung over it. It was over twenty feet thick and eighty feet high.

The gargantuan gate was just the first in a series of four, each one surrounded by dozens of arrow slits. It was nearly impenetrable. This was exactly why the Mai'Lang wanted control of it. They had already knocked down the first two gates at considerable expense—nearly thirty thousand men—to themselves and had returned in even greater numbers to finish the job.

Four catapults were wheeled behind the Mai'Lang army, presumably to occupy some of the defenders. Tovairsen knew that one of the forces set against each other this day wouldn't leave this battlefield alive and odds were his would be it. He shrugged, they had done all anyone could ask and more. They had killed twice their original number and he was proud to be standing here, leading this group of men.

In the sudden silence created by the Mai'Lang's halt, a sound like the wind passing through a narrow crevice ripped the air. On top of the wall, a blue circle appeared. It looked to be made of clear, liquid blue energy. The defenders stared at it, a few recognizing it for what it was. Out of it stepped two figures cloaked in dark blue, one tall, the other short and a golden light between them. The tall one turned and said something to the others and they shot off in a silver and gold blur down the wall and into the distance towards Bang'Lau.

The tall one floated majestically down to rest gently on the ground. He stood facing the hesitant Mai'Lang army among the thousands of corpses that littered the grass in front of the wall. He bent down and picked up a long spear from the grasp of a dead man. Hefting it experimentally, he admired its length. The Mai'Lang shifted nervously as the tall man eyed the spear, calm and silent. "Odin's Declaration of War," spears were often called, and the man seemed to think this appropriate. Then he threw the spear through the air towards the Mai'Lang lines. It disappeared into the clouds as thousands of heads followed its ascent. With a screech like a bird of prey diving, it rocketed out of the sky to impale the Mai'Lang General.

The assembled armies pried their eyes from the dead man in time to see the cloaked figure draw his sword and a metallic crossbow. His cowl fell down about his shoulder allowing his long white mane to flail in the light breeze. His blue eyes flared dangerously and all knew now who he was.

The Mai'Lang Army was standing face to face with the Fifth of Magi.

Danken began walking briskly towards the Mai'Lang who shifted nervously. When they didn't retreat, he unleashed *Stormcell* on them.

The marble-sized hail punched through armor like wet paper and lightning caused the ranks to separate, leaving huge sections of charred corpses in its wake. Next, he used *Gale* to scatter them even further before segregating them into groups with *Firewall,* immolating perfect grids into the unlucky.

The panicked Mai'Lang milled about helplessly until one among them took charge and ordered them to attack. Danken shook his head sadly, killing the man with *Magefire.* Still the Mai'Lang charged him. They did not charge through bravery or anger, but through pure, undistilled fear of the one they had been trained to hate since birth. He had been like them once, though it seemed so very long ago.

Tovairsen watched in awe as the scene unraveled. He knew the Mage intended to fight the Mai'Lang host alone but resolved that he would not have to.

"Colonel, you stay here with First Regiment. Everyone else with me!" he yelled.

Danken fired several devastating bolts of *Magefire* with *F'laare* clearing entire paths through the attacking force. Next, he called up several *Earth Elementals* from the ground to further occupy the attackers. Sheathing himself in *Magefire* from hundreds of arrows and the onrushing masses, he froze an entire portion of the army with *Icewall.* Fully a third of the Mai'Lang host were already dead, if not more but still they pressed in on him.

Firing off three last rapid bolts from *F'laare,* he rushed at the mob, *Mak'Rist* a flashing blue arc of death cutting through steel and armor as easily as flesh. They had no defense against him. He could see every move they were going to make long before they made it, dispatching them easily. He was tiring rapidly but kept fighting the waves of soldiers as if he was possessed. He felt his *Magefire* shield about to give out but would not stop fighting. For Amaria he would not.

The roar of one thousand Sendar coming to aid their Mage, was the final straw that sent the Mai'Lang running. They were picked off all the way off of the battlefield, their numbers drastically reduced. Tovairsen came cautiously over to Danken to check on him.

"Magus, are you all right?"

"Aye," Danken answered, trying to catch his breath.

"Do you require anything?"

"Food, water," Danken said between breaths.

"Aye," Tovairsen said, grabbing a nearby soldier. "You, get food and water, lots of it, on the double."

"Aye General," the man said, running back towards the wall.

"General?" Danken asked.

"Tovairsen, Magus. General Regerdotir is dead."

"I see. Well, thank you."

"Thank *you*, Magus. Without you, we probably would have lost the Wall today," Tovairsen said.

The food got there soon and Danken was his usual animal self as he inhaled it. When he had finished and rested a moment, he sent his *Stonespeak* into the ground. He found Swifteye and T'riel near a small village on the coast north of Bang'Lau. Marking the spot, he opened the portal.

Rascan watched in awe while Yardin orchestrated the Orcan squad's movements. He had given the older Commander every detail of his encounter with the Barakans to add to Yardin's own arsenal of knowledge. He had even ventured forth a few theories that Yardin seemed genuinely interested in. He continued to pay close attention to every minute maneuver for his future reference.

The Barakans had been spotted just offshore of Soling'Ta along with two hundred Darkwatch Shrakens. This altered the original plan slightly, as the Barakans would be following experienced warriors into battle. Yardin had no doubt that his force had also been spotted so he disguised his battle plan as a simple frontal assault.

The hundreds of sunken ships in the harbor provided excellent ambush cover for the Shrakens which they would certainly use. Rascan hazarded that they would use the plentiful Barakans as cover to distract the Orcans before ambushing them, with which Yardin agreed.

So, with this knowledge, the Orcans swam into Soling'Ta's harbor as if in straight attack formation. Rascan could almost hear the

Shrakens' teeth gnashing in gleeful anticipation. But they were Mistgarde Orcans and nothing they did was as it seemed.

As the Barakans moved to attack in a staggered diamond formation four groups high, the Orcans attacked with *Sonarblast*. The Barakans deflected it with their *Concussion*. As they did so, the Orcans suddenly split into squads of twenty and torpedoed into the sunken ships. The Barakans were left stunned for a moment before they began to comprehend what had happened. The Shrakens, too were caught off-guard because they had expected the Orcans to shy away from the ships, not attack them. The Orcans employed their *Cleansing* spells before entering the ships with concerted *Sonarblast* to counteract the Shrakens' *Stunspore* attacks.

Many of the hidden Shrakens were killed in the ensuing melee as they hadn't been prepared to defend. The Barakans rushed into a battle zone totally alien to them. The Shrakens and Orcans had lived this contest thousands of times to the point where they were born knowing how to fight the other. Completely swept away by the brutal efficiency of it all, the silver skinned Barakans were utterly destroyed in the ruined hulls of the sunken warships. They were merely fodder for the two ancient enemies, who killed them indiscriminately.

The Darkwatch Shrakens fought savagely and well but were simply outnumbered and outmatched. Rascan killed two frantic Barakans with his javelin and was surprised to find there was no one left to fight. He found Drylyn floating over three dead Shrakens, a superficial hook wound in her side and shredded netting hanging from her shoulders. He quickly cut her out and brought her to the makeshift sickbay that had been set up.

It was fairly full but one of the medics saw to her. She watched him sew up her side without so much as a grimace. Rascan raised an eyebrow at her unexpected toughness. She looked up at him halfway through the procedure and gave him a coy smile. He drifted slowly over and squeezed her hand gently.

"Doing well, Lieutenant Drylyn. That was quite a fight you put up out there," he said.

"Thank you sir," she answered as the medic cut her last stitch.

"All set Lieutenant," the medic told her. "Try to keep from making any sudden moves for about two weeks."

"Aye, thank you," she said as Rascan escorted her onto the beach, where he laid her on the sand to adjust.

Sendar soldiers came running from the city, cheering the Orcans' victory. Medics came with stretchers to take the wounded Orcans to sick beds where they could adjust to land in relative comfort. Rascan stood shakily on beach, overseeing the project. After a thorough search of all the ships, the rest of the Orcans came out of the water to adjust. Commander Yardin came to stand beside Rascan, feeling lightheaded from the abrupt transformation to land.

"Your plan worked to perfection, sir," Rascan said, staring into the city, which was now in full motion.

"Our plan, Commander," Yardin corrected.

"Aye sir."

"I see you are worried for Lieutenant Drylyn."

"Aye, for all those under my command, sir," Rascan answered warily, unsure of Yardin's direction.

"Aye, but for her especially," Yardin smiled slightly. "She is a fine, brave soldier and pretty as well."

"Aye sir."

"Good luck then Commander. You'll have your hands full, I suspect," Yardin told him, walking slowly off to supervise the effort elsewhere on the beach.

Danken looked on nervously at the tiny wooden shack on the edge of a high cliff. He had intended to come here right off, but the situation at Lundgarde had needed to be dealt with, so he had sent Swifteye and T'riel to watch over the shack's residents until he arrived. T'riel sat on his shoulder in rare silence.

Danken heard a beautiful song come from inside to comfort the piercing wails of a baby. He approached the shack slowly, cautiously, keeping an eye open for signs of trouble. When he reached the faded wood door, he opened it using *Breezesummon* and entered silently, using *Stealth* to silence the creaking floorboards.

A tiny, flickering fire illuminated the drab interior, casting long shadows around like pools of darkness. His eye was drawn to a bed where a Mai'Lang woman lay dead. It was obvious to him she had died during childbirth. A beautiful woman wearing a tattered red and gold cloak was kneeling on the floor with a tiny, Mai'Lang baby cradled in her arms.

His heart skipped a beat as her song faltered when she caught sight of him. Her burning green eyes showed no sign of recognition. He was left speechless for a moment as a thousand emotions and thoughts flooded through his head. His mouth felt dry and sticky and his jaw worked soundlessly as he struggled to force out the words crowding his throat.

"Amaria?" he asked softly.

She looked at him in anger now, clutching the baby closer to her breast. Danken took a step towards her and she recoiled from him, a soft hiss escaping from her lips. She backed against the wall, her eyes wildly darting about. Danken reached out his hand slowly towards her.

"Amaria, please, I'm here to help you," he said reassuringly, letting a calming flow of blue trickle into her. Before it could take effect though, she bolted out the door, blowing by Swifteye and T'riel. The Oracles had transferred her *N'famar* emotions to the child and erased her mind.

Danken followed her, anxiety ripping him apart. He was so used to being in control of every situation that his sanity was close to unraveling. She whirled to face him, clutching the baby like a security blanket in front of her. She slowly backed towards the cliff.

"Amaria, please let me help you," he pleaded.

"Stay away from him!" she screeched.

"I don't want to hurt you, you know that."

"Keep-Away-From-Us," she said fiercely.

"You have to fight him, Amaria. He's controlling you!"

"No!"

"Look at his eyes!" Danken yelled, pointing at the baby's glowing red eyes, but Amaria wasn't looking. He wasn't sure she was even seeing anything for what it really was.

Danken felt the Oracles burning in his cloak pocket as if in response to their master so near to victory. His eyes narrowed in anger at the thought. He reached into the pocket and grabbed them. Nervously, he rolled the scorching hot balls around, their odd textures scalding his palm.

Amaria continued her slow, steady backwards shuffle, inching ever closer to the edge. Danken eyed the sharp drop where the bright green grass seemed to run directly into the angry purple and gray sky. Sweat trickled down his forehead, stinging his eyes. She held the crying infant tightly to her, her knuckles white from strain. She was only a few feet from the edge now. Danken gritted his teeth in frustration. He knew he had to act soon but he just didn't know how. He searched desperately for the perfect solution but his mind was blank with panic.

"Amaria, I love you," he said, his voice breaking, "please, come back to me."

"Shut up!" she shouted.

Danken felt his grasp tighten on the three deadly Oracles. He knew what he had to do. He reached deep into the core of his being and built his power with a lightning fast crescendo. He felt it coursing through his veins like molten lava.

Suddenly he drew the Oracles from his cloak in a blur that ended with his hand straining at her. Smoke sizzled from his burning flesh and his eyes flared brightly. He channeled all of his built-up energy through the Oracles, focusing them on her and the baby. With a cry of pain, he released the energy into them. A thunderclap preceded a blinding flash of blue that made the whole scene disappear. Danken felt as if he were in the eye of a hurricane, a calm in the center of a vast, chaotic maelstrom of power.

When the light faded, he had to blink several times to get his sight back. Once this occurred, he looked up to see Amaria staring dumbly at the hysterical baby. She slowly rocked the baby until it was silent, humming a mysterious Elven tune to it. When it had quieted, she gently set the tiny bundle onto the soft grass.

Danken felt tears of relief spring to his eyes. His throat felt tight and he had trouble breathing. She stood slowly to regard him with her large, soft, knowing green eyes. The eyes she had dazzled him with. He saw tears running down her cheek, a small smile tugging at the corner of her lips.

"Amaria?" he asked quietly.

"I'm sorry, my love," she answered.

"You don't…"

"It's the only way," she smiled sadly. "We can never be."

"What are you…" Danken started to ask but was cut off as Amaria let loose a powerful burst of *Moonfire* at him that forced him to shield himself in *Magefire*. She then gracefully dove off the edge of the cliff like the most beautiful bird he had ever seen.

"Noooo!" he shouted, trying to use *Breezesummon* to catch her but it was too late. He ran to the edge of the cliff past Swifteye and T'riel who were staring down in shock. He turned to his *Avian* form as he leapt into the air, diving to the wave-swept rocks below.

As he reached the white-foamed water, he morphed back into his true form. He looked helplessly at her broken, lifeless body, her face locked into that same sad smile. Dropping heavily to his knees beside her heedless of the sharp rocks that cut into his skin, he held her. The waves crashed over him but he was numb to them. He looked to his hand where the Oracles had turned to dust and were blowing out across the ocean. He stared after them blankly, unable to comprehend how he couldn't save her. He held her long into the night, the cold water seeming to seep into his very soul. Finally, T'riel landed on his shoulder, letting gold energy into him to take away some of his pain.

"Boy must get out of the water before he freezes," she said.

"So what if I do?"

"Boy shouldn't talk like that," T'riel admonished lightly.

"Everyone I care for ends up dead. If you're smart, you'll leave while you have the chance," Danken said darkly.

"That will never happen." She sniffed and he stared at her.

"Aye, somehow I knew that would be your answer" he said, slowly getting up with Amaria's limp body in his hands. He used *Airlift* to lift himself back to the cliff's edge where Swifteye was awkwardly holding the baby. Danken used *Everwarm* to dry himself off but he couldn't get rid of the cold ache in his heart. He set Amaria gently on the ground.

"Thank you both for being here," he said solemnly, taking the sleeping baby, whose eyes were no longer red but the glowing green of an Elf. It looked up at him sleepily and then went back to its slumber after the hard, stressful day. Danken then noticed that its palms were no longer red either. The power unleashed through the Oracles must have erased them, he thought blankly.

"What will Boy do with it?" T'riel asked of the baby.

"Take it back to the Peak, I suppose."

"But it's Mai'Lang," she said.

"Evil isn't inherited, T'riel. It's taught. We'll teach this one to see the Light." He handed the infant back to Swifteye. "I need you two to keep it safe."

"Where Boy goes, One goes," T'riel stated flatly. Swifteye harrumphed his agreement.

"Not unless you can breathe underwater, kiddo."

"Boy is planning something," T'riel sulked.

"Aye," Danken agreed, opening a portal. "I'll be home soon."

"Promise?" T'riel asked, buzzing in front of his face.

"I promise," Danken agreed, ushering them through the portal. A whooshing sound heralded a blast of warm air from above him and he turned to see Tersandi and her fiery steed silently land on the cliff's edge. She was more beautiful than even his memories gave her credit for. Through his sadness and his loss, he was strangely at peace when he saw the Valkyrie. Guiltily he admitted to himself that Amaria had been right. They could never be. Not when his whole heart was pledged to Tersandi. A force of nature who would never reciprocate.

"You have lost much this day, Danken Sariksen," her sweet voice echoed.

"Aye, Tersandi, but it is good to see you again, nonetheless," he replied solemnly, trying to come to terms with the whirl of emotions in his head.

"Imagine my surprise when I realized that my Chosen was your mate. For what it is worth, I'm sorry for your loss, but she was needed on a higher plane. You have not lost all though Magus. Your sister, the one I vowed to look after is safe. She has found someone and her anger is fading. You will be reunited with her one day. Until then you must content yourself with that knowledge."

"Thank you for that," Danken said, refraining from asking her the thousands of questions in his head.

"I've sent many souls to Hela's embrace at the edge of your blade in recent months, even a select few have I escorted to Valhalla. You have been busy."

"Too busy by far," Danken replied bitterly.

"Perhaps it is time to give your blade a rest," Tersandi said softly.

"I only wish I could."

"End it. You had the right idea in your conversation with the Bearded One and Nymph," she said confidently. "You are the Sapphire Son. Your heart has always been your guide."

"You believe it will work?" he asked, realizing an instant later that she had used his Asgard name and confirmed that he was the one from the Foretelling, much as Sanngetal had.

"That is for you to decide."

"Aye. I just don't know if I'm strong enough. Everything I touch seems to be hurt."

"You have not hurt me, Danken Sariksen." She reached out and touched his hand and he felt a warmth flood through him making every emotion seem sharp as a razor.

"You are right, Tersandi. I should not have doubted you or myself. Pity is not my strong suit."

"You have done well so far. Follow your heart, it is pure. I have been watching."

"I thought you weren't supposed to take interest in the affairs of Midgarthe," Danken said with a sad smile.

"I'm not, but you make me feel what I have not for thousands of years and you seem to be worth the risk of Freyja's wrath. Remember your heart, Sariksen," she said as she disappeared. "Remember Hope."

"I won't forget, I promise," he said as he opened a portal. Picking Amaria up, he took one last look at her. "One way or another, I promise," he said, stepping through.

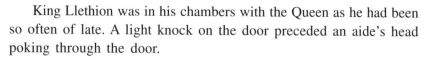

King Llethion was in his chambers with the Queen as he had been so often of late. A light knock on the door preceded an aide's head poking through the door.

"What is it?" the King asked.

"Sorry to disturb you, Sire, but you and the Queen are needed in Princess Amaria's garden."

"What?" the Queen asked.

"It would be better if you see for yourself, Majesty," the aide said, staring at the floor.

The Royal couple rushed into the garden, where they saw Danken kneeling with his head bowed. Using *Faunagrow,* he had made a small hole which Amaria floated peacefully over. He had wrapped her in the roots of a year-old sapling to let her become one with the garden she had loved so much. The stars seemed to be keeping vigil over them, the chill air a reminder of their loss this night.

"Gods," King Llethion breathed, touching his daughter's serene face. The Queen sobbed silently as Prince Andren came to stand at her side. Danken slowly lowered her into the ground and covered it up, leaving only the sapling in its place.

He kept his head bowed through it all, remaining silent. The King slowly walked over and placed his hand on Danken's head. Danken rose slowly, his blue eyes glaring dangerously.

"She died to save us all. I thought I had saved her but she was already gone. I..."

"It is all right, Danken," the King said, his voice broken. "It was meant to be. The Gods had need of her."

"I promise you, this war ends now," Danken bowed fiercely. The King nodded meaningfully as Danken opened a portal and stepped through without looking back.

CHAPTER 39
ENDGAME

ek'Sho was silent in the dead of night. The palace guards were alert because of the occupation of Mok, but their vigilance was wasted as a blue portal opened in the King's bed chamber. An angry Danken strode out of it and cast a *Firenet*—a derivative he had taken from the Sorcerer's *Firerope*—over the terrified Goblin. Once secure, he dragged the flailing King back though the portal, leaving his several concubines speechless.

The same thing happened in Isthok to the newly appointed Queen and in Do to the Giant King, as well as the underwater city of Sawtooth to Queen Darkfin. They were all thrown into the bed chamber of Emperor Stanlan'Kante at the Imperial Palace in Mai. The confused Impress was rudely thrown out and the doors magically sealed.

The five heads of state squirmed miserably in their unbreakable nets, shouting weak protests laced with fear. The palace guards pounded ineffectually on the doors and Danken silenced them with *Stealth*. He glared at the petrified rulers with open disdain.

"For thousands of years, an unspoken agreement has existed between the Sorcerers and Magi, that Royal families and other important statesmen were exempt from harm by either side. Attacks using Sorcerer or Mage magic were also forbidden. In this way only two battles have been fought between the Five in three thousand years. Dak'Verkat and you have broken that agreement, bringing the battle count of the Five to three and forfeiting your lives."

"It vass you," Queen Tarss of Isthok hissed. "It vass you who murdered sse Royal Family and all itss Nobless. You burnt out sseir eyess."

"Aye. I did you a favor, so shut your mouth before I rip that tongue out of it," Danken barked. "Now, I have brought you together on this night to propose a treaty."

"Pfwah!" Tarss scoffed before her air supply was cut off.

"I will speak, you will listen," Danken informed them, releasing his spell on the sluggish Queen's lungs. "As you know, your forces have been defeated at every turn. We control five major ports, Faust's Wall is secured and the Shrakens are retreating to Sawtooth, where they will be caught between the Mistgarde Orcans and the combined Mer'khan and Orcan armies chasing them.

"You have lost. If you send the Darkwatch to retake Soling'Ta, not only will you fail, but leave Mai open for the taking, as well. The Sorcerers are dead and so are your treacherously placed forces in the Northern continent. If you are wondering why Dak'Verkat's tower still stands, it's because he is being slowly digested by a Sea Dragon as we speak."

"If you are so confident of your victory, why do you not destroy us?" Queen Darkfin asked icily.

"Because there has been enough bloodshed in the last five months to last for the rest of our lives. Thousands upon thousands lost their lives for what? Land? Power? It stops now."

"Anda ifa wesa says it not a stops nowa?" King Mek'Lo asked in barely understandable Sendar.

"Then not only you but your entire family lines die. Then I take your cities anyway, one by one."

"Why for not Mage kill and make self King?" King Nog stupidly asked, repeating Queen Darkfin's questions as if not buying Danken's answer.

"All right. I'm going to say it slowly so you can understand it this time. I'm tired of war. Besides, eventually new Sorcerers will grow up and want what's theirs back and I'll have to fight another war."

"This is why we fight you, because you act weak," the Emperor said, shaking his graying head, his pointed black beard remaining immobile.

"And it's also why we win," Danken shot back.

"What are your terms?" Queen Darkfin asked.

"Simple, really," Danken answered, pulling a scroll from his sleeve. He unrolled it and placed it in front of the five. "You call all of your armies back to their homes. You cease state-sponsored piracy and raiding. You end the slave trade."

"Sounds like you get everything and we get nothing," Stanlan'Kante said, shaking his head in disapproval.

"Aye. What do we get?" Darkfin asked.

"Three things. Your lives, peace and access to selected ports after a six month evaluation period."

"You would give us access to your ports?" the Emperor asked unbelieving.

"*Select* ports. And aye, as long as the favor was returned. Say Shun'ka, Mok, Riss and Shaank to our Crask, Southport, Cona and Myr. A restriction will be placed on weapons and state technology but everything else will be fair trade."

"Seeing as we have no choice, and your concessions are more than I expected, the Empire of Mai'Lang will agree to your proposed peace treaty," the Emperor said after a long pause. He took the offered pen and signed his name. The rest resignedly followed suit, King Nog just doing as he was told, signing by his name with a barely legible 'x.'

Danken signed his name on the bottom line.

"Betray my trust and I will do far worse than kill you," Danken told them seriously. They nodded their understanding before being sent back to their home cities. Danken turned to the Emperor. "You are the glue that holds them together now that the Sorcerers have gone. I hold you responsible above all."

"The Duah Princess, did she make it?" the Emperor asked carefully. Danken's eyes narrowed dangerously at her mention.

"No."

"I am sorry. Dak'Verkat forced my hand."

"You excuses fall on deaf ears," Danken said tightly.

"As well they should. Please allow me to open my chamber doors. I have something for you."

"I don't need..."

"Please," Stanlan'Kante begged. Danken opened the doors, knocking the guards down the hallway, using *Gale*. Stanlan'Kante called to the Empress in Langjian. She looked at him quizzically for a moment before rushing off down the hall. "Please wait," the Emperor asked.

Not long after, the Queen walked into the chamber with an astonishingly beautiful young Mai'Lang woman, the guards keeping their distance. The woman wore an elegant black and red silk gown that complimented her long, shiny raven hair.

"What is this?" Danken asked warily.

"Allow me to introduce you to Hrafna'Verkat, daughter of Dak'Verkat. She has lain in a coma since I was a young man. She has no memory, but a desire to serve. It cannot erase what has been taken from you, but maybe you can find some use for her."

"I cannot accept a person as a gift," Danken said.

"I know that my land seems alien and evil to you, but these are our ways, how things have always been. If not as a concubine, than as a Blood Debt, as an advisor in our ways, as an ambassador between our people. Please allow me to atone for your pain and the pain of the Elven people with our own," Stanlan'Kante begged. Danken closed his eyes with a heavy sigh.

"Very well, as an ambassador."

"Aye, thank you."

"Do not let me down Emperor Stanlan'Kante," Danken said, opening a portal in the middle of the room. He looked at Hrafna, who eyed him anxiously. She stood and Stanlan'Kante embraced her, telling her of her new duties and of the future her people placed on her shoulders. She accepted them with strength, fervor and excitement, Danken observed.

He indicated that she should go through the portal first. With one last nod at the Emperor, he closed the portal behind him.

EPILOGUE

ife. It is an unknown road, fraught with potholes, crossroads and forks that lead to completely different places. What lies at its end is just as big of a mystery as what lies around the next bend. In the end, it rarely turns out how we thought it would when we were children, for a child does not see obstacles and challenges, only the final result. Not one among us can claim that they have seen the future, that they alone can weave or unweave the threads of Fate as they choose. The consequences of our actions can be predicted, but never guaranteed. They are far reaching and irrevocable, a constant that cannot be avoided.

All that can be done is to set goals and do everything in our power to achieve them while maintaining our beliefs and honor. To find what we have long searched for, to experience what we have only dreamed of will never come without a price. In every life, there comes a time when we must sacrifice what we want in order to obtain what we need, because life is a compromise of both. Every road had two sides. What good are material possessions and fame if one has sacrificed his happiness to attain them? There is a difference between being wealthy and being rich. Being wealthy means one believes he has the ability to attain happiness. Being rich means he has already attained it.

That being said, sacrifice itself has its limits and they are far too easy to overlook. The line between a noble sacrifice and a meaningless loss is thin, blurred and easily mistaken for the road to glory. It is not always wise and noble to forge your own way simply for the sake of notoriety or even individually. Sometimes there is a very good reason that the road less traveled, remains so. Sometimes when we get to the end of the road, we find that what we always thought we wanted, wasn't what we got. Sometimes what we got turns out to be even better.

–Archives Magus Gellar
This sacred year, 87
Age of Mystery

n his quarters at Mist Peak, Danken contentedly watched Dot play tag with the otter Rip over and around the sleepy-eyed Shard. She had become quite the animal tamer since she had arrived, even making friends with Lanaia's wolves. She hadn't spoken again since the night he had left but when Danken used *Stealth,* he sometimes heard her talking to the animals.

Tae now lived with Dot, and Lanaia was learning what it was to once again be part of an Elven clan. Dot was thrilled to have a real family but still spent more time than not outside with the animals. Maple was still her nursemaid and she and Danken had developed a close relationship since he had returned.

Hrafna had turned out to be one of the happiest, caring people Danken had ever met. She had won over most of the people in the crater with her quick smile and excellent Sendar. She had taken an instant affection to Jadn, the now five month old Mai'Lang baby. Danken had named him after the Duah word for 'hope.' Tersandi's influence on him, he knew. And in the child's green eyes, he could see Amaria.

Danken found himself dropping by several times a day just to talk to Hrafna. She seemed to enjoy his company as well and had been ecstatic when he had asked her to look after Jadn. He had gone to great lengths to make sure they weren't harassed for their race when she went out of the White Castle. He even had a meeting scheduled with Arn on that very subject later in the day.

Swifteye had become one of Danken's closest friends, even beginning to speak more often. He had elected to stay at Mist Peak instead of returning to Silverstaff. He had easily passed the test for Mistgarde and had stunned the assorted Dwarven Commanders with his unreal speed.

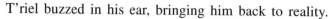

T'riel buzzed in his ear, bringing him back to reality.

"Boy will be late if he keeps daydreaming."

"I know," he said, hugging Dot and scratching the sleepy sabercat between his twitching ears. He left, heading for the War Room, where he found Arn and the assembled Mistgarde Commanders already in their seats. Also present were King Oreshatter of the Dwarves, King Llethion of the Duah, King Mashtor of the Vull'Kra, High Councilor Nordsen of Sendar and Princess Shonai of Orcana, in place of her ailing father. Prime Chancellor Tomar of Merkhandin was the only head of state missing, as his race couldn't leave the ocean. A scrying mirror had been created to allow contact.

They stood as Danken entered, standing in front of the five empty chairs at the head of the table.

"Please be seated," he said. "First order of business?"

"The Mai'Lang accords," the High Councilor said. "According to all reports they are nearly complete."

"Aye. Then our scheduled troop pullout will take place in two weeks as planned," Danken agreed.

They discussed other, more mundane issues for a short while longer before wrapping up their monthly council. Danken sent them all back through the portal, except for Shonai, who remained to talk with him.

"So how is your father?" he asked.

"Better. He'll be out swimming about before you know it."

"And Zoltaure?" Danken asked, knowing the Orcan had come out of his coma shortly after the war.

"Very good. My father made him a noble for his efforts to protect me."

"That's great! Now you two can marry," Danken exclaimed.

"Aye," Shonai beamed. "And I owe it all to you, Danken," she said, hugging him before stepping through her designated portal.

Arn was waiting for him outside the War Room with two men Danken recognized.

"Danken, this is Diedrik Pennsen and Myrisan Deathsong, both of Mistgarde Protectors Division."

"The inn," Danken smiled, clasping their wrists.

"Aye Magus," Diedrik said, rubbing his head at the memory.

"Pennsen," Danken nodded. "I thought I sensed something about you. What made you join the Protectors Division?"

"Myrisan here convinced me," Diedrik smiled.

"Aye, *that's* the reason," the Hafalf laughed.

"Anyway," Arn said, "as to what we discussed earlier, Danken, I'm assigning these two to Jadn. Hrafna also though she isn't the prime objective."

"Thank you, I can think of no one better," Danken said sincerely. Secretly, they would be watching her to ensure her continued loyalty to Sendar. No one would ever fully trust a Mai'Lang.

"They will be safe, Magus," Diedrik vowed.

"We will be their shadows," Myrisan agreed.

So it was that two weeks later, the forces of the Northern continent pulled out of the occupied cities. The Elven fleet under Admiral Kanumus and the Troll fleet under Admiral Magha, escorted the Sendar forces under Admiral Olafsen to Southport. There they met Admiral Luca Broderinsen's fleet and the Shun'ka fleet led by newly made Admiral Jarl Tamlinsen.

A massive parade was held in the large port city with people from all over the continent turning out to cheer the returning troops. Thousands of Mer'khan and Orcans crowded the harbor along with the ships of war. The celebration lasted the better part of a week.

Eventually, the exhausted, victorious troops went their separate ways back to their homes. The open-port agreement went into effect soon after and hostilities were put aside in favor of commerce that hadn't taken place for twenty years. Danken got together with all the people who had helped him along his journeys. They recounted tales of their glory with laughter and shared a moment of silence for the friends they had lost.

When it was over, Danken ported to his former stead outside of Lok Tryst, where Henrik and his wife had built a cozy farmhouse. He unobtrusively said a prayer over his mother's grave and then walked into the Pixian woods with T'riel buzzing excitedly all the way.

They stopped at the place where her parents had also been killed. While T'riel paid her last respects, a sudden commotion in the forest caused Danken to start and he turned to see Z'Nair at the head of hundreds of golden Pixies, like a thousand tiny candles. T'riel flew over to them and exchanged greetings.

Danken picked up that they had made a tenuous peace with the Gnomes for which he was glad. He listened to them chat awhile longer before wandering off. He found a clearing nearby that seemed to call to him. He continued to stare at it until T'riel broke his spell.

"What is Boy doing now?"

"T'riel, do you think your people would mind if I made something in this clearing?"

"One thinks Pixies would be honored. What is Boy planning to build?" she asked.

In response, Danken went into a trance, sending his *Stonespeak* into the ground. He called to the stone, asking for its assistance. He channeled his energy into it, molding it, shaping it to his will. The ground seemed to rip apart, groaning with displeasure at the disturbance of its slumber. Danken felt the power surging through him as if he was part of the moving rock. It spiraled up towards the sky unendingly, Danken caressing it into the shape he wanted as it went. When he had finished, the deafening rumbling came to its abrupt halt, the silence was a welcome reprieve.

He looked up at his Tower with a kind of euphoric satisfaction. It was one hundred stories high with rounded, random outcroppings and seamless crevices. It was pearly white, reflecting the sun's rays off of it in prismed blushes of color. At its zenith, were four spires in each of the cardinal directions surrounding one larger one in the exact center.

T'riel was flying slowly around it in shock. Soon there were thousands of similar golden orbs circling the Tower as well as a like number of short, bark-skinned Gnomes at its massive foundation. The Tower had no discernable door, but when Danken approached it, it allowed him to walk right through its solid rock exterior as if it were air.

Once inside, he marveled at its complexity. Empty rooms abounded throughout, waiting to be filled with artifacts from his travels or books of one sort or another. Their were no staircases, merely a wide corridor straight up to the top for him to float through. It seemed as if the tower was a reflection of his mind and he felt comfort enveloping him.

Suddenly he felt something else, a jaw-dropping power. The temperature dropped and Danken saw Sanngetal through his freezing breath. The one-eyed, red and grey-bearded being looked around the tower idly. He twirled his humongous spear as if it were a baton.

"I like it. It fits your personality. Modest, yet proud," he said, nodding his approval.

"Thank you, I guess."

"You have learned much in the past year, young Magus."

"Aye, and at what cost?"

"From the greatest losses come the greatest gains," Sanngetal told him, pacing around the room to inspect various things. "You would be a far different person today. Not a worse person, just not the leader you have become."

"Sometimes I think that would be better."

"Maybe for you, but not for the realms."

"Aye, maybe."

"Besides, think of all of the lives you have touched and made better through your strength. Without you, the world is still at war."

"Dak'Verkat. Is he dead finally?" Danken asked.

"That is not for me to say at this time."

"Why not? Why can you tell me certain things and not others?" Danken wanted to know.

"Even Gods have rules they must abide by."

"*Dwei.* So the peace I worked so hard to forge may just be shattered before it has a chance to flourish."

"Maybe. That is the way of the Dark. Chaos, power and instability. It is your responsibility to bring Order, justice and stability to the equation in order to balance it. That is the great truth of your life as a Mage, Danken."

"Aye. Thank you," Danken said, still unsatisfied.

"Your friend, Tok'Neth, may have the answers you seek, though."

"Tok'Neth?"

"Aye," Sanngetal nodded. he put his fingers to his lips and let out a deafening whistle. In response, a gargantuan horse with steaming nostrils and fiery eyes appeared out of thin air. Danken saw that it had eight legs instead of four. "Oh and Danken," Sanngetal said as he mounted up, "your parents are with me in Valhalla and your lost love is well in Ljossalfheim. They are safe. Worry about them no longer," and then the mysterious being was gone.

Danken stood in stunned silence for a moment before the words sunk in. A smile slowly crept onto his face which quickly turned to awe. He had been speaking all this time to the All-Father, Odin himself. Still shaken by the news, he left the confines of the Tower. T'riel was at his side in an instant.

"What is inside?" she asked, the assembled Pixies and Gnomes leaned forward to hear his answer.

"My mind."

"Boy's mind?"

"Aye, like I can walk around inside my own head."

"Whoa," she said simply.

"That's what I said."

Jet appeared then, in his customary wide black riding leathers, open at the wrists and ankles, impressed by the gigantic Tower. He had just finished visiting his sisters and the Sendar woman who had raised him in her new well furnished manor house complete with servants as Jet had ordered. He and Danken had not spoken since the battle atop Mount Taeria but Jet was as unafraid and implacable as ever when the Mage fixed him with a cold stare.

The Stormdogs' ranks had swelled rapidly after the war and he now controlled a fortified keep outside of every city in the Southern continent. As ever, Wytchyn drove him insane and gave him her heart in dizzying turns. Like now, when she had his teeth on edge while she spied on a rival guild called the Black Sails made of mostly Shrakens, including those that had deserted from the Stormdogs. She had last reported that Ureshk had found a very high place in their ranks. But that was for another day. Today he had to concentrate on not letting Danken kill him. He whished he had Katir'Tua and Wytchyn here with him though. Trust. He'd never thought he'd see the day when he trusted someone, let alone *two* people. Trust was pain, but Danken was death.

"You have nerves of steel, Jet."

"I know," Jet laughed, not nervously, he hoped.

"What are you doing here? Don't you have a crime guild to look after?"

"Just visiting is all. It is nice not to be recognized as Landar this far north. You haven't been idle, I see."

"No," Danken said simply, looking again at his Tower. Jet could feel the sheer power emanating from the man—no longer a boy. Neither of them were. See death enough times and soon your eyes lost that childhood mischievousness, curiosity and even imagination. What could you imagine that you had not seen before? He hoped he could find his imagination again someday. Someday. For now he would settle for closure.

"Listen, Danken. I know we'll never be friends, but I wanted you to know how sorry I was about Amaria. I can't claim complete innocence. Know that it is one of the few things in my life that constantly weighs on my conscience," Jet said sincerely and Danken merely nodded, afraid to speak.

"Do you remember that old rumor monger at the inn in Altae's Birth?" Jet asked finally.

"You mean the one you beat to a pulp?"

"Aye," Jet laughed. "And do you remember the stories he told of you being the one the Forest Folk call Darkperil?"

"Don't remind me."

"Well, he may have been telling the truth."

"What?"

"Look." Jet pointed and Danken followed his gaze to the Gnomes. They were no longer the color of trees and their eyes no longer glowed. They looked like tiny, round bodied Sendar. Laughing and cheering, they celebrated wildly, chanting in praise of Darkperil in an ancient

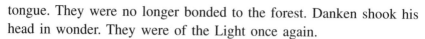

tongue. They were no longer bonded to the forest. Danken shook his head in wonder. They were of the Light once again.

"It seems you are right, Jet."

"You know, we're not so different, Sariksen."

"Oh?" Danken asked skeptically.

"You said so yourself back in that same inn. We both serve something greater than ourselves. We don't like what the other serves but we respect it. We both are orphans. The Orphan Mercenary and the Orphan Mage."

"Orphan?" Danken laughed. "I tell you what Jet. This day I will prove to you which of us serves the greater power." He opened a portal. Jet eyed him skeptically but followed him in, T'riel keeping silent.

They stepped out just outside of the Spirit Blades' compound. The two sentries stiffened and bowed hastily. He whispered in one of their ears. Not long after, Kierna appeared, followed by an older, dignified Mai'Lang Spirit Blade and the massive, black-dressed form of Regiment Commander Rekfoll who appeared from nowhere, carrying his short axe and constantly surveying the surrounding area for threats with his amber eyes.

"What is this Danken?" Jet asked irritably. "I told you, I swore an oath! You don't have to rub it in that you found out anyway."

"Shut up Jet." Danken told him, Jet gritted his teeth. He was not the Stormleader here. Most definitely not.

"Danken." Kierna smiled at him and scowled at Jet, an odd reversal. "I didn't think to see you again so soon." She clasped his wrist, the three blue rings on her sleeve marking her has a Temple Second conspicuous.

"Jet. I want you to meet someone." Danken placed his hand on the Mai'Lang woman's shoulder. She seemed both excited and reluctant at once. "This is Plentis'Rhan. Your mother."

Jet's face went slack and the two stared at each other for an eternity. He and Plentis began talking, each wary of the other.

"Kierna," Danken smiled. "I'll expect you at the Peak for Summer Finding Festival."